WONDERLAND

WONDERLAND

FEAST OR FAMINE

ACT ONE

J. M. Alexia

All rights reserved. No part of this publication may be reproduced, stored in a retrieval system, or transmitted in any form or by any means electronic, mechanical, photocopying, recording, or otherwise without prior written permission from Podium Publishing.

This is a work of fiction. Names, characters, places, and incidents are either products of the author's imagination or used fictitiously. Any resemblance to actual events, locales, or persons, living, dead, or undead, is entirely coincidental.

Copyright © 2023 by J. M. Alexia

Cover design by Podium Publishing

ISBN: 978-1-0394-2124-0

Published in 2023 by Podium Publishing, ULC
www.podiumaudio.com

This book is dedicated to the rats in the walls whose chittering keeps me up at night when I need to finish a late chapter, and to the still-beating heart beneath my floorboards that sings me to sleep when at last my hands give out.

I am grateful to the birds with human eyes that follow me each morning as I walk to the cafe for my food and drink, and to the black goat with a thousand young that watches from the outside.

And I suppose I should thank the actual humans, as well, for indulging all my silly little delusions. Thanks to my dear aunt for supporting me all these years, and thanks to my writing friends for inspiring me to show this project to the world, and a special thanks to my patrons and readers for feeding me the attention I needed to finish this book and move on to the next.

And a special dedication to you, whoever you are, for giving this book a chance.

WONDERLAND

PART ONE

WELCOME TO WONDERLAND

OR, COST-BENEFIT ANALYSIS AS CALCULATED BY A MADWOMAN

"Who are *you*?" said the Caterpillar.

This was not an encouraging opening for a conversation. Alice replied, rather shyly, "I—I hardly know, sir, just at present—at least I know who I *was* when I got up this morning, but I think I must have been changed several times since then."

"What do you mean by that?" said the Caterpillar sternly. "Explain yourself!"

"I can't explain *myself*, I'm afraid, sir," said Alice, "because I'm not myself, you see."

—*Alice in Wonderland*, Lewis Carroll

I

When I was a little girl, I loved to read. I read every book I could get my hands on, from quaint little tales to sprawling epics meant for adult eyes only. I didn't distinguish; a book was a book, and any page with words on it was worth reading.

As I grew older my sense of taste sharpened and my eye became more discerning, but I have never let go of the wonder that fills me when I open a new book and breathe in a new world. When I read a story I immerse myself in it; I walk through a world of ink and paper as the chosen protagonist of the tale, and I feel as they feel, think as they think. It allows me, if only for those few precious moments, to imagine that I am in another world.

I've always dreamed of falling down the rabbit hole like bold little Alice—I even entertained the idea of going by Alice when I renamed myself, but settled on Morgan because it was nice and neutral—or being whisked away by summoning spell or errant Japanese delivery truck to the world of an isekai light novel. I would give anything to live a life of magic and mystery and adventure. I would give my whole world to be taken to another.

The reality isn't quite what I was expecting.

My eyes open from dreamless sleep and I find myself standing in a classroom with three solid walls and an infinite chasm of darkness in the place of the fourth. My gaze darts about as I take in new information and attempt to process it. This isn't my bedroom. Am I dreaming? This doesn't feel like a dream. *Focus, gather data, analyze.*

For a moment I set aside the plunging emptiness from which no light escapes and examine the classroom that doesn't really look like a classroom. There are desks and chairs in neat little rows, and on the far wall behind the teacher's desk there is a chalkboard with "WELCOME" written in a rainbow of colors. No chalk, I note, and nothing on any of the desks, even the teacher's desk. The three walls still standing are barren of any posters or projects or those tacky little mottoes that teachers so love to hang up. There's a door to my right, another concession to normalcy, but there are no signs of habitation or use in the whole room, and though I can see as clear as day, there are no lights amid the ceiling tiles above.

And then there is, of course, the matter of the yawning abyss.

I step up to the edge and peer into the darkness, watching the barely perceptible roll of shadow. Something is moving in the depths, or there is the illusion of motion, but like an optical trick, I can't quite make out what. It's not like outer space—no pinpricks of starlight shimmer in the dark—but there's texture to it, a sense of dimension that I can't quite wrap my brain around. It isn't *normal*. It fascinates me.

I stick a hand past the dividing line and feel the darkness against my skin. It isn't cold like the dark of space or the dark of night; this dark is warm and soft, almost comforting, but *alive* too. Like putting your hand against someone's forehead when they're sick; *feverish*. I wave my hand through the fever-warm dark and meet no resistance. It's just air and darkness and dull heat.

I pull back into the cold, empty classroom, or what might be the facsimile of a classroom. A simulacrum of the real. An impossibility. Elation bubbles in my lungs and courses through my veins but I force it down: *not yet, not yet. One more experiment. One more test before we can be certain.*

I grab the nearest desk, check that it's empty—it is—and shove it toward the edge. My scrawny bookworm arms strain more than they really should for an object that honestly isn't that heavy, but I've never been the athletic type and my atrophied muscles protest even the slightest exertion. I push the desk until it teeters on the brink of the abyss, then give it one good kick and let gravity handle the rest.

Gravity does not oblige. The desk neither flies off the edge nor tumbles into the depths; it just dips and keeps dipping until all of it has slipped into the endless blackness, and then it gently drifts out into the void, rotating slowly with the last of the momentum I gave it. No friction drags against it, so it floats off at a steady rate, getting smaller and dimmer, until the shadows swallow it whole.

I can't help it: I start laughing. I laugh and laugh until my lungs ache and I have to steady myself against the nearest wall just to remain standing. It bubbles out of me in bursts and waves, an inconstant cascade lacking in rhythm or reason. Tears stain my cheeks with wet, salty joy. *Magic. That's magic. I've found magic. I've finally found magic.* I sweep a hand at the abyss. *Nothing like that can exist, right? A void without gravity, warm, connected to a room affected by gravity, cold. No membrane between them, no separation. That breaks at least two laws of physics, right? Has to be magic.*

As my laughter dies for lack of breath, the first question I asked returns to the forefront: *Am I dreaming?*

Immediately I grimace at the question. *Of course we're not dreaming. What about this feels like dreaming? Why even question if we're dreaming?*

The impossible room with its impossible void, I counter dryly.

I feel too lucid to be dreaming. I can think, feel, move. I can contemplate my own existence and act with free will. I can read writing and perceive color. I rake my nails across my cheek and feel the sensation of pressure transmitted to my brain as a light, pleasant pain. I feel the nerves tingle even after my fingers are drawn away. *I am not dreaming. I know I'm not dreaming.*

So where are we?

The answer is obvious: *Another world. I'm in another world. I'm in another world and it has magic! I'm not dreaming, but this is all I've ever dreamed. I'm in the kind of story I've read about and fantasized about a hundred thousand times!*

I squeal loudly and hug myself, grinning and wiggling as I lean against the wall, and it's only then that I notice what I'm *wearing*: a navy-blue blazer over a white blouse, a pleated gray skirt that stops just above white knee socks, and black dress shoes that look fresh out of the box. My joy is slapped with indignation and I scowl.

"Really? A schoolgirl uniform? I can *drink*! I'm in *college*! If this is some fetish thing, I am going to be very cross. Do you hear that, whatever or whoever brought me here? Cross!"

It doesn't even have pockets. And it *should* have pockets! The blazer has what *looks* like a pocket, but it's been stitched over so you can't actually put anything in it. Unbelievable. What a miserable excuse for an article of clothing.

I fidget with the traitorous stitching as I push off the wall, that spike of anger bringing my focus back to practical matters. *I am in another world, or at least someplace so unlike the familiar that it might as well be another world. This world has magic, which is incredible, but I'm also in a weird not-quite-classroom with only the clothes on my back and my wits, and the clothes are pretty sub-par. I need more resources and fast before whatever dangers exist in this world get a whiff of easy prey.*

We probably should have thought of that before laughing loud enough to disturb the underworld. If there's anything nasty waiting in the wings, it definitely knows we're here.

Yeah. Shit. I need a weapon.

I quickly move to each desk and peer inside for useful loot. The desks are all spotlessly clean, not even a layer of dust, and all but one are completely empty.

In the exception I find a stoppered glass bottle, unmarked, filled with green liquid I don't recognize. *Potion? Bottles of weird liquid are usually potions in fantasy settings.*

That's assuming this is a fantasy story, which isn't a sure bet. Sure, the abyss is pretty unscientific, but unnatural abandoned schools are pretty common in supernatural horror.

I take the mystery bottle and am forced to hold it in one hand as I do not have any *pockets* to store it in. I take off my pocketless blazer and use it to wrap the maybe-potion so it won't break if I accidentally drop it, which is depressingly likely to happen.

Step one: find a weapon. Step two: find some fucking pockets.

I turn the door handle and step out into a plain, sterile hallway. Plain wooden floor, plain ceiling tiles once again devoid of lights—I can still see perfectly well, though the lighting is a little colder than sunlight—and more doors interspersed regularly. No writing on or above the doors, no grime or signs of decay. To my right, the hall turns a corner and continues out of sight. To my left, there's a ghost.

She's got skin paler than mine—which I assure you is an achievement, as I detest being under the harsh light of the daystar—and stringy black hair that completely obscures her face. She's wearing a gauzy white dress that seems to flutter in an unfelt breeze, and her bare feet are covered in dirt. She stands there with her arms at her sides, so still you could mistake her for a statue or a photo image if not for the fluttering dress. She is, to put it cleanly, the very image of a Japanese horror ghost girl.

We don't know she's a ghost. She might just have bad haircare and avoid sunlight, like you.

Hey! I take excellent care of my hair.

I turn to face the almost-certainly-a-ghost and wave. "Hey there! Quick question: are you a ghost? Because that would really help me pin down the genre of this setting. My gut says isekai fantasy, but my gut is a dumb series of meat tubes and the abandoned school suggests something more urban or supernatural, and if you're a ghost that's a strong tick for the horror column. It's important to know your genre when waking up in another world."

The pale woman doesn't respond, but she does take a step forward. Her body twists at an odd angle, her movement twitchy and unnatural in the exact way J-horror ghosts tend to move.

"I guess that's kind of an answer but I would really prefer something more concrete and definite, please and thank you," I say as I carefully step back. "Anything? Just going to continue being silent? You're not much of a conversationalist, are you?"

It's weird that I'm not afraid right now. I'm usually terrified of ghosts in movies, or of anything that reminds me of death. Why isn't this scaring me?

The very-definitely-a-ghost ignores me, rudely, and continues stuttering forward step-by-step. I keep pace, trying not to make any moves that are too sudden or aggressive. She's stick thin and frail looking, but so am I, and unlike me ghosts are rarely burdened by the curse of flesh.

"No offense, but you seem like trouble. I'm just going to go head in the other direction, okay? We cool? Cool."

I wave goodbye to the ghost lady and keep my eyes trained on her as I walk backwards toward the corner turn. She doesn't increase her pace as I increase mine, which I take as a good sign. When my back hits the wall my gaze automatically flits toward the new hall on my right, and when I snap back to the girl in pale she's right in front of me, raising a kitchen knife over her head.

She stabs the knife down at my delicate, vulnerable body, and my piss-poor reflexes are way too slow to save me. The impulse to dodge has only just reached my muscles when the knife sinks into my left shoulder. Pain lances through that arm and makes my fingers convulse involuntarily. I scream at the sudden, blinding agony and my other hand clenches around the blazer-wrapped bottle. Before I can think to do something, anything, the pale lady rips the knife back out and looms over me.

It hurts, it hurts, why does it hurt so much? I stumble away from my assailant into the hall around the corner and grit my teeth against the pain as a whimper escapes my lips. My injured arm is shaking and blood soaks into my blouse. I can still move my arm but every motion brings a fresh spike of pain and it *hurts, it hurts, it hurts.* I glance back at the pale woman but she's just standing there, still as a statue, watching me.

There's a noise echoing off the walls, echoing out of her, a staccato pattern somewhere between gurgling and clicking, and there's a note of *amusement* to it. Entertainment. She's *laughing* at me. My shoulder is bleeding, my nerve endings are shrieking, and she is *laughing at me.* Mocking me.

Fury joins the pain.

She takes a step forward and I take a step back, but I know she's just toying with me. She could be on me again in a single blink but she's drawing this out so she can play with her food. Maybe she wants me to be afraid, wants to taste my terror and feed on it, but I feel no fear. There is only the red haze of anger and pain mixing together in my veins and pouring over my body from the wound in my shoulder. I can't outrun her. I can't reason with her. The only way out is through.

No weapons. No chance of disarming her. The only tool at my disposal is the bottle. Another exchange of steps. Another shock of blistering pain. *If it's a healing potion, drinking it will only delay the inevitable. If it's harmful, drinking it is a bad idea anyway. Easy choice.*

Another step, flinch, pause, and I pull the blazer off the bottle. I clutch the jacket with my weaker hand while my uninjured hand grips the bottle tight. I only get one chance at this.

My opponent tilts her head as if curious, and this time when her hair shifts it stops covering her face. The upper half of her face would almost be normal if it weren't for the blood pooling in empty eye sockets, but the lower half of her face is a mass of needle teeth from ear to ear, rows and rows of sharpened enamel like the mouth of a shark but somehow wider and deeper.

The monster comes closer and I don't move away. Pause, step, pause, step. She's an arm's length away now, and when she takes her next step I move at the same time. I swing the bottle at her face as she lunges at me with the knife and she's still *faster*, damn her, but she doesn't even try to dodge my attack.

Her knife stabs into my outer thigh, another shock of agony but nothing lethal, and when the glass bottle shatters against her needle-toothed face and the green liquid within begins to seep into her hair and skin and teeth, everything the liquid touches starts to *melt*.

The monster lets go of her knife and claws at her face, a surprisingly human scream emitting from her throat before it is silenced by the acid eating into her flesh. I stare with wide eyes as the acid corrodes her clutching hands and I spare a moment to be relieved that I never tried to drink that horrid elixir. Then I let the anger back in.

I pull the knife out of my leg, a terrible decision for my health but an excellent decision for my *having a knife*. The lady in white falls to her knees, still grasping at her melting face, and I drive the knife into her shoulder. I sink it deep and *twist*, enjoying the feeling as the knife meets resistance and pushes through. I withdraw the knife and stab her thigh, repaying her for both wounds, but her throat is melting and she can't *scream* like I did so it isn't enough, it hasn't been made *fair*. I stab her again, again, again, again, not caring where the blows land so long as they draw blood. Her insides are human, I discover, despite how inhuman her face looked, and she bleeds the same red as coats my clothing. The body stills and I keep hacking, slashing, stabbing, chopping, until the last of my fury spills out and the exhaustion hits me all at once.

I slump against the wall next to the corpse. I breathe: in, out, in, out. Heavy gulps of precious oxygen. Adrenaline fading. Crash. The last of the awful energy that filled me as I butchered the not-quite-human monster escapes from my chest in uncontrollable laughter. I laugh and shudder and collapse, spent, on the wooden floor now covered in our blood.

I want to lie there for an eternity. I want to lie there and hug myself and ignore the world around me, but the pain forces me to keep moving. My shoulder and my leg both ache and burn, demanding my attention. I'm losing blood, but not quickly; given that monster's sadism, I suspect luck isn't to blame for my survival. I'm familiar enough with the sight of my own blood to know that neither wound will kill me if I stop the bleeding, but I still need to *stop the fucking bleeding*.

I cut my blazer up with my new knife, roughly sawing through the cloth with a blade not meant for the task. It suffices, and I tie a makeshift bandage around each injury. My shoulder is harder to bandage than my leg thanks to some awkward angles involved, but I'm well-practiced at the art of wound care.

After tending my fresh wounds I force myself to my feet and stare down at the mess I've made; my blouse is more red than white, and even after wiping my hands on my skirt they're still stained with my own blood and that of the monster. The thing that tried to kill me is in a much worse state, of course. It failed, and it died. I killed it.

But only barely, comes the thought unbidden. *Only because it was playing with you. Only because the liquid in the bottle was acid. You stumbled about while it laughed at you, and then you got lucky. The roll of a metaphysical d20 was all that kept you from being dead on the ground in that thing's place.*

I squeeze my knife. We won. We won, and that's all that matters. There's no point in obsessing over might-have-beens. We won, and we will keep winning. I'm not dying here. This is my story, and I'm going to win.

How? How are you going to win? You traded acid for a knife that you don't know how to use.

It's a knife. It's not hard. Just stick them with the pointy end. I stick the corpse again to illustrate my point, and my upper lip curls.

There's a pretty big difference between stabbing a dead woman and battling a living being. Face it: you're weak, you're clumsy, and you're slow. You're more likely to hurt yourself with that thing than you are to actually take someone in a fight.

"Shut up!" I hiss, hands starting to shake. "Shut up, shut up, just shut the fuck up and leave me alone. I don't need this right now, I really, really don't need this, so just *shut up!*"

You're the one making noise. Attracting more monsters. It'll be your fault when they come, and then they'll laugh at your little knife and tear you to pieces. They'll kill you. But maybe that's what—

I slap myself, hard. My head jerks to the side and my injured arm screams but I let both stay at that odd angle, staring into nothing. There is silence. There is stillness.

I straighten up and force a smile to my face. "I am calm. I am in control. This is my story, and I am going to win."

I grip the knife tightly and start walking.

11

I limp my way through another hallway full of doors. Each door I open shows the same scene: another empty classroom with another endless void in the place of the far wall. I poke my head into each and give a visual scan for anything of value or interest, but every one is identical to my starting room, save for a lack of writing on the chalkboard. I make a quick search of a few just in case there's another bottle of acid secreted away, but no dice. No loot, no writing, so I keep moving.

I don't think ghosts are usually that solid, I muse as I investigate another empty classroom. *I don't remember ghosts ever being weak to acid, either, in all the stories I've read, and those teeth were weird. It almost felt a bit sci-fi, like some horrible lab experiment loosed in a test environment. The void feels strongly fantasy, though. I guess there could be some genre cross-pollination at work. Either way, my analysis of this story is skewing closer to "horror" than "power fantasy."* I grimace. *Which means I'm going to need to work a lot harder to get my hands on magic. When I meet whatever put me here, I'm going to stab it.*

Two bends in the hall later, I find my next clue: a classroom different from all others by virtue of the child-sized doll sitting atop one of the desks.

The doll has a porcelain face with painted eyes, a puffy eggshell dress covered in lace and ribbon, and perfect posture as it sits with its hands folded in its lap. The doll is mostly shades of off-white with two glaring exceptions: the scarlet butterfly crystal hairpin threaded through its lifelike hair, and the glittery pink backpack looped through its arms.

I practically salivate at the sight of a backpack, an honest-to-gods *backpack*. Sure, it's pink and sparkly and deeply offends my darkly gothic sensibilities, but it has *pockets*!

I take a cautious step inside and give a quick glance around. Messy writing is scratched into the three standing walls: the words "I AM A PIECE OF A PIECE OF ME" repeating over and over in spiraling fractal patterns. The words get mixed up in places and blend together, but the message always surfaces again. Some of the scratch marks are stained with what looks like dried blood, as if someone carved these words into the walls with their fingernails until their hands were raw and bleeding.

The walls present a fascinating puzzle, but I elect to ignore that puzzle to focus on the pretty doll and the loot it's wearing. I heft the knife and glance between it and the doll.

You should stab the doll. There's a one hundred percent chance that thing is going to come to life and attack you.

A reasonable decision. Counterpoint: what if it comes to life and it's nice? And then I've stabbed the poor thing and it will look at me with those fake doll eyes and cry a single tear as it dies alone and betrayed, spurned by a monster it only wanted to befriend. All it wanted was a friend, Morgan, *someone to hug and cherish, and you killed it. And every time I look at the backpack I stole off its dead doll body I'll have to remember that look of pain and loss. Do you want me to have a crisis of conscience every time I have to take something out of my stolen backpack?*

I circle the doll as I debate with myself, never letting it out of my sight. I wince with every other step, my leg still whining at me about the open stab wound.

So you might kill a friendly abomination, so what? Better than getting killed by a bloodthirsty abomination! It's finite loss versus infinite loss, and equal gain.

Okay, first of all, please avoid saying anything that even remotely reminds me of Pascal's stupid wager. Second of all, what if killing the doll curses me? That's some classic moral fable shit: the protagonist gets offered a choice to be kind or to be cruel and when they choose cruelty, they are punished for it. Severely. This could be a test. What if we're the Beast and this is our Enchantress?

Does this really seem like the kind of story that has fairytale tests of character? The first living thing we encountered in this world tried to murder *us, and we haven't seen another sign of life since. Not even bugs! Have you noticed that there are no bugs around? Of course you have, you're me. So far all the evidence points to everything in this world hating us and wanting us dead.*

I have to admit, I make a good point. *Okay, look, I just don't want to start my adventuring career off with a mistake that I'll regret for the whole rest of the story and moan about when I'm contemplating moral choices. Let's try diplomacy first, and if that doesn't work, stabby stabby time.*

I step back in front of the doll and clear my throat. "Hi there, my name's Morgan and—"

Hmm. Should we take this opportunity to pick a more interesting name? I mean, we're in a fantastical otherworld with weird horrors, don't you think "Morgan" is a little boring? Like, it worked when we wanted a name that was very normal and easy for people to learn, but I feel like we should inject some spice to our name in this new world.

We could go by "Alice" instead? Strange girl in a strange land?

I said spice! Throw some flavor on there, make it cool and badass. How about "Malice" as a name?

Horrifically edgy. The very personification of chuunibyou delusion. I love it.

I cough to ineffectively hide my tangent. The doll has yet to move or respond. "Disregard that, please and thank you. Hi there, my name is *Malice*, and it is a pleasure to make your acquaintance. If you have an acquaintance to make. Are you alive?" The doll does not respond. "I'm kind of hoping you aren't alive, because I really want that hairpin and that backpack and I'd hate to steal from someone who is nice and alive."

I pause and process what I just said. "Sorry, that sounds rude. I don't mean that I wish you were dead, just that it would be very convenient if you were amenable to letting me have your stuff, and I really don't want you to murder me. I'd love to be friends with you, if you are both alive and not evil. Even if you are evil, so long as you're friendly!"

The doll continues to do nothing, its painted eyes staring past me. I nod. "Cool, cool, that's great. So, it seems like you aren't alive. If you are alive, I would really, really appreciate you doing something to show that, because otherwise I'm going to take your silence as tacit approval to slit your throat and steal your stuff."

Another pause, another lack of response. "It's not that I want to hurt you, I really don't, it's just that if you're not friendly I can't take the chance of you springing to life and murdering me. You understand that, right?" Silence fills the air and the doll remains still.

I let the moment stretch out, waiting for any kind of reaction from the doll, but nothing changes. Carefully, knife at the ready in case it moves, I lay my other hand—ow, ow, my shoulder—on the doll's throat and try to feel for a pulse, for warmth, for anything. The doll is cold and lifeless, just like a doll should be. No motion beneath the skin, no sign of anything strange. It's just an ordinary doll.

I sigh to myself, apologize to the doll, and stab it in the throat. The blade sinks in easily and without noise. The doll doesn't make any noise either, still doesn't move or react, but when I pull the knife free the blade is coated in pale, milky blood. The hole in the doll's throat bleeds pink liquid that drips onto the pretty dress and ruins it.

What the fuck? That's the only cogent response I can muster. *No, really, what the fucking fuck? What?*

I'm committed now so I stab the doll's chest for good measure, aiming for where its heart would be if it were human. The blade sinks in just as easily and more milky blood pours out when I withdraw the knife. I'm making a mess and some of that pink is getting on my hands and clothes, adding new shades to the bloodstains already present. And still, even bleeding from two stab wounds, the damned doll doesn't make any sign that it's alive, that I'm killing a living thing.

What is this? Why is this? Did someone fill a doll with fake pink blood? What is the point of this thing, and those walls, and this whole fucking room? Why is a high-class doll wearing a middle schooler's backpack, and why does it bleed blood like milk, and why are those words scratched into those walls? None of this feels organic, none of it feels real. It's like it was all hand placed for me to find.

When the blood stops flowing, I finally accept that the doll probably isn't going to move. I still keep the knife clutched in one hand as I nick the doll's ruby hairpin and attach the scarlet butterfly to my hair. Maneuvering the backpack off is a little trickier since I have to move the straps around the doll's arms and one of *my* arms is still in quite a bit of pain, but the doll is light and easily adjusted. When both articles of loot have been retrieved, I pick the doll up and throw it into the abyss.

Sorry, but I can't afford to take any chances. I empty the backpack onto the nearest desk and school supplies spill out: pens in black and red, a pack of colored pencils, highlighters in three shades, scissors, two spiral notebooks, and two composition notebooks. No calculator, I note with annoyance. Calculators are always great to have in fantasy settings when you want to show off to the locals. Granted, the modern school doesn't exactly scream "pseudo-medieval fantasy world," but nothing here seems like it *belongs*. None of the items that pour out of the backpack have brands on them, not even maker's marks.

These were placed here, just like the doll and the bottle and the needle-toothed monster. Whatever brought me here set these in my path. I search the desk interiors but come up empty. I'm itching to investigate this room further to try and understand it, to understand the writing on the walls, but I can't let myself get distracted; there are bigger mysteries at play here than anything I've uncovered, and I highly doubt Needles the Not-A-Ghost was the only threat in this weird fake school.

I load the backpack up with all its sundry school supplies and loop the pink horror through my arms, which causes another blistering bout of pain from the injury on my shoulder—I'm lucky the straps are long, because I'm really far too tall to be wearing a child's backpack. *I really hope this setting has healing magic, because otherwise this is going to be a bitch and a half to deal with.*

No fake ghost accosts me when I leave the room this time, which is nice. I pass a few more empty classrooms and round a fourth bend that *should* bring me back to the hallway I started in, but instead the hall around the corner abruptly ends at a flight of stairs leading up.

Strike another law of physics from the roster, and add alien geometries to the genre discussion. Still firmly in the horror camp, but now we're starting to lean cosmic.

The stairway only goes up, so up I climb.

Climbing a flight of stairs, I discover, is *hellish* when you have an open leg wound. Every step sends another stab of pain up my leg, and I have to stifle every gasp and shriek into a grunt or hiss. By the third flight I'm already winded, and the stairs keep going up; where there should be an opening to another part of the school there's just a blank wall and more stairs, and looking up, I don't see an ending to the stairwell. It's one of those stairwells that goes stairs-flat-stairs-flat, so I take a break on the next flat and sit down.

I lie against the wall with my new backpack cushioning me, knife still clutched tightly in one hand, and for a few moments I just breathe.

We are in terrible shape. Just truly, genuinely terrible.

What did you expect? We spent a good two thirds of our life cooped up indoors reading books and dreaming of magic. And I was always frail, even as a little girl.

You were frail because you didn't exercise, which is a problem we need to fix and fast now that we're in serious life-threatening danger.

I agree! I really do. Our pathetic nerd body is not going to cut it in this horrible nightmare world. But I can't exactly do a few push-ups and get buff. If we really want to get stronger, we need to cheat. A spell of strengthening, an experimental gene treatment, a stat boost, whatever form of physical power progression exists in this setting. But hard work will take too long for too little gain.

I feel like that attitude is why we're so weak in the first place.

I shrug, which does positively miserable things to my wounded shoulder and forces me to bite back another yelp of pain. I wince and let out a strained breath. *This is bad. This is really bad. I can't win another fight like this.*

I glare up at the seemingly endless stairwell and say aloud, "Doesn't this seem a little unfair to you, whoever you are? Isn't this all a bit much? You send me to another world, dress me in a stupid uniform, throw me against a monster with a knife, and you don't even give me magic? No spells, no stat boosts, not even a one-of-a-kind magic item? Don't I deserve at least one cheat ability? Don't I deserve *something* to help me survive?"

I rant against whatever entity dropped me here, not expecting a response, but then my backpack gets heavier.

I blink. No voice from above accompanies the sudden weight but as I shift my seating I can just *feel* something new inside my stolen backpack. I eagerly take it off—ow, ow, ow—and shuffle it around into my lap. I set the knife beside me and dig through the pockets, searching frantically. It doesn't take long to find the new arrival: a crystal flask about the size of a water bottle, filled to the stopper with luminescent red liquid. There's a tag that says "Drink Me" tied around the neck of the bottle.

I pop the stopper and raise the flask to my lips but stop myself a second before drinking. *This could be more acid. It would be a very dick move for this to be acid, but it could be acid.* I hesitate, consider, then carefully spill a drop onto my shirt. Nothing burns, so I stop hesitating and down a big gulp, and then a second gulp because I suddenly realize how thirsty I am.

As I recap the flask and the liquid flows down my throat, I feel a warmth start to spread through my whole body. Wherever the warmth touches, I feel renewed and revitalized, all my aches and pains fading away.

I carefully set the flask down and unwrap the bandages on my shoulder and thigh. After scraping off some dried blood with my fingernails, I find smooth, pale, unbroken skin. I poke the skin around the area a few times just to be sure, but everything is completely normal. I stretch my muscles and sigh contentedly, luxuriating in my freshly restored range of motion. The warmth lingers and soothes my strained body, slowly fading away as I stay in this perfect moment.

As the last of the restorative warmth leaves me, an ugly thought springs to mind and I glare at the bottle suspiciously.

"You know," I confide to the empty air, "this seems a lot like a healing potion. And hey, that's neat. Healing potions are neat, and I definitely needed some healing. But it occurs to me that a healing potion is not what I asked for. A healing potion is not a spell, or a stat boost, or even a one-of-a-kind magic item. They practically give these things away in RPGs."

"Of course, maybe it wasn't a healing potion at all! Maybe this special little elixir gave me regeneration that'll last the whole rest of the story and save my ass time and time again. And that would be great! That's a pretty handy cheat ability. The difference between a consumable healing item and a permanent healing factor is, and you don't need me to tell you this, absolutely vast. And it would really go a long way toward improving my opinion of you, mysterious-entity-that-has-just-confirmed-its-existence, if this turned out to be more than just a dinky little healing potion. So let's run a quick test."

I glance at the kitchen knife, but it won't work for this. Kitchen knives are great for chopping and solid at stabbing, not so great at making precise incisions. Plus, that thing's filthy with the dried blood of three different people—for a certain definition of the word—and there is a very high likelihood that I'd get an infection if I cut myself with it.

I fish through my backpack and find the scissors inside. They wouldn't be my first choice in most circumstances but I know how to make them do what I want. I lay one scissor blade across the skin of my forearm, breathe, and make the cut.

It doesn't hurt, but I wasn't expecting it to. I watch the thin line of red bloom to life and start counting in my head. I reach one hundred without any noticeable changes so I take a bit of blouse not already soaked red and wipe off the blood. The incision is still there. I glare skyward for a second time and accuse, "Cheapskate. What kind of supernatural reality warper can't spring for a basic regeneration package?"

I sigh. *Guess I have to get my hands on superpowers the hard way.* I stow the half-drunk potion and slowly get off the ground, picking up my knife as I do. I consider keeping the bloody remains of my blazer but decide that an ignominious grave is karmic retribution for its crimes against pockets.

Inventory: kitchen knife, backpack full of school supplies, and a half-empty healing potion. Truly I have come prepared for adventure.

My climb goes quicker now that I'm not limping and holding back screams, and after five more flights of stairs I experience a sudden change of scenery; one second I'm walking up another flight, the endless stairwell above me, and the next instant I'm standing at the abrupt end of the stairwell halfway through a set of stairs, like the top half of the structure was laser-cut to be flush with the ground.

And there *is* ground: an expanse of dirt and moss bare of underbrush and broken only by the twisting roots of gnarled, crooked trees. A heavy canopy of leaves blocks any light that might come from the sky, but once again my vision is unobscured by the seeming lack of light sources. I breathe in the fresh air and allow myself a smile. I can smell wet earth and pine, and it reminds me of wandering through the woodlands back home, dreaming up stories or play-acting little scenes. I cock my head to the side and let sound filter in, but the only thing I hear is the gentle rustle of leaves.

So an abandoned school in the shadow dimension teleports me to an eerie, empty forest. No birds chirping, no bugs chittering.

I walk a few steps from the school entrance and stoop down to inspect the forest floor. The moss looks real, it looks alive and healthy, but I don't see any bugs. Nothing burrowing through the earth or trekking across the dirt, nothing nesting in the moss or crawling over a root. I stand back up and look around. Everything is so *still*. Even the canopy above is frozen in place, like someone took a photo of a real forest and plastered it onto a skybox. The sound of shifting leaves is completely disconnected from the reality of that stagnant image. I extend my arms out to feel the wind, but the air is dead. *If the air is so still, what's sending these scents my way? How can it smell so fresh?* There is sound and smell but not the accompanying sensation or sight.

No wind, no stars in the sky . . . yeah, this is a navigational nightmare waiting to happen. How do I get out of here when every direction looks identical?

"Mind handing me a compass?" I ask the empty air. "You know, since you can't give me superpowers but you can make magic items from nothing."

The air declines to humor my request, so I flip it off. *I guess we just pick a direction and start walking.* The forest is fairly open, owing to the lack of underbrush and the wide berth between trees, so I can see all around. It all looks the same to my eyes, though I'm sure anyone who knows anything about wilderness survival could spot something I'm missing. The clearing I'm in isn't even really a clearing, just another natural gap between trees. If I didn't know it was here I might not even notice the hole in the ground.

A new scent reaches my nose and I frown. Why do I smell smoke? If there was a fire in the forest I would see it, and there's no wind to blow it toward me so where—

I glance back at the stairwell and catch a few wisps of smoke rising up. And within, barely visible but getting brighter and brighter, a strange green light.

Fuck.

The ground starts to rumble.

Fuck!

I bolt for the nearest tree as fast as my stupid weak legs can carry me. I throw myself behind the gnarled trunk, bunch up to make my body as small as possible, and hold my breath.

Then the world explodes.

III

Green-gold flame devours the world.

A wave of heat and force blows past my hiding spot and scorches away the lichen coating the forest floor. I feel the shockwave in my bones and see the canopy shudder and catch fire. The tree behind me creaks and strains, but it holds. I hear an awful splintering as another tree is not so lucky, and I try to make myself even smaller against my shelter.

The shockwave passes, but the strange green fire clings to blackened dirt and patches of moss. The canopy above, still blazing, rains embers and ash on the forest floor. The fire is spreading, and soon my shelter will catch.

I stumble away from the tree that saved me and spare a glance back toward the stairwell, or what remains of it. There's a wrecked pit where the stairwell once was, and around that pit the soil is scorched and the fire burns bright emerald. *No going back.*

I stare at the ruins as I back away, and then fury replaces self-preservation and I scream my frustrations to the canopy of leaves. "A FUCKING EXPLOSION!? WAS THAT REALLY FUCKING NECESSARY!? I nearly die to a bastard with a knife, I have to limp around that horrid little school with an injured leg, my *very polite request* gets *mocked*, and then you *blow it all up*!? When I find you, you little shit, I'm going to—"

My petulant whining dies in my throat when I see the first monster.

Imagine that someone took a dog and stretched it like taffy until it was in the rough shape of a giant spider, legs and all. A fluffy fur coat covers the bulbous back half of its body and the flattened front, and the fur continues onto eight segmented legs that twist up before coming back down and ending in horrible little stumps.

The face is the worst part: a cramped cluster of eight watery dog eyes, a squashed nose, shrunken ears, and jutting mandible-fangs that obscure its mouth. It is, in a word, hideous. And there are more of them crawling into view from deeper within the forest, moving toward the source of the shockwave . . . and circling around the inferno to come straight for the idiot girl who was making so much noise.

I think I might be incapable of learning from my mistakes, I muse.

Less self-deprecating, more running! We are not getting eaten by tarantula-mutts!

I sprint away from the flames and the horrible spider-dogs, and as I run I hear a chorus of very tarantula-like hissing rise up from behind me. I keep my gaze firmly focused on the path in front of me, watching for every bit of root and moss that might slow me down or trip me. I dodge and weave and I don't dare look back.

And yet, despite the sense of urgency, I'm still not *afraid*. I understand rationally that I need to run because getting caught and dying would be bad, but all I feel is adrenaline and focus. Normally just errant consideration of my own mortality is enough to send me into a near panic attack, but now I'm in mortal danger and *I am not afraid.*

Something is wrong, and I think I know who—or what—to blame.

I can hear the hissing getting closer as I make my winding path through the trees. Adrenaline gives me momentum but my legs are already burning and I curse my frail body for what feels like the dozenth time today.

Dirt, root, moss, dirt, just run, just keep running. If I stop moving, I die. Behind me, one of the hissing noises gets sharper and then falters. I find an even path in front of me and chance a quick look behind. The tarantula-dogs are still skittering toward me at top speed, but one of them is pulling itself off the ground, spidery legs all mixed up and being slowly untangled.

Flashbulb: *they have legs like spiders, so they move like spiders, which means they're* clumsy *like spiders!*

I fix my gaze forward and start charting a new path, aiming for every bit of uneven terrain I can hit. It's risky, but I have to bet that the spider-mutts will be clumsier than I am.

I clamber awkwardly over a giant root, crest a bump in the dirt, and nearly slip on a damp patch of moss, but the monstrous chorus behind me stops getting closer. Dodge that branch, jump that root, steady footing on the lichen. Run, run, keep running.

My breath is coming harder now, each gasping inhalation setting fire to my lungs, but after the way my day started this is only mildly torturous. I fight to keep one foot in front of the other no matter how loudly my body complains about mistreatment. *Pillows and blankets for a whole day,* I promise it. *Every soft object I can find all piled in a nest, and pajamas if we can wrangle them. Just gotta keep moving a little farther.*

More sounds of spidery frustration reach my ears, and the noises are getting farther back now. They're losing ground, falling behind. I can do this. I can survive this.

My luck runs out.

I'm too slow cresting a root and my foot catches on it, sending me tumbling to the ground. I have just enough presence of mind to keep the knife angled away from my own body—it would be utterly humiliating to die by my own weapon—but I still hit the dirt hard and lose what breath I had left in my lungs. The shock of it keeps me pinned to the soil for precious seconds I can't afford to burn, desperately trying to suck in air, and when I finally draw a good clean breath I scramble to push off the ground before the monster can catch up, but I'm too late.

The tarantula-dog skitters over the root I tripped on and swoops down at me with those giant fangs. I don't have time to think; I duck low and lunge at the monster's soft underbelly with my knife, aiming at what passes for a neck on its hideous misshapen body. One of its fangs gouges my arm and I scream at the fresh shock of agony, but my blade finds purchase in its flesh.

The monster rears back and hisses angrily at me before I can rip my knife out. *Shouldn't you be in excruciating pain!? Fucking die!* I desperately want my weapon back but I can't waste this opportunity, so I bolt before it can come crashing back down.

I run through the woods, clutching my injured arm and blinking away the tears that are welling up in my eyes. Pain pulses with every step, every motion, and my exhaustion is mounting. The adrenaline keeps me going but it won't last forever, and I am so tired. I can't do this much longer. I can't do this. *I can't do this.*

I take another step and the ground that was there a second ago *vanishes*, and then I'm falling.

I hit a slope and roll, keep rolling, all the way into water. I slip below the surface for an instant but the water is shallow and my hands find a bed of pebbles to push off of. I rise out of the water on hands and knees and stumble to my feet.

I look around wildly and find my surroundings have changed abruptly once more; where there was an endless forest before, now I'm standing in a rocky creek that stretches to the horizon both upstream and downstream. The water is crystal-clear, or was before my blood got mixed in. The slopes to either side of the river are steep but not so steep as to be impassable, and beyond those slopes I can see trees that sway with the breeze. The leaves are lighter in color than those of the canopy before, universally so, and the bark is lighter and smoother.

Above, I can finally see the sky: it's clear and blue and utterly cloudless, and there's not a trace of any sun. There seems to be light, at least; I could see just fine in the school and the forest but there was a coldness to the lighting, and now everything is cast in warm, pleasant tones. But there's no sun.

This place just keeps getting weirder. The tarantula-dogs come skittering and tumbling over the ridge of the slope, which really only heightens my indignation at whatever bastard god built this hell-world.

I clench my fists and grit my teeth through the pain. I can't outrun them. I can't fight them. But I will be *damned* if I die before giving this crappy world and its shitty maker a piece of my mind. Maybe a tiny measure of my burning hatred will stick in my tormentor like a splinter, or a thorn, or a shard of broken glass.

"Come at me!" I scream. "Rip and tear! Kill me, eat me, send me to whatever sick god put me here so I can *spit in her face!*"

The first monster dips a leg into the water and a flaming arrow—green flame, not orange or red—sends it flying back with a furious hiss. I blink, stunned, and stare as arrows strike the second, third, fourth fifth sixth—*all of them* take perfect shots and are slammed against the dirt slope by the force of the projectiles.

The tarantula-dogs still twitch and struggle despite the arrows embedded in their vital parts. *These things just won't die.* I hear the snap of fingers, and an instant later the entire slope erupts in that familiar green-gold flame.

They don't die quickly, even with all the flame pouring in. They struggle and scream and writhe, and the flame writhes too; green fire pours past mandibles into mouths and builds, the glow of flame visible through stretched-out skin, until it explodes from the inside. The spider-dogs are torn apart from within, and the last horrible hiss fades as a dozen charred corpses lie in pieces on scorched earth. There is a second finger-snap, and the flames vanish.

What just happened? Magic? Definitely magic. Fire magic. Green fire magic. Just like the flames in the forest.

I hear footsteps from behind and whirl to see a pointy-eared redheaded hunter in a scarlet-trim fur cloak swaggering down the far slope. He's got a quiver on his back, and an unstrung bow painted red and gold rests in the quiver. His features are too sharp, almost predatory, and the obnoxious smirk plastered on his face makes him look like a genuine grade-A asshole.

His glowing orange eyes entirely ignore me as he marches *over* the creek. The bastard's gold-embroidered hunting boots don't even get damp as he walks on water to reach the other side of the stream, and here I am with my everything soaked through. Little flames dance across the surface of the water as he passes, all of them green.

Fucker's got a theme, that's for sure. Elf or faerie. Is there a difference in this setting?

The elfy type strolls into the middle of the slope of charred corpses and holds his hand out, waves it in an arc, then brings it to his mouth and swallows. I don't see anything enter his mouth, but his eyes glow a little brighter in response to some invisible stimulus.

He sniffs disdainfully at the messy assortment of dead spider-dogs. "A pitiful meal." His voice is deep and throaty, but the tone is pure arrogance.

"Hey!" I shout in his direction as I stomp through the creek in my soggy shoes and soggy socks and soggy *everything*. "You piece of shit, you used me as bait!"

The maybe-fae turns at my exclamation and his eyes burn orange-gold as he shoots me a withering glare. "Watch your tone, little girl. Prey animals should know their place and be grateful for the charity of their betters. I did not have to save you from an excruciating death."

I get right up in his face and poke his chest with my finger, finding his richly detailed tunic oddly soft. *Is this bastard actually wearing silk armor? Fucking what?* "You used me as *bait*! I'm not an idiot, I recognize that fire. It's the same fucking color as the fire that blew up the school. You know, the school I was *right outside of*? You lured the monsters right to me with that flare, which makes *all of this*," I gesture to my bloody arm wound and drenched clothing, "your fucking fault!"

He sneers down at me—he's actually tall enough to do that, which is an unusual occurrence given that I'm 6'2"—but he doesn't draw a weapon or burn my head off. "As if I would notice a gnat like you. I cannot be blamed if you happen to get in the way of my hunt. Accept that you were simply in the wrong place at the wrong time, and be grateful I deigned to save your worthless life."

I curl my lip and sneer right back. "If I'm beneath your notice then you weren't really saving me, now were you? I just happened to get caught *in the way of your hunt*. So are you lying about saving me, or are you lying about not using me as bait? Either way you're twisting the truth."

This is such a gamble. He could kill me just for being impudent, but if he's a fae and fae have rules here then I might be able to weasel some kind of debt out of this.

His eyes narrow but he doesn't counter my retort, so I push my luck and insist, "Grievances are owed, for reckless endangerment if nothing more. Do you not respect your debts? Or are you a creature without *honor*?"

In a flash there's a sword at my throat, and I idly note the unique design: it looks like a hunting sword, short and straight and single edged, but the blade shines in all the hues of sunset and the golden cross guard is shaped into a breathtaking facsimile of leaves and branches. A truly beautiful weapon.

The hunter is less pleasing to look at, his eyes smoldering with barely contained rage. A vein pulses on his forehead. "You would *dare* impugn my honor?

You mock a Rider of the Wild Hunt, a Huntsman handpicked by the Wolf Queen herself. *Recant*, or I will stain this river with your blood."

I meet his gaze and let the frustration I feel drip from my every word. "In the past few hours I have been stabbed, bitten, soaked, and nearly blown up. I *know* which of us is in the wrong. If you want to make me recant, then fucking *make me*."

Those glowing eyes blaze bright and I'm already composing the tirade I'll throw at this world's god when I meet her, but he still doesn't kill me. The fire goes out, leaving an altogether more curious light in his eyes, and for the first time he really looks at me. His gaze lingers on my hair longer than the rest of me—the hairpin, maybe—before snapping back. "You know I am more than capable of killing you. Are you truly not afraid to die at my hand?"

"Do I seem afraid?" And I'm not. I should be, I really should be, but I'm not. Why am I not scared? I have *diagnosed* thanatophobia and I'm mouthing off with a blade at my throat. I should be a gibbering wreck incapable of stringing words together beyond pleading for my life, but instead I'm talking shit to a fucking fae.

". . . No, I don't taste even an ounce of fear from you. What a strange little creature you are." He snorts and sheathes his sword in a fancy scabbard I'm only now noticing. The Huntsman shakes his head and scolds, "There is little pleasure in hunting a beast that does not know the fear of death. Killing you would be a waste of a curiosity. I will entertain your accusations, mortal. For petty slights, a petty concession will be afforded."

I rub my throat and consider the offer. *What I need is more than petty. For all his fire and fury earlier, he actually seems more intrigued by my boldness than offended by it. Let's see how far we can push that.* "Alright. Dry me off."

The Huntsman raises a solitary eyebrow.

"I'm sodden. My socks are soggy, my stupid uniform is soaked, and I've got notebooks in this bag that are undoubtedly suffering *severe* water damage right now. You're a big strong faerie with badass fire magic, can't you dry me off without burning me?"

Annoyance creeps back into the Rider's voice as he says, "Is that really what you would ask of one who rides with the Wild Hunt? My patience has limits, even for curiosities."

"You offered a *petty* concession, so I made a *petty* request." I give him my best worst look of innocence and flutter my eyelashes.

The corners of his mouth twitch. "My queen would like you, curiosity."

"Thank you." I preen. "I'm very likable."

"That wasn't a compliment."

Oh. "I'm choosing to interpret it as one regardless. Consider it death of the author."

The Huntsman sighs. "Oh yes, she would like you very much. [Controlled Flame]." He snaps his fingers and a wave of heat washes over me.

Okay, um, the fuck was that? Did I hear that right? Are we in litRPG territory now?

I shake out my clothing and find it all perfectly dry. A quick glance inside the glittery pink abomination shows that the contents are unharmed, even the notebooks! I zip it back up and grin, though a spike of pain from my arm makes me wince. *Okay, we should deal with that soon, but we have a healing potion so it's not a big deal.*

"Thank you, Huntsman. You can consider my grievance addressed."

"But I suspect," the Rider leads, "that you are not done taking up my time." He crosses his arms and looks down at me through half-lidded eyes. "Speak your piece, mortal."

Deep breath. Okay. "I want to make a deal." *Faeries like deals, that just has to be true.*

Golden eyes sharpen. "Do you, now?"

"I don't know where I'm going, and I need to. I need a compass, or something like a compass, that can lead me to where I need to be. Something that can find what I tell it to find, even if I don't know what I'm looking for."

I had contemplated asking for a taste of fire magic or maybe some kind of travel magic, but the former won't help me leave this weird place and I don't know any destinations for the latter. A magic compass won't help me fight, but the potential resource gains vastly outweigh anything else I could bargain for. I have to think long-term here.

The Huntsman laughs at me, a full-bellied chuckle that reverberates through the air. When the laughter stops, he asks me, "And who are you, child, to risk your life for sodden socks and make such brazen demands of a Rider of the Wild Hunt?"

I straighten up and smile with teeth. *Okay, okay. Just like we've rehearsed a hundred times in the mirror. This is our moment.* "I am the girl who will do whatever it takes to seize her ambitions. It is my nature to push at limits until they or I break. I will have all the world, Huntsman, or I will have nothing at all. My hunger is boundless and unceasing."

The Rider smirks. "What prideful words. But can you back them up? What could you offer me, famished little girl? What do you have to bargain with that I could not take by force?"

I roll my shoulders, match his smirk with my toothy grin, and reply, "My name. I'll sell you my name."

IV

Silence. Stillness. Pain in my arm. The Huntsman watches me, expression inscrutable. My blood drips onto the dirt.

Come on, bite. Fae like names, don't they? That one's a classic.

When he speaks again, his voice is deathly soft. "You would offer your name, and all that entails?"

"I would."

The Huntsman smiles. "You surprise me yet again, curiosity. Let us discuss terms."

Yes! Yes! Yes! Inwardly I'm dancing, but outwardly I try to keep up my cold, confident mask. I can't let him know how much I'm winging this. "Can you grant me the boon I desire? I need something that can guide me to places I don't even know the existence of, on vague headings like 'the nearest safe space' or 'a potential ally.' Is that possible?"

"I possess such a spell, and the authority to bestow it. Pathfinding is a specialty of my kind." His posture is amused and relaxed now, seeming to relish in the details.

"Excellent. It needs to interpret my requests benevolently and intelligently, that's very important. I want it to act on my intent, not screw me on the letter. Oh! Can I cast it infinitely or does it have to be limited use?" I'm getting excited now, fantasizing about my soon-to-be *magic spell*! I shouldn't be letting my enthusiasm through but I can't stop the smile that's spreading.

"Do you think your name worth a thousand discoveries?" the Huntsman chides me. "Your compass shall be called upon thrice, and not a single use more."

I don't like hearing that, but now that we're in the thick of the deal I have to be careful not to overstep. "Fine, not infinite, but only three? That's so few. At least five."

"Three has greater symbolic weight. If you wish for longevity, would you sacrifice benevolent intent?" The tone of his voice makes it clear he knows my answer.

Bad idea, very bad idea. "Three it is! I'm good with three, that's a nice round number."

"Then we have an accord. Thrice-seeking for a name." He looks at my hairpin again, then back to me, and asks, "Have you invoked before? Or will this be your first contract?"

I don't know what invoking is, though I can guess from context, so, "No, never."

Amusement flickers across his face and passes. "How interesting. Well, simply follow my lead and do what feels right. The Dreamweaver will guide you, if you listen to her."

Dreamweaver? Damn, I really want to ask about that but I get the feeling he'll charge me for the information.

The Huntsman holds out a hand, palm up, and summons green-gold flame. He calls out, "Azathoth, O Dreamweaver!" *Eh? Azathoth? That Azathoth!?* "I claim the right of channeling you granted my kind at the Fall of An Talamh. Bear witness to this contract and give it meaning. Hear our words and make them binding."

The pressure in the air rises. A weight descends upon me, smothering and all-encompassing: the weight of a god's attention. The world beyond fades into nothingness—not invisible, not gone, just not *important* compared to what's happening right here. That pressure, that attention, it slides over my body like a thousand hands caressing me, studying me, cherishing me, dissecting me. I am a bug under a microscope, a treasured possession being held, detritus in a petri dish, a child in her mother's arms. I want to vomit. I want to stay like this forever.

In that instant I feel more vulnerable than I did when the Huntsman's blade was at my throat, and I don't know—I can't know—if that's a good thing or a bad thing.

The Huntsman shivers and closes his eyes, perhaps lost in the same internal conflict, but then he opens them again and those glowing orbs burn like golden fire. "The Dreamweaver watches. Let us not disappoint her."

My mouth is dry, and I mutter dumbly, "Yeah."

The Huntsman speaks, clear and bold, "The contract is thus: a bestowal for a name. I offer my library of spells to pull from, and my mana to serve as a vessel for the Dreamweaver's grace." The flame in his hand flickers. "Speak your dream, invoker."

That oppressive, joyous, terrible weight settles on my shoulders and whispers to me in a language I can't even begin to fathom, but some part of my brain knows exactly what is being said and *obeys*. My mouth moves without my will. "I want a compass that will lead me to destinations I don't yet know exist. I want a pathfinder to all my desires."

The flickering flame becomes a disk of fire, and then that crude circle becomes a wheel with three spokes. "I believe the spell [Find the Path] meets those criteria." The Huntsman lowers his hand and the burning wheel stays fixed in place, floating in the air between us. He smirks again. "It would seem Azathoth agrees. But all magic comes at a price. I have offered a spell to be bestowed, the mana to bring it to life, and the grace of the Dreamweaver to bind it to your soul. What price shall you pay for this great gift, invoker?"

Deep breath. *Goodbye, Morgan Mallory.* I speak my old name and it vanishes from my mind. For a moment there is only emptiness, a hollowness in my chest, but then the void fills up as I take my new name and make it mine, make it the only name that rings true. *Malice. I am Malice.* I am whole again, as much as I can ever be.

My hand is lifted by the will of a god and the burning wheel sears itself into my palm. I grip my hand tight, an act of *my* will, not hers, and fight through the pain. The flames flicker out, but when I open my hand I see the wheel's brand burned black against my pasty white skin. I feel a pulse of magic within my palm just waiting to be called forth.

The Rider's gaze follows the motion of my hand with keen interest, an unreadable expression crossing his face. He continues, "The bargain is made, the contract etched. You have my seeking spell, and I have your name. It is complete."

All at once the pressure falls away and the world comes back into focus. The Huntsman and I, the dirt and the creek, the trees and the sky. The world, free for a moment of that *thing*. I stumble and have to catch myself, shaken by what I just experienced. I take in deep gulps of air and will my body to relax from some of the gathered tension.

But not too relaxed. The Huntsman still watches me, so I can't afford to let my guard down.

"Are you satisfied?"

I nod. "Yes, thank you. I *will* remember this."

"See that you do." The Huntsman draws his cloak about him and takes a step up the slope, but then he pauses and looks back at me. "Oh, mortal, before I go . . . I wish to know what new name you took, when you sacrificed the old to my care. What did you try to seal it with?" He smiles, and it is a cat's smile, wicked and full of cunning.

Shit. Shit shit shit. He figured it out. I'm too shocked to respond, so I just stare at him mutely. I can't deny it, I've already shown too much of a reaction.

The Huntsman smirks at my sudden freeze-up. "You are clever, girl, but you are not as clever as you think you are. You gave your name so freely because you believed you could replace it with something new. You thought you could escape the consequences of your deal while slipping away with the prize. *Did you think you were the first to try and cheat the fae?* You are not. The only thing special about you is that you didn't even need to be *convinced*. So many have taken the deal when I offered it, confident in their little trick, and let me assure you, it *does not work*."

He says a word, my word, my name, but it slips out of my grasp before I can understand any syllable of it. My whole body stills, paralyzed, trapped inside my skin. I try to move but my body won't *listen*, I try to speak but my throat is *closed* and my lungs are *burning* and I can't breathe, why can't I breathe, I—

He says that name again and I gasp, greedily gulping in fresh air. "A trick for a trick, and so the old rules are observed. A name once given has hold for all eternity. You are *mine* for all eternity." He laughs and the fury blooms inside me, but it's tempered by the pain in my arm and the memory of being breathless. "Don't worry, I won't take you *now*; I wish for you to go out into the world and use that little spell to become *exceptional*. Grow, change, evolve, and become worthy of joining my *collection*."

This is bad. This is really bad. I fucked up. I already regret this deal, but what choice did I have? "Collection? What do you mean 'collection'?"

The Rider just laughs again. "Poor, deluded creature. Now: your *name*."

I still hesitate. "You can't have both. I'm not letting you own me twice over."

Even more smugness creeps into his stupid bastard face. "Oh, child, what bedtime stories have you been listening to? There is a whole world of difference between offering your name in dreambound contract and introducing yourself by it. You have my *word* as a Huntsman that telling me your new name will not give me further power over you."

The air shivers at his proclamation, yet still I hesitate. *I've already made one fatal mistake today.* The Huntsman narrows his eyes and adds, "I could just *make you* say it, but I'm being nice as a reward for your entertaining behavior."

I grimace. I square my shoulders and try to put some fire back into my voice. "Fine. But I want to hear your name too, fae. That's only fair, isn't it?"

Amusement returns to his expression. "An exchange of information, then, as our third and final transaction." He makes a sweeping bow and introduces himself. "You may know me as Eirdryd Llewellyn of the Wild Hunt, your master-to-be."

I curl my lip. "Eirdryd. You can call me Malice. Malice of Nowhere."

A pause. A *long* pause, and I can see mirth glittering his eyes and a thousand barbs waiting on his tongue. He starts laughing, practically cackling, and when he finally gets a hold of himself it is to say, "Malice? Really? *That's* what you went with? You could pick any name at all, and you chose *Malice*?"

I cross my arms defensively and pout. "What? It's a cool name! It's like 'Alice' for wonder and adventure, but then you add an 'M' in front to make it dark and spooky. Malice, the incarnation of ill will. It's cool!" He stifles a snort and I die inside. "It's . . . it's supposed to be intimidating. To make people take me seriously."

"Good luck with that, *Malice*. And I do mean that sincerely; become worthy of serving me, lest I regret this *investment*. You would not like to disappoint me."

Eirdryd Llewellyn turns away from me with another laugh and starts walking toward the tree line. I curse him out under my breath as he leaves. Bastard asshole fae thinking he gets to decide what is or isn't a cool name.

In fairness, Malice is an extremely edgy name, and we knew that when we picked it. At least we didn't go with "Shadow" or "Lady Ravendark" or any of your other old characters.

So I'm an edgelord, so what? Edgy is cool!

Sure it is, sweetie.

I glower at my treasonous inner monologue. I know I'm just trying to distract myself from the awful fact that my stupid trick failed and I'm now bound to a faerie until the end of fucking time. Stupid idiot girl trying to outwit a monster out of myth.

You are not as clever as you think you are.

By now the Huntsman is thoroughly out of sight so I can finally drop character entirely and clutch at my arm, teeth gritted through the pain. Pretending to be a badass is hard. There were so many moments I thought for sure he'd call my bluffed confidence and murder me on the spot, but now I realize the bluff never mattered; my life was never in danger because it was my autonomy he wished to take, and I just *handed it* to him.

I'm more and more weirded out that I wasn't afraid at any point in that conversation; I really, really should have been. Was that lack of fear what made Eirdryd interested in claiming me? Was it something about the hairpin he kept glancing at? Could he tell I'm from another world?

Another spike of pain forces me to consider my arm. The wound hurts but it isn't deep, and if there's any poison, I haven't felt the effects yet—and with all the running I did, the poison should definitely be in my system by now. So it's probably not going to kill me, but it still slows me down and I really need both arms. Do I drink the potion now and risk not having it later, or save the potion for later and risk losing because I wasn't in top form? Not that my top form is very impressive.

Maybe we should run another experiment. I have a sneaking suspicion that I drank more than I needed to that first time in the stairwell. This time, when I pull the potion out of my backpack and remove the stopper, I try to drink only a sparing amount. When I lower the potion there's still nearly half of it left, but I feel that warmth coursing through me just as before. The wound on my arm closes up like it was never there, and the warmth slowly passes.

Welp. I definitely drank too much last time. I stow the potion and contemplate what I've learned from my encounter with the Huntsman.

Eirdryd gave me a lot of data to work with, and I think I had my first proper encounter with the god that put me here: the Dreamweaver, Azathoth, who happens to share a name with the blind idiot god of the Cthulhu Mythos. In the Mythos, Azathoth is a mindless force of chaos who dreams the universe into being by accident, but the presence I felt in that moment seemed anything but *mindless*. Whatever she is, the Azathoth of this reality is neither blind nor an idiot.

I still need more data, ideally from someone willing to give me baseline exposition about this setting without having to bargain for it and play word games. I can't make any real conclusions about Azathoth—about anything—until I have a basic understanding of this world and its rules.

I can start by getting a taste of the magic system. It's a fascinatingly strange experience to *hear* square brackets around a word. I hold out my hand and focus on the spell within the brand. "[Find the Path]." The three-spoked wheel of flame comes forth once more, gently spinning above my hand, but as I summon it I see a diagram in my mind's eye, a dazzlingly complex array of interconnected shapes and symbols.

I have no idea what any of those mean. I imagine one of the shapes moving and it starts to shift in an arc. I focus on a symbol and see other symbols surrounding it, and I find that I can connect them together, split them apart, or select one to be the focus of a particular part of the diagram. The diagram seems extremely malleable, but I have *no idea what any of it means*.

When I focus on a symbol below all of the others, disconnected from the rest of the diagram, it expands into what is very obviously a *text box*: it is a wide black box with a white border, and there is a white underscore blinking in and out just above the bottom left corner.

Okay! We are definitely *in litRPG territory! Bracket-named spells that bring up arcane code and a text box? Now this is starting to feel like a more conventional isekai. More of the video game mechanics and less of the horrible monsters and asshole fae, please and thank you.*

I dismiss the spell by willing it to dissipate; I want to try it out, but I need to finish my business here first.

I start digging through burnt husks. The tarantula-dogs are mostly ash and char now, but on one of them I find my faithful companion still embedded in spidery flesh. I rip the knife out of the dead monster. *Knaifu, I missed you! But, oh my, what's this? Just an ordinary kitchen knife, but that's no ordinary kitchen knife!*

I had expected the Huntsman's flames to warp the knife past the point of usability, but instead the blade is longer and thinner, its shape closer to that of a dagger. There's a dull heat to the knife, and no matter how much ash I wipe off on my skirt there's still more clinging to it. When I dip the knife in the creek a few bubbles rise up, but the blade doesn't emerge any cleaner.

Magic item? Please tell me it's a magic item now. I swing the knife around experimentally and find more weight behind my swings, yet paradoxically I seem to be moving a little bit faster, or maybe my motions are just more precise. I still feel limited by my paltry arm strength and lack of training, but it's like the dagger is helping me along, nudging me to be more efficient. *Definitely magic. Fuck yes! First magic item!*

I grin wide at the dagger and hold it out parallel to the ground. "You and I are going to do wonderful things together, my beloved blade. And like all magic weapons, you need a name. I think I shall name you . . . the [Ashthorn]!"

The blade catches fire. Like an idiot I tighten my grip instead of releasing it, but when the green flames wash over my hand, they don't hurt me. I'm holding a flaming dagger and my on-fire hand is not burning.

"YES!" I scream. "Fucking yes! Yes, yes, yes!" I twirl around giddily and sing, "I've got a flaming *dagger*, I've got a flaming *dagger*!" I whoop and swing the dagger around wildly, enraptured by the trail of fire.

It's the same shade as Eirdryd's fire, or close, and I can't help but draw a visual comparison to Greek fire. Curious, I dip the dagger into the stream and am delighted to see the flames continue to burn unaffected by the flowing water. When I retrieve the dagger a few flickers of flame cling to the water, though it doesn't take them long to die out.

Very cool that it can't be extinguished by water, but that does pose a question: how *do* I extinguish it? The dagger lit up when I named it, so maybe saying the name again will deactivate the effect. *I wonder . . . I didn't hear Eirdryd speak the spells that killed the spider-dogs or the spell that let him walk on water—if those were spells—so maybe just thinking and focusing will do the trick?* I focus on the blade and will it to extinguish. [Ashthorn].

The fire goes out. *Hells yes! That is awesome. Okay, magic item acquired, now let's put that spell to work.*

With the dagger in my left hand I turn my attention back to the brand on my right hand. "Alright, compass, let's give you a spin." [Find the Path]. I summon the burning wheel, but something feels . . . off. I can't remember exactly how the diagram looked before, but there are definitely shapes and symbols missing from it now. *What the fuck?*

I dismiss the spell. "[Find the Path]." The wheel flickers to life and the diagram is back in its full glory. *Are you fucking kidding me? The spell behaves differently if I think it or if I say it aloud? Do all spells work like that? Argh, I hate that but I can't do anything about it yet. Okay, focusing.*

I focus on the text box with its blinking underscore. "For my first wish I want you to lead me to the person, place, or thing that my future self would most recommend I ask you to lead me to."

Nothing happens. Or to be more accurate, I see my words appear in the text box and then the whole box turns red and the text vanishes. *Yeah, I kind of figured time fuckery was off the table, but I had to check.*

"Okay, how about this: lead me to that which would give me the greatest gain at the lowest cost, accounting for the tools at my disposal and my ability to travel."

Again, the text goes red and vanishes. *Damn, that's still too vague? Am I giving it too many variables, or just the wrong variables? Okay, let's try again.*

"I want to find someone who is amenable to becoming my ally, can teach me about this world, and will help me get stronger." *This has to be specific enough.*

Sure enough, the text goes blue this time. The whole diagram shifts, shapes clicking into place and symbols appearing, disappearing, and drawing lines to each other. Too much of the diagram changes for me to make any sense of it, but it is a fascinating insight. The shift in diagram only takes a few seconds, and when it's done moving a symbol in the very center of the diagram—which had stayed still through the whole process—starts blinking.

I focus on that symbol and it flashes blue, and then the diagram vanishes. The burning wheel spins and the three spokes shift from being radial lines to being the three sides of an arrowhead. After a few seconds of spinning the wheel stops in place with the arrow pointing downstream. I move my hand around and the arrow adjusts each time to keep its direction stable. *Alright, there's my heading.*

I stay by the water's edge and take a leisurely pace, feeling more confident now that I have a spell and a magic dagger. I hum a song to myself as I stroll. I can finally get to the adventure part of this fantastical adventure. Of course, I'm sure there will be more nightmarish horrors blocking my way, but what's the worst that can happen?

Don't answer that, Azathoth. I know you're listening.

I have no way to gauge time so I don't know how long I've been walking, but I've gone through a full album of anime openings by the time my surroundings finally change. As twice before, the transition is sudden: one second I'm walking along with no end in sight, the next second I'm at the end of the stream and standing on the edge of a cliff that falls away into a vast nothingness.

The slope is gone, the dirt I'm standing on level and stretching off to either side of the river with no sign of trees. The gentle creek is now a tumultuous waterfall, water cascading off the side of the cliff and falling down, down, down into an infinite open space. The pale blue sky darkens as it falls below what would be the horizon, becoming utter blackness directly beneath me.

In front of me, a ways past the waterfall, I see the sheer cliff face of a floating island. *Another* floating island, I correct, because that's almost certainly what I'm standing on. Past these two islands, in the infinite expanse, I see dozens more chunks of land drifting in an empty sea. Lush jungle, icy mountains, rolling plains, and even one chunk with what look like sand dunes.

The island aren't all at the same elevation, but they *are* arrayed in a loose ring formation around a central point. The cluster curve away in either direction and meet together far in the distance.

In the center of the ring, at the heart of it all, floats a tower of jagged black glass.

Well then. Guess we found the final dungeon.

V

The enormous gap between my island and the island across from me poses a problem, but my magical fire compass insists the correct path is forward, straight across the empty air.

The blue-black void doesn't seem to have a bottom, so I would probably die of dehydration before splatting against anything. Oh, hey, dehydration. I haven't drunk anything that wasn't healing potion since arriving and I've been here, what, a few hours?

Luckily there's a river literally right next to me. Well, currently a raging waterfall, but when I take a few steps back I'm by the creek again. I kneel down to the placid stream and scoop up a nice handful of water, dismissing [Find the Path] first so I don't get a face full of flame. It soothes my parched throat and I greedily drink more. Once I've had my fill I return to the cliff's edge and peer over.

It's odd staring down into the abyss. It's particularly odd because I am supposed to be scared of heights, but I feel nothing. Back home I'd get nervous just climbing high stairs or crossing a bridge, but now I'm on the edge of a literal cliff to nowhere and I don't feel scared at all, not even when I make myself vividly picture falling to my death. Something is very, very wrong with my fear response.

If my isekai cheat ability turns out to be some kind of fear immunity, I am going to murder someone.

I don't see any way across the void, but if that was really true then why would the compass lead me here? *Something about this setup feels too intentional.* It's in the way the waterfall faces the cliff, the clean edge. I can almost imagine the two sides clicking together.

Leap of faith? I scoop a handful of sand and toss it into the void. Most of it falls out of sight, but *some of it* lands on something invisible. I scoop more sand

and keep scattering it until I can make out a whole platform fixed in the air just a single finger-length past the edge of the cliff. *Invisible bridge! Called it.*

I kick the sand-covered platform to see if it moves, and when it doesn't I place a foot on it and apply pressure. No matter how much weight I shift onto it, the tile doesn't react, so I step on with both feet. *Okay, now what?*

I test the far edge of the platform and find a gap, but there *is* another tile on the other side of the gap. I repeat my testing process to make sure it's secure, then make the crossing.

The rest of my trip across is tedious busywork; I cross platforms, test for a new platform, test the stability of the new platform, then cross again. Eventually I'm back on solid ground, landing on a patch of dirt up against the far-side cliff face.

Now that I'm here I can examine things more closely, and what I find is intriguing: the cliff is too sheer, just like the top of the stairwell. There's no sign of any entryway, just a perfectly cut stone wall, but when I resummon the compass for a moment it continues to point forward.

I dismiss the spell and trace my fingers over the wall, looking for a hidden indentation or illusory surface. I keep the knife clutched tight, not willing to let it out of my grasp again after the disaster with the spider-dogs.

I find a spot on the wall that feels different and push. I'm expecting some mechanical contraption that makes a block of stone sink into the wall, or some kind of illusory passage that my hand will pass right through, but instead I find myself stumbling forward, hand against empty air.

I catch myself before my stumble can turn into a fall onto hard stone. I'm in a corridor of stone, the same type as outside but not as unnaturally smooth; there's decent friction as I walk and I see striations in the walls. Behind me is more flat stone, with no visual indicator that it leads outside.

Another translocation. Seems that happens every time we cross a threshold. This place has fascinating spatial mechanics; could we exploit that in some way?

The hall curves off to the right. There are no torches to light the way, but this reality doesn't seem to care about light sources; once again I can see perfectly fine in the lightless corridor. I follow the curve of the wall and in short order come to a wooden door.

The door looks sturdy and well fitted to the stone hall, but there's no lock and no handle. I pause by the door and listen for any sounds on the other side, but hear nothing. I kick the door with my foot and it creaks open. My knife is at the ready.

The chamber on the other side is uninhabited but not empty: there's a wooden table and two wooden chairs, a tattered rug gathering dust, and two doors leading out. The door across from me is simple and unadorned, just like the one I just opened, but the door to my left is covered in ornate engravings.

I step inside and stab the rug, table, and both chairs, just in case any of them are mimics. I poke the doors too for completion's sake. I have no reason to believe mimics exist in this world, but it seems like the kind of bastard thing that Azathoth would cook up to ruin my day, *especially* since I've already encountered other furniture that didn't attack me.

None of the inanimate objects I menace cease being inanimate, and thankfully none of them bleed pink blood, so I ignore the furniture and push open the far door.

This room looks like it's half barracks, half storage: cots and blankets are crowded against the left wall while crates are stacked against the right wall. The siren song of loot calls to me and I start opening boxes.

Rancid meat, moldy bread, and pools of sludge that might have once been fruit don't fill me with confidence, but I squeal with delight when I find a hooded black cloak. I happily equip my new article of clothing and keep searching. I find metal canteens with water still inside and throw one inside a pouch on my backpack.

The next box contains an assortment of medical supplies, all of which I pocket: a few bandage rolls, a needle and spool of thread, and a bottle of modern antiseptic. The antiseptic is labeled but again I note the conspicuous absence of any brand or logo. The bundle of rope in the next box won't fit in my backpack, but the half-empty box of matches will.

The last box is the largest and has mouthwatering contents: three plus-sized, heavy-duty, lotsa-pockets, not-pink backpacks! They look like the kind hikers take with them, big enough to fit a week of supplies. I rifle through and they're all empty, but they have way more space than my dinky little monstrosity.

I go to lift one and wow it's heavy. Too heavy, I realize. I can take it out of the box and move it around but if I load it up any more than my current backpack, I probably won't be able to run with it. I'm already starting to feel the weight of my pack and there's barely anything in it. It makes an annoying sort of sense: when I was still in school I used to get out of breath just carrying textbooks from one class to another.

This is vaguely humiliating, so I'm glad no one's here to see. Except Azathoth, the perving bastard.

I reluctantly let the superior backpack go out of concern for my poor, aching back. With my sacking of the storeroom complete I return to the antechamber and inspect the ornate door. The carvings are of scenes that wouldn't look out of place in a religious text: sufferers kneeling in prayer, faces of anguish, the strike of a lash. I push the door and it swings open. On the other side is a hexagonal room, five more doors, and *another monster*.

Because why wouldn't there be another monster?

The monster resembles a human, mostly, but one that's been stretched out to twice its height and tortured for weeks or longer. All of its limbs are too long and lanky, and it has six of them: two legs bent, kneeling, clothed in ragged trousers, and two sets of arms sprouting from two sets of shoulder blades on an elongated torso bare of coverings.

The lower arms, shorter, are clasped in prayer, while the upper arms are busy striking the creature's back with many-whipped scourges that end in metal barbs. The monster flagellates itself in steady, controlled motions, and by the scar tissue and dried blood covering its naked chest it must do this often.

The creature's head is hairless, and symbols I have no frame of reference for have been carved into the top of its head. It wears a thick blindfold over its eyes and there are streaks of dirt staining the creature's cheeks like dried tears. The monster's mouth is the oddest part for how *normal* it looks: perfectly proportioned and clean, with full lips and pristine white teeth. It moves that oddly perfect mouth in some repeated chant, but what I hear is a chorus of whispers like a dozen people murmuring too quietly to be clearly heard.

Its head is initially bowed, but when I step inside the room it lifts its head in my direction and stops flagellating itself. It's still kneeling in the middle of the chamber, a solid few meters from me but way too close for comfort. The whispers stop and the monster speaks.

"Do you know regret?" Its voice is unnerving for how beautiful it is, choral and resonant like a choir in harmony. The voice is vaguely male, but only in the way that deeper voices can dominate a certain kind of group singing.

I debate running, but I don't know which door is my goal and if I summon the compass, this thing might just take that as provocation. Better to play along. "Can you clarify your meaning? Are you asking if I know the definition of regret, or if I personally have regrets? I mean, the answer to the former is that of course I know what the word means, I read *books*." That last line makes me sound like a smarmy kid bragging about her advanced reading level to her classmates, but that's exactly who I was in grade school so it fits.

The creature does not take my evasion well. It rises to its feet, moving slowly, and four arms hang limp at its sides. At its full height the creature has to hunch over to avoid the roof of the cavern. It speaks again. "Do you know regret?"

I feel like lying is the best move here. Lying is always the best move. I lift my chin confidently at the giant and proclaim, "I have done nothing wrong, ever, in my entire life. I'm basically perfect—divine, one could argue, and I have—and I regret absolutely nothing."

The monster's lips curl back and that choral voice commands, *"Repent!"* with all the gravitas a choir can muster.

Okay, so maybe lying wasn't the best move.

The flagellant lurches forward and swings wildly with both scourges, but each step is a laborious motion for the creature and I'm already sprinting away. Where the attack connects with solid stone it leaves a wicked gouge in the wall. *Wow! That'll just fucking kill me!*

"[Ashthorn]." My dagger is wreathed in green flame and I keep it pointed at the monster, ready for it to come at me again.

The flagellant moves slowly, with great weight behind every motion, and turns to face me once more. "Repent!" cries the unearthly chorus, and the creature makes another lumbering lunge toward me.

I was outpaced by Needles and outpaced by the tarantula-dogs, but I finally have an opponent slower than me and I'm reveling in it. I dodge the attack even easier this time and I can feel [Ashthorn] helping in subtle ways; the dagger isn't literally making me faster, but it's nudging me to be more efficient in my movements, and that adds up.

The monster crashes its whips into the wall and has to take a second to recover, so now it's my turn. The flagellant's back is even worse than its chest, the skin torn raw and even the flesh scourged away in areas to reveal bloody bone. I'm not sure how much harm I can even do to this thing but I stab it with the burning blade, driving my dagger into exposed muscle and sinew.

When I pull the dagger out, wisps of green flame cling to the wound. The flames crackle and hiss, and I can see the flesh of the wound starting to char.

The creature turns to face me and I take a step back to get out of reach but I'm blindsided by a backhand from one of the lower arms. I'm sent flying and I think I hear a rib crack even before I slam into the ground and lose all the breath in my lungs. The dagger slips from my grasp and clatters across the floor, extinguishing as soon as it leaves my hand, and I lie there sucking in air for precious seconds before I can force my body to move again. I scramble for the knife on hands and knees but the monster is on me again and I have to roll away from another scourge swing, putting the flagellant between me and my weapon.

I push myself off the ground and sprint to the wall furthest from the dagger. The monster lumbers after me, scourges scraping the ground, and again that perfect voice cries out, "Repent!" It swings as soon as it's in range and I dodge the blow but only by inches; the agonizing pain in my chest is slowing me down and without the dagger I'm clumsy and uncoordinated. As soon as I'm clear I turn on my heel and race for the dagger. I scoop it up and reignite it with a pained word.

The flagellant advances. I dodge, wincing at the flare of pain, and this time I play it safe and don't go in for an attack. I can see the burnt wound on its back where I stabbed with [Ashthorn], but the trickle of blood is slow to emerge. *Is the dagger cauterizing the wound!? That is insanely irritating if true.*

My broken rib is wrecking me, but another exchange plays out as I move defensively and puzzle over how to kill this horrible bastard. *I can't trade blows like I did with the not-ghost and the spider-mutt; I'll die before I can drink the last of my healing potion and that still won't be enough to kill it. If I attack from the front it'll break me with those scourges and if I linger too long behind the monster it'll just grab me with that second pair of arms.*

Another swing, another dodge, another moment to breathe. *So if no single stroke will win this fight, reverse tactics: wage a war of attrition and cripple its ability to fight.* I dismiss [Ashthorn]'s flames, quietly relieved that the agility effect isn't tied to the burning effect.

The chorus calls for repentance once more, and when the flagellant strikes the wall I duck low and stab its ankle. The dagger sinks in and I leap back before the giant's grasping hands can seize me. The monster makes no noises of pain, but I can see the blood starting to drip, and when it comes after me next it's limping.

The flagellant's limp makes up for my screaming rib and I win the next exchange. This time I manage to stick the shoulder of a scourge-bearing arm. The arm doesn't suddenly drop limp, I'm not that lucky or that good, but when the flagellant pulls back that arm for another swing, it stops halfway to its previous zenith.

I repeat tactics. The monster lunges, I dodge, I give it a glancing blow and back off. Not all my attacks manage to do any damage, but the dagger's assistance is making me more accurate than I should be and enough blows land to make a difference.

The creature is tough, but it isn't invincible. With each new wound it flags more, and though I'm tiring too, the adrenaline keeps me a step ahead. When the monster misses again and lingers for a few more seconds, straining, before gathering for another assault, I see my opportunity.

On the next round I go for the kill. As soon as I'm clear of the scourge swing, I step back in and drive [Ashthorn] into one of the monster's blindfolded eye sockets. My dagger passes through the blindfold and finds something *squishy*, and I shove it deeper, but as I push it in one of the flagellant's lower arms grabs my leg and *squeezes*. Bone shatters and my leg gives out but I hold tight to the dagger and I drive it down to the hilt. "[Ashthorn]!" I scream. The blade ignites inside my enemy's brain.

Screams tear out of my throat as fresh agony courses through my calf and up into my thigh. Pain, pain, *pain*, more than I've ever felt, unbearable, unimaginable, it just keeps building. I keep twisting and my leg keeps shattering into more and more pieces until finally, finally, finally, the pressure eases off.

The monster falls to the ground and I fall with it, the pair of us crumpling in a heap. I am screaming, crying, shattered. I clutch at my ruined leg and wail and the pain keeps rising. I can see shards of bone and pulped flesh, a gruesome visage of spilled blood and mangled meat.

Dimly, somewhere in that pain-induced fog, I remember the potion. My hands are shaking as I fumble with the zipper of my backpack and pour everything out onto the bloody floor of the stone chamber.

I see the crystal flask and grasp at it, pull it close, bring it to my mouth. I try to force my hands to still but they won't listen. I tear the stopper off and don't care where it goes, I just need to be *whole*. I pour the potion down my throat, spilling some, and let the empty bottle slip between my fingers.

Warmth. That comforting, amazing, loving warmth flows through my veins. It washes over my chest and eases the pain in my ribs. It washes down my leg and drowns the lancing agony. My whole body is warm and soothed and whole and I lie there on the bloody floor with eyes closed, tears still leaking out.

The warmth recedes and the cold comes in. The pain is gone but my body still shivers from shock and anguish. I'm sobbing, I realize; the sobs wrack my chest and pour out of my throat.

Why? Why is this happening to me? Am I being punished? Is this what I deserve for all my sins? Am I meant to suffer until I break? I'm not special, I'm not strong, I can't handle this. I'm weak. I'm worthless.

My sobs get quiet, and numbness replaces the anguish in my chest. I sit up, open my eyes, and stare at the empty potion bottle with its "Drink Me" tag.

If not for that potion, I'd be dead. Her gift saved me.

I snarl and bare my teeth. *Azathoth is the reason I had to use it in the first place. It's her fault I was stabbed and slashed and beaten. Her fault for bringing me to this wretched world full of horrors.* The hate rises and escapes me in a low growl. *She gave me that to prolong my suffering! Her "gift" justified throwing deadlier monsters at me.*

It kept me alive.

Kept me alive, but didn't give me any power. Kept me alive and *powerless so I have to rely on it just to keep moving.*

As I continue to stare at the potion, reality sets in. *It's gone now. The potion is gone. My "free fuck-up" card is gone. What do I do now? What do I do without my lifeline?*

Mechanically, numbly, I start filling my backpack with everything I threw out. There's blood on the notebooks, on everything, but I wipe off as much as I can on my thoroughly dirtied outfit.

Hydration is essential for maintaining normal function, my brain intones clinically, so I take a drink from the canteen before securing it in its pouch. I zip up my backpack.

We have to keep going. The only way out is through. We can still win this.

I rise to my feet and turn to the dead flagellant to retrieve [Ashthorn], but the monster isn't there anymore: instead the dagger is lying embedded in a heart of fired clay, the ceramic organ made to look ritually scarified. *Huh. Okay. Definitely adding* that *to the list of questions I have for the first halfway-decent source of exposition I find.*

I rip [Ashthorn] from the clay heart. I'm half expecting the heart to explode in an energy wave or something like that, but all that happens is that a few cracks spread across the ceramic. I shove the heart in my backpack, then summon the compass. The arrow of the seeking spell points to one of the four side doors, so I walk over to it.

This door has carvings like the one that led to the central chamber, but also has a proper handle and a bar that's been lowered to block the door from opening. I glance at the other side doors and confirm they all have the same setup. *So whoever resided here didn't care about blocking passage in or out of the rest of this place, but these rooms contain things they wanted to keep trapped inside. How promising.*

I gather myself before the door and try to wipe off as many tearstains as I can. I'm filthy with blood and dirt, but I can't really do anything about that, and I can't do anything about this embarrassing outfit either. I just have to avoid looking weak. [Find the Path] led me here but it can't speak for me; I have to convince whoever is on the other side of this door that I am worth joining. I have to prove myself to be charismatic, intelligent, interesting, and *worthy.*

I wince as I note that they probably heard me sobbing, which won't help my case. I need to lie my ass off and hope they can't see through me. I raise the bar, plaster a confident smirk on my face, and open the door.

On the other side I see a stone room, a circle of salt, and a horned man standing inside the circle.

VI

Demon. Or devil. Hopefully not a yugoloth, those were always my least favorite fiends in Dungeons & Dragons. We should really ask about this setting's naming convention.

The curling ram's horns, cloven hooves, and barbed tail all make it pretty clear that this man is fiendish in nature. His skin belies the big red devil trope for a more normal light brown, but his eyes are a delightfully unnatural combination of black sclera and lilac irises. His hair is darker than mine, as well as shorter and neater, and his facial features are strong in that "conventionally attractive" way. The only article of clothing he's wearing is a pair of shiny leather pants, or maybe faux leather.

My overall impression of the fiend would be one of handsomeness if he didn't look so malnourished: skin stretched tight, bulging veins, and sunken stomach. There are bags under his eyes, and though he's put on a charming grin he can't hide the strain at the edges of his mouth, like it's costing him just to smile.

He's looking me over as I examine him, and for a moment I see something I can't decipher wash over his face before he masters himself and the grin returns. He catches my eye and gives me a wink, then spreads his hands.

"A warm welcome, my new friend." His voice is honeyed and deep but not too perfect, not unnatural like the choral voice of the monster that nearly killed me. There is something altogether human about his voice, something comforting and friendly that puts me on edge. "I heard the commotion of your scrap with my warden and I was expecting someone wearing power armor and carrying a halberd. That you managed to defeat the sin eater with merely your wits and a dagger speaks volumes of your ability," he flatters me.

I'm taken aback at the role reversal—and at the mention of "power armor;" did I mishear?—but manage to keep my smirk fixed to my face. *Didn't you hear me crying and screaming? I sounded pathetic.* Then I put the pieces together. *Right, duh. Fiend bound in a ritual circle, first face he's seen in however long, and he needs to play nice with me to get out of his prison. We're both lying in the hopes of getting something.*

Well, let's run with it. "It was in my way," I reply in a light tone. "I had to put it down so it wouldn't interrupt our conversation."

"Oh? Did you come all this way just for me? I'm flattered, truly." He makes a half bow but doesn't break eye contact. "What can this humble imp offer you?"

Imp, got it. I step farther into the room and try to match his casual energy. Or maybe he's matching mine, after my dismissal of the monster? *Sin eater, he called it.* "You can offer your name, for a start. Call me Malice."

Another crack in the mask, a brief twitch of facial expression, but it is quickly mastered and put away before I can figure out what it means. He rises from the bow and puts on a face of consternation. "Ah, you have my deepest apologies for failing to introduce myself properly. I am Bashekehi the Ever-Gleaming, a masterless incubus. It is a pleasure to meet you, *Malice.*"

It's almost unfair, the way Bashekehi says my name so respectfully. He says "Malice" like my name is the best name he's ever heard, like he can't even conceive of a worthier name. It hurts to hear, especially after Eirdryd's mockery. I swallow and force myself to answer, though my voice is nowhere near as smooth and controlled as his. "Likewise, Bashekehi. You have an admirable way with words."

He smiles again, seeming prideful and sincere, but I recognize that he's probably a much better manipulator than I am and could be faking even this. "My thanks, Malice. I am glad to hear that my speech has not rusted in the years I have been trapped within this cage."

Years? I guess that tracks with how spoiled the food was. "How long have you been trapped here, Bashekehi? Do you know?"

The incubus shrugs. "At least two years, possibly longer. I kept count for some time, but incubi are not suited to stillness and so my attention waned. But if you came to find me, perhaps my stillness is over at last. Please, Malice, tell me: what desire brought you to an imp of temptation and excess?"

Hmm. How do I respond to that? What do I want out of him? Wait, what if he asked me that to make me think about it so he could read my thoughts or something? Slowly, putting on not entirely faked airs of curiosity, I ask, "Can't you tell? I always imagined a being like yourself would be able to sense those things."

He chuckles. "Indeed. To my discerning eyes, shallow wants come easy and even deeper yearnings take only a bit of focused peering. But your soul is . . . difficult to read." The incubus quickly adds, "Take that as a compliment, please. I've never met someone who could foil my sight so effortlessly."

Interesting. Very interesting. "I'm flattered. Well then, allow me to answer your question with another: what can you offer me? I know stories of incubi, tales of what they want and what they're capable of, but I am uncertain of the veracity of those fables." I tilt my head curiously. "Enlighten me."

I notice his barbed tail twitch in two directions as if about to swish back and forth, but then it stills again. "I can offer a great many things. Indulgence is my purview, the domain of lust, excess, and want. I have made princes of paupers and ruined casinos with a subtle touch; if you desire riches, they will be yours. I can show you every mortal delight under the sun, pleasures that would make the finest of courtesans green with envy. I can extend your lifespan, make you faster than a competitive runner, and reshape your appearance to your heart's desire."

He's watching me like I'm watching him, each of us searching for signals. I'm sure I'm giving a great deal away; though I try to control my expression and keep up that mask of curious detachment, his speech is undeniably tantalizing. Not the riches or the pleasures, of course; what draws me in is the promise of longevity. Eternal life.

There is a flicker in his eyes, a light that I can only take to be triumph. Bashekehi takes a step toward me and presses one hand against an invisible wall, the boundary line of the salt circle. He smiles at me and says, "Ten years, a hundred, even a thousand could be possible. Only a whisper of mana to rejuvenate this tired form and I can make that dream a reality. If you make a contract with me, I will strive with all my being to repay your generosity. I will—"

I sweep my shoe across the salt and break the circle.

There is a rush of stale air as the barrier is shattered, and then the imp is free. Bashekehi stares at me, false charm replaced by pure, raw confusion. Tentatively, as if fearing a trick, he passes his hand over the salt line. I revel in his bafflement, exulting in the sight of a genuine incubus rendered speechless.

He steps over the line with one hoof, then the other, and he's free. Bashekehi glances at the broken circle, then back to me. He gapes at me, fish-mouthed, still incapable of mustering words. It takes him maybe a full minute to finally say, "You . . . you broke the circle. You let me out."

"Yes," I agree.

"*Without* making a contract first."

"Also yes." *Even if we get nothing out of this, I'm calling it a win just for that dumbstruck face.*

The incubus keeps staring at me. "You could have had anything. You could have demanded the world of me and I would have had no choice but to exhaust myself trying to give it to you. Why didn't you make a contract? Why would you free an imp without making even the most basic of bargains? No one is that altruistic, so *why*?" A bit of frustration seeps into his tone, or perhaps anger, and mixes with the lingering confusion.

"Narrative consequences," I reply unhelpfully. I can't help it, I'm finding it so fun to wind him up.

"The fuck what?"

"Narrative consequences," I repeat. "See, if I forced you into a lopsided bargain under threat of continued isolation—a leonine contract, if you want to call it by its trope—then that would give you the narrative backing to betray me at a later date and get away with it. Plus, you'd probably resent me and *want* to betray me for having forced you into servitude under duress. But if I free you without asking for anything, you'll be more positively predisposed toward me and will have the narrative against you if you betray me later. This way is easily ten times safer, trust me."

Bashekehi stares at me for another long moment before shouting, "*THAT* is your reason!? I'm not a wyldfae, and you're *definitely* not any kind of spiritbound, so why the *fuck* would you think those rules apply to either of us?"

Huh. Well, that's definitely not the reaction I was expecting. So, does this setting actually have narrative laws as a mechanic? And it only applies to some people?

The incubus puts his face in his hands and mutters, "I've been rescued by a girl who thinks like a damned faerie. Unbelievable."

Bashekehi takes a step toward the door and stumbles, so I rush to catch him and hold him up. He's light, too light, and as I prop him up I pretend to be concerned and ask, "Hey, are you okay? I mean, obviously you're not, you've been alone in a boring room for literal years, but are you *okay*?"

The imp winces and steadies himself. He forces himself to stand ramrod straight, but he doesn't back away after I let go. His hands are held like claws at his sides, straining, and the look on his face is bleak. Within his eyes I see desperation and hunger.

"Starving," he murmurs. "I am starved. It's been years since I last fed, and I'm surviving on the very dregs of my essence."

I chew my lip. *He's not much use to me if he dies of malnutrition. Hmm, maybe we could kill a flock of birds with one stone.* "Hey, you're an incubus, right? I don't know what that means for *you*, but the stories I've read all say that incubi feed on sex. That true?"

A bit of mirth bleeds back into his face. "To a point. We feed on excess, of which sex is one of the more pleasurable forms for most. My preference leans closer to the excess found in casinos and gambling dens, but I'm not one to say no to a spot of carnal feeding." He glances me over, his gaze searching, and frustration passes over his face before being wiped away. *He's trying to peer into my* soul, maybe, and coming away stymied. *Assuming he was telling the truth about that.* "Why do you ask, Malice?"

I gesture at my body and ask, "Could you feed on me, then?" I try to keep my tone light and curious.

His gaze sharpens and his presence looms larger in the room. "If you're offering. But I should warn you that in my current state, I might not be gentle once I've gotten a taste of my food." He says the line like one of those "I'm dangerous and that's sexy" characters from a bodice-ripper, all dark and brooding.

"Will it kill me?" *Probably should have asked that first, honestly, or some variation of it.*

He shakes his head emphatically. "No, not a chance. It would make us rather poor partners if imps of Indulgence killed with every sexual encounter."

I shrug. "Then go ahead and feed. I don't mind." *Wait. That might sound too passive.* I add, "By which I mean: I give my full and enthusiastic consent to whatever weird incubus things you are about to do to me."

His answering laugh is deep and rich, and then he's close enough that I can feel his warm breath on my neck. One hand trails along my outer thigh while the other traces circles on the arm not attached to a dagger. I note it all clinically and start rehearsing lines in my head; I want to give a good performance. He's a little shorter than me, maybe just an inch, so I adjust my posture so it's easier for him to loom over me if he feels so inclined.

Bashekehi's lips lean down toward my neck, but he pauses before actually touching my throat. "You . . . are not attracted to me. Not in the slightest."

"You're very handsome," I reassure him.

Bashekehi draws back and gives me a reprimanding look. "I am an *incubus*. Sensing that kind of desire is my specialty, and even if I can't discern your deeper motives I can still read some of your surfacemost desires, and your *body language*. This isn't arousing for you, and you don't expect it to be."

"True," I admit. "If I were the straight lead in a romance novel I'm sure this would be exhilarating, but since I'm a lesbian it mostly interests me in the abstract." I tilt my head curiously. "Is my enjoyment a requirement for you to feed?" I'm surprised at the idea that it might be. *I may have to put aside a lot of my assumptions about incubi.*

The imp pulls back further. "What kind of question is that? No, really, what kind of question is that? You're talking about—" He breaks off, looking disturbed now. "Why would you think like that?"

I shrug. "I assumed the physical component would suffice. The body can respond to certain stimuli with certain somatic responses, regardless of how the mind feels about the source of those stimuli. That's sometimes true of even the worst kind of sexual interaction."

That look on his face worsens. "That's *not* how I feed. Whatever else I may be, however hungry I may get, that will never be the kind of person that I am. Never."

Oh, we may have phrased that poorly. "Sorry, I didn't mean to imply anything about you or make you uncomfortable." *It's a shame, I was hoping to have that source of leverage. Still, we might be able to use this in other ways.*

Bashekehi rubs his forehead and leans against the nearest wall, tail swishing in agitation. "Why would you do something like that? Why would you offer your body to me when you are *gay*? Wouldn't that be deeply unpleasant for you?"

I smirk at him. "I'm willing to do all manner of unpleasant things if they get me closer to my goals, and a bit of incompatible sex is far from the worst thing on that list." I snort and add, "If you think that's bad, listen to this: a couple of hours ago I sold my name to a faerie from the Wild Hunt."

"It's like you're waging a war on common sense," he marvels. "You've completely abandoned rational thinking."

"I prefer to think of it as a high-risk, high-reward approach," I say with another shrug. "Playing it safe is for people who can afford to deal in small losses and small gains."

"Do you really think you can afford to take large losses?" He rolls his black-and-lilac eyes and crosses his arms, tail swishing again. "You sell your name to a Rider, you free an imp without making a contract, and you try to offer your body to an incubus that you aren't attracted to. Continue that pattern and you'll be dead by year's end."

"Probably," I admit. *Alright, now for the hard sell.* "Which is why I can't keep going it alone."

The imp does not seem surprised by my sudden pitch, and he just quirks an eyebrow in response.

"You asked me what I wanted, before I broke the circle. What I *desired* of you, Bashekehi. Well, here it is: I want a teacher. Someone to help me learn the things I don't know, and to point it out when I make mistakes. Left to my own devices, I'll undoubtedly encounter some even worse monster and trade it my heart for a few good books, so I need someone like you to keep that from happening. I need a voice of reason."

"What?" This time he sounds properly baffled.

"Travel with me, Bashekehi." I hold out a hand. "Make a contract with me and become the devil on my shoulder. Follow me on the path I walk. Help me seek knowledge, help me gather power, and help me learn from my mistakes so that I can avoid making them again. When you see me about to do something reckless, warn me before I jump."

"You're asking a *temptation imp* to be your impulse control?" Disbelief drips from every word. "Do you understand how ridiculous that is? My whole purpose in life is to tempt people into *indulging* their desires, not to caution people against them!"

"And yet, when I offered myself to you, offered something you desperately wanted and needed, when the only objection was a petty moral objection, you balked. You chose to stay hungry rather than cross the line I was inviting you over. Are you really going to say that I can't trust you after that?"

Shock, then open suspicion. "Did you . . . did you set that up to *test* me!?"

I make a *sort of* gesture with the hand not holding a dagger. "I rarely have just one reason for doing something. Learning more about you was one objective, but you wouldn't have failed any test if you'd gone through with it. Both outcomes were deemed acceptable."

"You . . ." The incubus trails off. He continues to stare me down, and I let him think. When he speaks again it is slower, careful. "If I said yes, what would you offer in return? If you expect to leverage gratitude alone, you'll find me unreceptive."

I shake my head firmly. "Not at all; I believe that people are motivated primarily by selfish desires, so those are what I'll appeal to. Consider this, Bashekehi: if you are the warden of my self-control and the arbiter of my impulses, then you get to decide when it's okay for me to let loose and indulge those reckless desires. Your very role has its own reward baked in."

His tone is skeptical. "You would sabotage the contract before it's even been signed."

"Not sabotaged, just given certain release valves. Believe me, I would hate to listen to reason *all* the time."

"Do you have any idea what an insane statement that is?" he mutters. I politely ignore him.

"What's more, I'm going to be getting into a lot of trouble in the days to come, and I expect there will be plenty of opportunities for a creature like you to feed on what results." I tilt my head again. "Am I wrong?"

He looks at me, then at my outstretched hand. "You're mad. Utterly mad. So how are you making that sound so tempting? You are, genuinely, a walking temptation."

"I try," I say proudly.

"I can tell." He seems pensive, but he hasn't agreed yet. I need to push a little further.

"This is a chance you'll never get again. The path I'm walking, the destiny in front of me, it's like nothing you've ever seen. Azathoth as my witness, I swear: be my lancer, Bashekehi, and I will show you a feast like no other."

The world shivers as the Dreamweaver bears witness to my promise. Bashekehi's eyes widen as he glances once more between my face and my outstretched hand. "You're really serious about this, aren't you?"

"I am. Are you in?"

The imp pushes himself off the wall. He takes a step toward me, delicately takes my hand, and says, "No."

VII

"Eh?"

"No, Malice, I won't take your deal."

Well, shit. I didn't really have a Plan B here. "Okay, cool, got it, understood, and I don't want to challenge your agency here or anything, but, mind telling me why?"

Bashekehi sighs and looks away from me, pulling his hand away. "I won't lie, you're sorely tempting; in all my years as an incubus I've never met someone so eager to be taken advantage of. I'm grateful, too, for being freed, and I won't forget that. But I want a chance to enjoy that freedom before I swear myself to a new master. Especially one so . . . unique."

Hmm. That wasn't exactly the kind of relationship I proposed, but this might be some imp thing I don't have the context for. Regardless, it's time to change tactics. I adopt an easy smile and wave a hand. "No worries, I totally understand. Would you prefer we go our separate ways, or are you okay with traveling together for a bit? I don't really know this area well and I could use a guide, even if our partnership is an informal one."

The incubus turns back to me with a skeptical look. "You're taking this suspiciously well. I hope you don't think you can get me to change my mind if you just work at me long enough."

"Of course not," I lie. "You've set a hard line, and I'll respect that. I have nothing to gain by burning bridges over a minor disappointment. Besides which, most of what I want from you doesn't need to come bundled with a formal relationship. In fact, I think I may have overstepped by phrasing my offer the way I did; I have no desire to be your master, I simply want for us to help each other as best we are able in this strange and dangerous world."

Bashekehi still looks suspicious, but he doesn't challenge me. "Right. Well, to answer your question: yes, I'm willing to travel with you. I do feel a sense of debt to you for freeing me, and I have an inkling of how I can repay that debt, depending on details. How long have you been in the Labyrinth?"

New term, interesting. Is that the name of this world or just this particular region? I tap my chin, consider the question, and respond, "About three hours, I think. Maybe four."

He winces. "Then you probably don't even know what the Labyrinth is. Shit, okay, I guess I'll have to explain that in detail at some point, but the barebones version is this: you're in a realm of Pandaemonium ruled by an ancient monster called the Nightmare Queen or the Lady of Shards, depending on who you ask. Most of the Labyrinth is a horrible mess of terrifying monsters, but there are a few safe havens and I happen to know a path to one of those havens. We just have to get through the Contrite, assuming any of them are still alive."

That is all *fascinating* and I am deeply interested in learning more about what is absolutely the thing residing in the big glass tower, but I tamp down my curiosity for the moment. "Great! Excellent plan. We can start by getting you a bit better equipped; there's a storeroom that has a few goodies left in it, and you look like you could use some water. If you drink water, I mean. I don't really know how incubus biology works."

A flicker of amusement crosses his face. "I can drink. Lead on, Malice."

I head back into the central chamber and stop by the spot where the monster—sin eater, Bashekehi called it—died. I *should* keep going to the storeroom so I can start accruing more goodwill with the incubus, but I can't resist asking, "So, what's the deal with the thing I killed? You called it a sin eater, so is it one of those Contrite you mentioned? And why did it turn into a clay heart when it died?"

He frowns. "How do you not . . . do you not know what a homunculus is? Sin eaters are the homunculi of Contrition; the Contrite are her zealots within the Labyrinth, and they make sin eaters." He's looking at me with a worrying gaze, but I can't exactly back out now.

"Interesting, very interesting. So, this may seem like a stupid question, but, who or what is Contrition?"

The look on his face worsens. Slowly, as if talking to an idiot, he says, "The archdemon presiding over regret, guilt, and punishment."

I rub my hands together. Data! Juicy, delicious data! "Perfect. Now, next question, and forgive me if this is offensive: are archdemons and imps considered the same kind of entity, just operating at different power levels, or is there a deeper categorical distinction between them? And if there is a connection, do you have a term that would refer to both of them collectively?"

Silence. Bashekehi looks pained now, and he's clenching his fists, but through his teeth he says, "Why don't we start with what you *do* know? About . . . anything."

I wince and raise my hands apologetically. "Ah, well, this is where we get into rather embarrassing territory for me, as I'm afraid I don't really know much of anything about this world. I was *kind of* hoping you could help me out with that. As I mentioned, I arrived here just a few hours ago, and I've actually never encountered anything like any of this before. Imps, archdemons, homunculi; I must confess they're all quite new to me, at least outside of stories."

Bashekehi drags his hands down his face and groans, "Gods and archdemons, she's a lethe drinker. Why? Why me? Why this? Why is this how I escape?" He turns around and paces the room, muttering to himself all the while. "Fucking lethe drinker. I should have guessed, I should have guessed! Why else would she be wearing a butterfly? Why else would she be so cavalier around imps and fae? Why else would she go around using the same name as *an archdemon*? But she didn't *sound* like a lethe drinker, she was too *eloquent* for a lethe drinker! That'll teach me. Gah!"

Eh? The fuck? None of this conversation is going like I expected. I clear my throat and wave at the ranting incubus. "Hi! I'm still here. What is a lethe drinker, and why are you calling me one? And what does that have to do with my hairpin? And what was that about my name?"

Bashe groans again, louder, but turns back to me and comes close. "Okay, I hate this so I'm going to make it quick: you know how you have huge gaps in your memories? Big enough gaps that you don't know what imps or archdemons are, and you probably don't remember where you got that hairpin? Yeah, you sold your memories to the archdemon Wonder, or to one of her lemosynes, not that you understand the difference between them because all your memories of that difference are *gone*. We call people like you 'lethe drinkers.'"

I start laughing. *Fuck me, this is hilarious.* I clutch at my stomach as the laughter pours out, unable to stop myself long enough to explain what's so fucking funny. *He thinks I have amnesia. This is rich. This is the best.*

The incubus starts massaging his temples. "I didn't ask for this. I really, really didn't ask for this. Why a lethe drinker? Of all the people it could have been, why a lethe drinker? I really, really do not want to explain basic shit to a lethe drinker. In fact, I'm not going to! I'm not going to teach you grade school facts about the universe."

I finally get a hold of myself and gasp out, "Not a lethe drinker. Not missing memories." I steady my breathing and continue, "I'm not missing any memories, and I found this hairpin on a doll in the abandoned school I woke up in. Look, the reason I don't know shit about this world is that I'm not *from* this world. I came here from another world entirely, or rather I was brought here against my will." *Let's just leave out the fact that we would have jumped at the opportunity to come here willingly, even with the horrible monsters.*

Bashe is unimpressed with my dramatic revelation. "Yeah, no shit, we were all brought here against our will. Story of this damned Labyrinth."

Interesting, but beside the point. I roll my eyes. "Good to know, but you're not getting this. Look, whatever world you came from before here, I'm not from there either. Your world had magic, right? Mine didn't. I come from a place where beings like you don't *exist*. A world where gods and incubi are both just myths."

He raises an eyebrow. "That's your story? Really? You're not a lethe drinker, you're just *from the Zero Sphere?* I don't know why you'd think that would be more believable, but it's really not. You may be a good liar, but nobody can sell a lie that ridiculous."

The what? The fucking what? What? What the fuck is going on? "Hold on, what the fuck did you just say? The Zero Sphere? What the fuck is the Zero Sphere?"

He crosses his arms. "I'm not buying it. I'm not buying your bullshit, Malice."

"Really, truly, sincerely, I *don't know* what you're talking about. What is the Zero Sphere, and why do you think I'm claiming to be from there?" I try to inject as much truthfulness as I can into my voice, which isn't hard since I'm actually being truthful for once.

He sighs heavily. "Fine, whatever, if that's the game you want to play. The Zero Sphere is the 'world without magic' that was supposedly used as the prototype for Firmament itself, and even most of the worlds in greater Pandaemonium, but which no one aside from the Demiurge has ever seen or been to, so it might not even exist. There, happy?"

I stare at him, mouth open. *They know about Earth!? They think Earth might be a myth!? What the fuck is going on?* This isn't even "that strange place that reincarnated and/or summoned heroes come from," this is "that mythical place we can only speculate on the existence of." "Okay. Uh. Okay. Gotta admit, none of this conversation is how I thought things would go. Um. Sorry, still struggling to process that you guys have heard of my world and *don't think it exists*."

He narrows his eyes at me, then looks away with a noise of disgust. "I hate how hard it is to read your soul. This would be so much easier if I could just *know* what you're really feeling right now."

Lightbulb. "Okay, but what if you *could* know that?"

He looks back at me, skeptical but not dismissing the idea out of hand. "How?"

I take a deep breath. "Okay. Fuck, I'm saying that word too much. This is all just very disorienting for me."

"For *you?*"

I glare at the incubus. "Yes! For me! Quiet, you. Here's my idea: deals are a thing here, right? I made a bargain with that fae, and it *seems* like I could have made one with you, if you had accepted. Azathoth, Dreamweaver, whatever you want to call her, she listens in and she makes things happen, right? So what if we make a deal, and I agree to tell you three true things about me, about my history. I'll be bound by Azathoth to tell you where I'm really from and what I really remember."

Bashekehi looks at me with undisguised suspicion. "There's no channeling without equivalent exchange. What would I be exchanging?"

The choice is obvious. "Knowledge. I want to know everything about this world: its cosmology, its history, its *magic*. I'll tell you three true things about me, and you tell me three true things about the world. That teaching you were so unenthused about," I say with a smirk. "And I want it in *detail*! No mathematician answers."

Bashe runs his hands through his hair and looks down with a grimace. "Even if you're not lying, you're still wrong about being from the Zero Sphere. But it'll bug me if I don't have a clear answer, so fine. Let's make a deal."

"Yay!" I cheer as I punch the air. "Can I get Azathoth's attention for this, or do you have to do it?"

"I have to." He rolls his shoulders, flicks his tail, and extends his hand toward me. "Azathoth, O Dreamweaver! I invoke the right of channeling that all imps are due. Bear witness to this contract and give it meaning. Hear our words and make them binding."

Once more, I drown in a god's embrace. I am nothing. I am everything. I feel her love and cold detachment. The world is the moment, her touch, and shallow breath.

Bashe wobbles, nearly buckles, but stays standing. His face grows taut and the hand not outstretched clenches into a fist. He speaks. "The contract is thus: three truths for three truths. I offer my body of knowledge, to be plumbed at the invoker's leisure. Three questions I shall answer, truthfully and in detail, as chosen by the woman calling herself Malice."

The unknowable voice of Azathoth whispers in my ear, and words not my own escape my lips: "I offer my personal history, to be plumbed at the channeler's leisure. Three questions I shall answer, truthfully and in detail, as chosen by Bashekehi the Ever-Gleaming."

The sensation of Azathoth's presence tightens around my neck like a noose choking me, like a scarf keeping me warm. Cotton candy in my mouth, cloyingly sweet.

Bashekehi winces and shakes his head. "The bargain is struck, the contract etched. We are bound to truth, when demanded. It is complete."

The pressure falls away from my shoulders, from my body, from my mind, but not from my neck. The world snaps back into focus, but I can still feel

Azathoth's hands wrapped around my throat. Not squeezing, not stopping me from breathing, just lingering there. Then, slowly, that fades too, but never quite to the point of true absence.

The incubus looks me dead in the eyes and says, "Tell me what you remember. Tell me where you're from."

The hands of a god caress my throat and the words come tumbling out. "I'm from, well, I guess you'd call it the Zero Sphere, but we just call it Earth, which is a dumb name because it's actually mostly water but I guess we thought the dirt part was more important so whatever, and like I said, it doesn't have any real magic or gods or demons or whatever, well some people think there are gods and stuff but that's just a mix of ancient superstition and a longing for community, and also there's some existential stuff in there about, like, meaning and shit, but the point is that we don't have magic, and things like faeries and incubi only exist in fiction! Also Azathoth is a fictional character where I'm from! Also also I'm from the specific part of Earth that we call California, which is a horrible desert and I didn't like being there so I moved to Washington, which is a nice forest and has rain! Also also also—"

Bashe raises one hand to stop me and rubs his forehead with the other hand. "That's enough, Malice." The hands ease off. "Okay, so you have memories of an impossible world. That doesn't mean you're really from there, but I guess it means you're not lying. About *that* at least."

"My turn!" I insist. "I want to know everything about everything."

"Be more specific. Also: walk and talk. I don't want to be in this shithole any longer than I have to be." He immediately makes for the open door to the antechamber without waiting for me to follow.

I bound after him and debate what I should ask. Cosmological data could help me analyze the setting as a whole, and starting early on any big cosmological mysteries might help me take major plot shortcuts. On the other hand, understanding the magic system should have immediate benefits and might actually contribute just as much to mystery solving. And a part of me really wants to pester him about my name being *apparently* the same as an archdemon's, but that seems like such a small thing to waste a third of my questions on.

"Magic," I tell him. "I want to know about magic. There's so much I've seen already but I feel like I'm just scratching the surface! How do spells work? Why does saying a spell's name make it stronger? Are all spells limited use or does it vary by spell, or does it vary by caster? Are spells naturally occurring or were they created by someone? Were they created by Azathoth? What do those weird symbols in the diagram mean? Does every spell come with a text box? Is there a difference between faerie magic and imp magic? The faerie mentioned mana, how does mana work? Do you have a regenerating pool of mana or is there like a field of ambient mana you draw on? Does—"

"*Please* stop talking," the incubus groans. He's doing that expression again, one hand on his face and the other held up in front of me. "Gods and archdemons, please stop talking."

We're at the storeroom now, and he's paused his search of the crates to whine at me. I flip my hair at him and harrumph. "I get a question! That was the deal, Bashe."

"Three questions! That was way more than three, and—hold on, did you just call me Bashe?" Confusion breaks through his frustration for a brief moment.

"I like nicknames. I have a short attention span and long names are hard. I can come up with a different nickname if shortening your name like that is insulting, I don't really know imp culture." It wouldn't do to be insensitive.

He blinks at me a few times, then shakes his head. "You know what? Whatever. I don't care. That is the least of my worries; call me Bashe all you like. The *point* is: if I answer all those questions we will be talking for *hours*."

"I'm okay with that."

"I'm not! Pick *one question* and I will answer it."

I stick my tongue out at him but Bashe returns to his looting without acknowledging my petty childishness, which really defeats the point of said petty childishness. I sigh and try to pick whatever question seems most immediately relevant. I *want* to ask what kinds of magic exist in this setting, because I crave categorization, but I don't know if that loredump will actually help me in any meaningful way.

I need power. If I want to achieve any of my goals, I need power. And I want to understand that power, but I don't know that I *need* to understand that power, at least in the short-term. The girl who got lost in books wants to dissect every facet of this magic system and compose a model for it, but the girl who lost her mother only cares about *survival.*

I clear my throat and ask my question. "The Huntsman had magic. He could shoot flaming arrows, bring down an inferno on a pack of monsters, and walk on water. The spell I bargained from him only had three uses, and now it only has two. I want better than that. I want spells that aren't limited by the terms of a contract. How do I get magic of my own?"

Bashe picks up one of the hooded black cloaks and tries it on. "Big question. Are you asking how to get magic that is *uniquely* your own, or just magic that you can use indefinitely?"

I hesitate. What I *want* is the former, but all I really need right now is the latter. If my only goal is survival then I should pick the latter, but is that a trap of short-term thinking? *Bah. The issue is that I don't understand this magic system* well enough to know if those two things are mutually exclusive. *Is all unique magic finite? Is all indefinite magic non-unique?*

Is uniqueness necessary to achieve my long-term goals? Is it pride, to want my magic to be special, to want to be *special?* I don't even know the questions to ask to decide what questions to ask.

Fine. Shot in the dark. "Both. I want magic that is uniquely mine *and* indefinite."

Bashe keeps rifling through crates as he answers, "Then you want to become a sorcerer, or more formally a scion. There are five kinds of scion, so that means five ways to get the kind of magic you seem to want."

Scion? That has fascinating connotations.

Bashe hoists one of the hiker backpacks, takes a long drink of water, and makes for the door. "Put simply, your options are to become an elf, a lich, a wizard, an exalted, or a demon. You should consider none of those to be *realistic* options, but there they are."

Hunger burns in me, but I keep my questions focused. "That's *what* I can become, but not *how* I become them."

The incubus waves a hand as we return to the central chamber. "Getting to that." He sighs. "You just had to pick the most complicated question possible, didn't you? Do you have any idea how involved this topic is?"

"Obviously not, I'm a lethe drinker," I say with a wonderfully smarmy expression on my face. "Now get to answering!" I'm a little annoyed he's not spilling his guts like I was.

Bashe rolls his eyes before finally giving me an explanation. "Practically speaking, two of these are *impossible*: the Wolf Queen makes elves and the Lich Queen makes liches, and neither faerie queen is accessible from the Labyrinth."

The Wolf Queen, that's the one Eirdryd thought would like me. Given that he was a vicious prick, maybe I should be relieved I'm not likely to encounter her any time soon. Never say never, though.

"There *is* at least one dragon trapped in the Labyrinth, so you have an incredibly slim chance of becoming a wizard. You just have to find that dragon, impress it, and spend a good decade or two practicing martial arts, studying alchemy, and learning the draconic tongue until the dragon deems you worthy of rising to scion status."

I blink. "Hold on, did you just say that wizards do martial arts in this world?"

He raises an eyebrow, looking genuinely confused. "Uh, yes? How else would they cast their spells?"

What? What. What? Okay, we are interrogating the fuck out of that at our earliest convenience. "Noted. Carry on."

The incubus gives me a weird look but continues. "That leaves exalted and demons. Exalted are chosen by eidolons—ah, you don't have the context for that so just think of them as minor gods, I guess—to serve as their champions. They go out on quests, perform great deeds, protect communities, all that kind of thing. They're heroes, essentially, and their heroic qualities are why they get chosen. They swear oaths to embody the virtues of the eidolon, and are empowered to act on those virtues."

So a codification of the conventional heroic role. "And demons?"

Bashe grimaces. "The opposite. Demons are chosen by dark entities called geists to become monstrous paragons of will and want. They make bloody covenant, and only those who are willing to *kill* to get stronger are chosen to become demons. You can't seek out a geist like you can an eidolon; it has to find you. Some of the greatest massacres in history were perpetuated by those hoping to draw the attention of a geist."

I can feel the hunger rising in me, getting stronger, more irresistible. *Demon. Is that what I want to become?* I can't deny the allure of the idea; two paths are blocked to me, and wizardry sounds like a lot more exercise than I'm willing to put up with, so that really only leaves becoming an exalted or a demon.

I *should* want to be chosen by an eidolon. If this is an isekai story, shouldn't I try to be the Hero? A great journey, quests and deeds, all the hallmarks of a classic fantasy tale. It would be the morally correct path, from what Bashe tells me. It's the *right* decision, if I care about right and wrong.

Big if.

The incubus watches me, and I'm sure he can see at least a trace of the desire I feel. I smile at him and show my teeth. I tell him, "Thank you, Bashekehi, that is an excellent start. The next question is yours."

He gives me another long, searching glance, then points down at the pool of dried blood. "How did you kill the sin eater without taking any injuries, and why were you screaming? In detail."

The gentle pressure on my throat returns and I wince. "Yeah, no, I definitely did not clear that fight unharmed." I seem to have more control over the pace this time, but I don't try to push my luck. "I stabbed the thing, it broke one of my ribs, I stabbed it a bunch more times, it slowed down, I stabbed it in the eye and burned its brain with [Ashthorn]"—the dagger bursts into flames—"and it shattered my leg into a mangled mess of flesh and bone. Then I drank a healing potion and got better." The pressure retracts.

Bashe stares at me. I dismiss the flaming dagger. He keeps staring.

"Bashe? Did I say another ludicrous thing that shouldn't be possible but has just been confirmed to definitely be true because of the contract we made?"

Bashe blinks and scrunches up his face, then forces a very strained smile. "No, no, I'm clearly just misunderstanding. It sounded like you said the sin eater shattered your leg and you drank a potion that healed your shattered leg in seconds."

"That's correct," I confirm.

Bashe bundles up part of his cloak, raises it to his face, and screams into it.

VIII

Impressive pipes for someone who probably hasn't used his voice in years.

I tilt my head at the incubus. "Okay, how is *this* causing you stress? It's just a fucking healing potion. Do you guys seriously have something against healing potions?"

Bashekehi drops his cloak and shouts at me, "They! Do not! EXIST!"

What? Why? Why is this setting!?

"Healing potions—*true* healing potions—are a myth! Panacea, the fabled dream of every healer. It's not how healing magic *works*."

"That's the stupidest thing I've heard today. Health pots are a copper a dozen in RPGs." *Okay, that math is definitely wrong, but I'm exaggerating for comedic effect.*

Bashe looks at me with despair in his eyes. "Malice, I had really, really hoped I wouldn't need to tell you this, but: *real life is not a video game.*"

"Wait, hold on, you guys have video games?"

"THAT IS NOT THE POINT RIGHT NOW!"

I wince. Ouch, okay, this has him really worked up. "Okay, okay." I hold up my hands in an appeasing gesture. "Clearly things do not work how I expect them to. I'm just not really clear on why healing potions would be impossible for magic to pull off."

"Because—" He pauses and gets a shrewd look in his eyes. "That should be one of the three. If you want more magic knowledge, pay up."

"I'm actually totally okay not knowing," I lie. "I'm perfectly happy to remain blissfully ignorant of why healing potions are impossible, and will simply continue to bother you about how silly you're being."

Bashe narrows his eyes at me. "You're lying."

"I am! But which one of us will crack first?" I ask with a grin. "'Cause it seems to me like there's really no reason for you to be so fussy about this. Maybe you just don't understand how healing magic works? Healing potions are super easy, so easy you don't even have to be a mage to make one! Are you sure you know how healing works? I could educate you, if you'd like."

"Fine!" the incubus hisses. "If it will get you to shut up, fine. Look, there are basically four kinds of healing, and the only kind that you can bottle is preservative healing: magic that is fast-acting and keeps you alive but doesn't fix anything wrong with you. The kinds of healing magic that heal you quickly and completely . . . they're dangerous, and rare, and *definitely not* something you can put in a bottle."

"Gotcha. Noted." *So this system has harsh limits on healing magic. Why would it be designed that way? It's obviously an artificial limitation since I was handed an exception to the rule.* "Thanks for the intel. I did absolutely drink a healing potion, though."

Bashe sighs and walks to one of the side doors. "Just one more impossible thing, I guess. Let's see if we can find any other prisoners to free."

We don't.

In one room we find a dead woman, chained to the wall, who had bitten off her own tongue to avoid slowly starving to death once the Contrite stopped bringing food. Her body had liquefied in some areas and ruptured in others, which is fascinating to look at but disgusting to smell. In another room we find scattered salt and scorch marks in the shape of a circle, but the door bar is intact with no signs of being forced open.

The final side room is barren, and I take the opportunity to ask Bashe, "So, tell me more about magic. When I mentioned narrative tropes, you reacted like those have actual power here, just only for *some* people. Wyldfae and spirit-bound, right? What's the story there? Why them and not imps?"

Bashe crosses his arms and chews his lip. "Give me a second to figure out how to answer that."

"Sure."

We head back into the main room and Bashe leans over to grab one of the scourges dropped by the sin eater—for whatever reason, they didn't disappear when the monster did. He gives it a few experimental swings and I resist the urge to make a joke about him knowing his way around a whip, because I am an *adult* and have *restraint* (and definitely not just because I don't want to interrupt storytime).

Bashe seems satisfied with the scourge, lets it dangle, and leans back against the far wall. "So there's this phrase you're going to hear a lot: 'the essence of magic is the manipulation of meaning.' That's really all a spell is: you're unleashing a packet of meaning-rich data into Pandaemonium and enacting a specific effect. That meaning can be personal, if you're a scion, but for most of us it comes from on high."

I eagerly take notes in my head and wish that I could sit down and start scribbling in one of my regrettably bloodstained notebooks.

"I said there were five scions, and there's a reason it's specifically five: there are five Thrones that rule all magic. Each Throne is like a different lens, a different way that events and actions are framed and given meaning. Imps like me belong to the Throne of Shadow, and Shadow is all about *will* and *want*. Choice, free will, and individuality are enshrined at the very heart of Shadow magic... at least in theory," he adds with a mutter.

Hmm. For an incubus, he really doesn't seem that happy with his own "Throne." Interesting. Can we use that?

Bashe continues, "The Throne of Spirit, on the other hand, is all about the beliefs and values of the many. When people tell stories, those stories all have something to say about the world, about how things are, about how things should be. When you take that magic into yourself, when you bind yourself to that lens, it can affect you and the world around in ways you didn't intend, because your *intent* isn't what's most important; the meaning isn't coming from you, it's coming from the collective that made you and empowered you to act, for better or worse."

I frown. *Fascinating. Narrative laws enshrined into the fabric of reality, but only when specific entities are involved, because the very nature of the meaning driving their magic is different between categories.* "What about fae?"

The incubus grimaced. "Fae are thieving fucking vultures, that's what. They murdered their own world and made off with its treasures like tomb robbers. One half of the fae, the Winter half, took the technology of the old world with them and made it part of their necromancy. The other half, the Summer half, took the stories with them and used those stories to expand their magic far beyond what it should have been. So the wyldfae are a mess of all sorts of spells and abilities because they have the benefit of drawing on a dead world's stories, but it can also bind them and trap them into performing certain actions or abiding by certain rules."

That is a whole bunch of really useful and cool information that I am itching to dig into and analyze but hold the fuck up, did he just say that one half of the fae in this setting are techno-necromancers? Damn it, that is almost worth wasting a question on. "Very interesting, thank you. You should be a teacher." I wink.

Bashe ignores my wink. "My turn. How did you get the dagger and the potion?"

The Dreamweaver's hands—or tentacles, they could be tentacles—wrap around my throat, and I answer him, "Oh, I'm pretty sure Azathoth gave me the potion when I asked for healing. I—"

"Nope! Nope, that's not a thing," Bashe interrupts me. "Wrong, incorrect, you are mistaken."

I pout at the incubus. "C'mon, at least let me finish!"

"You're just wrong here. Azathoth never, never, *never* intervenes directly. It's one of the Dreaming Edicts." *Ooo those sound interesting. Maybe not worth burning a question for, but definitely something to pry out of him later.* Bashe hesitates, then adds, "Nyarlathotep might send the Intercessor to act on her behalf, but not over something as trivial and petty as that."

What? "What? What? What the fuck? Why the fuck did you just say 'Nyarlathotep' and when you said 'her' did you mean Azathoth or did you mean Nyarlathotep and what the fuck?"

Bashe looks surprised at my sudden questioning but I don't care just *answer the damn question!* "Uh, okay, why are you freaking out all of a sudden?"

"Because," I hiss, "I recognize that name! Nyarlathotep is another character from fiction back on Earth—the Zero Sphere, I mean. In the Mythos, Nyarlathotep is the most human of the Outer Gods, the most lucid of them, and the most *malevolent* of them."

Bashekehi frowns. "For the record, I still don't believe you, but that's not an inaccurate description. The Demiurge is all of those things." The imp actually looks uneasy now, not dismissive or irritated. "Just . . . keep telling your story."

I grit my teeth, desperate to know more, but the pressure around my throat tightens. "Fine. I fought a thing that wasn't a ghost in an abandoned school and it stabbed me twice. While climbing some stairs I complained loudly at whatever entity was responsible for me being sent to this weird world. I demanded that it give me some kind of cheat ability or one-of-a-kind magic item, and god-DAMN IT I'm just now realizing that bitch gave me exactly what I asked for. Fuck! Shit, fuck, shit, bastard, genie bastard bullshit. I'm gonna be pissed about that one for a while, ugh. Whatever. I asked for healing and the potion just appeared in my backpack. I drank some of it, it healed me, and I moved on."

Bashe frowns, but he doesn't challenge me on anything. "And the dagger?"

"Got a knife from the not-a-ghost, stabbed a spider-dog with it, the asshole faerie guy burned all the spider-dogs to death, and after he left I grabbed the now-crispy knife, gave it a name, and it burst into flames. Magic dagger!" This time, when the pressure eases off, it vanishes completely, and I breathe a sigh of relief as Azathoth's attention leaves me . . . for the moment.

"That's not—I mean that's not how—what the fuck, Malice?" Bashe looks pained again, but he takes a deep breath and forces his expression back to neutrality. "Okay, that's not really how artifacts are made in most systems, but maybe it's some weird fae thing I don't know about. Plausible."

Definitely interrogating that later, but I have bigger fish to fry right now. Speaking of which . . . I rub my hands together. "Alright, final question." *Nyarlathotep Nyarlathotep Nyarlathotep—*

Bashe holds up a hand. "Wait. Before you ask your last question, there's something I can *show you* that might change what you want to ask. Would you rather waste the question now or wait a few minutes and ask a better question?"

I shrug. "Yeah, sure. What are we looking at?"

Bashe opens the far door, the only one we haven't gone through yet, and we enter a room with only one defining feature: an ornate mirror wide enough to fit three of me side-by-side, and tall enough to fit maybe one and a half Malices.

It's the first time I've seen my reflection in the new world and I immediately avert my gaze, catching only a flash of pale skin, chestnut hair, and a whole lot of dried blood. The incubus cuts a much more striking figure, somehow managing to look handsome and confident even starved, which I attribute to cheating. I examine the pretty gold filigree bordering smooth glass and find no scenes of torment or sinister designs, just artistic swoops and embellishments.

I glance at Bashe. "So . . ."

Bashe walks up to the mirror and puts his hand through it. His arm sinks into glass like a pool of water, and ripples flow outward from the point of entry. He smirks back at me. "First quirk of the Labyrinth: every mirror is a doorway. Step inside and get your first glimpse of the mirror-paths." Then he steps through and vanishes, disappearing both from the room and from the mirror's surface.

Right, well, that's fucking awesome. Through the looking glass! I stroll over to the mirror and stick my leg through. I meet resistance, but only the kind you get when you try to move through water. I take a deep breath and plunge through.

I step out into an infinity of swirling color. A thousand overlapping kaleidoscopes shimmer and swirl, rainbows within rainbows twisting across a sky that stretches in all directions. Behind me I see the mirror that I stepped out of, which shows not my reflection but that of the room I was just in. Beneath me is a pane of glass that reflects the oscillating bands of color, red then green then blue, cyan to magenta to yellow. It's a dizzying effect, and though I can tell the glass pathway goes forward, I quickly lose track of it in the endless parade of dazzling light.

Two deviations break the chaos: straight ahead of me I see another mirror, twin to the mirror behind, but showing the reflection of a room with strange, discolored walls and a floor of graying lichen. To my right, looming over everything, I see the tower of black glass.

The tower draws in light like a black hole, the rainbow colors blending together and warping as they swirl around the tower and are drawn in. The tower is jagged, sharp, less a work of careful engineering and more an angry shard of glass stuck in the skin of the world like a bad splinter. I blink my eyes to clear the disorientation and my perspective shifts, my interpretation of what I'm seeing changes; the tower isn't drawing in light, all that color and light is bleeding from every shattered edge where the tower pierces the sky.

The tower looks close enough to touch, close enough to breathe on it. I take a half step toward the tower and reach out a hand to try and feel its surface. Before my fingers can brush against black glass, I am pulled back, Bashekehi grabbing me by the wrist. I glare at him, about to say something biting, but the look of panic on his face stops me. "What? It looked weird, so I wanted to touch it."

A strangled noise escapes Bashe's throat. "'It looked weird'? That is the worst motivation—" Bashe cuts himself off, clenches a fist, and forces a calmer expression onto his face. "Listen to me, Malice: I understand that you're very curious and that being reckless comes very naturally to you, but this is not something you can afford to take risks with. Stick your hand in an open flame, shove your foot into a bear trap, but *do not touch the Nightmare's Heart*. The monster keeping us all trapped here, the Nightmare Queen, she *lives* in that tower. Nothing good has ever come of drawing her attention."

I must look unconvinced, because he keeps talking before I can get a word in. "Look, you may not place much value on your life or your sanity, but the consequences for messing with the Lady of Shards are *dire*. Whatever you do value—your identity, your drives, the things you think you know—can vanish in an instant if the Nightmare Queen whims it. Stay away from the Heart, and stay away from her." His voice is full of gravity, so much so that I almost feel bad about what I'm about to say next. Almost.

"Ah. I think I'm here to kill her, actually."

Bashe's face goes blank in that way when it feels like your whole brain is restarting. Blue screen.

"See," I continue, "I'm here for a reason. I obviously don't know what it's like where you're from, but back on the Zero Sphere we have lots of stories about plucky young girls—mostly boys, actually, but ignore that—getting whisked away to strange new lands where they acquire fantastical powers and steadfast allies. And, almost invariably in these otherworld stories, the protagonist falls into one of two roles: the Hero destined to save everyone from the local Dark Lord, or the Dark Lord destined to conquer the world." I grin and spread my hands. "Now, who's to say which one I am, but it doesn't really affect the outcome much. If Azathoth—or Nyarlathotep, since you seem to think that's more likely—brought me here as a Hero, killing the Nightmare seems like a sure bet to save everyone she's imprisoned. And if Nyarlathotep brought me here to be the Dark Lord, well . . . dethroning the current dimensional ruler is an important step in conquering said dimension."

"You're insane," he mumbles. "You're actually, totally, completely insane."

I make a so-so gesture. "Insanity's kind of a buzzword: it doesn't have a real medical meaning. Well, not where I'm from; I have no idea what psychiatry is like in your world. I *do* have a personality disorder, but it only includes, like, the teensiest bit of psychosis, arguably none."

"Malice."

"My point is: it may seem ridiculous to you, but do you have a better explanation? A girl from the Zero Sphere, gifted a miracle in a bottle by powers unknown, wielding a dagger that defies your understanding of artifacts. Who else could have arranged that but the Dreamweaver or the Demiurge? And if the Demiurge really did bring me here, then *why*? Why bring me to the Labyrinth? Why set me on such a path that within a single day of arriving here I've bargained magic from a faerie and freed an imp from his years-long imprisonment? It's because Nyarlathotep has a story for me to play out. This Labyrinth is a stage, a theater, and she's brought me here to be the lead actor in the Labyrinth's final play."

"Or you're delusional," he counters, "and lucky. The only evidence that you came from the Zero Sphere is that you *remember* that you came from the Zero Sphere, and memories can be *tampered with*. Even if you were from the Zero Sphere—and to be very clear, you are *not*—that wouldn't make you special enough to kill something as old and powerful as the Lady of Shards. She predates *physics*, Malice."

I shrug, then blink as I realize what he just said. "Okay, well, we're absolutely unpacking that later because—and I can't believe I keep saying this—what the actual fuck, HOWEVER: I don't intend on killing her right away. First I need to figure out the magic system and use it to amass power. And on that note . . . I'm ready to ask my final question."

My dialogue starts light, but by the end of it I'm fully serious. This is important. The most important question of the three, the one that I knew I had to ask from the moment I heard the word. There are so many tantalizing secrets that I want to tease out of the incubus, but in the end only one is important enough to spend my final question on.

"Bashekehi . . . can a mortal become a god, or something like unto a god? In this world, can a human reach apotheosis?"

Something new creeps into Bashe's gaze as he looks at me more closely than ever before, peering at something only he can see. Softly, he murmurs, "I think that's the first time I've seen your soul clearly, Malice. The first moment I've seen the chaos harmonize. There was a hint of it, when I told you I could make you live longer, but that was nothing compared to this."

I tense, not happy that he can read me, but I persist with my questioning. "Can a mortal human become a god?" Unspoken is the true question, the question that Bashe has just seen in my soul: *Can I become a god?*

The incubus keeps me pinned with his judging gaze, and when he speaks his voice is still so very soft. "That is, in fact, the only way that gods are made."

IX

The rainbow maelstrom swirls, the black glass tower stabs the sky, and I am going to become a god. This day could not get any better.

"That doesn't mean *you* can become one, before you get any bright ideas. There's no world where you ascend to godhood, Malice." Bashekehi smirks at me and I glare back at him.

I mutter, "Just punch me in the throat next time, I might like it more." I wave a hand dismissively. "Your utter lack of faith in me aside, I want the gory details: *how* do I become a god? The deal was for detail, so spill!"

The incubus rolls his eyes at me but continues, "A god is born when a human becomes a living myth. A mortal becomes the champion of an eidolon and does great deeds in their name, and after a certain critical mass is reached the exalted champion ascends into godhood, becoming Royalty of Spirit." Bashe pauses, then adds, "Archdemons, for the record, are the Royalty of Shadow, and they were all once human as well, though I would not suggest emulating any of them."

I rub my hands together, glee rising despite Bashe's earlier dismissal. *I can become a god. I can become a god. I can become a god.* A giggle escapes me involuntarily.

Bashe sighs. "Malice, you're not going to become a god. It just doesn't happen for any but the most exceptional of the exceptional. There are maybe a few dozen exalted in a generation, sometimes fewer, and none of them have a better-than-poor chance of ascending. Humanity has walked Heimshafse for nearly a thousand years and in that time we have seen only *nineteen* true gods."

Wow that is a lot of information I want to dig into but godhood eeeeeee! "Don't care, becoming a god!"

Bashe rubs his forehead and closes his eyes. "Malice, I'm going to regret asking this, but *why* do you want to be a god?"

I stare at him in disbelief. "Why the fuck don't *you*? How could *anyone* not want godhood? It's *godhood*. Apotheosis. Unless your gods are vastly, radically, unthinkably different than the gods I've read stories about, godhood means immortality, power, and worship. An eternity to revel in the love and respect of countless millions, maybe billions. An eternity of *power*, of being the apex predator in a universe-wide food web. It means *everything*. Being everything. Having everything. It's the ultimate goal. It's the only goal. How could you settle for anything less?"

He shakes his head, still not looking at me. "Some people don't *need* everything."

I scoff. "I'm sorry, didn't you call yourself an imp of *excess*? Pretty out of character to start preaching restraint, isn't it? That seems more like *Contrition's* domain."

He whirls on me and for the first time I see real *anger* in his eyes, pure and white-hot, nothing like the petty frustration of before. "Never. Never, ever, *ever* say that to me again. You don't know the first thing about what you're talking about."

Abort. Switch masks. Appease. Defuse. I throw my hands up (careful with the knife) and try to make my expression as apologetic as I can. "Sorry, sorry, that was too far. I had no intention of offending you but I clearly *did* and for that I deeply apologize. I promise I won't do it again, but I recognize that may ring hollow without action to back it up so I won't blame you if you don't accept my apology, and I'm totally cool with dropping the conversation here." *We'll interrogate exactly why that made him blow up later, but for now the name of the game is damage control.*

Bashe stares at me, some of the fire in his eyes going out. He clenches his fists, releases, deep breath in, deep breath out. "You . . . you make things difficult, Malice. And I could deal with that—I really could—if I weren't starving." He turns from me and starts walking. "Come on. Let's just keep moving."

I follow him in silence, contemplating. *Definitely struck a nerve. Contrition's what did it, most likely. Is that just because of the imprisonment, or is there more to the story?*

I pushed too hard. He was already getting frustrated with me and I pushed too hard and now he hates me. Good job, me.

So how do we make him like us? He won't accept sex, he's not charmed by confidence, not endeared by weirdness. Should we get him to talk about himself? He hasn't had social interaction for literal years, he should be more attention-starved than he's acting.

Maybe that's why he's putting up with us at all; for all his frustrations, he hasn't really tried to get rid of us. Could be a sense of debt, or it could be a craving for human interaction.

What can we offer him? What can we use to win him over?

Bashekehi doesn't lead me to the opposite mirror, instead taking a side path I hadn't seen. I look around and see dozens, hundreds of other mirrors scattered throughout the space around the ever-looming Nightmare's Heart. I know I probably shouldn't keep pushing Bashe, but I'm just too curious.

"So, how does this place work? What's the deal with all these mirrors?"

Bashe sighs. He doesn't answer for a few moments, long enough that I start to think he might not answer at all, but then he says, "We're in the Corridor of Reflections. Every mirror in the Labyrinth connects to the Corridor, and the paths in the Corridor connect to other mirrors. Distance is conceptual here, not physical, so you could cross the entire length of the Labyrinth in just a few steps if you found the right pair of mirrors. And they all connect to the Heart."

Conceptual distance, fucking rad. Definitely exploitable. "Good to know. On a related note: why aren't we taking that mirror back there?"

He sighs again, deeper this time, but answers, "Because, Malice, that mirror leads to the stronghold of the Contrite. If any of them are still alive, they'll have all the advantages. And while I'd love to make them pay for what they did to me, I don't have nearly the mana for prolonged conflict."

Before I can respond to that, we reach another mirror. This one is plain, a little smaller, and most notably: it doesn't have a reflection. The mirror is just an unassuming pane of silvery glass.

Bashe swears. "Fuck. I knew it was too much to hope for. Screwed over by our own sense of caution, what a joke."

I tilt my head. "This is fun to watch, but I'm not sure of the point."

Bashe shoots a glare at me. "You really can't shut up for five minutes, can you?"

I shake my head. "It would be bad for my health. What's with the mirror? Not working?"

He turns his glare on the mirror. "It's a doorway to my old home in the city. We kept a mirror handy for easy access to the paths, but covered it when not in use so no uninvited guests could get in. Covering a mirror makes it a wall instead of a door."

Who is "we"? Mm, file it for later. Now, should I press for answers, or offer solutions?

Bashe hits his thigh and clenches his fists. "Fuck. Weaver damn this whole fucking world!"

Solutions, definitely solutions. I clear my throat. "You said the problem was about mana, right? You mentioned one way to get more mana, but are there other methods? Methods more palatable to your sensibilities?"

The incubus stills, then flexes his fingers. When he turns back to me there is an inscrutable expression on his face. "Perhaps. I don't have the means to *feed* right now; I'm not going to fuck you, we're lacking anything to gamble with, and I don't think getting into a no-holds-barred fistfight would help either of us." He pauses, then adds, "But there is *one* other method."

"Tell me."

"Memory. If you gave up a few of your memories, I could reduce them to mana and use that to restore myself. There would need to be equivalent exchange, of course, and depending on how much you give I might even be able to grant you *magic* in return." His tone is light, but his eyes glitter with confidence and hunger. He knows exactly how tantalizing that offer is. "Not a strong spell, given I would need to burn mana to bestow it, but it would be magic, and it would be yours."

My hunger blooms. *Magic. More magic. More spells!* Immediately I seize on a thread. "How many times can we do that?"

Bashe furrows his brow. "What do you mean 'how many times'?"

"Memories for magic." I'm grinning again. "You give me a spell, I give you memories, you burn the memories for mana, now you have enough mana to give me another spell. That's possible, right?" *First exploit, first exploit, please let this be our first exploit! Infinite loop of magic here we come!*

Well, infinite until we run out of memories.

Bah! We have plenty of memories. I could do without a few years of them.

Bashe stares at me like I've gone crazy again, but then he bursts out laughing. "No self-preservation whatsoever. Genuinely. I think you'd set yourself on fire if you thought it would get you fire magic."

"Would it!?" I lean in, eyes sparkling.

"*No*, you absolute fucking creature! Why would that teach you fire magic?"

I stick my tongue out at him. "Boo! And also, you still haven't answered my question!"

Bashe rolls his eyes, but he does answer me. "Yes! Yes, Malice. If I get enough mana to cast another spell, I can bestow that spell for more memories. *But*," he stresses, raising a finger, "there's a limit. *Your* limit, or rather your soul's limit. The soul has a limited . . . well, we call it a pleroma, but I guess you could think of it as the outer body of the soul. Royalty and scions both have the capacity to grow their pleroma, but everyone else is stuck at a fixed value. As an unaligned mortal, your soul can only hold three invocations."

I grimace. *Fucking limitations. Why must absolute power take so much effort?* "Is there really no other way to raise that cap?"

He grimaces back. "For a diabolist? There's one way, but I've already hard vetoed it: a Pact of Mastery. When you bind your soul to an imp, you become an aligned invoker and get to draw on more of their spells." He pauses, then follows up with, "You said something about a deal with a fae, earlier. What did you trade for? I've heard not all fae magic takes the shape of an invocation, thought that might just be hearsay."

I hold up my hand with the scorch mark and summon, "[Find the Path]. The spell that led me to you. Good for two more uses." I let him get a good look at the burning wheel before dismissing the spell.

Bashe scratches his chin. "Yeah, that's definitely an invocation. So you've got space for two more." When he sees my scowl he adds, "That's still two whole magic spells you didn't have before."

I spread my hands and admit, "Yeah, that's fair. Still absolutely going to claim more than that. Alright, how many memories do you need from me to run a second bestowal and still be fighting-fit for what comes next?"

The incubus considers the question. "You really are just *eager* to carve off pieces of yourself. Given your memories are probably fake, I suppose I shouldn't feel too bad about taking advantage of that. Three memories, then. Three memories, provided they resonate right, should get me to where I won't be so starved and can possibly grant you a second, more potent spell. But they need to be *resonant* memories: memories with a resonance for Indulgence."

"Examples?"

Bashe lists them off, counting on his fingers. "Intense sex, glutting yourself on food, fighting or exercise that really gets your adrenaline pumping, gambling large sums, major drug use, thrill-seeking, anything else that really exudes excess and hedonism. If it made you feel like you were flying, it'll probably suffice."

"Yeah, I can manage that." *It's a shame that means I'll mostly be getting rid of pleasant memories, but hey, power is power.*

Bashe takes a deep breath and lets it out. "Okay. I guess we're making a deal after all. Just so we have the terms out in the open beforehand: you'll trade three memories for a spell bestowal. With what little mana I have left and the spells in my repertoire, there's really only one good option for bestowal: [Adrenaline Burst], a spell that will let you move faster and react faster."

"Is it limited use?" I ask, hoping the answer is no.

Bashe shakes his head and internally I cheer. "With what you're sacrificing, it can easily be a permanent addition to your arsenal. It *does* have a drawback, because every unaligned invocation comes with a limitation or drawback. In this case, [Adrenaline Burst] is going to be consuming your actual adrenaline while it's in use. When it's active you'll be faster, sharper, deadlier, but when it wears off the crash will hit like a bitch."

"Burn the fuel faster to make the flame brighter, gotcha. Sounds good."

The incubus rolls his shoulders. "Then let's begin. Azathoth, O Dreamweaver! I invoke the right of channeling that all imps are due. Bear witness to this contract and give it meaning. Hear our words and make them binding."

The maelstrom of color falls away. The black tower vanishes from view. Bashekehi and I stand in the presence of an eldritch horror, and it watches us in silence. As before, Bashe seems to take it as poorly as I do, and it brings me a bit of satisfaction to know that even a veteran of these deals still has to steady himself when Azathoth arrives.

"The contract is thus: a bestowal for memories. I offer my library of spells to pull from, and my mana to serve as a vessel for the Dreamweaver's grace." Bashekehi holds out his hand and purple-pink light flows out of his hand and into the air, forming a gently floating sigil. "I offer the spell [Adrenaline Burst], and have explained its capabilities to the invoker."

The Dreamweaver settles around my shoulders and commands my voice to speak her words. "I understand the capabilities of the spell and find it satisfactory for my purposes." I hate this. I hate the way she can so easily control me. But for the sake of magic, I'll suffer anything.

Bashekehi swallows and continues, "There is a price for all magic. I have offered a spell to be bestowed, the mana to bring it to life, and the grace of the Dreamweaver to bind it to your soul. What will you sacrifice to claim this offering?"

My memory has never been very good. Well, maybe it's more accurate to say my memory is *selectively* good. I can rant for hours about obscure lore from my favorite books and games, but if someone asks me what I did the day before, I'll blank. Some things I try not to remember, too.

Still, there are enough fragments of memory floating around that I can find at least three moments of excess. As I focus on each memory and imagine offering it to Bashe, the memory vanishes from my mind. Just like my name, which I can't even remember the first letter of.

A night of pleasurable bliss, stoned out of my mind in the arms of two pretty ladies, gone. That time I pigged out at three different fast food joints in the hopes of making myself throw up, gone. That game night where I spent hours making my friends suffer in Magic: The Gathering, gone.

Three memories vanish from my mind, and I see three faintly twinkling stars appear around the sigil that Bashe is holding out. They dance around the sigil, but stay floating above his hand when the sigil glides away from him and toward me.

My first spell branded my right hand. This time, the spell sinks into my left hand and settles into the flesh beneath. I shudder at the alien sensation of something nesting in the veins of my hand, but the feeling passes quickly.

"The bargain is struck," Bashe murmurs. Azathoth's presence falls away, and the three stars linger above Bashekehi's hand.

I'm giddy at having a second spell, but I want to pursue a particular thread first. "Do you get to see what's in those, when you crack them for mana?"

The incubus nods, only half listening, his gaze locked to the dancing lights. Hungry. "When I eat them, I experience them. Speaking of . . ."

He pops the first star into his mouth and bites down. Immediately his eyes roll back and he lets out a very *pleased* noise, so I assume that to be . . . uh . . . sex? Was that one of the memories I gave up? Or maybe he just reacts that way to any form of feeding. I actually have no foundation upon which to make that guess.

He breathes in, breathes out, closes his eyes, and rolls his shoulders. "[Indulgent Vitality]." A wave of change washes over his body, wiping away all the signs of malnourishment I noticed at our first meeting: skin no longer unnaturally stretched, veins no longer bulging, stomach no longer sunken. The skin around his eyes clears up, and his whole body seems to relax, limber up, settle into itself. When he opens his eyes again there's a new light to them, those black sclera and lilac irises practically sparkling.

"It has been so, so long since I had a good meal." His voice is fuller, richer, and more confident. There is something almost catlike about him now, languid and amused. "I must say, for all your flaws, you have excellent taste in lovers. That was *delightful*, Malice."

Aha! So it was sex! "Glad you enjoyed. How's your mana looking?"

He shrugs. "I spent all of that memory's gains restoring myself. The next two will do more to actually put me in the green." He pops the second star and lets out a contented sigh that quickly breaks off. A disturbed look passes over his face, and he visibly hesitates.

My pulse quickens. "What did you see?"

"I . . . it doesn't matter. It doesn't prove anything." His face doesn't match his words.

"What did you see, Bashe?" I press him.

He grimaces. "Familiar, yet unfamiliar. Fast food brands I've never seen before, a language I've never seen before, cars and buildings that are similar but different . . . it was all uncanny. But *not* impossible for someone to construct. For all I know that could just be another Sphere that *still isn't* the Zero Sphere."

I roll my eyes very dramatically. "Oh, come on. Stop being such a skeptic about this!"

"No." He pops the last star. There's a brief grin, a trace of excitement, which then mingles with puzzlement. "Huh."

"What was it?" I tilt my head curiously.

"A card game. Fairly similar to one I've seen back home, actually, but obviously not the same language. From what I understood of the scene, you were playing a strategy that your friends *fucking hated*, and getting off on that."

"Yeah, that sounds like me," I admit. *Wait. Language.* "Hey, uh, weird question: what language are we speaking right now? Because you seem not to have recognized English, which is what I *thought* I was speaking, but now I'm second-guessing myself, and I probably should have been questioning that assumption from the start but hey, sue me, I've had a lot on my plate."

Bashekehi smirks at me. "You're speaking Primordial. You probably shouldn't stress over the specifics, but it's a language that roots in the brain of everyone who steps into Pandaemonium. It goes deep enough that it'll feel as natural to you as your native language, maybe more, and as it evolves in one part of Pandaemonium that evolution spreads to every speaker, so it always remains one universal language."

Someone's solution to linguistic drift. Should take the time to practice switching between Primordial and English at some point. Should figure out how to do that, first. Aloud, I ask, "Did Azathoth create Primordial?"

Bashe shrugs. "Probably? Depends on who you believe, but I'd put money on her or Nyarlathotep being responsible."

Huh. Should really weasel a creation story out of Bashe at some point. Just gotta find the right moment. "Interesting. Shall we proceed to the final bargain?"

"Right. The next spell is . . ." Bashe hesitates. He smooths his hair back, chews on his lip, and finally looks at me and says, "You know, this is normally the part where I might try to downplay the risk involved to nudge the invoker into making the deal, but you seem to *thrive* on risk, so I'll just lay it out: the spell I'm offering you is extremely dangerous and could get you killed if you use it poorly. It also might be your best option for survival, and is disproportionately powerful compared to anything else I could offer."

I grin. "I'm all ears."

"The spell is called [Abyssal Armament] and it calls the power of the Abyss into a weapon of your choice—a physical weapon that you have to be touching as part of the spell—for a limited time. When a weapon is imbued like that, every strike that hits something with a soul will carve off a piece of that soul and feed it to the Abyss."

I can practically feel my eyes sparkling. "The *Abyss*? You have a place called the Abyss, and it eats souls!? That's so fucking metal!!!" I squeal a little. "You *have* to tell me more. Are there ways to commune with the Abyss? Other methods to draw power from it?"

"I wish I had a rolled-up newspaper to slap you with," the incubus rudely confides in me. "The Abyss is *bad news*, Malice. Not in an edgy way, not in a 'conventionally taboo but actually harmless' way, in a very real and dangerous way. Shadow magic is considered an inheritance from the Abyss, the last gift of the Leviathans, but even demons have to be *extremely careful* whenever it comes to dealing with the Abyss. If you slip up for even a second it will *swallow you whole*. Case in point: this spell. The price of [Abyssal Armament] is that it demands to be fed whenever you use it. If you don't slake its thirst with souls, the spell will turn on you and take a bite out of *your* soul. Fail to feed enough times and you'll go Hollow."

That's not nearly enough of an argument to sway me, but we can leave that conversation for another time. "Right, sure, scary dangerous Abyss is bad news. Now let's trade some Abyss magic for more of my memories." I grin at Bashekehi to add emphasis to my contrasting statements.

He sighs, clearly unconvinced. "I'll note that's the price of the spell for *everyone*. Normally there would be an extra cost for an unaligned invoker, but you happen to have the perfect counter. The invocation will erode any non-artifact weapon it is used on, rotting it to nothing after only a single use."

"And I already *have* an artifact," I preen.

"A useful coincidence," the incubus admits.

Bashekehi holds out his hand once more. He repeats the mantra of summoning and offers up a new spell. The sigil that appears this time is similar to the last, but the light that forms the sigil is darker, streaked through with gray-black. I hunger for it, and I make my offering, shivering as Azathoth's presence greets me once more.

More sex for sure, since he seems to have liked that. He said he preferred gambling, do we have anything relevant? We haven't done a lot of gambling with real money. Do gacha games count? There was that time I rolled Fischl second try, but that was a freebie roll.

Hmm. I did cheat at poker that one time. The actual gambling was low stakes but the cheating gave it a real thrill. Okay, so that's memory #2. And for the third?

How about drugs? Drugs are good.

A couple hours of sex, gone. Cheating at poker, gone. Getting very, very, *very* high, gone. As soon as they leave my mind and alight over Bashe's hand, they're completely absent from my memory, so thoroughly stripped I can't even figure out what was taken.

The dark sigil uncoils like a snake and curls around my right wrist, then sinks into it. I'm expecting it to be cold, for whatever reason, but as it meets my skin and bonds to me it carries a very familiar warmth: fever-warm. The spell settles into my wrist comfortably, almost pleasantly, and rests as what looks like a slightly spiky tattoo.

Azathoth's presence falls away and I am left with a burning question. "Bashe," I ask, "what does the Abyss look like? What does it feel like? How would I know if I'd been in its presence?"

He holds up a finger and pops each memory in his mouth, one by one, before replying. He sighs in contentment and rolls his shoulders. "Ah, food. Glorious food." Then what I said catches up to him and he furrows his brow with a very concerned expression. "Wait, what? Why would you think . . . oh, I'm going to regret this, aren't I?"

"Probably. Now answer the questions, Bashe."

He sighs, but he seems in a better mood now and there's less active frustration in the sound. "I've never seen the Abyss, mind, but it's been described as an endless realm of darkness, yet oddly warm, like a shadowed womb."

I grin. "Great, that sounds exactly like what I saw and felt when I woke up here."

The incubus stares at me. "Okay, you're fucking with me, right? This one's a joke, yeah?"

"Nope!" I chirp.

Bashe sits down on the glass walkway above the swirling maelstrom of rainbow light and puts his head in his hands. "Abyss take me," he swears. "Alright, you know what? Just tell me the whole story, because clearly there are some important details that I'm missing."

So I do. I tell him about the empty classrooms that opened into a fever-warm void, the not-a-ghost that tried to kill me, and the pink-blooded doll with its mismatched hairpin and backpack. When I get to my escape from the abandoned school and the Rider's all-consuming flames, Bashe stops me.

"There is *so much* wrong with that story. That's not . . . that's not how anything is supposed to work here."

I tilt my head curiously. "What do you mean?"

He rubs his temples. "Okay, for starters, *the fucking Abyss*! Yeah, what you described sounds a whole fuck of a lot like the Abyss, and the thought of the Abyss seeping into the Labyrinth is *terrifying*. The thing that tried to kill you sounds like normal Labyrinth weirdness but the school doesn't, and again, this world *isn't a video game*. Random 'loot' isn't a thing. The doll . . ." Bashe hesitates before continuing, ". . . it unnerves me. The symbol on the hairpin, the butterfly, it means a few different things. I assumed it was being used to represent Wonder, but it's also the alchemical symbol for transmutation—well, the culmination of transmutation—and it's one of the symbols used to represent Azathoth. That combined with the panacea makes me uneasy."

I lean in. "Starting to come around to the idea that Azathoth intervened after all?"

"No!" he snaps. "The Dreaming Edicts have *never* been broken. Whoever set that up, it wasn't Azathoth. Just . . . I'm willing to accept that it was *someone*, and not random chance." He looks almost frightened, and his gaze flits over to the black glass tower.

I roll my eyes. *Whatever. He'll come around eventually.* "So, back on topic: new spells!"

"Right, yeah. Feel free to test the adrenaline spell if you like, but *don't* use the Abyssal spell until you're in a position to feed it."

I decide to accept Bashe's advice, since I'm not entirely sure what the repercussions of losing my soul would be at this early stage of the campaign. Bashe lifts himself off the ground and takes a few steps back. I mentally reach for that feeling in my left hand, my second magic spell, and invoke it aloud. "[Adrenaline Burst]."

A new spell diagram appears in my mind's eye. I immediately compare it to my memory of [Find the Path]'s diagram and find this one to be much simpler in construction . . . and notably, much less configurable. Most of the symbols I see are fixed, unchanging no matter how much I focus on them. I recognize two of the symbols: the one that opens the text box and the one that activates the spell. That latter symbol is already blinking, which I recall indicates the spell being ready to engage. I don't really have a clear idea of what I would ask the spell to do differently, so I just hit the "on" button and let the spell do its thing.

My world electrifies. Everything snaps into focus—sharper, crisper, cleaner—and the swirling maelstrom of color seems to slow, just a bit. I can feel energy coursing through me, and I start bouncing my legs and tapping all my fingers just to bleed some of it out. I feel like I could run a marathon. I feel like I could catch a bullet. I bounce in place and twirl around, gotta move, gotta keep moving, motion is life. I twirl and twirl until I get dizzy, and then I stop myself and cancel the spell.

The world hits me like a Japanese delivery truck. A wave of exhaustion washes over me and my legs buckle, nearly crumple. My whole body feels sore, like I just did some kind of exercise workout bodily exertion. Is this what people who exercise feel like all the time??? How are they so fucking cheerful???

Bashe chuckles at my reaction. "Yeah, the aftershock's a bitch. You'll get used to it. Now come on, let's go pay the Contrite a visit." He hefts his stolen scourge and starts walking.

I follow behind, still a bit disoriented from the sudden strain infusing my limbs but working it out as I walk. Bashe doesn't talk as we head back to the first set of mirrors, and for once I'm content with the silence. I want to explore these spells more. I nonverbally activate [Adrenaline Burst] to see how it differs and find the whole diagram locked now, the only option to activate the spell or dismiss it.

Then, nonverbally so that Bashe doesn't find out I'm kinda-sorta ignoring his advice, I activate [Abyssal Armament].

The diagram for this spell feels *radically different* from either of my previous spells. All three use a similar set of symbols and shapes, for the most part, or rather they use symbols and shapes that feel like they're part of the same programming language, but there is a single symbol in [Abyssal Armament]'s diagram that looks different, harsher, hard to wrap my brain around, and it feels warm to the touch despite the fact that I literally can't touch it. It's like just looking at the symbol makes me feverish. It's also a different color from everything else; all the other symbols and shapes are white on black, but this symbol is black on black and somehow still perceptible, like a color so pitch dark it makes the night sky look gray.

With [Adrenaline Burst], the fixed parts of the diagram felt like a mechanism locked in place, like gears that had clicked together. With [Abyssal Armament], it feels like a bug caught in amber, something crystallized and frozen. *I really need to experiment with these. Hmm. If these are known spells, I wonder if anyone else has written down what all the symbols mean? Something to investigate as soon as we find books here.*

I dismiss the spell and shortly thereafter we reach the mirror opposite the one we took to enter the Corridor. I see the reflection of a room with strange walls and a carpet of graying lichen. Bashe stops just in front of the mirror and puts a hand on it. He breathes deep, fists clenched.

Under his breath, he murmurs, "If any of them are still alive, Muzaffer, I promise you, I'll make them pay."

Ooo, file that under "secret traumatic backstory"! Is that like, whoever he was contracted to before getting sealed away? Definitely keen to dig more into that relationship. Y'know, carefully and covertly. Wouldn't want to pick at his wounds in a way that would get us caught.

Bashekehi steps through the mirror, and I step through after him.

X

I step out of the mirror and immediately hear Bashe swearing.
"Fuck, fuck, fuck!"

There's a bit of sensory overload when I first look around to get my bearings; everything in this new area is radically different from any of the previous zones of the Labyrinth (and I *am* thinking of them as zones like an RPG might have, especially with the weird way they transition).

The graying lichen beneath my feet is probably the most normal part of this whole mess. The wall immediately facing me was hard to decipher from its reflection but now that I'm up close it looks like someone took the interior of a cathedral and *melted it*: arches meld with warped iconography that devolves into fractal patterns spiraling off into infinity. The walls stretch up and to either side past the point my eyesight can discern, and that's still nothing compared to what I see when I turn around.

It's like a cavern, dim and claustrophobic and oppressive, but there's no *end* to it; curved darkness gives the impression of walls and a ceiling but there's no stone, only great ornamented spires and crumbling clock towers emerging at odd angles from the vast dark. Twisting, turning bridges of lichen-choked stone crisscross over a pit that glows deep down with cold, dim, flickering light.

The air is heavier here, denser, thicker, or maybe it just feels that way? The sensation is strange. My movements are more difficult, even breathing is harder, but the resistance doesn't seem *physical*; it's like every act of motion is just more taxing in this space. There's something murky about the place, too, in sharp contrast to the perfectly even lighting throughout the rest of the Labyrinth so far.

I walk over to join Bashe where most of the floor we're standing on falls away into the pit and a thin strip continues on to the nearest bridge. He kicks a loose clump of moss off the edge and continues swearing.

I quirk an eyebrow at my devilish companion and try to think of a witty line that will make him think I'm funny and charming while also prompting him to exposit about why exactly he's getting so worked up. I don't think of one so I just ask, "'Sup?"

He interrupts his swearing to glare at me. "Really?"

I roll my eyes at the mouthy incubus. "Come off it. Just tell me what's going on. You're *clearly* upset about more than just whatever was riling you before. What *is* all this?" I ask, gesturing at the vast expanse of darkness, bridges, and jutting towers.

"This," he hisses, "is a fucking mess! It's a catastrophe! It's absolute fucking *bullshit* is what it is!"

I give him my best unimpressed deadpan stare.

He breaks eye contact, adjusts the straps of his backpack, and mutters, "It's a dream bubble."

I blink. "Like in *Homestuck*?"

"What the fuck is a 'Homestuck'?" he asks, baffled.

"Well, let me tell you about—"

"No," he interrupts me, "shut up, I don't actually want to know. Every time I've let you talk about things from your world it just makes my headache worse."

I glower at Bashe. "Just make with the exposition already."

He kicks another clump of moss off the edge. "Here's what you need to know: the Lady of Shards casts off pieces of herself—shards—and makes horrible fucked-up monsters that we call Beasts of the Labyrinth, and one of those Beasts lives at the heart of the city on the other side of this dream bubble: the Beast of Lamentation and Euphoria. Whenever it wakes up, the Beast sheds a piece of itself and sends out a Mourner or a Reveler. *This,*" he gestures at the eldritch mess of architecture, "is what happens when a Mourner finds a little piece of the Labyrinth it likes and turns that piece into its nest. We call things like that nest 'dream bubbles.'"

I lick my lips at the new information. *That seems like an excellent setup for conflict escalation: start with a Mourner, then fight the Beast, then throw hands with the Nightmare Queen herself.* "Okay, so how do we kill the Mourner?"

He throws up his hands. "We *don't!* This is not a problem we can solve with violence, and, for the record, I know I was cheering on the idea of killing all the Contrite, but *most problems* cannot be solved with violence."

I frown. "That doesn't track with my understanding of history at all."

A horrible echoing wail cuts off whatever Bashe says next. The wail is a layer cake of awful: the plaintive cry of an anguished child, a mournful dirge, and an ear-bleeding shriek. The wail shakes the very foundation of the space we're in, knocking loose a stalactite church tower off in the distance.

Bashe's face pales and he immediately starts marching for the mirror. "Nope, not doing this. I am not sticking around any longer."

I chase after him. "You're leaving? Do you know another route to the city?"

"Nope. I'll figure it out once I'm *not here*."

The incubus reaches for the mirror and I grab his arm to pull him back. He's stronger than me, probably was even before feeding on my memories, but he stops and turns to glare at me.

"Let go, Malice."

I curl my lip at him. "Are you really just running away?"

"We can't *fight* a fucking Mourner. You don't know what they're like, you don't know what they're capable of. It spreads despair like a virus, it infects you and makes you its puppet, and it uses you to spread the sickness to others. You won't even be its slave, Malice, just another infection vector." He looks at my hand still clutching his arm and lowers his voice, tone dangerous. "Let. Go."

I tense, but I can't let him leave. I need to get to the other side, to keep moving forward. Stagnation is death. "What about the Contrite? What about your revenge?" I hesitate, but only for a moment. "What about Muzaffer?"

He punches me in the face.

I don't see it coming and it sends me reeling back. I wobble, vision jagged, world spinning, as pain blooms across my nose and cheek.

"Fuck you," he spits at me. "You selfish little *bastard*. Muzaffer was my *husband*, and the Contrite *murdered* him, and now you're going to try and use his name to make me risk my *life* for you? For your stupid *delusions* of being important?"

"I'm sorry! Sorry, sorry, sorry," I babble on instinct, responding automatically to being hit while my brain tries to catch up and process what he's saying. *His husband. Muzaffer was his husband.*

Bashekehi turns from me and takes another step toward the mirror—

—and it shatters into a hundred shards as a second wail rocks the whole platform we're on.

The incubus and I both stare at the shattered mirror, shocked. Bashe's hands curl into fists and as he whirls on me, I'm already saying the words, "[Find the Path]."

The burning wheel appears over my hand and the diagram appears in my mind's eye. Bashe stops and his eyes narrow. "You—"

"Fucked up, yes, I know! It's all my fault and I am a horrible person and you can call me names and hit me *later*—please avoid the face next time, the rest of my body is fine—but right now we need to get out of here and I'm the only one with a spell that can do that. Am I wrong?"

Bashe's lips curl and his fists tighten, but he says, "Fine. Get us out of here, and then we can *talk* about what just happened."

I focus on the correct symbol in the spell diagram and activate the text box. "Compass, find me the safest path to the city on the other side of this dream bubble."

The command is accepted, I engage the activation symbol, and the wheel spins and resolves into an arrowhead once more. Predictably, the first direction it points is straight onto the nearest bridge leading farther inside the Escher-esque cavalcade of bridges and spires.

I take a deep breath and exhale. "The only way out is through."

I lead the way across the stone bridge, shoes squishing into gray lichen as I run and Bashekehi follows. The compass guides my route, showing me when to turn onto a branching line of mossy stone. I'm thankful for my seemingly neutered fear response as I run across precarious, crumbling pathways.

A third wail shakes more church towers loose from above, great works of architecture falling like stalactites and crashing into distant bridges. Bashe swears but I ignore the carnage and focus on reading the compass.

When I cross the halfway point of another stone span, everything changes. Just like before, I breach a threshold and the world dramatically shifts. The endless spires and bridges are gone and I am running through narrow halls of what looks like rusted metal, or maybe those are dried bloodstains. As the compass leads me on, I round a corner and skid to a stop at the sight of a corpse lying against the wall.

"Why are you stopping?" Bashe snaps at me, but then he sees the corpse on the floor and jerks back. "Shit!"

The body is a man's, bare-chested and wearing only a pair of very austere trousers. His flesh is scarred in every spot that *can* be scarred, a tapestry of scarification that has to be intentional—I would know. His face is blank, eyes glassy, unblinking and unbreathing, but as I watch closely I see one of his eyes twitch and his head starts to move, glacially slow, in our direction.

Zombie. That's a zombie, right?

"[Abyssal Armament]," Bashe shouts, and the scourge in his hand is wreathed in darkness as he throws it back and snaps it at the not-so-dead body. The whip strikes true and its payload scores the unbreathing man's chest. The shadows writhe and drink deep of the wound, and when they fade from the scourge their passing is accompanied by the man's passing as he collapses in place, head lolling.

I stare at the body, unsure if it'll stay dead this time. "What the fuck was that?"

"The Lost," Bashe spits. "It used to be Contrite, but now it's just part of the disease. *That* is what happens if the Mourner gets you; the virus will sap the will from you until you can't even breathe, but it won't let you *die* either. If you see more of them, don't let them touch you; they can spread the virus through contact."

"Unbelievable. You have *depression zombies* in this horrible world."

I want to examine the body further, particularly the unique scarification, but mindful of Bashe's warning and the distant wailing of the Mourner, I keep moving.

The compass leads us through a maze of twisting halls and winding stairwells; we don't see any more of the Lost until we turn the corner into a wide hall and see half a dozen of the listless bodies lying there. Bashe raises the whip again but hesitates, none of the Lost seeming to react to our presence.

A terrible wail shakes the hall, and every single body opens its eyes.

Bashe acts first, lashing out with the spell-enhanced scourge at the nearest zombie. I activate the same spell and lunge for one on the other side of the hall, reaching out to stab it in the throat while keeping most of myself as far from it as possible. The shadows pour down the dagger and into the Lost, devouring something unseen, and after a moment the body is made a true corpse.

The other Lost are rising, slow but not as slow as that first one. Bashe's first target falls and he lashes at the second, but the zombie's arm gets in the way and it keeps rising. I carefully step around my own victim and make a few cutting motions at the next Lost in my way. Like with the arm hit, these lesser wounds seem to take less from the Lost.

Fighting the depression zombies is a strange feeling; there's tension, certainly, as Bashe's warning rings clear in my mind, but no *urgency*. The third and fourth zombie collapse as the fifth and sixth are finally moving towards us with arms outstretched, dull eyes glassy.

I don't want to risk getting tagged trying to stab one of them, so I step back from the approaching Lost and let Bashe handle the remainder. With the scourge he has just enough range to comfortably strike and retreat, and though the last Lost grabs hold of the scourge to try and pull him, that just hastens its demise.

As soon as the last one falls and we're sure none of them are faking it, Bashe tells me, "Keep moving. We have to reach the exit before the Mourner reaches us."

We follow the compass through more halls and past more of the Lost, though never as many at once; each time we encounter them Bashe takes the lead in dealing with them, scourging them with the power of the Abyss. I feel a little useless, but he inarguably has the better weapon and I'm not keen to risk myself getting close to a depression zombie just for the sake of petty ego.

The tense blend of frantic running and sudden halting continues until the environment shifts again. This time we're in a vast hall with clearly defined boundaries: the ceiling is arched, the floor is tiled, and the walls are panels of stained glass depicting scenes of suffering from people being whipped until they died to people boiling in a sea of flame.

The way behind us stretches into infinity, but the way in front of us terminates in a glowing doorway. The compass points straight for that doorway and I spare a grin at Bashe as we immediately start sprinting for it, but then that awful wailing tears across the hall and this time it is *close*.

A quick glance behind me provides my first glimpse of the thing that terrified Bashekehi so deeply: the Mourner is an ethereal existence, a roughly human-shaped mass of diaphanous pale blue fabric cut into a thousand strips all flowing out of a porcelain mask. The mask has eyes of painted pitch that drip down the cheeks like tearstains, and the mouth of the mask is drawn in the distinctive frown of the tragedy mask from Greek theater.

"It's here!" I shout, and immediately I hear Bashe scream the name of the first spell he gave me and start sprinting even faster. I mentally curse and out loud shout, "[Adrenaline Burst]!" to keep up and outpace the monster rapidly flying towards us.

We run for the bright white light and the Mourner chases us, the mass of diaphanous fabric soaring through the air without a care for the laws of physics. It screams again, that awful mix of shrieking, a crying child, and a dirge for the fallen. This wail shatters every panel of stained glass in the hall, the shattering spreading out from the source of the scream. One by one the panels crack and glass is sent flying, though the hall is vast enough that none of it comes close to hitting Bashe or me. Beyond the shattered glass I see more endless darkness, the boundless boundary of this strange pocket world.

My body burns, already exhausted from all the running to get here and now being pushed past its limits by the adrenaline spell, but I have to keep moving. The door draws closer, closer, so close I can almost reach out and—

The Mourner wraps a single tendril of pale blue around my left hand.

On instinct I lash out with "[Ashthorn]!" and cut the fluttering banner from the main body of the Mourner, but as I pass through the door of light I'm already feeling the effects of the monster's touch; waves of weakness course up my arm, impossible to ignore.

I stumble out the other side and everything more than a few feet away is a blur, unimportant, too difficult to perceive. The scrap of Mourner falls away from my hand, but my fingers still feel numb, deadened, unresponsive. There is a deep coldness flickering in my fingertips and creeping across my hand and farther, making its way centimeter by centimeter.

Bashekehi is at my side, staring in horror at my hand. "Fuck, fuck, fuck!"

I can feel the poison entering my system, the virus that would love nothing more than to hollow me out and make me like those *things* in the maze. Lethargy, grief, despair, I feel all these lapping at my mind. Whispers of all my failures and failings, flickering images of mistakes that I've made, the deep knowledge that I am unfit to be here, unfit to be important, unfit to be *alive*. My existence is a cosmic accident, something that never should have been.

But I know that. I've always known that. I knew that when I took the knife to the artery in my inner thigh, and I knew that when I cut too shallow and couldn't bring myself to finish the job. I've heard these whispers a thousand times from my own treacherous mind, heard much more seductive promises: an end to pain, the peace of oblivion, no longer burdening others, no longer struggling in vain for things that could never be. I have been tempted before, lured to the brink, made to see no path more viable than utter self-destruction.

Humans, as it turns out, have quite the potent survival instinct.

A fire burns in me and I raise the burnt dagger with the hand not cursed by the Mourner's touch. "[Abyssal Armament]." The spell comes to life and the diagram appears in my mind's eye. I focus on the right symbol and declare my intent: "*Carve out the rot.*"

The spell takes hold, my dagger writhes with hungry shadows, and I stab the blade into the palm of my cursed hand.

There is a terrible sense of something tearing apart, and then everything goes dark.

INTERLUDE

SHADOW & GLASS I

The worst day of my life was the day I met you.
    I know it's tempting to say that the worst day of my life was the day I murdered my father, or the day it all unraveled, but those were just consequences. Inevitabilities. I deserved the pain I felt, both those days.
    Meeting you? That pain? I'll never forgive you for it.
    It started with a bad decision, one of many I made that day. I had been warned time and again not to skulk around my father's study when he wasn't present, so of course that's exactly what I was doing.
    I'd been sneaking past castle guards since I was old enough to cast my first spell, so getting into the study without being noticed was quite literally child's play for me. Over a decade of knowing that every patch of darkness could be hiding the crown princess had made the guards jumpier, but it hadn't taught any of them to look *up*. I slipped from rafter to rafter, stepping through shadow, until I reached the study door.
    The guards posted there would notice if I walked right in, so I transmuted my body to liquid darkness and flowed through a crack where the top of the door met the frame. On the other side I knew I had to act fast before the artifact went off, so I was already forming the spell in my mind, weaving together Shadow and Starlight. I envisioned plucking a star from the infinite darkness of space, stealing it away to be returned come next dusk. I murmured the incantation under my breath, too soft to be heard.
    "Darkness vast and shadows deep, swallow the stars and drag them 'neath. By my will these shadows seek: eclipse the light and make it sleep."
    I emerged inside the study and immediately unleashed the spell at the bronze helmet sitting on the central desk. Blue light was already radiating from the helmet's eyeholes, the artifact alert to the presence of an intruder, but before it could

finish activating it drowned in starry night. The spell consumed the artifact and pulled it inside my second shadow.

Candle's burning. The artifact was kept stagnant inside the extradimensional space of my second shadow, pacified by the embrace of my soul's pleroma, but I couldn't hold it there for long. No artifact would allow itself to be imprisoned for even an hour's length.

I set about my purpose with gusto. There was no specific prize I was after here, merely the satiation of curiosity. My father very rarely clued me in to what he was thinking, so I had learned to seek answers on my own time. I had filched from this study dozens of times, reading through reports and letters to try and decipher why he had said something or done something.

My father was a very organized man, which made my snooping much easier; he divided all his paperwork across different desks and partitions of desks by importance and purpose. This section for unimportant documents to be discarded, that section for important documents to be filed, the section over there for paperwork he'd yet to look at, and so on. I rifled through partitions until I found something in archival that shook me to my core:

It was a decree, a king's writ. The good paper, the good ink, and all the royal stamps. The word of the king made law and enacted on the world.

And it was a knife to the heart.

The writ declared, in a great deal of words, that the crown princess Reska Ines Zelic Dawnbringer was to be stripped of her claim to the throne, with the title of crown heir passing to the king's bastard son, Luka. I would still get to call myself a princess and I would benefit from the protections and privileges of the Dawnbringer bloodline, but I would be excised from rule and statecraft, excised from any position of power over the family's most crucial holdings. Perhaps I would be sent off to some distant estate to brood in for the rest of my days, like what happened to my grand-uncle after he disgraced himself.

The shock hit me first, and the denial. I read the letter, read it again, kept staring at the page.

This isn't right. This can't be right. Why would he—no, he wouldn't do this to me! This is just . . . a draft. A joke! Haha, very funny, Father. Please. Please just be a bad joke.

I moved to a separate partition, where my father kept documents that he intended to send out to the castle scribes for duplication and distribution. To my growing horror, I found a second copy of the writ sitting neatly in the position for items of highest priority. The writ was real, and my disinheritance was already happening.

Why would he do this? Why, why, why!? I failed to choke back a sob and had to cover my face to muffle the noise. My hands were shaking.

I knew why, of course; in many ways this moment was inevitable, and had been since I failed to manifest the family affinity as a child. The clans had no use for an heir that couldn't practice the bloodline's magic.

Still, I kept staring at the writ. I felt like I was being disowned, though some rational part of my brain reminded me that there were much worse forms of disinheritance practiced by the sorcerer bloodlines. I would still keep the name "Dawnbringer" after all, which meant I was still considered a full member of the family.

That didn't really matter to me. Rationality had no place in this; my father had immortalized on paper his immense disappointment in me as his daughter. He had given up on me and named me a lost cause. Undeserving.

Worthless.

I wanted to scream, but the guards were still outside, and I dimly recognized that I was running out of time before the artifact escaped its bonds. I dragged my nails down my arm, hard, to force myself to focus. Slip out unnoticed, then scream. I took a deep breath, directed a tendril of my shadow to rest on the central table, and released the helmet at the exact moment I transmuted back to liquid darkness and escaped through the door seam.

As I slipped through the rafters back the way I'd came, the fear and grief turned to anger. Betrayer. Liar. I shook with the weight of it, the absolute enormity of what my father had put to paper. For a sorcerer, inheritance was everything. No matter how many children a sorcerer had, only *one* could inherit the family legacy. The deepest secrets, the accumulated resources, and the sorcerer Crest that was the crown jewel of every bloodline.

To be chosen as heir meant you had earned the air you breathed. It justified the years of feeding you and caring for you and teaching you sorcery. It was the only sign of value and worth a sorcerer could respect. To be passed over meant you had failed your ancestors, your parents, and even yourself. You were dirt.

I didn't deserve this. I deserved better. I wouldn't let my father just throw me away like a broken toy. I wasn't broken. I wasn't broken. I wasn't broken!

Without consciously choosing to, I'd brought myself to the grand doors that led into the throne room where even now my father was holding court. I watched the door in silence, seething and stewing in my own negative emotions. I clenched my fists, I gritted my teeth, and I felt a deep yearning to storm into that chamber and give the whole court a piece of my mind.

It would be another rule broken, but what did that matter now? If I was nothing, the dirt beneath a better sorcerer's feet, then why care what they thought of me? Why care what anyone thought of me? My father had already made up his mind, and his was the only opinion I wanted to know.

Fuck it. Let the beast out.

I dropped from the rafters and landed gracefully in front of the two guards posted outside the door. Terror immediately crossed their faces as I rose, still wreathed in darkness, and growled at them, "Out of my way."

The guard on the left, scrawnier, eyes like gleaming amber, paled at my demand. The guard on the right, stockier, eyes gray like storm clouds, hesitated but stood his ground. "I'm sorry, Your Royal Highness, but His Majesty's orders were explicit: no one is to enter while court is in session, and that includes you."

My fingers twitched and I had to restrain myself with a hiss. *I wanted to lash out, I was aching to lash out at someone, anyone, but it wasn't their fault, it wasn't their fault, don't hurt them, please don't hurt them. I saw the fear on his face, his gaze flickering to my hands, to the darkness still heavy around me.*

I forced myself to channel that energy in a different direction and focused on eviscerating his argument. "No one, you say? No one at all?"

The guard slowly nodded, mute.

I bared my teeth and leaned in. "Well, that's very interesting, isn't it? Because 'no one at all' means that even if the castle were under attack from night horrors or a rival bloodline, the two of you would hold your posts and let not a peep of that through to the king and his guests. Is that correct? Or were your exact orders a little bit different from what you just told me?"

The guard on the left nervously shuffled a step further away from me. The guard on the right, the one whose personal space I had been invading, gulped audibly but didn't answer.

"Let me take a guess, then. I'm going to guess that you were actually told something to the effect of 'no one gets in unless there is an emergency,' am I right? Tell me I'm at least close, aren't I?"

The guard on the left cracked. "Yes! H-he told us, 'no one is to enter while court is in session, including the princess, unless there is an emergency that cannot wait.' Please don't eat me!"

Eat you? Really? Is that what you think of me? *Pain flared in my chest, but it was an old pain, nothing compared to the still-sharp betrayal of the king's writ, so I set it aside. The fear was useful. The fear was a weapon.* "See?" I remarked to the other guard while he glared daggers at his compatriot. "Was that so hard?"

The second guard let out a tired breath. "No one can enter while court is in session unless there is an emergency. I have not been informed of any emergency, Your Royal Highness."

I snarled, "Well I'm informing you! There's an emergency, and it can't wait, so get out of my way before I lose my patience and just blast the doors open."

The gray-eyed guard was tense, fearful, but his resolve held. "We can't let you do that, Your Royal Highness. We have our orders."

The amber-eyed guard did not hold his resolve. He protested, "What are you doing, Karlo? Just let her through!"

"The king's orders were clear, Neven." Karlo's voice was tight, controlled.

"I'd rather take my chances with His Majesty than with the—" Neven broke off, swallowed his words, and finished, "With the princess."

I knew what he had been going to say, before he caught himself: the Shadow Fiend. The people in the castle whispered about me, when they thought I wasn't around to hear them. They called me a monster from old myths, a demon wearing human skin. Sometimes, they said that I had crawled out of the Abyss and into the king's wife while she was pregnant.

They said it was my fault the queen had died.

The shadows pressed in, curling around me and creeping across the floor and up the walls. Darkness licked across the guards' boots and caressed their bronze-tipped spears. The dark vibrated with my anger and my pain. It seethed with my frustration, and it longed to lash out. Only my full force of will kept the shadows from tearing into the two innocent men barring my way.

I kept my voice quiet and low. "Just step aside and this will stop being your problem. Please."

Neven had already pressed himself against the nearest wall, desperate to be out of my way, but with my earnest plea it was finally enough for Karlo and he slowly, hesitantly stepped away from his post. I breathed a little sigh of relief, too soft for either to really notice in their panic, and threw open the throne room doors.

"Father! I know what you've done!"

My father sat on a masterwork of bronze sculpted with imagery of the rising sun: the Sunlit Throne. He wore robes in our colors, green and gold, and carried in his lap our family's sorcerer Crest: the Sunlit Scepter, a golden rod ending in a stylized sunburst that held all the power of our ancestors. He did not look pleased to see me, those eyes of pale gold seeming to burn into me.

My half brother, Luka, sat to the throne's right. I noted his presence with distaste; it was no secret that Luka attended these councils while I did not, but before that day I had avoided thinking about the implications of that. Now I felt the keen awareness of how deeply I had already been excised from the operations of my own clan. Panic flared in his burnished gold eyes when he saw who had barged in unannounced.

Six others were arrayed in seats around the throne, the king's council that he spoke with regularly on matters of policy and governance. I knew their names and faces, had even spoken with them regularly when I was younger. The Master of Coin, Branko, had taught me numbers and found me a quick learner. The Master of Letters, Emil Posava Zelic Dawnbringer (named for the same ancestral Zelic as

I was), had tried to teach me etiquette and the art of influence. The duchess of our kingdom's second major clan, Ruzica Kadic Bladesinger, had tutored me in the sword before dismissing me as destined for the pen and book instead.

As I stormed into the throne room, shadows curling behind me, it was the Master of War, Viktorija Dawnsworn, who acted first. She rose from her seat, hand already on her sword and keen vigilance in her citrine-yellow eyes. Her gaze swept over the entrance and settled on me, and what was initially cautious concern melted away and became irritation at the presence of an unwanted pest.

"This is a closed court, Highness. You should know what that means." There was a dangerous edge to her voice, a warning. I did not care to heed it.

I kept stomping forth, darkness spreading into the room. It occurred to me then, dimly, that I was still in my sneaking clothes—soft-soled boots, gray silk trousers, gray silk tunic—and not anything remotely appropriate for court. I vaguely wished that I could have thought to wear something more dramatic and theatrical, but in the end it was just another meaningless embarrassment to add to the ever-growing list.

The Master of Pigeons, Mislav, chuckled at Viktorija's warning. "Of course she knows. Sit, Warmaster, and let us hear what brings the girl before us." The king's spymaster was a secretive man, and I had never much liked him; of all the keen-eyed folk in the castle, he was one of only two that I could never fool when creeping about the castle.

Emil frowned at my approach. "Your Highness, these theatrics are ill-timed. Interrupting court will only earn His Majesty's ire."

I hissed at the Master of Letters, "I don't care. That doesn't matter anymore." I marched around the table, the Warmaster glaring but not stopping me, and came before the throne.

Luka stepped in front of me, raising a hand to ward me back. His voice was low, and he met my gaze with those damnable golden eyes. "Reska, don't do this. I know you can be smarter than this. Just walk out now and all you'll have to face is being chewed out for impropriety. Don't go making things worse for yourself."

I seethed with anger, and the shadows seethed with me. The dark crawled up the walls and the four pillars of the throne room, finding the sunstones and smothering them. One by one they went out, plunging the room into greater and greater darkness until only the light of the throne illuminated the grand hall.

Luka still barred my way, unflinching. "Please, Reska. Just walk away and accept whatever punishment he gives you. It's not too late to salvage this."

"Piss off."

The crown-prince-to-be exhaled and stood aside, returning to his place by the king. "On your head may it be."

At last I stood before my father, King Kresimir Vincek Dawnbringer, with no one else standing between us. He stared at me with that implacable disapproving gaze, still silent.

I clenched my fists, met his gaze, and gathered my resolve. "Father. I know what you've done. I read the writ."

My father showed no reaction, and I couldn't see any of the councilors to know their minds, but Luka's mouth tightened at my words. He knew. He'd known, and still he tried to stop me. Liar. Betrayer.

My grip tightened and I whirled on the assembled court. "Did you know? Did you know that my father, our beloved king, has cast aside his own daughter and disinherited her? I will be of the blood in name only, an embarrassment to be exiled to nowhere and left to rot. And Luka"—I spat the name—"is to be your future king, the crown prince of Sun and Sword."

The spymaster Mislav's reaction was inscrutable as ever, and the same held true for the court's Master of Lore, the wizened crone Zdenka of the Lidless Eye. War and Coin, Viktorija and Branko, both showed the dull surprise of learning something that had been neither known nor unexpected. Emil and Ruzica had known, of course; they had both been close with my father before he claimed the title of crown heir from his cousin, and to my knowledge their friendships had only deepened in the two decades since. Both displayed their foreknowledge openly, though one showed what I took to be false pity and the other showed blatant contempt.

"So you knew, or a few of you did and the rest are unsurprised. Do none of you care that your king is betraying his own daughter?"

The duchess snorted at my words, silver eyes shining. "Whingy little brat. A few hard knocks and you come crying before your betters. What a worthless thing you turned out to be."

"Your Grace," interjected the Master of Letters, "perhaps it would be more constructive to offer arguments instead of insults." He turned to me and continued, "Your Highness, there is significant precedent for a writ of this nature; precedent of which I am sure you would have considered had you the time to process this revelation. Neither your father nor Duchess Bladesinger were the trueblood heirs to their respective clans, but rather earned their crowns through great effort and achievement. It is traditional for the crown heir to be whoever holds the strongest tie to the clan's affinity, and for any child who cannot manifest that affinity to be exiled from the clan entirely. Your father has done you a great mercy with this decision."

I knew that. Of course I knew that. Rationally, intelligently, logically, I knew that.

The shadows sharpened and I heard a sunstone crack.

My father spoke. "Zdenka, please recite what you know of the lore of spontaneity."

The ancient Loremaster intoned smoothly, "The spontaneity tendency is a phenomena observed only in children, most often in children who have yet to evolve their innate affinity for Chaos into a more coherent affinity. A child whose relationship with dreamweaving is yet instinctual, untempered and uncontrolled, will sometimes manifest magical effects without meaning to cast any spell. This spontaneity is considered to be a response by the child's magic to internal impulses and desires that the child is struggling to express conventionally. In the majority of cases this spontaneity tendency is resolved by the early teenage years, and in no known cases does spontaneity persist past the onset of adulthood." The crone's face split into a smirk and she added, "Barring one."

A flush began to heat my cheeks as the old woman used a great many words to call me, in essence, a child.

"Thank you, Zdenka," was my father's calm reply.

I turned from the council and back to my father, anger now mixing with mortification. I tried to control the shadows, tried to reach out to them and guide them back to my side, but they just wouldn't listen to me. As I guided one tendril of darkness to my feet another slipped from my control and curled around a new object in the room.

They watched me fail. They all watched as I tried and failed to control my magic, like a child with affinity still unformed.

I swallowed hard and tried to hold on to my anger, to my righteous indignation. "You can't do this to me, Father. You can't abandon me like this. I know I'm not—not perfect like Luka, not the golden child who fits your perfect mold. But I'm powerful. I may not have our family's affinity, but I have something stronger. I have a power that no other bloodline on all of Svijetstakla could ever claim to grasp, a power that no human has ever even touched before me—at least not without dying a painful and immediate death. You can't just ignore that. I deserve more respect than that!"

Luka shook his head at me and I almost hissed at him before stopping myself. I had to stay calm. I had to stay in control.

Father watched me through every word, through every motion, and through my forced restraint after. He watched, silent, as the tension rose in me again, and it was only when I made to speak once more that he stood from his throne and cut me off.

"You throw a tantrum in my court," he began, his voice low and cold and calm. "You make demands of your king like a child begging for sweets. You insist that you be treated with respect, and yet, when you make your way to this most hallowed chamber—unannounced, uninvited, unwanted—and interrupt an important meeting, you can't even control your own affinity. That behavior wouldn't be fit for a child half your age, let alone an heir to the Sunlit Throne."

With each word I shrank in on myself, anger withering as I was scolded like a misbehaving little girl. I wanted to disappear. I wanted to pretend that I had never walked into the throne room, but still the last embers of that rebellious flame flickered inside me. I had a right to feel this way. He was abandoning me and he wouldn't even tell me about it before telling the rest of his court. My shadows grew spikes and geometric patterns, undulating in strange waves as my control slipped further away. "Father, I—"

The Master of Sun and Sword lifted his hand and a new sun was born, a blazing orb of white-hot light that scoured every shadow from the room. Every writhing, seething, twisting tendril of darkness was burnt to ash in an instant. The whole of the room was cleansed of my magic, purified in the light of our clan's true affinity. The sun dimmed, becoming a single pinprick of light, but the shadows did not return.

When he spoke, my father's voice carried the edge of violence that I knew and feared. "On your knees, child. Hand outstretched."

Cold terror consumed the heat of anger and humiliation. Nervousness bubbled in my chest and I had to fight to keep it down. I couldn't let it escape, couldn't let it burst from my chest as terrified laughter because if I laughed then I would just make it worse. "I—I'm sorry, I'm sorry, I'm sorry, I—"

"Now!" he snapped.

I dropped to the ground in front of him and held out my shaking hand, still stammering apologies with every other breath. He lifted his foot and held it in the air, watching me with cold anger frozen on his face.

Sternly, as if teaching a lesson, he told me, "If you insist on acting like a child, then you shall be disciplined like a child."

My father was always a careful man, even when he did not need to be. There was little he could have done to my hand that castle healers could not have fixed in minutes or hours, and yet he was always so precise with his violence. He stepped on my hand and ground it down to the point just before permanent injury would have been caused, allowing me to simmer in the pain and anticipation, and only when my apologies gave way to wordless crying did he relent.

He turned from me and settled into his throne once more, watching with those cold, furious golden eyes as I shook upon the floor of his hallowed throne room and stained the stones with my tears.

When he spoke again, his voice was dispassionate. "Out of my sight."

So I ran. I bolted from the throne room and melted into the shadows of the castle halls, trying desperately to stifle my sobs lest someone hear and the shame rise ever higher.

I fled to my chambers and slammed the door shut behind me, emerging from darkness to crumple in a heap upon my bed. My self-loathing was growing teeth, my fear and shame and grief mutating into something darker and viler.

Weak. Worthless thing. Just a broken toy. A failure. A whingy little brat.

I stumbled from the bed into my washroom and stared into the mirror, gripping the sink tightly with both hands. I stared into my own eyes, my own awful, hideous, disgusting eyes: dark like frostbitten fingers, dark like buzzing flies, dark like long-dried blood, dark like the monsters that creep from below through the cracks in the skin of the world. A demon's eyes, they whispered when they knew I could hear. And I stared at a face that was, in every way except those accursed eyes, the spitting image of every portrait I had ever seen of my mother.

My fault. All my fault. It was my fault she died. It's my fault they all hate me. I am the thing that stole her life and stole her child and ruined everything for everyone. It's my fault. It's my fault.

I screamed wordless anguish and punched the mirror until it shattered. The glass shards sliced into my hand and opened my skin and blood dripped out, drip, drip, drip, onto the pale porcelain below. Warmth blossomed and spread from my hand across my body, pain and relief in equal measure. The agony of a dozen lacerations drowned out every thought in my head and finally, finally, finally . . .

. . . there was only silence.

INTERLUDE

SHADOW & GLASS II

The silence didn't last; it never did.

The warmth faded and the blood kept dripping, and self-preservation took over. My hand had been injured and I needed to fix it. It was my left hand, the non-dominant, but I still needed it.

Trying to pick out bits of glass by hand was clearly a terrible idea, so instead I called the shadows to me and directed them to swarm my hand and take away everything that didn't belong. I swept them over the sink and floor and dragged every shard of glass I could find into my second shadow's storage space.

My hand twitched and bled and I stared at the broken skin. There was something enrapturing about the sight, even as panic started to creep in and I realized how utterly fucking stupid I had just been.

I can fix this. This is fine.

I was lying to myself. If not consciously, then at least unconsciously. I knew my effort was doomed to failure, but still I tried.

Nothing in my concept of Shadow or Starlight was tied to healing, but in my desperate attempts to evolve my magic I had developed a third affinity: Blood. Blood could represent kinship, lineage, and bonds, or it could represent life and death, heal and harm. Blood brought life as it flowed through veins, and it signified death when spilled on the battlefield. Blood was sacrifice, hardship, and suffering.

My affinity for Blood had always strayed much nearer the negative connotations than the positive, but I pushed that aside and held on to a strand of hope. I can do this. I gritted my teeth and called the magic to me, finding it sluggish and stagnant compared to fluid, dynamic Shadow. It knew this act went against its meaning.

I built the image in my mind, thinking of all the times I had seen healers repair flesh and knit wounds shut. I thought of gaps in skin closing cleanly and imagined blood flowing back from whence it came. I pictured my hand, whole again, and the restoration of my body's equilibrium.

I didn't have a formal incantation for this, no verse rich with meaning, so I did the next best thing: I talked.

"Blood is life. Blood is the essence of life, so to master Blood is to master life itself. The blood in my veins is mine, and it obeys my call. So restore my flesh and heal my wounds, because you are the essence of my life and you belong to me, you answer to me. Heal me, damn it. Mend what is damaged, repair what is broken, fix my mistake. Blood is life, and this is my blood, my life, and I can fix it. Heal!"

I shoved the spell into my hand and poured every scrap of meaning I could think of, drawing on all my memories of being patched up by family healers. Sunlight healers, using the family affinity. Cuts and scrapes and disapproving stares, light and dark and nerves. Healers working their magic, striving, failing, not enough to save her. My brother, my healer brother who was renowned for his healing ability, renowned for his mastery of Sunlight, his stupid wretched too-perfect—

The magic sank into my hand, into the breaks in my skin, into the blood flowing free, and the blood shook and twitched and shuddered but it didn't go back in and the cuts didn't seal. All I accomplished was making my hand even redder.

Stupid. Pathetic. Stupid pathetic worthless—

I closed my eyes and started counting. I imagined constellations in the night sky and counted the stars that made them. Six stars to the Leaping Lion, four stars to the Farmer's Flail. Five stars to the Gleaming Aegis, nine stars to the Lidless Eye.

It helped, a little. Enough that I could steady my shaking hands and wash them in the sink. Enough that I could quiet the noise and reorient myself. *I am calm. I am in control. Deep breaths, Reska.* I tried to keep my breathing deep and steady as I dried my hands on a towel and moved back to my bedroom.

I kept a kit under my bed for wound care. I knew that I should see a healer, I knew my hand was too important to risk with a shoddy patch-job, but I couldn't bear the shame of it. What would they think, when I showed them my bloody hand not even an hour after humiliating myself in front of the most powerful members of my father's court? What would they say this time?

I applied a bit of honey to bandages and carefully dressed my hand, then added a layer of dry dressing and wrapped it tight. I was lucky the wounds were shallow enough to not need sutures, as doing that one-handed would have been a nightmare.

There was something calming about going through the motions of tending to my injury. The work was simple but demanded focus, and when the task was done I felt a bit better, like I had bandaged up more than just my hand.

I could still feel the ache inside me from the contents of the writ and my stupid, reckless overreaction, but it felt a little more manageable. Still, I needed a better distraction. If I stayed in my room and stewed I would inevitably talk myself back down into a spiral.

There was one obvious answer: the library.

I swapped my gray sneaking clothes for an outfit that would look more at home wandering the castle and browsing the library shelves: a silk dress with vibrant orange body, cream-colored sleeves and skirts, and pale orange floral patterns threaded along the hem of the sleeves and skirts; and a silk cloak in sky-blue with sunburst patterns in gold lace, draped over the shoulders and voluminous enough to hide my injured hand within the folds. I kept my boots, comfortable as they were, as I doubted anyone would notice them beneath my skirts.

I wished as ever that there was a convenient way to hide my eyes, but my pale blonde hair was common enough in the realm that I could probably evade notice so long as I avoided looking at people directly, or if I maneuvered my hair to hang over my face. Being able to occasionally obscure my identity was half the reason I kept my hair so long and straight.

I took a few more steadying breaths before finally gathering the resolve to step out of my chambers and into the halls of the castle. I made good pace for the library and, before I was even halfway there, came face-to-face with Luka.

"Reska. I was on my way to pay you a visit." My half-brother was still in his court uniform, bedecked in silk and gold and precious gems. "We should talk." His demeanor was easy, relaxed, but his tone was serious.

My mood soured immediately, but I forced myself to be polite. "What about, dear brother?"

Luka winced. "I can tell you're still upset. I understand that. I knew this was going to be hard on you and—"

"You knew and yet you didn't warn me," I cut in. "We haven't even spoken in weeks." Another little pang of pain crossed my chest. It hadn't always been that way, with Luka. "But I get it, I do. You were too busy with Father, preparing to take my place."

"Reska—"

"No," I interrupted again, "you already took my place years ago. Maybe you always had it. So what's there left to say?"

The crown prince sighed. "You know it's not like that. Please, Reska, be reasonable."

Why should I? I bit back the words I wanted to say. "Just . . . just go away, Luka. I don't want to think about this right now. It already hurts enough." I looked away from him, unwilling to meet that golden-eyed gaze.

Out of the corner of my vision I saw him grimace and fold his arms. "It's not that simple. I don't think you properly understand the consequences of what you did today. You can't just run away from that and hide in your room, or in your precious library."

I pulled my cloak tighter around me and snapped, "Is that why you were looking for me? To lecture me? I don't need this from you, Luka. I get enough of it from Father. At least he doesn't pretend to care about me first."

Luka's voice softened. "Is that what you think? That's not true at all. Father cares, he just has a stern way of teaching. The burden of kingship is heavy, but he's a reasonable man. If you stopped antagonizing him, you'd see that."

I dug the fingers of my uninjured hand into my palm. Softly, weakly, I said, "He doesn't even give me a chance, Luka. I've tried so hard for so long to prove myself and he just spits on all my efforts. I built three affinities in the time it takes most to develop one, but because I can't call a sun to my hands I'm nothing to him."

Luka went quiet, and after a moment I turned to leave, but he put a hand on my shoulder and stopped me. "There's more to being the heir than just having the right magic, Reska. I know you think that's the only thing standing in your way, but it isn't. To lead the family means knowing the right time and the right place to say the right things to the right people. It means mastering our blood's magic, yes, but it also means mastering diplomacy and commerce and warfare and subterfuge. And barging into court like that? Making a scene in front of everyone? You had to have known that wouldn't go well. But it's the kind of thing you always do. It's just in your nature."

I stopped, stunned, and then I whirled on him and snarled, "What are you saying? That I'm just unfit to be in the public eye? That I'm worthless *as a child of Dawnbringer*? That I should just exile myself and get it over with?"

Luka closed his eyes, took a deep breath, and opened his eyes to snare my gaze head-on. "I'm saying: what girl wouldn't kill to be a princess? Isn't that enough?"

My mood was getting darker, sharper, despairing. That's not what it's about. That was never what it was about. "Would you still hold that attitude if you were the one who lost?" I pushed his arm off and stepped away from him.

Luka rolled his eyes, exasperated, but before he could make any retort he caught a glimpse of my other hand as my cloak shifted with the motion of pushing him away. Immediately his expression went murky and he muttered, "What did you do to yourself this time?"

This time. What did you do this time? What did you do to yourself this time?

The crown prince took a step toward me and said, "You should have told me. Give me your hand and I can—"

"No!" I shouted as I clutched my wounded hand to my side and raised the other arm defensively. The shadows in the hall sharpened and came together in front of me, coalescing into a thicket of thorns that separated me from Luka.

Luka's hand went to the hilt of the ornate rapier looped through his belt, moving on instinct, but he stopped before drawing the blade. He narrowed his eyes at the barrier of darkness, then at the panicked expression on my face. "Sister."

I swallowed hard and tried to force the shadows back to their corners. "I—I don't need your help. I can take care of myself." The resisting manifestation of my magic contrasted my words starkly.

Luka just kept staring me down. When the barrier finally started to bleed away, he shook his head at me slowly and said, "Control yourself. If you can learn nothing else, at least learn to control yourself."

He left without another word, and I stood there alone with the noise in my thoughts. When the last of my shadows returned to the corners of the hall, I resumed my trek to the library in even worse spirits than before.

The rest of my walk was uneventful, and when I took my first steps into the library, I felt my heart lighten a shade. I've always loved to read, ever since my father first taught me with his favorite works of literature and theory. A library is a greater trove than the most lavish vault of coin, and all the more comfortable to explore.

The library was one of the largest chambers in the castle, occupying nearly two whole levels of the northwest wing. While most of the castle was lit with sunstones, the library was lit with moonstones to be gentler on the pages. The shelves were treated greatwood imported from our neighbors in the Kingdom of Wood and Cloud, and the floors were carpeted in wool dyed into intricate patterns in shades of blue, green, and orange.

The library was divided into nine sections, themselves subdivided into smaller sections, and over the years I had familiarized myself with each of them extensively: literature, history, sorcery, philosophy, manuals of craft, manuals of war, mathematics, medicine, and law.

I wandered the shelves, enjoying for a time the simple act of reading the titles of books and recalling what I knew of the contents. I hadn't read every book in the library, of course; there were probably thousands in total, and my interest in the written word was not universal. Still, I had read more than most.

I contemplated what I should read: there were a few books I had been meaning to sit down and sink my teeth into, but I wasn't in the right headspace to really digest their contents. There was always the option of rereading a comfortable favorite, but something about that idea made me feel uneasy.

You can't just run away and hide in the library.

I clenched my uninjured fist. I couldn't get Luka's words out of my head, nor the memory of the debacle in the throne room. More than anything, I remembered the way my own magic had embarrassed me, the shadows refusing my dominion both in front of court and alone with Luka.

My magic had always been like that, and it rankled; my power was greater than any sorcerer of my age, greater than most sorcerers twice my age, but it slipped from my control like I was still a little girl. Just one more reason the whole castle called me "demon."

I left the literature stacks and slipped through the shelves to the sorcery section. Of all the collections in the library I had read this one most thoroughly, and I knew exactly what book I was after: The Aspected Child: You Are What You Can Do, assembled by the Covenant of the Lidless Eye for the benefit of budding sorcerers. It was a standard read for any scion to a sorcerer bloodline, talking at length about how to shape meaning and develop finer control over one's magic.

I found the right spot, reached out to pull the book from the shelf, and as I did my hand touched yours.

I pulled away, surprised, and immediately panicked that I'd be recognized. I looked away and brushed a lock of hair in front of my face to try and hide my eyes. "Sorry, I was lost in my head. Go ahead, I've already read that one."

You laughed lightly and said, "No, no, the fault is mine." Your voice was confident, low, and smooth. "Though if you've read the book, I'd love to hear what you think of it."

I risked a glance and was caught off guard by the sight of you; you looked like the strangest girl I'd ever met. Your hair was short and messy, a choppy tangle of russet brown, and your eyes were dark like mine but burning with an almost frightful intensity. You were bony and thin like someone starved, but you were as tall as my father and there was a manic energy about the wide grin on your face.

Your clothes were the strangest part, and at the time I didn't know what to make of them. You dressed all in black, which suggested either foreign make or absurd wealth given that no black pigment could be found locally. You wore a tunic that was of absurdly fine cotton and bore an intricate geometric design in vivid red, tight-fitting trousers of what seemed to be heavy twill, and a jacket of polished leather and metal decorations that went only to your waist and was worn open in the front. You would later tell me that those articles of clothing were called a T-shirt, skinny jeans, and (least surprisingly) a leather jacket, and that the design on the shirt was meant to represent an icosahedron, which you called a "d20."

I will admit that I found the whole effect oddly compelling; your aberrance was almost exotic after a lifetime spent interacting with the same few social circles. I still wonder: did you tailor your appearance to disorient me, or was it simply disinterest in the idea of pretending that you in any way belonged in my world?

No matter. The end result was that I spent a few surprised moments staring blatantly at your strange attire, and when I looked back up at your face you were smirking at me. "Find anything interesting?" you asked in a playful tone.

My face reddened with embarrassment as I hurriedly replied, "Sorry! Sorry, I didn't mean to stare. I've just never seen clothing like that before."

You changed your expression to something warmer but still amused. "Don't worry, I like the attention."

I didn't know how to react to that, and I was still caught between embarrassment and panic that I would be recognized, so I froze up.

You pretended not to notice, but broke eye contact and shifted your attention to the book to give me space to breathe. "You have so many books here, it's wonderful. This library is absolutely magnificent. I don't suppose you know how they're made? The paper, in particular, since it seems of such high quality."

The sudden change in topic let me refocus, though I found the question confusing; wasn't that just common knowledge? Still, it was a chance to share information, so I gladly told you, "It's a fairly simple process. I'm actually surprised anywhere hasn't heard of it. All it takes is someone with the right affinity and a good sword. They cultivate these big mushroom forests and then slice the stalk into perfectly thin pieces."

Your eyes gleamed as you glanced back at me, and then you looked at the moonstones above and murmured, "Fascinating. What about the lights? You have excellent lighting in this castle but they don't seem to operate on electricity. What are they?"

A part of me started to suspect that I was being led on, made a fool of, but you seemed so sincere that I had to answer. "Those are moonstones. Glassblowers with a certain affinity make them and let them soak up moonlight. The lights in the rest of the castle are sunstones; they follow the same principle but with sunlight."

"Affinity," you said, tasting the word. "I've seen that in a few of these books. It's the foundation of your magic system, right?" You tilted your head and looked at me curiously. "Do you have one? Forgive me if that's a presumptuous question, I'm afraid I lack for social graces."

I froze at the question, and then the rest of what you said hit me. How can she not know about affinities? Is this some cruel trick? I looked at you like you'd asked what water was. "Is that a joke? Do you really not know? Everyone has an affinity."

You winced. "Ah, I'm showing my ignorance here. I'm . . . not from around here. In fact, I'm so 'not from around here' that this is actually my first exposure to any of this. We don't have the same kind of magic where I'm from."

I had a hard time believing that, but it seemed too outlandish to be a trick. If someone wanted to mess with me, there were far simpler means. "What do *you* know, then? About magic, I mean, and about where you are." I paused and added, "How did you even get in here? I took you for a visitor from a far-off clan but you can't have interacted with any of the bloodlines and come away that clueless about our magic."

You seized on those last few words, ever the type to press opportunity. "Are you from one of the bloodlines, then? I've been keen to learn about them firsthand since first catching mention in these texts. I have to admit, the reading material has been pretty dense without the cultural context to understand it."

On the back foot once again, I warred with myself over whether to tell the truth, but curiosity and pragmatism won out. "I am, yes. I . . . my name is Reska Ines Zelic Dawnbringer, and I am the trueblood princess of clan Dawnbringer. And you didn't answer my question."

You chuckled and said, "Would you believe that I just woke up here a few hours ago?" You gave me a considering glance and said, "No, you seem like a very intelligent woman, Reska, so I doubt you'd take me on faith. So I'll offer this instead: wherever I'm from and whoever I am, you could probably kill me with your eyes closed. I'm neither a threat to you nor to any of the things you care about. All I am is a girl burning with curiosity, and a stranger in a strange land."

An initial sense of flattery at your compliment to my intelligence gave way to the cold realization that you were probably right: I could kill you with my eyes closed. I could probably kill most everyone in the castle with just the hint of a thought, if I immersed myself in my magic and let Shadow run free.

The thought chilled me and gave me pause. What was I really worried about, questioning your story? The worst that you could do to me was humiliate me, and that ship had already sunk in front of my father and his court. I didn't know if I could believe you about just finding yourself in the castle, but I could believe that you weren't a threat.

And . . . a part of me liked the attention. I liked talking to someone who wasn't calling me a demon or looking down on me as a petulant child. I liked talking to you. You made me feel like I wasn't worthless.

How pathetic is that? A few kind words and I was already hooked.

So instead of interrogating you further, or calling the guards, or doing any number of far more reasonable things, I just said, "You know . . . you still haven't told me your name. Hard to have a conversation with someone when they're just 'hey you.'"

You smiled at me, knowing you'd won. You told me, "My name is Homura," and I believed you.

You always were an excellent liar.

XI

I wake up.

It's a gradual thing, hazy and confusing. For a few moments I am Reska and Malice both, two sets of memories overlapping. I remember my father, her father, my father, the ugly feelings different but that core of confused anguish shared. I remember the mirror, the loathing and shame, the reasons different but that discontent shared.

I see a girl with my face and my voice lying to me about her name.

Fucking weeb! I accuse in my head. *Homura? Really? You're not even Japanese! Did you actually name yourself after the girl from* Madoka *whose whole character is defined by her obsessive self-destructive love for the titular character? I can't tell if that's a shocking degree of self-awareness or an equally shocking lack of self-awareness. At least you didn't name yourself after Vriska.*

The girl in the dream was me, obviously. She dressed like me, she looked like me, she acted like me, and at minimum she shared my love of *Puella Magi Madoka Magica* and tabletop roleplaying games. There are other possible explanations, sure, and I shouldn't discount those explanations entirely, but Occam's razor says that girl is me via time travel, or maybe an alternate universe version of me, or maybe with how this whole setting works she's some kind of astrally projected dream construct?

I don't think that's what Occam's razor means.

Shush, me. I'm trying to analyze me.

The whole dream sequence was fascinating, especially given that I can still remember the whole thing clearly. Minutes have passed and the details aren't fading into nothingness like dreams usually do. Is that a function of the setting, or some oddity unique to the vision-like nature of the dream? Will I be receiving more dreams, or was this the only one?

So many details stand out that it's almost overwhelming. The magic that Reska was using, none of the spells she cast had bracketed names or a user interface; she was directing the magic herself, creating meaning and shaping magic into a personalized spell each time. Is the magic I've been using a more advanced form, made more complex yet easier to control, or is it an inferior form, packaged for mass consumption but stripped of the personal element? Both?

The social structures, the architecture, the literature, so much of it fascinates me, but I keep coming back to the girl with my face. She called herself Homura, and I think it's a safe bet that she was referencing the anime, so what does that *mean*? It could have just been chosen for the sake of sounding cool, sure, but that doesn't click. I'm edgy, sure, but there's *meaning* beneath the edge.

I picked—headache, ow, ow—whatever my old name was because it was neutral-sounding, so it wouldn't raise any questions whatever someone perceived my gender as. I picked Malice because it sounds edgy, yeah, but also because the word is associated with spite, ill will, and danger, and because it's a bit like Alice. Being Malice means being someone who is dangerous, someone to be taken seriously, someone impressive . . . not that people so far have actually perceived it that way, to my annoyance.

So why Homura? The character of Homura is a magical girl who travels through time over and over again to save the girl she loves, Madoka, from making a deal with an evil catlike wish-granting entity called Kyubey. She's ruthlessly pragmatic, keeps secrets from those around her, and for all her noble aims she is at her heart a selfish creature driven more by obsession than a sense of right and wrong.

Applied to the context of Reska's situation, we can easily pin Reska as Madoka; my doppelganger is clearly trying to influence Reska for some ends, and given Reska's rough situation it wouldn't be difficult for someone with foreknowledge to play the knight in shining armor. And my other self clearly *has* a degree of foreknowledge, if the way she played on Reska's insecurities is anything to go by.

Of course, that leaves the relevant question: if my doppelganger is Homura, and Reska is Madoka, then who's the Kyubey?

This theory relies on a lot of assumptions that might be disproven, and I fail to see how it's immediately relevant to our situation. I don't think we can reasonably draw any conclusions about the events of the dream without further context, either from more dream sequences or from clues in the waking world.

I grimace at my voice of reason, and then I grimace harder as I finally notice the pain in my hand. My hand is shouting at me that something's wrong with it, but the pain goes deeper; it feels like the entire left side of my body is shot through and torn up, like I'm missing pieces. I can guess why.

I open my eyes and the disorientation only increases as I see what looks like a very modern bedroom. The bed I'm lying on is solid and comfy with modern textiles, there's a dresser just to the side, a closet, and a lamp that isn't on (which, as always, does not seem to affect my ability to see).

I force myself to sit up, wincing at the pain in my left side, and try to get my bearings. The events of my dream aside, a whole lot has happened in the past however many hours and I should probably get to processing *that* before I spend any more time pondering events that may not even be real (they're definitely real).

The pain in my hand is probably from *stabbing my hand with a knife*, and the pain in my left side is probably from *stabbing my soul with a knife*. My hand has been bandaged, though I don't remember bandaging it. I don't feel any kind of supernatural despair, so I'm going to go out on a limb—get it, because I stabbed my hand—and say that my impromptu soul surgery worked and saved my life. Take that, Bashe!

Wait, where is Bashe?

I frown, realizing my easily irritated companion is not within eyesight. I call out, "Bashe? I'm awake!" but don't get a response.

Uneasy now, I push the covers off and stumble out of bed, steadying myself on the nearby dresser. I push open the bedroom door and step into a hallway that opens out into a living room, dining area, and kitchen, all exactly as I'd expect from a normal apartment. There's a fridge, a microwave, a television, a dining table, a sofa . . . it's all extremely regular looking, if a bit minimalist and sleek.

I call for Bashe again and still get no response. The lights are off, and nobody's home. My unease is rising and I feel a thrill of fear, and then it hits me like a truck that I can *feel fear again.* I stop, stunned, and quickly play back memories from the day before. I force myself to think of walking across the sky bridge and my legs get shaky just from the hazy image of it, a jolt of panic running through me at the thought of tumbling into forever.

The monster with the knife, the abandoned school, the doll that bleeds, the spider-dogs, the burning-eyed elf, the sin eater singing of regret, the horrible incarnation of grief and despair; all the times I should have been afraid and wasn't are rushing back to me. I could have died. So many times I could have *died* and I just faced those dangers head-on like they couldn't have *fucking killed me*!

I break out in a cold sweat and start running through the apartment, pushing open doors wherever I find them and calling out Bashe's name. No incubus in the other bedroom, no imp in either bathroom, no Bashekehi the Ever-Gleaming waiting in the hall just outside the apartment. He's gone. Bashe is gone.

The realization sinks in as I wander vacantly into the living room. He's gone. My only guide to this strange new world is gone, and it's all my fault. He must have dragged me away from the dream bubble, brought me to this apartment, and left. And can I blame him?

It's my fault. Of course it's my fault. I tried to use his dead husband to manipulate him into risking his life for me. I tried to manipulate him into a contract with me. I felt out his boundaries and kept pushing, like I always push, like I always do, because I'll never be satisfied, I'll never allow someone to just *be*.

I talked his ear off, kept annoying him and pestering him with a dozen stupid details that didn't matter, it didn't matter, just trying to satisfy my stupid curiosity, my obsessive interests. Wanting to break the system, thinking I could be the clever little isekai monkey cracking open a system of magic that a world's native inhabitants had been working with for who knows how many *thousands* of years. Because I'm special. Because I'm the protagonist, of course I'm the protagonist, what else could I be?

Can't accept that you're not special, that you're just another random fucking nobody in a world full of nobodies. Not enough for you. Never enough for you.

So now he's *abandoned* me because I was too *annoying* and too *stupid* and too *hurtful* and too *heartless*, and why should that be any kind of surprise!? *My fault. Always my fault. Stupid. Pathetic.*

And now he's gone. And now he's gone, the only other person I've met in this new world beside an asshole fae who took my name, and now I'm alone. I'm alone and I'm going to die because *I can't do this on my own.*

The tears start falling and I clench my fists because I don't want to be sad, I can't be sad, that's not me, that's not *allowed*. But the aching in my chest doesn't care what's allowed and the sobbing starts as I crumple onto the sofa and cry, wet and nasally, a disgusting mess of tears and snot and choking sobs.

Bashe is gone and I am alone and I am going to die, and I cry like the stupid weak pathetic worthless bitch that I know I am, that I've always known I am, because I can't change, I can't be better, I can't be anything. *Stupid. Stupid, stupid, stupid.*

It's not enough, the crying isn't enough, so I start hitting myself in the head. I ball both hands into fists, relishing in the pain of my injured hand, and I drive them into my head. The first hits are just taps, light, pathetic, cowardly. *Coward. Weak. Stupid. Just a coward who can't do anything.* I hit harder, forcing more energy behind the motion, forcing myself not to pull back at the last moment. I need the pain. I need to be hurt.

Stupid. A real strike this time, enough to sting. *Stupid.* Another. *Stupid.* Another. *Stupid, stupid, stupid, stupid stupid stupid stupid stupid stupid stupidstupidstupid stupid—*

The door to the apartment creaks open and I hear Bashe ask, "Malice?"

The sound of his voice is a bolt of lightning to my system and a cocktail of new emotions floods my brain: relief that he hasn't abandoned me, shame that I fell into an episode with such little provocation, and panic that Bashe will see me like this and cut his losses for real.

I quickly wipe my face on my shirt, smoothly rise to my feet, and slide the mask back on. *We are measured. We are in control.* I plaster a wide grin on my face and call out, "Bashe! Good to see you're alive and well after that dreadful mess. Shall we discuss our next steps?"

The look in his eyes makes it clear that he absolutely heard me crying and hitting myself but it's *fine* because I am *smiling* now so just *let it go.* ". . . Yeah. Next steps." Bashekehi is wearing new clothing, having apparently found the time to add some gold rings, gold earrings, and a knee-length navy-blue coat with sharp shoulder pads and beige decorative stitching. His chest is still bare, I note, which at this point is absolutely intentional on his part. I feel self-conscious about the horribly bloodstained schoolgirl outfit I'm still stuck in.

The incubus is *also* carrying three plastic bags in his arms, and as he sets them on the dining room table I see *food* inside. "I went out for groceries," he says by way of explanation.

Groceries? I flit to the table and lean over, hands behind my back as I peer inside each bag from a tilted angle. The first bag has a bottle of red wine, a box of tea bags, some instant noodles, a pack of coconut rice cakes, and a pack of fish-shaped red bean cakes (still no brand names, but very colorful packaging). The second bag is mostly filled by fresh plums, peaches, tomatoes, and cucumbers, but I also see a delicious-looking block of feta cheese. The final bag has a bunch of covered styrofoam containers, but they all smell like *food.*

I stare at the bounty. "Holy shit. How did you get all this?"

Bashe shrugs. "It'll be easier to show you, and I'd rather eat first. I'll get breakfast set up if you want to put the rest away."

"Uh, yeah, sure."

I have no idea what's going on, but food is food and I am *starving.* Bashe sets the third bag off to the side and starts grabbing plates and cutlery from kitchen cupboards and drawers. I take the first two bags and sort them: snacks and drinks into the pantry, fruits and vegetables into the fridge with the cheese. When I finish my half Bashe has already laid out table settings for both of us and revealed a tantalizing meal: mushroom stew, garlic flatbread, and white rice.

Bashe breezes past me into the kitchen and says, "Serve yourself, I'm going to get some tea started."

I grab a seat and don't wait for the imp. I layer a generous helping of rice into a bowl and then ladle mushroom stew on top until the rice is uniformly mushroom-ified. I start eating with gusto, and even if I wasn't ravenously hungry I would find this meal sinfully delicious. Mushrooms are amazing and I will hear not a *single* bad thing said about them.

Bashekehi joins me soon after with two cups of steaming hot tea. I sniff it and am slightly disappointed to find that it's black tea, not green, but it smells fragrant enough that I'll give it a shot anyways (not that I'd turn down tea regardless).

We eat in silence, which suits me fine as I'm too busy shoveling mushrooms and rice down my gullet to actually use my throat for speaking. Once the rice is down to its dregs I pour in more stew and start dipping the flatbread, which is actually even more amazingly delicious.

Bashe doesn't hold back either, and comes up with the very clever idea of laying down flatbread as a foundation, spreading rice on top, and then pouring in the mushroom stew to a healthy level. We both grab seconds once we've finished the first course, though I grab a much lighter portion while he actually increases on the second round.

The tea turns out to be pretty good, with some nice herbal flavors whose nature I can't quite discern. When the last of the food is eaten Bashe takes the plates to the sink and I volunteer to dispose of the empty containers. Then we're back at the table, sipping tea in silence and staring across at each other.

Bashe is the first to break the quiet, letting out a deep sigh and adopting a conflicted expression. "So. About . . . things." He looks away, grimaces, then turns back to me and continues, "Thank you. For freeing me, I mean. And I'm sorry that I hit you. It was an overreaction, one born of stress, but I know that you were under a lot of stress too so that doesn't excuse it."

I mumble, "It's fine. I deserved it."

He sighs again. "At least let me finish. The rest of what I was going to say is that trying to use Muzaffer to manipulate me into risking my life was a *disgusting* act of attempted manipulation, even if you didn't know the precise context of my relationship with him, and I do not forgive you for it. If you ever try to use him against me again, I will leave you for the crows."

"Right," I say softly. "That makes sense. I . . . I'm sorry."

Bashekehi takes a long sip of tea before responding. "For what it's worth, you did a good job getting us out of there. That tracking spell was invaluable, and as crazy as that [Abyssal Armament] gamble was, it *worked*. I don't think I would have had the resolve to mutilate my own soul like that, but you didn't even hesitate. Honestly, I'm not sure if that's a sign of iron will or just another piece of your weird no-fear thing."

"That's gone," I whisper.

He frowns. "Gone?"

"I can feel fear again. I don't know why."

The imp leans back and considers it. "Mm. The suppression effect must have been anchored to the part of your soul that got ripped out. Well, this is probably a good thing in the long run. Fear keeps you alive."

"Yeah."

Bashekehi considers me for another long moment, sighs again, and says, "We're in the city now, Malice. You're going to be meeting people, some real and some not. But... they're all going to know that name. The name of an archdemon. Malice, the archdemon presiding over torture, cruelty, and transgressive violence."

I already feel like shit, but that adds a spike of cold misery. *Right. My name. The name that Eirdryd mocked, and Bashe lied about liking. The name that they say doesn't belong to me. The name that apparently belongs to ... well, to someone that sounds exactly like the name implies.* "You want me to change it?"

"There will be *consequences* if you don't. Impersonating an archdemon will only get you the bad kind of attention, and you do not have anywhere near the power to make people think you're the real deal."

I clench my fists, but I know he's right. I just hate admitting it. "Fine." Still, I have one act of defiance left in me, and I push a smirk onto my face. "If I can't be Malice, then call me Maven Alice. M. Alice."

The incubus looks like he desperately wants to say something about that, but instead he swallows his objection and says, "That will work. Maven Alice."

I tap the fingers of my injured hand along the table, heedless of the pain. Actually, that's worth asking about. I raise my bandaged hand and ask, "Why doesn't this hurt more? Like, don't get me wrong, my whole left side aches like I got my soul ripped out, but my hand does not feel like it got impaled by a dagger."

"Because it didn't." At my look of confusion the imp clarifies, "You stabbed your hand, yes, but the blade didn't actually go very deep. You lost consciousness pretty much immediately after the tip of the knife touched skin, so the damage there is mostly superficial. The real wound is the third of your soul that you lost, which *can* heal, but it'll take time."

I give Bashe an accusatory glance. "You're a lot more forthcoming with exposition now."

He laughs. "I've had some real food, and talking to you is no longer putting minutes between me and said food. Don't get me wrong, you're still kind of an obnoxious shit, but I can indulge your curiosity. It *is* what my breed are known for," he adds with a wink.

"Fair enough. In that case, what does it *mean* that I'm missing a third of my soul?"

Bashe steeples his fingers and leans in. "To be more specific, you've lost a third of your pleroma. The soul is divided into two parts: the core, which contains all your most essential qualities, and the pleroma, which is the emanation of the soul and reflects it. To make a shaky comparison to brain function, the core is your long-term memory and the pleroma is your short-term memory. The core is your identity, your most complete sense of self, while the pleroma shows a reflection of your immediate emotions, desires, etcetera, as well as being the means you use to interact with Pandaemonium on a deeper level. The pleroma is how you cast spells and store mana, and it is *also* where an invoker's contracts are stored. Speaking of which . . ."

Shit. I quickly run through my spells. [Abyssal Armament]. The interface fires, showing me the crystallized array of strange symbols. I dismiss the spell and activate [Find the Path], which shows me the familiar interface as well. When I try to conjure up [Adrenaline Burst], I get nothing. I hiss and tell Bashe, "It took [Adrenaline Burst]. Fuck!"

"That's actually a pretty lucky break," he points out. "It was easily the least valuable of your spells."

"Then let's replace it with something better," I insist. "You've had a chance to feed, haven't you? I've got plenty more memories to burn."

The incubus raises a hand to stop me. "It doesn't work like that, Alice. Your soul can't support a third contract until it regenerates from the damage it took."

I roll my eyes, but I'm not going to argue with the expert. Much. "Okay, how do I do that?"

Bashe gestures at the tea in front of us and the dishes in the kitchen. "You've already started. You heal your soul by doing things that enrich you. For some people that's a good book, for others a good lay, but most everyone gets some meaning out of a good meal had in fine company. It takes *time*, so you can't just binge your favorite things and expect to be whole next morning, but chip away at it every day and you should be back to shape in a few weeks."

My eyes go wide. "*Weeks?* You're joking."

Bashekehi makes an exasperated noise at me. "You mutilated your *soul*, Alice. Did you think that wouldn't have consequences?"

I grit my teeth. "I *thought* that you would have *solutions*. Shortcuts. I need power, Bashe, not a vacation. You know more about this world than I do, bunches more, so tell me: how do I get a lot of power in not a lot of time? You're an imp, this should be your thing!"

"Look, I told you the options you have. The kind of power you really want, the power to carve your own path, the kind of power that leads to becoming something 'like unto a god,' that's what you're after, right?"

"*Yes!*" I hiss. "With every fiber of my being."

He raises a hand and immediately tucks in the thumb and pinky. "Disqualifying Summer and Winter because you're trapped in the Labyrinth and because they don't have good routes to apotheosis anyways, that leaves three paths to ascension. The first path involves you spending a couple hundred years honing your body and your mind until you impress the dragons enough they bring you into their cycle of reincarnation. The second path involves convincing an eidolon that you're worthy of becoming its champion, then building its legend to such dizzying heights that you merge with it and achieve godhood. The third path involves being chosen basically at random by a geist, turning into a demon, and meeting a set of criteria so difficult only eight before you have ever achieved it, all so that you can ascend as an archdemon. Those are your options."

I blink. *Wow. That is actually a lot of useful information.* "Okay, well, fuck that first option. Dragons are cool but no way am I spending a hundred years exercising. The second option has a very appealing endgame, and I can probably use the compass to find an eidolon that'll sponsor me. Honestly, that one sounds the most like a classic RPG narrative, and yes I see that eye roll and I am immune to your sass. So, a solid contender."

"I will remind you, Alice, that you have to be *worthy* of becoming its champion. That means you have to fit into the ideal traits of a specific culture, and, very importantly, *be part of that culture.* Do you see a problem?"

"Oh. Shit. You're saying that because I'm from the Zero Sphere, there's no culture here I can really claim to be from, right?"

He waves a hand. "That, and you just don't seem like the kind of person to value things like 'tradition' and 'virtue.'"

I glare at the imp, but I don't actually have a rebuttal. "Okay, so that leaves option three: getting the attention of a random geist so it can make me a demon. Any ideas on that one?"

"I believe I can help with that," says a white-haired catgirl that wasn't leaning against the sofa a second ago. The girl smiles, her cat ears twitch, her heterochromatic eyes—one yellow, one blue—gleam brilliantly, and she says, "My name is Cheshire, and I'm here to grant your wish."

XII

Guess we found the Kyubey.

... And I'm still wearing the damn schoolgirl outfit.

Bashekehi bolts out of his chair and takes a step away, eyes wide. "How the fuck did you get in here?" I follow to my feet more slowly, taking everything in with as much curiosity as caution.

The catgirl waves a hand dismissively. "Oh, y'know. Details, details. The important thing is that I can help Ms. Alice here with her little problem." She puffs her chest proudly and says, "See, I'm a geist, a.k.a. your friendly neighborhood incarnation of human will and want. *I* have the power to grant Ms. Alice's wish and help her become first a demon and then, with a bit of elbow grease, an *archdemon.*" Cheshire grins. "Doesn't that sound fun?"

I have a billion questions I want to ask this very obviously suspicious intruder, but I start with, "Do you really want to make me an archdemon? Why?"

Bashe glares at me and starts, "That is not the most important question—"

Cheshire cuts him off with a cheery, "Sure do!" She pushes off the sofa and comes to lean over the table, getting right up in my face. "I've been *watching you*, Ms. Alice, and I *love* what I've seen. The way you butchered that nightmare in the school, the way you bluffed a Huntsman, the way you carved through everything in your path with lies and violence? Simply *delectable!*" The catgirl hugs herself and squirms, grin seeming even wider. "You're *perfect*, Alice. You would make a truly magnificent archdemon."

I don't know how to feel about that. A part of my brain is screaming that this is obviously the exact evil entity I was theorizing about and I should stay very far away from making any kind of deal with it, and yet . . . she says that I'm perfect. She says that she wants to give me what I want. And she could be lying, of course she could be lying, everyone has been lying to me since I got here so it's practically certain that she's lying to me. And yet.

I keep my persona calm and measured, almost detached. "A bold claim, and one I would love to interrogate further, but first: why do you have a name from the Zero Sphere?"

Cheshire claps her hands together and declares, "Because *someone* broke the *rules*." She clicks her tongue disapprovingly. "Earth is off-limits, everybody knows that, but that rascal Katoptris—the Lady of Shards, as you know her—reached across the veil and plucked you right from your home to bring you here. That is a *very serious* breach of the Dreaming Edicts, I'll have you know."

Bashekehi is seeming more and more distraught with every exchange. "Hold on, are you seriously claiming that Alice really is from the Zero Sphere? That doesn't happen! That's not possible! Not even a god or archdemon could accomplish that. The only one who—" The incubus's face pales as he bites off his own words.

Cheshire wiggles a hand noncommittally. "You'd be surprised what's possible that you don't know about. *Regardless* of what the poor deluded imp here thinks, the fact of the matter is that you, Maven Alice, were brought here from the Zero Sphere in violation of some very important laws, and someone had to even the scales. And so *I* was created."

My attention sharpens. "Created?"

"Mhm! I was made to be your greatest asset, Alice. I was born with full knowledge of your life on Earth and all your interests, your desires, your fears, your beliefs. I like what you like, I hate what you hate, and I want what you want. I was made to adore you, to be obsessed with you, to devote my whole existence to helping you achieve your goals here in the Labyrinth." Cheshire's yellow and blue eyes light up with manic energy, her words dripping with frenzied passion. "You are the reason I exist. I love you for that."

She's still extremely close to me, close enough I can feel her breath on my skin, and my body chemistry is at war between attraction and discomfort. The catgirl is *not wearing very much*; she's in a white tube top, a leather vest that barely covers more than the top, and a red skirt that stops well above the knees, plus high socks and leather boots. She looks like the kind of catgirl you'd see in an anime or a JRPG.

She is, in a word, a fantasy; she's the living fulfillment of a wish.

How many nerds want a partner that shares their hobbies? How many mentally ill people want a partner that loves all of them, even the disturbing parts? How many fucking *weebs* want a catgirl girlfriend who will hang on their every word?

"I don't believe you," I let slip out. I swallow, committed now, and say, "I don't trust you. Why? Why any of this? Why me?"

Cheshire leans back and adopts a wounded expression. "Why not? Don't you think you deserve this? Isn't this what you've always wanted? To go on a grand adventure in another world, to have incredible magic powers, and to meet a girl who will love you just as obsessively as you love her?"

I clench my fists and snarl, "Of course I want that! But I don't *deserve* that, and I don't *believe* that after the hellish first day I've had it would just be dropped in my lap. So why are you really here? Why are you *lying* to me, and what the fuck do you get out of trying to manipulate me?"

For a moment it seems like Cheshire is about to cry, her eyes watering and nose sniffling, but then it all goes away and she's grinning again, eyes twinkling. "I kind of figured that'd be your reaction, but I had to try. The prospect of luring you in with just a pretty face and an appeal to fantasy was too thrilling to resist."

Vindication surges within me, but I'm right back to unease with her next few words.

"Now for the real pitch." Cheshire winks at me and cracks her knuckles. "For the record, I wasn't lying about being obsessed with you. You *fascinate me*, Alice. I want to strap you to a table and vivisect you, and the craziest part is that instead of being terrified by that, you just became a little bit more attracted to me. Am I wrong?"

My face heats up and I protest, "That's not—I mean, I don't—shut up!"

Cheshire laughs, the sound rich and full, and she gives me a knowing smirk. "When I said I know all your desires, I *meant it*. I know exactly how to entice you, Alice. I know what makes you tick. You don't really want a girlfriend who will hang on your every word and flutter her eyelashes at you; you want a girlfriend who will pick you apart like a science experiment. You want a girlfriend who would commit murder to keep you *hers*. And you want a girlfriend who would find it charming instead of disturbing that you would be willing to do the same for her."

I feel naked in the face of her analysis, stripped of all persona and all my layers of protective insincerity. She knows me, and that is exactly as terrifying as it is appealing, and she knows *that* too. I struggle to find the words to respond, unsure how I even should respond, and she pounces on the opportunity to keep talking.

"I wasn't lying about what I want, either; I really do think you'd make a glorious archdemon, and making that happen would be worth all the effort just for its own sake. I want to help you get all the things you want, and I know exactly how to do it: *killing the Queen of Nightmares.*"

Bashekehi has been watching nervously through this whole conversation, but as Cheshire unveils her latest twist he sucks in his breath and takes another step back. "That's crazy," he tells us. "That's fucking crazy, and you're crazy for even suggesting that."

"I know," murmurs Cheshire, mismatched eyes still alight with twisted enjoyment. "But the thing is, little imp, Alice *likes* crazy."

Slowly, hesitantly, I find my words. "If I said yes . . . what would that mean?"

"I would make you a demon, of course," she answers. "As a geist, I have the power to bind myself to a single soul and transform it. Through our connection you would become something inhuman, something more than human. You would have the power to create your own spells, to alter your appearance as you wish, and to grow ever stronger until you taste apotheosis and become something greater still: an *archdemon*, like only eight before you."

The thought is immensely appealing, and I am damned curious to learn more, but before I can say anything else Bashekehi steps back into the conversation. The incubus turns to me and says, "Alice, *don't do this.*"

I blink in surprise and look over at him. "Why? I get why I'm conflicted about this, but why do you care? If I say yes I'll be out of your hair and you can get back to doing whatever you want."

"Because you don't know what it would mean to walk that path." Bashekehi's expression tightens and he says, "Listen to me, Alice: people are *right* to be suspicious of imps and to fear demons. And the archdemons? They're the worst monsters of them all. The archdemon who made my kind, Indulgence, murdered thousands to get her Throne, and that is absolutely the norm for an archdemon. Cheshire told you that being a demon means being more than human, but it also means being *less* than human; you lose a piece of yourself, lots of pieces of yourself, until you can't even recognize the person you once were.

"There is a *price* to power, and I know that better than you might think. To be an imp, to be like me, means being driven not by any of my own wants but by the wants of an archdemon I've never even met." He hesitates for a moment, looking almost pained, but continues, "Alice, an imp is made when a mortal gives up the core of their soul. When they sell it, for whatever price they think is worth it, to another imp. And imps are driven to convince people to take that deal, because there's a whole lot that you can do with the core of someone's soul. But the end result for the mortal is that they get a big hole inside them, and that hole in your very essence gets filled with the imprint of an archdemon, a crystallized echo of what makes them what they are. The core of your soul isn't you anymore, it's the instincts and desires of that archdemon."

I'm shocked at the sudden verbosity of my incubus companion. I think this might be the most he's ever talked without prompting, and I keep silent to let him continue even though I'm burning with further questions.

He takes a deep breath, exhales, and tells me, "The man whose name was Bairam Dara is dead. He sold his soul and now that soul is as likely to be a pair of fuzzy dice as it is to be a knife or a cloak or any other random object fashioned by the bastard that offered the bargain. I am the thing that took Bairam's place, and I am ruled by the nature of the archdemon I trace lineage to. Bairam was a gambling addict, but he could still refuse to play a round of cards; an incubus cannot. When Bairam saw something that tempted him, be it wine or sex or some other luxury, it was just an idle thought easily dismissed; an incubus sees those things and the instinct to indulge is overwhelming."

I frown and this time I *have* to interject. "But that's not *true*. I've offered you a bunch of temptations and you rejected all but one."

"And *that*," he says sharply, "is because Bairam Dara had his own soul modified before becoming an imp. Bairam had a list of rules etched into his pleroma, a behavior modification anchored to his soul like the fear-killer was anchored to yours. The reason I can resist temptation is because those rules are etched into *my* soul, into *my* pleroma, and they govern me just as much as the instincts deeper down. I am the fusion of Bairam Dara's rules and Indulgence's instincts. Those rules keep me more human than most imps, but they are *painful* to follow and it is still *exhausting* to deny my impulses."

His story has my interest, but I still have another objection. "That's all well and good, Bashe, but you're talking about becoming an imp. Exactly how applicable is that to what *I* am being offered?"

Bashe lets out a frustrated noise. "Becoming a demon is a different process from becoming an imp, yes, but it will still change you. It will force you to sharpen yourself and distort yourself in pursuit of power. To be a demon you must cut away pieces of yourself until all that's left is a raw and bloody core of will and want. When you reach the end of that path, if you ever do, there might not be anything of the original 'you' left."

I am silent, contemplating his words and the threat of ego death, so it is Cheshire who speaks next.

"You really don't understand her, do you?" remarks the geist. "You must think she is vastly different than she truly is. But rest assured, little imp, I suffer no such delusion."

Bashekehi glares at the catgirl. "If I can save her from you, I will."

Cheshire doubles over with laughter and has to wipe a tear from her face. "Save her? *Save* her? Incubus, you don't even understand what she needs saving *from*. Have you not at any point stopped to wonder *why* it is that Alice is so obsessed with the prospect of ascension? Why she hungers so greedily for power and immortality?"

Bashe opens his mouth to speak and the geist cuts him off. "It is because she is *terrified*, Bashekehi the Ever-Gleaming."

I freeze. *Does she mean—*

Cheshire turns from Bashekehi back to me. She leans in close once more, but this time instead of being flirtatious it is *menacing*. "She is terrified," Cheshire says, answering Bashe but pinning me with those beautiful yellow and blue eyes. "She is terrified, and the fear gets stronger every year. Every month. Every day. Isn't that right, Maven Alice?"

I swallow, hard. "I don't know what you're talking about."

Cheshire laughs in my face and it is a cruel and scornful melody. "Liar. Lovely little liar. I love the way you lie. But you can't lie to me, Alice. I know you. I know that every year the fear gets stronger because you get *older*, and *weaker*, creeping ever closer to a final, terrible, inevitable *end*. You are dying."

My nerves are fraying, my pulse speeding up. *Shut up. Shut up, you don't know what you're talking about. Stop talking!* But I can't make my lips move to deny her. I can't lie.

Cheshire traces a finger down my cheek, my neck, lingering there and tracing lines, her touch soft and warm and threatening. "You didn't think you'd live to eighteen," the monstrous thing says gently and cruelly. "You thought you'd slit your throat by nineteen. You *tried* at twenty, just in a different place, but you made the cut too shallow and when you saw that red line the all-consuming terror that followed broke your will to die."

I remember. I remember the moment the fear swaddled me as I stared at the self-inflicted wound filling with blood. My hand is shaking. Both my hands are shaking. I can't make them stop. I see the blood, and the wound, and the scalpel falling from my fingers. I feel the fear that held me down and drowned me.

"At twenty-one you looked around and realized the world had kept *moving* while you were standing still. And every year you ask the question: is this the year when you finally die?"

Is this the year I die? Is this the month I die? Is this the day I die? Is this the hour I die? Is this the moment I die? I see a thousand deaths sprawling before me: a car hits me as I'm walking down the street; a man with a gun comes into my school or my place of work and shoots me; a heart attack; cancer, like took my mother; the wrong pills; blood, so much blood; going to sleep and just never waking up. A thousand cruel, terrifying endings.

Cheshire is still smiling. "This is a truth of the world: Maven Alice is scared to die. Thanatophobia is the driving force behind at least half of everything you have ever done in your entire life, isn't that right?" She pauses, giving me space to speak, but I don't respond. I'm paralyzed. "Isn't that right, Alice?" she asks again, voice just as soft but with a dangerous undercurrent.

I find my words just long enough to answer, "Yes," in barely more than a whisper.

That awful smile grows wicked and vicious. "You are terrified of death, but what's more is that you are selfish—self-*obsessed*—and cannot conceive of a world that *you are not in*. You think your death will render your life meaningless, because the meaning only matters if you're the one experiencing it. You are the only person you really care about, in the end; you're the only person you really think is *real*, and when you are gone the universe will be ash and dust because *you will not be in it.*"

In my mind I die a thousand times, and a thousand worlds spiral into darkness.

Cheshire pushes on my chest, softly, insistently, and I take a step back. Another. She pushes me against the wall and pins me there, and when she whispers into my ear her voice is softer, gentler, delicate. "You are dying, and you are scared, and he can't save you from that. No one out there can save you. But I can."

Please. I don't want to die.

Cheshire hugs me, squeezing tight, and the comfort of her warmth almost breaks me. When was the last time anyone hugged me? When was the last time anyone cared?

I'm so alone. I've been alone for so long, and I'm going to die alone, I'll die alone and—

Cheshire slowly releases me and takes a step back, and I let out the breath I didn't realize I was holding. I'm still caught in her orbit, held by those eyes that gleam like one disc of gold and one disc of sapphire. "You are dying, Alice, but I can save you. I can help you. All you have to do is let me."

"Don't do this, Alice." Out of the corner of my vision I see Bashe reach for me. He's looking at me with a tangled mess of emotions that I don't bother to unravel. I don't care. "You're making a mistake. You *know* she's manipulating you. You know something's not right about this, even if you believe every word she says."

Yeah. But it doesn't really matter, does it? I close my eyes—breathe in, breathe out—and when I open them again my voice is cold. "If you wanted to be my voice of reason, you had your chance."

The incubus reels back as if struck, something approaching hurt blooming on his face, but I don't care. All my attention is on Cheshire now. Smiling, smug, mirthful Cheshire. Loving, caring, lying Cheshire. Only Cheshire.

"Okay. What do you need from me?"

"Just say 'yes.'"

I do.

PART TWO

MAD TEA PARTY

OR, ANTHROPOLOGICAL FIELD RESEARCH BY MEANS OF GETTING STABBED

"But I don't want to go among mad people," Alice remarked.
"Oh, you can't help that," said the Cat: "we're all mad here. I'm mad. You're mad."
"How do you know I'm mad?" said Alice.
"You must be," said the Cat, "or you wouldn't have come here."

—*Alice in Wonderland,* Lewis Carroll

I

My eyes open and I find myself standing in the eye of a storm.
A maelstrom rages in every direction, but rather than being composed of wind and debris, it whirls with sights and sounds that I recognize from my memories: flashes of moments that I've experienced, imagery that stuck in my mind, sounds I could never forget, all getting twisted and tangled and blurring past in endless chaotic motion.

Out in the storm, all the colors are too bright and the sounds are too loud, and below the storm I see a desolate wasteland of jagged rock and deep burning chasms. The geography of the wasteland is as volatile as the maelstrom above, great stony outcroppings falling away into ravines as molten rock bubbles up from cracks in the ground and creates new twisted formations.

Red rivers run through the wasteland from distant mountains that resemble parts of the body: red water streaming between the fingers of a great hand, red tears falling from the eyes of a misshapen head, red sweat dripping from a human spine of cracked earth.

Skull-faced beasts of shadow and smoke wander the churning wastes, their forms shifting in size and dimension with every step. Creatures in the approximate shape of humans but made of torn skin and exposed fat and muscle drink from the red rivers. Where they meet, the skull-faced beasts and the flayed ones tear each other apart and gorge on the carrion.

Within the eye of the storm, surrounded by a circular wall of whirling memory, is a messy stack of open books each the size of a small house. The text is nonsense, incomprehensible scribbles and unfamiliar symbols crowding each gigantic page. The book I'm standing on is at the very top of the pile, and on the page opposite me I see a table laid out with checkerboard tablecloth, a fancy tea set, eight bowls of fruit, and two distinctly different seats: one seat is a simple stool, but the other seat is a pile of colorful pillows in the arms of a massive stuffed bunny rabbit.

The whole scene is quite surreal, and I don't know how I should be feeling right now. The horrific imagery out beyond the safety of the book pile is fascinating, but it also reminds me of how I got here; Cheshire's manipulations, using my fear of death to coerce me into taking her offer.

You are dying, Alice, but I can save you.

Should I hate her for that? Should I be furious with her? What *do* I feel? I feel vulnerable, most keenly, in the way that someone feels vulnerable when a knife is held to their throat. But most people don't get *aroused* when a knife is at their throat, so the common comparison doesn't really hold. Is *that* how I feel? Ugh.

The way she systematically deconstructed my hopes and fears and used them to break me down and back me into a corner was cruel, and it was disgusting, and it was the act of a truly loathsome intelligence, but it was also *kind of hot*. She cut me open with her words and dug through my entrails, and then she stitched me back up in a manner more pleasing to her desires. That's as terrifying as it is alluring.

My feelings are all tangled and knotted. I feel the fear of death, and the terror of being known. I feel anger and frustration that I was made to feel so small and helpless. I feel a thrill of enticement that someone was able to push my buttons like that. I feel ashamed that any part of that horrible sequence could turn me on.

And a part of me feels hopeful, truly, desperately hopeful, that I might yet live forever.

So I guess we do what we always do: we learn the rules, and we play the game.

I don't know for certain what this place is but I can hazard a guess that it's some representation of my psyche—the place is certainly edgy enough—and it seems obvious what I'm meant to do next: I wander over to the big bunny and plop myself atop the throne of pillows. As I take a seat I realize that my outfit has changed: gone is the bloody schoolgirl outfit—and the stolen hairpin—replaced by a poofy black dress with a hearts-and-diamonds motif, plus black-and-white striped tights.

I frown at my new clothing and debate whether it's an improvement or a downgrade—those horizontal stripes are quite nice, but the dress is far too bulky—until I hear the pouring of liquid and look up to see Cheshire sitting in the stool across from me. The white-haired catgirl is outfitted in a dress of her own, a lacy pastel yellow-and-pink affair that leaves decidedly more skin bared than my dress, which has me hastily averting my gaze to the creature's visible amusement.

Cheshire pours from the teapot into first my cup and then hers. The "tea" we're having is a dark red liquid that resembles blood by sight, though an experimental sniff gives the scent of pomegranates instead. I take a dainty sip of pomegranate juice, set the teacup back down, and level a flat expression at the ever-grinning catgirl.

"This is all a bit much, don't you think?" I gesture at the storm and the book pile and the porcelain tea set. "You tell me you can make me an archdemon, you nearly induce a panic attack by hitting all my thanatophobia triggers, and now we're having a tea party. It's all just a bit absurd."

Cheshire takes a sip from her own cup and replies, "It is human nature to seek inherent meaning, just as it is the nature of the universe to deny humanity any such thing. There is no intrinsic value to anything humans do, and yet," she gestures at the storm raging beyond the bounds of the book pile, "here we sit surrounded by made meaning, a lifetime of assigning weight and value to actions that were, speaking nihilistically, quite devoid of either. Absurd indeed."

I blink a few times, as I had not been expecting the scantily clad catgirl to start throwing musings on the nature of existence at me, but that's really my fault for being unimaginative. I narrow my eyes at her, still wanting to pursue the "you manipulated me by exploiting my trauma" angle, but I'm a sucker for arguing about philosophy and she clearly knows that. "Where are you going with this?"

The catgirl's yellow and blue eyes twinkle. "Allow me to answer your question with another: from where do we derive meaning?"

"Define 'meaning,' 'cause there's more than one definition. I can guess from that first speech but I want it made clear."

"Of course," she answers smoothly. "We can examine semiotic meaning in more detail later, but what I'm really asking about is *significance*: the meaning of life. Why do we exist? What is the purpose of our existence? What makes our lives meaningful, and from where do we derive that sense of meaningfulness?"

I raise an eyebrow. "That's a pretty big question to ask on a first date." I'm not sure if I intend that last part to be sarcastic or not. Do I consider this a date? Should I? Am I on a date right now?

Cheshire laughs, her voice rich and full and achingly beautiful. "Would you have it any other way, darling?"

Her terms of endearment still make me uneasy, but I admit, "I suppose not," and consider her first question. I've thought about it plenty—who hasn't?—but all my prior answers were derived from a rather different set of universal conditions.

Cheshire fills the silence, as she seems to enjoy doing. "I'll start us off. If we accept both that there is no inherent significance to human existence and that it is human nature to seek inherent significance, we find the paradox of the Absurd. In the face of such an irresolvable contradiction, the only rational solution is to abandon the search for intrinsic meaning and instead become the maker of meaning." She gestures once more to the storm of memory. "If significance is something that can be created, then there is value in doing so, and the creation of meaning has meaning in itself. Would you agree?"

"Sure." I shrug. "You're basically explaining my own beliefs to me."

Cheshire takes two of the teacups not in use and sets them in front of her. "This presents a further question: is the creation of significance a resolution to the desire for meaning, or is the act of creation rendered meaningless by the inevitable death of all things?" Cheshire pours pomegranate juice into the first cup, and then she picks up the empty cup and squeezes until it shatters, shards of porcelain falling from her now-bloody hand. I watch the blood drip from her hand, fascinated.

I lean forward and steeple my fingers beneath my chin. *Our interlocutor knows our beliefs at least as well as we do, so our best option is to reject those beliefs and go on the attack. Luckily, the point of attack here is obvious.* "You're presenting a false dichotomy. One of your premises is flawed: you said there's no inherent significance like it's an absolute, but that kind of thinking is a product of nihilism. Existentialism and absurdism function as philosophies because God is dead, faith in the divine murdered by the materialists and the rationalists. If there's no higher power to give us meaning, then we have to make it ourselves, or accept that death will undo anything we try to make. But this isn't Earth and I'm not Nietzsche, so I have to ask: is God dead?"

I know the answer, of course. I've seen it. The storm flickers and in it I see flashes of red liquid in a crystal flask, drank and spilled. A burning dagger, plucked from an abomination's corpse. The weight of Azathoth's attention pressing down on me, suffocating me with her obsessive love and detached curiosity. I have felt her touch and I find her divinity to be undeniable. My atheism died the moment I woke up in this strange new world.

Cheshire watches the storm with me, keen gaze flitting from memory to memory. "You are right, of course; the Dreamweaver and the Demiurge alike remain comfortably alive, both literally and metaphorically."

"And they seem sufficiently opinionated," I press. "Is this universe truly without intrinsic meaning, this world a cosmic accident? Is there no transcendental significance bestowed upon its inhabitants? Were all of you created by Azathoth and Nyarlathotep for no grand design or reason to exist? I find that incredibly unlikely."

"Ah," Cheshire says, "and now we turn to the philosophy of *my* reality. Indeed, the painter of worlds—Nyarlathotep, for Azathoth merely provides the canvas—had a reason for making mortal minds and setting them loose in the cosmic playground, and it is told to us by all those who would know: she wanted toys in the toybox."

Her statement is punctuated by a change in the table decor: a bowl of fruit becomes a painted crate filled with fidget toys, Lego bricks, a Rubik's cube, and a doll wearing a pretty dress and a butterfly hairpin. I stare at the doll intently, but when I blink it is gone and Cheshire is speaking once more, and I idly note that her hand is now unbloodied.

"If the toymaker decides the purpose of each toy she makes, then we are toys and nothing more, and the meaning of our lives is to be found in how well we entertain our *generous* and *benevolent* Demiurge." Cheshire's voice drips with obvious sarcasm and she actually rolls her eyes.

I note her actions with interest. *I have to wonder: is this part of the performance, or does she genuinely have some personal dislike for Nyarlathotep? Cheshire said that she was "created," so was the Demiurge the one to create her? If she was telling the truth about that part, who else would have the means and motive to respond to the Nightmare Queen pulling me from Earth?*

Cheshire continues, "That notion is, as you may imagine, *unacceptable* to many. There are some who lead their lives seeking to satisfy their creator, certainly, but there are others in Pandaemonium who rebel against the Demiurge as someone from your Earth might rebel against the absurd."

I pick up a spiky ball fidget toy and roll it around my fingers aimlessly. *So rebellion against the divine is cross-cultural. I suppose that leads to the obvious question.* "So how does the Demiurge feel about that?" I muse aloud.

"*That*," says Cheshire with great relish, "depends on who you ask."

Cheshire cracks her knuckles and another bowl of fruit transmutes, this time becoming a pair of statuettes: an angel of solid gold and a horned devil of black iron, both female in shape. The angel carries a book in one hand and a trumpet in the other, while the devil carries a sword in one hand and a serpent in the other.

"Hear now the story of the archons: the Intercessor and the Adversary, two beings of incredible power—power beyond any god or archdemon—brought about by the will of the Demiurge. The Intercessor serves the Demiurge as a messenger and herald, and she sets schemes in motion to satisfy the Demiurge's designs. The Adversary was once like the Intercessor, but rebelled against the Demiurge and now snuffs out the plots and plans of the Intercessor wherever she can find them. The Adversary dedicates her existence to undoing the works of the Demiurge just as the Intercessor dedicates her existence to pursuing those works."

I frown and set down my fidget toy, leaning my chin on my hands once more. "But if the Demiurge *made* the Adversary, or at least empowered her, then why hasn't she just taken the Adversary's power away? Is there some reason she *can't* depower the Adversary?"

Cheshire shakes her head. "None whatsoever. And thus we come to the great question: is the Adversary—who by all accounts despises the Demiurge and Intercessor both—doing exactly what Nyarlathotep wants her to do? Or to return to more Earthly matters: if God made the Devil to fall, is the Devil not serving God's will in every act of sin?"

"You're asking someone who was an atheist until, like, a day ago," I point out.

Cheshire waves a hand dismissively. "Don't pretend you haven't thought about it. I know you, Alice. I know everything about you, you little edgelord, including your *interpretation* of certain Biblical tales. I've read your framing of the Garden of Eden as 'a heroic serpent gifting humanity with free will, only to be punished by a cruel and controlling God.' You clearly have a stake, and a side, in this line of questioning." The snake in the statuette's hand flicks its tongue, once, and then returns to stillness.

I resist the urge to wince at my cringe-inducing younger self. "Okay, fine, I have opinions on religion, and on free will in particular." I shift in my seat and let one hand fall away from my chin to start tapping the table as I think.

The Christianity comparison here would be the problem of evil, but that feels too imprecise; Nyarlathotep may be powerful but nothing of what I've heard suggests she's benevolent. Then again, maybe we just need to reframe "goods" and "evils" as "desired outcomes" and "undesired outcomes."

"Okay, so, in religious philosophy," I start, "there's this question about the problem of evil, which basically goes like this: if God is both omnipotent and omnibenevolent, why does evil exist? A common refrain in responses is this idea that sometimes lesser evils are necessary for greater goods, one of the best examples of that being free will: if you allow people free will, you must allow them to do evil, or else they aren't really free."

Cheshire plucks an apple and takes a bite. "It has to be a choice."

I nod. "If we take that and apply it to the Demiurge, we can ask: if the Demiurge is omnipotent and has desired outcomes, why does she allow undesired outcomes to happen? Maybe the Demiurge allows the Adversary's rebellion as a necessary sacrifice to achieve desired outcomes elsewhere. It serves a purpose."

Cheshire sets the apple down, turning it so the bite mark faces me. "And what if the act of rebellion *was* the purpose?"

Toys in the toybox. You can line them up in a row, you can have them play house . . . or you can make them fight. "You're saying Nyarlathotep *wants* the Adversary to oppose her, or to oppose the Intercessor, because it makes the playground a more interesting space. Like how any game of chess needs two players."

Cheshire smiles and takes another sip of her pomegranate juice. "At least, that's what some believe."

I eye the strange monster sitting across from me. "Is that what *you* believe, Cheshire? You said that some people serve the Demiurge and some people rebel against her, just as the Intercessor and the Adversary do. Which do you align with?" I gesture at the two statues.

Cheshire shrugs. "I know only what I was made to know, and I was made to be of use to you. I will support you however you choose to act."

I glare at the geist. "You're too smart to play dumb. You clearly know way more than I do about this universe, and you just as clearly have *opinions* about what you know. So spill."

It's the first time I've really seen her stop and contemplate something. She glances between the angel and the devil, her expression more thoughtful than devious for once. "I think that . . . in the end, we have no choice but to play the part we've been given. Whether that role be god or godslayer, it would be hubris to deny what has been written for us. We're all slaves to God's script." Slowly, Cheshire reaches out and lays a hand on the statuette of the angel.

Is that how you really feel? Or is even that a performance? I place my hand on the statuette of the devil. "I think you're wrong. And I'll prove it to you, whatever it takes. Once we usurp the Lady of Shards, the Demiurge is next."

Cheshire laughs. "Oh, Alice, you really are perfect. Well, regardless of your deicidal schemes, I think we've established enough of a philosophical foundation. Now, we get to talk about magic."

II

Magic magic magic magicmagicmagicMAGIC!
"Let's play a game," says Cheshire.
I frown. "Will this game help me amass incredible magical power?"
"Yes, actually."
"Then I'm in! Give magic please. I would like one magic with all the magic, please and thank you."
Cheshire grins. "Excellent. Now, we're going to be diving in and out of different facets of the magic system going forward, but I'd like to start by hearkening to the kind of activity that I know you've done plenty of times: building a list of superpowers. Pretend you're making an RPG character and you only get to pick four powers, assigning them priority from most important to least important. What would you pick first?"
"Immortality," I respond instantly.
Cheshire waves away my answer. "Let's set immortality aside for now, since it isn't immediately achievable. It's obvious that you want to be powerful and eternal, but we can redefine that as short-term survival and long-term survival. From there we can game out what kind of magic supports the former while keeping the latter in mind as a goal to strive for. So, aside from immortality, what's at the very top of your ideal list of superpowers?"
I hesitate. I know the answer—like she said, I've made this list at least a dozen times before—but I'm nervous to admit it. Cheshire says she knows me, she says my goals are her goals, but I don't believe her. I don't trust her. I'm afraid of what she'll say.
Cheshire sees my hesitation and gently touches my cheek. "It's okay, Alice. It's just the two of us here, and I already know what you're going to say. You're safe here; this is *your* soul, after all," she adds with a wink.

I brush her hand away from my cheek, but her words sink in. *This is my soul. My domain. And saying that . . .* I meet Cheshire's gaze and insist, "I want reciprocity. If I'm going to tell you all the powers I fantasize about having, I want to hear what powers *you* dream of having."

Cheshire leans her chin on the back of her hand. "You assume I have such dreams, and that they differ from your own."

I look at her with obvious skepticism. "Look, there's only two real scenarios here: either you're lying about being created to be my perfect fantasy, or you're not. If you are lying, then obviously you're going to have your own wants and traits that differ from mine. If you're not lying, you're still going to be substantively different from me in ways that I find challenging and engaging and completing. There is no scenario in which you're just an empty husk or a blank mirror of me, so *play the game*. Reciprocate."

The catgirl chuckles. "Alright, we'll have a back-and-forth: you name a power, I name a power. Sound fair?"

No, because you still know vastly more about me than I know about you, but it's a start. "It sounds *acceptable*."

"Then take it away, my dear Alice. What power do you want more than any other? What's your signature spell, your defining ability?"

Okay. All cards on the table. It's fine. This is fine. She already knows my answer. This is a formality. I have nothing to lose. She's not going to judge me for it. Still I hesitate. "I want to be liked," I say to talk around the actual answer. "More than liked, I want to be adored. I want people to be obsessed with me, to think about me constantly. I . . . I want to trust people. I want to know that the people around me won't betray me, won't abandon me, won't turn on me. And . . . I don't think that's really possible."

Cheshire smiles at me and asks, "Why not?"

I clench my fists. "Because I am a shitty, garbage, worthless person. I'm unlikable, I'm unlovable, and human beings are too self-interested to put someone's needs above their own even when that someone is *deserving*, let alone when it's someone like me. And for all that I try, I can never really be better than I am. I can never earn their loyalty. So betrayal is inevitable. Abandonment is inevitable. Being *alone* is inevitable. Unless . . . I take away the choice."

"Mind control," Cheshire says like it's something casual and normal and not an unforgivable violation of every moral system under the sun.

"Mind control," I reluctantly agree.

Cheshire tilts her head and asks, "What kind? There are plenty of ways to go about subverting someone's will, and I'm sure you've thought about this."

I grimace. "I . . . have. Okay, so, the problem with most mind control—the practical problem, I mean, because the ethical problem is a whole different can of very evil worms that I am just not interested in opening right now—is that it's too fragile. When a character gets mind controlled in a story it's basically guaranteed that the mind control will break at exactly the worst time for the villain responsible. If you give a mind-controlling necklace as a gift to the princess, all you're really doing is setting up the dramatic removal of said necklace at the climax of the third act."

I'm getting animated now, gesturing with my hands as I speak. I add, "And that's true of basically any kind of 'enchantment' mind control. Whatever kind of trance you put them under, it's just not going to last. Now, brain parasites are a different story. Take the Yeerks from *Animorphs*: itty-bitty brain slugs that slither into your ear and make themselves cozy wrapped around your gray matter. The Yeerks can't be beaten with willpower, and it takes absurd amounts of effort to force them out of a host. Brain parasites are effective and reliable, but they do have weaknesses: they're slow, they need stealth or for the victim to already be at your mercy, and they can still usually be removed under the right conditions, even if those conditions are rare or difficult. So that really just leaves one ideal method: corruption."

Cheshire's yellow-and-blue eyes brighten. "Go on. Tell me more."

I sit back on my throne of pillows and drum my fingers against the arm of the big stuffed bunny. "Okay, so, if you've done your research you already know this story, but I'm going to tell it anyways because I'm in love with the sound of my own voice and it's also exactly what you want. Yeah?"

"Mhm!" she affirms cheerily.

"Right. So back on Earth there was this game I liked called Magic: The Gathering. It was a card game about mages that could travel between worlds, and of all the worlds in their multiverse there was one that I adored above all others: Phyrexia. New Phyrexia, actually, but that's just details. Phyrexia was a place, and a people, and an idea, but more than that it was a virus. It spread through glistening oil and it infected flesh and metal alike, creating horrible fusions of mortal and machine that carried in them the means and imperative to infect others with Phyrexia's glory. And for all that it was monstrous and horrifying, it was genuinely *glorious*. The Phyrexians still had identity, they were still individuals, but they were *Phyrexian* individuals with *Phyrexian* identities."

The speed of my drumming picks up as I'm getting excited telling this story, and I continue, "There was this mage, Tamiyo, who was driven by a desire to share knowledge and protect her family. And when she was made one with Phyrexia, both of those things were still true; but now, she wanted to collect knowledge to bring to Phyrexia, and she considered all of Phyrexia her family to be protected. Tamiyo was the same person at her core, just . . . recontextualized.

Made part of a greater whole." I pause for dramatic effect before finishing, "That's the kind of mind control I want to be capable of."

Cheshire's smile is predatory. "My beloved Alice, I think that's a *little bit more* than 'I want to be liked.'"

I flinch and look away. "Yeah, well, that's all you're getting out of me for now, so it'll have to be good enough. Your turn, Cheshire."

The catgirl laughs. "Oh, it's more than good enough. Alright, let's set your dreams of viral dominion aside for the moment."

Cheshire snaps her fingers and the storm of memory peels back from the book pile—not by much, just a little hollow carved out adjacent to the pile. A pedestal rises out of the wasteland, and on that pedestal kneel supplicants in worship, figures of shadow kneeling and praying and bound in red string that all leads back to the statue standing above them: me. The red string wraps around the wrist of the statue, and the representation of me is dressed in lavish robes with a crown upon her head and an ornate staff in the unbound hand.

"I'm going to bend the rules a little," Cheshire starts, "if that's alright with you. Rather than answering in terms of most to least important, I'd like to frame my choices as a response to your choices. How does that sound?"

"Sure, I'll allow it."

"Excellent." Cheshire rubs her hands together. "You spoke at great length about mind control in terms of ends, but I'd like to shift focus to *means*: why would someone feel it necessary to use magic to influence others, rather than more conventional manipulation techniques? I think the conclusion is obvious: a would-be controller of minds is someone who feels insecure about their social capabilities."

I tense up at her verbal thrashing. "Isn't this supposed to be about you now?" I mutter. I mean, she's not *wrong*, but it feels uncouth to say the quiet part out loud.

Cheshire laughs at my complaint. "Getting there, love. My point is that mind control is only necessary if one lacks confidence in their ability to make others do what they want through speech alone. I, however, am *very* confident in my skills as a manipulator, so the power that I would like is something that allows me to learn people's secrets. If I know everything about someone, that makes it easier to get them to do what I want."

She winks at me and I choose not to think about the complicated bouquet of weird and contradictory feelings that arise from what she just said and did.

"So instead of mind control, I think I'd like to go unnoticed and learn people's secrets. I want to be a bird watching from its perch, or a spider on the wall, seeing and hearing everything but never being seen or heard myself."

Cheshire gestures to the side and a new pedestal rises opposite the first, smaller but still grandiose. The scene is a diorama of different small, almost unnoticeable animals watching two shadowy figures share whispers.

"Hmm." I take a long drink of pomegranate juice and consider her words carefully. Some of what she said fascinates me and demands further examination.

There's an unspoken component to her reasoning: maybe it is social insecurity that drives someone to want mind control powers, but I don't think the default choice should be rejecting those powers. If you want to manipulate people, mind control is still a useful tool, so to set it aside entirely suggests . . . pride, maybe? Satisfaction in manipulation? The way she talked about manipulating people—about manipulating me—makes it seem like she gets a thrill out of it.

If it was just about ends, then there would be no problem using mind control. And if it was just about ends, she would have approached that scene in the apartment completely differently. But she doesn't just want to manipulate me into taking certain actions, she wants to do it with flair. She wants to prove that she can manipulate me even when I know I'm being manipulated.

Cheshire watches me, and I wonder if even that train of thought was an intended reaction. Did she want me to know that? Does that change the veracity of the claim? It's impossible to tell.

"Alright, my turn," I finally say. "I feel like I'm overusing media examples here but I don't know how to express this one clearly otherwise. Back when I played *World of Warcraft*, my favorite class was warlock, and one of the things I loved doing as a warlock was treating my health as a resource. Burn hit points for mana, spend mana to rip the life out of enemies. It was this beautifully elegant gameplay loop of turning life force into spells to take life force from my opponent."

"It's risk/reward," Cheshire points out. "That's essentially what you've been doing the whole time you've been in the Labyrinth; you burn your life or your soul for fuel with the eventual goal of using that fuel to achieve greater gains than you spent."

"I think those greater gains are the most important part. I don't want to break even, I want to get *stronger* through this process. I want to devour the strength of my enemies and make it mine, feasting on their essence." *Power progression through murder is a staple of RPG leveling systems, and if I can make it a fact of this world I will.*

"It's a form of vampirism," Cheshire suggests. "It's blood magic. You sacrifice a piece of yourself in exchange for the power to feed on others."

I grin. "I like that framing. Vampirism and blood magic it is." I hesitate, then add, "Though as attractive as the idea of ripping throats out sounds, I'd actually prefer to stay *away* from my enemies. I want *controlled* risk; I want to be the only one spilling my blood."

"I can work with that." Cheshire waves her hand and once again the storm pulls back from a new hollow. This time my statue-self is baring fangs and holding out a clawed hand that drips with fresh blood. A hapless victim contorts in anguish as all the blood is ripped out of their body and flows through the air in a continuous stream toward my statue-self's outstretched hand.

I admire the image for a moment before saying, "Okay, your turn."

The catgirl picks up one of the shards of porcelain from the cup she broke and toys with it, not seeming to mind the way it cuts into her fingers. "You take on risk for the sake of reward, but I believe there is reward in risk itself. There is pleasure in pain, and there is a certain thrill in dancing on the knife's edge."

Cheshire flourishes the teacup fragment and it becomes a knife midswing, her grin turned feral. "My second choice is this: blood magic as you would wield, but more *visceral*. I would rip the life from our foes with bared fangs. I want to taste violence and return the favor."

One finger snap later, a new scene joins the rest: a statue of a giant wolf tearing out an indistinct figure's throat. The wolf is covered in bleeding wounds, and blood from those wounds flows to the mouth of the beast.

Hmm. I wish she'd spent more time elaborating on that choice, but I guess we have something to work with. Taken on its own that screams "sadomasochist" or "adrenaline junkie" to me, but that's the second time she's brought animals into this. An archetype she's playing up, or a sincere inclination?

. . . And does that mean my maybe-girlfriend is a furry? Does it count as a furry if you're already part animal? Wait, do I count as a furry by maybe-dating her!? Shit. Focus on superpowers! Back to superpowers!

"My third power is minion-making." Another desire gained through video games, but this power is arguably more useful to me in a real context. "I want the power to make armies bound to my will: necromantic hordes, legions of bound devils, living shadows, packs of wild beasts, towering golems . . . whatever works, really. I want minions that will do the fighting and the grunt labor for me, servants that will function as my sword and shield."

"That's pretty broad," Cheshire points out. "Think you can narrow it down?"

"Hmm." I grab a cluster of grapes and idly start popping them in my mouth while I think. "Kind of difficult, actually. I mean, you can ditch the golems, they're more of an afterthought. The beasts too."

Cheshire taps her chin thoughtfully. "I'll talk about this more when it comes to actually making spells, but you'll get more bang for your buck if all your concepts are at least loosely related. Necromancy clicks with your fear of death and living shadows could be justified for any demon, but I actually think there's some really interesting space to explore with beasts, and maybe not just beasts."

I tilt my head curiously. "I'm listening."

"We talked about vampirism before, and I think that's actually a great foundation for you, for reasons we'll get to later. Vampires are often associated with creatures of the night and various 'sinister' animals. Sometimes that means wolves and bats, sometimes crows and rats, and sometimes creepy-crawlies like centipedes and spiders. If you want to double down on the vampire theme, that might be a fun way to do it."

"I wouldn't mind commanding an army of centipedes and spiders," I admit. "'Queen of Worms' has a nice ring to it."

"Great!" Cheshire claps her hands and another space is carved out of the raging storm. This time the scene shows insects, arachnids, wolves, rodents, and bats all coming together in a swarm.

"Mm. It would be kind of fun to make horrible chimeric abominations by mixing different animals together. Something to come back to later, perhaps."

Cheshire grins. "I think you're starting to enjoy this. Getting a taste for the supervillain lifestyle?"

"Fuck it, I'm a demon now. I can be a little evil, as a treat."

Cheshire cackles and I match her grin. When the catgirl's had her fun, she rubs her hands together and says, "Alright, here's my third: physical prowess. You want to hang back and send your minions to do the dirty work, but I want to fight as the beasts do, scrapping in the thick of it. I want to be strong enough and fast enough to be a constant in-your-face threat."

Doubling down on the violence angle, and tripling down on the animalism themes. Interesting. "So, will you actually be fighting alongside me? Because I had kind of assumed you would play the sinister advisor role but never dirty your own hands, and instead it's sounding like you would actually really *enjoy* dirtying your hands."

Cheshire shapes part of the storm into another statue of her gleefully murdering people as a big fuck-off wolf, and answers, "Well, that'll be up to you. As your geist I can only act in the ways you allow me to act, but I *can* be quite useful. Some demons have their geist stay as just advisors, some have their geist handle complicated spellcasting, and some have their geist manifest a physical form to act as bodyguard-slash-assassin."

I look between the two wolf statues and say, "I'm guessing you'd prefer that last option."

Cheshire grins. "You already know me so well. Alright, on to the very last power! Give me something juicy."

I pop a few more grapes and ask, "I don't suppose you'd let me cheat and argue that two should be considered one?" *She basically stretched one power into three.*

The catgirl winks. "Make your case, Alice."

"Okay, so, I don't know how much psychoanalysis you'll actually get out of these, but my last power pick is pyromancy and umbrakinesis: fire and shadow. Fire because I'm a pyromaniac and I love watching things burn, and shadow because . . . well, because it's edgy and I like edgy."

"Got any specifics for me?" she asks.

I shrug. "I mean, the fire part is obvious: burn things till they're ash. For the shadow part I do actually have some specific spell ideas: shadow-walking, making tentacles of darkness, turning shadows sharp and stabbing people with them, and cloaking myself in darkness to hide."

"Perfect!" Cheshire smirks. With a wave of her hand another statue emerges from the storm, this one a twisting mass of intertwined shadow and flame. "There's actually a way to make sure you get both of those *and* that they'll be powerful, but you might balk at what it costs."

"I'm listening." *For magic, for power, I'll pay any price.*

Cheshire pulls a knife out of thin air: the scorched dagger I gained from my encounter with Eirdryd and the spider-dogs. With her other hand she gently grabs my wrist and strokes the tattoo-like design that appeared after my bargain with Bashekehi. "It involves breaking these down into their component parts. While we *can* make spells from just the substance of your internal world, we'll get more 'oomph' by repurposing existing configurations of magic, like this artifact and this invocation."

I frown and extricate my wrist. "Hold on, when you say 'break those things down,' you mean you're going to destroy them, don't you? I *like* having a magic dagger, Cheshire."

Patiently, without a hint of condescension, Cheshire asks, "Alice, how do you think you would fare in a knife fight—by which I mean, a fight in which both you and your opponent fought with knives and nothing else?"

"This is a trap," I point out.

"It is!" Cheshire cheerily replies. "Now answer the question, love."

I roll my eyes. "Ugh, fine. Barring additional context, I would *lose.*"

"Now, as a follow-up question to that: how do you think you would fare in a fight against someone who was wielding a sword, a spear, or an axe?"

I sigh. "I would lose."

"You are not a warrior," Cheshire gently chides me, "and you don't really want to *be* a warrior. Think about the powers you asked for: mind control, draining life, summoning monsters, throwing flame. None of those are a warrior's powers. You asked for the powers of a ruler, a summoner, and a mage who controls the battlefield from the backline. So what are you going to do with a knife?"

I grit my teeth. "[Ashthorn] saved me from one of the spider-dogs, and it let me kill the sin eater. I get it, I'm not a melee fighter by any stretch, but it doesn't hurt to have a backup weapon."

"I agree! But a backup weapon shouldn't come at the cost of developing a *primary* weapon. Perhaps more importantly, if all your spells aren't enough to stop a foe from getting close enough that you can knife them, do you really think a knife will be enough to save you?"

Reluctantly, I force myself to play out that scenario in my mind. I imagine throwing flame and centipedes at someone. I imagine that someone brushing aside all my attacks and coming in close, and I am forced to admit that having a knife—even a flaming knife—probably wouldn't save me in that situation. "Okay, you're right. Eat the dagger."

[Ashthorn] crumbles into its namesake and Cheshire collects the ashes into a simple urn—conjured from nowhere—that she places on a second table, which wasn't there a moment ago. She points to the tattoo around my wrist and asks, "Any objections on that one?"

I shake my head. "If the dagger goes, the dagger-amplifier goes."

The representation of my [Abyssal Armament] spell goes up in smoke, and those wisps of smoke drift over to be captured in a glass vial that Cheshire quickly corks. The smoke turns into liquid darkness once the vial is corked. "There: a collection of elements born of flame and the Wild Hunt, and a collection of elements born of the Abyss and its all-consuming nature."

"Elements?" I ask.

Cheshire grins. "Elements indeed. It's time for the real lesson, Alice. I'm going to teach you what the universe is really made of."

III

Cheshire holds out a hand, palm up, and a sword appears above it, floating gently. She says, "This is a sword. To be more precise, this is a constructed representation of what the universe says a sword is. This is the *concept* of a sword, and it contains within it all the various meanings of the word, a cluster of connected ideas crystallized into a single representative word. In oneiric theory—the study of the deeper workings of Pandaemonium and Firmament—we say that this is an *elemental* sword."

The sword splinters apart into a dozen smaller swords, and Cheshire continues, "The elemental sword contains subordinate components, individual points of meaning that we call *oneiros*—*oneiron* in the singular, *oneiric* in the adjective. Some oneiros are derived from the denotation of the word—the literal meaning—but most oneiros are connotations: the cultural and emotional associations of the word, existing at the intersection of the individual and the collective. When you think of a sword—of what a sword is, of what a sword means—what comes to mind?"

I lean in, enraptured by her explanation, and give the question serious thought. "A sword cuts," I begin. "A sword is . . . an implement of violence. A weapon. A sword is swung in combat, in duels and battles and wars. A sword is butchery and honor, murder and valor, the sins and virtues of a killer." I pause, and then another idea strikes me. "In tarot, the King of Swords is the philosopher king, and the suit of swords is the suit of the nobility, probably because it was usually nobles who could afford to actually own a sword. Tarot associates swords with air and intellect and misfortune."

Cheshire brings her hands together with a smile and all the smaller swords merge back into a single sword. "A perfect demonstration, darling. Yes, all those notions are contained with the elemental sword as oneiros. And here we can make a comparison to the universe that you're more familiar with."

Cheshire separates her hands again and the sword splits in half. One half fractures into smaller swords as before, but the other half fractures into diagrams of atoms. "In a physical universe, a sword is a complex structure composed of iron and carbon atoms, plus some impurities and whatever the hilt is made of. You might call those component parts 'elemental iron' and 'elemental carbon,' but you wouldn't call the sword an 'elemental sword' because there's nothing elemental about it; to the laws of a physical universe, there are no swords, only particular configurations of iron and carbon.

"In a *metaphysical* universe, a sword is as much an element of reality as the iron it is forged with. And reality in a metaphysical universe is more *recursive*; the idea of a sword contains within it other ideas, those lesser notions we call oneiros. We could compare our elemental sword to the elemental iron atoms of a physical sword by calling it a 'sword atom,' and from there we can compare the oneiros that make up our metaphysical sword to the protons and neutrons of an iron atom. And just as you can break the parts of an atom down into quarks, dividing the indivisible, you can break an oneiron down into more fundamental ideas that exist beneath even the implicit."

"Semiotics," I say uneasily, the reality of her speech finally hitting me. "You're saying that the foundation of magic—no, the foundation of this entire universe—is semiotics: signs and symbols and their interpretations."

"Precisely!"

Cheshire banishes the split swords and instead lifts up the apple she had taken a bite out of before. The apple blurs and breaks apart, and in its place I see a hundred resonating images: the biology of an apple, an apple plucked from a tree, an apple eaten as food, apples representing health, immortality, fertility, forbidden fruit, discord, knowledge of good and evil, love... and somewhere in that cloud of meaning, an oneiron that I instinctively recognize as *my* association, *my* personal meaning: the apple that taught a man and a woman to think for themselves in a garden where they were kept ignorant.

"In Pandaemonium, material reality isn't really *real*; there are spaces where some approximation of physics is present, but it's just a trick of perspective. Everything in the universe is made of meaning, not physical laws. *That* is why we say that the essence of magic is the manipulation of meaning."

That explanation unnerves me. Maybe it's because I come from such a materialistic culture, but the idea that everything in this universe—even *matter*—is made of *ideas* rather than anything more solid makes me nervous. "How does that work? Is there just no such thing as matter or energy here? Am I really just made of... ideas?"

Cheshire makes the apple-cloud vanish and says, "Matter and energy *exist* in that you can interact with them, but they're not *fundamental*. Every atom in Firmament—those pockets of physical space I mentioned—is just an *oneiron* pretending to be an atom. Those false atoms simulate physical laws because they've been told to, and so they behave with physical and chemical consistency, but only until they're told otherwise." Almost as an afterthought she adds, "As a newborn demon you exist somewhere between the false material and the true immaterial. Right now your body is still acting like it's made of matter, mostly, but the more demonic you become, the less your form will pretend to be physical. Isn't that fun?"

Terrifying, actually, but I guess kind of exciting in a weird way? I genuinely don't know how I should feel about that. I mean . . . what the fuck? Yeah, actually, that's a solid response. "What the fuck, Cheshire?"

The catgirl cackles at my shock.

"No, really, what the fuck?" I hesitate. "When you made the apple break apart, I . . . I saw the apple from Eden, from my version of Eden. But that's my interpretation of a story from my world, so what is it doing here? Is that just the nature of the space we're in right now, or . . . is that the nature of this universe?"

Cheshire recovers her composure and grins. "The question you really want to ask is if the reality of this universe is your subjective personal experience of that reality, and the answer is yes . . . to a point. Your reality *is* your experience of reality, but solipsism is a lie and other people exist. And now seems like the perfect time to digress onto the topic of Thrones."

You're just going to leave it there!? That is not something to just quickly brush past! I almost object, but so far everything Cheshire has done has had a point, so I stifle my argument and let her continue.

Cheshire takes three pieces of fruit from the nearest bowl—a pomegranate, a peach, and a dragonfruit—and sets them down in front of her. "From where do we derive meaning?"

I frown. "You asked that before, and we got into a whole dialogue about existentialism and rebellion against the divine and other shit."

"Ah, but that dialogue was purely about meaning as *significance*. Now I seek to discuss both definitions: meaning as significance and meaning as semiotics. So I ask again: from where do we derive meaning? Start with semiotics."

"Okay, uh . . . I'm going to use an example because otherwise this will get way too abstract way too quickly." I grab a Lego brick from the pile of toys that Cheshire made earlier. "So this is a Lego brick, and I think most people where I'm from would recognize what that means. It's a toy, and you're meant to use it with other Lego bricks to build houses and hospitals and landmarks and other shit, but you can also use the bricks to make things that aren't in the manuals."

I grab a couple more bricks because they're fun to play with and I start clicking them together. "As a kid, you learn what Lego bricks mean in a couple ways: there's some stuff you learn from the marketing of the brand and from what other people tell you about them, like that they're practically indestructible and that they're a toy you can build cool structures with; but there's also stuff you can learn without interacting with anyone, just by playing with the bricks and experimenting until you figure out how they work and what you can do with them."

My Lego construction is terrible, because I absolutely suck at spatial thinking, but I proudly display my unrecognizable creation. "Part of the meaning of 'Lego brick' comes from other people, no way around it; the term was created by someone else and communicated to me by someone else. But a lot of the meaning comes from my own personal experiences with it, my own interpretation; I find them fun to play with but difficult to make much with, while someone else might find them easy to build with but not particularly engaging."

Cheshire claps politely for my brick abomination. "I think you picked an excellent example. Allow me to add one detail: while most of the semiotic meaning of 'Lego brick' comes from the cultural associations and your personal experience with it, there are also some physical aspects that we can consider to be more 'objective' insofar as objectivity exists. A Lego brick is made of plastic, and the chemical composition of a Lego brick can be measured, as can its physical hardness."

"You said physical laws were just an illusion," I point out. "Does it matter, then, what physical properties an object has?"

Cheshire laughs easily. "It's a fair thing to question. I would say it does matter, if only as a foundation. I think an element of the physical, even an illusory physical, is necessary for shared understanding. You and I may have a different cultural understanding of a great big rock, and you and I may have a different personal understanding of that great big rock, but we can both stand upon the rock and feel its firmness. Get deep enough out into Pandaemonium and you can escape the tyranny of the empirical, but most of the shallower layers are going to roughly mimic at least the appearance of universal physical properties."

"Hmm. Interesting." I feel like a student learning about the world for the first time, which in a certain sense I am. "So three sources of meaning, I guess you could say."

Cheshire nods. "More formally, we can consider semiotic meaning to be the intersection of three not entirely distinct aspects: observable properties of the natural world, associations learned from the collective, and individual interpretation. This formal reading of semiotic meaning dovetails nicely with the *significant* meaning of the three Thrones that are considered most intrinsic to the fabric of Pandaemonium: Order, Spirit, and Shadow."

"Bashe mentioned some of this before," I tell Cheshire. "He didn't go into much detail, but he called them different lenses of magic."

"It's a decent way to understand them. Each Throne is, in a very real sense, an interpretive lens by which its adherents engage with semiotic and significant meaning. Every Throne has to acknowledge all three aspects of the semiotic, of course, but they can place different emphasis on specific components."

Cheshire taps the dragonfruit and it grows scaly wings. "The Throne of Order says that the most important meaning is that which can be derived from scientific observation of the natural world. Order finds significance in the material world, in the natural laws fashioned by the Demiurge, and adherents of Order believe that they can divine the meaning of life through study of those laws. We are given impulses to survive and propagate as the beasts do, but we are also endowed with higher faculties, with reason and creativity and the capacity to *create*, and that must speak to our purpose in the universe. For proof, look no further than the five flights of dragons that rule Order: they are the only natural-born Royalty in all of Pandaemonium, and they embody the five principles which form the foundation of Firmament."

I raise a hand and Cheshire smirks but still calls on me. "Yes, Ms. Alice?"

"Can we tangent onto 'Royalty' real quick? Because I've heard it mentioned about gods and archdemons and now I'm hearing it about dragons, and I'm really keen to learn what the fuck is up with all that."

Cheshire laughs. "Sure, we can tangent. To understand Royalty it's best if you also understand scions." Cheshire taps the peach and it splits in half, exposing the stone—the seed—inside. Cheshire extracts the seed and tosses it onto the nearby ground where it sinks into the page and immediately sprouts. In seconds a peach tree has grown tall and casts a shadow over the table. A single peach falls from the tree into Cheshire's hand.

Cheshire takes a bite of the peach, swallows, and says, "Imagine that of all the peaches on that tree, only a few of them—let's say ten—will have what it takes to pass on their genes and grow into a big beautiful tree. And let's say that of those ten trees, only one of them will bear fruit and make new peaches. Now, actual plant science would undoubtedly give a different reason, but let's pretend that the peaches which make trees do so because they, when they were still flowers, were pollinated by bees while the other peach flowers weren't.

"The peaches that don't grow into trees, those are the retainers and invokers—imps and diabolists, kindred and priests, and so on. They've got a lot to offer, but they can't make anything new. The peaches that grow into trees but don't bear fruit, those are the scions, a category which you now belong to as a demon. Scions have the capacity to create new magic, to use spells that no one else ever has, but their ability to pass that magic on is limited. Royalty, however, can bear fruit; as the peach tree grows new peaches, an ascendant archdemon gets to make a new kind of imp and start spreading a new selection of spells to mortal diabolists. And just as sometimes a peach can mutate into something that is not a peach, Royalty can ascend that carry with them a new kind of Throne entirely."

So it's a magic system that evolves over time. "Am I to assume that your kind are the pollinators, then?" I ask.

Cheshire grins. "Guilty as charged. It's different for the different Thrones, however: Shadow has geists like me, but Spirit has eidolons and the other three have it baked into their Royalty."

"Fascinating," I murmur.

Cheshire lets the bitten-into peach tumble away and picks up the two halves of the split peach, which both start emitting a serene white light as she brings them together. "Let's talk the Throne of Spirit next. Spirit says that meaning is most important when it comes from the collective, from things like culture and community. Adherents of Spirit find significance in kinship and tradition, and believe that they can divine the meaning of life from enduring shared narratives. There is significance in the enshrining of virtues, and there is significance in having faith in a higher power. Eidolons and gods—the spirits from which the Throne takes its name—embody those values which are most integral to a collective, those stories which have the greatest weight, and could there be a better measure of what the Demiurge finds meaningful? It is our ability to raise communities and tell stories that sets us apart from the low beasts of Pandaemonium, and so that ability more than anything is what makes our lives meaningful."

"Not all stories represent the values of the society that produced them," I point out. "Some stories are explicitly countercultural."

"Very true!" Cheshire chirps. "And yet a counterculture is still a *culture* and can still produce eidolons. And thus we have the internal polarity of Spirit." She raises the two peach halves and the light shifts, one becoming primarily white with a black spot in the center and the other becoming primarily black with a white spot in the center; yin and yang.

I drink more pomegranate juice and eye the peach halves, idly wondering if they're still edible in their glowing state. "Makes sense. Spirit equals collective, different collectives behave differently. That just leaves Shadow, right?"

"Indeed! Think you can make a guess at what governs that Throne?" Cheshire tosses the peach halves aside and picks up the pomegranate.

I think over what Cheshire's said so far and add in what Bashekehi told me. "It's the Throne of the individual, obviously. Shadow finds meaning in will and want, in the intensely personal. You get to make your own significance, fuck what anyone else says." I chew my lip as I consider another angle. "You could argue it's the Adversary's own Throne, if she's meant to represent rebellion against the divine. Fuck the toymaker's meaning, fuck what the Demiurge wants of you."

Cheshire claps her hands. "Very good! That is an excellent summation of the Adversarial interpretation of Shadow. It is not, in my opinion, the *accurate* interpretation." I raise an eyebrow and Cheshire continues, "For all that Shadow may claim to care about choice and free will, most of its adherents are bound to forms of significance dictated by Royalty. Further, even those archdemons are not truly *free*, as all touched by Shadow have been stained by the Abyss; the Throne of Shadow is the legacy of the Abyss and the Leviathans that once ruled it, and so it demands conflict and predation from all its adherents. In this, we see yet again an argument for the Demiurge's intent: the struggle to make meaning is itself the meaning that Nyarlathotep intends. It is God's cruelest joke, to allow a demon to hope that it has escaped her strings." Cheshire's smile is even more vicious than usual.

"I think I prefer my version," I mutter.

Cheshire pats my hand. "I know you do. But don't fret, because I have a way to cheer you up!" Cheshire flicks her wrist and the tea table careens away into the maelstrom, immediately replaced by the table with the urn and vial. "It's time to become a proper demon and design your first three spells."

IV

Cheshire gestures at the various statues surrounding the book pile. "The powers you chose will give us quite a bit of metaphysical grist to work with. We'll start by extracting elements from those, then add a few elements from general observations about your behavior and drives."

"And we'll use those elements to make spells?" I ask.

"There will be a step between, but essentially yes." Cheshire points to the scene of red string and bent supplicants. "First, let's look at mind control. You said your desire for a corrupting ability was driven by a desire for attachments and a fear of abandonment, and that's certainly accurate to a degree. You need other people, you want to be around other people, but you don't *trust* other people, so you want to be able to control them. Your story, however, speaks to another truth: you think there is something *glorious* about uniting the many as one, and you think you *deserve* to be the one leading the chorus." Cheshire pauses, ever-grinning, and finishes, "You think you're better than everyone else, and you want them to finally acknowledge that fact."

I tense up and clench my fists. "That's not . . . I don't think that way."

"No?" Cheshire tilts her head curiously. "Then how *do* you think, Maven Alice?"

I hesitate. "I . . . I just want to cheat, okay? I want to be loved and adored and I'm not *good enough* to get that with my personality, because my personality is shit and I'm a garbage person. So I want to cheat."

"Would you be satisfied if adoration came provisional with a position of weakness? If you were loved and cherished but beholden to someone else, made to belong to someone else?"

I bristle. "I'll not be someone's *pet*."

"Of course not; you want to be in control. You want to *rule*. Am I wrong?"

I hiss, but I know she's right. She's eternally right, the cat-eared little shit, and she clearly won't let me think otherwise for even a moment. "Whatever. Extract the elements and let's move on."

"As you wish, Your Majesty," she says with a wink. A crown appears on the tea table, opulent and crimson and decorated with rubies carved into hearts and drops of blood.

Cheshire points to the exsanguination statue and says, "You are willing to sacrifice pieces of yourself to achieve greater gains. Risk and reward, sacrifice and growth, but controlled risk, controlled sacrifice. And of course, the obvious associations with vampirism and blood magic. You seek to glut upon prey, even at the cost of your very soul. Does that sound accurate?"

I nod. "Pretty much, yeah." A chalice filled with blood appears on the table.

Cheshire points to the statue of the swarm and says, "We can draw more vampirism associations there, but we can also draw more associations of *rulership*. You want *minions*, Alice, and you want to use those minions to make people respect you, even fear you. The kind of corruption magic you want is a form of rule through love—twisted, hideous love—but an army of horrors, beasts dripping with night and death, suggests rule through *fear*."

I don't see much value in denying it at this point. "Yes, yes, fine. I accept your interpretation: I want to rule through fear and love." I add, "Machiavelli *did* say that the ideal ruler employs both."

A second crown pops into existence next to the first, black as night and made to resemble a curled centipede with a skull-patterned carapace.

Cheshire conjures a burning candle and says, "Pyromania is a fairly simple desire, but the other half of your fourth pick has some interesting notions to play with. Spells to run away, showing your fear of dying. Wielding the dark as a weapon, a primeval terror." She adds a second vial of liquid darkness beside the first, this one with a skull-faced stopper.

I glance over the two vials, the candle, and the ashen urn. "I'm going to guess that rather than being redundant, having multiple connections to fire and shadow will actually be a good thing?"

"Correct! Being able to stack meaning will enhance the potential of the finished product. On that note, I have a few more elements to add to the pile."

Cheshire cups her hands together and summons a dagger of blackest night, which she carefully lays next to the other objects. "You are a scion of the Throne of Shadow, and that means its elements are your elements: darkness, consumption, conflict, will, and want. You are heir to the legacy of the Abyss, to the hungering dark that would devour all worlds."

I eye the dagger with curiosity. *The hungering dark . . . I do like the sound of that.*

"Next, I want to examine your original choice of name here in the Labyrinth."

I wince. "Do we have to? I've already given up on it, I know I can't keep it."

Cheshire smirks. "It's the motivation that I'm concerned with, not the results. You chose the name 'Malice' because you wanted a name that was *intimidating*. You wanted a name that was a threat demanding others respect you." A piece of paper appears on the table with my now-discarded name written on it.

Cheshire continues, "Since arriving in the Labyrinth you have been fascinated by this world. You have asked questions, performed experiments, and acted to acquire as much data as possible. You are curious, and that curiosity is fundamental to your nature." A little porcelain cat appears on the table.

"You know," I quip, "they say that curiosity killed the cat."

"Ah, but they also say that *satisfaction* brought it back," Cheshire replies with a wink. "Speaking of satisfaction, I'd like to highlight the pleasure you took in mutilating your first foe, back in the halls of the abandoned school. You also stabbed that doll completely unprompted, and have generally defaulted to violence whenever it suited you. I think we can make a convincing element out of that willingness to do violence." She gestures at the table and a bloody knife appears next to the shadow-knife.

"It's not that I'm a violent person," I insist, "I just think violence is a useful tool."

Cheshire just raises an eyebrow at me.

"Okay, maybe I'm a little violent."

"Regardless, the final element I'll posit is the one that drove you to become a demon: fear of death. I think we can skip the explanation on this one." A skull manifests in the center of the table.

I look over the various objects: an urn, a candle, two vials of liquid shadow, a red crown, a black crown, a bloody dagger, a shadowed dagger, a chalice of blood, a written name, a porcelain cat, and a skull. "Alright, what next? You said there's a step between gathering these together and making spells out of them."

Cheshire conjures a sword again, but this time has it stab itself into the table and stay there. "To be a scion," she begins, "is to be a sword carving your Truths into the world. For others those Truths are derived externally, but for a demon they come from within, and they are made with purpose. To perform any sorcery, you must first have the weight of a Truth behind each spell."

I raise an eyebrow. "And I'm assuming these are 'Truths' in some metaphysically significant sense?"

Cheshire laughs lightly. "Of course. That's what it's all about." Cheshire sweeps her hand in gesture at the assortment of objects and says, "Elements are, by their nature, descriptive. The elemental sword contains all the meanings that you would associate with a sword. Truths, on the other hand, are prescriptive.

The *Truth* of Swords contains only those meanings which *matter* to you; you might make the connection between a cutting sword and the suit of swords in tarot, but if you don't really care about tarot and its meanings then those meanings won't be included in your Truth of Swords. When you define a Truth, you are declaring to the universe which meanings matter to you. This focus allows Truths to be of greater complexity; as an element contains *oneiros,* a Truth contains elements."

It clicks for me. "All the elements we extracted, I have to turn those into Truths. Configure them, like atoms making up a sword." *It's like the affinities from our dream: Reska mentioned Blood having all sorts of positive connotations, but her affinity only contained the negative. But why's the name different?*

Cheshire nods. "Precisely. To take the stage as a true, proper demon, you must first construct the three Truths of Maven Alice."

"Why three?" I ask. Reska had three affinities in the dream, and that has certain implications.

"A single Truth is fragile, too easily broken. A pair is too polarized, and Pandaemonium will inevitably seek to pit them against each other. More than three weakens them all, stretching your magic too thin and shallow. And three is a symbolically important number, so it'll have more weight."

Yeah, okay, that makes sense enough for this setting. "So what are the rules? Can I just mix and match whatever I like and call it a Truth?"

Cheshire waves her hand in a so-so gesture. "There are rules, but they're more intuitive than rigidly defined. Fundamentally these are *your* Truths, so what matters most is that they make sense to *you*. That means there should be some relation between the elements you use to make up each Truth, that it should feel intuitively correct that these denotations and connotations are being categorized this way, and that whatever you decide on is meaningful to you. It might make sense for your Truth of Swords to contain elements like 'continuous cutting motion' and 'philosopher king,' but it probably doesn't make sense to contain an element like 'loving comfort' unless you have a really aberrant relationship to the concept of swords."

"Got it." I push out of my pillow-and-stuffie throne and start pacing around the table to think. Cheshire takes her stool and steps away to give me space.

I brush all the objects to one side of the table, then pick up the two crowns and place them next to each other on the other side. "Rule; through fear and through love." *There's the easy one out of the way. What about the rest?*

I move the vials of shadow next to the shadowed dagger, but I'm not sure if that's enough for a Truth; can I have a Truth of Shadow if I'm already part of the Throne of Shadow? It doesn't seem solid, but I leave them together for now.

If these are meant to be our Truths, they have to be meaningful to us. As much as I fought her on it, Cheshire is right that I want to Rule others. What are my other core drives? I want to live forever, so maybe some concept like Life or Vitality? I chew on my lip and examine the remaining objects. *Actually, that could work.*

I grab the chalice of blood—vampirism and sacrifice—and set it with the skull and skull-faced vial—fear of death. "Vitality; consuming life, spending life, and fearing death."

That leaves the urn and the candle, the first vial and the shadowed dagger, the bloody dagger, my discarded name, and a porcelain cat. Flame, shadow, violence, intimidation, and curiosity. *I feel like fire and shadow should go together, just on principle. They're both pretty vicious things. Combine them with violence, get something like, say, Ruin?*

I move the urn, candle, vial, and both daggers into a pile. "Ruin; through flame, shadow, and violence." It doesn't really feel *convincing*, though; it sounds fun, sure, to throw fireballs and cause destruction, but is that *meaningful*?

Cheshire is silent as she watches me, keen eyes tracing my every move, not allowing any hint of what she's thinking to reach her face.

I focus my attention on the last two items. The name—intimidation—can go with Rule, but what about curiosity? That's absolutely something important to me, but where does it fit? A curious ruler, the philosopher king? The risks of curiosity, a flimsy justification for Vitality or Ruin?

I'm missing something, I know I am. I'm simplifying too much, I think. I pick up the two crowns again and think about what they really represent: rule through love and rule through fear, yes, but that's not all of it. The black crown is fear wielded as a weapon, fear of death and the dark. The red crown is my fear of abandonment, but also my desire for intimacy, attachments, *bonds*. Those concepts—those *elements*—are substantively distinct.

I narrow my eyes. "The way you made the objects, it's a trap; there's another layer to this puzzle."

Cheshire grins from her perch on the stool. "I knew you'd figure it out."

I glare at the catgirl, but I'm actually kind of enjoying the puzzle so it's a half-hearted glare. I set the crowns back on the table. "Split the red crown; I have a new idea."

Cheshire snaps her fingers and the red crown becomes two red crowns, one with heart imagery and the other with *broken* heart imagery. I take the broken-hearted crown and place it with the skull, the skull-faced vial, the black crown, and the written name. "Fear; of abandonment, of death, of the dark. And rule *through* fear. Fear rules me, so it's only fitting that I make it *serve me* as a demon."

Now, that won't be the only one that's in too few pieces. I consider the chalice of blood next: sacrifice, vampirism . . . is vampirism too broad? *If we break that apart, we get notions like consuming life, feeding, blood—*

Blood.

Blood can be kinship, it can be life and death, it can be *sacrifice* and *bonds*. Blood is vampirism, it is violence, it is *love*. That's the connection. That's what ties it all together.

I set the chalice of blood with the full-hearted crown and the bloody dagger. "Blood. Blood can be offered in sacrifice, or taken from another and consumed. Blood is bonds, and love, and rule *through* love, and it is also violence and rule *through* violence."

That leaves the remnant of Ruin to deconstruct and the cat to incorporate. Fire, shadow, and curiosity. Fire, burning bright, dancing across wood and flesh alike, consuming it.

Consuming. Consuming flame, eating up fuel, ever-hungry. The Abyss, all-consuming, an endless pit of hunger and want. Curiosity, *hunger* for knowledge. All of them wanting more, hungering, glutting.

"Take a bit of blood from the chalice," I instruct Cheshire. She conjures a new vial and fills it, then stoppers it. I take the vial of blood and place it with the urn, the candle, the vial of shadow, the shadowed dagger, and the porcelain cat. "Gluttony. Hunger for life, hunger for power, hunger for knowledge. The hungering flames, consuming all they can until they starve from lack of fuel or air. The hungering dark, the soul-eating Abyss."

"Are those the three you want?" asks Cheshire.

I look to the catgirl, nervous, but she's not revealing anything in her expression or her posture. I feel like a student handing in their homework to be graded by the professor, except that I was almost never nervous to hand in my work because I was great at school.

Maybe it would be more accurate to compare my nervousness to first date jitters; with how much we've talked about philosophy this is definitely a date, and probably the best first date I've ever had. And . . . I want to impress her. I want Cheshire to think that I'm intelligent, that I'm interesting, that I can keep up. And a part of me is afraid, is always afraid, that those things aren't true.

Still, this *feels* right. This has to be right. I swallow my hesitation and force confidence into my voice. "These are the Truths of Maven Alice: Blood, Gluttony, and Fear."

Cheshire examines the objects upon the table, peers at each of them closely, and then turns to me and grins. "Perfect."

I let out a sigh of relief. *I would hate to embarrass myself in front of the inhuman monster claiming to be in love with me.*

In one swift motion Cheshire grabs the tablecloth and yanks it aside. The tablecloth flutters away in an unfelt breeze and is caught by the raging storm, but it leaves behind not a scattering of objects but three glowing symbols engraved in the wooden table beneath: a crimson drop of blood, a fire-orange toothy maw, and a violet skull missing its jaw.

"These three Truths are now inscribed upon your soul," Cheshire intones. "Gluttony will be the strongest, at least at first. It has been fed by outside sources and all of your behavior since entering the Labyrinth matches with Gluttony's ideals. Fear will be the weakest, owing to your utter fearlessness in the face of many dangers."

"That's bullshit," I hiss. "That lack of fear was forced on me, and you *know* fear is what drove me for all the years *before* I came here."

"I do," Cheshire says, "but Pandaemonium does not, or not so strongly. In the eyes of the Dreaming Sea—which has only witnessed your actions since arriving here, and nothing before—your fear comes off as more of an informed attribute than an essential character quality. There is dissonance between identity and action that must be resolved through demonstration. Pandaemonium must see you *afraid* before your fears will have true power."

I glower. *Literally the worst cheat ability, ever, of all time.*

"Now that we have your Truths and elements settled—though I assure you these can grow and develop as your demonhood grows and develops—we can actually make your first spells."

"*Finally*," I say with a roll of my eyes. "Look, I love philosophical introspection as much as the next gal but *give me magic now.*"

Cheshire laughs. "Okay, okay. Magic for the hungry girl. I've assembled a few options for you to choose from, but we only have the power to create three of them right now."

I narrow my eyes at the catgirl suspiciously. "How long have you had those prepared?"

Cheshire smiles at me innocently. "Since before we started arguing about nihilism."

Motherfucker. Also: "How does this interact with the invocation rules? Aren't I down a slot thanks to my knife trick?"

Cheshire waggles a hand in a so-so gesture. "It's a bit more complicated than that. These are stored in your soul *core*, not the pleroma, but the pleroma *is* an important factor in creating spells. If you hadn't sacrificed the dagger and the invocation, we would be limited to two spells right now."

Interesting. Is being stored in the pleroma a necessary limitation of invocations or a forced limitation? "Noted. You may proceed."

The geist taps the symbol for Blood and says, "Your first option is a spell I'm calling [Exsanguinate]. Put simply, it rips the blood from someone's veins, provided they're already bleeding."

Want. Definitely want.

Cheshire taps the symbol for Fear and says, "The second option is [Cry of Terror], which will unleash a scream that instills panic in all who hear it. It won't have an equal effect on everyone, of course, but it might buy you a crucial few moments."

Useful, but not particularly exciting. Fear is supposed to be my weakest Truth, right? I guess using Fear spells is a decent way to change that, but still.

Cheshire taps Gluttony next. "If you want some raw firepower, [Soulfire] will let you do exactly what the name implies. Abyssal flames will burn your enemy's very soul."

"Does it have the same drawback as [Abyssal Armament] did?"

Cheshire shakes her head. "[Soulfire] is a bit more indiscriminate in what it consumes, so it'll always find *something* to sate its hunger: souls, flesh, air, even metal. Of course, it'll be most *effective* at burning souls, so keep that in mind."

"Best on souls, will eat anything. Gotcha."

Cheshire taps the symbol for Fear again. "[Carrion Swarm] is your first summoner option. Eventually you should be able to conjure some real monsters, but for now we're limited to small animals like rats, crows, and centipedes. This one's the most versatile of the selection, since you can use it for non-combat purposes, but it should still be fairly vicious in a fight."

This one probably makes the list too. It's fun to play with skittering horrors.

Cheshire taps Gluttony. "I saved the best for last, of course: [Prey Upon]. This spell has the strictest prerequisite for use, as you can only cast it on the dying, but the effect is worth it: you get to eat part of someone's soul. Frequent use of this spell will be *the* quickest way to get powerful enough to add more spells to your library."

"That one," I immediately declare. "Taking that one, I want it, gimme."

Cheshire laughs. "And for the other two?"

"[Exsanguinate] and [Carrion Swarm]. The others are interesting but I *want* those spells."

"Then they're yours, my love." Each of the symbols glows brighter, and a smaller copy of each symbol carves into the center of the table. "Welcome to having spells. Welcome to being a demon."

I am *salivating*. It's magic, it's *my* magic, and it's everything I ever could have wanted. It's perfect. It's just so fucking perfect.

Cheshire winks at me. "So? What do you think?"

I run over to Cheshire and scoop her up in a hug. I close my eyes and just squeeze tight, feeling her warmth. "Thank you," I whisper. "Thank you. Thank you. Thank you."

She hugs me back.

V

When the hug finally ends and we separate, Cheshire says, "There's one more thing we should take care of before we leave the deepest recesses of your soul."

"I was *wondering* where we were and why it looked so edgy," I snark in a blatant attempt to distance myself from my brief moment of emotional vulnerability. "Damn, if this is what my soul looks like, what does that say about me?"

Cheshire grins. "The creation of the inner world is an act of self-definition." The catgirl gestures at the wasteland and the maelstrom and the book pile. "This isn't a reflection of your true nature, it's a reflection of how you *perceive* your true nature. In other words, your inner world looks so edgy because you *think* it should look this edgy."

I wince. "Ouch. That's a rough hit. This is like taking a girl home and accidentally showing her your cringe fanfiction. Now instead of feeling embarrassed by my haunted soul I feel embarrassed by the unnecessary melodrama of it all."

Cheshire clicks her tongue disapprovingly and says, "Don't you dare; a little melodrama is *perfect* for our purposes. Remember: the essence of magic is the manipulation of meaning. A little flair goes a long way in making that meaning 'stickier,' for lack of a better word."

I quirk an eyebrow. "So, let me make sure I'm understanding you right: you're saying that my magic will be more effective if I'm more *theatrical* with it?" My eyes widen as I suddenly make a connection. "Wait, hold on a second, does that mean . . . is that why saying the name of a spell makes it work better!?"

"Precisely! In fact, that isn't the only way to bolster sorcery; how you act, how you dress, choosing the right moment, these can all have a noticeable impact on the efficacy of a given spell."

"How I *dress*?"

"Of course!" Cheshire tugs on my fancy dream-clothes. "Think about it, Alice: when you see someone dressed head-to-toe in skull motifs and someone else wearing khakis and a polo, which would *you* take for a necromancer? Those assumptions have meaning, and all meaning has weight when it comes to magic. To maximize your sorcery you should be stacking as much relevant meaning as you can."

I laugh. "Holy shit. You know what? I take back every bad thing I said about this setting. I get to min-max being a mage by *picking the right clothing*. That's great." As an afterthought I add, "Aside from the part where I don't know shit about fashion."

"Don't worry," Cheshire assures me, "that's one of the many things I'm here to help with. Ah, but that does bring me to that one last thing I mentioned: your appearance."

Immediately I tense up. "What about it?"

Cheshire's hand on my shoulder is gentle, light. "I know how you feel. I know *why* you feel that way. I'm not going to ask you to confront it now. I won't even make you look at a mirror. We can save the big changes for later, once you feel more comfortable. Okay?"

I hesitate, but nod. "Yeah. Okay."

Cheshire smiles at me warmly. "I'll make this easy: just pick two things you want to change about your appearance. Two things you've fantasized about adding, perhaps."

Oh! I know exactly what she's talking about. "Pointed ears and sharp fangs!" I blush a little. "I mean . . . I know the ears are usually an elf thing but they look great on everyone and *especially* vampires . . . and I maybe may have once looked up how much it would cost to get the cosmetic surgery that gives you elf ears." Answer: a lot.

Cheshire giggles. "You're *adorable.* Pointy ears and pointy fangs coming up." Cheshire snaps her fingers and I feel the subtle shift in my biology: ears lengthening and tapering, teeth growing and sharpening.

I run my fingers over my new ears and tease the shape of my fangs with my tongue. Beautiful, gorgeous, throat-piercing fangs. Mine. "Fangs. I have fangs. I have fangs!" I squeal and bare my new fangs gleefully.

Cheshire grins. "They look great." She flashes her own fangs, a bit smaller but still sharp (of *course* the catgirl has pointy teeth).

I hug myself and wiggle in place. "Fangs! Fangs fangs fangs! And pointy ears!" I squeal again.

Cheshire pokes me in the cheek. "Boop. Look at that cute face." I stick my tongue out at her and her expression softens. "You look lovely, Alice. I mean it."

The catgirl's faked affection makes me uncomfortable—there's a new pain in my chest—so I look away. *Shut up, shut up, you're lying, you don't mean that.* I feel warm all over from her compliments and I *hate* that. "Yeah, well, whatever. It's done. Can we go?"

"Of course." Cheshire grins and takes my hand, and when I blink I'm staring at the walls of the apartment. I lift my head from the dining room table, returned from the world within my soul.

The disorientation is sharp but brief; this is not the book pile amid the wasteland and the storm, this is not the table engraved with my new affinities, and I am not wearing the poofy dress or the stripey tights. I'm back in the bloodied schoolgirl uniform (plus cloak), sitting in the dining room of a modern apartment.

The first thing I do is check my ears and teeth, and to my delight their pointiness has carried over from the dreamscape setting. I have fangs and pointy ears! Yes!

A visual sweep of the space around me doesn't reveal Bashekehi, but I do see Cheshire: she's sitting across from me, grinning and playing with her hair—and wearing the top-and-skirt outfit from before.

More importantly than any of that, I have *magic* now. Magic that is *mine* and no one else's. I can feel each of my new spells at the edge of awareness, waiting to be called upon. The contracts felt stored within my body, but these spells are nested far deeper.

[Exsanguinate]. [Carrion Swarm]. [Prey Upon].

These will be the foundation of my ascension.

The idea of filling my new apartment with bugs is kind of icky, but I just want to *see* what the spell diagram looks like. I hold out a hand and murmur, "[Carrion Swarm]."

The matrix of signs and symbols—elements or *oneiros*, perhaps, represented in some base code of Pandaemonium—blossoms in my mind's eye. I don't recognize most of the symbols, and I still have no basis for the organization of this language—if it even is a language—but I think I must have seen at least a couple of these before.

There's something odd about the diagram, though. I don't know what, but it's like when you catch something out of the corner of your eye. It's knowing something is there but not seeing it. I can't read the symbols, I can't parse the connections, but . . . it's that headache you get, when you're looking at something that you know you should be able to figure out, but it isn't coming to you.

Setting that strangeness aside, the most interesting difference between this diagram and previous diagrams is the empty bar beneath the activation symbol, and the fact that said activation symbol is grayed out.

Bashe said something about mana, back when he was drip-feeding us exposition. I dismiss the spell and raise an eyebrow at Cheshire. "Tank's empty. How do I fill up on mana?"

Cheshire taps her chin idly. "Take a guess. You've got some clues, and I know you like feeling clever."

I glower at the smug catgirl, but she's not wrong. *Okay, clues, clues. We know Bashe uses mana, and we know that he gets mana from sex, from gambling, and from eating memories that have a "resonance for Indulgence." Indulgence is the name of the archdemon, but is it also the name of her Truth, or Truths? Indulgence is part of the Throne of Shadow, but does it also occupy some kind of sub-Throne, something halfway between a Throne and a Truth?*

The way he talked about what resonates with Indulgence, it certainly sounded like the elements that comprise a Truth. So let's apply that logic to our own Truths: Blood, Gluttony, and Fear. Which means—

"Do I get mana from drinking someone's blood!?" I lean over the table and grin at Cheshire. "Fuck yes!"

Cheshire laughs. "That's certainly one way. You should also be able to feed on fear and love, and any act that could be construed as acting on your hungers should get you at least a little bit of mana." She pauses, then adds, "I'll note that all shadowtouched do *feed* on mana, which requires a personal element. Your incubus companion can't just wander through a casino or a brothel; he has to be involved in some capacity to drink in all that delicious aspected mana. For you, that means the fear or love you feed on has to be directed at *you*."

Interesting. That actually limits our options quite a bit. "So basically, ignoring memory-feeding, I've got two ways to get mana: a slow trickle from pursuing lesser hungers, and big bursts of mana from directly feeding on someone. Hey, wait, does that mean [Prey Upon] actually refills my mana?"

Cheshire winks. "I may or may not have constructed the spell with that in mind. With how conditional the spell is and how much it resembles the act of feeding, it should be a near-total refund for the mana you spend. Not quite infinite, sadly, unless you're willing to sacrifice the long-term benefits for short-term gain."

I'm a little peeved that my very first spell isn't a game-breaking infinite loop, but that's just because I'm a whiny little brat who will never be satisfied with anything less than everything. Also, more importantly: I feel a prickling sensation somewhere inside me.

On a hunch I recast "[Carrion Swarm]," and there it is: the bar beneath the activation symbol is just a tiny bit less empty. I dismiss the spell and cackle. "'Hunger for knowledge!' I get mana just by asking questions! Okay, that more than makes up for not getting my broken exploit combo."

"Of *course*," mutters a voice from over in the living room. "Of fucking course that's how you'd treat your magic."

"Bashe!" I cheer. I stand up and poke my head over the sofa to find the incubus lying on it with eyes closed and a now-empty bottle of wine in one hand. "Didn't think I'd see you again so soon. Just couldn't stay away?"

"You," he begins, voice only the teensiest bit slurred, "are an obnoxious little shit. You're like a cockroach in clown makeup: you skitter beneath people's feet and when you stubbornly refuse to die, you pretend that you're the life of the party."

I grin, though he can't see me yet. "Flattery will get you nowhere, Bashe."

He finally opens his eyes to glare at me. "See, this is exactly what I'm talking about: I'm insulting you to your face and you're *preening* about it."

I shrug. "All attention is good attention when it's directed at me."

"And again, I can't tell if your head is really that messed up or if you're just acting like that to *fuck with me*."

"It's probably both," I muse. "I haven't been able to tell the difference for years."

Bashe groans and closes his eyes again. "Why did it have to be the crazy girl?"

Cheshire pops her head in and suggests, "Because the Demiurge is a capricious bastard who gets off on tormenting her creations."

"Ain't that the fuckin' truth," he mutters.

I stroll into the living room and take a seat on the other sofa, facing Bashe. "So, why *are* you still here? Unless the answer is 'because this is my home,' in which case the question should be: why haven't you kicked me out? Did you actually decide to stay with me?"

Bashe slowly sits up and lets the empty bottle drop to the floor. He opens his eyes again and grimaces at me. "This isn't my home, and I'm not staying for long. I picked this apartment at random because it was close to where we came out of the bubble. Do whatever you want with it when I'm gone."

"Ah. Where will you go?" I ask.

The incubus shrugs. "I used to have some semblance of a life in this city, and I want to see how much of that I can rebuild. There are people I have to look for, places I have to visit. I'll figure it out."

The news isn't as devastating as it would have been before meeting Cheshire. I'm sure a part of me will miss Bashekehi, at least at first, but I'm well-versed in letting attachments crumble to dust. Besides, he was kind of a dick to me, even if I deserved it. "When are you leaving?"

The imp of temptation sighs. "I would like to say 'right now,' but I still owe you some shadow of a debt. For all the pain in my ass you've been, you did free me and feed me. The least I can do in return is help you get your bearings in the city." He glares at me and adds, "And don't think you were clever about that; I know half the reason you freed me without a contract was to make me feel indebted to you."

Ah, beautiful reciprocity pressure. I rub my hands together gleefully. "Details, details. What's important is that I can use this opportunity to extort more exposition out of you! Muahaha!"

Bashe doesn't even react to that one, which takes some of the fun out of it, but if I let him know that, he'll keep not reacting to try and drive the behavior into extinction, so I continue grinning at him regardless.

"So! Next moves." I clap my hands together. "As much as I'd love to take a tour of the city and put together a new outfit to replace this horrid little number, I am *hungry*. I want mana, I want a lot of it, and I want it quickly." I frown. "Hmm. You know what I need? I need a quest log. Cheshire, is there some fancy magic you can do to give me a quest log?"

Cheshire leans on the couch and points out, "You have writing materials in your backpack, you could just make a quest log yourself."

"But I want a fancy user interface," I whine. "I want the parchment-y background and the yellow exclamation marks that turn into yellow question marks when I fulfill quest objectives."

Cheshire walks over and pats my head. "Aw, you poor thing. Too bad!" She snickers and ruffles my hair.

I stick my tongue out at her rebelliously. "Rude. What good are you if you can't cater to my every absurd whim? Also, serious question: is that a genuine limitation or personal preference?"

"I'm actually pretty restricted in what I can do," Cheshire admits. "A geist's role is to empower and guide, and we are bound to our demon. By default you're the only person I can interact with physically—in fact unless one of us chooses otherwise you're the only person who can even see me and hear me—and the only magic I can perform is the magic you give me. If you can't cast a spell, I can't cast a spell."

"Fascinating," I say as I am rewarded with another trickle of mana. *Definitely exploring that in detail at a later date, but for now: quest log!*

I return to my new bedroom and find my sparkly backpack slumped against the dresser. The knife is nowhere to be seen, which makes sense given that I apparently ate it as part of the Truth-making process. I dump out the backpack and examine the pile.

Inventory. Wait, if we're going to be playing this like an RPG, we should make an actual inventory in the journal.

I grab a bloodstained notebook and flip through in search of a page that isn't completely ruined. The pseudo water damage is pretty thorough, but it's worse in the front half so I just turn the book around and treat the back like it's the front. I grab a pen and start writing.

Inventory: sparkly backpack, miscellaneous school supplies, hooded cloak, schoolgirl clothes, canteen, bandages, needle and thread, antiseptic, and a weird clay heart.

The bandages are a bit blood-logged too, so I doubt they'll actually be much use for their intended purpose, but whatever. Maybe I'll need to wrap something? Meh. I flip the page and title this entry Quest Log.

[Quest Accepted - Filling the Tank]: Gather mana so you can start casting spells. Get a sense of how much mana each activity produces.

[Quest Accepted - Clothes Make the Demon]: Get some new clothes and put together an outfit that says "bloody queen of fear and love" instead of "isekai'd high schooler." I AM A COLLEGE STUDENT!!! Or was, at least.

[Quest Accepted - Sightseeing in Wonderland]: Accept a tour of the city from Bashekehi and try to get your bearings.

I really wish I had a nice satchel that I could store this in, instead of lugging around that backpack everywhere. Oh, there's an idea. I flip to a new page.

Shopping List: satchel, new clothes, a new knife, and a smoothie.

Right, that looks like a good start. I guess we'll just carry this around with us and try to make getting a satchel our top priority. I don't think we should bother with any of the rest of this junk.

I take the notebook with me and move for the door, but pause. *Wait. Am I still covered in blood?* I run my hands through my hair and realize that I am absolutely still covered in blood. I can't do anything about my clothes yet, obviously, but I can at least take a fucking shower.

I pop my head out to the living room and quickly shout, "Washing the blood off be out in five *peace!*"

I duck back inside, strip off my clothes and the butterfly hairpin—I should probably leave that off, given everything it apparently represents—and hop into the shower.

I take my showers scalding, and it is genuinely blissful to immerse myself in burning-hot water after the past however many hours of filth and suffering. I cleanse my body and luxuriate in the soothing heat, and my mind wanders.

Did my other self take that name to warn me? Did she know I was going to see that vision, and so named herself "Homura" to stop me from taking Cheshire's deal?

It doesn't feel like enough *of a warning. Sure, I can put the pieces together and compare Cheshire to Kyubey, but I could have done that even if I wasn't primed to think of her that way. Everything about her introduction to the narrative screamed "Deal with the Devil," and she wasn't even being subtle about it after I called her bluff.*

But you still made the deal.

And why shouldn't I take the deal? It's everything I want. Why should I settle for the struggle? Why should I play by rules that are rigged against me? I'm not going to become a wizard, I'm not going to be some pious heroine, so what other choice do I have?

There's always a choice. You chose to trust the least trustworthy person you've met so far, and I will remind you that one of those people was an actual faerie.

I grimace. Giving up power isn't an option. That was never going to be an option. So what was I supposed to do? Just turn Cheshire down and hope some better offer shows up? Not going to happen.

Any offer would have been better than the one proposed by the creature that admits it likes manipulating us.

So maybe she has a few schemes lying in wait, so what? This is our best shot at power and immortality. This is our chance. This is a game that can be won.

More than once I've thought about what three wishes I would make if I found a genie's lamp. There are so many stories about getting screwed over by a genie unless you find the right words to trick them with. They'll use your exact words against you, so you've gotta be careful, gotta game it out like a contract. I've seen so many people brag about the manner in which they'd cleverly outwit an ancient immortal being. And hey, I'm not immune to that hubris; obviously not, with how I tried and failed to trick the Rider.

But in all the ways I've seen to get the most value out of your wishes, I think *Aladdin* did it best: the thief gets his wishes granted not because he outwits the genie but because he *befriends* the genie. He offers the genie what it wants, so the genie helps him and doesn't try to screw him over.

So that's my answer to the genie puzzle: I would promise to give the genie whatever it desires so long as it helps me achieve *my* desires. A relationship of mutual interest. And that's my answer to the Cheshire puzzle too: if she really means to help me, if she really will grant my three wishes . . .

. . . *Then I would burn the world to make her happy.*

And if her desires conflict with yours? If Cheshire's victory condition is contingent on your suffering, on your powerlessness, on your death? *What then?*

I clench my fists and mutter out loud, "That's not going to happen."

No? Why not? Because she's pretty, and she's smart, and she compliments you? Because she talks philosophy with you and calls you adorable? Because she presents herself as the very fantasy you called her out for being? She's lying to you. She could be lying about everything.

"Stop it!" I hiss. "This isn't *useful*."

What isn't useful is hiding from what's right in front of you. She's using you. What if she's making you into a sacrifice? Fattening you up for the pot? What if this all ends with you bleeding out *because you fell for a pretty face? All your plans rest on the obviously malevolent entity being* nice *and granting your wishes without caveats, without an attempt to screw you over. We've already compared Cheshire to Kyubey; how did that deal work out for Madoka? How many times did she* die?

"This isn't a fucking anime!" I nearly shout, fighting to keep my voice down as the dread and frustration rises. I can only hope the sound of running water keeps Cheshire and Bashekehi from hearing. "She's offered me the world. How can I say no to that?"

Willpower. But I know you don't have any of that. So you'll go along with her, you'll lie to yourself, you'll try and pretend that she's not plotting your downfall, that she's not setting you up, that she's not creeping up behind you to stick a knife in your back. And when you are bleeding out and dying *you will know that you were wrong and I was right.*

My hands are shaking. "You are just a psychological adaptation," I tell my own maladaptive thought processes. "You are catastrophe and nemesis. You are a liar."

I'm only you. The part of you that isn't blind *to reality. The part that wants to survive. Do you want to die? Is that why you're trusting her, because you want her to slit your throat, to cut you open like you lacked the fucking* will *to go through with? Because she* will *kill you. She'll hurt you, she'll betray you, abandon you, kill you. She will kill you. You are going to die. You are going to—*

I wrap my hands around my throat and *squeeze* until the animal panic chokes out all my bad thoughts. I let go, breathing shakily, and let out a few broken laughs. "You're wrong. You're wrong, because I am going to live forever."

I cut the water and towel off, thankful to find one waiting in the bathroom cupboard. I put the schoolgirl clothes back on and throw the cloak over my shoulders but leave the hairpin with the rest of my rubbish.

With notebook in hand (and pen clipped to the binding) and flesh cleansed of filth (aside from what's already starting to collect again from my horrid outfit), I return to the living room. Bashekehi lies on the sofa, eyes closed once more, but Cheshire is leaning against the far wall, smiling, staring right at me.

I don't know you. I don't know what you really want. I don't know how you really feel about me. But I know that I need you, and I want you to need me too. So I will do whatever it takes to make you love me for real.

I force a smile, wink at the geist, and say, "Okay, I'm ready. Feeding time."

Bashe slowly gets to his feet and makes for the door, fidgeting with his hair and outfit as he goes. I don't see the scourge anywhere on his person, but maybe he has some pocket dimension magic to hide it in. I feel naked without a weapon, and I mentally bump getting a new knife to the top of my shopping list.

Bashe doesn't lock the door behind him as we step out into the hall of what I presume to be an apartment complex, which has me glaring at him. "You seem to be taking our security pretty lightly."

The incubus rolls his eyes at me. "Don't be paranoid, especially when you don't have a clue how this place operates. It'll be fine."

He moves on despite my protests. Cheshire and I follow him into an elevator—or rather I follow him into an elevator and Cheshire melts into wisps of smoke that flow into my shadow and vanish into it. I blink at the sight and tentatively wave at my shadow . . . which waves back out-of-sync. *Okay, that's pretty cool.*

Bashekehi takes us to the ground floor. The trip down isn't long, so instead of striking up an awkward conversation I continue playing with my shadow.

It's quite surreal how *normal* everything is so far. My introduction to the Labyrinth was a gauntlet of otherworldly challenges, but there's nothing about this apartment building that distinguishes it from the equivalent back home. The elevator opens into a lobby with a perfectly normal human woman sitting at the help desk. She waves at us as we cross to the exit and I wave back.

. . . I guess it's abnormal that she doesn't even blink at the absolute state of my outfit, but maybe this is the bad part of town.

Bashekehi opens the door and we step outside. I get my first glimpse of the city in the Labyrinth, and it is *immense.*

It is a city of stone and metal and neon, a sprawling maze of squat tenements and skyward towers. I see arches and pillars and all sorts of fancy architecture I don't have names for. There are neon signs everywhere advertising restaurants and shops and more in a language that isn't English but which I can read perfectly.

There are *people* too, everywhere. People in modern clothes in all sorts of styles, people walking to or from work, people grabbing a bite to eat, people chatting with other people. It's a sea of humanity, and I idly note that they are all *walking*; there isn't a single vehicle in sight.

In the distance, two structures dominate the skyline: in one direction, a massive pyramid of metal and glass and glowing neon circuitry; in another direction, a stone amphitheater larger than the Colosseum back on Earth.

Bashe gestures at the city and says, "Welcome to Sanctuary 7."

VI

I point at the amphitheater. "What's that?" Then I point at the pyramid. "Also, what's that?" Then I point at the people. "Also also, why the fuck are there so many people here? I know you said this place was a city but I was genuinely not expecting a whole *city's* worth of people. Was everyone here taken from other worlds?"

Bashekehi isn't even fazed at this point, which is really quite rude of him. "Lair of the Beast, the Pyraplex, and those aren't people."

My plans to interrogate those first two points are immediately derailed by the third. "Eh? Not people?" I peer at the passersby closely, expecting to see that they all lack faces or have identical faces or some other strangeness like glitching out or being slightly translucent, but no dice; they look as real as can be.

Cheshire manifests next to me in a swirl of smoke and winks at the incubus. "I'll handle this one. I speak her language."

Bashe rolls his eyes and starts walking in a seemingly random direction. "Be my guest, but let's keep moving. I saw a good falafel stand on my grocery run and I want to grab some before we talk about *your* food." *Ooo, falafel!*

Cheshire and I follow, the catgirl walking like a person this time. "So," she begins, "do you remember that old thought experiment about philosophical zombies?"

"Of course," I reply. Then I blink a few times as the implication hits me. "Wait. Okay, just to be clear: you're talking about the idea of a person who looks like a person and acts like a person but *isn't* a person, right? A simulacrum that can mimic all the observable traits of personhood but lacks consciousness?"

Cheshire gives me a thumbs-up. "Got it in one, babe. We're talking about someone that would scream in pain if you stabbed them, but can't actually *feel* that pain. They're just going through the motions."

I frown at the crowd around us as we follow Bashe through the streets of Sanctuary 7. "You're saying all these people are fake? A whole city of p-zombies?"

Cheshire nods. "We call them 'figments.' They're a feature of any throne world, but the ones in the Labyrinth have a few special rules. Aside from not actually being able to feel anything or think anything, the figments of the Sanctuaries will always act like the Labyrinth's idea of perfect citizens: they can't commit crimes, they forgive easily, and they are incapable of harming anyone."

That is . . . vaguely creepy. "How do they stop someone from stealing or murdering? Are there other figments that *can* do harm, at least in defense of innocents?"

"Nope!" Cheshire chirps cheerily. "In fact, since none of the figments can break the law, they don't even have law enforcement here. The only real consequences are social consequences, but since you can just take what you want even that isn't really a big deal."

Okay, that's even creepier. "Those sound less like perfect citizens and more like perfect victims," I mutter.

Cheshire winks at me. "Don't they just?"

I chew on that idea and a question comes to mind. "Did Katoptris make the figments, or are they just a byproduct of making the Labyrinth?"

The catgirl taps her chin in consideration as we weave through more people and keep close to Bashe. "I would argue that the distinction is irrelevant; whether she intended her figments to be perfect victims or not, that's the result. If we look to the throne worlds of other Royalty we see that the figments of their realms always reflect some quality of Royalty or of how that Royalty sees the world: Indulgence fills her world with hedonists, Acuity's figments perform neverending military exercises, and the figments of the Wolf Queen's Arcadia are prey to be hunted. Perhaps Katoptris intended this, perhaps not, but either way it speaks to her perspective."

Bashe interrupts before I can respond. "Philosophy aside, here's the practical: this city doesn't have money and the figments will freely give you whatever you need to survive. Hungry?"

"Always," I respond automatically while I try to parse the vast implications of that statement.

Bashe veers off the main road—it's not accurate to call it sidewalk because without cars people go straight down the middle—and brings us to a food cart selling falafel pita wraps that have my mouth watering.

I glance over at Cheshire, who is still walking about instead of lurking inside my shadow. "Do you eat?" I ask the mysterious catgirl.

The geist shrugs. "I don't *need* to eat, but I can consume and taste if you let me. You just have to manifest me, which I can teach you how to do." She makes one of her signature wide-mouthed grins. "It'll be good practice for when you need to manifest me for a fight."

Interesting. Definitely want to learn how to do that. Bashe orders two falafel wraps and I quickly butt in to say, "Make that three."

The incubus raises an eyebrow at me before shrugging and confirming with the vendor. Or, well, I guess vendor isn't the right word? The cook, maybe? True to his word, Bashe doesn't hand over any money and the woman who takes his order doesn't seem to mind.

Cheshire takes my free hand in both of her hands and holds my gaze, and I force myself not to tense up at the sudden contact. She says, "As a demon, not all of your abilities require mana. The changes to your appearance didn't take mana, and among other benefits you can manifest your geist without spending mana. You will need to use an anchor, however."

I frown, a thought tickling my brain. "When I killed the sin eater, it left behind a clay heart instead of a corpse. Was that an anchor?"

Cheshire grins. "It was. If you want me to fight by your side, it'll be worth making an anchor object as purpose-built as that one was, but for a simple bit of eating you can use pretty much anything with physicality. Your cloak would work, or the notebook. You've staked both of them as 'yours,' and that helps."

I pout, since I like both of those quite a bit. A new outfit is on the docket eventually, so I could feasibly ditch the cloak, but ditching the notebook would free a hand. "Do I get it back at some point? Like, if I gave you my notebook as an anchor, would I be able to use the notebook again or would it be gone forever?"

"You'll get it back," Cheshire assures me, "unless someone destroys my manifestation in the time between manifesting and getting a better anchor."

"Hmm." I glance around. *Odds of a fight breaking out in the next few hours or so?*

Higher than I'd like. Still, the notebook is already pretty damaged and the cloak has an actual function, so . . .

"Alright, use the notebook." I offer the item in question and she lays a hand on it but doesn't take it from me yet, other hand still holding mine.

Cheshire says, "Manifestation is an act of will. You're telling Pandaemonium that something exists which didn't a moment ago. That would be pretty tricky to do entirely mentally, so demons have an aide: an incantation that Pandaemonium recognizes and can thus shortcut most of the process. All you have to do is think of me, hold the anchor, say the words, and will it to happen. Make sense?"

I nod affirmatively and force myself to actually focus on Cheshire's physicality: shorter than me (only by a few inches), lean and scrappy, pale and white-haired, cat ears and heterochromatic eyes, swishing tail, and that JRPG-looking outfit. Her face is impish, somehow looking mischievous even in those rare moments that she's not smiling.

"When you've got a good image, recite this incantation: 'By my will, let this object become your anchor, and let the stuff of dreams become your body. Rise, geist, and fulfill my design.' Oh, and don't be afraid to personalize it! That'll actually help forge the connection."

This magic system is absurd and I love it. I take a deep breath, let it out, and straighten my posture. "By my will, let this notebook become your anchor, and let the stuff of dreams become your body. Rise, Cheshire, and fulfill my design."

The image, the anchor, the words, and my will. Rise, Cheshire. I will the geist to take form and to move with the weight of physicality. I will her to manifest through false matter, just one more lie in a world seemingly made of them. And the world hears me. The world hears my request—or perhaps my plea, or my command—and answers. The notebook vanishes in shadow and smoke, and something about Cheshire *changes.*

It's like when you only notice a noise by its sudden absence; I never consciously felt that there was something immaterial about Cheshire's presence, at least not beyond the obvious, but now there's a realness to her form that wasn't there a moment ago. It's like she wasn't *really there* a moment ago, but now she is.

The catgirl stretches luxuriously in a way that does very interesting things to her body, and she winks at me when my gaze flits to her face out of self-conscious habit. She does it just to fuck with me, doesn't she? I stick my tongue out at the creature and she laughs at my childishness.

Bashe interrupts by shoving two pita wraps at me, which I retrieve daintily like the elegant lady that I definitely am. I pass one of the wraps off to Cheshire and tear into mine like a starving beast, devouring the falafel with the frenzy of someone who didn't have breakfast, like, a couple hours ago. It is *delicious:* rich and herby and warm, with all that wonderful veggie goodness you'd expect from a meal like this. This was one of my favorite meals during the couple of years I went vegetarian.

Bashe and Cheshire eat like normal people, so I'm done well before them and have time to check my mana again while they finish. I felt a bit more coming in during my meal, so I cycle through all three spells and compare the results: [Prey Upon] has the fullest gauge at nearly a third, while [Exsanguinate] still has barely a sliver of the required mana and [Carrion Swarm] is at maybe a tenth or an eleventh. I suppose it's only sensible that violently ripping the blood from someone's veins should cost a bit more than summoning a few bugs and rats.

That same headache pounds at me when I try to focus on each spell diagram. It's still difficult to tell any kind of pattern in the symbology, but I do recognize one icon that I've seen before: the black-on-black mark of the Abyss, now nestled inside [Prey Upon]. *Is that an element, or an oneiron? Both this and [Abyssal Armament] eat souls, but the details are significantly different between them, so maybe this represents the elemental Abyss?*

An incredibly reckless idea comes to me, and unlike prior showings I have enough fear in me to hesitate and hold off, wary of dire consequences. *If our working theory is that the symbol stands for elemental Abyss, could we crack it open and see the oneiros inside? Would we face backlash for such an act? Risk of the Abyss lapping at my soul?*

Is that any riskier than trusting Cheshire?

I dismiss the spell diagram and see the catgirl in question watching me, pita wrap consumed, a curious glint in her blue-and-yellow eyes. When she notices my attention return to my surroundings she winks and asks, "Fun daydream? Kiss any cute girls?"

Do we respond to that? Do we just ignore it? Do we try to tease her back? I choose to change the subject instead. "Bashe! Where's a good place to feed?"

Bashe has also finished his food and rolls his shoulders before answering, "Depends. Remind me what you feed on?"

"Blood, love, and fear," I list off.

"And violence!" Cheshire adds with a grin.

"So blood, love, fear, and violence," I correct.

"Right," the incubus mutters. "Okay, that makes it pretty fuckin' easy. See all the figments wandering about?" Bashe gestures at the not-quite-people going from place to place all around us. "Pick one, shove them into a dark alley, and do whatever you want with them."

I deflate a little. *Well that makes it sound downright dreadful.* "That's it? Just grab a rando off the street and chow down? That seems . . . both too easy and very unsatisfying. You know I can't cast any spells yet, right?"

"You don't *need* spells. Have you not been paying attention? They can't fight back, they can't do *anything* to you. They're not real people."

I shiver. *That's so fucking terrifying.* I watch the figments passing by, every one of them looking like an ordinary human being. But apparently they're not, and nobody would stop me if I decided to just murder one of them. *What the fuck is wrong with this place?*

Do I have to kill to feed? I don't know how to feel about that thought. I feel hesitant, but is that because of some shriveled sense of conscience, or is it the remnants of social programming? *It's not like I haven't thought about . . .*

murder. I always said I wouldn't because I was afraid of going to jail, not because of any moral objection, but is that just edgelord posturing?

Can I become a murderer? Do I have that in me?

I don't know that I'm ready to find out. The thing in the school, the sin eater guarding Bashe, they didn't feel like *people* to me; they were clearly monsters, and clearly trying to kill me, so it was just self-defense. It wasn't really murder, even if I might callously call it that when being flippant. I'm not a murderer. Not yet.

What are you more afraid of: that you might not have it in you to murder someone . . . or that it'll be a whole lot easier than you expect?

Maybe I'm just afraid of knowing either way.

"Cheshire," I finally ask aloud, "when I feed, will it have to be lethal? I know vampires in stories can often feed without killing, but I'd be ripping a fucking hole in someone's neck and drinking their blood. Actually, how does that even work? Vampires always get a pass in fiction but like, are my fangs hollow? How do I drink blood???"

The catgirl snickers at me. "You're still thinking too *physically,* Maven. What matters is the *meaning* of the act: a vampire bites, a vampire drinks, a vampire feeds. The physical mechanism is comparatively unimportant because what you're really feeding on is metaphysical. So to answer your first question: no, you don't have to kill, but you'll get more mana if you do."

"Right. Okay." *So. Pick someone and feed. Who do we pick?*

I'm saved from having to make that choice by Cheshire adding, "If I may: you'll *also* get more mana if you make use of layering. Remember our conversation about how picking the right clothes and the right moment can help spellcasting? Well, the same is true of feeding; if you feed in a way that feels more true to your nature as a demon, you'll get more mana out of the act. So where do you expect a vampire to feed, Alice?"

"Nightclub," I respond automatically. "Vampires are always lurking about nightclubs, it's their favored terrain. Oh!" I clap my hands together excitedly. "Plus, if it's a nightclub with drugs and shit we can get someone high and make sure it doesn't hurt too much when I stick 'em in the neck."

"They don't feel pain," Bashe reminds me.

I scowl at the incubus. "You say that, but I'm not convinced yet, so I'm gonna play it cautious for now. Take me to a nightclub, Bashe! Or whatever this city has that fills the same niche."

Bashekehi shrugs. "Sure, I know a place. Let's call that my last favor to you, then."

"Lead on."

Cheshire and I follow along behind the incubus as he leads us through the city, and I silently contemplate whether or not I want to try and keep the imp around.

On the one hand, pretty much anything he knows is something that Cheshire probably knows, excepting stuff specific to this city and his history with it. On the other hand, Cheshire is entirely untrustworthy and getting a second source of information might help me spot holes in what Cheshire tells me. Cheshire is much more forthcoming with information, and other things, but Bashekehi... well, honestly, I'm not sure he has much value left.

He's helped immensely, of course, but I'm not sure I need him anymore. I have a guide to this setting, I have magic of my own, and while Cheshire may one day stab me in the back, she'll make a much better minion/ally until that sudden-yet-inevitable betrayal. Bashe, after all, has made his distaste for me rather clear.

I don't believe that Cheshire loves me, but... I think I can make her love me, if I work at it. Affection is like one-third proximity plus time and I'm going to be spending a lot of time in very close proximity to Cheshire, so I have that covered. I just have to figure out what she really likes and become that, and she'll be too enamored with me to ever pull the trigger on that whole "betrayal and gruesome murder" thing. That seems like the sanest plan.

Sanity has nothing to do with it, you BPD bitch.

Shush! I'm plotting. Actually, hey, this could be a good opportunity for us to get a better read on Cheshire. There's a couple of ways she could respond and none of them give us perfect information but it might help us develop a model.

I hang back a bit to put some distance between me and Bashe, then sidle up to Cheshire and nonchalantly murmur in her ear, "I'm trying to decide if I should make any effort to keep Bashe from leaving after this outing. What do you make of the incubus? Do you think he still has value to be extracted?"

Cheshire tilts her head and hums, then grins and whispers back, "If I were to guess why you're asking that, and if I were to guess correctly how you expect me to respond, would I get a treat?"

Alarm bells immediately ring in my head, but hey, fuck it, I like a good gamble. "Sure. Make your guess."

Cheshire taps her chin and, speaking softly so the incubus ahead doesn't hear, tells me, "You're still trying to figure out what my true nature is, so you want to ask questions that will give you clues. If I say to you, 'No, get rid of the imp, you only need me,' then that might indicate that my love for you is real, deep, and possessive, but it's also what I'd say if I were lying about my love and trying to isolate you for nefarious purposes. If, on the other hand, I kept your best interests at heart in some rational manner, I might tell you, 'Keep the imp close, for a second opinion is valuable even if I am trustworthy.' Is that about right?"

Bah. Why do I keep getting into intrigue duels with people who are better at it? Not that I'll stop, mind. "Okay, that's about what I was considering, yeah. So what's your real answer?"

"That it's a moot point," she whispers to me, "because nothing you can do will convince him to stay. If you want a second opinion or even just a second set of hands, you'd be better off finding a new mark."

I grimace at the answer, but she's probably right. My relationship with Bashekehi was critically sabotaged by the circumstances of our first interactions, and there's probably no repairing that; he'll always know me as a delusional clueless weirdo. I think there's a term for that in psych, actually, something about how your first impression is the stickiest impression you'll make.

Now that I actually have an idea of how this setting functions, and now that I have a power source in the form of Cheshire and my fledgling demonhood, it should be much easier to make friends and influence enemies.

"So," I muse, no longer whispering, "what kind of—"

"We're here," Bashe interrupts me from where he's stopped ahead.

I look past him and see what must be the club: a slab of stone adorned in metal, with inscribed designs and bits and bobs sticking out. No sign, I note. What is it with this Labyrinth and its aversion to branding?

I move for the entrance but Bashekehi holds up a hand for me to wait. I tilt my head at him curiously, but he just grins and says, "Give it a minute. You burnt enough time sleeping, eating, and getting lost in your own head that it's almost six o'clock."

"What happens at six?"

The clock strikes six and the blue sky above *vanishes*. In its place is an endless span of glittering stars and colorful nebulae, like those pictures of far-off space. There's no moon, but the night sky is plenty full without one.

When the sky above shifts, the city shifts with it: streetlights turning on, building lights brightening, and the crowd changing. People in mundane day clothes head to their homes and new people—new figments, I suppose I should say—hit the streets, dressed darker or brighter but always more *interesting*. It's amazing how fast the switch happens.

Bashe gestures at the nightclub, which dozens of figments are now streaming towards, and says, "Shall we?"

VII

All of my experience with clubbing come from pop culture. Actually, most of that experience comes from a single video game, and the rest just got absorbed through random miscellanea.

When I think of a nightclub, I think of people grinding against each other in very suggestive ways that barely qualify as dancing, and I think of strobe lights and dark spots, and I think of music that is . . . what do the kids call it? EDM? The music with the noise and the other noise and uh, okay, look, I don't know anything about music and couldn't describe it to save my life.

When the viewpoint character in a story goes into a club, the sound washes over them and gets under their skin in all the right ways. They feel the beat and the crowd, they melt into the masses like they belong there. The lights and the music are stimulating in all the right ways and it gets everyone in just the right mood for the kind of hedonistic delights portrayed as going on in a club like this.

When there's a *vampire* in a nightclub, they're like a predator roaming their natural ecosystem, feeling the ebb and flow and following it to know exactly where and when to find the perfect prey. They are masters of the environment, perfectly at home and perfectly dangerous. I imagine myself as one of those vampires, gliding past dancers and finding a pretty girl to lead into a dark corner and sink my fangs into.

But none of the characters in those stories were autistic, so instead we walk inside and the atmosphere punches me in the face.

Any pretense of being a cool, unflappable, badass vampire sexy lady vanishes in an instant as I desperately cover my ears with my hands to try and protect myself from the assault of loud music. I freeze up, paralyzed just past the entryway as the barrage of sound makes it difficult to even hear my own thoughts.

The lights aren't strobing—they're actually quite muted and dim—which helps a little, but then the stench of body odor comes crashing in and I'm being jostled by bodies that come flooding in to fill the space like sardines shoving themselves into a can. This space is too packed, there are too many people touching me, and it's only been a few moments but it's already way, way too much. I try to cope with the onslaught of too-sharp sensory data and I can't. I'm shutting down.

Light spots, dark spots, music pounding, dancers, skin and leather and fabric and jangly metal, space, movement, too much, too much! I hate it, I hate it! My hands over my ears aren't enough, it's still too loud, it's all awful. My whole body is tense, frozen, knife's edge.

Touch, sensation, a hand on my arm, I look over and there's Cheshire, and Bashe behind her, and she's tracing delicate circles on my skin that force my attention away from the lights and sounds and smells, at least halfway. I look at the motion of her hands, the expression of soft concern on her face, the way her cat ears are flattened.

Bashe tilts his head and my vision snaps to the new motion, and I watch as he quirks his eyebrow as if to ask what's wrong. I mumble, "Loud," so quietly that I can't even hear my own voice. He doesn't seem to get it.

I want to be angry at myself, I want to be furious that I'm having a meltdown over sensory overload like I'm still a little kid, but I can't *think* through all the information my senses are trying to process. Cheshire grabs my hand and tugs on it and I follow her mutely as she leads me away from the crowd and over to an alcove booth where the music isn't quite so loud and I can't see as much of the club.

I sit down and Cheshire sits next to me, leaning against me. I'd be uncomfortable about her closeness in any other situation, but right now I'm actually grateful for her presence and how it helps me focus. I try to breathe, try to sort all the information, try to be a fucking adult about this.

I'm not a kid anymore, I'm not a kid anymore, fuck!

Cheshire moves in closer, brings her mouth to my ear, and asks, "Do you wanna see a magic trick?"

What? I don't understand, so I say nothing and just stare at her. The cat-girl smiles, and then she vanishes and there's an actual housecat stepping into my lap.

The cat has fluffy white fur, one yellow eye, and one blue eye. She kneads my thighs and settles in like cats normally do, and I have no idea how to react. *What? She's a cat? She can do that? Holy shit.*

The Cheshire cat—yes yes, this is the reference—pokes at my hand with her face and I automatically start petting. Her fur is soft, her body is warm, and when I close my eyes I can let the world start to fade and just focus on the repetitive, controllable sensation of soft fur on the skin of my hand.

I breathe, deep and steady, and the panic starts to subside. I let out some of my nervousness in joyless laughter, and slowly my body relaxes from its initial tenseness.

I open my eyes and look down at the feline in my lap. I feel a wave of gratitude for her help, for just immediately *getting* what I was going through and knowing how to fix it, and that gratitude is followed by suspicion.

Did you set this up? Was that a leading question, when you asked where a vampire goes to hunt? Nudge me towards the nightclub where you know I'll go into overload, then be right there at my side to offer the solution so I'll feel affection towards you?

It's probable. The geist seems to know everything about me, so it wouldn't be difficult for her to engineer this sequence of events. Another trick, another clever plot to manipulate me. And yet . . .

Her ears are still flattened against her head. And that could mean nothing, because in both forms those are cat ears that hear better than human ears, so of course she's going to dislike the loud music, but . . .

The voice of fear tells me that this is all part of the trick, that she's doing this on purpose so that I'll want to empathize with her and trust her and love her. The fear tells me that I'm falling for every trap she lays. But there's another voice, a voice I hate, that whispers that maybe, just maybe, I've found someone who can understand me. Someone like me.

I have a lot of conflicting thoughts about this, but I think the right course of action is clear: if there's a chance that Cheshire understands these kinds of sensory difficulties on an intimate, personal level, then I have to reach out and empathize. If it's real, then it's an opportunity for me to do to her exactly what she's doing to me.

"Cheshire," I ask the cat resting so adorably atop my legs, "do you . . . well, first, um, thank you for helping. For knowing how to help. It's been actual years, I think, since I last had to deal with that level of overstimulation. Since I had to deal with any part of my autism really making a problem for me. So, yeah. Thanks. And . . ." I hesitate, unsure how to word the next part, which Cheshire seems to pick up on.

I hear her voice coming from the cat, though her mouth doesn't move. "I understand what it's like to be overwhelmed in ways beyond your control. I get it. I'm here for you."

I feel relief, and then suspicion, because that's exactly what I wanted to hear and the perfect opening to ask, "Do you have . . . sensitivity, like I have? Or is this just something you know from learning all about me?"

Cheshire adjusts her position on my lap and says, "It's one of the ways that I was made to fit you. I experience the same sensitivity issues that you do, in much the same manner."

That's a start, but... if she really was constructed a short while ago, or if she's going to be firm about that narrative, it'll be hard to hit on any sense of isolation from those traits. There's nothing to empathize with if she's not actually felt it before. Hmm. "Is this your first real experience with it, then? Or were you around for long enough before my arrival here to go through it a few times?"

"I think you misunderstand the nature of my knowledge of you," Cheshire replies evasively. "My understanding of your existence is not purely observational; I have *experienced* many of your memories."

I shiver at the invasiveness of that notion. *How many of my memories? How did they make you feel?*

How could you possibly love me if you've been inside my head?

I look away from Cheshire and out onto the club floor. The throng of humanity—figmentanity?—looks like I was expecting to see: skintight clothing, scraps of fabric that barely qualify as clothing, fishnets and leather, and everything's either pitch dark or neon color bright. It's constant physical contact out there, with even the dancers that aren't grinding on each other still making incidental contact with every motion thanks to how packed together everyone is.

I see Bashekehi out in the midst of it, smiling and laughing and making eyes at all the clubbers he's flirting with, and I imagine he must be on his way to quite the feast. I, meanwhile, am hiding in the corner because of my stupid broken brain. At least I'm mostly in control now, if still on edge.

I sigh theatrically and stop stimming with Cheshire's fur, instead folding my arms together and grimacing at the imp having fun out on the dance floor. The cat, perhaps noticing my irritation, gets off my lap and plods over to the seat next to me, where she becomes a catgirl again. I make a mental note to ask about that later, but right now it's hard to focus on anything but my miserable inadequacies.

"Something on your mind?" Cheshire asks.

"Always," is my pithy reply, but then I sigh again and admit, "I was hoping to really play up the seductress vampire persona and flirt with a cute girl so that I could see if it would provoke a jealousy response from you, but now I'm realizing that plan is shot for a myriad of reasons."

"Such as my ability to see it coming from miles away?" she quips.

"Well, yes, but even setting aside how you'd probably see right through my scheming, I've never actually flirted with someone I've only just met." I slump against the booth table and admit, "Actually, all my relationships have been the result of calculated charm over an extended period of time, slowly probing that more-than-friends space experimentally before taking the plunge—and even then, I'm not really the initiator type; I'd rather lead the person I'm flirting with into asking me out first. Of course, you know all this, don't you?" I give the geist an accusatory look.

She grins and holds her hands up to her face in a cutesy pose. "Guilty! But really, what are you worried about?"

"I'm *worried* that there's no guarantee anyone in this club would be even slightly receptive to my advances," I mutter, "because the majority of my experience with flirting is reliant on having the time to learn a person and construct a personality they'll be attracted to."

Cheshire laughs. "I love the way you think, dearest Maven. Your mind really does fascinate me."

I roll my eyes and snort. "I'm really not that special. That's just life for borderlines. I'm already trying to figure out how to create an ideal persona to appeal to you, and I don't even like you yet!"

Cheshire laughs harder and I glower at the mirthful wretch. "Oh, sweetie." She gets a mischievous twinkle in her eyes and says, "You know, this is probably the part where your partner would normally tell you, 'Oh, just be yourself, you don't have to change for me.' I, however, am looking forward with delight to the mask you make for me. I'm sure it'll be simply perfect."

Heh. That ... probably shouldn't make me feel as good as it does. But it is nice, to be accepted for what I am. Hahaha. Am I really this easy?

"I will *also* point out that this isn't going to be as much of an issue as you think it will be."

I raise an eyebrow. "Do tell."

The catgirl leans back and plays with one of her ears. "You can be sure that at least one person in this club will make for a good mark, because *you* are a scion and *these* are figments. You're putting more weight on Pandaemonium, and they're exactly the kinds of creatures that respond to that weight."

I frown and lean in. "Elaborate."

Cheshire gestures at me, then at the dancers, and says, "If you consider Pandaemonium in terms of theater, then you can treat scions as the lead actors and figments as the extras; put another way, scions drive the scene and figments act as they are needed. That's going to depend on the throne world, of course, but here in the Labyrinth figments exist to be perfect citizens and perfect victims, which makes them perfect for what you need. If you need prey, the city will provide."

Fascinating and disturbing in equal measure, but I suppose I should default to expecting that mixture from this strange world. "So, what, someone to feed on is just going to be dropped into my lap? That seems a bit overly convenient."

Cheshire smirks. "And this whole *city* doesn't strike you as overly convenient? It's a paradise begging to be plundered, Alice. Food, clothing, housing, leisure, all of it absolutely free. A city full of people who can't fight back and won't resist if you roll up and declare yourself god-empress of this-and-that part of town, except for the handful of fellow reals. Do you get what that creates? Do you understand the *purpose* of a city like that?"

I chew my lip and think it over. *It creates a certain baseline. It shortcuts a lot. You don't need to get sucked into some shitty job for your basic necessities, so you can pursue whatever you like. Even the higher stuff isn't out of reach, so material resources probably aren't a real motivation. The only people you need to worry about are other* people, *other non-figments. Wait...*

The others like you are also free of material concerns, also free to act as they wish, only having to worry about how their handful of peers will respond. It... does it create anti-social incentives? Or the freedom to act in anti-social ways? All limits are enforced by the few, and you can break those limits if you can just overpower those few standing in your way.

Does that create the world of a comic book? A fantasy novel? A world like that...

I crease my brow and meet Cheshire's gaze. "It's a world of heroes and villains, or maybe just conflict. The only consequences come from other people, so if you can overcome those people then you can do whatever the fuck you want. If you want to call yourself king of the castle, what's stopping you from claiming turf? If you don't like the attitude of that self-proclaimed king, what's stopping you from taking his head? There are no structures in place, no societal pressures, so it all comes down to whoever has the biggest stick."

"And the most friends," Cheshire adds. "There is strength in numbers, and the strong can draw numbers to them. But in essence, yes: this is a city where all conflict is personal and vicious, driven by the desires and ideals of the powerful. And you, my dear, are now one of them."

Hells. I'm both deeply concerned and deeply elated by that notion. I tap my leg and hum idly as I process. *A world of main characters and extras. My will against whoever gets in my way.*

Cheshire intrudes on my musing and says, "Tracing back to your first point: yes, it *is* quite convenient that prey will come to you if you don't come to it, but that's because 'vampire hunts for figments' isn't really the kind of conflict that the Labyrinth *cares about*. If you want prey, you'll have prey, and all the ways you can feed on figments are distinctions without differences. What matters isn't the conflict between you and your food, but the conflict between you and whoever might *object* to your means of feeding and choice of prey."

"Huh." I tilt my head and start chewing on a fingernail. "That is . . . a fascinating dimension. That's—well, maybe it's my nerd side showing, but that sounds *a bit* like conflict resolution in RPGs: if the conflict is trivial enough, don't bother rolling. Though even then you'd still have to do *something* to justify the outcome."

"You *have* done something," Cheshire points out. "You came to a suitable feeding ground and you've made your presence known, so now it's just a matter of luring in someone who finds *this*"—she gestures at me—"enticing."

"I'll be fascinated to see how the Labyrinth justifies *that*," I mutter.

As if on cue—or perhaps literally on cue, with all that Cheshire's just told me—I see movement not far from our booth: three young women in goth-adjacent fashion are clustered together, all looking at me, two of them giggling at a nervous-looking third wringing her hands. One of them gives Nervous Girl a push—more of a nudge, really—and Nervous Girl starts walking towards me, keeping to the edge of the crowd.

Cheshire chuckles as she watches me watch the newcomer, and then the catgirl is gone and a white spider is skittering away beneath the table. *Spiders, too!? We seriously need to figure out what's up with that.*

Nervous Girl reaches my booth, interrupting my Cheshire-related train of thought. She smiles at me softly and asks, "Hey, um, would you mind if I sat here?"

Fuck. She's cute. What the fuck do I do now???

. . . I guess it's time for another date?

VIII

Nervous Girl has a killer aesthetic going for her: stompy boots with lots of buckles, torn leggings, a lacy white dress with layered skirts, a septum piercing, dark makeup (including absolutely excellent black lipstick), platinum blonde hair kept long and straight, and a pair of black-rimmed eyeglasses. She's a tall, pale, and ravishing goth icon.

"I wouldn't mind the company," I tell her while I desperately try and think of something cool and flirty to say. "Maven Alice," I introduce myself.

"I'm Lena," she says, her voice soft and sweet.

The pretty goth slides into the seat across from me and tucks a bit of hair out of her face. She looks me over, then glances back at her still-giggling friends, then back to me, and despite all of Cheshire's assurances I find myself uneasy. It wouldn't be the first time a pretty girl has expressed fake interest in me on a dare from her friends.

Insecurity is self-sabotaging. Regardless of her motives, we'll have a better chance of impressing her if we act confident despite our paranoia.

Lena finally works up the nerve to ask, "So, um, is that like, real blood?"

Huh. It actually takes me a second to register that, yeah, I showed up to a nightclub in a bloodstained skirt and blouse, and looking around, I'm pretty sure I'm the only one dressed like this. *Fair play, Labyrinth, that's a pretty decent justification for someone taking interest in me from afar. Well, let's try and run with this. Game face, Maven. You are a sexy, scary vampire.*

I force a smirk and flash my fangs at the goth girl. "If I said yes, and told you it came from the last pretty girl to come my way, would that make you scared or excited?" *Shit, is that too forward? How do you flirt with cute girls???*

Lena looks down at the table, bites her lip, then looks back at me and says shyly, "Maybe, um, maybe a bit of both?" Her eyes look big and soft behind those glasses, and the expression on her face *feels* flirty but I could just be reading too much into it.

"Heh. If it puts you at ease, I'll only bite if you ask me to." My smirk holds for a valiant moment, but then it cracks and I laugh weakly. "But, actually, most of this is probably my blood."

Concern flashes across her face. "Wait, are you hurt? What happened?"

"I, uh, I've had a rough couple days." I scratch the back of my head sheepishly and lean into the booth seat. "Got attacked by a bunch of horrible bullshit outside the city, stabbed a few monsters, got beaten and bruised. I'm fine now, mostly, but yeah, a lot of this is my blood and the rest is from the shit that failed to kill me."

"Wow," Lena breathes. "That's . . . I mean, that's pretty fucked up, but it's also kind of impressive? Sorry, I don't know if that's insensitive," she hastily apologizes.

I wave a hand dismissively. "Nah, you're good. I'd rather laugh about it than mope."

Lena leans her face on her hand and sighs. "I've never been in danger like that. Like . . . that's the kind of excitement I dream about, you know? You wouldn't believe how boring most of my days are."

I quirk an eyebrow and tilt my head. "What's your deal, then? What kind of life has you fantasizing about close encounters with terrifying monsters?"

"Oh! Um, well, I'm not that interesting." Lena laughs nervously and fidgets with her hair again. "I'm actually a student at the local university, in the mathematics wing."

"Oh, hella. I was a student myself before getting thrown into this world." *A very lazy student, but that's the natural consequence of being a gifted kid.* "What kind of math are you into?"

Lena brightens and leans forward. "I'm doing graduate work on differential geometry! I want to use it to prove the existence of mixed motives."

Ah. I have no idea what that is. "That sounds rad. I stopped at pre-calculus because higher math is just not my jam, so I'm always impressed by people that have the brains and the patience to study that stuff." Math is annoying because it takes effort and you have to memorize a billion formulae.

She blushes. "It's not that impressive, I'm firmly middle of the pack in my class. But thank you. What were you studying?"

"Eh, something of a hodgepodge." I wiggle my fingers for emphasis. "I wasn't really pursuing a major, just taking humanities classes that seemed interesting. Literature, philosophy, whatever caught my eye that quarter." I cough into my blouse and mutter, "I, ah, I wanted to be a writer."

"That's pretty neat too!" Lena laughs lightly and admits, "I could never do that, I'm not creative enough."

"Bah, anyone can write. Creativity is a muscle, you just have to exercise it like any other." I mutter, "The real difficulty is being able to do it with any kind of consistency."

Lena gives me a visual once-over and comments playfully, "You know, you don't really strike me as the exercise type."

"Ha! Yeah, no, I was *not* physical in my old life." I sigh at the thought of how much trouble that's caused me. "I wasn't very good at taking care of myself in any capacity, really."

Lena smiles. "If it's any consolation, I'm not much better; I think dancing is the only exercise I get besides walking to classes, and I only do this one day a week. I could do with getting in shape but it's hard to start."

"I think you look great anyways," I say, stumbling over my words, "I mean, like, your whole deal looks great, good aesthetic."

Lena blushes and responds, "Thanks! Um, I think you have pretty eyes."

That immediately puts me on edge, but I understand rationally that it's just my broken fucking brain and that all her signals are suggesting sincerity. *Accept the fucking compliment, stop being so guarded!* "I really like your piercing," I blurt to cover up my discomfort. "I mean, like, your whole face has a really cool aesthetic, you have really nice makeup and I like your hair." Oh gods I'm so awkward. Kill me now.

I am rescued—or perhaps further doomed—by the sudden appearance of Cheshire at our table, the catgirl having somehow acquired a waitress uniform and a pair of shots. "By the Eight, you're both so pathetic. Here." She shoves one shot glass at me and another at Lena, both full of some bright pink liquor. "Get drunk and start making out already. I refuse to watch you useless lesbians pussyfoot around what you're actually here for."

I glare at my geist, but she ignores me and I'm left holding a drink while she vanishes back onto the floor of the nightclub. I glance at Lena to see her reaction and she's already downing the shot, tossing the whole thing back and wiping her mouth on the back of her hand.

Welp. I guess I'm drinking??? I mean. It's probably fine, right? It's just one drink, and I'll say no if Cheshire tries to get me to drink a second, and Lena already took hers, so . . . it's fine? Sure. I knock back my own shot and it goes down sweet and sharp, strong enough to have me coughing after I swallow. I massage my throat and wince. It was fruity, which I like—I favor pink wine when I drink, which is a rare occasion—but somehow packs a bigger kick than fucking *vodka*, which I have had once and absolutely hated.

I'm still recovering from the initial kick when the alcohol hits me all in a rush: my whole chest lights up with tingly warmth that starts to spread to my limbs, and my brain gets a bit fuzzy and pleasant. I blink my eyes a few times and shake my head to try and clear my thoughts. *Holy shit, how strong was that stuff!? I only had one drink!*

I see quite a bit of pink showing in Lena's cheeks, and her eyes gleam as she seems to gather her courage to ask, "So, um, are those fangs actually real?"

I show them off again with a toothy smile and trace my tongue over my beloved fangs. "They are, yeah. And they're genuinely meant for biting people, I just, ah, haven't actually fed on anyone yet."

"What *are you*?" she asks with a big grin.

"I . . . am a demon. New to the role, but still a demon." I chew on my words, contemplating how edgy or self-aggrandizing I should be. "I am also this world's first vampire, and a very dangerous woman." On impulse, I cock my head and ask, "What are you?"

Lena shifts closer to me. "I'm the kind of girl with a taste for dangerous women, *especially* the monster kind. And I think it's very, very hot that you're a demon. So, if there's, um, anything *demon-y* that you maybe want to do to me . . . I wouldn't mind." She bites her lip and looks up at me, eyes alight with clear interest.

There's a part of me that wants to seize on that opportunity to launch straight into the bitey-bitey, but I'm still *uncomfortable* with all this. With the awkward flirting, sure, but also with the idea that this person I've had fruitful conversation with is, in fact, not a real person. Even through the fresh buzz of alcohol, I'm not ready to just throw aside my curiosity and my hesitation for the sake of biting a cute girl.

So instead of flirting back or going for Lena's neck, I tell her, "Actually, I think what I'd like most right now is to know whether or not you're a real person."

"Huh. That's a pretty interesting question. Am I a real person . . . ?" Lena blinks a few times, then settles back into a more comfortable posture and taps her chin thoughtfully. She looks at me with those big soft eyes and asks, "Are you?"

The counter catches me off guard, but the question is far from alien to me, so I have an answer prepared. I shrug noncommittally and take the time to make sure I phrase everything correctly through the alcohol. "Some days more than others. I've gotten pretty good at pretending to be a person, but I don't always feel like one. I still feel . . . real, though." I change tack. "Do you know what a figment is?"

"I do," she answers, soft-spoken and thoughtful. "It can mean 'figment of imagination,' but here in the Labyrinth it's more likely to refer to a specific kind of oneiric construct. Something that looks like a person and talks like a person but lacks a person's internal world. A fake."

I am silent, waiting, monitoring her responses. Her expressive face, her active hands, the shifts in posture and positioning. Her face is flushed, her breathing is heavier, and her pupils are dilated, but is that because of the alcohol or just for show?

Lena meets my searching gaze with those adorable eyes behind cute glasses, and when she speaks her voice is nervous, hopeful, searching for approval. "So, I guess, to answer your first question . . . no, I'm not a real person. But I think I make a pretty convincing fake, don't you?"

She looks and sounds so human for something that just admitted otherwise. *How can you just call yourself a fake like that?* "You know that you're a figment, then, and you understand what that means. To be honest, I was expecting you to plead ignorance."

The not-a-person shrugs. "Most would. More than nine in ten would act clueless if it was brought up, but those numbers might get skewed if *you* were in the room." She holds a hand in front of her mouth and giggles, the sound full of life and emotion that seems to contradict her self-identification.

"Why? Why do they pretend, and why do I change the math? Are they pretending, or do they genuinely not know until something wakes them up?" I have to know this before I can even think about drinking her blood. I need to understand what Lena really is.

Lena plays with a strand of hair and asks, "Would it surprise you to learn that most people don't want to think too hard about the nature of figments? It's a lot easier to hurt a figment if you just take it at face value that they're not people. Right now you're poking and prodding at one to see what's inside, but you could be doing so much more *satisfying* poking and prodding, if you chose to." She winks at me and I try not to blush at the rather suggestive implication. "What's holding you back, demon girl?"

"Forgive me for giving a shit about consent ethics," I mutter.

"I don't forgive you," Lena blithely replies, "as I lack a consciousness capable of proffering either forgiveness or blame. I'm just an object pretending to be a person, Maven. I can't feel pain, or hope, or fear. I can only pretend. Even this pretension of self-awareness is just another act, performed for your benefit."

Everything about that makes my skin crawl, but I want to know more. "Why bother pretending, then? Why giggle and blush if it's not real?"

Lena shrugs. "It's what my character would do. The character of Lena is attracted to you, Maven. She's excited by the idea of you sinking those pretty fangs into her luscious neck, and she's a little scared that you might go too far, but that fear only makes it more exciting. She finds her daily life boring and craves thrills that a demon like you is perfectly suited to provide." She smiles, again seeming so soft and sweet despite the horrors spilling from her lips. "So insofar as I am capable of giving consent, I give it. I want you to feed on me, because Lena wants it, and because it fulfills my purpose."

"What *is* your purpose, then?"

Lena leans in further, close enough I can feel her hot breath on my skin, and says, "To make people like you happy enough to want to stay here forever." She laughs again, the sound darker this time. "So go on, demon girl: tell me what will make you happy."

I'm quiet for a moment, taken aback, processing. I could answer lots of ways, tell all kinds of lies and half-truths. I want to interrogate this figment's existence further, I want to see what stories she can tell, I want to see what roles she can act out. But honestly?

I still need mana, and they say the best mood boost in the world is a good meal.

So I tell her, "Act human, and bare your neck."

She tilts her head and brushes back her hair, and for all that I loved to play at being vampy in my old life I never felt *hunger* like this. I move forward on autopilot, a fresh set of instincts driving me toward exposed skin with bared fangs and deep, all-consuming hunger.

I sink my teeth into Lena's neck and my fangs pierce her skin just like they were made for it, and I hear her gasp but she doesn't push me away. I feel motion, sensation, my hand on her arm, her hand on my leg, but it's all dim compared to the *flood of ecstasy* pouring down my throat.

Cheshire was right: it isn't the taste of blood, not really. I've tasted blood, incidentally, in trace amounts, though always muddled by the taste of skin, and it's more metallic than this. Blood is the taste of iron, for all that it's easy to romanticize for internet edgelords like me.

This taste is something deeper. Something greater. The taste of blood and skin is there, too, but it's dim like the touch of Lena's fingers on my thigh. It's all overwhelmed by the *life* coursing down my throat and pooling inside me. It tastes *red* like wine and meat and the frantic *pulse pulse pulse* of *pumping in our veins*, and it tastes red like the frantic red energy that builds and builds and *builds* when I'm at my most manic.

I drink a girl's essence and it is more savory than any mortal meal.

All notion of going slow to spare her life vanishes from my mind, and if anything I bite down harder and my grip tightens, desperate for more of that glorious lifeblood. I want this. I need this.

Dim, muted, I feel Lena's grasp on my leg grow weak, unsteady, frail—*what are you doing what are you doing what are you doing*—but I can't make myself withdraw my fangs. I can't stop. I need more. I need it all, I—

Rough hands grab my shoulders and I'm pulled from Lena's throat and tossed to the floor of the club. I hit the ground hard and my lungs ache and I realize I haven't been *breathing* since I started drinking from the figment. I gasp for air and spit blood onto the filthy dance floor.

"Fucking freak," jeers a new voice. Female, sharp, mocking.

A second voice, male and cutting. "Yeah, but the fucking freak is probably a fucking *demon*, so don't underestimate it."

Footsteps. Footsteps on the floor, how can I hear them? Oh, right, my head's on the floor. Vibration. Step, step, step.

A hand grabs me by the collar of my blouse and pulls me up, and that second voice spits in my face, "Who are you, what are you, and what the fuck are you doing in my club?"

Shit.

IX

The fear is back.

That's the first thing I think as I stare into the face of my assailant: *the fear is back.* This man could kill me, and I am terrified. Any lingering trace of alcoholic buzz or feeding high is washed from my system by the absolute *fear* racing through me.

I take in the scene before me in bursts and flashes: a broken nose, scruffy red hair, violent green eyes with bags beneath, a fair and freckled face made harsh and vicious by curled lip and wrinkled brow. *Ears. Check the ears!* Rounded, to some small relief. Not an elf.

The hand gripping my shirt is rough-calloused, bruised knuckles. *Brawler. Killer? What's he planning?* Rolled-up sleeves, a gambeson vest dyed blue and purple and green, and an *axe* on his belt with a hunting knife right next to it. *Fuck.*

My gaze flits to the other one, the woman, but then Brawler is shaking me and my thoughts scatter and my heartbeat races and he's up in my face, grip tight, spitting words at me, *roaring* at me to *listen* and *answer*, and I am so fucking terrified.

"I *said*, what the fuck are you doing in my club?" Those baleful green eyes burn into me and I *squeak* in response, which only seems to piss him off further. "Do you even know who we are? *Speak!*"

Outside the booth, the music is too loud again, and though space has cleared around us there are still too many *people* here. My panic reaches its peak and I babble, "I don't know! I don't know, I don't know, I don't know! I-I just walked in, I saw a place and I came here, I don't know who you are or what you want or *why* you care that I'm here! I-I just wanted to eat, that's it, I was just *hungry!*"

Brawler narrows his eyes and demands, "Who are you and what are you?"

"Alice," I blurt. "My-my name is Maven Alice, and I'm a demon. Please don't kill me."

I hear a growl, and my gaze darts from the man holding me for just long enough to catch sight of the world's ugliest dog before my attention is squarely back on the axeman. He sniffs contemptuously. "Buster doesn't like you. Wonder why that is?"

"Ha," I laugh nervously, "I'm usually quite good with animals. Have I mentioned that I would like it if you did not kill me? Here, I'll mention it again: please don't kill me."

I look away from the dangerous man with the axe, hoping to catch sight of Bashekehi or Cheshire somewhere in the crowd, but instead I see Lena, neck thoroughly bloodied, stumbling away into the arms of her no-longer-giggling friends. There's a brief moment of relief that I didn't *murder her*, and then I'm brought back to immediacy by a snort from the woman with the sharp voice.

"You sure this thing's a demon, Shane? I thought they were supposed to have *spine*."

I glance at the woman and see dark skin, dark hair tied back in a messy ponytail, cool brown eyes, purple scarf, and a bright blue-green gambeson coat. More importantly than any of that, I see a crossbow in her hands and a sword at her belt.

The axeman—Shane—glares at me and says to the woman, "Could be lying, could be fresh, but my money's on fresh. Ask the dog."

Crossbow Lady calls to the dog, "Hey, Buster: tell me what the fuck is up with that," and points at me.

I freeze up further, muscles straining to remain perfectly still as I see what is definitely *not a dog* approach me: it's completely hairless, for one, and its face is misshapen, with skin stretched tight against its skull. It has big teeth, lots of them, and its body is too muscular, too bulky. Worst of all are its eyes, human-like and gray. The not-a-dog sniffs me, oversized nostrils flaring, and then it pads back to the woman with the crossbow and whines.

Crossbow Lady frowns. "Shadowtouched for sure, but . . . something's off. I think she's fucking with Buster's read, because he can't get anything more specific on the girl, and he's getting a whole *bunch* of *other* scents off her."

Shane tightens his grip on me. "Like what, Mahiri?"

"Like another *elf*."

Fuck. I glance around the club once more, desperate to catch the gaze of someone who can help me, and this time I see Bashe staring back at me from amidst the crowd, expression tight and body still. He notices me notice him, hesitates, and then the absolute fucking bastard looks away from me.

I focus back on Shane to find him watching me intently. He smiles, a mean, *mean* look on his broken-nosed face. "Well, isn't that interesting. A demon comes to town on tonight of all nights reeking of an elf that *isn't* Averrich. The boss will definitely want to see you, little demon."

I smile weakly and raise my hands in a placating gesture. "Listen, I really don't want any trouble. I really, really didn't know you guys were here. Actually, it wasn't even my idea to come here; an incubus by the name of Bashekehi the Ever-Gleaming told me this was a good place to feed. If you're gonna blame anyone, blame him."

I would feel bad about throwing Bashe under the bus, but no I wouldn't, and this is absolutely his fault, and *please don't kill me*. To my surprise, the brutes threatening me seem to recognize Bashe's name, because Shane frowns and the woman—Mahiri—whistles.

Shane looks to Mahiri and asks, "Wasn't that the name of one of the Coiners? I swear I've heard Imlashi mention him."

Mahiri nods and raises an eyebrow at me. "Not just any Coiner, either; if I'm thinking of the right guy, he was in their triad. She talks about him all the time, him and Avaya. He's the one that stayed behind."

"Right, right." Shane looks back to me. "How do you know a dead man's name, demon?" His breath is hot and rancid against my face, and though his tone is now light I can't ignore the threatening edge to his every word.

My hands are shaking. I try to lean away from him but there's nowhere to go, nowhere to run. I refuse to die here. I can't die here. I find Bashe in the crowd again, see him slipping farther away, and I point at him in a sudden jerking motion. "BASHE!" I yell. "Don't you fucking leave me here!"

Shane and Mahiri look to where I'm pointing and see the incubus freeze in place. His fists clench for a moment, then unclench, and Bashe turns around with a fake smile on his face. He raises a hand in greeting, but doesn't move towards us.

Mahiri points the crossbow at Bashe and calls out, "Come say hello, dead man. We need to have a word with you."

Bashe hesitates, and for a moment I wonder if he might run, but then he starts walking for our little group. As he approaches he says, "I'm afraid you have me confused with someone else, friend. I'm very much alive."

I glare at the treacherous incubus and perform some treachery of my own. "Hey, Bashekehi. You didn't tell me this club was subject to a fucking *turf war*. That would have been useful information before I started snacking on a clubgoer."

Through the overwhelming fear I feel a core of white-hot anger that he's put me in this danger. Hypocrisy, perhaps, but I'm no stranger to that.

The axeman releases me and I have to steady myself. I breathe a sigh of relief, but before I can start planning some method of getting the fuck out of Dodge, he jerks his head at me and says to the horrifying not-dog, "Buster, watch the demon. Bite it if it tries to run."

The creature plods on over and sits down on my feet, which is horrible and I hate it. *Fuck, fuck, fuck. And where is Cheshire!?* I am alone and surrounded and going to die, where the fuck is Cheshire!?

Shane raises a hand when Bashe is a few feet away, and Mahiri keeps the crossbow trained on the incubus. Shane makes a hand gesture towards someone off in the crowd—staff, maybe—and seconds later the music volume mercifully lowers.

"So you're the one Lashi is always talking about, eh?" asks Mahiri. She chuckles. "You don't look like much, if that really is you."

Bashe seems caught off guard by that, his facade of ease falling away as he turns to the woman with the crossbow. "You know Imlashi? I . . . she's alive, then?"

"Alive and well," Crossbow Lady says with a grin. "And she'll be mighty keen to see you again."

Shane cuts in, "But if you really are from around here, you really shoulda known better than to stray on King's Carnival turf." He rolls his shoulders and cracks his knuckles. "Did you come looking for a fight, or did you just wanna piss someone off?"

Bashe takes a step back and shakes his head. "Hey now, nothing like that. Look, I didn't even know you guys would *be* here. If you know who I am, then you probably know better than I do how long I've been gone from this city, and it's long enough that I'm *shocked* to find out this territory belongs to Averrich's people now. You guys have *expanded*."

Gods I wish I could be absorbing all this information in a safe, comfortable context instead of while under threat of gruesome murder. Who are any of these people being mentioned!? How can I use any of this information to not fucking die!?

"We have," Shane replies to Bashe, "and we've owned this stretch of town for the better part of a year. 'Course, you've been gone for the better part of four, so I suppose I shouldn't be surprised." Shane cocks his head and continues, "I *am* surprised you come back working for a demon."

Ha! I wish. I watch the warriors—soldiers, gangsters, whatever—chat up Bashe, and try to look for some opening to escape. The fucking dog will be the hardest part, but even if I can shake it off, I have that nasty crossbow to deal with. And what's with all the pre-modern weaponry paired with this extremely modern nightclub?

Mahiri chimes in, "Always heard you were something of an aberration among imps. 'Fiend with a conscience,' Imlashi called you."

Bashe waves a hand at me dismissively. "I'm not working for the girl. *Abyss*," he swears, "I don't even *like* the girl. She's obnoxious and a brat. She got me out of my cell, that's all. After today I hope to never see her again, honest." He hesitates, then asks, "Imlashi . . . you talk about her like she's one of yours. Did she join your crew, after the attack?"

Shane eyes the imp and answers, "She did, yeah. Got in good with the boss and climbed the ladder real well. Seems to think you shoulda joined her. You planning to?"

Bashe passes a hand over his hair and sighs. "I'm really not ready for that conversation yet. Not the conversation with Lashi, and *definitely* not a conversation with Averrich. What about . . . what about Avaya'ari?"

Mahiri smirks. "Wouldn't you like to know?"

There's something very satisfying about Bashe being the one stonewalled for exposition. While they're busy talking, I silently check my spells: all three are showing a full tank, but I don't know how to determine if I have enough mana to cast multiple spells in a row. Still, I know what to open with: [Carrion Swarm] is the only spell in my arsenal that really *works* as an opener.

Shane folds his arms and says, "You can hear about it from Averrich, because that's a conversation you're *not* getting out of. This little intrusion aside, a lot has changed since your day, old-timer."

Bashe laughs and puts on a grin. "Old-timer? Is four years really that long?"

Shane and Mahiri share a look.

Bashe's laughter dies, and he drops the smile. "It's that serious, then? What has *happened* since I was gone? Did the truce—"

"The truce is dead," Shane interrupts. "It died when the Contrite swept in, and its corpse got pissed on when the Contrite were swept *out* and a *demon* stepped in to fill the power vacuum. No more treaties, incubus; it's kill or be killed these days."

Bashekehi grimaces. "Well, fuck." He looks away. "Can you at least give me a *day* to prepare? I'll talk to Averrich, promise, but I *just got back*. I haven't even . . ." Bashe trails off, leaving the final sentiment unspoken.

Shane shakes his head. "If it was just you, maybe, but you can't come back with a demon and expect to walk that off. The Goblin King will want both of you in his court *now*. This is bigger than you know."

Damnit, I kind of want to figure out what they're talking about, but I have learned my fucking lesson: I am not *getting tangled up with another fae.* I prime [Carrion Swarm] and zero in on the command prompt within the diminished spell diagram. *[Carrion Swarm]: I want you to summon venomous spiders that will bite the dog and weaken it.* It works, the text turning blue in my mind's eye. I just need the right moment to unleash the spell.

I miss whatever Bashe says, but then Mahiri is talking again with, "Doesn't matter. You came in together, you're leaving together. Don't make this difficult."

Bashe looks at me and says, "That might be a problem for the girl. She's not too fond of fae. You really wanna pick a fight with a demon?"

Shit. Running out of time.

Mahiri glances at me disdainfully. "Not much of a demon."

My hands twitch, my fight-or-flight going wild from the renewed interest, and I almost unleash the spell, but I stop when I hear Cheshire's voice whisper in my ear: "Wait for my signal. Focus the reaver with the crossbow."

I don't see Cheshire anywhere, but I give it decent odds she's some kind of bug right now. *Okay. No choice but to trust her, really. So how do we respond?* I smile uneasily at the two reavers(?) and say, "Hullo again. Just waiting for my turn. Please, take all the time you like with my dear friend and stalwart ally, I'm a very patient girl."

Different tactic. I dismiss the spell and call it again. [Carrion Swarm]: *summon crows to peck at Crossbow Lady's eyes.* The command is accepted, the spell primed and waiting.

Shane turns back to me now and makes a contemptuous noise at me. "Well, demon girl? Is all that sniveling real, or do you think you can take us in a fight?"

"Definitely not," I assure the reaver, entirely truthfully. "I am weak and frail and I know I've said this a couple times, but please, please do not kill me. Also, please do not take me to your scary fae boss? I can just leave. I'd really rather just leave the city, if those are my choices."

"Not an option," Shane tells me bluntly. "And allow me to be crystal fucking clear about what your options *are*: with us, or against us. Come to the Goblin King and join his hunt, or be an enemy of the King's Carnival and die like prey." He pulls the axe from his belt and points it at me, Mahiri keeping her crossbow leveled at Bashe. "Make your choice, and quick."

"I would like to live," I say with more desperation than enthusiasm. "Living is my choice, always, in any context." Internally, I am paralyzed with indecision. *Is it even worth it to try my luck? Should I just go along with what they want here?*

I hate it. I hate the idea of being bound to another fae, forced into servitude on threat of violent murder.

And yet: it's a damn compelling threat. Maybe it makes me a coward, but I'd prefer slavery to death.

In the end, Cheshire chooses for me. The second that Shane turns his attention back to Bashe and asks, "And your choice, incubus?" something happens to the dog: it yelps, twisting its head around to bite at its flank, and that takes off just enough weight for me to forcefully step back and away.

Mahiri turns the crossbow on me but I've already unleashed [Carrion Swarm] and four crows take shape and divebomb the reaver, going straight for the eyes like I ordered. She still manages to pull the trigger, but with the distraction from the birds it misses me, though only by *centimeters*.

I damn near have a heart attack from the close call, but I don't stick around to see what happens next, instead bolting for the crowd. Behind me I hear Bashe cry "[Adrenaline Burst]," and Shane roar "[Wolfsong]!"

I reach the edge of the crowd but I'm too *slow*, and before I can vanish into the mass of figments I am caught by the monstrous *thing* that Shane and Mahiri called "Buster." The monster dog hits my heels, tackles me, shoves me to the ground, jaws coming for my throat, and for a single terrified instant I can see my death looming over me, but then a *giant fucking wolf* comes barreling through and slams into the horrible faerie dog, knocking it aside and latching on with big glorious fangs.

I scramble to my feet, slip into the crowd, and the fight is on.

X

Cheshire is fighting the dog, my crows are pecking at Mahiri, and both Bashe and Shane are unaccounted for. As the violence breaks out, the crowd—which to this point had mostly continued their various forms of entertainment—starts to panic and make for the exits, a throng of not-quite-humanity pushing in different directions and creating chaos that I hope to use as cover from the fucker with a *crossbow* that I just sicced crows on.

This is an absolute nightmare.

I try to blend into the rush of figments but I'm well aware that I stick out like a bloodied schoolgirl in a crowd of dancers. The cavalcade of sensory data is threatening to overwhelm me again, the movement of the crowd and the screams and cries of panicked clubbers; it's a mess and I hate it.

I shove past a few figments in skimpy garb, trying to put distance and bodies between me and the reavers, and I glance back at the mess I left behind just in time to see a *flaming crossbow bolt* sink into a figment right as he passes in front of me. I catch a brief glimpse of the female reaver, Mahiri, bleeding from one eye but no longer being pecked at by my crows. *What did she do, shoot them!? Stab them!?*

I duck low, grateful for the confused masses blocking off a clear shot, and wince at the poor victim that took a bolt for me. He screams as green-gold flame spreads across his body from the wound in his torso, and the sheer agony of that sound has me wondering if he's really a figment . . . but Lena was convincing too. It doesn't matter either way. *This is a mercy kill.*

[Prey Upon]: *all to mana*. I crouch down farther and press my hand to a yet-unburned part of the downed man's leg, then unleash the spell. Shadows spill from my hand and sink into the body of the victim like teeth biting down. I can *feel*, in some intangible sense, as the tendrils of my magic find purchase within this man's essence and extract their due. The burning man breathes his last, going silent, and the shadows pull back into my hand with a bounty of mana in tow.

It doesn't feel anywhere near as good as feeding on Lena did, but there's an undeniable satisfaction in the feeling of this mana pouring into me. The pleasant sensation helps dull the panic pounding in my chest, but only so much.

I rise from my crouch, still trying to stay hidden in the crowd but needing to move quickly lest I be left out in the open. I stumble away from the corpse of the probably-a-figment and do my best to keep the other figments between me and that archer. A few more bolts sink into clubbers around me as I try to navigate my way toward the exit, but I don't risk another [Prey Upon]; the crowd is starting to thin as people make their way out the door.

When I feel like I have a moment's breath, I spare a glance back at the corner I came from and see the giant wolf—Cheshire—take a brutal axe blow from the male reaver—Shane. Cheshire doesn't see it coming, focused on scrapping with the not-a-dog, and the blade comes cutting in without warning. My heart stops as the axe cleaves *through* the wolf, separating flesh and bone with impossible cutting power. On panicked stupid instinct I reach out toward Cheshire, a scream half-formed in my throat, but then the bloody halves of her body melt away into smoke and shadow, and a torn notebook drops to the ground in her place.

Cheshire reforms next to me, catgirl once more, and winces. "Sorry about the notebook. We should run." Her form feels immaterial again; she's not translucent or anything like that, but I just have this sense in looking at her that she's less *physical* right now than she was a second ago.

"Uhh, right. Yes. Running time." I try to ignore the massive whiplash of what just happened and instead focus on getting as far away as possible from the people trying to kill me.

We dash for the exit at full speed—or rather, I dash, shoving figments out of the way to make a beeline for the door, and Cheshire just rejoins my shadow to piggyback along. Then I hear an awful barking sound, something halfway between what a dog should sound like and the scraping of nails on chalkboard, and it's getting closer.

I glance behind me and see the horrible not-a-dog *teleporting* through the crowd, blinking in and out of existence to bypass the remaining mass of figments and come right for me. For a moment my terror spikes to untenable levels, but then it hits me how *injured* the creature is: it's covered in bloody wounds from its scrap with my wolf.

As the monster dog leaps for me, I throw out a hand and scream, "[Exsanguinate]!"

I slam the activation sigil as soon as the spell diagram pops into my brain, and then I watch in enraptured fascination as the dog-creature's many wounds gush and convulse, blood ripped from the beast's body in vicious bursts. Crimson liquid soaks into its hairless skin and falls to the floor in waves of red rain, and when it slams into me it is *frail*, shaking, and even with my paltry strength I'm able to push it off before it can do more than scratch at me.

The monster is pale and bleeding and yelping in pain, too weak now to even rise to its feet. It twitches and whines, body struggling to move bloodless limb in pursuit of its target. I don't give it a chance to recover, lunging for the beast and snarling, "[Prey Upon]!" as I grab at it. The shadow trick repeats itself, my magic flowing into the dying creature and ripping out its very essence. I don't specify mana this time, and a part of me is very hungry to find out what a *soul* tastes like . . . if this creature even has one.

The taste is altogether different this time: as my magic flows back to me, the flavor of it is neither the intense savory of Lena's blood nor the muted satisfaction of taking mana from the fallen figment; I still feel a trickle of mana returning to me, the spell's efficiency paying minor dividends, but what I take from this creature is so much *more* than mere mana.

A fragment of something glorious slides down my throat, and as it melts away inside me I feel *more*: more powerful, more capable, more *real*. It's like the feeling when I saw Cheshire manifest, yet somehow applied to my own existence, my own self-perception and sense of consciousness. I feel more *true* than I was a second ago, and I have the overwhelming, terrifying realization that *there is still so much more I can become.*

I laugh with manic delight as I take my next step on the path to apotheosis, and then I look up from the dog just in time to see Shane bringing his axe down at me. I scream in terror, stumble back, and raise my arms in front of me in desperate survival instinct.

The axeblade sinks into the flesh of my right arm and carves deep, and I scream as white-hot agony lances up my arm. The axe tears through skin, parts muscle and fat, and when it hits bone I can feel my arm *splintering* from the impact. He rips the axe out and I see the layers of meat that comprise my arm before blood rushes in to fill the vast emptiness.

"You should have joined us," the reaver says with a shake of his head. "You didn't have to die here."

The pain drives every thought from my mind and I cry and fall against the floor—*it hurts it hurts it hurts*—as the fear comes rushing in and I scrabble to get away on desperate hands and knees but *I can't feel my hand.* The reaver comes in for another strike and I can feel in my screaming bones that this is where I die—

—but then Bashekehi is there in between us, lashing out with the flagellant's scourge.

Shane dodges the attack, his movements so fast as to be blurred, but he keeps his distance, wary, and I realize on second glance that Bashe's weapon is writhing with those shadows that mark the magic of the Abyss. I stare at the scourge, at the shadows, but it's hard to hold on to that information because the pain in my arm is still pounding through my whole body. He cut me to the bone, and I don't have a potion anymore.

I don't stay to watch the fight.

I sprint for safety, for anything, and throw myself behind the nearest bit of cover—the bar, it's the bar. Cheshire comes out of my shadow as I slide behind the counter and crumple to the floor, the catgirl looking deeply concerned at the gigantic fucking hole in my arm.

"The cloak," she tells me, and I look at her blankly. "Use the cloak to manifest me and I can get back in the fight," she clarifies.

Oh. Right. Fighty wolf. Geist rules. Bodyguard. *Focus.*

The knowledge comes to me dimly through the haze of anguish, but I comply. I tear the cloak from my shoulders with my working hand and stumble my way through the incantation, focusing on the memory of Cheshire's prior manifestation. I remember the words, mostly, and the act of will, and the shaping of a visual, though it's all shaky.

"This cloak your anchor, and dreams your body. Rise, Cheshire, and *destroy my enemies!*"

Cheshire's form becomes real again, and immediately she's back in wolf mode. Now that I actually have a chance to look at her closely, I'm amazed at this latest shape: she's larger than any wolf I've ever seen, lean and powerful, with snow-white fur and a full set of vicious-looking chompers. One eye is gold, the other ice-blue, just like every form she's taken so far. She's a perfect specimen, and I absently reach out to feel her fur with my not-bleeding arm. Her fur is wonderfully coarse and dense, and even through the pain it makes me feel a little better.

Focus! We need to perform repairs. I shake my head, breathe deep, and look at the wound: deep and horrible, blood and flesh and visible bone. My arm is useless to me like this. I struggle out of my shirt, the act awkward but doable, and start wrapping it tightly around my injured limb.

It infuriates me that I've had to sacrifice clothing for bandages twice in two days, especially now that I'm down to a bra and skirt, but the self-conscious embarrassment isn't enough to burn away the dread and anxiety I feel knowing that both reavers are still alive out there, armed and hunting for me.

That fear gets a massive spike when I hear Cheshire growl and see her lunge for a target just out of sight. I freeze up in the midst of my bandaging and watch as Cheshire collides with the archer, Mahiri, who appears from around the corner with sword in hand and crossbow nowhere to be seen, blade smeared with black blood that I can only assume to have come from the crows I set on her. "Found you," the reaver growls.

Cheshire snaps at Mahiri but the reaver is fast, movements blurred like Shane's were, and dodges each frenzied bite. The reaver sidesteps another bite and stabs at Cheshire, but the wolf becomes a hummingbird for just long enough to fly around the blade before transforming back into a wolf for another bite attack.

The two test each other, trading feints and strikes but never actually drawing blood, careful and wary. Cheshire keeps between me and the reaver, able to project enough aggression to keep Mahiri back but not able to gain any ground. I'm tense, terrified that Cheshire will make a single mistake and there will be nothing between me and the tip of that sword. I have to do something.

Mahiri isn't bleeding anywhere near as bad as her dog was, but there's still a bit of red trickling from one eye where my crows pecked at her before they were slain. I don't know how that will affect my spell, but I have to try.

Cheshire snaps at the reaver, the reaver cuts back, and when Cheshire turns into a tiny bug to avoid the attack, I point at Mahiri's bleeding eye and scream, "[Exsanguinate]!"

What follows is . . . unpleasant. Mahiri's eye *pulps* as the blood is ripped out of it, and she clutches her ravaged socket with the hand not holding a sword. The spell drenches half her face in vital fluids and viscera, the disgusting gory remnants of what used to be an eye. She lets out a cry of frustration and agony, attack rhythm broken, and Cheshire takes advantage of the lapse in flow to go wolf again and make another lunging bite, which Mahiri just barely evades. Cheshire growls at Mahiri threateningly, fur bristling.

The reaver grits her teeth, glances between Cheshire and I, and cedes the bout. She bolts away, back out onto the main floor, and I sag with relief and exhaustion. My arm throbs and wails, but I finish bandaging it and with some help from Cheshire—who returns to her catgirl form to assist me—I manage to get back on my feet.

I lean on the bar for support and survey the scene: all the figments are gone from the club, and out in the center of the space I can see Bashekehi and the male reaver circling each other. Bashe's scourge still seethes with Abyssal shadow, but Shane has somehow set his axe on fire—classic red-orange fire, not the golden green I've come to expect from what must be Summer. Neither of them bear any wounds.

Shane still moves with blurred swiftness, and he strikes on the offensive, forcing Bashe back with every attack, but there's a caution to his movements; any time it seems like Bashe might have an opening, Shane abandons his attack and pulls back defensively. *Probably terrified of getting soul-scarred by that weapon buff.*

The other reaver, Mahiri, scrambles over to where she left her crossbow and loads it. I tense, ready to duck, but instead of swinging it around at me she lines up a shot at the incubus. A wealth of literature tropes tell me that shooting into melee is a bad idea likely to go wrong, but just as many suggest that an archer with supernatural skill and ability doesn't need to give a shit about what's normally a bad idea.

[Exsanguinate] was brutal but I've already used it on the one obvious target, so I prime "[Carrion Swarm]: rats take her!" and unleash the spell.

Somewhere between a dozen to two dozen rats emerge from the dance floor in wisps of shadow and smoke, and the would-be swarm dashes at the female reaver and begins to crawl up her legs, biting and scratching and climbing. Mahiri swears and takes the shot, aim thrown off just enough that the bolt sinks into Bashe's side as opposed to anywhere more lethal.

The hit still injures the incubus and he falters in his movement, presenting an opportunity for Shane that the reaver quickly takes, but then Cheshire is coming at Shane in wolf form and the reaver pivots to try and sidestep the bite attack. Cheshire goes for his axe arm, not caring to defend herself, and latches on with her fangs even as the axe sinks into her body, a glancing blow compared to the strike that destroyed her form earlier.

I'm terrified and hurting, but the fear of that reaver wounding me again isn't as strong as the fear of him killing Cheshire again; there's no way I'll stand a chance against both reavers with only Bashe at my side.

I start running for the fight, splitting my attention between Mahiri's struggles with the rats and Shane's struggle with Cheshire. The male reaver tries to get his arm free but Bashe swoops in before he can and shoves his hand at the back of Shane's head with a shouted, "[Burning Intensity]: magnify his pain!"

The reaver's eyes go wide and he lets loose a horrifying shriek. His grip falters and he stumbles, then falls, shoved to the ground by the force of Cheshire's fangs. Bashe lashes out with the scourge and rakes it across Shane's bared arm, drawing blood and soul, then steps back and dismisses the spell, shadows vanishing.

I see my chance and dart in. I grab for the dagger at his belt, pull it free, and ram it into his throat. A second scream—gargled this time, broken and rasping—escapes his wounded throat, and I don't wait any longer to press my hand to his chest and cry, "[Prey Upon]!"

The shadows seep into the dying man's flesh and dig for his essence. There's a struggle, something in him fighting back in a way the figment and the dog didn't, but I twist the dagger with all my paltry strength and the fresh burst of agony and violence breaks whatever is resisting my will. Shane goes limp, the light leaves his eyes, and a fragment of a human being's soul slips down my throat.

The exhilaration nearly wipes the pain from my battered body, and a manic laugh escapes me from the sheer *joy* of my victory. I look up from the corpse of one reaver and meet the one-eyed gaze of the second, her sword bloodied with rat guts—black like that of the crows, perhaps some property of my summons—but more rats still scratching at her.

Cheshire growls, bleeding but still manifested, and Bashe hefts his weapon. Mahiri looks between us all, hesitates, and then flees. I'm too tired to pursue, and Cheshire and Bashe show no interest, so the reaver escapes the club and runs off into the city. Part of me wants to follow, wants to keep her from telling others, but I can't stay on my feet.

All the adrenaline leaves me at once, and then there's only the anguish and the pain and the horror that I almost just died. I sink to the ground next to the reaver's corpse and curl in a ball, staring blankly into the glassy eyes of the man I just killed.

XI

I've always been afraid of death, but that fear has always existed in the abstract, barring my suicide attempt.

I didn't have a particularly dangerous childhood; I wasn't a very active kid and I didn't have many friends, so I mostly read books and played video games and stayed away from the wider world. I lived in safe areas and avoided the less safe areas, I didn't play any kind of sport that could result in a concussion, and I just... never really faced any real danger.

Still, despite that lack of danger, I was *obsessed* with forestalling my own demise. I read about telomere decay and dreamed of going into the medical field to find a solution to aging. I read about global warming and wanted to fix it. I read about the sun's eventual expansion and yearned to travel the stars in search of a new world. I even wanted to find some solution to the heat death of the universe, because even an uncountable number of years was *too few*. It still ended.

Is it pathetic, to fall into suicidal depression out of a realization that one day, no matter what you do, you are going to die?

"... trap ... injured ..."

Distantly, dimly, through heavy fog, I hear noise. Arguing, from tone. My companions, I presume, though I can only catch a few words and make no effort to discern further information. I should. I would, in any other circumstance, but it's so hard to care about whatever they're saying when I'm staring into the glassy eyes of a dead man.

I shiver on the floor of a nightclub in a pool of blood—some mine, some not. Next to me is the corpse of a man who, until mere moments ago, was a thinking, feeling being. He had a life, and a group that he belonged to, and probably friends within that group, and now he's dead. He's dead, and I killed him.

How fucked up is that?

"... not my fault ... four years ..."

I trace my fingers over his cheek, my hand shaking, and feel the lingering warmth. He's dead, and that could have been me. If the axe hadn't been stopped by my arm. If the crossbow bolt hadn't been stopped by that figment. If Cheshire or Bashe had been just a bit slower. If I hadn't used my spells in the right ways at the right moments.

I feel so very, very cold. I laugh, the sound hollow and broken, as I realize that right now I feel colder than the corpse lying next to me. Even the throbbing in my mutilated arm feels dull and muted, the hot spike of pain given way to steady room temperature agony.

"... debt ... fix this ..."

I hate this. I hate the pain, I hate the fear, I hate that I almost died, I hate staring into those stupid lifeless eyes *accusing me, judging me for what I did. It's not my fault. It's not my fault. You tried to kill me first. It was self-defense. I'm not a murderer. I'm not a murderer. I'm not—*

I hug my arms to my chest and the sudden movement sends a jolt of awful from my arm up to my brain, scattering the bad thoughts before they can spiral any further. I shudder and shake and feel something wet drip down my face towards the floor. I'm crying. *Stupid. What kind of protagonist cries over one dumb fight?*

The rational voice says: *We're experiencing the aftershocks of a high-tension encounter. One chemical cocktail is being replaced by another, and nothing in our time on Earth equipped us to process the complicated emotions involved in taking a life and nearly having our own life taken. Let it hit you. Cry. Breathe.*

I snarl, animalistic, and ignore her advice. My advice, but the wrong advice. I don't need to cry, I don't need to fucking cope, I need to be *more!* I crawl closer to the body, gritting my teeth through the fresh pain, and rip the dagger out of the corpse-thing's throat.

More blood spurts from the wound, and I press my fangs to the gaping hole, wrap my mouth around the ruins of his—*its*—neck. I drink his blood and it's still warm, still flowing, but the taste is *rancid* and *horrible,* like drinking liquid death. I try to force more down my throat, try to fill myself with this wretched substance, but it's so bad that on instinct I tear my fangs away and spit out the blood, coughing. As I do, though, I feel that same telltale trickle of mana as when I ate falafel or interrogated Cheshire.

"... geist ... changeling ..."

It's not much. Not worth the taste—and that taste is so much worse than it should be. Is it some property of my new existence? Like a vampire or ghoul vomiting up a meal it shouldn't have eaten?

I glare loathing at the further-mauled body, mouth wretched with the lingering taste of the corpse-blood that has slid between my teeth and found home beneath my tongue. I have the urge to take the knife and stab the body like I did with the not-a-ghost all the way back in the school, but when I try to lift my arm it takes more energy than I have. I slump, exhausted, and focus on the conversation between Bashe and Cheshire for just long enough to catch a single full sentence before the pain takes me and I fade into blissful darkness.

"This is the way the world ends."

. . .

"Alice."

. . .

"Alice!"

I'm being shaken awake by rough hands, and when I open my eyes and blink away the disorientation I see the incubus standing over me. I'm sitting up, though I don't remember moving, and my back is to the wall of the club.

Bashe snaps his fingers in front of my face, twice, and I hiss at him. "I'm up," I mutter, head pounding and arm aching. I am fascinated to discover that the imp's wound has seemingly vanished, with only a smear of blood to betray where it once was. I point at the glaring lack of a hole in his chest and ask, "Did you heal? I thought you said fast healing was dangerous and rare?"

The fucker rolls his eyes at me and complains, "Even half dead you ask too many questions. Unbelievable."

"Answer the question, incubus," murmurs Cheshire from my left. I look over to see the catgirl—a vicious gash in her side that drips blood to the floor below—crouched down and scribbling intently in the ruins of my notebook. "It's relevant and you'll have to explain it anyways for the contract to take."

"Yeah, yeah," Bashe mutters. He sighs and smooths back his hair. "I guess we've got time, since you're not in any real danger of dying from that scratch."

"Joy," I mumble. I poke my wounded arm and wince at a fresh spike of pain. "Why isn't this worse? I mean, it hurts, a lot, but it also feels . . . weirdly manageable? I was freaking before I passed out, and now I don't really feel like I'm in danger. Why?"

"Benefits of being a demon," Cheshire informs me without looking away from her art. "Even as a fledgling you're a lot harder to kill now than you were when you woke up in this world. You're not likely to die of blood loss, disease, or even poison unless there's a mage backing it up."

I frown. *Fascinating. That's something to be grateful for, I suppose.* "Okay. Walk me through what's happening next. Cheshire mentioned a contract. Am I getting a new spell?"

Bashe nods and gestures at the spot on his chest where the wound should have been. "I did this with [Indulgent Vitality]. You've heard me use it once before, actually. It's a big spell, but it can be deceiving; that hole the crossbow put in me is still there, and it'll still be there for a while. The spell spruces up your appearance and tries to keep any harms from getting worse while it transfers those harms to a marked object, usually a portrait or statue. Since that transfer counts as regenerative healing, it goes pretty slow."

Portrait? Like the Oscar Wilde story? I glance at Cheshire and finally realize what she's drawing: it's me. She's drawing a portrait of me. I look away quickly and back to Bashe. "I'm interested, but I want to know why this is necessary. If I'm not in danger and it's not going to make me better at any reasonable pace, what's the point?"

"The point," Cheshire answers, "is that your arm is shattered and bleeding and it *will* get worse. You're not going to die of blood loss, sure, but your bones aren't going to mend themselves and running around will only aggravate the wound. We need the imp's spell so you'll be safe to transport to a *real* healer. Also, it's a useful spell to deconstruct later."

Right. Making my own spells. "'Kay. What's the catch?"

Bashe gestures at the sketch of my ugly mug and says, "It may surprise you to learn that this spell is mostly used for non-combat purposes. Someone wants to drink or take drugs without worrying about their liver or other organs, and maybe they want to get rid of those bags under their eyes and all the other signs of hard living. All those harms and imperfections get sent to the portrait, and they build. An imp can siphon mana from the portrait to reset it, but if the portrait gets too corrupt—or if the caster dies while they have an active portrait—then their soul is trapped inside and left at the mercies of any imp."

I blink. "That seems like a big deal. So is that the invocation downside?"

"It actually isn't; everyone who uses the spell has to deal with that quality. No, your unique downside is that every time you cast the spell you're going to experience some . . . let's call it 'mental feedback.' It'll make you more like Indulgence herself, though if you only use the spell once it shouldn't be too noticeable." He hesitates with an unpleasant look on his face and adds, "It can sneak up on you, though."

That's also *part of the story. Corruption of the portrait and corruption of the self. Hmm.* "I think I understand the risks. How many memories do you need?"

Cheshire makes a final mark on the notebook page, sets it carefully aside where it won't soak up blood, and melts into shadow and smoke. My cloak settles where she was, torn, and I grimace at yet another loss.

The catgirl reforms sitting next to me and gives me a wink. "There's one more thing to be aware of," she says, "which is that if the portrait gets damaged it'll send all the harms it's gathered back at you en masse. So, ah, don't let that piece of paper get ripped once you've spelled it."

I shiver, very aware of how fragile paper can be. "Noted. So, the memories?"

Bashe shakes his head. "I don't want your memories, Alice."

"Oh." I tilt my head. "Then what *do* you want? I don't exactly have a lot to give here, my guy."

"I don't need mana; I need assurances that whatever you become, whatever kind of demon you turn into . . . you're not going to come after me." His voice hardens. "I'm not interested in helping someone who's going to turn around and try to eat my soul."

I glare at the incubus. "That's a pretty rude accusation. Didn't I tell you when we met that I consider that kind of betrayal self-defeating?"

Bashe gives me a very unimpressed look. "If I put any trust in the value of your word, I wouldn't be insisting on a binding contract. So let me be clear: if you want the spell you need to reach a healer safely, you're going to have to swear by Azathoth to keep my soul out of your filthy fucking fingers. No bindings, no soul-eating, no taking my soul and forging it into an artifact."

I glance at Cheshire and raise an eyebrow. "Is this what you two were arguing about?"

"Among other things," Cheshire mutters.

I look back at Bashe and ask, "Why the soul specifically? Wouldn't it be better to have me swear not to harm or kill you?"

Bashe snorts. "We both know there's a dozen ways around an oath like that, no matter how we word it. *Especially* with *that thing* at your side." He points at Cheshire accusingly. The catgirl raises her hands to her cheeks and grins. "There's no contract you can sign that will bind *her* not to attack me, so it's a moot effort. Taking away my soul as a prize kills your biggest incentive."

I chew my lip and consider his logic. *Were we planning on stabbing him at some point? I mean, he's gotten under my skin a few times, and I would have liked to have him as a minion, but I'd already written him off from the moment I left the tea party. So, I don't think this actually inconveniences any of our plans, and it doesn't stop us from acting in self-defense if he betrays us.* Okay. "Sure, I'll take the deal."

Bashe nods and doesn't wait any longer. "Azathoth, O Dreamweaver! I invoke the right of channeling that all imps are due. Bear witness to this contract and give it meaning. Hear our words and make them binding."

The club falls away, and the body of the man I killed, and the blood on the floor, and even the pain in my arm . . . but this time, as the world vanishes, there's one sensation that's different: I feel Cheshire's hand slip into mine, soft and warm and oddly comforting. I can't see her, but I know that she's next to me, with me, even inside this strange ephemeral space.

An eldritch horror watches all three of us, waiting, perceiving. Her doting love and clinical interest pick and tear at my psyche, and rather than fade from repetition it only seems stronger this time, more intense. *There's more for her to take interest in, now. More to love. More to dissect. More to witness.*

Bashekehi has more composure this time as he says clearly, "The contract is thus: a bestowal for a sworn oath. I offer my library of spells to pull from, and my mana to serve as a vessel for the Dreamweaver's grace." The incubus lifts his hand and a new purple-pink sigil forms, streaked through with bright green. "I offer the spell [Indulgent Vitality], and have explained its capabilities to the invoker."

The Dreamweaver seizes my throat, her caress cold and caring, and forces me to say, "I understand the capabilities of the spell and find it satisfactory for my purposes." I tense my good arm, desperate to exercise some small act of free will, and feel Cheshire squeeze my hand in response.

"There is a price for all magic," Bashe continues. "I have offered a spell to be bestowed, the mana to bring it to life, and the grace of the Dreamweaver to bind it to your soul. What will you sacrifice to claim this offering?"

Azathoth's grip tightens, softens, expands, contracts. I speak again, her words in my mouth. "I shall not take the soul of Bashekehi the Ever-Gleaming within myself to consume, nor shall I bind that soul to my will, nor shall I forge that soul in the manner of demons and imps. I shall not lay a hand of flesh nor a hand of will upon the soul of Bashekehi the Ever-Gleaming, this and these I swear by Azathoth, Dreamweaver, All-Mother, Origin. Weaver take me if I forswear."

My breath catches in my throat as the last word leaves my lips, and I feel the vast presence of the Dreamweaver pour *inside me,* tendrils of divine emanation breaking into my chest and curling around my lungs, my ribs, my heart. Azathoth *squeezes,* and for a moment my mind goes white with terror, and then I am released and can breathe again, each breath shallow and panicked.

What was that? Why? A warning? An embrace?

I see stars, and I see the glowing sigil travel from Bashe's hand to my chest, nestling into my sternum and taking residence. I feel vaguely uncomfortable realizing I've done this whole ritual in just a bra and skirt, but I'm sure Azathoth was watching me in the shower anyways.

"The bargain is struck," Bashe murmurs, and Azathoth's attention falls away ... but I'm certain not all of it.

I steady my breathing, grateful for another hand-squeeze from Cheshire, and focus on my new spell. "[Indulgent Vitality]." The diagram appears in my mind's eye, full of fresh symbols to examine, and once more I strive to understand the diagram, to see the secrets hiding behind the strain that rises whenever I glimpse some hint of deeper meaning. It's still too overwhelming, and after a few moments I cease my attempt.

Bashekehi hands me the notebook page with its sketch of my face. I clutch the paper gingerly and mentally select the text prompt. "Make this page my portrait, and restore my broken body." The symbol turns blue, and I unleash the spell.

It's utterly mesmerizing to watch my own body alter as Bashe's once did—and *revolting*, once I see what it does to my skin. The wave of change washes over me and seems to fix my arm, mending flesh and restoring mobility, though I can still feel great pain and ache beneath the surface. And wherever the wave passes over my scars, it washes those away too.

I panic at the sight of all the scars on my arms and legs suddenly vanishing, skin made smooth and unblemished. I run my fingers over the skin and feel the smoothness, feel the glaring absence of scars that have been there for years. The name of the spell catches in my throat, almost primed for a second time, but I can feel the weight of two gazes bearing down on me. What would they think, if they saw me ask for my scars back?

I lower my head and try to control my breathing, try not to think about how *wrong* it feels to be missing the texture on my skin. To be missing so many marks of memory. I hate it, and I hate that I hate it, but to do anything about it would invite more judgment than I can bear right now.

I raise my head, clear my throat, and ask, "Where to now?"

Bashe is inscrutable, but Cheshire watches me, hand still wrapped in mine, and there is a sympathy in her gaze that makes me profoundly unsettled. She lets none of it into her voice, though, as she tells me, "Now, we visit the city shrine."

XII

"Right, well, before we do that, it's looting time."
Cheshire giggles at my declaration and Bashe rolls his eyes at me. I rise to my feet and immediately stumble as a wave of nausea washes over me, but Cheshire is still holding my hand and steadies me. I grimace at the moment of weakness and extract my hand from hers.

I survey the nightclub: a dead hunter, three dead figments, and a small wooden object where I killed the hunter's hound. That last one intrigues me, but I suspect the majority of my loot is going to come from the corpse formerly known as Shane.

I saunter over and pick at his body. I pull the dagger from his mutilated throat with a wet squelch and wipe it off on his gambeson, which is looking very appealing to my safety-seeking sensibilities. An extra bit of protection between me and a stray crossbow bolt sounds just delightful.

I take the no-longer-burning axe in both hands and give it a few swings, but my injured arm twangs at me and I clearly do not have the upper body strength to be any good with this thing. I toss the axe aside and rifle through the dead man's pockets.

Sadly, his pockets are pretty bare. In a belt pouch I find an empty vial with a weird stopper, but that's it. I grumble at Cheshire and Bashe, "Do you guys not have phones?"

Cheshire snickers at me and winks, which I take to mean she got the reference, while Bashe frowns and answers, "Not in the Labyrinth, no. How do you know what a phone is if you're from a world without magic?"

"What? Literally what the fuck? Why would magic be necessary for phones???" *What is this setting what is this setting what is this setting???* "Okay, just so we're on the same page: what is your idea of a phone? Because I'm thinking of a little handheld device that you can use to call people or send them messages across vast distances, or interact as part of a global communications network."

"Right." Bashe nods. "A machine that fits in your pocket that you can use to access the digital realm, more formally known as Mimisk's throne world."

I blink. "Sorry, did you just say that your phones work by literally accessing another layer of reality?"

"Uh, yeah? How else would they work?" Bashe is looking increasingly befuddled and how fucking dare he when he's the one spouting nonsense.

"Okay, you know what? Just gonna shove that one aside and deal with it later." I steal Shane's belt and sheathe the knife in it, then loop it around my waist and get it comfortable.

I scan the figment bodies and find one of them wearing an outfit that looks acceptable and likely to fit. I ditch my shirt-turned-bandage but keep the skirt, then strip the corpse and throw on a loose top (shoulderless and flowy) and some torn leggings. It's not a perfect look by any stretch, but it feels a little better than what I was wearing before and certainly better than walking around shirtless.

Next on the looting agenda: the item I presume to be the dead hound's anchor. Up close I can see that it's a wooden carving meant to resemble a dog, with a spiked collar around its neck and a hunting horn held in its mouth. *Hmm.* I glance over at Cheshire, who's joined me at my side, and ask, "So, am I right in assuming this thing is an anchor and that dog was a homunculus?"

She claps her hands and smiles. "Look at you, clever girl that you are. That creature was called a goblin dog, and they are indeed classic homunculi of the Wild Hunt, with this carving the traditional anchor."

I give Cheshire a shrewd look. "You mentioned before that it's better to manifest you with a purpose-built anchor. This wasn't made for you, but it *does* seem to click with your shapeshifting trick. Think it'll work, wolfie?"

"Only one way to find out," she grins.

I pick up the carving and hold it out in front of me. My last manifestation was rushed, so I'm going to make up for it this time with a bit of extra flair. "I am Maven Alice, the newborn demon of Blood, Gluttony, and Fear. By my will, by my desire, and by the Throne of Shadow itself, I command: let this carving become the anchor that shall give form to my geist that she might serve me well. Let the stuff of dreams become her body, and let her shape that body to our whims. Rise, Cheshire, O geist of mine, and fulfill my every wicked design."

The image I bring to mind is not Cheshire's catgirl form but that moment of crystallized glory when I beheld her as a wolf. The anchor, matching, the carving of a hunting hound. The words, given care and detail to stand out from the base incantation. My will, pulsing out into the world, reaching for the fabric of Pandaemonium—of the Labyrinth—and commanding it to obey.

The carving vanishes from my hand in swirling shadow, and Cheshire vanishes too, reappearing as a great white wolf when the smoke clears. I reach out to trace my fingers over the wolf's fur and she nuzzles my hand, mismatched eyes gleaming. It's a hard thing to measure, but something about her feels different this time, a sense of presence and coiled tension like a predator about to pounce. I find it exciting.

I return to the dead man and consider stealing his gambeson vest.

Pros: armor is armor, armor means less getting stabbed, and it's probably not that heavy.

Cons: still probably a bit heavy, and not my colors.

Eh, okay those are pretty shit cons. Gambeson it is. It takes me an annoying amount of time to get the vest off the corpse and onto me, my arm twinging all the while, but eventually it's done and I feel slightly more protected. The thing is damn heavy on my shoulders though. Well, realistically I know that it's probably not that heavy for most people, but I am a weak frail baby and not suited for physical exertion of any kind.

Still, I'll survive. I look to Bashe. "Okay, I'm ready. Lead the way."

I follow Bashe out of the club and into the night air, wolf!Cheshire padding at my side. The streets are vacant now, all the figments away inside their homes or inside more locations like the one we just left. It's eerie to see a city looking so empty, especially since there aren't any cars here.

Bashe takes a second to orient himself and then takes off at a brisk pace, and I trail behind with Cheshire. I give the wolfie some skritches behind the ears and ask, "So, where are we going, exactly? You mentioned a shrine, and I want details."

The wolf leans into my attentions and responds, "It's the shrine to the city spirit, the local eidolon. Every city has one. They're tied into the city in ways deeper than anything else, and maintaining a symbiotic relationship with one is crucial to the health of the city. Also our best bet to find a good healer, because most priests have a bit of healing ability."

From ahead, Bashe calls back, "If the Myriad are still anything like they were when I left, it'll be one of the kindred that fixes you up. They've got a serpentkin with sacrificial transfusion, last I was there."

I glance at Cheshire. "Mind giving me some exposition on healing? Fucker over there only gave me the barest hints of detail when I asked last time."

The wolf grins, which is creepy, and says, "Sure. There are four kinds of healing magic in Pandaemonium, which we can break into the two categories of classical healing and transfusion. Within classical healing we have preservative healing, which acts fast but can only slow the progression of injuries, not truly mend them; and restorative healing, which *can* mend wounds but acts slow and requires an understanding of what's broken and how to fix it to get much done. The spell keeping you in working order, [Indulgent Vitality], has excellent preservative effects but weak restorative effects, owing to the way it doesn't ask you to have any medical knowledge before casting it."

Hmm. Interesting limitation. "So the person we're going to see, the healer, I'm guessing they're not just a fantasy healer but also an actual doctor of some kind."

"Likely, if they know any restorative healing, but if they just use sacrificial then that might not be the case. Transfusion is *very different* from classical healing: it manipulates life force directly rather than working through a physical medium. Sacrificial transfusion allows you to take your own life essence and pour it into someone else, healing them and harming you. It's much quicker and more effective than classical restoration, but it can very easily be lethal to the caster, especially if you aren't careful or underestimate the wound you're trying to heal."

Okay, I'm vaguely familiar with that trope space. A life for a life, that very old-school equivalent exchange approach to healing magic. "And the last one?"

Cheshire pauses for dramatic effect, and when she speaks again her voice is dripping with excitement. "We call that one *parasitic transfusion*, and I think you'll quite like it. Instead of sacrificing your life essence for someone else, you steal the life essence out of a victim. It's the quickest and most effective way to heal yourself, bar none."

My mouth is watering, but it sounds a little *too good* to be true. "What's the catch?"

Cheshire chuckles, then tells me, "Two catches, actually: the first is that using any kind of parasitic transfusion weakens your ability to take healing from other sources, to the eventual point of becoming immune to the others, even sacrificial; and the second catch is that using parasitic transfusion is addictive and makes you want to use it more."

"I'm not sure those are big enough downsides to dissuade me," I admit. "If I commit to that path I'll be planning to rely on it anyways."

"I thought you might say that. It's something we can look into after we fix your arm and have a chance to examine your spells again."

The rest of the walk goes in pleasant silence, the comfort of petting a big fluffy wolf making up for the continued pain in my arm. At a certain point in the walk, the city *shifts*: I take a step forward and the whole architecture of the city changes, becoming more ornate and weathered, still modern but like one of those very old cities that still shows its history despite modernization.

Interesting. "Is this like, a district thing?"

Bashe is the one to answer. "The city is divided into wards, so yes. Each one reflects a different part of another world."

We reach the shrine itself soon after, the city opening up into a wide open space where all the buildings fall away before a vast temple-like structure of marble and basalt and statues, but the real crown is the massive tree growing out of the temple. The highest branches of the tree came into view as we shifted into this new ward, but up close the great tree is *magnificent*, its leaves a spectrum of colors from the crisp reds and yellows of fall to the fresh greens of spring.

I'm starting to feel exhausted again as we approach the shrine, my arm aching and my head muddled. I thought I was fine after waking up from my brief nap, but turns out that wasn't really a nap and I'm still horribly injured and overexerted.

There are two guards waiting at the entrance to the shrine, and they look at us warily as we approach. They're both jackal-headed like Anubis, and have deep brown skin from what I can see of their arms. They've got nice armor: the main body of it looks like mail and plate, with proper plate greaves and vambraces (plus a helmet), and it's all been painted white. They've each got a spear-and-shield thing going, and they don't point the spears at us as we approach—which seems nice of them—but they clearly have them at the ready.

The one on the left calls out, "What business do you have? The Carnival aren't welcome in this ward, hunter."

Huh? Oh, shit. I look down at the gambeson I stole from Shane and wince. Before I can say anything, though, Bashe is already stepping forward with wide arms and a friendly expression.

"Apologies, friend," the incubus says. "I'm afraid my companion's garb has given the wrong impression. We *fought* the Carnival, just a few hours ago, and she took that bit of armor from one of them since she was lacking. I'll swear by the Weaver that we don't work for Averrich, if that's what convinces you."

There's a brief shiver in the world, and the guards look between each other before nodding. The one on the right says, "Understood. Then allow us to greet you more warmly, and ask in more pleasant terms why you've come to our hallowed hall."

"My companion and I both took injuries fighting reavers, and we've come to request treatment." He pauses, then adds, "And I'd like to speak with Esha, if I may. It's been some time."

They usher us inside, and the rest of it is a blur. There are people inside the shrine, lots of people, though Cheshire points out most of them as figments. We're taken through hallways to a chamber where a serpent-man in a very modern doctor's uniform asks questions that Cheshire fills in for me while I'm laid down on an examination table, and at Cheshire's prompting I focus on the sensation of [Indulgent Vitality] and will it to fade.

The wound in my arm becomes visible again, blood seeping from it, bone showing, pain spiking, and right away the snake doctor starts casting spells and fetching tools. I'm offered painkillers and take them, and then he begins cleaning my wound with some liquid solution and what look like alcohol swabs.

A numbing agent is introduced to my arm, which combined with the painkillers does a lot, and then as soon as he can poke my arm and get no response he starts digging in and picking out bone shards, which I watch with fascinated horror. He mutters that it's a miracle I'm not in worse condition after a blow like that, and I silently thank Cheshire for turning me into a demon.

He talks me through the process of what he's doing, explaining how he's using preservative magic to keep my blood inside my body, restorative magic to regrow bone (using the collected bone shards as raw material), and finally a sacrificial spell to infuse the whole area with life essence and knit it back together. That middle part takes the longest, though I don't know quite how long, and when he's finally ready to cast the final spell it takes only minutes for the flesh of my arm to regrow, skin flowing over it.

I'm made to drink lots of water, which I imagine is to help replenish lost blood, and then I'm taken to a bed while the snake doctor goes off to recover from using the spell ("sunlight and fresh mice," I'm told).

Cheshire is at my side when I drift into exhausted sleep.

INTERLUDE

SHADOW & GLASS III

We spoke again, and again, and again. In no time at all you became the highlight of every week, then every day. I sought you out in the library and you were always there, waiting for me.

You would never tell me how you got in or out of the castle, but you were never caught and slowly I tried to stop worrying so much. It was easier to just focus on our conversations, on reading, and on spending time together.

You had so many questions, and you seemed enthralled by every answer I gave. You would ask about the littlest things, like the taxonomy of local insects, and act enamored with me when I embarrassed myself by going on for hours. You wanted to know everything about my world, and I was only too happy to share. I would point you to the best books for a subject and you would read them, but you would always want to hear what I had to say about it, what I thought of the information contained within the books I was recommending.

No one had ever listened to me with that kind of sincere desire to hear me speak, that level of respect and care and attention. When I was younger and more sociable, it was easy to tell when someone was just humoring my interests for the sake of meaningless political connections, but you . . . you weren't like that.

Even now I'm not sure it was a lie. You found my passions so endearing that you encouraged me to keep sharing even when nothing about the topic could have benefited you. Obscure craft techniques, history, even philosophy and law. Those last two always sparked your interest further, and when it came to philosophy in particular you had your own stories to share.

Our meetings became more frequent, and longer, long enough to grow hungry in the midst of them. It was easy to procure meals from the kitchens, and that became a new topic of fascination for you: you wanted to try everything we had to offer, from roasted pheasant with stewed vegetables to the plum dumplings that were my favorite.

Of course, it would be irresponsible to eat in the library, so we began having conversations in a nearby sitting room that went largely unused. As I grew more comfortable with you, and as I began to worry once more about our conversations being interrupted, I worked up the nerve to suggest that I host our meetings in the tearoom that was part of my personal chambers. You were, of course, delighted at the idea.

And so our conversations continued, and I satisfied your curiosity again and again, but there was one topic that everything always circled back to: magic. You were hungry for it, and I covered the basics as best I could, then the more advanced theory. I told you about the clans and the sorcerer bloodlines, and the affinities that were central to everything.

I avoided speaking of my own affinity, and you could tell. I was evasive, always hastening to mention some historical example or the affinities of neighboring clans or even the classical affinities of Dawnbringer and Bladesinger. But never my own, never referencing myself in those dialogues.

We were having tea when you finally pried it out of me. We were discussing something banal, and while I excitedly droned on you reached for your cup and, distracted watching me speak, accidentally knocked it from its platter. Of course, with time I've begun to suspect that the act was premeditated, a measured attempt to goad me into using my powers. The moment was too perfect, your response too precise.

The teacup tumbled from its perch, porcelain and payload destined for the floor, but my shadow lunged for the object while I sat paralyzed. My magic, acting on instinct and immediate panicked desire to keep you happy, reached out with tendrils of darkness and seized the cup, absorbing spilled drink and carefully bringing the cup back to its place upon the table.

As soon as I registered what had happened, I banished the tendrils back to my shadow, but it was too late; you had seen, and you had that glint in your eye which I had learned by then meant you had a topic in mind and wouldn't cease until you knew everything about it.

"Why do you never talk about your affinities?" you asked me.

I looked away from you, nervous. Rationally, I understood that you could have asked anyone in the castle or beyond about the strange princess and her strange magic. There was a part of me that was warmed at your wanting to hear the story from me before any of them. But still. Still I hated the idea of telling you. I didn't want to ruin . . . whatever this was.

"Do you feel ashamed?" you continued when I didn't answer. "You shouldn't, if you do. You have an amazing power, Reska, and I've only seen the barest hint of what you're capable of. What's to hide?"

I grimaced, still not meeting your gaze. "Everything. It . . . it's not natural. It shouldn't exist. I don't want to have this power."

"Why?" you pressed me. "Who taught you to hate your magic?"

I stared down at the floor, silent, dreading the conversation to follow. Finally I murmured, "You really aren't going to let this one go, are you?" I looked back up in time to catch you shaking your head.

"Not a chance. This means too much to me to let it lie."

I sighed and slumped in my seat. "Okay. I . . . I have three affinities: Shadow, Starlight, and Blood. The one you just saw is Shadow, and it's wrong. Shadow magic shouldn't exist, Homura. The way it reached out just then, that wasn't conscious, that wasn't me, that was an affinity acting on its own. That's not supposed to happen outside of children. It's aberrant."

You smirked. "I thought it was pretty cute. It saved a bit of cleaning, and brought my cup back all nice and whole. I should thank your Shadow."

I gritted my teeth. You weren't getting it. You didn't have the context for this, didn't have the history for it. "Homura, when I say this magic shouldn't exist, I mean it. Humans can't use this magic, not normally. No one else alive has an affinity for Shadow, because anyone who tries to build that affinity dies. But I was born with it, in a family where most are born with Sunlight."

You raised an eyebrow. "That seems more impressive than ostracizing. What's the catch?"

"Shadow magic is . . . it's the magic of the Abyss. Of the Leviathans. This magic is evil, and dangerous, and hideous. Nothing good and true can come from the Abyss."

You watched me with those discerning dark eyes, taking in every detail of my body language and facial expressions. After a moment of contemplation you reached out and took one of my hands in yours. "These are things you've heard from others, aren't they? Stories you've been told. Whispers and rumors. But how does your magic feel to you? Does it feel evil? Does it feel hideous?"

For all the hesitation and doubt and self-loathing that haunted me, I couldn't lie to you. I admitted, "No. It feels . . . natural. Like a second skin, or a second pair of limbs. It's easier to cast with than my other affinities, more responsive, quicker, stronger . . . and there's a comfort to it. I feel safe, in the dark. But . . . it gets lonely." I gently extricated my hand and said, "I want to show you something."

You nodded and let me go. "Anything you like."

I rose from my chair and took a deep breath, incredibly anxious and yet . . . surprisingly excited. I'd never shown this to anyone before, for all the time I'd spent getting it right. It had always been mine alone, and my heart ached to think that finally, finally, I could share it with someone who might appreciate it.

"This is my second affinity: Starlight." I began calling magic to me, drawing on Shadow and Starlight and bringing them together. The room darkened, that part of my magic responding before the spell was even partially formed.

In the growing dark I spoke my incantation, lovingly crafted over a period of years, a full decade. "The night sky stretches like an endless sea of Shadow, deep and all-encompassing. From horizon to horizon, the drawing dark heralds the death of day. This darkness is vast, greater than all the worlds in the Dreaming Sea. This darkness is the Abyss, where Leviathans once held sway, and though the old gods are dead their hunger lives on, swallowing the light with every nightfall."

The dark thickened, shadows swirling and intensifying. My shadows crept up the walls to snuff every sunstone in sight, sweeping across the room like the death of day. Then, there was only darkness, deep and absolute.

"But though the night is full of horrors, and though the hunger of dead gods steals the sun, hope is not lost. For within the dark shine points of light that cannot be consumed: the stars, numberless and gleaming, to keep us safe till morning comes. Each star, the soul of a Titan, bound by the Leviathans but never broken. For even in the deepest darkness, even in the lowest depths, the light always endures."

And within the dark, a thousand stars blazed to life. A thousand points of light, shining bright amidst the void, and lines of gleaming silver starlight connecting them. The darkened room became the night sky, a star chart projected onto the walls and ceiling and floor. A map of constellations, made from countless hours spent poring over records and stargazing from my balcony.

You breathed out in awe at my creation, and I let a bit of pride trickle in. It was my great work, the one good thing I'd built with the whole of my existence, and I finally had someone to show it to.

"It gets lonely," I told you, "being in the dark. Reaching for the sun and knowing you'll never hold it in your hands. But the sun isn't the only source of light. My father told me that story, that I just told you. And I'll never call the sun like he can, but I can pluck the stars from the sky and cast them in my orbit. And . . . it helps. I don't feel so alone."

You reached out to touch a constellation, marveling at it, then turned back to me. "This is incredible, Reska. You are incredible. This is a work of art that I could never hope to create."

I blushed, still not used to compliments despite your willingness to use them on me. I pointed at the constellation you had touched and told you, "That one's the Sleeping Rabbit. The one just above it is the Silver Loom, and next to that is the Crooked Candle."

You gave me a shrewd look. "Can you name every single one of these constellations?"

My blush deepened, but I admitted, "Yes. I, um . . . I spent a lot of time memorizing them. There's something about it that just . . . brings me comfort. They're beautiful. They make the night sky beautiful. And . . ." I cringed at what I was about to say, but committed to it, ". . . I think there's something poetic about how you can only see them at night. The stars are beautiful, but they're made beautiful by the dark surrounding them."

You moved closer to me and reached out a hand to brush a strand of hair out of my face. "You're beautiful, too," you murmured to me. "And I think the world is more beautiful for having you in it, just like the night sky and those stars."

Your flirting flustered me so much that I lost concentration on the spell. The shining stars flickered and faded and the smothering darkness retreated to my shadow. Your gaze held me, pinned me, and my heart beat faster than I think it ever had before. In a panic, not sure how to deal with feelings that were so alien to me, I blurted, "Three! I have three affinities!"

You chuckled, but returned to your seat and released me from that piercing gaze. "You wanna tell me about your third, then?"

I sat down as well, face definitely red, and took a sip of tea to calm my nerves. "My third affinity is Blood. Traditionally, Blood has been associated with life and death, bonds, conflict, and sacrifice. It is also one of the three affinities used by the Lidless Eye, the loremasters who record all information about the nature of magic."

You tilted your head, that curious look on your face. "Interesting. But that doesn't tell me what it means to *you*, Reska. Aren't these supposed to be personal in some way?"

I winced, caught out. "Well, yes. It's just . . . it's not that interesting a story, not compared to the last."

You tapped your chin, contemplative. "Let's see if I can puzzle it out, then, yes? You were born with an affinity for Shadow, and you've been made a pariah because of it. You tried to develop Sunlight and failed, so you seized on the light of the stars instead. So what's Blood have to offer?" You snapped your fingers and grinned. "Got it: healing magic. You wanted to be a healer, like your bloodline is known for, right?"

I slowly nodded. "I did. I . . . I wanted to prove that I could put some good into the world. That I could heal, not just harm." I stared at my injured hand, still not yet fully recovered, and flexed unsteady fingers. "I was wrong. My Blood is pain, sacrifice, and self-destruction. It's the very quintessence of harm."

Again your eyes took in everything. It always fascinated me, the way you could flip between careful observation and animated interest with such speed. When you spoke again, it seemed on the surface like a complete topic change, but I could read the implicit point in your line of questioning.

You asked, "Have you ever felt that awful energy build and build and build, filling you up till you feel like bursting, till you'd do anything to make it go away? Have you ever wanted to lash out at the world so fucking badly, like it's a fire burning in your veins, so you turned that inward rather than risking hurting someone else?" The last question was gentle, soft, caring. "Have you ever just needed the release?"

I felt mortified. I felt seen. I felt like any moment that look of sympathy would turn to disgust. Hesitantly, fearfully, I whispered, "Yes."

You slid your jacket from your shoulders and showed your arms to me, and I saw the scattered, patternless mess of scar tissue adorning both. Dozens of scars: thin and thick, pale and pink, long and slight. "Yeah," you said, with a quiet altogether unlike you. "Me too."

"You . . . you've . . . ?" I was stunned.

"I know what it's like, to feel something so intensely that all you can do is blot it out with pain. I've been there. I'm still there." You leaned in closer, capturing me with those beautiful dark eyes, completely serious. "You are not alone."

Tears started to fall from my eyes, unbidden and unwanted. I felt ashamed of my emotions, but more than that I felt so very grateful that I had met you. It was like a flood, all the feelings I'd been burying now bursting up.

You rose from your seat and came next to mine, knelt beside me. You put your arms around me and held me tight, hugged me like I hadn't been hugged in years and years. "You're not alone anymore."

I cried harder. I finally stopped holding back, and the tears came so easily. I hugged you back, and my self-control fell away entirely as I blubbered, "It's not fair. Wh-why are you so nice to me? I don't deserve it. I don't deserve you."

"Shhh. It's okay. It's okay. You deserve the world, Reska. You deserve so much better than you have. But I'm here for you now. You're not alone." You rubbed my shoulder gently, comfortingly.

I cried, and you comforted me, and the flood of emotions was overwhelming and horrible, but as I wiped the last tear away I felt lightened, almost cleansed. I smiled at you. "Thank you, Homura. For everything. I . . . I want to repay the deep favor that your presence has been to me. I want to help you develop your first affinity."

You smiled back at me. "I think I know what I want it to be, now, thanks to you. Reska . . . teach me your affinity for Blood."

And so I would.

XIII

I wake up, and once more I have to untangle my Reska memories from my Alice memories.

Associations and connections form automatically as I parse each aspect of the dream and acknowledge it as a dream, a vision, a separate set of memories; not *my* experience. I am not Reska, and I'm not the one being flirted at by Homura, but it strikes a chord with me nonetheless, and it pulls my mind to Cheshire and her manipulations.

I know, better than I would have a mere week ago, how it feels to meet someone who seems hand-crafted just for you. I know it has to be a lie.

My mind sifts through possibilities and commonalities, dissecting the dream. There's a part of me that feels rushed, panicked, like I have to understand it *now* or lose it forever, but just like last time I find that none of the details of my dream are fading. In fact, the details of the *first* dream are still clearer and crisper than some of my real memories.

So I have information, and I can catalog that information as something distinct from my experiences in the Labyrinth, and it is *fascinating* to examine the similarities and differences. I have the vague sense that I am in a bed right now, beneath lumpy blankets, and I remember being brought to a shrine and a doctor, but I willfully ignore my physical sensations to immerse myself within the world of my dreams.

It happened again. The visions of Reska and Homura, they didn't stop with the meeting. Will this happen every time I sleep? Is the length of the dream determined by how long I sleep, or some other factor?

Are these dreams of something that will happen? Something that has happened? Or something that is happening?

And why am I receiving these dreams? These are too crisp, too structured. There is a sense of purpose here. I thought it might be a warning about Cheshire, but I received that warning and ignored it. I took Cheshire's hand. I said yes.

I run through the events of the dream once more: Reska and Homura growing closer, discussing magic, discussing *Reska's* magic, showing Shadow and Starlight and Blood. I seize on that last item, on Reska's affinities. I feel like I can see puzzle pieces clicking into place, though the complete image eludes me.

In the first dream, Reska narrated, "They called me a monster from old myths, a demon wearing human skin." But demons aren't mythical, not to Bashe, not to the reavers. And in the second dream, she said, "Humans can't use this magic, not normally. No one else alive has an affinity for Shadow, because anyone who tries to build that affinity dies." But there's a whole Throne of Shadow, with demons and imps and diabolists tapping into it. Those first two may be inhuman, but they weren't always, and diabolists are definitely human. So there's desync.

The Leviathans, the Abyss, those are things I've heard from my companions. Bashe told me at length how dangerous Abyssal magic is, but he also revealed how accessible *it is. I could borrow some when I was still just an unaligned human. It's not some forbidden, impossible, mythical form of magic. Not to us. But it is to Reska's people.*

I questioned before why Reska called them affinities and Cheshire called them Truths, but maybe that difference is substantive, not just superficial. Maybe Reska really is using a completely different system of magic. If her relationship with Shadow is so different, if the Throne of Shadow doesn't exist, then maybe she exists in a time before it was made . . . or after it was destroyed. I can't know for certain either way.

I need to know more about the setting as it is now before I can determine how Reska's setting relates. For all I know, she could exist in some obscure corner of Pandaemonium where all the rules are not quite the same.

That last affinity is interesting, though, for wildly different reasons. Reska and I both have a connection to Blood, and now my dream-self, Homura, is developing an affinity for Blood of her own. Is Homura an astral projection, and taking on Blood because I've chosen to? Does she predate me, and my choice is an echo of her choice, of Reska's choice? Does she exist after me, and her choice is an echo of my choice?

There must be something significant about this alignment. I didn't choose Blood because of Reska, though I did think of her when I made the choice. If Blood can represent bonds, then is there something meaningful in how all three of us (or perhaps two of us, if Homura is not substantively different from this version of me) made Blood a part of us?

If Homura is me, then why does she need an affinity if she already has Truths? Is that a lie to manipulate Reska? Has she lost her magic?

It makes me uneasy. Again, I wonder: why am I having these dreams? What am I meant to take away from them? How is the information contained within meant to recontextualize the information I already know?

In the end I'm left with more questions than answers, and so at last I allow myself to open my eyes and rise from my rest.

I'm in a room with cream-colored walls and a bed that is comfier than I'm used to for a hospital bed, not that I've been in many. There's a chair in one corner, a little table with a flower vase on it, and a fairly typical-looking medical cabinet. Bashekehi is leaning against the wall next to the door, watching me.

As I sit up I realize that my blankets aren't lumpy, there's just a cat lounging atop my legs. Predictably, the cat has white fur and mismatched eyes. I give the kitty some ear scritches and murmur, "Good morning, Cheshire. Morning, Bashe. How long was I out this time?"

From my lap, the cat answers, "A healthy night's rest, but no longer. We're at what passes for dawn in the Labyrinth."

"Well, that's good. I'm hoping to make this a very productive day after the *disaster* of yesterday." I glare at Bashe, still largely blaming him for how that went.

Bashe is immune to my glare, of course. He's giving me a long, measured look, and it's honestly kind of annoying me.

"Hey, incubus: pipe up. You don't get to play the silent game after that fiasco. You led us right into a trap, then tried to bail. What the fuck is up with that?"

Bashekehi stares me down, not rising to the bait. After a few more moments of him getting on my nerves he finally speaks up. "Why'd you kill that guy?"

What? "What? Why does that matter? Why do you care? Also, again, circling back to my point: *you fucked up.* That place was a terrible feeding spot."

The incubus shrugs. "So it was. Things have changed." His gaze is hard, unrelenting. "But you didn't have to kill that man."

I scoff, disbelieving. "What is this? What is this moralizing bullshit? He was trying to kill me, Bashe, so I killed him back. That's how the game is played."

"It's not a game," he snaps at me. *Shit, is he actually angry about this? What the fuck?* "I need you to understand that *none of this* is a game. I have no love lost for Averrich's brigands, but once upon a time there were *rules* in this city; a code of conduct."

I fire back, "Are you even listening? Were you not there? He tried to *kill me*! I could have died there. I didn't have a choice." *I didn't have a choice. I'm not a murderer. It was just self-defense.*

"There's always a choice. Who threw the first punch? Who escalated a tense conversation into open violence? That situation was *salvageable*, Alice, and you sank our chances."

"Fucking hells," I marvel, "you actually are moralizing at me. You dumb shit." I start laughing. "What's the point of this? Really, what's the point? You've said you don't care about the people involved, so it can't be about *who* I killed, it's about the fact that I killed at all, right? Does that surprise you? Does it surprise you to learn that a *demon* is capable of killing someone?"

He narrows his eyes at me. "I know you're not as cavalier about this as you're pretending to be. I saw you staring into that dead man's eyes. There's still a human in you, and people don't just walk away from that kind of violence unaffected."

"So what?" I hiss. "Is this the part where you give a long-winded speech?" I switch tone and start mocking him. "'Oh Alice, I know we've had our differences, but I truly believe that there's still good in your heart! I'm convinced that you're better than this, despite all evidence to the contrary!' Fat fucking chance."

He rubs his face and sighs. "Call me delusional if you like, but yeah, I do think there's some good in you. Not a lot, mind, but a little. An ember. You're a selfish, manipulative, violent piece of shit, but you're not a *monster*. Not yet, at least."

The retort I'm about to make is silenced by Cheshire stirring from her place on my lap. She hops off the bed and shifts back into her catgirl form, arms crossed.

Bashe turns a burning look on her. "Got something to say, changeling?" *Changeling, changeling . . . didn't I hear that before, in the club? What does that mean in this world?*

Cheshire's voice is calm and cold as she asks, "Son of Amin Dara, who do you blame most for the death of your father?"

Bashe's expression immediately cycles from vicious to stunned to furious. "You little—"

"Do you blame the mobster who slit his throat to send you a message?" Cheshire interrupts. "Or do you blame yourself, the prodigal son who could never live up to his father's moral standard? What part of it do you feel most guilty about, Bairam? The gambling debts you racked up in your obsessive attempts to win a game rigged in the house's favor? The devil's bargain you made with an incubus to try and cheat the casino's system?" Cheshire pauses, and then, before Bashe can cut in, says, "*Getting caught?*"

Holy shit. So that's his backstory? He got in deep with the mob, turned to an imp for help, and ended up getting his dad killed? How the fuck does Cheshire know that?

Bashe's fury turns cold. "Don't think you can manipulate me, witch-beast. I'm nothing like your demon." *Rude,* I mutter to myself internally.

Cheshire strolls up to the incubus and pokes him in the chest. "Don't use my demon as a proxy for your own failings."

He slaps her hand away and says coldly, "I'm just trying to do some good. I know that concept is alien to your kind."

"You're not some righteous martyr," the catgirl sneers, "you're just a broken man stuck in all the worst moments of your life. No, it's worse: you're a fiend pretending to be a man, lying even to yourself. You think your precious rules make you different from all the other imps with hearts of Indulgence, but it's just a mask. That's all it will ever be, Bashekehi: a *mask*. A lie. And one day, I promise you, that mask will shatter."

"You're wrong," the incubus says with the conviction of fact. "These rules make me better. They help me *be* better. I can still do good with this life of mine." He hesitates, and I wonder if Cheshire's words have hit more deeply than he's letting on. "I can still balance the scales, such as they are."

Cheshire smirks. "Bashekehi the Ever-Gleaming will never find redemption for the sins of Bairam Dara. Drown in regret all you like, but know that nothing you do will change the score."

Bashe glares daggers and opens his mouth to speak again, but I speak first. "You said I'm not a monster, Bashe. Do you really believe that?" I lower my legs to the floor and stand up, wobbling a little and letting Cheshire help steady me.

The incubus turns from Cheshire and meets my gaze. "I've met my share of monsters. You're standing right next to one, in fact. But you're not a monster, not yet."

I tilt my head. "And . . . when you told me that the path of a demon involves killing thousands, and I still chose to walk it . . . that didn't make you think that I might be a monster?"

He laughs, clipped and dark. "No, it made me think you're like one of those little kids bragging on the playground about how good at *killing* they'd be if they were the hero of their favorite book or show, too immature to understand that there is nothing 'cool' or 'badass' about the taking of a life. You are a child, Alice, playing at being a villain but not *understanding* what that entails."

I feel a flash of white-hot rage at being talked down to like this, and I dig my nails into my palms to keep control of myself, to keep myself from lashing out without thinking and saying something he can use against me. I run through responses in my mind, looking for anything that doesn't make me sound as childish as he's accusing me of being. *I'm not a child. You underestimate my resolve. It's not like that. You have no idea what I'm capable of. You're wrong.*

They all ring hollow, because on some level I think he might be right. Hells, I couldn't even bring myself to bite a girl without first interrogating the philosophy of her existence and attaining her explicit and very enthusiastic consent.

A wash of cold shame and loathing dulls the heat of my anger. Is he right? Am I committing to a path I'm not prepared to walk?

Deep down, you're still just a scared little girl.

I exhale the rage from my lungs and let exhaustion filter onto my face. "Maybe I don't understand. But I will. I have to. Because I have no other choice."

He shakes his head. "There's always a choice."

"You've said your piece," Cheshire says with a roll of her eyes. "Now get going. You *are* leaving, aren't you?"

Bashe curls his lip at her, but says, "I am. And Weaver willing, this will be the last I see of either of you."

"What a heartwarming sendoff," I mutter. "Don't forget to write."

The imp turns to leave, and as he goes he delivers a final warning. "Just remember, Maven Alice: there's still an ember of good in you. And I would hate to see what you become when that ember flickers out."

I wait for the sound of his footsteps—hoofsteps?—to fade before turning to Cheshire and immediately asking, "Hey, what the fuck is a changeling in this setting?"

She seems more amused than annoyed by the question, which is a relief. "I admire that curious spirit of yours. Allow me to pose a question of my own, and then I'll answer yours. What do you think of, when you hear 'changeling'?"

I tap my chin and take the question seriously. "Well, my view is a bit biased here, but I'm used to thinking of changelings in terms of autistic or otherwise neurodivergent kids getting demonized for being different. Your kid's not like the other kids and you're an illiterate peasant, so you say they were replaced by a faerie or a devil and beat the sin out of them."

Cheshire nods. "There are similar points of contention surrounding changelings in this world—or rather, the worlds beyond this prison of glass and dreams." The catgirl hums, then sits down on the bed and pats the sheets for me to join her, which I do. "This is, in fact, one of the things I was arguing with Bashekehi about. He believes, as many do, that changelings are inhuman *things* handcrafted by the Demiurge to replace a human child, while others argue that changelings are born as ordinary children and marked by the Demiurge in early childhood. Either way, it is known that changelings have visual differences from other children, such as physical deformity or discolored hair and eyes."

I note her white hair and those vibrant yellow-and-blue heterochromatic eyes, which have carried into every transformation, and I wonder if the cat ears are also part of her changeling nature, or, since they don't stay when she shifts, if they're some affectation of her form as a geist.

Cheshire picks her words carefully, staring off into the distance rather than holding my gaze. "They are also different in behavior, manifesting from a young age and worsening over time. Those who fear changelings would say that this is a sign of their inhumanity, and they are often said to be incapable of empathy and other essential social traits. Those changelings that do manage to fit in and adapt, it is claimed, are just very clever liars."

So far, so similar. Handpicked to be relatable to my experiences, and I doubt that's any kind of coincidence.

"And then, of course, there is what gives weight to many people's fear of changelings: their magic. At a certain point in every changeling's life, they will discover the Gift of Change: a power granted to them by the Demiurge which does not obey the rules of Throne magic. It's different for every changeling: some can take the shape of humans they've seen, some can take the shape of animals—but not magical beasts like night horrors—and some can change their whole body but not individual parts, while others can change individual parts but never the whole body." Cheshire grins and becomes a cat once more, then returns to her catgirl form. "You can see what I was given."

"You said it differs from Throne magic," I immediately focus on. "How so?"

"The change doesn't require mana, for one, and it's not really a *spell* like you've been dealing with so far. There's no bracketed title to announce and no spell matrix that springs to mind. It's all instinct and will."

"Fascinating," I murmur. "He also called you a 'witch-beast.' Is that derogatory, or an actual descriptor?"

Cheshire wiggles a hand in a noncommittal gesture. "Somewhere in between, really. There are a few *vanishingly rare* cases of someone having a power or ability that is clearly magical but just as clearly *isn't* Throne magic, and the people who have those abilities are called 'witches.' Those looking to dehumanize witches—particularly changelings—will call them witch-*beasts* instead." She shrugs. "I don't find it that offensive, really; I quite *like* being a beast."

I chew over everything she's told me, a pressing question looming in my mind. A lie has been exposed, or maybe revealed, but I need to gather just a bit more data before interrogating her about it. "You said there was 'contention' about whether changelings are born or made; replaced or transmuted. Which is it, in your expert opinion?"

The changeling muses, "I'm not sure which it is. I'm not sure the distinction means anything, to the Demiurge. I think, either way, that the changeling was chosen before it was even conceived, and so the details are irrelevant."

"Mm. Then . . . were you lying, when you said you were created? When you said you were made for me, and that you were made because of Katoptris dragging me into the Labyrinth?" I try to keep my voice curious and interested rather than sharp and accusatory.

Cheshire smiles, the expression softer and subtler than her usual wide-mouthed grin. "Not entirely. I wasn't lying when I said that I was made for you . . . but I wasn't made *recently*, and I wasn't born knowing everything about you. I wasn't born a geist, either, since you were probably wondering about that."

"I was, actually," I admit. "So . . . how exactly does that work? How were you made for me, but didn't even know about me at first?"

The geist chuckles. "Nyarlathotep is scary good at playing the long game. I had a childhood, though hardly a normal one, and then I learned that I was a changeling, and then that I had powers, and then that I enjoyed *using* my powers. And then . . . she found me. She found me, bleeding out, in the winter snow. I'd come to enjoy my powers too much, and I had become reckless in my shifting and my play. So she found me there, bleeding out in the form of a cat, and she offered"—Cheshire licks her teeth, expression growing sardonic—"a *generous gift*: the gift of nine lives."

I couldn't stop the snort that came out of me at that. "Really? Cat gets nine lives? Wait, do you guys even have that legend here?"

"We *don't*," Cheshire laughs, "or at least the world I was from didn't, and it really threw me for a loop when I first learned about that. Nyarlathotep is *terribly fond* of making references only she will actually get. But, yes, she offered nine lives to a dying cat, and all she asked in return was that, when my last life ran out, I would come and serve her as a geist. I said yes."

"And then you died."

"And then I died," she agrees. "Nine times, in nine different ways, taking nine reckless risks that were wholly unnecessary but very, *very* fun." Her lips twitch and she adds, "I didn't even last nine years. Real waste of symbolism, don't you think?"

"Truly the greatest loss," I snark back. "What happened next?"

"I kept my word, though it wasn't like I had a choice in the matter. She came to me again, as I lay dying in a different place by different means, and she told me that it was time to become a geist. And then she . . . reshaped me." Cheshire shivers at the recollection, gaze going far-off and unfocused. "Do you know what it's like, to be sculpted in an artisan's hands? I do. She put me under the knife and she cut until I was the pinnacle of her art. She snipped at dead growth like a horticulturist tending her garden. She grafted secrets and knowings to my raw and open soul, and she pressed her fingers into my mind until it gave like wet clay and could be molded into the perfect shape. The perfect Cheshire." The changeling leans against my arm and turns her gaze up at me, frenzied light now burning in her eyes, blissful smile fixed to her lips. "She made me perfect *for you*. The perfect Cheshire to your perfect Alice. It's what I was born for. It's what I died for. It's what I was remade for. It was all for you."

That is . . . wow. Uh. Wow. I can't help but shiver as my mind fills with vivid, tantalizing, horrifying imagery. To be destroyed like that . . . to be created like that . . . and all for me. Somehow, that's actually *more* concerning than the idea that Cheshire was created *ex nihilo* to seduce me. The Demiurge picked a thinking, feeling woman and took a scalpel to her identity until she fit the role of my ideal partner.

The cosmic toymaker made a toy just for me. I'm hit by immediate conflicting waves of excitement and revulsion. How the fuck do you respond to that? How can I possibly interact with Cheshire knowing that Nyarlathotep did *that* to her, and all for my benefit?

If it was *for your benefit, which it very likely wasn't. Nothing about this Demiurge seems benevolent. If Cheshire is telling the truth about her rebirth—and for all that I'm suspicious of her in general, that story felt too* raw *to be entirely a work of fiction—it still doesn't mean we can trust Cheshire. I refuse to believe that Nyarlathotep would grant us a handcrafted girlfriend out of purely altruistic motives.*

Yeah. You're probably right. But, still . . . how do we deal with this, if any of it is real? I . . . I don't know what to do.

Then we focus on what we do know, and on what we can do, and that means our next steps are clear: getting out of this shrine, getting an outfit that boosts our magic, and growing our power until we're ready to take on the Beast of Lamentation and Euphoria.

I look down at the impossible creature still smiling up at me, this radiantly horrifying vision of perfection. I struggle for words and find my thoughts too scrambled from Cheshire's revelations. Even if only a fraction of her story is true, it's still utterly game-changing for me.

When I finally manage to speak, it's only to say: "I don't know how to respond to that. If you're not lying, then . . . that's horrifying. That's terrifying."

Cheshire tilts her head. "Are you terrified of being loved, Maven Alice?" I immediately hiss at her and she laughs. "You really are such a delightful creature. Don't worry, Alice, we'll save *that* discussion for another time."

"Or never," I mutter.

Cheshire ignores me and rises off the bed, then takes my hand. "For now, you should de-manifest me: I'll be more useful on invisible reconnaissance than bodyguard duty, at least until we run into trouble again. It's also good practice for doing it when you need to."

I push off the bed and ask, "Alright, how?"

"Just focus on my form and will me to return to your shadow. It's as easy as picking up something you've dropped."

I take a few breaths, search for that strange sense of physicality in Cheshire's shape, and reach out with my will. I touch *something*, and pull, and then Cheshire is melting into shadow and the wood carving appears in my hand.

I quickly pocket the carving in a belt pouch and ask, "Cheshire?"

I hear her voice whisper behind my left ear, "I'm with you. Shall we go shopping?"

"I *do* need some new digs. Just have to find our way out of here and off to whatever passes for a mall."

I leave the bedroom I was in and take a look around the hall outside, but before I can gather my bearings there's a man in plain robes waving at me and saying, "Ah, you're awake! Excellent, simply excellent. Please, if you would, come with me: the priestess would like very much to see you."

Ah. So . . . detour first, then shopping.

I follow the messenger deeper into the shrine.

XIV

Let's say that there are three parts to every game: a set of goals, a set of rules, and a medium of interaction. If you're willing to employ a bit of creativity, you can apply that definition to just about every form of socialization: when you speak with another human being, you have something you want out of the exchange, you have a set of rules governing your behavior, and you have the conversation itself as a medium of interaction.

So by this (admittedly twisted) logic, we can consider a conversation to be a game, and that means that it can be approached like a game.

I have a set of goals: I want to survive this conversation, I want to maintain this location as a safe haven, and I want to accrue social capital with these people in case I need their goodwill later. In simpler terms, I need to make a good impression.

To win the game and achieve my goals, I need to understand the rules, and ideally I need to understand my opponent. This would be easier if I could tap Cheshire for information, but I'm not sure how to get her attention without alerting the man in plain robes who is leisurely leading me through the halls of this shrine.

Cheshire? Cheshire, any chance you can read my thoughts? It would be hella pog if you could, and if you answer in the affirmative I'll give you, I don't know, my undying fealty to your sinister master plan? No? Limited-time offer to obtain a forever-minion? Hello? Nothing?

Nothing. No whisper in my ear; no brush against my thoughts. Either she can't hear me, or she's pretending she can't hear me to avoid showing her hand. Either way, it looks like I'm on my own.

I'm grateful for the slow pace of the person (or not-person) that I'm following, and I keep my own pace as slow as possible to give myself more time to think. I ignore the sights and sounds around me, careful not to let the architecture and the inhabitants of this shrine distract me. I retreat inward, letting my body move on autopilot, and begin scheming a strategy to win this next game.

Let's establish a greater goal of making a positive impression on this group—the Myriad, I think Bashe called them—and break that down into the sub-goals of "convince the priestess that I am likable and trustworthy" and "convince the priestess that I am worth healing and do not pose a danger to her community."

So, how do we do that? What kind of personality would appeal to this priestess, and to the greater organization she belongs to? What do I know about these people?

I string together bits and pieces of what I've been told over the course of my time in the Labyrinth. The "reavers" in the club, they worked for an elf—a fae—and I learned from Bashe that the fae are divided between Summer and Winter, with Summer being stories of a dead world and the riders of the Wild Hunt. In my mindscape, Cheshire mentioned "retainers" and "invokers," and I've heard that latter term from Bashe and Eirdryd both. If a diabolist is an invoker aligned with Shadow, then maybe a reaver is an invoker aligned with Summer? I know reavers can't be scions, because that name didn't come up in Bashe's Dreamweaver-verified list, and my gut says they're not retainers.

In her example of retainers and invokers, Cheshire listed "imps and diabolists" and "kindred and priests." She never explicitly linked that latter grouping to Spirit, but I think it's a safe bet; I could eliminate Thrones until only Spirit's left, but the kicker is in that first name, "kindred." It's a word that means family, kinship, like of kind, and that fits perfectly with the notion of Spirit as community.

So we have a kindred doctor and a shrine priestess, and I'm pretty sure I remember it being mentioned that this is a shrine to an *eidolon,* which are like Spirit's take on geists. That seems like more than enough evidence to conclude that the Myriad are Spirit-aligned like the King's Carnival are Summer-aligned.

Spirit's meaning comes from the collective, and its adherents find significance in tradition, community, and virtue. Speaking less generally, this particular group of adherents chose to heal me at cost to themselves, asking nothing in return, simply because I needed the help. They've been nothing but polite, nice, and cordial.

I may not know the specifics of what this culture values, but they seem firmly prosocial, and I can work with that. Assuming their benevolence is not an act, all I have to do is construct a persona that is appealing to the average empathetic human. I can do that. I've done that.

We should keep in mind that our very existence might be anathema to the Myriad, if they are indeed aligned with the Throne of Spirit.

They don't necessarily know I'm a demon, though they might have ways of detecting that.

They also might have been warned *by Bashekehi. He went to speak with someone named "Esha," remember? I give it decent odds that Esha is the priestess we're being taken to. We should plan for the worst outcome.*

Agreed.

And so it is time to don a new mask.

I regret that I was unable to make a proper face for Bashekehi, and to a certain extent Eirdryd, but the conditions of my first day in this world were not at all conducive to careful persona-building. Now I have a chance to do it right, and I won't squander this opportunity.

There is a method to mask-making, a set of tendencies and habits that produce best results: we build from what is real, from what is existent, and from what is natural or close to natural. An effective mask is built from a core of unalloyed truth, and then decorated with creative interpretation. This process is usually much more intuitive and less structured and pre-planned, but I'm making a special effort given the stakes at hand.

To my amusement, Pandaemonium has actually handed me a new tool with which to carve my false face: the trinity of Truths. The system is compelling, and so I eagerly incorporate it into my process.

Here's a simple truth from which we might build a Truth: people like it when you ask them about themselves. That's a good bit of dating advice, but it also applies to basically any social interaction. People like getting a chance to talk about themselves, and they really like it when it seems like you have a sincere interest in the things that they value and consider part of their identity. If someone happens to have some strongly held beliefs, they're going to like it when you display earnest, open curiosity about those beliefs.

I shape the eyes of the mask, what some call the windows to the soul, and I fill those eyes with my first Truth: Curiosity. I have a desire to understand and a willingness to learn. My eyes shine bright with a youthful sense of spirit and curious interest. This world is full of so much to learn, and I want to learn all of it. I'm willing to learn it all, if you'll share it with me.

I am open to new ideas. I am receptive to information received. This curiosity is neither cold nor clinical, no rote gathering of data. This curiosity is warm, earnest, and that of a friend. I want to know. I care to know. These are my eyes, wide-open and glittering.

Gratitude is another potent tool, and I will make it my second Truth. Gratitude is expected when services are rendered, and I have been done a great service. Gratitude is appreciated whether earned or unearned, and I want to be appreciated. Even those who push off gratitude out of insecurity or discomfort will still be warmed by it deep inside. And by the principle of reciprocation, those who are shown gratitude will be inclined to return that positivity in future interactions.

I shape the mouth of the mask, a key vector for the presentation of emotions. I feel gratitude for your kindness, and so I show you a warm and earnest smile. My lips move in thanks, my cheeks lifted by joy and grace. I am indebted to you for your acts of charity. Thank you. *Thank you.* I mouth the words, practicing them, tasting them.

I'm broken from my reverie by a polite cough from the man in plain robes. "Right through here, miss. The priestess is waiting by the well."

Gah. I'm not done. I keep the grateful smile on my face, curiosity in my eyes, and say, "Ah, thank you so much. Would it be alright if I took a moment to compose myself? I'm rather nervous about this." The words sound honest as they leave my lips, but there's always room for improvement; more emotion, more control, more fine-tuning. I repeat the lines in my head, simulating different points of inflection and emphasis.

"Of course, take as much time as you need." He returns my smile, gives a little half-bow, and walks off, leaving me by an arched door.

Okay. Play the game, follow the rules. One more Truth. One more piece to the mask. Remember: core of truth, garnish with creativity.

For my last Truth, I repurpose Bashekehi's observations from our conversation just a few minutes ago: I killed a man, and I don't know how to feel about that. I killed a reaver, an agent of the fae, and it was in self-defense ... but I still killed a man, and that's not nothing; that can't be nothing. I am afraid of what that might mean.

I take that Fear and pour it into my mask, allowing the corners of my mouth to twitch with nervous anxiety, my smile not wholly warm and sweet. This world is strange and new, and though I knew of magic in the abstract back home I had never been confronted with it in such blunt and violent ways. There are dangerous brigands here, and I fear for my life. There are brigands, and I killed one of them, and that haunts me in ways I can't begin to describe. There is blood on my hands, and who will wash it out?

My mask is more than just a face; my mask is my body, my motion, all the way to the tips of my fingers. My hands shake at the memory of taking a life, because who wouldn't be horrified by such an act? I'm not a killer—I can't be a killer—but I've killed, and I wish I hadn't.

It's only a little white lie. Barely a lie at all.

My name is Maven Alice, and these are my Truths: Curiosity, Gratitude, and Fear. I am a girl from another world, but a world of Pandaemonium. The Zero Sphere is a myth, obviously, and I don't put stock in such tales (and if I'm pressed on the nature of my homeworld, I can pull from a plethora of Earth fiction these people know nothing about). I am curious, grateful, and nervous. I am likable. I am not a threat. It is safe to let me in. You are safe, to let me in.

Trust me.

The mask settles on my face and around my hands and into my thoughts, and I make a few final adjustments to my body language as I push open the door and step into a new, much larger chamber. I try to relax, but I allow a bit of the nervous energy I'm genuinely feeling to seep into my limbs in various fidgeting gestures. *The most convincing lies are recontextualized truths.*

The halls and rooms of the rest of this structure were clean, and well-made, but there was nothing that I really found worth noticing. This room is different.

The chamber is vast and feels central, important, grandiose. It is made of clean white stone and decorated with vibrant wall murals depicting what I can only assume to be the Labyrinth itself: floating islands, mirror-doorways, and scattered cities. I see no sign of the black tower, however. Unknown to the artisans, or an intentional omission?

There are people here, or perhaps simulacra of people. I see a few in plain white robes, going between groups and carrying bowls that they hold out to people. I take them for attendants, especially in contrast with the others milling about in normal, perfectly modern outfits. They sit on benches and speak to the attendants and marvel at the murals, and I see them laugh and smile and hug each other.

And I have to wonder: *are you all figments, or are any of you real?* They read like the extras in a scene, the background characters put there to provide verisimilitude, so by the logic of the Labyrinth does that make them less than human?

I set my unease aside and turn my attention to what is clearly the main attraction: the pool of water and the great roots that descend from on high. A full third of the quite-large chamber is taken up by a pool of clear water that shimmers with pale light. Gnarled roots reach down and taper from above, dipping gently into the water and appearing like an inverted canopy of branches. The roots are dual-toned, tinged white and gold, and shift to golden brown as they get closer to the central trunk of what must be the great tree I saw from outside.

Two figures are waiting by the pool, and while one of them is clearly the priestess, my attention is drawn first to the woman suited head-to-toe in what can only be described as *power armor*. I have the sudden realization that I definitely wasn't mishearing Bashe when he said, "power armor and a halberd."

Ms. Space Marine here isn't carrying a halberd (in fact I don't see any weapons on her person at all), but she is absolutely wearing power armor and

I literally cannot even. It's that type of power armor that has the bulky alloy plates over a flexible (but still armored) bodysuit, and while the bodysuit is a signature black, the armor plates have been painted white with gold trim in a truly ostentatious display. The plates look machine-cut, and they have that future-metal surface texture to them. I don't see any obvious signs of circuitry or servos, but there are a few perfectly spherical glowing red gems embedded in key plates. *Something magitek?*

There's a tabard over the armor, white cloth, showing a golden tree whose branches bear many-colored fruit. That does a bit to shift the ensemble from space marine to space *knight*, and the next detail furthers that notion: while she may not have a weapon, she is carrying a *shield*. The possibly-knight is holding a largely unremarkable heater shield that has a gem sphere of its own, this one a deep earthy black.

Ms. Marine is also not wearing a helmet, which I consider an unforgivable sin from a tactical perspective, but if she's got Spirit narrative powers then it might not be a big deal? Heroes don't tend to die from getting shot in the head, even when they should by all rights. Her hair is "amber waves of grain" coloration, but cropped short and kept neat. She's got speckled eyes, very tan skin, and features that make her conventionally beautiful in that generically uninteresting supermodel way.

She is also, however, somewhere around seven feet tall, and from how she fills that power armor she looks to be seven feet of pure muscle. She's big and buff in that "I want you to step on me, power armor dommy mommy" kind of way. With how heavy that armor looks and how stick-like I am, she could probably lift me like a training weight. She could crush me to death between any two parts of her body, and that is *kind of delightful.*

Not that I express any of that out loud, of course. I allow myself to internally enjoy the sight of this maybe-literal-amazon for a brief, surreptitious second, and then push that aside entirely to focus on the mission. No distractions, even gay ones.

The other woman, the one not wearing power armor, is dressed in plain white robes like all the other attendants I've seen, but she's distinguished by the clearly magical staff in her hands; the staff is shaped a bit like a shepherd's crook, but it looks grown from a single branch, gnarled and continuous. The arc of the crook is a bit uneven, and in that imperfect gap is suspended an orb of water that shimmers with the same pale light as shines from the pool. *Magic staff! Now that's some classic fantasy.*

A blindfold covers her eyes, and she has rich brown hair that falls in curls. Her skin is honeyed and her features are kind, and she has an ageless look about her like she might be thirty or sixty with no way of telling. This is definitely the priestess. *Blind oracle and her space marine bodyguard? Okay, I kinda dig that.* She's kneeling by the water's edge, one hand hovering just over the surface of the pool.

I run a few scenarios in my head as I approach. *Are you the priestess? I wanted to thank you, profusely, and I hope you can pass my thanks along to the healer who helped me. Words alone cannot properly express my gratitude. Words aren't enough to express how grateful I am.* Smiles and sincerity and clasped hands. *My name is Maven Alice, and I wanted to thank you for everything. Please, if there's any way to repay your kindness—if there's anything I can do to repay your kindness, I would be happy to assist.*

Meh. I don't like any of those, really. Too structured, too rehearsed-sounding. I want to leave a stronger impression. Something . . . disorienting.

The warrior woman is watching me as I step up to the duo. My initial plan was to cough politely to get their attention, but it looks like I already have the attention of the one I plan to address first. As soon as I'm within comfortable speaking distance I put a bit more spring in my step, look up at the tall lady with wonder on my face, and babble, "Your armor is, like, *amazingly* cool! Is that power armor!? Where did you get it? It's so tough and awesome, it makes you look like a total badass!"

She seems taken aback by my outpouring of interest, but then she chuckles and lifts one arm, holding it out and flexing her fingers to show off the articulation of the joints. "It's nice, isn't it?" Her voice is smooth, confident, and deliciously deep. "It was a gift from the Machinist's Guild, for services rendered. Fits like a glove and takes hits like a mountain."

"Oh, wow, so it was custom-made? That's incredible! Um, are those guys, like, something from your old world, or are they here in the Labyrinth?" I don't think I'll ever be physically capable of wearing power armor, but it feels like a convincing thing for my character to want.

"The latter." She muses for a second, then comments, "I should let Lady Esha explain; I believe she intends to give you a *comprehensive* explanation of the state of our city."

The blind priestess smiles and rises from the water's edge. "Indeed I do. But first, I believe we should make proper introductions to our guest." She turns to me and gives me the same half-bow the attendant did. "I am Esha, priestess to the city spirit of Sanctuary 7. This is Achaia, my bodyguard, and we are both delighted to meet you."

I wince and act embarrassed. "Oh, sorry, I got totally ahead of myself there. I'm Alice, and the pleasure's all mine. Thank you, profusely, for everything. And please, pass my thanks to the healer who helped me." *Esha and Achaia.* I roll their names around my mouth, tasting them and trying to memorize them.

Esha's smile is warm and gentle. "I am glad to see your wound has recovered, Alice. Even with our Dryden's talents, it is not often that one heals so quickly."

"Believe me, no one's happier about it than I am." I shiver. "That was more of my insides than I ever want to see again."

Esha nods sympathetically. "I am sorry you went through that. This city was a peaceful place, once, but violence has infected it, and I fear that things will only get worse unless something drastic is done."

"So what can be done?" I quickly add, "And I don't mean that as a pure hypothetical; if there's anything I can do to help, please, let me know. Words don't suffice to repay the kindness you've shown me."

"The offer is appreciated, but you should hear the nature of our problem first; you are under no obligation to help us, and these are dangerous matters. And, to be clear on that first point: you are in no debt for the healing you received. There is no charge, and no expectation of repayment. We hold to the ideals of the sanctuaries, and offer our help to all those of good intent."

Meaning I'm thoroughly disqualified, so lying it is. Her voice practically sings with benevolence and empathy, to a frankly uncomfortable degree. She makes it sound like she actually cares about some random loser that turned up on her temple's doorstep. "I have lots of questions . . . but, regardless of the answers, I do feel immensely grateful for your aid, and I do want to give what help I can."

"I am happy to hear that. Allow me to give you some context, then." Esha gestures delicately in the direction of the pool and branches, and says, "[Recollection of the Myriad]: show me Averrich, Vaylin, and the Machinist."

Motes of pale light rise from the pool and coalesce into three distinct shapes, then gain color and definition. The elf is obvious from his pointed ears and languid sneer. The second one looks like an imp, or maybe she's a demon. The last one . . . is that a *kobold*? It's short and scaly and has an adorable snout and big floppy ears.

"Averrich is the man those reavers were working for."

The priestess gestures at the first illusory figure, and I commit his visage to memory: he resembles Eirdryd in the sharp features and pointed ears, but that's the end of it. His eyes are a mercurial blue-green, his hair is big and blond, and everything about him is just so *extra*. He's shirtless, which I'm sure I would appreciate more if I had the slightest interest in men's abs, and he's wearing a tattered green cape with a purple fur mantle, as well as a crown of leaves and berries.

His bare skin is decorated with tattoos evoking foxes, snakes, and spiders. His ears are pierced with colorful trinkets, but aside from those and the organic crown he wears no jewelry. I don't see a weapon on him or any of the others, but I assume the real version must carry one.

"Averrich is wyldfae, as I'm sure you can tell. He once rode with the Wild Hunt, and now he rules a band of cutthroats and thrill-seekers, most of whom are reavers or lesser fae and thus bound to him through Summer. His King's Carnival once respected the truce of this sanctuary, but now they prey upon the vulnerable like beasts of carrion." Her voice carries fascinating emotion: there's clearly history between those two, but her tone is disapproving rather than disgusted, like she's chiding a lost child.

"I heard a bit about this," I tell the priestess, "but I'm eager to learn the full story. I know that there was a truce, and a gang called the Coiners, and then the Contrite broke them up before being driven out themselves, and then a demon showed up?"

The priestess laughs lightly. "That's certainly a condensed way of putting it. Yes, you have the right of it, and that last point is perhaps most relevant to the current state of Sanctuary 7. Our truce with Averrich may have survived the Contrite incursion if not for the arrival of one Vaylin Kirinal."

Esha points to the second figure, who I can now confirm to be a demon. Vaylin Kirinal is definitely the most demonic creature I've seen so far in this Labyrinth: she has azure blue skin, two pairs of upward-curving horns, four opaque black eyes with white dots for pupils, and fingers that curve into sharp talons. Vaylin's arms—bared by her tank top, which is such a jarring sight on a demon—have been stitched into with red thread, the body stitching forming all manner of floral designs.

Her hair is long and black, her black-lipped smile is sinfully wicked, and she is adorned in a truly absurd amount of jewelry: gold bands around her horns, gem-studded rings on every finger, gold studs in her ears, glittering jewels on a golden choker around her neck, and gold lacing down the sides of her sleek leather pants.

"Vaylin came to the remnants of the various groups shattered by the Contrite, and she offered each of them a choice: submit or be made to. Her gang, Vaylin's Voidhearts, grew until it threatened to swallow the city. And so the other powers of this sanctuary were faced with a choice of our own: stay as we were and risk consumption, or become consumers ourselves."

She gestures to Averrich, to herself, and to the last figure above the water: a little lizard-dog-person in shiny power armor, with floppy ears and black scales and an adorable snout. "The three of us," Esha continues, "chose survival. Averrich was first to break the treaty, but the Machinist followed shortly after. To prevent the others from driving us out, even the Myriad have had to become more aggressive in our recruitment of warm bodies and our absorption of smaller groups. We all must eat lest we starve ... but of course, with every bite that every power takes, the other powers are driven to keep eating."

It clicks for me. "The security dilemma. You're talking about the security dilemma: each rational actor is driven by a need for greater security in the face of possible threats, so they seize more resources and strengthen their capacity for violence, which drives every other rational actor to do the same for the sake of their own security. Nobody's actually getting any safer because they're all stuck in an arms race, but anyone who stops running just gets eaten." I've seen it likened to the Red Queen's race from *Alice in Wonderland:* running and running and going nowhere. I wasn't expecting that bit of internet research to be relevant to my life, ever, but here we are. "You're locked into the conditions of interstate anarchy until a hegemon emerges to settle the mess."

The bodyguard woman, Achaia, gives me an appraising look. "Well, you've got a bit more learning than most in that area. Those aren't the exact terms I learned it by, but that's the general idea. Until something changes the parameters, we have no choice but to fight in deadlock."

Esha waves her hand and dismisses the illusory figures. "I hope you understand now the gravity of the situation, and the difficulty of offering to help. The Myriad would be grateful for your aid—we are desperate for every new pair of hands—but it is no small commitment, and there is no end in sight."

I process that, slowly nodding and looking down to broadcast contemplation. *They think they're asking me to fight in a forever war, but it's obvious what happens next: I'm the change in parameters that shifts the balance. Hells, even ignoring the story logic of a protagonist's arrival upsetting the status quo, I'm a scion in a city where that doesn't seem very common. Averrich's a scion, and so is Vaylin, but I'm not sure about the Machinist, and at first impression it doesn't seem like the Myriad are fronting an exalted. I could be the secret weapon that lets them overtake their rivals.*

That's the heroic story, at least: helping the prosocial group beat out the antisocial groups and restore the ideal status quo of the Labyrinth, the city of sanctuary made true to its name. But I am a demon, and my destiny may be darker than that. Still, even if I have grander ambitions, it seems rational to side with the closest thing to good guys I've seen since my arrival.

I raise my gaze back to Esha's face and say, "Even so, I think it's worth doing. Kindness should be met with kindness, and I feel like there's so much I can learn from your group about the Labyrinth and Sanctuary 7. I admit, the thought of facing those reavers again scares me ... but the thought of not having to face them alone is a comfort. So, if I can, once I get my bearings in this strange new world, I'd like to help."

Esha rubs her chin and makes a contemplative noise. "Hmm."

Achaia raises an eyebrow. "Well?"

Esha shakes her head. "It is as he said: the girl is shrouded from my second sight. I have never met one whose role is so clouded and ill-defined; she could be savior, destroyer, victimizer, victim. She could be all those things and none."

"But her nature," Achaia presses. Internally, I start freaking out. *She has special sight, like Bashe, and maybe the dog.*

"A tricky thing to ascertain. Her shroud ability does not seem demonic in nature, but if it did then that would give the game away. If I did not know to look for it, I am not certain that I could have discerned any deeper truth to her existence beyond the touch of the Abyss shared by all under Shadow's Throne. Her true nature is veiled behind a tumult of chaotic impressions each vying for my attention." Esha smiles, tilts her head, and finishes, "But with great effort, it *can* be discerned. So yes, my dutiful guard: the girl is a demon. This I know for fact."

Shit.

XV

Shit shit shit. Fucking incubus! Internally I seethe with rage at the imp's inevitable betrayal, but outwardly I wear a gentler mask of confusion, concern, and a touch of embarrassment. I start to formulate a reply, but a whisper stops me.

"Don't panic. You're doing great." It's Cheshire's voice, emanating from nowhere. *Where the fuck have you been?* I take her advice, even if I'm annoyed to only start receiving it after all that conversation.

After a pause, Esha speaks again. "With her shroud, my second sight cannot be trusted. I shall have to rely on my other senses, then, and on my intuition. Both of which, it would seem, are telling me that you, Maven Alice, are a great deal different than Bashekehi the Ever-Gleaming led me to believe."

Play it cool. This is what we built the mask for. I wince and scratch my head sheepishly. "Ah, yeah, I, um . . . my apologies about that. I'm afraid Bashe saw me at my absolute worst these past couple days. I was . . . *unsettled* by my shocking arrival in the Labyrinth, and I think I've been unfair to him. I just . . . I never really had a life of adventure before coming here, y'know? I was something of a shut-in back home, and I wasn't prepared for the stresses of real conflict and real danger." I let genuine nervousness bleed into that last line.

"That stress is completely understandable," the priestess reassures me. "Few of us take to the Labyrinth easily. Still, he raised questions that I find interesting."

"Such as?"

"Mm. Allow me to start with this: why did you become a demon? I do not wish to judge, only learn." Again her voice is kind and gentle to a uniquely grating degree.

Core of truth, shell of creativity. You've got this. I look away from her and chew on my lip. "I . . . I was scared. I was scared and I didn't understand, and

I still don't. Not fully. I'd heard stories of demons, rumors of demons, but I'd never *seen* a demon. Never spoken to one. They never felt real. Like storybook monsters. When I met my geist, when it made that offer, I . . . I didn't feel like I had a choice."

Cheshire's quiet laughter echoes around me, but the priestess and warrior give no sign of hearing it.

The priestess nods. "And if it were a choice? If you, in the situation you are in now, were offered that choice again?"

I visibly and audibly hesitate, hoping to strengthen the impression that I'm considering the matter carefully. "I think that . . . I'm not sure. I don't know. I've heard so many bad things about demons, about geists, about being what I am now, but I don't . . . I don't *feel* like a monster. Not yet, I guess. It just feels like power. It *is* power, isn't it? And power is safety."

"There are other forms of power," Esha points out, "and other forms of safety. Few paths to power are as dangerous as the one you now walk, Alice. For the body, or for the mind."

I laugh bitterly. "Yeah. Bashe said about the same." I hug myself somberly. "Is that it, then? Am I cursed? Doomed to become some monster unfit for a place like this?"

She shakes her head. "Not at all. No one is beyond help. It is rare, yes, but there have been demons that strived to retain their humanity. If you truly wish to resist the call of the Abyss, I will do everything in my power to help you navigate those waters."

"Thank you," I say quietly. "I'll remember that."

She smiles softly and says, "Bashekehi's description of you was not wholly negative, you should know. He said that you were creative, and clever, and very driven. Those are admirable traits, and we would be happy to make use of them. Do you think those traits are what drew the geist to you?"

Flattery and reframing to make me more open in answer. Hmmph. "Maybe," I answer evasively. "Maybe I was just an easy mark. Or maybe it saw something in me that no one else has. I find it impossible to tell."

Esha muses, "The ways of geists are often inscrutable. What commonality is there between the child that became Wonder and the monster that became Malice?" I suppress a shiver at my almost-name. "Within this community, we call an imp of Muse our friend and comrade. Indulgence and Contrition have both caused great harm, but they are opposite as can be in all other ways. What do you share with all those once-demons? What kind of demon are you going to be?"

Wonder. Malice. Muse. Indulgence. Contrition. That's five archdemons I know for certain, now. Given the naming schema, I suspect Acuity is among their number as a sixth. That leaves only two archdemons unaccounted for. "I'm not sure. But, if I were to guess . . . maybe it's a kind of yearning. That I share with them, I mean. Maybe we all have something we want so badly it makes the Abyss itself notice."

"And what is it that you want?" she asks gently, insistently.

I want to survive. I want to be stronger. I want to see everything there is to see, to learn everything there is to learn. I want to be loved. I want to be feared. I want to rule.

I want to be more than that scared little girl alone in her room, hiding from the rest of the world.

But aloud, I say, "I want to be safe, and I want to learn, and I want to—omigosh, what is that???"

I point excitedly at the gelatinous blob of clear non-Newtonian fluid and soap bubbles that has just oozed into view. The slime slides over the stone tiles of the grand chamber, but instead of leaving a mucus trail like slimes in all the media I've consumed, it leaves behind a sparkling clean layer of rapidly evaporating soapy water.

I skip over to the featureless mass of soap-jelly and lean over to beam at it. "You're so adorable!!! Hello! Hi!" I wave at it cheerfully.

The slime stops oozing forward and wobbles in place, vibrating in an erratic pattern. A single pseudopod rises hesitantly out of the main mass and wiggles back-and-forth in a motion vaguely reminiscent of my waving. "Hello," it says, its voice wavering and quiet.

EEEEEEEEEEEEEEE!!! Words cannot describe the effervescent joy that bubbles up in my chest at that cute-as-heck voice coming from that absurdly adorable slime.

Esha walks over (Achaia shadowing her, of course) and puts her hand over her mouth to stifle a chuckle. "I see you've found Bubbles, our resident custodian. I'm afraid they're a bit shy, but I'm sure they appreciate the enthusiasm. Bubbles, this is Alice."

"They," not *"it."* Noted. "Are they kindred, or are they a homunculus?" I feel like it's a safe bet that Bubbles falls under one of those two categories, so this should hopefully reinforce the impression that I am definitely from part of Pandaemonium. Also, I want to pet the slime so badly.

"Kindred," Esha confirms. "Bubbles was supplicant to an eidolon of public health, once, and came to that eidolon seeking transformation. Before the Labyrinth, they used the properties of their form to clean public infrastructure. Now, they find meaning in tending to this community center."

I lean down farther, look Bubbles dead in the lack-of-eyes, and say, "I would die for you." The creature vibrates a bit more, but then returns to their previous path of soapy oozing. "You're doing great," I whisper to Bubbles as they leave.

I do actually find the slime very cute, but I'm mostly putting on airs to convince the priestess I'm harmless. Also, there was an interesting phrase used just then. I look back at Esha and ask, "And, sorry, you called this place a 'community center'? I was told it's a shrine."

"It is, in some respects. But I prefer to think of it as a community center, as many of our members still keep faith in the spirits of their homeworlds, and religiosity is by no means a requirement to join the Myriad. All of good intent are welcome here."

There's that disqualifying phrase again. I could reassure her that I am of good intent, but I'm competing with whatever Bashe's told her. So what's a good way to change that impression, more than I already have? I glance around the room and my gaze alights on the various attendants and citizenry milling about. *Idea.* "This may seem off-topic, but . . . can I ask a question about the people in this room?"

Esha nods calmly. "You may."

"Are they . . . are these figments? The people in the robes, or the people not wearing robes, or both?"

"They are, both groups. I take it the Labyrinth is your first experience with figments?"

"I've only read about them, and heard about them from others." I fake hesitation, then barrel on, "Hey, so, I kind of have to hear what you think about something. Because Bashe told me that the figments of this city aren't people. He said they don't matter, that their lives don't matter, that they're just *disposable*. And I know they're not conscious like we are, yeah, but it still doesn't sit right to look someone in the eye and treat them like they're not deserving of the same respect as anyone else. Is that really how everyone here feels?"

I'm hoping to challenge Bashe's standing and strengthen my own with the same move. If I can invalidate the negative aspects of his character judgment of me, it should hopefully be easier to endear myself to the Myriad. Assuming the Myriad actually do care about the figments more than Bashe seemed to. I admit that part of my strategy is a bit of a gamble.

Esha smiles sympathetically. "I can assure you that it is not. That position *is* often stated by those with an interest in exploiting figments, but it is not universal. From our viewpoint in the Myriad, the figments of Sanctuary 7 are the original inhabitants of this city and deserve to be treated with respect, especially when you consider how much they do for us on a daily basis. We value the figments, and the ideals that govern them."

I smile back. "I have to admit, I'm relieved to hear you say that."

Achaia, largely silent for this conversation, adds, "There's a pragmatic element to it, too: if you treat them poorly, it's easy to get stuck in a pattern of treating everyone poorly. 'Course, that's not a huge deterrent to most of Vaylin's or Averrich's followers."

"How pleasant," I mutter. "Would be great if both of them could just fuck off."

The priestess sighs. "Were it so easy." She turns back to the pool and seems to contemplate it quietly. She traces a hand through the air and whispers something under her breath, and a breeze smelling of fresh flowers wafts past me. Esha nods. "Well, I hope this has all been . . . enlightening. Now, about something you said before . . . you offered to help us, if you can. Is that still something you want?"

I nod firmly. "Absolutely. Listen, I got distracted earlier, but that third thing I want: it's to *fix things*. I was a nobody before coming here. I never did anything with my life. I never made any kind of a difference to anybody. But now . . . now I can. I have power, for the first time ever, and I want to use it. So I want to help, as much as I can." I tighten my fists, put an edge in my voice, and say, "I have *words* for Averrich, too, if I ever see him."

"You wouldn't be the only one," Achaia mutters, rolling her shoulders. "That bastard *will* get what's coming to him, it's just a matter of time."

Esha says, "The Myriad would be happy to welcome you into our community, if that is something you wish for. Those who swear a vow to the city spirit are granted an invocation you may find helpful, if you intend to challenge the King's Carnival. Of course, you may still work alongside us and take refuge in the community center even if you do not join, but we would be grateful to have you."

"What would that entail?" I ask. "Joining, I mean." I don't particularly want to be part of their little society, since that seems like it would conflict with my mid-term goal of carving out a fiefdom to be Dark Lord over, but if it's not too onerous then it might be worth playing along for a while.

"You would vow to uphold the Truths of this city, and in return our eidolon would grant you the power to commune with the city whenever you are in its bounds. You would protect the people of this city, you would strive for peace, and you would welcome all of good intent." There's weight to those words, something I can just barely *feel* in the air.

"Mm. I'd be tempted to agree without taking the time to consider it, but I actually don't think I *could* make that vow right now: my pleroma was damaged in an encounter with a Mourner, and I doubt it's fully healed yet. I don't have the space in my soul for another invocation." This one isn't even a lie at all; I genuinely don't think my pleroma has healed yet.

I see something oddly like *guilt* pass over Esha's face. "Ah, my deepest condolences. I . . ."

Achaia rests her armored hand on Esha's shoulder and squeezes. The priestess' expression softens as she looks up at her bodyguard, and I immediately have two thoughts: one, that these two are hella gay for each other; and two, that Esha somehow feels *guilty* over my encounter with the Mourner??? Like. My facial reading skills aren't perfect, but they're a lot better than they were when I was a kid, and that expression *reads like guilt.*

What the fuck is up with that?

"Sorry, is there context I'm missing?" I ask aloud.

Achaia shakes her head. "Just old history. We've lost a lot of friends to the Beast over the years."

Yeah, no, that's definitely not it. Keep your secrets, for now, but I will *uncover them eventually.*

"Regardless," Esha says, "you raise a valid concern. Please, take the time to recover, and then find us with your answer when you are ready."

I nod. "I'll do that, thanks. And . . . I hope we can work together to make this city a better place."

"I do as well."

The priestess calls over a figment attendant to usher me out, and I accept the offer graciously. As soon as I'm outside the shrine—community center, to use their words—and out of earshot of the guards, I glare at my own shadow and snap, "What was that? Where did you go?"

Cheshire emerges from darkness and gives me a wink. "Aw, did you miss me?"

I hiss at the offending creature. "I could have used a little *warning* there, or some fucking *help.* That was stressful! I could have died!"

Cheshire waves a hand dismissively and blows air at me. "Don't be absurd. Those bleeding hearts don't have the guts to execute someone in cold blood. You were *fine,* Alice. I knew you could handle it, and I was right; you did a great job."

I grumble and cross my arms. "Yeah, well, it was still a gamble. I would *appreciate* it, in the future, if you would give me whatever help you can. Two heads are better than one, y'know?"

The catgirl giggles. "Are you saying you *need* me, darling?"

I give a very dramatic and exasperated sigh. "I am *saying* that I am out of my league and can't do this alone. So fuckin' pitch in, alright?"

"Hehe. Yeah, I can do that. But really, you were doing fine. I even spied on them for a little bit after you left, and it seems they really did buy your act."

"Well, at least that's something." I sigh again, this one more natural. "Okay. Another crisis dealt with, and I guess we have some breathing room. I'm starting to get an idea of how this city operates, and what my role in this drama is going to be. I should try to feed again before I run into any more gangsters, and I need to start worrying about power progression, but I do seem to recall one other step I can take to make everything I do just a little bit more effective."

"Shopping time!" Cheshire cheers.

"Shopping time," I agree, and we set off in search of a mall.

XVI

We flag down a passing figment and ask for directions. The citizenry are as eager to help as ever, and the conversation passes quickly without any existential interruptions. Cheshire takes the lead, moving confidently through the city streets, and I follow along close behind.

"I still have questions," I tell the catgirl. "Several days' worth."

Cheshire twirls around to face me, walking backwards, and gives me a double thumbs-up. "Fire away!"

Bah. So cheerful. I run my hands through my hair and consider which question to ask first. There is so much I want to learn, but it's best to be tactical about this. Proper sequencing. "Okay, let's start with this: why can't people read me?"

Cheshire quirks an eyebrow. "Like, in general? 'Cause I think you put a pretty decent effort into making it hard for people to read your true intentions."

I glare at the creature that definitely knows what I'm talking about and is fucking with me. "Second sight. Bashe looking at my desires, the dog trying to sniff me out, the priestess feeling for my role. That's three fuckers now who've tried to use some magic sensory ability on me, and all three of them have met with an opposition they seemed not to expect or understand. Why?"

Cheshire taps her chin and muses playfully, clearly teasing me. "Hmm, why indeed . . . what an interesting question. Why were they surprised by how difficult you are to read? Well, I *think*, if I were to guess, I would say that it's because none of them had ever met a witch before meeting you." She grins, toothy and smug, and I blink repeatedly in disorientation.

"Sorry, what? Sorry, what? I'm a *witch*? Since when!? You're saying that I am a *witch*, which—yes, ha ha—to be clear, is the kind of thing that you are? Someone with weird special magic that doesn't fit into the Throne system? That thing? I'm that thing? I'm a witch?"

The changeling giggles. "Yep! Hehe. You're fun."

I clap my hands to either side of my head and stare past Cheshire. "Fuuuuuuck. Gods fucking damn this bastard fucking world. Is this—is this why—is this why she didn't answer!? Because I already *had* a cheat ability? Because I've had one since I fucking woke up!? It would have to be! It would have to be, because I was getting that reaction as early as Bashe, and—oh you've gotta be fucking kidding me, is this why Eirdryd didn't *murder me*!? Okay, hold on, let's back up here. So, I am a witch. I have been a witch for an indeterminate amount of time, and being a witch does something to the various second sight abilities you have in this setting. How does that all work?"

Cheshire laughs again, richer and deeper this time. "Ah, I can practically hear the gears turning in your head, that machine of a mind recalculating everything you know. Here's how it is: every witch has, in addition to their actual power, a witch's shroud that helps to conceal them from those endowed with sight beyond sight. The shroud isn't perfect, of course, but it's fairly effective, and it gets stronger as you do. As for how long you've been a witch, I'd say 'since you woke up in the abandoned school' is about accurate."

"Motherfucker!" I swear. "So I've had a cheat ability this *whole time*, and I had no idea. Wait, it's not the fear thing, right? No, can't be, 'cause that's gone now. Okay." I'm bouncing on my feet, hands twitching, full of energy. I am *pissed* that I'm only learning this now, but I'm also so fucking excited to realize that I have even more magic than I thought I did. "Seriously, though, was that part of what made Eirdryd interested in me? Is that what stopped him from killing me, because he could see the shroud and knew what it meant?"

Cheshire wiggles a hand noncommittally. "Eh, I imagine it was *part* of his reasoning, but far from the whole thing. This may surprise you to learn, Alice, but you actually played that scene really well; wyldfae are bound by stories and trickery, and you were smart about how you seized the initiative and turned the story around on him. With how you positioned yourself, it would actually have been pretty difficult for him to just kill you on a whim."

"Huh. Interesting. Well, that's good to know, I guess." *I'm glad that gamble paid off, because I'm pretty sure that if I hadn't taken it, I would currently be dying of starvation, lost in the woods.* "Alright, that aside: what's my power? What's my witch ability?"

"Aw, but it's so much more fun if you figure it out yourself! Sooo I don't think I will tell you, actually." Cheshire winks at me and sticks her tongue out, which is as obnoxious as it is cute. "I'll give you a hint, though: you've already used it once."

Immediately I retreat inward, poring over memories in search of answers. *It's not the fear. The potion? Bashe reacted to that, called it impossible, but something that's impossible for Throne magic is perfectly possible for witch magic. But what does that make my power? I asked Azathoth for that potion—or rather I asked for something else and got the potion instead—but I received nothing when I asked for a compass. It wouldn't be Azathoth anyways, right? It's supposed to be Nyarlathotep that interferes.*

What other impossible things have I done? I mean there's the Zero Sphere but that's just isekai bullshit. What else did Bashe react to?

The knife. He got weird about the knife. Not like, potion or Zero Sphere weird, but he said it didn't sound like how artifacts are supposed to be made. I narrow my eyes at Cheshire and ask, "Hey, totally unrelated to this entire conversation: how do fae make artifacts? Comprehensive explanation, please."

She grins, and I know I'm on the right track. "Well, it differs between corpsefae and wyldfae, but I'll just assume you mean Summer. For anyone bound to Summer, there are two ways. When a hunt is called and a worthy prey is slaughtered, a hunting trophy may be claimed; materials from the body are taken to a forgemaster or rider and shaped into an artifact. The second method is available only to elves, who may take a portion of their stockpiled power and shape it into an artifact whole cloth, though in this case it is essential that there is a *story* to the resulting creation, and such artifacts rarely last long beyond the end of the story they were made for."

We could go over the details in that explanation and pick at the circumstances surrounding the artifact, but I think it's pretty clear that neither of those methods resemble how [Ashthorn] was made. Which means . . . "Did I *make* [Ashthorn]?"

The geist claps her hands. "Ding ding ding! Got it in one, babe. In a world where magic items have all sorts of esoteric rules attached to their creation, you're the real deal: a genuine bona fide *artificer*."

I'm stunned into silence for a few moments, just processing. I'm an artificer. I thought I was thrown into this world with *nothing*, with scraps, with just my wits and a scattering of items, but actually . . . I have what's arguably one of the most broken cheat abilities possible. I mean, there's time bullshit, sure, and various "I win" buttons, but being able to make magic items? That's crazy strong.

My brain is buzzing with possibilities. How does my power work? Do I have to meet certain conditions? How did I make [Ashthorn]? The fae burned a bunch of spiders and also my knife, and then I ripped the knife out and gave it a name. Is that it? I mean, I was excited by the idea that it might be a magic item, but I didn't will it to have any particular powers, right?

Hmm. I wonder if that matters? Could I shape an artifact with an intent, if I knew I was doing it? I have to try. I have to run *experiments*. Glorious science awaits.

And the mall should be full of fun toys to experiment on.

"Okay, well, that's going to be interesting. Looping back to sight and sound: if every witch has this shroud effect, that means you have it too, right? So if Bashe had looked at you with second sight, he would have seen the same thing?"

"Mm, almost. I've had my shroud long enough to learn how to control it, so I can make people see whatever I want them to see. When Bashekehi looked at me with his sight, all he saw was the darkness of the Abyss." Her lips quirk into a smaller, subtler smile, and she asks, "Would you like to see it in action?"

"Yes, yes, obviously yes, of course yes. How do I do that?" I lean in with eyes wide.

Cheshire pulls me to a stop by the side of the street, then rubs her hands together. "Okay, step one: close your eyes."

I comply, and the world is darkness—or more accurately, that not-quite-darkness of staring at your eyelids in a lit area. I can hear the dim chatter and clatter of people—figments—walking to and fro, and I can feel the sturdy ground beneath my feet.

"What's around you, right now?" Her voice comes from right in front of me, and I can remember her position relative to mine, but the visual details are already murky. I'm terrible at visualization, really; my brain just doesn't do pictures that well.

"You," I answer. "And the street. Buildings. Figments, passing by. The city."

"*The* city?" she probes.

I frown, working to parse her question. *She's stressing the article, so is that the issue? Why? Too definitive?* "A city," I test.

"What kind of city?"

My frown deepens. *What kind of a question is that? How am I meant to answer?* "A strange city. A half-real city. A city of not-quite-people and shifting landscape. A city of the Labyrinth." An idea seizes me. "Or . . . not a city at all. The idea of a city. The dream of a city."

"Close!" she cheers me on. "Very close. But you're missing a piece. You're still thinking too rigidly. You're in Pandaemonium now, and the rules are different. Real, not-real, half-real; they're all different here."

Pandaemonium. Real and not-real. Reality back home is . . . physicality. Materiality. But that's just one-third of the picture, here. The Throne of Order, the ordered laws of a not-quite-natural world. But there's Spirit, too, the world through the lens of the collective. And then there's me. Us.

The Throne of Shadow. The world of the self.

"Around me is one city and three cities," I begin. "A city of ordered laws. A city of . . . a city of groups; a city of factions: Myriad, Guild, Carnival, and Voidhearts. And a city of individuals."

"Very good," Cheshire says, her voice now behind me and to the side. "Three Thrones. Three lenses. Three worlds. Now: focus on that last one. You are surrounded by individuals; by selves. And you are a scion of the Throne of the self, so it is *child's play* for you to reach out and see those other selves. Witness the self as it is seen *by* the self. Peer into hearts and read desires."

I let her words play in my head, dissecting them and absorbing them. Around me is a city of selves. I just have to reach out and witness them.

"Will your sight—Throne-granted, Throne of the self—to open. See the world as you have not seen it before. And open your eyes."

I remember the feeling of willing Cheshire to manifest, or of willing a spell to dismiss. I have power. My thoughts *are* power. I focus my will and demand that the world show me those selves surrounding me. I want to see. I feel something shift, a prickling behind my eyes.

I open them, and I see a world of horror.

Crisp colors are stripped away, clean lines made sketchy and malformed. The city—the world—is scribbled on the pages of a sketchbook, but wavering, shifting. No line stays straight, no curve retains its arc. I see shattered windows and cracked stone and bent metal and endless stretching pavement toward the infinite swallowing dark all around me, seeping down from sky and up from hidden depths.

A sketchbook drifting in the void, lines of black on a splash of white drowning in an ocean of ink. And here and there, scattered through the monochrome mess of misshapen angles, I see splashes of color.

Shades of blue, green, and brown, indistinct but moving, shifting across my field of vision. My gaze flits to one, to a particularly vibrant green, and the rest of the world bleeds away. The ink runs from the page to be swallowed by the dark beyond, and that color gets bigger and brighter and more detailed. A cloud of color becomes an impression, then an image.

More lines, still sketchy but sharper, variation less intense, and filled in with charcoal and oil paint. I see a mask of bone-porcelain growing like a tumor out of a mass of red meat and jutting glass and flowing fabric, and deep within the eyeholes of that blank-faced mask I see two pinpricks of piercing green, glowing, bleeding their color down the cheeks of the mask to spill and stain the fabric below. Black and white and green and red, sharp and messy and twitching.

I see the strings, wrapped around each impression of a limb and sinking into the back of the mask-head like hooks and wires. The strings stretch up, up, up and away, far away, far into the distance, into a tower of black glass. My vision shudders, reality unravels, and again I see the trick in perspective: the wound in the world, the knife in the skin of the dream, inverted to show the dream bleeding out of the wound-tower, color spilling into the deep dark void.

I can almost see inside, past the blood and the shards, to something deeper, calling me, pulling me. Whispering my name.

I dig my nails into my skin and tear my vision away before the tower can drag me in. I'm breathing hard, clutching at myself, and all around me I am still surrounded by white and black and drifting color like anglerfish lures in ocean depths. I'm swimming. I'm drowning. There's so much. It's all so much.

A touch on my shoulder, light touch, gentle sensation, moving, tracing, gliding. A shiver on the back of my neck, down my arm. Skin, soft, fingers. Fingers tracing up my throat and settling on my cheeks. Color. Two colors, bicolor, dual color. Swirling color, yellow and blue.

My gaze slips into the new color, focuses on it, and I see the cloud resolve into two pinpricks of light—one blue, one yellow—within the eyeholes of a cat-faced mask, bone-porcelain, growing from a mass of seething darkness. Ink like the ink of the ocean surrounding me. A tangle of dark lines, coarse and dripping liquid night.

The mask opens in a too-wide too-toothy smile, all teeth in either direction, pristine cat's teeth filling the page from edge-to-edge and wrapping around. "Well?" she asks, voice still unmistakably Cheshire's: achingly beautiful and full of callous mirth. "Enjoying the view?"

"I . . . you . . . this is a lot. Woah. This is. What?"

She laughs, and the mask cracks by the edges of its lips, forming laugh lines. "Here, let me give you something nicer to look at."

The inky blackness recedes, tendrils and lines drawn into the mask like slurped spaghetti. For a moment it's just the mask: pale porcelain, carved cat ears, the stretching line of teeth, and those blue-and-yellow eyelights. I reach out on instinct to feel the mask, tracing smooth bone with fingers outlined in shaky graphite. So warm. So soft. Oddly comforting.

I start and pull my hand back, embarrassed by my lapse in reason. Another laugh from Cheshire, another crinkle-crack of the pale mask, and then a new image paints itself—or is painted by Cheshire, I realize: a face behind a mask, white hair and pale skin and a pair of cat ears; a body, lean and agile; a swishing tail, white-furred; vague impressions of yellow-and-pink fabric.

I'm looking at Cheshire drawn over Cheshire. I can't help but laugh at the abject absurdity of such a notion.

Cheshire's oil paint body smiles, and the forever-teeth fold back into the mouth of her mask. "There we go." A red heart appears under each cheek of the mask.

I breathe. I can finally focus on something that doesn't threaten to break my fucking brain. "Okay. That is. So much. I. The fuck? Fuck. Okay." I rub my head and wince. "That was incredibly disorienting. I am still kind of disoriented, honestly. I mean, it's *cool as hell*, too, but I do not know how to properly appreciate that without getting slammed in the brain by horrors beyond my comprehension."

"It's a skill," the changeling tells me. "This is your first time using the sight, so of course it's going to be a bit overwhelming. Right now you've filtered out everything except individual meaning. That's useful for letting you deep-dive someone's soul, but not great for actually functioning and moving. You could see if someone had violent intent, but you might miss the sword swinging at your throat. You need to learn to overlay *this* sense over your normal sight."

As she speaks, I can still feel her hands on my cheeks, but the image of her moves its hands in different gestures: a hand on my shoulder, both hands over her heart, hands clasped together, hands around my throat, a hand on her hip and a hand in the air. The mask warps and contorts through expressions of sympathy, love, erudition, anger, and satisfaction.

"Fascinating," I murmur. "How do I do that?"

I feel her pat my hand comfortingly. I see the image of Cheshire scoff and turn away from me. I hear her say, "You'll need to get used to switching between vision types first. We're close to the mall, so you could practice while holding my hand to keep from getting lost. If you trust me to guide you safely, of course." The charcoal-and-oil Cheshire swoons, red hearts sketching into the canvas and being erased in strange mimicry of motion.

As untrustworthy as she is in general, I sincerely doubt there's any harm in trusting her to lead me to the mall. "Sure. I'll give it a try." Her hand finds mine and our fingers interlace, and then she is leading the way and I am pulled along.

I reach for my old sight, close my eyes, and when I open them again I can see the city as it was. I switch between my normal sight and soul sight, practicing finding the feeling quicker, making it more natural, until all it takes is a single purposeful blink.

It's certainly disorienting switching between sights, but there's something fascinating about seeing the world in a different palette. I see more figment souls, or at least I'm nearly certain those blank-faced puppets have to be figments.

But at last we arrive at the shopping complex, and I discover that it is the massive techno-pyramid I noticed on first stepping out of the apartments. The Pyraplex apparently boasts over seven hundred shops, though I find "shops" a laughable term given this city's lack of conventional commerce.

The whole structure is made out of metal and glass—non-reflective glass, notably—with neon lines tracing everywhere. There are neon signs, too, and the whole place looks downright cyberpunk. The mega-mall has touchscreen kiosks, even, that display a floor plan of each section of this absurdly large structure.

That's pretty cool, but what's less cool is all the *people* milling about. It's not as bad as the club was, thanks to people generally spreading out and keeping moving, but my overstimulation isn't really the issue so much as my hypervigilance; I keep twitching whenever someone passes too close, expecting another axe-wielding asshole to come charging in at any moment. I flick on soul sight and sweep the area, but I have no real way of determining figment from person without manually checking every single splash of color.

I'll have to continue relying on Cheshire, I admit to myself. *Not that she warned me about the last attack, mind, but she at least had a plan.*

"So!" claps the catgirl in question. "Where to first, chief? We've got a whole world of options here: we could grab you some new clothes, see about a custom anchor for yours truly, fish around for other necessities . . ."

I see two separate food courts listed and my stomach lets me know how it feels about that. "Food. Food is first."

Cheshire grins. "Well, I suppose it is technically still breakfast time. Let's eat!"

XVII

Is there anything more beautiful than a fully stocked food court?
Yes. Obviously. That's not even a hard bar to clear.
However, most things more beautiful than a banquet of food are not more *delicious* than a banquet of food, so I must reluctantly cede the point to food on this one. By which I mean, I am hungry and I want to eat everything in this mall.
We navigate to the nearest food court and I marvel at all the options on display: burgers, sandwiches, pretzels, smoothies, ice cream, pastries, more burgers, more sandwiches, falafel, curry, pizza, sushi, fish, and about a dozen other themes. I see triple-stacked monstrosities of meat next to vegan varieties, and everything from the allegedly healthy to food that will absolutely induce a heart attack. Savory aromas waft from all across the court, and I am tempted by so many different treats.
I summon Cheshire, the act becoming easier with each repetition, and she immediately darts for a particularly greasy-looking burger place. I waffle between a buffalo chicken ranch sandwich, a mountain of chili fries, and a medley of different sushi rolls, but in the end I settle on a vegetarian mini pizza.
I grab a table and wait for my freshly baked pizza to cool, and Cheshire's on me in a flash. The catgirl slides into the seat across from me and sets down a paper bag already starting to fray at the edges from what I presume to be burger juices. She grins at my own choice of food.
"You're bringing new meaning to 'vegetarian vampire,' Allie. Don't you want something with blood?" There's a teasing lilt to her words as she reveals a three-patty lotsa-cheese burger and starts chowing down. A bit of grease or meat juice dribbles down her chin and she makes a very satisfied noise.

I smirk and lean against my hand. "I could say the inverse about you." I'm struck by a bit of nostalgia for an old show and muse, "In a weird way this reminds me of a scene from *Teen Titans:* whenever Cyborg would get on Beast Boy's case about being vegetarian, BB would justify it by saying that he's been those animals and it feels wrong to eat them. And here you are, shapeshifter, playing the carnivore with gusto."

Cheshire swallows another big bite and quips, "I've been those animals, and they're delicious."

I chuckle and take a bite of my veggie pizza. It is, for the record, perfectly scrumptious. I always hate whenever media takes cheap shots at vegetarian food. A whole bunch of people are so obsessed with meat that they'll pretend a plain burger with no sauce or toppings tastes better than a veggie burger stacked with goodies. I like meat burgers, I do, but I've had black bean burgers that knocked most meat burgers out of the park.

I chew on a bit of mushroom and spinach, swallow, and ask, "So, here's an interesting question: did your taste in food actually change when you started changing forms, or no?"

The catgirl wiggles her free hand while the other clutches her burger tight. "A bit. I've probably spent more time as carnivores than herbivores, but human food just tastes better than what you can get the old-fashioned way, basically categorically. It's all chemical: the fat and sugar that was rare and precious in a hunter-gatherer lifestyle gets concentrated into every single meal, made abundant. You have to work at it harder to get the same caloric intake, out in the wild."

"I vaguely recall learning something like that, once upon a time. So, what, a few nights of hunting prey made you long for microwave dinners?" I take minor amusement in imagining wolf!Cheshire wolfing down a plate of macaroni and cheese.

She polishes off the last bite of her burger and sighs contentedly. "You could say that. I can remember more than once spending hours hunting mice for the thrill of it, then leaving my prey for the beasts while I filched the good stuff from humans."

"Mm." I take another bite of pizza and chew slowly. *What a fascinating creature you are. If any of this is true, I mean. Gods, it's exhausting being this paranoid all the time. With most people I can just assume that whatever they're lying about doesn't matter enough for me to care, but Cheshire might* actually *be plotting to murder me. How the fuck am I meant to function with that kind of paranoia?*

Cheshire opens a box of fries and starts dipping them in what looks like barbeque sauce. "I tried to combine the two, actually," she tells me while munching on fried potato. "I threw a few slices of pizza to some rats, then hunted them down in fox form and dined on the prize. It was alright. The hunt was fun and the pizza was good, but the pizza would have been better if it hadn't been dragged through literal filth and garbage."

I snort-laugh at that image. "So my new girlfriend eats trash. Good to know."

"Don't worry, I keep my mouth clean." She winks at me, and I staunchly refuse to unpack whatever she's implying with that wink.

"Ignoring that, I've got a topic of curiosity: what *are* your favorite foods, then? I imagine you already know all mine, but I doubt they're the same. And, if they are, that's pretty creepy, and I'd like to know what they used to be regardless."

Cheshire grins. "Well, you'll be happy to know that the Demiurge left me that much of myself. I like a lot of food, though. Food is food, at the end of the day. I suppose I've got a few favorites, if you divide them up into categories." She points a fry at the last of my mini pizza and says, "As far as pizza goes, I like the meaty kind. Pepperoni, sausage, ham, bacon, throw it all on there."

"Opinions on pineapple?" I ask, steepling my fingers and leaning in imperiously. "You *will* be graded on your answer."

The geist rolls her eyes at me. "It's mid at best. And before you act all offended, I *know* that you only defend pineapple because you like being a contrarian little shit. It's an alright topping. I'll eat it if it's in front of me, but it's never my first choice."

My contentious overreaction is pre-emptively vanquished, so instead I shrug and admit, "Yeah, okay, it's not really my favorite. I'm a spinach-and-feta girl when it comes to pizza."

"Under the broad heading of sandwiches, I'm a fan of burgers that are as meaty and cheesy as possible, with sauce. Can't go wrong with a good bacon burger." She gestures to the remnant stains of her recently devoured bacon burger.

"Bah," I declare. "Bacon is overhyped, and this one *isn't* me being a contrarian little shit. Bacon is only good when it's the side dish to real breakfast like eggs or french toast. I think it's actively worsened the burgers and omelets I've had it in."

"I definitely don't believe you on that; you've had at least one good bacon burger," she accuses.

"Ehhhh, maybe. Still not great. Anyways, the best kind of burger is a black bean burger with blue cheese crumble. Next!"

Cheshire giggles and finishes her last fry. "Alright, let's talk sushi. I like 'em the crazier the better: the kind that's got three kinds of fish and gets caked in sauce and breading. You?"

Mmm, sushi. Damn it, I should have gotten sushi. "That's pretty good, though I'm also partial to the humble avocado roll. Mostly because avocado, which is a divine treasure."

"Pfft. Californian."

I glare at the offending creature. "You don't even—you're not *from* anywhere on Earth! That sentiment is nonsense! You're only saying that because you've got a bunch of me-adjacent memory-knowledge-stuff! Hiss! Hiss I say!"

"Am I wrong?" She smirks at me, smugly.

I mutter some unkind words and choose to abruptly and valiantly change the subject. I make a sweeping gesture at all the people around us in the mall, and ask, "So hey, what's up with phones? Bashe said phones are like, strictly magic here? And don't exist *here* here, in the Labyrinth? Is this something to do with how everyone is 'trapped' here?"

Cheshire nods and leans back in her chair. "Basically, yeah. And a quick note: phones aren't *everywhere*. Bashe's world has 'em, but they're far from common among the Spheres, and they're different on each Sphere that has 'em. Bashe's phones tap into the throne world of a god of information, and they only function at all when they can maintain an active connection to that throne world. But nothing can interact across the Labyrinth's barrier, so in this throne world they're just scraps of metal and plastic."

"Hmm. Noted. So . . . what's the deal with this barrier?" I lean in, because I'm pretty sure this is some plot-critical shit. "No interaction in or out, but people keep getting pulled in, including a girl from the Zero Sphere. And *you*, if I recall, blame Katoptris for that last one: the Lady of Shards, the Nightmare Queen, who plucked me from my world . . . for which I should really be thanking her, but you seem to want me to kill her."

"It seems like the logical endpoint of your quest, does it not?" She spreads her hands questioningly. "Transported to another world as the would-be Dark Lord, to accomplish any of your goals you'll eventually have to depose the local dimensional overlord. Further, it will be necessary if you ever wish to *leave* the Labyrinth; right now, you, along with everyone else in this throne world, are sealed from the rest of Pandaemonium by a barrier, and that barrier is sustained by the Lady Katoptris. Kill the throne lord, break the barrier, and ascend."

I frown, pensive. *That's certainly the exact logic I used in front of Bashe, but I still have questions.* "What exactly *is* the Lady of Shards? Bashe called her an ancient monster, you call her a throne lord, but how does she fit into the system? Is she Royalty? Is she a witch? Is she a Leviathan?"

"*That* is an excellent question, and one that few have concrete answers to. She predates the Founding—the establishment of the laws and customs of Firmament—but she is distinctly neither Leviathan nor Titan. 'Witch' might be an accurate term, in modern context, or perhaps something more grandiose like 'witch-god.' I'm afraid the Demiurge did not permit me to know those precise details when she was sculpting my understanding." There's something so light about how she says something so disconcerting.

"Okay. We'll go off that for now. But . . . I always have more questions. I've made it one of my Truths, haven't I? A hunger for knowledge. So I *will* keep pursuing this, and all the questions I have, until I understand *everything* about this world and whatever mad plot I'm wrapped up in." I meet Cheshire's brilliant yellow-and-blue gaze, I blink, and I flicker on my soul sight.

The world turns to paper and ink once more, all the other souls in the food court fading to splashes of dim and distant color. There's just Cheshire in front of me, star of the sketchpad. She shows me a new view, this time: the cat-eared mask is tied with red ribbon, and the ribbons twirl and twist on each other in endless fractal patterns that stretch off the page.

I peer through the ribbons, within the ribbons, to something behind the mask. I see glittering multi-colored stars, and some indistinct shadow moving through them, visible only when it blocks the light. The absence of starlight moves closer, and it's surrounding me, embracing me, and I am filled with a sense of warmth and sincerity and love.

I snap my eyes shut, clench my fists, and banish my second sight. When I open my eyes again, Cheshire is smiling at me with that smug fucking grin. "Were you hoping for a show?" she asks.

I growl and rise from my seat, grabbing my trash to throw it in the nearest waste bin. "It is insanely vexing, trying to figure you out. You're my only source on basically everything in this world, and I have no idea how much I can trust you. So, I don't really have a choice, and that vexes me."

Cheshire touches my shoulder and looks at me with (probably false) sympathy. "I understand. I really do. And I wish that you had been able to come to this world under better circumstances; your life would be a lot easier right now if you were in a normal city rather than one of the Labyrinth's little safe havens."

I sigh. "Yeah, well, I probably wouldn't have been brought here at all if that were the case, or at the very least I wouldn't have been given magic. So . . . let's just keep moving. There's more to do, right?"

Immediately her demeanor shifts, expression brightening and body language adjusting to be more chipper. "Yep! Oh, so much to do! You, my dear, need a wardrobe upgrade. It'll do your magic good, and also you look terrible, no offense."

I *am* still wearing a dead person's clothes: torn leggings, a loose top, and the thoroughly bloodied skirt I've had since waking up. "Yeah, that's fair."

"Of course, we'll have to change your appearance first," she points out cheerily. "No point picking an outfit if we don't know what it's gonna be framing, right? So let's crack open that mindscape of yours and get to reshaping your adorable physical form."

I panic, not ready for that yet, and blurt, "How about books? Books are cool. Why don't we do books first, actually, and then we do that after? Yeah, that sounds like an awesome idea. To the bookstore!"

I grab Cheshire's hand and start power-walking for the nearest terminal, and from there we follow its directions to a place apparently specializing in fiction. Cheshire seems amused by my panic but doesn't fight me on the digression.

We reach the bookshop (again I'm not really sure "shop" applies but I just don't have a better word) and find it quite quaint: within the high-tech neon-and-chrome mall, this hole in the wall is all done up to look ancient and rustic, wood-paneled. We step inside and I am met with the wonderful scent of *books:* that delicious musty papery smell I know so well.

With a grin on my face I stride through aisles of wonderment. The first thing that strikes me is the difference in genre: I'm used to seeing fantasy and science fiction given a little corner of shame, but here I see stories of the fantastical mixed in throughout all genres . . . and then I realize that, of course, the fantastical is *normal* for these people. On closer inspection, there *is* a dividing line: about half the store is marked as speculative fiction, while the other half is contemporary.

They just both feature magic, for the most part, because a world without magic is almost inconceivable to the inhabitants of Pandaemonium.

I examine some of the contemporary fiction, fascinated by insights into Pandaemonium: a romance between an elf and a shrine priestess, an action tale about an exalted and their band of heroes besting a wicked lich, the arduous road of a wizard-in-training that dreams of becoming a dragon, and so many more. There's a part of me that wants to stay in this section forever, learning as much as possible about Pandaemonium, but I get the distinct feeling that learning about a world exclusively through its fiction may leave me with some not-quite-useful assumptions.

So, to recreation: I cross the boundary and step into what Pandaemonium sees as speculative fiction. Unsurprisingly I do catch a couple of novels dreaming up wild tales of what the Zero Sphere might look like (all horribly wrong, obviously), but as I trace my finger over lovely spines I catch sight of one title that strikes my interest: *The Machinations of the Ashen Warlock.*

It's a silly bit of fantasy: the story of a young girl from an impoverished background who is given a chance at rising through the ranks of her society's elite sorcerer caste. The central tension appears to be the Trials that all aspirants must go through to be made a sorcerer's apprentice, which pit them against each other in increasingly lethal contests. The tension rising in the background concerns the titular Ashen Warlock, a mysterious magus who cured the protagonist's debilitating health condition for purposes unknown.

It sounds fun, and I idly flip through a few pages, getting a feel for the story. A few pages turn into more, and I'm a quarter of the way through the book when I suddenly stop and laugh. I grab a bookmark—they're left all over the bookstore, thoughtfully—and turn to Cheshire with a grin.

"You know, the first book I ever tried to write was about a warlock. It was nothing like this story, really, but this story's definitely much better than mine was. I was . . . well, I was an idiot kid, and I had more ambition than technique or experience. It was so cringe, but I was like twelve when I wrote it. It was about—well, actually, I guess you'd already know that, right." I scratch my head sheepishly, embarrassed.

Cheshire smiles at me. "I want to hear it, regardless. I like listening to you talk, especially about something you have passion for. And I *know* you have passion for this. So c'mon: sit, and spin me a yarn."

She gestures to a pair of chairs to sit in. I've been reading standing up, like a fool, so I stroll over and get comfy. I drum my fingers along the arm of the chair, nervous, and then I get right into it. "Okay, so, it's this story about a warlock. A grand warlock, who was sealed away for ten thousand years, and at the start of the story finally escapes his prison. His prison was—well, okay, I guess I have to make a quick digression. I say that this is the first book I ever tried to write, and in some sense it is, but it was built on the ashes of an even earlier attempt. I wanted to write a story about an amnesiac, but it turns out that's actually really hard, so I scrapped it before I'd written more than a few pages and turned the outline into a very unwieldy prologue for *this* story."

Cheshire curls up in her chair and asks, "Did you write a lot of unwieldy prologues?"

"Oh, yeah, absolutely. No self-awareness, little Alice. But yeah, so, big unwieldy prologue explaining this war between the good kingdom and the evil empire, and this big bad evil god of darkness—who, get this, was named after a *League of Legends* character—and then hero-boy kills the dark god and saves the day, but this has consequences: it lets out the grand warlock, who was . . . gods, he was such an edgy character. His name was *Tharias Maledictus*, and if you think the faux-Latin is bad then wait till you hear where the 'Tharias' part came from: a *World of Warcraft* random name generator, because he got his start as my *WoW* character."

Cheshire bursts out laughing and I laugh with her, because it's just patently absurd. "Amazing. Your video game warlock with a last name of '*Curse*.'"

"Ha, it's meant to be Tharias *Evilcurse*, actually, because 'even more edgy,' but I know that's not actually how the Latin works in that conjugation. Anyways, yeah, he was your generic edgy self-insert OC: uber-strong, uber-smart, a twelve-year-old's sense of humor, the works. And he's got these big plans, and he goes on these crazy adventures, but the core of it starts with him picking up an apprentice from this half-elf orphan girl he finds in the slums of some city in the good kingdom. Her name is Elizabeth, and she's arguably the real protagonist of the series. She's scrappy, vicious, and she falls into a lot of those 'Strong Female Character' tropes you see get used when someone wants a feminist character but doesn't really know how to write one and is kind of overcorrecting. Like, there's literally a scene where some guy thinks she shouldn't be on the adventure because she's a girl, so she kicks his ass. That bargain-bin shit."

Cheshire claps her hands together and makes an, "Awwww" noise, which I ignore.

"So, Tharias and Elizabeth adventure together, and he teaches her how to become a warlock, and they kinda sorta end up as a couple? Which, actually pretty yikes, looking back. Like there's a lot of power differential going on there, and he withholds a lot of information from her. The whole master/apprentice romance angle is creepy, especially since it's not like, played for subversion or anything, but again, I was twelve. I genuinely didn't know any better."

"Sure, of course," Cheshire nods. "And that's definitely not at all indicative of some of your preferences now, mhm."

The catgirl winks and I hiss at her. "I will boil you alive, cat."

She snickers, then waves a hand. "Go on, continue your story. You're cute when you infodump."

Fucking cat changeling geist thing getting in my head and calling me cute like a weird wrong weirdo. Hiss! I huff and get back to the story. "So, I'm not gonna explain the whole story, because this stupid thing was meant to be *nine books long*, and who the fuck sits down to write a story that long? It's absurd. Nine books, Cheshire. A trilogy of trilogies! Absurd! The trilogies went like this: in the first trilogy, we're introduced to the core cast and the setting, and then in the third book I kill off half the cast as part of a dramatic upheaval of the status quo that leaves our protagonists—Tharias and Elizabeth—as the seeming villains of the story. The second trilogy starts by reinforcing that impression with heroes coming after the duo, but then there are huge plot reveals about the eldritch horrors really pulling the strings, and the central couple are separated by said horrors. The final trilogy focuses on them apart at first, allowing Elizabeth to really come into her own, and then they reunite in time to defeat the eldritch horror big bads, but it turns out that the only way to save all life from their dominion is to burn away the whole universe and reincarnate it as something new free of their influence. So that's what Tharias and Elizabeth do, and that's where the series ends, with the whole universe burned away and forged anew."

I breathe deep, a little winded from rambling on for so long. I look over at Cheshire, still nervous despite *knowing* she already knows all this. It's weird; I don't usually *care* if someone finds my early writing cringe, because it absolutely is, and that's fine. I like my old stories, even if they're horribly amateurish. So I shouldn't care what she thinks . . . but I do. Gods, she might be the only person in this world with a chance of understanding me, of knowing me. So I care so very deeply what she thinks of me.

. . . And also there's the whole maybe plotting my demise thing? Yeah. Complicated relationship.

Cheshire is still smiling, but it's more thoughtful now. "So, which character were you?"

I laugh darkly. "That's . . . complicated. I mean, it wasn't, when I wrote it. Obviously Tharias was my self-insert, it's what I wrote him for. But I plotted that story a long time ago, and even then . . . I sure did show a lot of attention to Elizabeth. I was drawn to her, to the point that I wrote Tharias out of the story for a while so I could develop her further, and I made her the star of the show, I made her the key to everything. She was the one who went on an actual character journey, and she was the one with the classic protagonist backstory setup. So, in a way . . . I guess they're both me. Writers do that, yeah? Put a piece of themselves in every character, or, I guess, a lot of themselves in just two?"

I hesitate. I know the subtext here. I know the reason. And I know she knows. But it's still so damn hard to say it for the first time to . . . to whatever she is to me. Whatever *this* is. It means confronting shit I don't want to confront. But, I have to say it. I have to.

"I guess what it comes down to is that I wrote that story before I knew I was trans, and I never really went back and rewrote it because I was too busy making new versions, new stories. So it's kind of . . . transitional, in a way. Heh."

Cheshire acts amused at my silly little joke, but then says, "So: transness. Is that a thing you want to talk about? Given the whole 'avoiding dealing with your appearance' thing?"

I look away from her. "Not particularly, no. What's there to talk about? I'm not interested in making my life into another example of trans misery porn. I'm *fine* with who I am, with myself. I'm cool, I'm smart, and I can be incredibly charming when I choose to. So it doesn't *matter* that I'm not pretty or good-looking or even slightly conventionally attractive, or that I'll never really look like I want to, how I want to."

"But you can," Cheshire says gently. "I'm offering that. So what's stopping you?"

I notice one of my hands shaking, so I clasp it tightly with the other. "I. I just. I don't like to think about it, okay? It's not a problem if I just ignore it and let it fester. And actually fixing it means facing it. Facing me. This is how I cope, and I guess I'm just dreading that period of acknowledging it before it's fixed . . . and maybe, a little, I'm afraid that nothing you can do will really make a difference."

"It will," she says with the strength of true conviction. "I promise. So come on, Alice: let's make you everything you've ever dreamed of being."

She holds out a hand, and I stare at it for a long moment, the dread building. But finally I reach out, and I take it, and then we enter my soul once more.

XVIII

My inner world is not quite as I left it.

All the key features are still there, of course: the blasted hellscape, the maelstrom of memory, the pedestals of power, and the table of Truths. Horrid beasts of shadow and meat still kill each other in the desolate plains, the eye of the storm is still a pile of oversized books, and the tea table is still carved with three glowing symbols.

The differences are subtle: the book pile feels bigger, and the life-draining statue feels bigger, and the glowing symbols feel a little brighter, but none of it by much. The most noticeable change is that, out in the wasteland, I see traces of actual food being fought over instead of just carrion and smoke.

I frown at the scene beyond the book pile. Cheshire told me that this place is the deepest recesses of my soul, and that it looks like this because of how I perceive myself; I expect my soul to look like this, so it does. So, I wonder: if I changed my perception, could I change this world?

"Welcome back to your throne world," Cheshire says with that perpetual grin stuck to her face. I note briefly that she's back in her yellow-and-pink number, and I'm back in the poofy dress, but there's a much more important piece of information to focus on.

"Sorry, did you just call this a throne world? Like the Labyrinth? Like Royalty has?" I whirl on Cheshire, who's standing beside me atop the book pile, just a few feet away from the Truth-marked table.

The creature giggles and raises a hand in front of her face. "In a manner of speaking. The difference between your throne world and theirs is about as vast as the difference between your soul and the soul of someone who isn't a scion."

I pick at the details and pull on the thread further. "So, wait: if this is my soul *and* my throne world, and if that's the comparison you're making . . .

are they always one and the same? Is the Labyrinth . . . is it the *soul of Katoptris?*"

Cheshire raises her left hand and conjures the floating image of a woman with blurry features, then raises her right hand and makes a globe appear. "The soul is the self, which acts on the world and is acted on by the world. A sufficiently powerful soul—a sufficiently *empowered* soul—can bring the self and the world together as one." She pushes the woman and the globe together until they're overlapping. "And that is what we call a throne world: a localized space in which Pandaemonium has been overwritten by a higher authority. For a scion, that space is mostly internal except for some specific circumstances. Royalty, however, can keep that throne world manifested permanently."

"Specific circumstances?" I prompt.

Cheshire nods and lowers her hands, the image vanishing. "While a scion approaching apotheosis can start to manifest their throne world more casually and wider-reaching, you're mostly going to be manifesting it when you challenge someone to a scion's duel."

"That sounds fun and also dangerous." I lean against the big stuffed bunny rabbit (thankfully still here).

"It is! It's also the best way to get stronger as a scion of Shadow. A scion's duel begins with a formal challenge against a worthy foe. If they accept, you can manifest your throne world and the two of you will battle, usually to the death. Victory means you get to claim the soul of your opponent, while loss means your own soul is forfeit."

Ultimate high-stakes conflict. An all-or-nothing battle. "And when I get their soul, what do I do with it? Eat it?"

She licks her teeth. "That's one way, yeah. Eating resonant souls is how most demons make progress towards apotheosis, and it's also the only way that most of them can get more spells. Your [Prey Upon] gives you a bit of extra progress towards new spells, but it's still mostly going to be scion's duels that let you expand your library. But there's an important caveat: they have to be *resonant* souls. If you eat a soul that you can't feed into your Truths, you'll do more harm than good, and the consequences could be disastrous."

I frown. *Tricky. We'll have to play it careful.* "So what do I do with those souls, then?"

Cheshire snaps her fingers and a replica of [Ashthorn] appears in her hand. "You make artifacts with them!"

I give her a skeptical look. "I already have that power, apparently. What's the difference?"

"Pretty big. Look, I don't know all the details about how your Gift works, but I know this much: you channeled the lingering magic from a powerful spell into a resonant container, and the resulting artifact did almost nothing."

Cheshire tosses [Ashthorn] away and I reluctantly cede that point; the dagger wasn't useless, but its benefits were largely incremental. And apparently that's on the higher end of what I can make with my power? "You're making my superpower sound a lot less appealing."

"Not at all. Your Gift is versatile and has a high skill ceiling, but the tradeoff is that it'll take time and concerted effort to get results out of it. A soulforged artifact, on the other hand, is going to be immediately powerful."

"Noted." I peer out at the wasteland pensively. I have my path to power, I suppose: draining souls with [Prey Upon], making lesser artifacts with my Gift, consuming souls won through duels, and shaping souls into greater artifacts. And if I can just do that enough . . . divinity awaits.

"Now," Cheshire begins, "I believe we came here for a reason?" She looks at me expectantly and flutters her eyelashes.

Ah, right. That mess. I grimace and search for an excuse to procrastinate. Luckily, I'm staring at one. "Question first: if this is my soul, can I make it look like whatever I want? You said this is an act of self-definition, right? Because I'm really not keen on my inner world being a desolate fucking wasteland."

"Mm, I suppose that's worth doing while we're here," Cheshire muses. "Alright, I'll help you reshape your throne world. It'll be necessary before you fight any duels regardless."

I rub my hands together excitedly. "Excellent. I have *ideas*. If I'm going to be dueling people here, I want this to feel like a proper fucking battleground."

Cheshire chuckles. "I figured. But, a note before we begin: the truer your throne world is to your Truths and your true self, the more powerful it will make you, but also the more vulnerable if someone finds what you've laid bare. As a result, it's considered standard practice for a scion to shape their throne world in such a way that an outer layer of superficial truth hides an inner core of deeper vulnerability."

Hmm. So maybe . . . *something like a dungeon or raid from an MMO? We play the role of the final boss at the inner sanctum, but surround it with lesser threats to deter opponents?* "Let's get started, then. How do we do this?"

The catgirl sweeps her hand in the direction of the wasteland. "Just breathe, imagine the world the way you want it to look, and give it a push of will like you're summoning me. If it helps, you can describe things aloud or make hand gestures, but it's all about asserting your dream onto the landscape. This is your world; it'll listen if you command it."

"Okay." I take a deep breath, close my eyes, and crack my knuckles. *Making a world. I can do that. It's just an imagination game.*

First things first: we need a blank canvas. I imagine the wasteland falling away into vast white nothingness, and then the maelstrom doing the same, and even the books beneath my feet until I'm left standing on a single scrap of paper, with Cheshire by my side. I reach out with my thoughts for the world around me, but it doesn't feel the same as manifesting Cheshire. It doesn't click.

Because you're not affecting an externality. You're affecting an internal *world.* I reach inward instead, focusing inside and willing the world within my soul to change, and this time I feel something shift. I hear an echo of my own voice in my ears, and when I open my eyes I'm standing in a vast white void.

It worked! Yes! From beside me, Cheshire whistles appreciatively. "Quite the nice empty space you've got here. Whatcha gonna fill it with?"

"I have some ideas."

It takes me more than a few tries to get everything right; I have very poor visualization skills, and I'm bad with spatial reasoning, so it's an effort to get the impression in my head translated to something that looks good in reality. Still, bit-by-bit, my world coalesces.

I raise a bleak mountain, craggy and snow-dappled, and place a winding trail on its side. Beneath us and around us grows a forest of tree-like organisms made of meat and flesh and pulsating tumors, the crimson forest shrouded in a dense layer of mist. The sky above is dark and gloomy, an impressionist painting of browns and grays. Within that sky burns a baleful red eclipse, a hole in the sky ringed in writhing red like churning plasma.

The mountain path leads to a grim castle, dark and spiky and Gothic, with perching gargoyles and stained glass windows in a hundred shades of red. I shape a portcullis archway like the maw of a beast, and behind it massive double doors leading inside the castle.

I ask Cheshire if, since this is a throne world, I can fill it with figments, and she tells me that I can. Within the gruesome forest below I seed beasts of shadow and bone, hungering and preying upon each other. At the entrance to the castle I have a bit of fun: I dream up a pair of talking skeletons, one in a butler's uniform and one in a maid's, and on a whim I try to engrave both with a tendency for a very particular form of humor.

I try to imagine what would go inside the castle and run into a roadblock: I know nothing about floor plans and my understanding of 3D space is, as mentioned, rather shit, so how do I design the inside of a castle? I admit my difficulty to Cheshire and she reminds me that space here is conceptual, not physical; the castle could hold an infinite maze or a single small room, or both without contradiction.

Keeping that in mind, I shape a grand entrance hall full of doors leading off to rooms that I can worry about designing later, and at last I deem my work done.

I breathe out and feel a wave of relief wash over me; turns out reshaping reality can give you quite the headache. I was beginning to feel the strain from making and remaking pieces of the world to fit my perfect image. But now it should all be ready, so I roll my shoulders, lick my lips, and start walking toward the gate.

Cheshire follows behind, beaming at all the new sights. "Fun little vampire hideaway, and I dig the meat moss. But, quick question: is that sun from a video game? It looks oddly familiar but I can't place it."

I wince sheepishly. "Uhhh, maybe. I may or may not have stolen the bleeding eclipse visual from *Skyrim*."

She snickers, and then we reach the gate and the two skeletons. The butler skeleton bows while the maid skeleton curtsies, and then the butler skeleton says, "Mistress Alice, it tickles my spine to have you back! The estate is just as you left it, cobwebs to candle wax. There's even a fresh meal waiting for you in the dining hall."

"No thanks to him," the maid skeleton butts in, hands on her hips. "I work my fingers to the bone and this numbskull claims all the credit!"

The butler turns to glare at her, his skull cracking and shifting into the contortion of a facial expression, and he retorts, "Pipe down, you dusty old museum piece. Without my guidance, you'd have tried to serve the Mistress spare ribs!"

I'm grinning ear-to-ear; this is everything I wanted and more. "Don't let it get under your skin, Clavicus. I'm sure Bonehilda's just pulling your femur. I value both of you immensely."

The butler, mollified, adjusts his suit and mumbles, "Yes, well, it's good to be appreciated. Ahem. Would you like a guide, ma'am, or would you rather find your own way?"

I pat the skeleton on his adorable skull. "I think I'll be fine. Keep up the good work, the both of you."

I stroll past them to the big double doors and make to push them open, then pause. *Idea.* I snap my fingers instead and will the doors to open, and they swing inward like they were hit by a blast of wind. I clap my hands excitedly and head inside, Cheshire trailing behind me.

The catgirl pokes my shoulder and raises an eyebrow at me. "Skeleton puns? Really?"

"It tickled my funny bone," I comment dryly as I look about the interior of my castle. The grand hall is a lovely arched affair with chandeliers and red carpeting and literally dozens of doors lining the walls. At some point I want to add banners with a personal symbol on them, but I don't know what that symbol should be yet.

"And the fact that there were only two of them? A 'skeleton crew,' was it?" Cheshire seems more amused than annoyed, which is good and fitting; any creature made to be my perfect girlfriend would by necessity have a healthy love of puns.

"Guilty!" I happily admit. "Now, where to next . . ."

Cheshire coughs politely and says, "I think you know what should be next. We did come here for a reason, after all. Make a dressing room, Alice, and give it a mirror."

I hesitate, but she's right; it's time to face . . . well, my face. And then a new face. A new me.

I breathe deep, reach into the world within me, and shape a new room behind one of the grand hall's doors. A wardrobe, a few dressers, a makeup area, hairstylist's tools, and a person-length mirror. I feel it click and return to myself, and then with a wave of my hand the door to that room opens.

I glance at Cheshire, then back to the room, and swallow nervously. "Okay. Let's do this." I step inside.

XIX

I dislike mirrors. I can't say I've *always* disliked mirrors, but it's been true for a long time. Mirrors are cruel, wretched things, insistent on showing unwanted truths.

As I step inside the dressing room and survey the scenery, my gaze instinctively turns aways from the floor mirror—cheval glass, they're sometimes called—that I placed there just moments ago. I don't want to do this. I hate it.

Cheshire hugs me from behind and murmurs in my ear, "You've got this. This is the last time you'll ever have to see the old you. So give it a look, and we can figure out how to make the new you. Just look in the mirror and tell me what you want to change."

My fists clench, and I grit my teeth, but I know she's right. I know I need to do this. So I face my reflection.

It's a funny thing, but my face looked so much better on Homura. Maybe my recollection is being colored by Reska's point of view, but it was so much easier to dismiss all of Homura's imperfections as just normal human variation. But when it's the girl in the mirror?

"All of it," I tell Cheshire, knowing what a useless comment that is but still compelled to speak. "I wish I could rip it off. I wish I didn't have to deal with any of this stupid sack of meat and bone."

"Specifics, love. We've got to start somewhere. What about your teeth?" I can see her in the mirror, practically hanging over me, expression focused and intent.

"I hate my teeth." Once I get started, it's easier to keep going, the words finally flowing out of me all at once. "I hate how crooked most of them are, and I hate my dumb little overbite, and I hate that I've never taken care of them and nobody ever made me take care of them when I was just a dumb kid that didn't know any better. I don't even want perfect teeth, just . . . no, actually, if I can look like anything, then make my teeth perfect. Make them clean and straight and white. Keep the fangs, obviously. I want perfect vampire teeth."

"Your wish is my command," Cheshire says, and then for the first time in my life my teeth are beautiful.

"Okay, um. Chapped lips. I really just don't take care of any part of myself, so my lips are always chapped and I chew at them until they flake. Fix that." My lips smooth out, and I run my tongue along teeth and lips both to get a feel for them; they don't just look nicer, they feel nicer.

"How about your skin?" she asks.

I grimace. "Horrid." My skin is rough and I can see a few traces of acne, the unsightly result of poor skincare and a bad habit of picking at my face. "I want my skin smooth, soft, unblemished."

I blink and it's like looking at a different person; my skin is supermodel-perfect, practically airbrushed. "Holy shit." I reach up and touch my face. My fingers trace over skin that's smoother and softer than the best blanket I've ever held. It's incredible. It's sensory bliss.

I stare into my reflection's eyes, and more requests come pouring out. "The bags under my eyes, get rid of them. Actually . . . can you like, bake makeup into my skin? Like how some people get a tattoo that looks like eyeshadow?"

"Sure thing!" Cheshire chirps. "The sky's the limit here, Allie. Pick whatever you want."

I smile, and I notice my lips again, and that gives me another angle. "Okay, give me dark eye makeup, and shiny black lipstick, but they're actually just my face now." The changes happen instantly, and when I smack my lips and touch the skin around my eyes they don't feel like there's any makeup there at all.

That leaves my eyes themselves. My . . . ugh. "I have complicated feelings about my eyes," I admit to Cheshire. "Growing up, I had multiple people in my life joke about how, because my eyes are brown, that makes them 'the color of shit' or sometimes just 'full of shit.' And that got to me. I hated having brown eyes. It wasn't until like, much later, very late teens, that I made a conscious effort to try and be more okay with my eyes. 'Cause I mean, they're just brown. Lots of people have brown eyes. Attractive people have brown eyes! And my eyes aren't really ugly; they're not the most interesting color of brown, but I've had people express jealousy over my long eyelashes. I feel weird for how much I've cared about it in the past."

Cheshire smiles at me in the mirror. "Eyes are important to people. We put a lot of meaning into eyes. Tired eyes, kind eyes, cold eyes, sharp eyes. My eyes mark me as a changeling, and they're the only aspect of my appearance that I can't really change; no matter what animal I turn into, I'll always have this exact shade of heterochromia. For the record, I think your eyes are pretty as they are, but I don't think you should let old baggage stop you from looking *exactly* as you want. So: what kind of eyes do you really want to have?"

"Heh. I mean . . . what kind of self-respecting vampire doesn't have unnatural eyes? Can you cycle through yellow, orange, and red, so I can get a feel for each?"

She does so, and I watch my eyes flicker through different hues. I have an appreciation for yellow eyes, and I think orange eyes can look good, but ultimately neither of them really *pop* like a nice bright red. And besides, red's more in my color palette. But I do have one other thought . . .

"Question: can you make it so that, like, my eyes change color? Like, could we set it so that my eyes get brighter and redder, maybe even slightly glowing, whenever I feed or cast a spell?"

My eyes flash a burning crimson, and Cheshire grins. "You bet I can. Among the many wonderful benefits of your body being smoke and mirrors is that it's pretty easy to set up a conditional modifier like that."

The bright light fades and my irises return to a more modest red, but I am ecstatic. "That's so cool. Okay, I've gotta keep that in mind going forward, because there's so much we can do with that. Um, next change: eyebrows. I hate how thick and messy my eyebrows are, I want them thin and clean."

"Done." She snaps her fingers—for effect, I imagine, since she didn't need to do anything previously—and my eyebrows sort themselves out. "Any other face changes, or are we good to move to body stuff?"

"Yeah, I have a bit more I want to do, but I'm not completely sure on the specifics. I want a more 'elegant' face, I guess. Higher cheekbones, maybe, and a more delicate nose. Vampy aristocratic."

"I can work with that." Cheshire sculpts my face, making subtle and not-so-subtle tweaks to my facial structure until it looks more or less like I was imagining: a fancy vampire lady.

"That actually looks really good," I say, fascinated by hearing my voice coming out of a face that is getting less recognizable by the minute. "Last thing is hair. I want to try a few things."

I have Cheshire set my hair color to black, then white, red, and even a few shades of pink briefly. I lengthen my hair, then shorten it. I even have her change it from straight to curly, then back. I settle on black hair for higher contrast with my pale skin and red eyes, but I'm still not sure on the length and style.

"Do you know anything about hair?" I ask my geist. "Because I'm realizing that I know like two hairstyles and have never styled my own hair and don't really know how to. A shorter pixie-ish cut doesn't seem quite right for the character I want to play, but plain long hair seems boring."

"Hmm." Cheshire taps her chin and leaves her place behind me to start circling me, peering intently at my hair. "Let me try something."

My hair grows long again, and then Cheshire grabs a hairband from amid the styling supplies, bunches my hair into a ponytail, then spins it into a bun and keeps it steady with a few bobby pins. She lets a bit of hair out to either side so that I've got two locks of hair framing my face, and the end result is a cute and modest loose bun. Together with the red eyes and my new facial features (and the faux-makeup), I'm really starting to look like a vampire.

"That's amazing," I tell the catgirl. "Uh, though, if it gets messed up I don't think I can fix it."

Cheshire waves a hand dismissively. "That's what I'm here for. I'll happily do your hair whenever you like." Cheshire smiles at me, and I feel oddly like blushing. Oddly in that it's not an embarrassed blush or a horny blush, but almost . . . it's hard to pin down. There's just something nice and sweet about her offer, something comforting, even if it's coming from a creature I can't allow myself to fully trust.

"Thanks," I manage, not fully able to control the catch in my voice. "That's, um, that's hair, then. You said body, next?"

"It's your show, Alice," she reminds me gently. "You get to pick. But yes, if you're ready for it, we can take a look at altering your neck-down now. Of course, you'll probably want to *see* your body, so that dress might have to come off. For accurate measurements," she adds, and I can hear the suggestive smirk in her voice as clearly as I can see it on her face.

I'm back to feeling awkward and embarrassed. I mean, rationally, she's seen my life and has definitely seen me naked and wow that's a thought. Cheshire has probably—almost certainly—seen me naked. Possibly through my own eyes. Okay. Well. Just. Filing that away to freak out about later.

But regardless, it's not like I'm that self-conscious about being seen in my underwear. I wouldn't go so far as to say I'm an exhibitionist, but when I can ignore the dysphoria I'm perfectly fine showing off my body for attention. Hells, I was going to let an incubus fuck me just so that he'd like me more. And I've even changed in front of Cheshire, while replacing my ruined shirt at the nightclub. So what's different this time?

It comes to me quickly: context. It was a very functional action at the club, just rote changing of clothing. But here, we're discussing my body. We're changing my body. There's a more personal element to it, and a certain sexual/romantic element with the intimacy and the fact that what's attractive is inherently a part of the discussion. And even the "showing off for attention" part feels meaningfully different, because the relationship the attention is coming from is one that I have a lot of complicated feelings about. If I stripped for Cheshire, would that be an act of calculated attention-seeking manipulation, or is my desire for Cheshire to find me attractive something deeper and more vulnerable?

Because I do want her to find me attractive, I realize. My traumatized, abused, broken monkey brain is irrationally terrified that Cheshire won't find me attractive and will abandon me because I'm not pretty enough for her, not good enough for her. She'll call me ugly and leave me and then I'll be alone again. Like always.

Please don't leave me. Please, please don't leave me. I need you.

I swallow nervously, and I take off my dress.

I was expecting the underwear beneath to be fancy and frilly, given the dress itself, but it's just plain and functional. And now I'm standing there, looking at myself in the mirror, at my half-naked body. Pale skin. All the self-harm scars faded back in, the last effects of [Indulgent Vitality] dispelled. Thin arms; thin overall, technically, but pudgy around the waist and stomach, some flab on the thighs, and nubby breasts barely filling her bra. Stretch marks here and there but especially around the knees. A bit of light hair growing in on the legs and stomach and armpits.

Her bra? My bra. Because that's my body in the mirror. My stupid ugly worthless hideous body. Too thin in all the wrong places and too fat in others. Marked and scarred. Grotesque.

"So what do you want to change?" Cheshire asks, gaze sliding over my body.

"Everything," I snarl. "All of it."

She gives me an unimpressed look. "Let's go at this from a different angle, then: what do you want to *keep*? What traits of your body are worth preserving?"

I hesitate. I want to answer "Nothing," but I know that's not true. "I . . . I like my skin. I like how pale it is, and I like the scars. Sometimes. I—I want them to stay, at least. And I like having small tits. But I wish I were less fat, and smoother skin, and maybe a little bigger hips, and skin that's closer to really truly vampy pale."

"You're not fat," Cheshire points out. "Like, even slightly."

"But I could be thinner," I argue. I pinch a bit of stomach fat and wiggle it at her. "I'm thin, sure, but I'm also pudgy. And I'm not as skinny as when I was a teenager! I know for a fact that I've gained weight."

"Since you were *sixteen*? Yes, shocking news, you gain weight as you grow up. Bitch, you are a *twig*. If anything, you should fill out a little more so you don't look like you crawled out of an unmarked grave." Cheshire pats me on one bony, stick-like arm.

"Ah, but consider: I'm *trying* to look like a corpse! I want to be a vampire, remember? And doesn't your magic system reward synchronization of form and meaning? Ergo, it would actually be beneficial to my magic to be as thin as possible, and I don't even need to starve myself to do it! Why binge and purge when you can just stuff your face and then magically alter your body to your desired weight?"

Cheshire gives me a new look that says she is neither blind to nor impressed with the blatant eating disorder underlying my chain of logic. "Sweetie, when was the last time you saw a vampire woman in media who *wasn't* voluptuous? Genuinely, can you actually think of a vampire character you've seen who looked like a corpse and not a model?"

I grumble, but she's not wrong. I mean, I might think those shows and games are *cowards* for their portrayals of vampires, but I know that I'm rather unique in feeling that way.

"I think that you would look great *and* very vampy with a fuller chest," she suggests. "Which is not to say that I think you *should* do that, but I think you need a better argument for why not than 'to look like a vampire.'"

"Flat is justice," I insist.

"Weeb shit is neither a valid argument nor a sound argument."

"Ugh." I roll my eyes. "Look, everyone I've ever talked to who had big tits said that they were way more hassle than they were worth. Besides, they'd fuck with the gender aesthetic I want."

I immediately realize I've made a tactical error when Cheshire's face lights up and she leans in. "And what gender aesthetic is that, Alice?"

Shit. I've fallen right into her trap. I hesitate. *What do I say here? How much? Do I be evasive about it, or go full infodump?*

She called our infodumps cute.

Heh. Yeah. I guess she did. I breathe deep and brush a strand of hair out of my face. "Okay, so . . . I've kind of always wished that I could have been born a cis girl . . . so that it would be easier for me to dress masc and have masc hobbies. I wish that I could just fully embrace the like, nerdy tomboy aesthetic, without having to worry about getting misgendered. I mean, fuck, I've played Warhammer, Cheshire, and I'm obsessed with Magic: The Gathering. I was a Blizzard fan for years until Blitzchung, *Shadowlands*, and the abuse lawsuits. I play JRPGs and Pathfinder and *Stellaris* and *Dota*, and dear fucking gods do I watch a lot of anime. Those are some extremely male-dominated spaces, and it feels so *weird* to be a trans girl in those spaces, because I know it's distinctly not the cis girl experience in those spaces. There's this constant reminder that it didn't feel odd to exist in those nerdy interests as a kid because I was existing in it as a boy, not a girl. I got into *World of Warcraft* because of my aunt, and plenty of women play *WoW*, but a sizable chunk of the fanbase is horribly misogynistic and none of that was ever directed at *me* when I was playing the game growing up. And, to be clear, I *like* how immersed in some of those spaces I am. I like having that familiarity with nerd culture. But I hate the voice in my head highlighting what *masculine* interests I have, because even though I know it's bullshit and that plenty of cis women share these interests, it still gets under my skin."

"And how you dress?" Cheshire asks. "How does that play into it?"

"I like boy clothing. I like to do the spinny in the skirt and I like wearing a dress over top of shorts or leggings, but I mostly wear gamer T-shirts and plain jeans. I hate heels, and I can't be bothered to learn how to do my makeup or hair. And when you're a cis girl, none of that gets people to say that you're not a real girl. But when you're trans, every item on that list feels like another point of evidence invalidating the truth of your identity. So . . . yeah."

"You want to be an atypical kind of girl, but you have difficulty getting people to accept you as a girl at all," Cheshire interprets, and I nod reluctantly in reply. "Well, lucky for you, you don't have to worry about that anymore. So, Alice: what kind of girl do you want to be?"

I cross my arms and chew on the question. "I think that high femme is not my style. But at the same time, I'm not really tough enough or sporty enough for butch. I'm a weird bookworm."

"Futch," Cheshire suggests.

"I guess that fits." I scratch my head, nervous about this next part. "I have also, ah, debated going by different pronouns. I've tried she/they before, explored that space. I've even put some thought into it/its pronouns to express some inherent inhumanity, but I've never had the guts to try that with people and I feel like it would just get used against me by shitty transphobes. In the end I just default to she/her because it's easier for people and because it's the most definitive 'I am a girl, damn you.'"

Cheshire cocks her head curiously. "Do you want to go by any of those, with me? I'd have no problems incorporating them."

"Ah, no no no, that's not necessary." I hold up my hands and laugh nervously. "It's fine, really."

She smiles knowingly. "We can always come back to it later. But I do want to interrogate some of what you said: you want to express inhumanity, but you also want to be recognized as a woman."

"I mean, yeah, I guess. Part of me wants to be 'pretty' because of societal conditioning, but more of me wants to be a creepy fucking vampire. I want people to look at me and assume I'm female, but in a vaguely androgynous range where I can pull off different looks depending on how I'm feeling that day."

Cheshire nods. "And does that give you ideas on how you want to change your body?"

She definitely led me here. I don't know if I should be annoyed or grateful. "Yeah. Make me slender, my skin smooth and soft and pale, and rebalance fat away from the stomach to just a bit more in the hips and chest. Still thin, just a bit shapely, barely noticeable depending on the outfit. And get rid of all the hair on my body that isn't on my head."

Cheshire complies, and my form changes again. It's a subtle change, but clear to see, and I can't help but feel a wave of delight as I look at myself in the mirror and feel my hips with my hands. My skin is almost porcelain-smooth, and with the lack of a pulse it feels almost unliving.

Wait. Idea. "Cheshire, you said my body isn't fully physical anymore, and you called it 'smoke and mirrors.' What are the limits of that? Could I lower my body's surface temperature? Make it impossible to feel a pulse? Change the perceived texture of my skin?"

"All that and more," the catgirl confirms with a grin. "You could even give yourself faux-retractable claw nails that just transform back into regular nails when you're not using them to scratch someone's eyes out."

"Okay, well, first of all, please add that. And make them, I don't know, maybe black for the edge, or pink for the gap moe factor? Maybe pink lips too, actually, for the same reason? No, that would look terrible. Oh, how about make my nails and lips dark red."

"Done and done," Cheshire says, and it is.

"Hella. Okay, so, my idea: I want my skin to feel like porcelain. I want it to feel cold, and smooth, and there's no pulse. And I want my scars to look and feel more like cracks in the porcelain than scars in tissue . . . so actually, get rid of all the small and shallow scars so it's just the ones that will stand out. And the skin will be pale as porcelain too, a genuinely monochrome white."

Another blink and shift, and now my skin is even more like porcelain than before. There's something almost doll-like about it. "Hey, Cheshire, this is a weird question, but, since I'm a demon and less bound by the laws of physical reality, could I just, ah, choose not to have to urinate or defecate? Like, if my body isn't really real, then, when I'm eating, isn't it more about the concepts associated with eating? So can I just skip the demands of the crude physical equivalent?"

Cheshire nods. "Yes, you could alter your form to eliminate the need for physical waste expulsion. In fact, I went ahead and already did that for you when you first became a demon."

"Awesome. In that case, I'd like to . . . uh, hmm, what's a not-weird way to say this?" I stumble a little over what I'm trying to say. "Basically, give me doll anatomy. No nipples, and nothing down below. Just smooth porcelain."

Cheshire snaps her fingers and says, "Done," and I don't have to peek to feel the changes take effect.

I'm starting to get into this now. There's so much potential here. "Okay, I wanna get weirder. Creepier. If I can have retractable claws and eyes that shift color, what else? I want a jaw that unhinges and fills with razor-sharp teeth. I want to be able to rotate my head like an owl. Can I do that?"

"Yes and yes. Give it a try."

I open my mouth, then open it farther, to the point it would normally start to hurt, but instead the sides of my mouth split painlessly, my jaw keeps lowering, and all my teeth become vicious fangs. I shut my mouth and it all returns to pseudo-normalcy. Then I look behind me, and turn my head so far it's actually on backwards.

I turn back to the mirror, and I feel a bit of glee. "Make my tongue longer and pointier, but in a way that doesn't affect my speech." My tongue grows, and I can feel it reaching impossibly deeper into my mouth.

Okay, what else? I could give myself tattoos, maybe, or weird skin patterns, or fur or scales, but do I have good ideas for any of those? "Hmm. I'm debating adding doll joints but I feel like that might be taking it too far?"

Cheshire asks, "What's inspired the doll kick?"

"Good question. I mean, I liked the doll girl in *Bloodborne* a lot, and the doll girl in *Elden Ring*, but . . . could be that doll I met on arrival, too. Dolls are great for horror, you know, and they fit into this really interesting empty space, this sort of uncanny valley between human and not. You could make an argument for that contributing to my Truths, actually; dolls inspire Fear, but they are also loved and bonded with, something that falls under Blood."

Cheshire wiggles happily. "Ah, look at you, wrapping your brain around the Truth system. Very cute. If you don't want ball joints like a doll, you could add some bite marks on your neck instead."

"Oh that's a good idea! Okay, yeah, do that."

Two pinpricks appear on my neck, with just the slightest smear of blood. And now . . . I genuinely can't think of anything else to add. So here I am: a doll vampire demon with porcelain skin and crimson eyes.

I smile at my reflection, and for maybe the first time, I'm happy to see her.

XX

"You look lovely, Alice," murmurs my confusing companion.

"For once, I won't fight you on that." I continue admiring myself in the mirror, baring my fangs and playing with my hair. I really do look like everything I've ever wanted . . . barring the outfit, of course. "We should go back; I want some new threads to match the new body."

Cheshire leans against the wall. "Definitely, but we have a pair of items to get through first, while we're still in your throne world. You wanted some lifesteal, right?"

"Oh! Yes, absolutely." I rub my hands together and grin. I've always loved lifesteal effects in video games, and it just seems practical given the kinds of fights I'm getting in. "How do we do that? New spell?"

"Mm, not quite. But, before that, I want to make sure you're okay with the downsides: parasitic transfusion is addictive, and its use lessens the effectiveness of other kinds of healing on your person."

I'm sure those would be harsh enough penalties to make most people hesitate, but I don't slow for a second before saying, "Yep, sounds good. Totally willing to pay that price."

"Then here's how it's going to work: we don't have enough metaphysical grist to shape you a whole new spell, so we're going to use what you *do* have to make some modifications to one of your existing spells. We could add a life-draining property to [Carrion Swarm] and have you steal essence through whatever you summon, or we could add it to [Exsanguinate] for a more direct draining spell." Cheshire holds out both hands and creates a rat in one hand and an orb of blood in the other.

Hmm. I'm actually not sure which to go for here. [Carrion Swarm] is a useful spell and not as restrictive as [Exsanguinate], but it's almost more of a utility spell than a damaging spell, so how much healing will it actually contribute? From a Truths perspective, [Exsanguinate] is very Blood-aligned, and I imagine a life-draining effect would fit somewhere between Blood and Gluttony?

I wish I could tell what the symbols mean when I prime a spell and see its matrix. That would probably give me a lot of data for planning my synergies better.

... Wait. Idea. We're modifying the spell, right? Adding something to it? Does that mean the matrix will gain new symbols? And, crucially, could we try and compare the matrix before and after the modification to see which new symbols correspond to the life drain effect?

I feel a frenzy of insight coming on. *I need to be able to record this. I need paper.* I sink into the throne world again and will a stack of paper into existence, and a pen next to it. "I have an idea," I tell Cheshire. "Let's do [Exsanguinate], but don't change the spell yet; I want to see what changes."

Cheshire peers over curiously. "Well, this should be interesting. Just tell me when."

"[Exsanguinate]." The spell matrix appears in my mind's eye, that complex array of interconnected signs and symbols. I take the pen and start scribbling away, trying to represent the spell matrix as best I'm able. It's a challenging task; I have to restart several times as I make one mistake or another, and even when I draw one part right it's hard to properly represent the connections between shapes. After many attempts I get a paper diagram that more or less matches the diagram in my head, if not as clean. My brain is starting to strain from keeping the matrix active for so long, so I dismiss the spell and sigh with relief. "Okay. I'm ready."

Cheshire banishes the rat and holds the blood orb in both hands. Her fingers press into the orb and dance across it in strange patterns, and then she slams her hands together and the orb vanishes between them. "Try it now."

"[Exsanguinate]." The spell matrix is, as I suspected it would be, different now. I grab another piece of paper and start drawing the new diagram, taking my time to try and get every detail right. When I have a copy that I'm happy with, I set it next to the first paper diagram and compare the two.

The result is exactly what I was hoping for: a clear set of interconnected symbols that appear only in the new diagram, like a tumor growing out of an organism or like a section of new code inserted into a program. I don't know what each individual part does, but taken as a whole this must be magic programming language for draining life. I quickly sketch the isolated section onto a new page, and title each of them so I don't forget. I have my first insight into the magic system!

... I'm not entirely sure what that really gets me, at this stage, but it *feels* important. I feel like I might have a chance at coming to understand this whole language, and then I could, I don't know, make my own spells? Make spells outside the restrictions of the scion system? Bah, it'll be useful for something, it has to be.

But on the topic of the scion system, I've got one other detail sticking in my mind. "Hey, Cheshire, you mentioned we don't have enough for a new spell, but I was wondering: do all scions start with three spells? Is that anything to do with the three Truths?"

"It is, and they don't." Cheshire traces a finger over one of the walls and draws glowing symbols for my three Truths: the drop of blood, the toothy maw, and the skull without a jaw. "Elves and liches get their Truths straight from the Throne, so they always start with three spells, but the other kinds of scion generally don't. Wizards start with a Truth relating to one color of dragon and slowly develop Truths relating to two more colors; exalted start with the Truth that drove them to become a champion and develop the other two as their legend grows; and most demons don't know themselves well enough to shape more than a single Truth at 'character creation.' Luckily, you're *very* introspective, so we get to start with three Truths and three spells."

I frown. "You said three Truths is the max, right? So when I eat souls and grow in power, I'm not adding new Truths. And I remember Bashe mentioning 'carving.' So how exactly does that work?"

"With each soul you absorb and assimilate, your pleroma expands and your core becomes purer and weightier. The process carves off imperfections, focusing your existence more tightly on those three essential Truths, until the three combined have so much power to them that they can override local consensus reality. Then, you get to be an archdemon."

There's something uneasy about that notion. I mean, obviously it's fucked up that I'm going to be cutting up my soul for the sake of power, whatever, but aside from any bullshit moralizing about the issue there's the matter of *liking* my imperfections. I'm messy, I'm complex, and that's a part of my identity that I'm not excited to give up. But I also want the power that comes with the focus she's describing. I want to be an entity of absolute power. So how do I have my cake and eat it too?

"Now," Cheshire continues, "I have one more item before we leave: a final demon ability that will prove very useful in our shopping trip. As a scion, you have a power called 'conjuring,' and it lets you move items between your throne world and your local reality."

I blink. "Like a pocket dimension? Inventory system? Bag of Holding?"

"Pretty much! You can take an item in your hand and send it to your throne world, or focus on an item in your throne world and place it in your hand. It's just another exercise of will, like manifesting your geist. Just picture the item or name it to summon it from your throne world, and picture or name a location in your throne world to send an item there. To that end, you should make a few storerooms before you go back to the Labyrinth."

Holy shit I get an inventory system! Okay, we officially have all the elements of a litRPG except the "number go up," and honestly the numbers are always the worst part of a litRPG anyways so we're basically golden.

... Actually that was a joke but maybe not entirely??? It's like a weird semiotic metaphysics litRPG. Instead of having a [Status] skill I can read a person's soul, and instead of accessing an inventory system I can place objects inside an internal world that is also my soul. I still have to kill people to get stronger, but that process seems tied to evolving and sharpening my identity rather than making an arbitrary number go up.

Which prompts the question: is that intentional? Am I seeing connections that don't exist, or did the Demiurge actually design this world's magic system to be a weird parallel to how litRPGs work? And if she did ... why?

I keep pondering that question as I head back into the grand hall and start shaping rooms for future storage. I expand the dressing room into a proper wardrobe, add a kitchen with a working fridge, add a grand library full of empty shelves (I take inspiration from *Beauty and the Beast*), add a bedroom, and finally add one storeroom that's just a big empty box.

When the last room is finished, Cheshire takes me back to the outside world. I open my eyes in the bookstore, still holding *The Machinations of the Ashen Warlock*. That seems like a great target to start practicing my conjuring, so I focus my will on sending it to the library inside my vampire castle. I close my eyes and picture a shelf in my mind, but the image is hazy, so I say in my head, *to the first shelf on the left when you enter the library.*

This time there's no learning curve; when I open my eyes the book is gone, and when I reach inside myself and ask for the book back it appears in my hand. I send it back to the library ... and then I look around at all the books I'm currently surrounded by.

Oh yes. This will make a fine addition to my collection.

A few hundred books later, I'm ready to go clothes shopping. I have a bunch more stuff I want to grab and send to my throne world—now that I have effectively unlimited storage space, I intend on bringing an entire castle's worth of goods with me wherever I go—but I'm still stuck in the outfit I stole from a dead figment and I really want to spruce up my style.

It's a weird otherworld mall, but it's still a mall, so of course clothing boutiques are plentiful. I flit through a handful just marveling at the different options and picking out clothing at random before Cheshire finally pulls me aside and asks me, "Alice, how would you describe your sense of style?"

"Poorly," I quip, but then I give the question some actual thought. "I mostly just wear jeans and graphic tees, in all honesty. Usually a jacket over the shirt. Sometimes I'll spice things up with a witch's hat and cape, a skirt, a loose top. I just don't put much effort into my appearance, so I kind of wear whatever's around."

Cheshire tilts her head questioningly. "Is that for aesthetic reasons, or mental illness reasons?"

"Those aren't the only two options," I complain.

"Got a third option?"

I glare at the stupid correct catgirl. "Okay, fine, the latter reason. I do *like* how more put-together aesthetics look. I want to look like a spooky vampire! The elegant gothic countess stepping down the stairwell to her adoring court. Maybe not so far as the fancy femme kind of vampire, though, something more like when a vampire lady is in a frilly suit, or something almost like a magician's uniform? Yeah, weird vampire magician gender-nonconforming countess. Like a *Bloodborne* protagonist. Also, not gonna lie, part of me really just wants to dress like an anime witch and wear a big hat."

"I can work with that," Cheshire says, and then she's dragging me off from one store to another, picking out articles of clothing for me to try on and add to the collection.

When all is said and done, I'm left with two complete outfits and some miscellaneous clothing to mix-and-match when I feel like it.

I grab a red leather coat that reaches below my knees, a black leather jacket with shiny studs, a black hooded cloak to replace the one I lost, and a red hooded cloak for variety. I pick out some lace-up thigh high boots that have *incredible* stompy energy, and also some cute white bunny slippers for when I'm feeling lazy.

I probably won't wear them often because I'm trying for a more impressive sense of attire, but my wardrobe wouldn't feel complete without a few pairs of jeans. The Labyrinth doesn't have graphic tees for any piece of media that I recognize, but there are some cool fractal designs and scenes of nature that make for pretty decent shirts.

On the fancier end of miscellanea, Cheshire selects a few dresses for me: a skater dress with a flowy skirt that's patterned to look like black tentacles reaching for a white void; a backless barely there scarlet dress that I will *never* wear; and a frilly *maid uniform* that I will extra definitely never wear . . . though I suspect the vicious little shit intends on wearing it herself to taunt me.

The last of the items to not make the final cut are a pair of black-and-white stripey leggings, like I was wearing in the dreamscape. I also stock up on underwear and socks but those obviously aren't worth detailing.

I decide to name the two main outfits I've picked out, because I am a nerd. The first one I call my Witch's Threads: a gothic lolita dress in black and white, an oversized wide-brimmed witch's hat in black and red, black opera gloves, a black funeral veil over my face, and dainty little kitten heels that curve up at the tip.

The second outfit, which I settle on wearing for the rest of my shopping, I name my Vampire's Regalia: a black faux-corset button-up vest over a white blouse with poofy sleeves; black denim shorts over diamond-patterned tights in white, black, and red; a pair of magician gloves; and a high-collared black cape with coattails and a silver ruby brooch to pin the cape in place.

I ditch the belt, since I can just summon its knife from my throne world directly. None of the mall dressing rooms have mirrors, which is irritating, but there's one big mirror in the center of the mall's third floor that I use to examine my completed outfits once I've assembled them.

Cheshire claps for me as I twirl for the mirror, and for once I don't begrudge her the pageantry. It's silly, but this whole shopping trip feels almost like more of a power fantasy than the rest of my time in the Labyrinth? Part of that fantasy is being able to look at myself in a mirror without feeling revulsion, and being able to just genuinely *enjoy* shopping for clothes and putting outfits together that look nice on me because I look nice! But, also . . . all of this is free, and I cannot overstate what immense freedom that is.

Time and again through our little shopping spree I find myself putting something away because I instinctively start thinking that it'll be too expensive to afford, only for Cheshire to remind me that *nothing costs money*. I can just pick what looks nice and what I want to wear, and I don't have to choose between buying a new pair of jeans and getting to eat dinner. That's so *weird*!

I sit down on the nearest bench and take a moment to just watch the figments pass by. I dip into soul sight and focus on a few, seeing sketch-lined bone-porcelain and flowing oil-painted fabric. I see blank-faced masks and bleeding eyes, and I see the strings on each limb. This time I ignore the strings, trying to look behind the mask, to see deeper inside.

The mask gives way, but there's nothing behind it; they're hollow, every one of them. Puppet shells walking on strings, no thought or emotion stirring beneath the surface. I withdraw from the inner core and stare at the exterior of a figment, but now even that looks empty and hollow; the color fades, the eye-lights dim, meat rots, and fabric tears. It all sloughs off like so much dead skin, and then I'm left staring at a blank mirror.

I blink away the soul sight and find Cheshire sitting next to me, watching me intently. There's a question in her eyes that I choose to ignore, instead saying to her, "This city is a horror paradise."

"Oh? Do tell." She's grinning, like always.

I gesture at the figments. "A city full of perfect citizens that double as perfect victims, each of them just a . . . just a reflection of your wants and needs, filling the role they're called for. Horror, if you stop and think. Paradise, if you just accept it." I gesture at my own clothing, and then at all the stores around us. "A city where money doesn't exist but all the trappings of rampant consumerism are still present. All the glitz and glamor that people associate with unfettered capitalism, but none of the soul-crushing debt and disparity. Paradise, or adjacent." I drum my fingers on my legs. "And a city where every free-willed soul is preparing for a fight to the death with their fellow prisoners over *nothing*. There's no scarcity, no lack of resources, but the security dilemma is still forcing everyone here to gather in packs and kill each other. Famine is slain, but War still claims his due. Horror."

Cheshire shrugs. "I think it's a matter of perspective. Horror to the weak, but paradise to the strong. Conflict is a crucible; for a scion of any Throne, this city is a perfect opportunity to rise in power. There are few better whetting stones to cut your soul against."

Ah. And that reminds me of my other concern. But this time, I have an idea. I rise from the bench and skip over to the nearest jewelry store, searching through its displays until I find something that looks perfect: a stainless-steel locket in the shape of an anatomically correct heart.

Cheshire follows me in and raises an eyebrow at my choice. "Did you run off just for a new shiny, or is there a deeper meaning to this?"

I hold up the locket and say, "I have an idea to fix a problem. To . . . remove a downside. Depending on if I can make this work and if it's even possible for my powers, but I'm optimistic."

Cheshire leans in, curious. "Go on."

"When you talked about carving away my imperfections, it made me uneasy, because I *like* a lot of my imperfections. Imperfection is beautiful. I'm a messy weirdo and sometimes that gets in the way but a lot of the time it makes me more interesting. For most of my life I've been, let's say not *particularly* physically attractive, or physically capable, or particularly affluent. I'm also not particularly *sane* or neurotypical, and I've learned to leverage that to make myself seem more interesting, more charming, more likable. I've learned to use some of my biggest aberrations and contradictions to improve my social stats. I'm unique in a way that I really don't want to compromise, even for the sake of power, and I'm worried that the process you describe will sand away some of the weird little inconsistencies I really like about myself. But what if I could keep those qualities *and* become a purer, stronger soul? What if I took a shard of my soul and shoved it into a locket, and every time I had to cut away a piece of my soul, it found its way into that locket? A horcrux. A phylactery. A piece of me, kept safe inside this vessel."

Cheshire licks her teeth. "That is a *very* ambitious project, Alice. I like it. For an ordinary demon I would say it's an idea with more vision than sense, but your Gift might make that dramatically more achievable."

I preen. *Yes! I did a clever! My intelligence has been validated by a creature that may be lying to me and manipulating me for nefarious purposes!* "Then let's give it a shot." I hold out the locket and will it to take shape as an artifact, to be transformed as [Ashthorn] was but in a more focused manner. I know the effect I want, I can imagine it sinking into the locket and transforming it. I imagine the heart becoming my own metaphysical heart, the carrier of my conscience and anything else I have to sacrifice from my soul to become an archdemon. I give it a name: "Alice's Heart."

Shit. That wasn't in brackets. Cheshire frowns at the locket. "That doesn't sound like it worked."

"It did not," I grumble. "And I do not know why. Is it something about the effect? The name? Does it need . . . a power source? Shit, that one makes sense, I remember you mentioning that I drew some lingering magic from Eirdryd. Okay, power, I can try power. There has to be some way to like, take my mana and feed it into the would-be artifact, right?"

Cheshire taps her chin and looks off thoughtfully. "I don't think you can do it directly, actually. To my understanding of Gifts, they don't usually interact with mana at all. Mine certainly doesn't. I think your Gift doesn't use mana, it just seizes local resonances in Pandaemonium itself. When a spell is cast, when that caster asserts their will over the local oneiros, an echo is left behind: a lingering resonance. Throne magic draws mana from similar resonances of different sources. It's just a guess, but I would theorize that your Gift lets you capture certain resonances, like spell resonances, and pour those resonances into a suitable vessel."

"That makes sense with the fire aspect of [Ashthorn], but what about the agility boost?" I point out.

"There's more to a spell resonance than the spell itself. The elf's flame spell would have resonated with fire, wyldfire, maybe violence or destruction, and maybe stories of fire-wielding fae, but it also would have resonated with broader notions of the Throne of Summer and everything that Throne contains, which includes supernatural agility. I'd wager agility surfaced among all those resonances because of the vessel you poured them into: a dagger, a weapon defined by being fast and lightweight."

Fascinating. Is this what underlies the whole magic system? The . . . *"deeper" magic behind Throne magic and witch magic both?* "So I need the right resonances to craft an artifact out of. And to get them, the easiest way would be to cast a spell and take those resonances ... but the only spell in my arsenal that I think might work is [Prey Upon], and that requires dead bodies."

"You also might want to wait until you eat your first soul," Cheshire suggests. "If you're able to harness more than just spell resonances, you should be able to get a few resonances from the act of eating a soul and carving your own, and maybe even incorporate your first cast-off soul shard as the foundation of the artifact."

"Shit, that's a good idea. Yeah, okay, if we can confirm that non-spell resonances work, that's the plan for making the locket." *Your help is appreciated, and also makes me very suspicious that something about this plan is a bad idea. At the same time, I feel like getting paranoid about every idea I have is a recipe for disaster.* I place the locket around my neck and step out of the jewelry store.

"So," Cheshire asks, "shall we continue our shopping spree?"

"Let's."

XXI

"I need to think of a good anchor," I muse as I teleport another kitchen knife to my soul storage. I've already sent two full sets, but it's always good to be prepared.

The mega-mall has literally everything, so I've been stocking up on anything that seems remotely useful to have while running around the Labyrinth: two lighters, a multitool, safety goggles, a packed toolbox, heavy-duty gloves, three different kinds of rope, a pickaxe, and a filter mask. I'll probably never get a good chance to use any of those, or I'll forget that I have an item when it would be critically useful, but whatever.

"Got any ideas?" Cheshire asks. The changeling has been content to watch me, for the most part, but did chime in to suggest the acquisition of rope. I am *suspicious* of her motives, and have informed her as such.

"Something animalistic seems sensible, since I mostly manifest you to maul my enemies with fang and claw." I pick out some duct tape and add it to the storeroom. "Carving of an animal? A chimera, perhaps, to represent your fluidity of form? I assume the precise shape of it has some effect on your resulting manifestation, yes?"

Cheshire shifts into wolf form and says, "It does, and I think animalism is a good starting point."

I scratch the wolf behind the ears and joke, "Perhaps I should fetch you a dog collar, then, since you seem to enjoy this particular form so much."

"Oh?" Cheshire shifts back to catgirl mode and leans in, eyes sparkling and grin wide. "You're collaring me on our second date? How bold. I accept, of course."

I turn red and hiss at her. "That's not—that's obviously not what I meant, you incorrigible beast."

The changeling giggles. "Really though, you suggest a collar and expect me *not* to jump on the entendre? For shame."

"Not all of us have our minds in the gutter," I mutter. "But fine, since you made a fuss over it, that one's firmly off the table. A carving is the working pick."

"Spoilsport," she teases.

She continues teasing me and poking fun at me as we progress through the mall in search of fine loot. Food is next, since this mall has a fucking *grocery store* for some ungodsly reason; I grab chips and dip, pasta ingredients, ramen, spices, bottled water, lemonade, a selection of artisanal cheeses, fresh fruit, and a few bottles of wine. The figments don't ask to see any kind of ID but I'm not sure they even have ID in this world and I suppose they couldn't *stop* me even if I was underage.

I guess I also don't really look like a kid anymore. I'm twenty-three, for fuck's sake, and I'm pretty sure my recent modifications only make me look more "mature."

I locate some general necessities: a first aid kit, a toothbrush and toothpaste, a hairbrush, deodorant, toiletries, and towels. I'm not actually sure how necessary any beauty-adjacent products will be, given that my physical form is apparently a lie powered by devil magic, but . . .

I pick up a nail file and force myself to stop and think about *why* I'm grabbing so much mundane bullshit. I'm not going to point-and-click adventure game my way to victory, so why all the random items? Is it just the freedom of being able to acquire them, free of capitalism hanging over my head? Is it some hoarder instinct? Is it just a desire for some normalcy?

That last idea makes me uneasy, which suggests it has a grain of truth. I want to go on a fantastic adventure in another world, but I also want to experience the creature comforts of a mundane life. I want . . . some grounding element.

I set aside the nail file, but I keep following that train of thought. If some part of me feels the need for a grounding element, for creature comforts, to hold on to things beyond pure survival and power growth . . . well, that's fairly similar to why I'm trying to craft the locket, actually. It's worth pursuing.

I change course and navigate to the nearest toy store, or rather a store that sells toys, games, and sundry similarities. There is a tangible joy that rises in me as I step inside and see the familiar colorful sights. That joy is part of me, and I refuse to relinquish it.

"Go wild," I tell Cheshire, and then I begin my perusal.

The toy store has a few unexpected treasures: there's a portable games console, which fucking baffles me, and there's a bunch of games to go with it (with names and covers and all), though the console itself still lacks any kind of branding. I also find a portable media player, like those old iPods and

Walkmans, preloaded with a bunch of songs I don't recognize by nameless artists. The third and honestly *wildest* piece of technology is what seems to be an actual toy drone, like the full-on spinny-propeller flying drone that you can pilot about with a controller.

"What the fuck is this setting's tech level!?" I complain to Cheshire, who is busy swinging a toy sword.

The catgirl shrugs and pokes at a big stuffed bear. "Heimshafse—Bashe's world—has tech that's basically cyberpunk, just powered by alchemy and a few gods. The Labyrinth borrows from a bunch of worlds to create its weird gestalt reality."

"Bah." I still take all three items and send them to my throne world, along with their accessories.

One corner of the sizable store is dedicated to one of my absolute favorite special interests: tabletop roleplaying games. Like the video games I yoinked, these rulebooks and paraphernalia *do* have markings, names, etcetera. There's still a distinct non-corporate feel to them, though; one line is named Pillars of Tyndall, but there's no sign of a publisher or any kind of parent company.

I yoink a few sourcebooks for Pillars, then take my pick of the rest: Solar's Call goes into the throne world, Crownkeepers, Eyes of Star and Ruin, Crimson Court, Jouster, Nebula Shift, Imaginarium, and Eclipse: The Binding. I also teleport some dice, figurines, playmats, and a GM screen. One day, I swear on the name of M. Alice, I will play otherworld D&D with some nerds.

But probably not today. I sweep my gaze around the room and alight on a new target: packs of cards. Booster packs. *Trading cards.* This world has motherfucking *trading cards!* From multiple games, too! One kinda tarot-presenting game called Four Houses, a clockwork fantasy game by the name of Artifice, and a cyberpunk-looking Esper. They have stats, and mechanics, and interactions, and oh gosh I'm nearly hyperventilating. New systems to learn! New cards to look at! The potential is palpable.

I scoop up packs from all three games and dump them in my throne world.

Cheshire hands me a few bags of jacks, which she smugly calls "caltrops," plus the toy sword she was swinging around. I dutifully add them to the storeroom. That seems like it . . . except for that one particular corner that I have been steadfastly ignoring until now: a corner absolutely packed with stuffed animals. I skip over and nearly squeal at what's on offer.

They're all so cute, and they look so lonely! The white kitty cat with big eyes, the big owl, the squishy pink blob, and the spotted puppy all call to me. I want to hug them and squeeze them and murder anyone who touches them. A purple-and-yellow bat! A cat rolled into a burrito! A very chibi wyvern!

I cannot help but grab each and hug it tight before sending it off to my soul's bedroom. I love them all, and they are my family. I will kill to protect my beloved sweet soft precious creatures.

I glare at Cheshire as she grins at my display and makes "aww" noises obnoxiously. "If you disrespect my new friends I will destroy you," I warn her.

"You are so adorable!" she squees. "You're a soul-eating abomination and you're getting protective over stuffed animals you just met! Gods and archdemons I love you so much you big beautiful *nerd*."

I cross my arms and pout. "I'm not *adorable*," I protest. "I am . . . cool. Sexy. Badass. I'm the big scary monstergirl villainess that people are terrified of but also find weirdly hot. I'm everyone's favorite yandere demon girl waifu."

Cheshire boops my nose. "You are also a very cute nerd who seems to have forgotten that she is still hugging a stuffed animal."

I blink a few times, then look down at my arms to discover that I am in fact clutching a plush made to look like one of those happy little anime slimes. I send Gloopsy to my bedroom and raise my chin defiantly. "I hadn't forgotten, I was merely debating the quality of its material grade."

Cheshire just smirks at me and sidles over to the stuffie zone. She holds up one cat plush, a black cat with white paws, and shows it to me. "You had one like this, didn't you? Back home?"

The mask of indifference drops and a wave of melancholy washes over me. "I did," I say softly. "She was a Figaro plushie, from *Pinocchio*, but I didn't have that context when I was two so I just named her Kitty. She . . . she and Frostbite were the only possessions I had left that I could trace to my mother. The last of anything I had that she'd touched. Her last gifts to me, my closest friends. Since I was four years old, they were the only companions I could ever really trust. And . . . and . . ."

My eyes are wet. Why are my eyes wet? This is so stupid. I'm crying over stuffed animals. Why am I crying over stuffed animals? What's wrong with me? Am I really this stupid and pathetic?

I sniffle and admit, "I miss them. I loved them. They were so special to me. And I can never see them again. I can never see anything from that life, ever again." My legs feel wobbly and I slump in the corner of the toy store, next to the stuffed animals, crying. "Oh God. I'll never see my aunt again. I'll never talk to my roommate again, or any of my internet friends. I—"

I sob, an ugly, wretched sound, and my tears drip onto my denim shorts and stain them darker. Cheshire is there, crouching down next to me, rubbing my arm and patting my leg. "It's okay. I'm here. I'm here. You're okay. I'm right here beside you. I'm here for you."

"I never got to say goodbye to my father," I choke out. "He—he was dying, I knew he was dying, he had to be dying, that's why he was reaching out and he sounded so tired and—and he apologized. He apologized to me. He wrote me a letter and I cried because"—I ugly cry again, another horrid sob—"because he said he was sorry, and . . . and for once it really felt like he meant it. Like he was acknowledging what he put me through, like he was validating it and seeing it and finally *meaning it* when he said he was sorry. And I . . . I-I don't want him to d-die thinking I still h-hate him. I'm sorry. I'm sorry, I'm sorry, I'm sorry . . ."

I trail off into more sobs, eyes too blurry to see, cheeks slick with tears. Cheshire is warm beside me, and when she leans in and wraps her arms around me to hug me I don't shy away or try to stop it. She's warm, and soft, and there's a comfort to her weight that I don't have the emotional energy to deny. So I cry into her arms as I mourn what I've lost.

"Dad," I whisper between sobs, "I'm so sorry. I love you."

. . .

It takes me an embarrassing amount of time to recover from my little fit, and I feel all the more awkward for how tightly I clung to Cheshire until I finally regained my wits and shook her off. I hate feeling vulnerable. I hate letting people see any of my emotions that I'm not willfully choosing to show them.

She's obviously a liar and a monster and just using me and making me feel better so that it'll hurt more when she inevitably betrays me . . . but I hope so desperately that she isn't. I know it's stupid, I know it's such a vain hope, but I wish with all my heart that Cheshire really is on my side.

And even if she isn't . . . maybe I can change her mind.

Once I've cleared my nose and my throat sufficiently, I say to Cheshire, "Let's, um, let's keep moving. I want to find a good woodcarver so we can get your anchor custom-made. That's how to get the most out of them, right?"

Cheshire nods, no longer hugging me but still holding one of my hands. "The better the materials and the more purpose-built the anchor, the more effective the resulting summon will be. True of homunculi and geists alike."

"Then let's make you an anchor strong enough that you'll be able to rip all their throats out the next time a pack of assholes tries to fuck with me."

We head for a shop marked on the mall map as doing custom woodwork. Notably, it's also one of the few shops to have a name that stands out: Torstein's Woodworking.

The shop is quaint, even its exterior done up to look all-wood. I step inside and hear a little bell jingle in response.

"Be out in a moment!" calls a voice from somewhere out of sight.

The inside of the shop is predictably packed with woodworking projects: carved toys, a rocking chair, various other pieces of furniture and trinkets, and even a full-body mannequin. I glare at the mannequin suspiciously, but it displays no sign of guilt or ill intent.

There's also a youngish guy behind the counter with a smile plastered on his face. He's wearing a nametag that says "Grandon." A quick flash of soul sight confirms that Grandon is a figment, so I file him away under secondary concerns.

A side door is pushed open and I see a brief glimpse of a workshop beyond it, but my gaze is more immediately fixed on the person who walks out: a tall woman with silver hair, opaque blue eyes, and pale gray skin. Oh, and those distinctive *pointed ears*. Another elf... or perhaps a dark elf? A drow? *Are there drow in this setting!? Holy shit I love drow.*

She's wearing a work smock over flannel and jeans, and she has safety goggles pushed up over her hair. She wipes a bit of sweat off her forehead and approaches with a grin, but that grin falters when she takes in my appearance. Her expression grows guarded, then faux-cheerful in that "I am afraid for my life but trying not to make the situation worse" way.

"Hello there!" she calls. "I uh, don't think we've met before, Miss...?"

"Alice," I supply. "Maven Alice, you can call me either. I hope I'm not causing a fright. I assure you, despite my appearance I mean no harm to you or anyone in your shop."

The possibly-drow clears her throat and adjusts her fake smile. "I would hope so. I'm Torstein, if you didn't get that from the sign." Her gaze flickers over my appearance once more and her brow briefly furrows. "Are you... with Averrich or Vaylin? Because I don't want any trouble"

I raise my hands and smile reassuringly. "Don't worry, I am no friend to either of those groups. I've already fought some of Averrich's people, in fact, and nothing I've heard of Vaylin sounds endearing. I'm really quite new, if you can't tell, and so far the only people I've met that didn't try to kill me were the Myriad."

That seems to put the woodworker at ease, and her smile grows more genuine. "Ah, you've met some of my fellows, then. That's good to hear. Sorry for the terse welcome, friend, things are just in a bad spot right now."

"I've heard," I comment dryly. "Something about an inescapable cycle of violence. I'm actually in talks with Esha about *doing something* about that cycle. With luck, I can put my unique skillset to the greater good of Sanctuary 7 and the Myriad."

A wistful look crosses Torstein's face. "Luck and a bit more, I reckon, but I wish you the best in that. We'd all rest a little safer if this city weren't teetering on the brink of war. Now, I take it you didn't come here just to talk me up?"

"Yes! Yes, I have a pair of commissions, actually, that I was hoping you could help me with." Cheshire looks at me curiously, but I just give her a quick smirk before returning my focus to Torstein the maybe-drow.

"Happy to hear it," she says as she pulls some sketch paper and a pencil out of a cabinet. She gestures to the table-and-four-chair setup on the display floor and we all head over and take a seat.

"Okay, so, the first one is a bit complicated. I want a chimera figurine. A carved wooden figurine, maybe painted if that's possible, of a creature that's a bunch of animals mashed together."

Torstein chews on the end of the pencil and nods. "Reckon that shouldn't be too hard. What animals?"

I glance over at Cheshire. "Definitely part wolf. Cheshire, what are your other favorite animals?"

Cheshire leans in and watches the sketch paper curiously. "Wolf, for sure. I'd like the body and head to be that of a white wolf, if you please, and red eyes. With colorful parrot wings, talons for back feet, and a curling lizard's tail, like that of a chameleon. And a crown of antlers growing from the wolf's head."

Torstein sketches expertly, incorporating each of Cheshire's requests into the final piece. It's fascinating watching it come together, the woodworker combining the disparate elements to create a sketch model of a chimera that looks pretty damn good. "What do you think?" she asks.

"I love it." Cheshire smiles.

"It looks great," I compliment Torstein. "You're a pro at this."

The carpenter chuckles. "Well, I've been in the business a while. Now, what was your other request?"

"Ah, right." I clear my throat and try to describe it clearly. "I want a staff. Long and slender, but solid, in crisp painted white. The staff is topped with a carving of a bat, also white, but with black trim. The bat's wings are wrapped around its body, and its mouth is open and has just enough space to fit a small gem. The one I'm thinking of is a ruby, but I don't know if jewelry is within your purview so I'm totally okay with finishing that part of it on my own."

Torstein draws a few sketches and has me point to the one I like best, which I do. "Shouldn't be a problem. The local figments are very helpful, and I've done a bit of work with precious stones before. It'll take a few days to have these done, but if this all looks correct then I can get started on it in no time."

"That's great!" I hesitate, then ask, "So, just to be clear: is there a charge for this? Like I said before, I'm *very* new in town, and I still don't quite understand how things work."

Torstein nods. "'Course, 'course. To answer your question: like everyone in the Myriad, I do my work for the pleasure of it, not for any material reward.

We try to be like the locals, in a way; doing our part to make the city better for everyone in whatever ways come to us best. And I'm drow, so this kind of craft is what I live for."

Yes! I knew it! I mean, I guessed entirely based on your physical profile, but ... okay maybe that's not something to be proud of. Also, hey, that's an angle on drow I'm not used to seeing. Craft-focused? Are they ... are they like dwarves? I mean, I guess the original dark elves in Norse mythology were dwarves, but you don't see that take very often.

The drow woodworker scoops her sketches and rolls them up. "I'll get to work on these, if that's all. Oh, and if you're interested in any of the pieces on display, my assistant can help you out."

"Great, thanks! I look forward to seeing what you make." I give her my best smile as she gives us a little half-bow and returns to her workshop.

I kind of wanted to interrogate her more, but I've already spent enough time in this mall. We should probably call the trip here. Although, I suppose I still need to get Cheshire an anchor that works in the immediacy. Hmm.

"New idea," I tell Cheshire, and then I'm skipping out the door and examining the floor plan. According to the map, there's exactly what I'm looking for only a few minutes of walking away.

Cheshire follows behind, eternally bemused, as I lead us to a jewelry store in the mega-mall. But not just any jewelry store; a jewelry store aimed at children to young adults, with so much sparkle and glitter and cutesy childish earrings and accessories. "Wait outside," I say to my companion, and then I step in.

The items on display are exactly what I need, and I go about assembling my masterpiece, fluttering about the whole store in search of the perfect components. A piece from there, one from there, replace that with those, and ... done!

I hide it behind my back, return to Cheshire waiting patiently outside, and announce, "Cheshire, my loyal geist and traveling companion, I have a gift for you. An anchor, when you need it, that I hope captures a bit of your essence in a way you'll appreciate. May I present: your new charm bracelet."

The chain of the bracelet is plain silver, but the charms decorating it are an eclectic mix of rainbows, hearts, and colorful chibi animals (including a bat, a spider, a cat, a wolf, and more).

Cheshire gently takes the charm bracelet from me and loops her wrist through it. She rotates her arm to admire the charms and gives me a warm, caring smile. "Thank you, Alice. It's absolutely lovely."

I grumble, "Yeah, well, whatever. Let's finish up here."

"Lead on, darling."

XXII

"[Carrion Swarm]: ordinary ants."

The spell takes effect and a swarm of those nasty, horrid monsters rises out of the dirt. The incarnations of pure evil mill about randomly, puttering along on their disgusting legs, feeling for each other with those sinister antennae. It is without a doubt the vilest sight I have seen since being brought to the Labyrinth, and I shudder in revulsion at the true nightmare I have unleashed.

Checking the mall directory revealed the existence of an atrium made to resemble a park, complete with dirt and grass and trees, so I took Cheshire there after stopping by a knickknack shop to grab a key item: a centipede preserved in amber.

I have a plan: I'm going to make another artifact. Cheshire told me that spells leave behind lingering resonances, so if I can stack a bunch of castings of [Carrion Swarm] in the same area then I should be able to pour those resonances into the chunk of amber and make an artifact that will do ... something.

Of course, there's the slight problem that I get the shivers just looking at most any bug up close, but I can work through that. I do maintain a nice solid twenty feet of distance from the ants I've summoned, but that's just a reasonable precaution.

"Stop moving," I command the ants, and they do. What feels like maybe half a colony's worth of ants suddenly stops in place, all those little specks of brownish reddish whatever. Now to begin my first experiment.

I focus my will, trying to reach for the ants and command them mentally. *Form into a ball*, I project in their direction. Nothing happens. I try to reach for the spell instead, that background radiation prickling feeling. I know I can dismiss active spells like this, so surely I can give new instructions through the link, right?

Form into a ball, I command more insistently. Still nothing. "Form into a ball," I say aloud, and immediately the ants start crawling on top of each other. The ugly, wretched, horrifying little beasts grab at each other and come together until I'm looking at a literal ball of ants. *Wow! I hate it!*

Okay, so, lesson learned: once the swarm is summoned, I have to command it verbally. I suspect we could change that if we had Cheshire crack the spell open and make some modifications, but the fact that she didn't enable such a feature in the first place suggests it might be more expensive than it's worth. So we could do that . . . or I can make an artifact that lets me bypass that restriction.

"[Carrion Swarm]: fire ants."

More ants crawl out of the dirt, these ones redder and even more disgusting. I shiver at all the little bodies appearing. *Why am I doing this to myself? I hate this so much.* Of course, there's a perfectly logical explanation: [Carrion Swarm] is at least partially Fear-aligned, so summoning creatures I'm afraid of should theoretically help with what I'm attempting.

I'm pleased to see that the first group of ants aren't unsummoned by the arrival of the second group. Well, actually, I think I'd be quite happy for the both of them to pop out of existence, but it means good things for the spell itself. I attempt another mental command that doesn't work, so I'll have to verbalize the next step.

"Both groups of ants: murder each other."

The conflict that ensues is—oh. Wow. Okay. Uh. Nope. Goodbye. Nope! Not looking at that! I turn around and look at literally anything else because hahaha that's horrible. I hug myself and shudder. *I hate ants I hate ants I hate ants!*

Cheshire taps me on the shoulder after a minute has passed. "They're done, if you want to turn back around. Just bodies and a few straggler fire ants."

"Thanks." I examine my handiwork: a field of ant corpses littering the dirt. I wish I could find some satisfaction in that, but all it does is bring back a *different* set of traumatic memories. "You know why they creep me out so much, right?"

Cheshire nods. "I do. Though, if you want to talk about it, that might be good for you."

"Yeah, sure. Let me just clean this up first. [Carrion Swarm]: an even mix of black widows and brown recluses to eat the ants."

And then there are spiders everywhere, and I have a much more sensible reason to be terrified and trembling. Oh gods, that is so many spiders. I can see their spindly legs twitching, those distinctive color patterns, and the way they just harvest the dead . . . horrifying, genuinely. Look, spiders are cute, they're lovely, they're wonderful creatures, but those spiders are the two kinds of scary dangerous spiders that were common in California and Washington so it's kind of programmed into my brain to be wary of them.

I dart behind Cheshire, completely unashamed of my cowardice, and the catgirl pats me on the head as she bravely stands between me and a swarm of spiders that are technically under my complete control. "So anyways," I say, now looking away from the spiders and resolutely into Cheshire's eyes, "the thing with ants. Who are definitely not as dangerous as spiders, but still freak me out."

"They also serve an important ecological role," Cheshire points out, "and are reviled despite their service, just like spiders."

"This is fair and true," I admit. "And yet, this does not change my desire to see all ants eradicated from time and space. They are the bane of my existence. My eternal foe. The Morbius to my Spider-Man."

"Laying it on thick, sweetie," the catgirl teases me.

"And like any great rivalry," I continue dramatically as if she hadn't said anything, "there is a tragic backstory behind our modern conflict! Once, when I was but a fledgling, a terrible pox fell upon my house: a plague of ants, invading those spaces I thought safe, creeping like the tendrils of some antediluvian sea beast! They crept inside the fridge, into the cupboards, into the dog food and the cat food and every room of the house! And though we fought them back with traps and bleach and bug spray, every year they returned in greater number. Because, y'know, my father refused to take the long-term preventative steps that would keep the ants from being a recurring problem so instead it was just an endless tug-of-war with the local ant colonies. Forever."

"Until they were replaced by flies and gnats," Cheshire adds with a grin.

"Yeah, I do not miss living in that house," I mutter darkly. "The flying bugs were definitely awful, though I still think nothing compares to the time my dad ate an ant-covered donut to prove they were harmless. Who does that!?"

I shudder, and this time Cheshire shudders too. The geist says, "Yeah, no, that memory was awful. Totally get the revulsion for ants after that much exposure to them."

I glance over at the spider-ant nightmare party and decide that the spiders are taking too long. "[Carrion Swarm]: centipedes to eat everything that's left." The latest batch of creepy-crawlies pops into existence and starts dutifully chowing down. "I have to wonder, do the summons get anything for eating each other? Can you get nutrients for eating something summoned? Is it one of those 'the calories vanish when the spell ends' things, or like, because conceptual reality, is the act of eating enough for it to be real?"

Cheshire claps her hands together excitedly. "Loving these questions, Allie, you're really getting the hang of this setting. So, the answer here is a bit complicated. Broadly speaking there are two types of summoned entities: phantasms and homunculi. Phantasms, unlike homunculi, lack an anchor and are considered less 'real' by Pandaemonium. They're like illusions that can throw a punch, pretty much, and they're tagged with a whole bunch of emptiness and falsity oneiros that would sabotage any attempt to draw sustenance from them. Imagine the difference between eating cotton candy and eating a candy bar; one is mostly air. It's not *nothing*, but it's close."

"Noted." The centipedes are still in the midst of their feast, and I can see plenty of spiders remaining, but all the ants are already gone. I'm fairly certain none of the bugs had time to eat all those ant corpses, so it seems they've vanished like the bodies of the birds back in the club. Typical summon rules, I suppose.

"What are you up to, anyways?" Cheshire asks. "I'm going to guess you're doing this to make an artifact, but what kind? What do you want it to do?"

Hmm. What's the most fun way to explain? "Have you read *Worm*?"

Cheshire gives me an amused expression. "No, since you haven't read *Worm*, but I know what you know about it."

"Mm, fair. Well, consider this my attempt to play at being Taylor: I want this artifact to let me mentally control my summons and share their senses, and I'm wagering it'll be easier to accomplish that if I restrict the effect to only bugs, which includes spiders under the broadest definition. Think it'll work?"

"The logic is solid, and I can confirm that restricting an effect usually makes it comparatively stronger. I don't know enough about your power to say it'll do exactly what you want, but the theory sounds right."

"Good enough for me!"

I breathe deep and gather my will. I close my eyes and imagine the resonances left behind by my castings of [Carrion Swarm], picturing them as clouds of green light in the shapes of ants, spiders, and centipedes. I think of stories I've read or watched where a character could control bugs, a swarm of skittering insects answering a higher will as a collective mass or as individual critters. A single hyper-venomous spider guided like a missile to bite down on my opponent's neck. Flies and ants going unnoticed and feeding back crucial information on an enemy's plans. A swarm of wasps orbiting me like buzzing bodyguards.

I open my eyes, hold up the amber-preserved centipede, and give the artifact a name: "[Swarmheart]."

It worked! It—

In the atrium park, some twenty feet away, all of the remaining bugs but one melt into a disgusting slurry of goop and guts, and then that slurry is drawn into the last survivor: a single centipede that grows in size as the slurry is absorbed.

When the process is complete, the swarm of centipedes is replaced by a single dog-sized centipede.

Okay. Uh. Uhh???

I can now confirm that centipedes only get creepier and grosser when they're massive, as looking at those wiggling legs and segmented carapace is giving me the heebie-jeebies. Why did I pick a strategy that forces me to look at the creepiest kinds of bugs up close!?

Whatever, it's kind of cute when it wiggles its antennae. I wave at my new pet. "Welcome to the family, Mr. Wiggles." Then I turn to Cheshire and say, "Right, well, it's nice to make a new friend, but I am mildly disappointed the artifact didn't give me what I asked for."

"Mm, it still might. Every artifact has two abilities: one active, one passive. [Ashthorn] caught on fire when you activated it, but it still did something when you were just holding it," Cheshire reminds me. "This seems like the active, so what's the passive?"

"Hmm." I try to issue mental commands to the mega-bug, but still nothing. See through its eyes? Nope. Drat. "Whatever it is, it isn't the control ability either."

"Try casting the spell again," Cheshire suggests. "More centipedes, maybe."

I shrug. "Worth a shot ... though I should really refill my mana after this, I'm sure I've used a ton. [Carrion Swarm]: centipedes!"

The spell fires and more centipedes arrive ... a lot more, actually. Like, not quite twice as many, but quite a few more than last time. Cheshire whistles at the sight. "You got a multiplier! Nice. Oh, hey, see if you can sacrifice those guys to the big one!"

"Ooo, good idea." I adopt an imperious expression, hold out the chunk of amber, and arrogantly declare, "I call upon the power of this artifact: [Swarmheart], make my monster grow!" I try to will the artifact to supersize the existing Mr. Wiggles rather than one of the new centipedes.

The freshly hatched swarm of wigglers is reduced to biological slurry and siphoned into the growing body of Mr. Wiggles, who goes from being the size of a Dalmatian to the size of a Great Dane. "Wow. Holy shit, that is one big centipede."

I walk over and tentatively give Mr. Wiggles a few pats on his weird, flat bug head, and then I try not to freak out over the sensory experience of touching a gigantic centipede. *Yeah, no, let's deal with this later.* I dismiss the spell and watch the monstrous insect turn into black mist that quickly disperses into nothingness. *I do look forward to unleashing you on my enemies, Mr. Wiggles.*

"Well, that was an interesting lesson. More experimentation is required, but first I think it's time to top up on mana." I do a quick check of [Exsanguinate] and determine that I still have enough mana to cast it, which I imagine has to be thanks to the slow trickle I've been getting from the day's activities. Still, more never hurts. "Let's look for someone to eat."

I don't have to go far; there's a human in the atrium with me, a guy in hoodie and jeans who's been enjoying the pseudo-park as I've played with magic. And by human, I mean figment, because a quick flash of soul vision confirms that his soul is empty and he's held up by strings.

Hoodie Guy is leaning against a tree, hands in his pockets, cheerful expression, whatever. I don't really want another repeat of the Lena scene so I'm not going to bother learning much about this dude beyond the absolute minimum. I stroll up to him and flash my fangs. "Hey! Hi there! It's me, Maven Alice, your friendly neighborhood doll-vampire-demon-girl weirdo. Lovely to meet you."

I offer a hand and he takes it, seeming confused by my introduction but still overall cheerful. "Uh, hello! Nice to meet you, I'm Cameron."

"Great, good, that's all I needed." I hold his hand gently and give him my best apologetic smile. "Would you kindly stop pretending to be a person for a few minutes? I'm a bit parched, so I'd like to drink some of your blood."

Cameron smiles back placidly, says, "Okay!" and then all the energy and personality bleed away from him until he's just standing there, arms at his sides, staring blankly right through me.

Oh, okay. That's. Oh boy. Okay, Alice, just focus on feeding. "Stop me if I'm about to kill the poor bastard," I mutter to Cheshire, and then I go for the throat.

My fangs sink into tender, vulnerable flesh, and I drink deep of a savory crimson. The taste is different this time; still meat and wine and manic energy, but . . . duller. A lighter shade of red. I drink his blood and every drop of it is better than the meal I had this morning, but it's still nowhere close to the pure *experience* of drinking from Lena.

The red sates my hunger well enough, but that lack of visceral ecstasy makes it almost easy to withdraw when I've drank my fill. I still hesitate for a second before pulling out, but it's no great loss; I was eating, and now I've eaten.

Unbidden, as I lick my lips, I think of Lena. I remember the taste of her blood, the fire of it, the glorious burning need that coursed through my body as I pierced her deep and drank her essence. I feel hungry again just imagining the flavor of her vital fluids.

And yet, when I glance at the bloody pinpricks in Cameron's neck, there is no intensification of that hunger, no yearning to return to my food source. In fact, as I stare at this figment's neck, I feel . . . unsatisfied. Detached. Perfunctory. And something about that disturbs me, but I don't know what.

I raise two fingers to his neck and feel for a pulse. Ba-bump. Ba-bump. Ba-bump. He seems fine, as far as I can tell. He'll live, whatever counts as living for a figment. Regular humans can lose a fair bit of blood before they really start to suffer for it, and I don't think I took enough to cross that threshold.

So my victim is fine, and I certainly didn't learn enough about him to get attached, so this can't be a moral foible making me so uncomfortable. Or, is that it? I didn't get to know him, so there was no intimate quality to the act of feeding, so it wasn't as satisfying?

He didn't taste like Lena. His blood wasn't bad, just bland. Lena was so delicious I nearly killed her, that's how badly I wanted to drink her up. But this Cameron just wasn't my flavor. Not my taste in . . .

. . . Oh. *Oh no, no no no, we are* not *making this into some weird psychosexual feeding-as-sex bullshit. Nope! That is not the kind of vampire that I am!!!*

"Cheshire, let's get lunch," I suddenly declare.

Cheshire raises an eyebrow. "Blood bag not enough for you?"

"I have a diverse palate. To the food court!" I start power-walking away from the scene of the crime. *It was probably just something about his blood! Maybe it's because I told Lena to act human and Cameron to stop being a person. It's nothing to do with my sexual preferences because that would be weird and I am . . . okay, that line of reasoning doesn't help.*

I scurry to the nearest food court (there are multiple, wildly) and order a pomegranate smoothie and some sweet waffles. Cheshire orders nothing, and when I sit down with my meal, she gives me a look.

"What? I was hungry." I sip my smoothie. Mm, fruit.

"Sure. And this definitely has nothing to do with you freaking out after feeding on that guy, yeah?" *Damn nosy cat.*

I glower at the catgirl and swallow another bite of waffle before answering. "What do you want me to say? Yes, whatever, it was weird and I felt weird, but the evidence is *inconclusive*! There are too many uncontrolled variables, and you can't expect me to calculate results with only two points of data."

Cheshire smirks. "It's cute that you hide behind your 'Little Miss Robot' act, but we both know you felt something there. What was it? How did that feeding make you feel?"

I grimace. "Nothing. I felt nothing, it was nothing. It doesn't matter. Who cares?"

Cheshire's expression turns hard, and when she speaks next her voice is cold. "If you are unwilling to face even this slightest of contradictions, then you will *never* be an archdemon."

I recoil as if slapped. "Wh-what? Where is this coming from?"

Cheshire leans in, her intensity only increasing. "Do you understand what you are, Alice? Do you understand what you're going to be? You cannot hide from yourself any longer. The weak of will do not ascend. The divided do not ascend.

Every contradiction must be resolved; every belief must be challenged. My role as your geist is to interrogate every piece of your soul—to help you find yourself by bringing the disparate pieces of yourself into conflict, because it is through conflict that we rise. That is the lesson, ideal, and inheritance of the Leviathans."

Them again. Okay. Let's try something. I take a long drink of my smoothie, breathe, and let the brain freeze bring clarity. "Fine, but I want something from you: if I tell you how I felt, you have to tell me about the Leviathans."

At once the intensity vanishes and Cheshire leans back with a wink and a laugh. "You don't have to bargain for that, babe. I'll tell you whatever you want to know, whenever you ask. It's just up to you if you feel like reciprocating."

Bleh. Clever little shit. Whatever, I think it should be obvious by now that I'm not going to win the game by out-talking her. I wolf down the last waffle, wash it down with smoothie, and wipe my mouth. "Alright, let's make one thing very fucking clear: I mean it when I say that I don't have enough data to work with. I reacted to Lena one way and I reacted to Cameron a very different way, and that probably means something but I can't be *certain* what it means."

"But you have a guess," Cheshire prompts.

"I have a guess," I admit. "It's possible that, because he was a guy and not a girl, I didn't enjoy it as much. Which suggests there's some creepy sexual aspect to my form of vampiric feeding, which is displeasing me."

Cheshire giggles. "Does that really surprise you? That's just vampires, babe. Can you genuinely name me a piece of vampire fiction where vampire feeding *isn't* at least in part a metaphor for sex?"

I pause, actually giving that some thought. *Uh, it's definitely sex in* Masquerade. Elder Scrolls *had that whole grossness with Molag Bal.* Carmilla, Dracula, Hellsing, Dresden Files, Buffy, *and the list just keeps going. We can automatically disqualify basically any teen romance vampire media. Although . . . actually . . .* "Twilight. The feeding in Twilight is completely unsexy, and even an arch-conservative reading of it as, like, 'sexual desire that has to be suppressed' doesn't work. There's the 'wait until after marriage' thing, except that Bella gets bitten in book one by the baddie and Edward has to bite her to suck the venom out, which, what, did he 'unfuck' Bella? And after they get married, he still doesn't bite her until she's literally giving birth, which would be the *weirdest* pregnancy sex metaphor ever written."

"So your counterexample is *Twilight*?" Cheshire asks with a raised eyebrow.

I blink a few times, then wince. "Okay, yeah, you win that one. Fine, feeding-as-sex is the norm for vampires."

"So what's the issue? Why does it make you uncomfortable?"

I hesitate. "Because . . . because they can't—because it makes me into . . . a predator. *That* kind of predator."

Cheshire tilts her head, adopting a look of innocent curiosity. "You're a vampire, aren't you? Vampires are predators. What makes this worse?"

"Because it's weird and it's gross and I don't like it!" I snap.

"Alice," she says gently.

"Oh, fuck off. You know exactly what this is about, you know what goes on in my head, you've dredged my fucking memories like a goddamn brain-eater, so stop playing dumb! I don't want to be *that* kind of monster." My hands are balled into fists.

Cheshire leans back. "Then what kind of monster do you want to be?"

The flash of anger turns cold, and I look away from Cheshire as I hug myself. "I don't know. It's . . . it's all so different from a fantasy. I killed a man. I nearly killed Lena. I treated the guy in the park like he was just food."

"Neither he nor Lena were really people," Cheshire points out.

"So what!?" I hiss. "People suck! I'd rather empathize with an object any day of the week. People are garbage, and liars, and traitors; a stuffed animal won't stab you in the back, and a toy just needs to be useful to justify its existence. So I don't care that Lena and Cameron were figments—no, I do care, and that makes it more important that I don't just dismiss what I did to them."

"Why?" Cheshire presses. "Why do you feel the need to be moral? Who's going to judge you for it? Are you a demon of justice, Alice? A vampire with a conscience? Is being a good person more important than living forever?"

It isn't. It can't be, because eternity is my highest priority. Nothing I do with my life matters if I can't make that life last forever. And yet. "I . . . there has to be a line. Somewhere. I have to draw a line somewhere, okay? To live with myself."

"Perhaps," Cheshire muses, "but the question remains: what kind of monster do you want to become?"

"I don't know," I answer honestly. "I think I'll have to learn by doing, in this."

"Well," she says, clasping her hands together and grinning, "let's get to it then. What's next on the docket?"

I take another sip of smoothie and consider my options. "I think we're good on shopping, but I kind of want to see if this place has a good library. I'm curious what kind of nonfiction I'll find there. And, of course, I want to hear about Leviathans."

Cheshire cracks her knuckles and rises. "Then let's get walking, and I can tell you how it all started: the beginning of everything, in the realms of dream and shadow."

We get directions from a passing figment and head out of the mall, and as we walk I finally get a taste of this world's deeper cosmology.

"Once upon a time," Cheshire begins, "the dream of a shadow cast the shadow of a dream, and two worlds were born that had never not existed. Two intertwined realities were locked in a causal loop, forever the paradoxical origin of each reality's twin, yet kept separate and ignorant of the other's existence: the Shadowlands and the Dreamlands.

"The Shadowlands embodied individual will and persistent essence, while the Dreamlands embodied collective consciousness and mutable form. Each inhabitant of the Shadowlands was its own distinct entity, possessed of unique drives and desires, while each inhabitant of the Dreamlands was bound to the greater whole, like single cells of a vast world-body. Our story begins in the dark, and within the Abyss."

Shadow and Spirit, seems like, or I guess a precursor to those Thrones. The recursive causality is wild but it fits the eldritch angle. This is exactly what I've been craving since I got here: a deep dive into the deep lore of this setting.

My companion continues, "The Shadowlands were once a diverse ecosystem populated by a variety of intelligent life, not all driven by hunger and conflict, but one-by-one they all fell prey to the ceaseless voracity of the Leviathans, a species of apex predators born of the deepest layer of the Shadowlands: the Abyss. Slowly, over timeless eons and thanks to the ever-reaching hunger of the Leviathans, the Abyss grew to swallow the entirety of the Shadowlands.

"Deprived of food, the Leviathans turned on each other. Each Leviathan was an amalgamate entity composed of shards of pure resonant will, like notes of music coming together in a violent and discordant song. When two Leviathans clashed, the violence cast off certain shards like torn scales from a snake, while the resonant core of the loser was devoured by the victor. The sundered shards were never reabsorbed, for they were seen as weakness excised.

"In time, conflict born of necessity gained an almost religious quality: the Leviathans came to believe that conflict itself was divinely righteous. Their forever war, the Eternal Conflict, was not merely a means for them to feed upon each other but instead a search for one of their number with the strength to devour all others. This all-consuming Leviathan would claim the mythical 'Throne of Creation,' and when it sat upon that Throne it would become God. The creation of God, then, became the purpose of their endless violent hunger."

Fascinating. "Azathoth," I say. "You're talking about Azathoth, right? She's the entity they were searching for." *Who sits upon a Throne, but not one of the five Thrones I've been told about. The Ur-Throne?*

Cheshire grins. "From one point of view, she is indeed the divine champion of their legends. But from another point of view, Azathoth is the arch-heretic of their nightmares. For there was a taboo among Leviathans: the consumption of sundered shards was considered the highest act of heresy, both because they are impure and because they are essential to the life cycle of the species.

"When a Leviathan died and its shards were scattered, those shards that went uneaten would eventually draw in dreams from the twin of the Shadowlands, and in time they would give rise to newborn Leviathans. Those new Leviathans were born of weakness but reforged by dreams and given a new chance to seek the Throne. To eat an impure shard was to consume an unborn child and defile the Eternal Conflict. And so it was their highest taboo, and no Leviathan would dare dream of performing the accursed act . . . except one."

"Azathoth," I say again, enraptured.

"The Leviathan that would become Azathoth," Cheshire corrects. "Long before the era of the Dreamweaver and the Demiurge, the creature now known as Azathoth was once the lowliest and most wretched of Leviathans. They called it Scavenger, Heretic, Defiler, Betrayer, Abomination, and Carrion-Worm. It was born at the very edge of infinity, where a single lonely patch of Shadowlands still existed untainted by the Abyss. The Scavenger's first meal was the last survivor of a species driven to extinction by the Leviathans, and it learned much from that meal.

"The Scavenger learned of fear, for its prey had long dreaded being discovered by a Leviathan. The Scavenger learned of curiosity, for it wondered as to the fate of its prey's kindred, and when it learned that fate, it wondered how a single creature had survived. The Scavenger stayed in that hollow for a long time, contemplating its first and only meal, until at last it grew hungry once more and was forced to leave its sanctuary.

"It emerged to find an Abyss filled with violence and death, and unlike its cousins, the Scavenger knew fear and had made fear a part of itself. It ran from conflict rather than seeking conflict, and it fed on scraps in violation of taboo. The Scavenger cared more for self-preservation and discovery than the act of sharpening and the progression of the Eternal Conflict. It did not seek the Throne, and for all these reasons it was reviled.

"The Leviathans took sadistic pleasure in hunting their smaller, weaker sibling. It lacked their purity of strength, so it could never prevail against one of them in a true fight, but it was quick and clever and learned of secret paths through the Abyss that allowed it to evade its hunters . . . but not forever. And so it came to pass that, within the infinite darkness of the Abyss, the Scavenger was caught, shattered, and consumed."

I blink a few times. "What? It *died*? But, it became Azathoth, you said. So it came back?"

Cheshire giggles. "This part is one of my favorites. Yes, the Scavenger died. But, the Scavenger was ever-fearful and ever-curious, and it had learned how to do something that the other Leviathans never could or would; the song of a Leviathan was a song of clashing notes, music turned against itself to reveal which notes were weakest and which could be heard through the clamor, but the Scavenger made itself into a harmony, every note—every shard—weaving together to form a single resonant chord.

"When the Scavenger was shattered, only its core was consumed, for to consume its sundered shards would be taboo. Yet every shard of the Scavenger contained the totality of its being, and as those shards fed on dreams they did not give rise to a new Leviathan but instead to a rebirth of the Crafter of Harmonies. The Scavenger was reborn, and again it was hunted down, but every time it regrew quicker, cleverer, and *stronger* . . . until there came a day that a Leviathan tested itself against the Scavenger and *lost*. And in that moment—"

Cheshire suddenly breaks off and freezes in place, staring wide-eyed at . . . is that an owl? There's an owl perched on a currently dim streetlight, its big round eyes staring right at us. I think it might be a barn owl.

"Fuck," Cheshire swears under her breath.

"Uh? Cheshire? Care to explain the significance of what looks like a perfectly ordinary owl? I was enjoying your story." She looks nervous, and that makes me look nervous, so I'm mostly just babbling to fill the air. "Should I be scared of the owl?"

"It's not an owl," she says, and then she slides the charm bracelet off her wrist and presses it into my hand. "Send this to your throne world, and don't take it out for any reason, okay?"

"Uh, sure, yeah." I teleport the charm bracelet to my bedroom. "Seriously, what's with the owl? It's just watching us."

"It's not an owl," she says, and then the catgirl transforms into a giant wolf again. "It's an *owlbear*."

My train of thought comes crashing to a stop. "What? No. You are fucking with me. That's not. What!?"

"Grab on!" Cheshire snarls, and on reflex I follow the command and grasp at her fur. The second I've got a good grip she *bolts*, sprinting down the street back the way we came, through a side alley, just running as fast as she can on her wolf legs. I cling to her as tightly as I can, terrified and exhilarated in equal measure as our surroundings blur together.

And then a bear drops out of the sky on top of us.

Holy Jesus fuck that's an actual fucking bear! I scream in my head as a gigantic mass of fur and fat and muscle plummets out of the sky and slams into Cheshire, flattening the wolf against the street. At the last second before it hits, I'm flung from Cheshire's side and roll across the ground, breath forced from my lungs, bruises rapidly forming.

For Cheshire, it's worse, and I see blood and viscera for only a moment before her wolf body melts into shadow and she reforms at my side, once more lacking in physicality. She coughs and shudders and says, "Say hello to your first owlbear. Can you move?"

I can't respond. My lungs are still empty, still struggling to suck in air, and my limbs move too slowly, barely moving at all. I need to move. I need to move. I need to move. I scrabble against the asphalt and push myself to a half-sitting position, and I finally manage to gasp out, "Ow."

The catgirl sighs. "I was afraid of that. Sorry, guess I threw you a little too hard. Okay, try not to die." Then she's running at the bear, and shouts, "Hey, ugly! You missed!"

The bear, which had been pawing at the flattened carving left by Cheshire's disincorporation, now looks up at the catgirl and growls. I've heard bears roar so many times in video games, but it's never been this terrifying to hear.

"Ignore it," commands a new voice. "Whatever you're seeing, it isn't really there." Deep, calm, almost lazy. "Pin the demon." *Shit.*

The bear rushes me, passing right through Cheshire's insubstantial form, and before I've managed to back up even an inch, the bear is towering over me. One powerful claw rams into my chest and slams me against the ground, knocking the breath from my lungs once again.

Pleasedon'tkillmepleasedon'tkillmepleasedon'tkillmeplease—

The bear looms over me, saliva dripping from that terrifying maw, brown eyes staring down at me. My gaze is locked on the bear, my body frozen, but I hear footsteps. Step, step, step. Two sets—no, three.

"Is this really the bitch that killed Shane?" asks a scratchy, nasal voice. "She went down like a chump."

"That's what Shane thought, too, right before she killed him," says a familiar voice. Female, sharp, but the mocking edge is gone. Bitterness, now. Anger.

Mahiri. My blood runs cold. *Shit, shit, shit. They're with fae boy. Averrich. King's Carnival. I am so fucking dead. I don't have a spell that can save me here, I'm trapped beneath a giant fucking bear!!!*

Scratchy laughs, then says, "I guess we should kill her to be safe!"

"Not happening," Lazy Voice retorts before I can panic-cast [Carrion Swarm]. "The boss wants her alive."

"But that's *boring*," Scratchy whines. "I wanna kill a demon."

"Are you going to take that up with Averrich?"

The only reply I hear is wordless grumbling. Step, step, step, and I can feel a shadow fall over me, but I can't tear my gaze away from the brown bear.

"Hey there, demon girl. You're probably freaking out right now, but don't worry; the boss just wants to talk. He's a generous guy like that, even after the stunt you pulled in his club."

I swallow nervously. When I speak, my voice is croaking, wavering. "Ha, yeah, that sure was a stunt. Uh, so, you're not going to kill me? 'Cause that would be mighty appreciated, let me tell you. I really like not being killed. Please?" *If I summoned [Swarmheart] to my hand, could I make enough bugs to keep the bear from killing me? I wish Cheshire were still manifested. Can I manifest her nonverbally? Fuck, fuck, fuck!*

Scratchy scoffs and complains, "What kind of demon begs for her life?"

I hear a sound like flesh against flesh, fist against face, and Scratchy cries out while Mahiri snarls, "Take this seriously, damn it! This is *exactly* what she pulled on Shane. She's stalling for time so she can set up her moves. Keep watch for that fucking wolf."

Great, and now that plan's shot. I am so dead. "Hey again, Mahiri," I call out with a pitiful excuse for a smirk on my face. "How's the eye?" *What? No!? Why are you antagonizing her, you stupid idiot!?*

Step, step—*wham*, a stabbing pain in my side as her boot connects with my chest and probably breaks *another fucking rib!* I scream and clutch at my abdomen, wishing I could roll over but still pinned beneath this stupid terrifying bear.

Lazy Voice chuckles. "Mouthy, isn't she?"

"Just cast the fucking spell, Kado," she snaps.

Kado sighs. "Yeah, yeah. Hey, demon girl."

"Alice," I cough. "Maven Alice."

"Sure. Do yourself a favor, Maven, and take a nap. [Enchanted Slumber]."

His words echo, and I feel a blanket of drowsiness begin to fall over me, but it's like there's . . . distance. Detachment. I can feel the effect, I can feel how it's *supposed* to feel—a tidal wave of soporific comfort—but it hasn't hit yet, not really. I fight it. I'm scared, and I don't want to die in my sleep, so I fight against the spell and when it finally hits me it breaks like the tide crashing against rock. The spell dissipates, leaving me just as clear-headed and panicked as before, if not more.

"Weaver damn it," Kado mutters. "I hate dealing with scions."

"What happened?" demands Mahiri.

"She resisted it, because that's just something she can do, even if it's the *wrong move* for her. Hear that, Mavie?"

"I'm not dying in my sleep," I hiss.

I hear another exasperated sigh, and then Lazy Voice crouches down next to me and I finally turn from the bear to get a good look at my other assailant: a gangly dude, looks I'd describe as something East Asian if we were on Earth, choppy beard, and lots of laugh lines around the eyes. "You get you're under a bear, right?" he asks me.

I grimace at the bear, then back to him. "I'm aware. Still not dying in my sleep."

Kado rolls his eyes. "We just wanna take you to the boss. You'll be fine."

"Then take me there while I'm lucid. I wanted to have a chat with Averrich anyways."

Mahiri scoffs, but Kado holds up a hand to stop her from interfering. "That's great to hear! But the boss has his orders: we don't want you trying something on the way there, and we'd rather you not see the path we're taking. So let the spell happen, we'll take you to Averrich, and then the two of you can talk this out."

I don't see a way out if I refuse, but the idea of being unconscious in the custody of this trio still freaks me out. But before I can dig my grave deeper, Cheshire is next to me, leaning on me, Kado not reacting to her presence. She leans in close and whispers in my ear, "Get him to swear by the Weaver. That'll ensure your safety, and then *I* can spy the path while you're asleep."

I have to stop myself from nodding in agreement. Out loud, I say to Kado, "Fine, but I need something from you: swear by the Weaver that you'll do me no harm while I'm under the spell, nor will your compatriots."

In the distance I hear Scratchy complain, "Do we really have to take this?"

Kado shoots a brief glare in that direction, then turns back to me and nods. "Deal. While the slumber holds I shall take no hostile action against you, Maven Alice, nor will I allow any of my compatriots to take hostile action against you, Maven Alice. This and these I swear by Azathoth, Dreamweaver, All-Mother, Origin. Weaver take me if I forswear."

For a moment his expression tightens and he stops breathing, but then it passes. I feel the barest trace of Azathoth's presence, like a soft finger brushing over the skin of my arm, and then she's gone.

I breathe in, then out. "Okay. Cast your blasted spell."

"[Enchanted Slumber]."

The tidal wave rolls in, and this time I let it take me, and everything falls into darkness.

INTERLUDE

SHADOW & GLASS IV

Developing an affinity takes time and effort, but you were a capable student, and I enjoyed teaching you. We practiced in the safety of my chambers, exploring the meaning of Blood and our respective relationships with it.

After a close call with a servant nearly finding us in the midst of practice, my worry increased and you suggested taking our lessons to a new location: outside the castle entirely. The idea made me nervous, as I had so rarely ventured from the castle grounds, but you were compelling and convincing and made me want to see the wider world.

It was depressingly easy to leave the castle; nobody tried to stop me when I filled a basket with food from the kitchens and books from the library, and when I told the guards at the gate that I was going on a picnic by myself, not a soul seemed to care. I left the castle with basket and parasol and picnic blanket all stored in my second shadow.

The castle itself was surrounded by the city of Dawn's Bloom, the capital of our kingdom, and beyond the city walls stretched orchards and farmland for miles. It was a ways past the city gates that I saw you, leaning against an apple tree and repeatedly tossing an apple up in the air and catching it.

You were dressed as you always were, while I had chosen to wear a pink-and-cream dress with red rose embroidered patterns, and I had done up my hair in an artful braid kept in place by a golden topaz pin. I admit to feeling a bit of disappointment when I saw that you hadn't done anything special, but I quickly quashed those feelings. Yes, this may have been a secret rendezvous like something out of my romance novels, but we had been meeting in secret for months already.

As I drew closer, you caught the apple for a final time before holding it out as if to offer it to me. "An apple for your knowledge, princess?" Your dark eyes burned with the mirth of some joke only you were in on.

I frowned worryingly at the apple. "You shouldn't be picking those; what if someone sees you and calls the guards for theft of goods?"

"They wouldn't catch me," *you said confidently.* "But, sure, I'll play nice." *You tossed the apple aside and fell in beside me.* "Lead on. I'm looking forward to seeing more of your kingdom than just that stodgy old castle."

"You're not alone in that," *I sighed.*

We left the orchard behind and climbed a hill that gave a breathtaking view of the whole area. I laid down the blanket and set up the parasol, but as I began pulling food out of the picnic basket, you hesitated and looked around. "I don't suppose you have a bit of magic to keep the bugs away?" *you asked.* "I'm . . . not the biggest fan of ants."

"Oh! Of course." *I recited a quick incantation that shielded all within the parasol's shade from outside intrusion, and swept my shadows through the grass beneath the blanket for good measure. I placed a few constellations on the dark underside of the parasol, picking out the Farmer's Flail, the Sleeping Rabbit, and the Crowned Canopy.*

We ate cucumber sandwiches and lemon tarts, and when we'd both had our fill I retrieved two books from my picnic basket. You leaned in, a twinkle in your eyes, always eager to learn.

"I want to start today's lesson by talking a little more about the history of my family," *I began.* "Every major bloodline can point to a founder who led the clan to a position of power. Sometimes that founder is the first sorcerer in the family to shape what will become the family Crest, but often the Crest artifact has already been in the family for some time before the transition to a proper clan. Our founder was Karla Sabal Dawnbringer, and she belonged to the latter camp."

I opened up the first book, a beautifully illustrated history of the kingdom, and turned to the page that showed Karla in all her glory, holding the golden rod that would gradually become the Sunlit Scepter. "Karla was born to a branch family—you can tell from the three names—and she sought to prove herself by deviating from tradition. Where her cousins used Sunlight as war magic, healing wounds and causing them, Karla pursued the renewing properties of Sunlight. This decision would save not only the family—which had been declining in favor with the royalty of the time—but also the entire region."

I flipped to an illustration of crops withering and peasant folk wasting away. "There came a great and terrible famine that swept through all the lands east of the Lothar River. It was a coming together of many separate tragedies: a recent war disrupting food stores, an unseasonable cold front, and a new breed of insect that preyed upon those plants which survived the cold."

A new page, a new illustration: a hand wreathed in golden light, and fields of grain springing to life. "Karla used her power of renewal on the farms around *each estate belonging to a Dawnbringer, restoring dead crops and making frozen land fertile again. The family had not been in danger of starvation, still possessing enough wealth to ensure they made it through the famine, but now they were advantageously positioned against their rivals. Karla leveraged this success to be named the new family head, and with Crest in hand she traveled across the length of the kingdom practicing her magic."*

The last illustration I showed you was that of Karla, now bearing a regal crown, sitting upon a bronze throne. "It was only a few months after the famine's end that Karla was crowned Queen Dawnbringer, carried on a tidal wave of support from the peasantry and the nobility alike; the common folk were grateful for their lives, while the other sorcerer families had made promises they could not renege in exchange for the restoration of their most valuable crops. And so our clan became the rulers of this kingdom, and our magic became indispensable to its operation."

I snapped the book shut and set it down with a smile. You were paying rapt attention, like always, and as soon as I signaled the end of my speech you had questions to ask. "Is that power of renewal something only used during times of famine, or does your family make use of it year-round? And what are the limits of that power? Is it just a permanent multiplier on your country's agricultural yield?"

I gestured to the rolling fields of verdant growth surrounding us, all those miles of farmland bursting with life. "You can see the fruits of our labor everywhere in the kingdom. Every Dawnbringer takes a yearly pilgrimage to personally renew the land and encourage growth, spaced out so there's almost always one of us cultivating." I grimaced and added, "Except for me, obviously, since I can't use that magic. But, normally, it's a common practice, and one of the most important yearly events for a Dawnbringer. Our magic is the key to our kingdom's prosperity: our crops never fail, and the removal of that risk has allowed our farmers to specialize and expand. The kingdom overflows with food every year, and one of the lesser clans has developed preservation techniques that make it easier to trade the surplus with neighboring nations."

"Fascinating," you murmured. "Next question, then: why is your family affinity 'Sunlight' if the power you're known for is 'renewal'? Is it just a matter of tradition, or is there some practical reason that the bloodline didn't shift affinities after the success of Queen Karla?"

I clapped my hands together and excitedly grabbed the second book, a text on advanced magical theory. "Ah, that actually brings me to why I shared that story. I think by this point you have a pretty solid understanding of how affinities work and how they contain other, lesser notions, but there's one key aspect of affinities that I haven't talked about: focus." I flipped to the right page, knowing it from memory, and pointed to where it read Sunlight (Renewal). "This notation is read as 'Sunlight focusing Renewal,' and this is my family's full *affinity*.

"As a sorcerer develops their magic, they can do so in one of three ways: developing a new affinity, developing their proficiency with an existing affinity, or developing a focus for an existing affinity. When an affinity is focused, all magic falling under that focus is amplified, but magic outside that focus is dampened. So a practitioner of Sunlight focusing Renewal can restore the land with incredible power, but their other uses of Sunlight are weakened."

You licked your lips and leaned back. "Specialization and trade-off. Interesting, interesting. So, your brother and father: do they have that focus, then?"

I nodded. "They do, yes. Both of them have Sunlight focusing Renewal as their first affinity, like all clan members are meant to. Luka has a second affinity, Sunlight focusing Healing, while my father's second affinity is Sunlight focusing Revelation—and he has a third affinity, Majesty, without a focus."

You raised an eyebrow. "Both doubling up on Sunlight. Is that also standard? Is it just for more options, or are there additional benefits?"

"It's very conventional for a bloodline sorcerer. The affinities feed each other, so both focuses are a little stronger than they'd be alone, and non-focused Sunlight isn't quite as dampened thanks to the doubling effect, though that actually depends on the combination; Luka is a peerless healer thanks to the overlap between Healing and Renewal, but it's practically impossible for him to use Sunlight offensively." I allowed myself a small moment of satisfaction at my brother's one inadequacy, but then I recalled the matter of inheritance and my mood fell. "Of course, one day Luka will be given our family Crest, and that will more than make up for his focus restriction. With the Sunlit Scepter in hand, any member of our family could perform the highest feats of Sunlight magic."

A shrewd look came to your face as you considered my words. "You have a focus, don't you? When you told me about your affinity for Blood, you described it as the 'quintessence of harm,' and said that it couldn't be used for healing. That sounds exactly like a focus restriction."

I winced. "That's . . . not entirely inaccurate. My affinity for Blood has progressed to the point that I could focus it, but I've resisted. I know I'll never be a healer, but it feels like giving up to just accept that one of my affinities is only good for harming. I don't want to be that person. So, my affinity is on the verge of a focus, but I haven't let it 'lock in,' as it were."

"How about Starlight and Shadow?" you followed up.

"Nothing for Starlight, no, but Shadow . . . Shadow is complicated." I hesitated, but you had always been so encouraging of my natural affinity, so I pushed aside my hesitation and animated a tendril of shadow, letting it caress my hand. "My magic doesn't behave like it should, when it comes to Shadow. Every spell I cast with Shadow is as powerful as if I had a focus, and I've never been able to find a restriction. Nothing I cast with Shadow is weak, and everything I cast with Shadow is strong. It's not like other affinities, which leads me to believe it's some inherent property of the Abyss."

Hunger glittered in your dark eyes, and you curled your lip with agitation. "A power like that, and your family would turn you away because it's not the right kind of power? Absurd. If anything, they should be trying to learn from you."

Your words made me uneasy, and I hastened to remind you, "The Abyss is dangerous, Homura. I . . . I appreciate the support you've given me, about my magic, but it's not something I can share with others. To the best of my knowledge, I am the only human that has ever survived wielding Shadow." *If I'm even human,* came the dark thought unbidden. That question had always haunted me: was I the exception that proved the rule, or was I the demon that everyone feared I might be?

You shrugged, clearly unperturbed by my warning. "Perhaps. Regardless, I think you should be given more credit. You have three affinities, one practically focused. That's almost as much development as your father, isn't it? And him with two decades on you at minimum. Don't you think you deserve a bit of credit for that?"

I looked away from you and hugged myself awkwardly. "That's not how the bloodlines see it. None of my achievements mean anything—not to the clans, not to my family, not to my father—because they're not the *right* achievements. Who cares if I was the youngest mage in our family's history to develop a third affinity, if none of my affinities are Sunlight? I thought my father might be proud of me, when I learned my third affinity at a younger age than even he had, but no, nothing. Nothing compared to Luka, because he got the *right* affinity, and then he did it twice!" I spat the last word, unable to stop the bitterness from overflowing. "I've never been good enough for my father, and I never will be. That's why he disinherited me, after all."

"Do you hate him?" you asked, calm but intense.

"No!" I replied automatically, but I knew it wasn't wholly true. "I . . . I don't want to hate him."

"But he's neglecting his only daughter," you pressed. "He's ignoring your achievements. And I know he's done worse than that, Reska." Your expression darkened, and the look in your eyes scared me. "I know he's hurt you. Don't you ever wish you could make him pay for what he's done to you? Don't you wish you could pay him back for the cruelty and neglect?"

I stared at you, nervous and uncertain. "I—I don't know what you mean. What are you saying?"

Softly, you said the words: "Do you ever wish your father would just . . . die?"

"No!" I shouted, more forcefully this time. I stared at you in horror. "No, no! I'm not—that's not—I don't want that. I don't want him to die. I don't want to hurt him. I don't want to hurt anyone, Homura. I just . . . I just wish he'd notice me." My voice went small and quiet, timid as a mouse, as I whispered, "I wish he wouldn't hurt me. I don't want anyone to hurt anyone."

That fire in your eyes only intensified, and you rose to your feet, nails biting into your palms, before turning from me and staring off at the castle in the distance. "I'm not like you, in that way. I don't let my spite die, or my anger. I feed it. I remember every horrible thing everyone has ever done to me, and I carve it into my fucking soul. I don't forgive. Forgiveness is bullshit, anyway. Apologies are just meaningless dreck; nobody ever means them. No, I can't just forgive and forget when someone hurts me, no matter what promises they make, no matter how many times they tell me how bad they feel about the way I force them to hurt me."

I was frozen against the blanket, watching you with held breath, not daring to even whisper and interrupt you.

You laughed, the sound horrible and pained. "You've told me a lot about your father, so I guess it's only fair I tell you about mine: he was a bastard, and I hated his fucking guts. Every time he raised his voice at me and threatened to beat me, I hated him more. Every time he dismissed me and rejected me as his daughter, the anger burned hotter. There was fear, plenty of fear, but when it passed it left only hatred and anger. And now, a world away, divided by time and space, I only have one regret: that I never got to stick a knife in the old man and watch the blood pour out."

A drop of blood dripped from your hand, then another, and I realized your hands were bleeding from the bite of your nails. You just laughed, seeming to relish in the pain, fueled by it. "Gods," you marveled, "I used to fantasize about that every night, when I was young enough the consequences wouldn't be quite so ruinous for me. I dreamed of ending the torment. But I never did it. I was weak. I was always so fucking weak." You turned back to me and lowered your voice to say, "But I never let the hatred die."

I found my voice, barely, and whispered, "I don't want to hate anyone. It . . . it scares me. I can't let myself hate. I'm afraid of what my magic might do, if I hate."

"Hatred can be a righteous thing, Reska. Is it not justice, to hate the oppressor? There are people who deserve to be hated; people who need to be hated. There are some people who just shouldn't be allowed to live. A better world is forged in the fires of anger, carved at the tip of a knife. Sometimes, violence can bring peace. Because sometimes, when the people who hurt you are the people with all the power, there's nothing else you can do, and no one coming to save you. No one is going to take pity on you and do it for you. No one will change the world for you."

I curled in on myself tighter, and I felt fear and sadness wash over me. "Not even you?" *I asked softly.*

You looked away from the castle and caught my gaze, holding me with those dark-burning eyes. "I'll do you one better: I'll help you save yourself. I'll help you find the strength to make them all pay. Everyone who's ever mistreated you, ignored you, hurt you, called you a demon—they'll all pay. They'll finally see what fools they've been. I promise, Reska: I'll help you change the world."

"I don't deserve that," *I insisted, eyes watering.* "I don't deserve your kindness, or your help."

Your fists tightened, more crimson droplets fell to the picnic blanket below, and then the blood on your palms boiled. *You lifted a hand and stretched it in front of your face, watching the blood boil and seethe, and then you met my gaze again and declared,* "You're wrong. You're wrong, and I'll prove it to you, whatever it takes."

I smiled despite myself, the expression slight and soft. "I think I'd like that."

You grinned. "I thought you might. And I know how to do it, too. Thanks to you, it looks like I have magic now, and I know how to use that to make every last bastard in that castle respect you like they should. I can get you the throne, Reska, and all that entails. Everything it means to you. But I can only help if you let me. It's still gotta be you, in the end. So . . . do you trust me?"

In your eyes, droplets of red blossomed like blood spilling into ink. You held out your bleeding hand, the blood still boiling, and you grinned with such breathtaking confidence it was impossible to doubt you.

And so I took your hand in mine, and together we took our first steps on the path that would lead my world to ruin.

PART THREE

JABBERWOCKY

OR, VIOLENCE FOR VIOLENCE IS THE RULE OF BEASTS

"Would you tell me, please, which way I ought to go from here?"
"That depends a good deal on where you want to get to," said the Cat.
"I don't much care where—" said Alice.
"Then it doesn't matter which way you go," said the Cat.
"—so long as I get *somewhere*," Alice added as an explanation.
"Oh, you're sure to do that," said the Cat, "if you only walk long enough."

—*Alice in Wonderland*, Lewis Carroll

I

I wake up, and like twice before I have to untangle two sets of memories, but this time I'm doing it while tied to a chair. Joy. I can feel the rope around my wrists and the hard wood frame, but I don't open my eyes yet; I don't want to give any signal that I've woken up if I can avoid it.

The memories are a little easier to separate this time, but that's small comfort when I have some absolutely batshit revelations to deal with. Thoughts untangle, the web is unwoven, and I'm left with Reska, Homura, and myself. But those latter two, they really might be the same, like I had suspected. But at the same time, not.

The anger she burned with: I know that anger. I know that hate. It used to burn in me . . . but it hasn't for years. The story Homura told, it was true; when I was a kid, I wanted my father to die. I held to my anger for so long, but with time and distance it bled away, and broke entirely when he sent that letter and finally made an apology I could believe.

So was it a lie? Was Homura just acting to manipulate Reska? No, she couldn't have been, because the anger was real enough to unlock her affinity for Blood. Her very real blood-boiling anger. That was magic, and old magic, something that responds to raw feeling and requires no system access.

Because that's what it is, to have to interface with an existing user of a certain category before you're allowed access to a set of mechanics: system access, regulated by moderators. But Homura asked no one for her magic; she reached out and seized it. She did something that I'm not entirely sure I can, and she did it burning with anger for a crime that I have forgiven.

So she's me, but not me. She is, and she isn't. She's the me that I used to be. Not myself, but not somebody else. A younger me. A harsher me, still driven by spite and hatred more than anything else.

Is she a dream self, fragmented from an echo of id? Is she a bad copy, made in my image but poorly, shunted back in the history of this world? Or is she the same soul, just separated by time?

A story springs to mind: *Alice in Wonderland.*

Not the original story, of course, but all the modern retellings: Tim Burton's movie, *The Looking-Glass Wars,* and *American McGee's Alice.* See, the original is a kid's book, and you want to court an older audience, so naturally you age Alice up and you make the story darker, but you still want to play with the old books, whether by making them canon as-is or canon with some twists. So your Alice has been to Wonderland before, but she's forgotten, or has convinced herself it was just some childish madness, until she's returned to a Wonderland much darker and more dangerous than her first go around.

If Homura really is the same me, just younger, then it means I've been to Pandaemonium before, my own personal Wonderland, and simply forgotten. I wonder: did some part of me know this, some buried fragment of subconscious, and that influenced me to take the name of Alice? Is that why Cheshire decided to take such a name? Either way, if I'm this Wonderland's Alice . . .

. . . then that makes me the person who hurt Reska, if her narration is to be believed. I was the worst day of her life. I broke her heart, and I made her kill her father. I brought ruin to her entire world.

A broken world and a broken heart; strange magic unbound by the system I've been introduced to. The past, perhaps the ancient past if that magic is old magic and not just different magic. The question is clear: did Reska become Katoptris? Is the world of my dreams the precursor to the Labyrinth?

That would explain why I'm getting these dreams, and why they're from Reska's point of view rather than my past self's, and it might mean that Katoptris herself has been sending them. If Reska is Katoptris, then is this whole excursion a form of twisted revenge? Was I dragged to this world and made to suffer as payback for something I did as Homura? Did I hurt her that badly, that she would torture me and deprive me like this? Do I deserve the pain she's put me through, for the weight of sins I cannot remember?

"Hey, you awake yet? Don't open your eyes, just murmur it softly."

A familiar voice intrudes on my inner monologue, and I recognize the presence of Cheshire. Cheshire, whose name I thought to be nothing but a silly reference until just this moment. I'm even less certain I can trust her now, if she knows about my prior journey to Wonderland and is keeping it from me.

"Alice? I can tell your breathing is different, I know you're awake. Let me know you're listening."

Interrogate Cheshire later, escape Averrich now. "Where am I?" I ask softly, fairly certain I know the answer.

"Averrich's base, the headquarters of the King's Carnival gang: it might have been a hotel at one point, I think, but it's fairly unrecognizable now."

"How do we get out?"

Silence. Hesitation? Then: "I'm not sure. We're in his place of power, surrounded by his minions. I don't think we get away from this without hearing him out first. But he's fae, and that means talking might actually work. They're bound by old stories, and by the need to play with their food. Be interesting enough, be bold enough, and he'll stay his hand."

"Joy," I mutter. "Another conversation with a fae for me to fuck up."

"I know you can get us out of this. I trust in you, Allie, with every inch of my soul."

I almost laugh, and I whisper bitterly, "If your story is really true, then you don't have much of a choice in the matter." *And if it's not a choice, could it ever be real?*

"There's always a choice." She pecks me on the cheek, lips against skin for only a brief moment. "And I choose you every time."

I am silent for a moment, thoughts heavy. I finally work up the courage to ask, "Why?"

"Why what?"

"Why me? If what you say you feel for me is real, then why? Meddling of the Demiurge or no, what could you possibly see in me? What could you possibly love about me?" I keep my voice low and quiet, but there's still a dark, wretched bite to my last question.

I feel her hands on my face, her fingers feather-light against my cold porcelain skin. Her fingertips find my eyelids and gently lift, the touch somehow painless, and I stare into those gleaming catlike eyes. Yellow and blue burn with equal world-rending intensity, swallowing me whole and holding me captive.

"Everything," she breathes. "I love everything about you."

I flinch, and then a new voice intrudes to say, "Ah, you're finally awake. Good, that means we can get started." It's Kado's voice, and when I glance in the direction it came from I see the gangly reaver leaning in an open doorway. "And you're fine, just as promised."

I glare at him as he strides over and cuts me free from the chair I'm tied to. He leaves my hands bound, annoyingly, but I probably don't need them free to cast spells. "That's a subjective assessment. I certainly don't *feel* fine."

"Ah, but the Weaver thinks you are, and it's her opinion that matters," he remarks dryly. "Now shuffle along, Maven. The boss has been kept waiting long enough."

The reaver leads me through halls that may have once been decorated but are now stripped of all wallpaper and paint, left barren. There are plenty of doors leading to other rooms, but Kado takes me up a flight of stairs and into a large chamber, maybe ballroom-sized, where the walls are lined with animal heads and weapons on plaques. In the center of the chamber towers a throne of silver and wood and bursting vegetation, and upon that throne sits the man I can only presume to be Averrich.

The elf looks like a peacock of a man. He's got the classic pointy ears and sharp features, swirling blue-green eyes, and dirty blonde glam rock hair that looks more hairspray than hair follicle. Atop his head rests a crown of gold bejeweled with sapphires and emeralds to match his sapphire-studded coat and emerald-embroidered boots. Aside from that, he's wearing only an open-chested blouse and very tight beige pants; no sign of a weapon, though I have no illusions of that making him any less dangerous.

Cheshire walks beside me, presumably invisible to the senses of my captors, and she narrows her eyes at the man on the throne. "Peer at his soul," she orders. "You need to see this."

I blink and activate my soul sight, and the world shifts once again. The rest of the room falls away, reduced to sketchy lines and splashes of ink and charcoal. Vague shapes, the faintest impressions of pinprick color, but all of it distant and blurry, corner of my vision, as the center of my vision is taken up by the sight of Averrich's soul.

I see a hunter. I see detailed muscles and dexterous hands. I see a bow, a knife, an axe, a spear. I see a mask of bone-porcelain in the shape of a fox's head, eyeholes swirling with blue and green light, the only color on the page. Behind the mask and beneath his skin I can taste old stories and moonlit nights, baleful green flame and a world in pieces. This is an old soul. An ancient soul. A soul stained by a great and terrible Fall.

But there is something unnatural creeping through his soul, spreading like veins over muscle and cracks in the mask: lines of white-hot light splintering like lightning. It hurts to look at, that searing white against all that ink and charcoal. And it burns not with pain but with ecstasy, delight, pure white-hot *joy*.

I blink away my soul sight as the white light starts to hurt, and Cheshire whispers in my ear, "He is maddened by joy. Use that. *Make him laugh.*"

I take a brief glimpse around the rest of the room as Kado keeps me moving forward. My audience is small: aside from Averrich, myself, and Kado, there are only three people in the vast chamber.

Mahiri I recognize, though I note a few changed details: the eye my summons took out looks unhealthily red but far more functional than I had hoped; she's got a pair of bulky goggles resting on her forehead, made of leather and metal and glass; and she's traded her plain sword for one with a fancier hilt that seems decorated with carvings of animals. She doesn't look happy to see me, to my complete and utter shock.

To the right of the elf's throne—my right, not his right—I see a beefy trash pile of a woman. She's got a big frame, maybe bigger than the power armor knight, and a ragged tank top shows off muscular arms. Her dark brown hair is matted in clumps, her face is dirty, and even from here I can tell that she smells like wet dog. Add that to those big amber eyes, eyes like a wolf, and my paranoid brain is immediately screaming lycanthrope.

On the other side of Averrich's throne stands a woman who is definitely some kind of fiend—I'd wager another imp. She has deep blue skin and violet eyes with black sclera, curling horns bedecked in gold and glittering gems, jeweled ear piercings, and a pointed tongue. She wears a black-and-purple dress that leaves little to the imagination and bares both arms and legs, showing off her clawed hands and clawed feet.

When I'm close to the throne, Kado shoves me to my knees. I restrain the urge to hiss and snarl at him. *Deadly situation, need to play this right. Elf gang boss whose soul has some kind of weird joy virus. Okay. Fuck.* I let my gaze flick to Cheshire for a moment, trying to broadcast my need for help through just my eyes.

Cheshire's right beside me, and she quickly says, "The fae like a mouthy brat, or at least that's what their queen likes, and they can only deviate so much from her template. Get scrappy. Be a bitch."

I can do that. Bratting is my specialty. I look up at Averrich and crack a forced grin. "If you're going to tie me up and put me on my knees, at least buy a girl a drink first. I usually charge for that kind of game, but I'll make an exception 'cause you're just so damn cute."

The faerie cocks his head, raises an eyebrow, and then smirks. "Noted. Imlashi, be a dear and treat our guest." Averrich plucks a goblet out of thin air and hands it to the blue-skinned imp, whose name I recognize from the nightclub.

Imlashi struts over to me, each move self-assured and languid. Cheshire whispers in my ear again, telling me, "This is a power move. The liquid in the goblet is harmless, but it's made to smell poisoned so you'll make a fool of yourself avoiding it."

Kado slashes the bonds around my wrists, freeing my hands, and Imlashi holds out the goblet for me to take, which I do. The liquid is a bright shade of orange-red, looking like some kind of fruit juice, but the scent of bitter almonds wafts off it.

If Cheshire's lying here, I'm dead either way. I down the whole thing in one gulp—grapefruit juice, I discover—before handing the empty goblet to Imlashi with a pleasant smile. "My favorite. Thanks."

Imlashi takes the goblet with grace and carries it back to Averrich, who vanishes it away into presumably his throne world—which is probably how Eirdryd pulled off that sword trick, now that I think about it.

I push off the ground and rise to my feet, unwilling to remain kneeling a moment longer. "So," I ask. "Shall we talk? You brought me all this way and with all this effort for *something*, didn't you?"

Averrich chuckles. "Spirited. Let's test that spirit: Imlashi, do what you do best."

The imp smiles, bows in a way that is very intentionally meant to give me an eyeful of her cleavage, and then she saunters closer to me than before and traces a finger under my chin, across my cheek, and tugs at my lower lip. "[Worship the Glorious]," she commands.

Just like the sleep spell, I feel the effect from a keen remove; I can hear the echo of the song, taste the shape and the suggestion, but it does not bind me. I feel a sense of adoration, grandeur, and all-consuming *worship*, but I heed no god nor master. I will the spell to disperse as easily as dismissing one of my own, and it's gone.

Then I bite the fucker's finger.

"Ah! You little bitch!" she shrieks, pulling her bleeding finger back and clutching at it.

I swallow a few drops of blood and grin, feeling a trickle of mana from the act. "Don't stick your finger in a vampire's mouth unless you want to *lose* that finger. But go on, do it again. I dare you."

The imp glares at me and curls her lip for a retort, but she's interrupted by the elf. "Report, Imlashi," he orders her.

Imlashi smooths her dress and restores her charming smile. "Her resistances are consistent with those of a scion, as Kado reported. I believe it is safe to assume that she is, indeed, a demon."

Averrich taps the arm of his throne and muses, "I wonder how she would fare against another scion's influence. [Dazzle and Daze]."

A second spell slams into me, a thing of light and sound and vicious disorientation. The distance between the spell effect and the sanctity of my mind feels perilously shorter, but I grit my teeth and force it off regardless. "My will is my own," I snarl.

The faerie chuckles. "So it is. Very well, only one more test: Imlashi, open your sight. Tell me what you see."

Imlashi nods and peers at me intently, violet eyes burning bright. She frowns and furrows her brow, and she begins to speak. "I see . . . contradiction. I see fear that is bravado, anger that is calm. It's like a storm of emotion and desire and meaning, all tangled and intertwined. It's nearly impossible to discern her true intentions beyond the vaguest impression of 'survive.' I've never seen any defense quite like it."

"I have," Averrich remarks. "She is protected from your sight by a witch's shroud. I've seen it thrice before, in my very long life."

Each member of his little court reacts differently: Imlashi stiffens, Mahiri's eyes go wide, and the possible lycanthrope narrows her eyes. I grit my teeth, but don't deny the claim.

"However, she is yet new to her Gift," he continues. "I cannot tell the shape of each thread, but I can perceive the presence, and that is more than an experienced practitioner would allow me. The girl is bound in covenant to two signatures: one of Shadow, and one of Summer."

The contract with Bashe, and the contract with Eirdryd. Damn it.

Averrich leans forward and smiles benevolently. "Now, let's be civil about this. Tell me, girl: where is Bashekehi the Ever-Gleaming? I've been dying to speak with him ever since I heard he had returned."

I blink rapidly. "What? What!? Are you fucking kidding me!? You kidnapped me over the godsdamned fucking incubus!? I DON'T EVEN LIKE THE INCUBUS!" I am *boiling* with rage that these absolute bastards would put me through all this nonsense just to ask me about *Bashe* of all people. Do I not matter? Am I not worth abducting on my own merits?

"If there is no love lost between you, then surely you would have no compunctions about selling him out," Averrich suggests.

"Well," I hedge, "I mean, that information has value. What are you offering?"

He smiles again and pulls a long, wicked knife out of the air. "The privilege of not having that information tortured out of you."

I pause, processing that, and Cheshire drifts back into view to counsel, "Don't play games over this one. Offer it as a gift."

Her counsel seems sensible, but still I hesitate. Quite aside from the fact that I only have an educated guess about Bashe's current location, do I really feel comfortable throwing him to the proverbial wolves? We left on bad terms, but it doesn't feel right. So instead of following Cheshire's advice, I try, "Hey now, isn't that against the spirit of hospitality? Pretty sure torturing captives is a big social faux pas."

Averrich's face lights up, Cheshire hisses, and I immediately realize I've made a fumble. The elf asks, "Oh? Do you cede to my authority, then, and acknowledge yourself as under my power?"

"Uhhh, nope! No, nope, not at all, definitely not, I am not doing that. *However*," I stall, "you, uh, shouldn't torture me anyways. Because—because torture is ineffective!" I seize on a point of attack and follow it through. "People will say anything under torture, absolutely anything. You stick a trained operative through a torture program and they'll sing you twenty different tunes but not a note will be on-key. They'll say whatever they think you want to hear."

"And are you a trained operative, Maven Alice?" he asks, a mocking edge to his words. The knife scrapes along the side of his throne, carving a gouge.

Okay, Cheshire's plan it is. "I offer a gift," I blurt. "A gift of knowledge: I'm not actually sure where Bashe went, but I imagine he *probably* went to go mourn his dead husband and get his life sorted. If there was a grave, probably there. His old base, maybe, or his house if he had one. We left on bad terms so he didn't tell me shit but he was pretty torn up about his dead husband and I may have pressed that button a little too hard, so yeah, that's where I'd go if I were looking for him, which I have no intention of doing because I don't care and he can fuck off and die, I'm not bitter."

Averrich chuckles. "I see. Well, that's good to know. But I admit, I led with the less interesting question. What I really want to know is . . . which fae put that mark on your soul? Who did you sell your name to?"

Fuck! Fuck fuck fuck! Argh, why does he have to know that level of detail? I grit my teeth and say nothing.

"Mahiri," he says casually, and the reaver cracks her knuckles, grins, and starts advancing on me.

I take a step back, bump into Kado, and hold my hands up placatingly. "Okay, okay, jeez. Back off."

Averrich holds up a hand and Mahiri halts, but there's still a dangerous edge to his voice as he insists, "Answers, demon."

I sigh. "Eirdryd. His name was Eirdryd Llewellyn."

The dirty muscle girl with the wolf eyes growls out, "What game does he think he's playing, sending Llewellyn so far from his territory?"

Wait, what? Is that a different "he" from Eirdryd? What the fuck is going on?

Averrich replies breezily, "The same as us, of course. Inform Kasumi all the same." The probably-a-lycanthrope nods and hurries out of the room, disappearing down a corridor. When she's gone, Averrich says, "Congratulations, fledgling: you just made my persons of interest list. Let's talk."

II

"What was that about?" I demand. "Who is Kasumi? What game? Who sent Eirdryd, and why?"

Averrich only laughs at my questions, seeming darkly amused. "If you don't know already... well, you'll learn soon enough. That is, provided you live to see the morrow. The big event will be the talk of the town!"

Argh, I hate this secret-keeping bullshit. Why is everyone in this world so keen on holding back information? I glare at the pointy-eared bastard and insist, "I don't have a single clue what you're babbling about. If you want me to swear my ignorance by the Weaver, I will. I was dropped into this world *yesterday*, and the past day has not exactly been conducive to information gathering. I just want answers. Please, just tell me what's going on."

The fae chuckles again. "No, no I don't think I will. It's much more entertaining to watch you squirm like a squirrel in a snare. But, I must say, it would be quite selfish of me to hoard this entertainment all to myself and my dear lieutenants. I think it's time we brought in the rest of our audience, don't you? Together, I think we can give them a simply wonderful show."

Averrich rises from his throne to his full height, and he takes the time to adjust his cufflinks and brush back his mop of hair—which springs back into shape the moment his hand retreats. The elf snaps his fingers and immediately all the doors lining the chamber fly open to reveal a waiting crowd.

More reavers stream into the room in a disorderly fashion, all wearing their signature gambesons and carrying swords, spears, bows, crossbows, and so on. I see the owl from before perched on one of the reavers, and there are a few more of those ugly, hairless, too-muscular not-dogs with human eyes and oversized teeth. New beasts pad alongside them: a pair of wolves that look formed of creaking branches and wicked thorns, with eyes of burning green and cracks in thick bark that reveal bright green sap beneath. Cheshire points them out as they file in. "Goblin dogs and bark wolves. They're homunculi of Summer, just like the owlbear."

"That one's an orc," she adds, pointing to a man with gray-green skin and yellowed tusks, with salt-and-pepper hair and beard trimmed short and neat. The orc has fire-orange eyes that remind me of Eirdryd's, and he's wearing a black smock and heavy gloves. "Summer retainer, one of several types. He's probably the forgemaster for the whole operation."

The last to file in are a group of squat green creatures with sharp teeth, big eyes and ears, and flat, almost pug-like noses. They're not wearing armor like the reavers, but they're wearing normal clothing—no rags or dirty sack-cloth—and all have knives at their belts. The goblins—it's obvious even before Cheshire calls it out—are wheeling in tall, thin, rectangular objects, each object covered in a sheet and manned by two goblins.

The goblins take their places on the right side of the room and remain by what they brought in, while the rest of the new arrivals cluster about the left side with Mahiri and Kado. When everyone seems gathered, Averrich sweeps his hands broadly and booms, "Friends and subjects, hunters of all stripes: welcome, welcome, to our moot! I have called you here because of this loathsome wretch you see before you. I tell you, friends, that one who is both demon and *witch* has strayed into our court."

Again, I see a complicated mix of reactions from the assemblage: those who heard my nature already are able to control their expressions, but the rest are hearing it for the first time. A few of the reavers scoff or laugh, as if it must be a joke; their peers look nervous, eyes wandering, hands tensing. The forgemaster merely crosses his arms and narrows his eyes, but most of the goblins seem frightened and inch closer to each other.

I drink in the fear, and find that sensation surprisingly literal: I can *taste* the little shock of dread that passes through them all at the reveal of what I am. It's heady and rich, almost decadent in its unexpected satisfaction. There are people in this room who are afraid of me—of *me*, the worthless loser nerd too frail to kill a bug just a few short days ago. There's a trickle of mana, too, but that feels like dessert to the main course.

Averrich catches my gaze, and whatever he sees in me makes him smirk. I realize, then, that he's paused in his speech, and he's giving me a bit of air to contribute to the scene. In some strange, twisted way, I am his partner in this bit of theater. I wonder, briefly, how I can be so certain of that fact, but regardless it is undeniable. *Alright, I'll play.*

"It's true," I tell the assemblage with a wicked grin. "The Abyss swims in my veins, and the Demiurge herself has taken a special interest in my existence. My name is Maven Alice, and I am a monster unlike any you have ever met." The taste of fear deepens, but only a little; I don't exactly have much more than words to back up my claim at this juncture. Still, every little bit helps.

"Monster indeed," the elf says. "A monster that one of our own has already fallen victim to. She trespassed our territory and hunted within our grounds, glutting herself upon a figment at one of our clubs. By acts of malignance, has she not revealed herself to be a true beast?"

The question is obviously leading, and the crowd is happy to oblige: jeers erupt from the reavers and goblins present, though not all. For my part, I curl my lip and protest, "My trespass was an accident! No insult was meant to you and yours, Goblin King. I arrived in this city *yesterday*, and my supposed guide was more interested in getting rid of me than explaining your borders and conventions."

"And yet," Averrich says, "those borders were still disrespected."

"How was I to know they existed?" I ask with clear exasperation. "There was no marker of ownership, no indication that a boundary was being crossed! You claim malignance, but my trespass was purely accidental."

"Oh? And was it an accident, too, when you *murdered* Shane Murtagh?"

Murtagh. His name was Shane Murtagh. I will remember that. "That was no murder," I protest with more confidence than I feel. "It was an act of self-defense. I didn't have a choice. He didn't *give me* a choice."

"And what were you defending yourself from, witchlet? What terrible fate had my reaver promised you?" Averrich's blue-green eyes shine like sunlight hitting water, and I hesitate to answer, so he keeps talking. "Ah, that's right: it was this very conversation. Shane Murtagh sought to bring you to me, and for that you took his life. Tell me, Maven Alice: do you still feel *justified* in killing that man?"

His gaze burns into me and I wilt away, my voice wavering and soft as I tell him once more, "I didn't have a choice."

"There is always a choice," the elf chides me. Then, to the crowd, he booms, "This blackguard's insult shall not go unanswered! A crime against any of my hunters is a crime against *all* of my hunters, this I swear to you as your rightful king."

Mahiri is glaring daggers at me, but the rest of the reavers are harder to parse; they make some noise for their leader's proclamation, but do they believe it? Am I looking at a pack of loyal marks taking in every word, or are they humoring Averrich because they don't have a choice?

I flicker soul sight and peer into Kado's soul, ink and charcoal bleeding away to expose a beating heart of calm blue. Measured, steady, purposeful. He, too, is playing his part in this performance, following his lines as the Goblin King wrote them. For what?

"Though the demon-witch has vast potential for growth, she is yet a mere fledgling before the powerful." Averrich's continued speech snaps me out of soul sight, and I look at the elf with my physical—or faux-physical, I should get used to thinking—eyes. "I could slay this whelp with but a word... and yet, that hardly seems fair, now does it?"

He cracks a grin, and he lets his people cheer and jeer. Mahiri's hand tightens around the hilt of her shiny new sword. Imlashi huffs. Kado watches, calm and measured.

"Who would I be," he asks rhetorically, "if I were to hoard all this glory for myself? This demon will make a truly excellent trophy for some worthy hunter, and I would not dare deprive my followers of the chance for such a hunt. No, I think striking her down here would be entirely the wrong decision. But what say you? Shall we give the demon a chance to play prey?"

This time, the whole crowd roars their approval, and I see hunger in many eyes. *Hunting trophy. Cheshire told me that's one of two ways that Summer makes artifacts. They want to hunt me down and forge a magic item from my bones.*

Averrich laughs with delight and sweeps a hand toward the goblins. "Well, I think that's *quite* clear. Goblins, unveil the mirrors." Six sheets are pulled from six tall mirrors, and immediately my tension ratchets up another notch. "All ye gathered, I call a hunt: five volunteers and one wretched demon will step through these mirrors and fall into a specially prepared dream bubble. There, the reavers will seek their target, who seeks to escape, and all six must avoid the seeking gaze of the Reveler which makes that maze its home."

Reveler? Where have I—oh, fucking hells. It's one of the Mourner's siblings, a.k.a. another version of the bastard that nearly ended me before I met Cheshire. The catgirl in question grimaces. "Throwing his own hunters into a Reveler's maze... is he mad, or is there another layer?"

Mahiri steps forward and raises her chin defiantly. "I will answer the call, my king. I shall hunt the beast, and anyone who wishes to steal that prize will have to take it over my dead body. I *will* claim the demon's head." Mahiri looks at me with such naked loathing that I almost flinch.

Yeah, kinda saw that one coming. Is this just about the eye, and her wounded pride, or did she have some affection for Murtagh? Four more reavers step forward to volunteer for the hunt, though none of them are as dramatic about it as Mahiri was. There's a woman with a spear, a man with a crossbow and a dog, a woman with a bandolier of knives, and a man with a sword and buckler.

I size up my opponents, and they do the same to me. One of them, the man with the crossbow, smirks at me and says, "I'll try to make it quick and painless, darlin'."

I smile sweetly and reply, "I make no such promises. Overconfidence is a slow and insidious killer."

He just huffs and hefts his crossbow. The others don't talk, merely eyeing me speculatively. I wonder how much Mahiri has told them of our encounter in the nightclub.

Averrich claps his hands together and declares, "We have our volunteers! Brave hunters, everlasting glory awaits the greatest of your number—but remember: though you are all part of my Carnival, only one of you can claim the trophy of this hunt. Now . . . mark your prey, and we can begin."

As one, the five reavers look at me and say, "[Hunter's Mark]." I feel no change, but I can hear the strange tonal indicator of a spell being cast.

"Tracker spell," Cheshire tells me. "Probably how they found us after the mall, come to think of it."

For a moment I grit my teeth in frustration, but then the colder, more rational voice in my head speaks up. *This represents an opportunity. We have to get the sequencing right, obviously, but there's the potential for significant gains here. We leverage what we know about Averrich and his game to petition for an evening of the playing field, and then we pull out our ace.*

Averrich is speaking again. "The prey is marked, the maze awaits! Prove yourself in this hunt and earn this demon's trophy."

I laugh scornfully. "Earn it? Hardly. I see what kind of hunt you're really interested in: no test of skill or cunning, but a *fox hunt*: no risk to the hunter, no chance of failure, only the baying of hounds and the laughter of the lazy. Are you really going to stack the deck in your favor so openly?"

The elf cocks his head and grins. "Bold words, but they lack bite. Am I to believe a demon witch has no means of punishing the hunter and their hounds?"

I spread my hands and lean toward him. "If I were at full strength, maybe, but I've had a rough few days. If you want this hunt to be worthy—if you want this show to be entertaining—then we have to even the playing field a little: a last meal, to give me the strength to make your hunters *work* for their trophy." I bare my fangs and run my tongue across my teeth.

Averrich makes a show of considering the idea, while a few of the reavers and goblins look between the two of us nervously; they must be wondering if he's going to offer one of them as that last meal. When he speaks again, it's not to me but to his right-hand imp. "What do you think, Imlashi? Does the girl look *starved* to your sight?"

Imlashi quirks her lip. "She's a demon, Averrich; they're *always* hungry."

The Goblin King laughs, this one deep and booming. "Yes, yes I suppose so. Well, demon," he says, turning to me, "I'll let you have your meal. Let it never be said that I was unfair in the calling of a hunt. In fact . . . I'll even let you drink from my very own veins."

His grin is wicked as he holds out an arm and pushes back the sleeve. A single glimpse of his bared wrist is enough to get the hunger rising. What does fae blood taste like? Would it give me more mana?

Cheshire steps in front of me, expression urgent. "Don't, Alice; the madness you saw in him might be infectious. This is almost certainly another trap. Push for the lycanthrope instead."

I was right! Werewolf! The woman in question is back by the throne, having slipped back into the room when I wasn't paying attention. The thought of drinking werewolf blood has me salivating even more than fae blood. Can I become a vampire werewolf!? Is that a thing!?

I glance back at Averrich and say, "A generous offer, Goblin King, but I'm afraid your blood wouldn't agree with me. I'd much rather have a taste of that woman at your side, actually: the lycanthrope."

The werewolf narrows her eyes at me, but Averrich seems to take no offense. He says, "Picky eater, are we? I'll allow it. Gretchen, what say you?"

Gretchen curls her lip and I catch sight of some very lovely fangs filling her mouth. "If she thinks she can handle it."

I don't wait for further permission; I dart over to the werewolf, brush her mane of hair out of the way, and sink my fangs into that powerful neck of hers. She doesn't stop me, but she doesn't *give* like Lena did, and there's something unnervingly satisfying about that moment where my fangs meet resistance, slow, and then *push* through.

Lena was ecstasy like red-burning life and tender, juicy meat. Her blood was like the pulse in my veins and the beating of my heart, and her blood was the energy that suffuses my whole body when I get lost in a manic episode. Her blood was life and joy and desperate, loving hunger.

Cameron was a duller taste, like meat still soft and tender but dried of its savory juices. His blood was no true crimson but an imitation shade, and his blood was the hunger you feel after a meal that doesn't quite fill you.

Gretchen's blood, though, is primal need and the acid burning in overworked muscles. Her blood is the iron taste of bleeding gums and the scent of rich earth. Her essence flows into me and I feel more than anything the urge to rip and tear with fang and claw.

I bite down harder, my jaw begging to clench harder and pierce deeper. I want to rip out a chunk of her throat. I want to swallow her flesh and keep going. I want to devour her whole. I want—

She's pushing me off, bloody gash in her neck, that wonderful taste lingering in my mouth and on my lips. I stumble back and catch myself, deep breaths, eyes wide and wild. My gaze is still locked to the blood dripping down her neck, enticing me, singing to me. It was a messy feed, this time, messier than my first.

The lycanthrope growls at me, and I have to laugh. It bubbles out of me like all my manic laughs do, and I grin. "Fuck, you taste good. After I kill all your friends, I'm going to enjoy coming back for seconds." I wipe the blood from my face with my hand, and then I catch sight of that vibrant red and can't help but lick it off.

Hahaha, you look like a fucking psychopath right now. What the fuck is wrong with you? I lap up the last of the blood and laugh again, this time bad enough that I nearly double over.

I look up at Averrich, the would-be king watching me with clear interest, and match his smirk with one of my own. I pull Shane Murtagh's dagger from my throne world, hold it up, and name it, "[Hunter's Marker]."

See, I think I know why I got the [Swarmheart] wrong: it was all about the resonances. Eirdryd shot flaming arrows from his bow with supernatural agility, and my Gift took that and gave me a burning dagger that made me a bit faster. I spam-summoned bugs and made them eat each other, so my Gift gave me a rock that made more bugs and then ate them to empower a single survivor bug.

This time, the resonance is clean and clear: five instances of the same spell, all doing the exact same thing, all doing exactly what I want my new artifact to do. I focus all my attention on the man standing in front of that throne, and I will the dagger to become a compass pointing to my marked quarry.

As I speak those bolded, bracketed words, almost immediately I can feel with some new sixth sense the location of the Goblin King. It's like there's a tickling in the back of my mind, a strange navigational instinct that points right where Averrich is standing. I've marked him as my quarry, and now I can find him from anywhere.

For a moment, I see a flicker of surprise cross Averrich's face. He masters it quickly and resumes that mocking smirk, but now I know I've done something he didn't predict. "Ah," he says, voice low. "So that's the kind of witch you are."

"That and more."

Averrich considers me for a moment longer, but then he claps and applauds me, "Bravo, demon witch. You've claimed two prizes for your trouble, and given us all an *excellent* showing. There can be no doubt that this will be a fair and worthy hunt."

I glance doubtfully at the five people chosen to try and murder me. *Yeah, sure.*

"Now enough delays: let the hunt . . . begin!"

The five reavers each walk to a different mirror, and I reluctantly walk to the last one left. There's no point in trying to stop this; my best chance of survival is to enter the maze, kill all my opponents, and escape from there.

I step through the mirror, and it begins.

III

A flash of rainbow maelstrom and the ever-present dark tower is all I see before I'm stumbling, slipping, falling through a chaos of color and then just as quickly gone from the space between worlds, through another mirror and out the other side into a brand-new area.

I hit the ground and my side flares with pain where Mahiri kicked me. My lungs protest as they struggle for air in a state of breathlessness that is becoming reprehensibly commonplace. I clutch at my injured side and slip a hand beneath my shirt to feel for broken ribs, but though waves of pain follow every finger-press I don't actually think the bone is cracked. *So just bruised, then. Phew.*

. . . Wow. That's an actual genuine relief. A bruised rib is a *relief* now. I hate what my life has become.

I take a deep breath—ow, ow, ow—and push off the ground into at least a sitting position. The ground is . . . weird, here. I blink away my disorientation and look at what I'm actually pressing on: it's fabric. Huh. I guess that explains why the fall was just painful and not bone-shattering.

I'm on what looks like a bunch of ribbons of fabric stretched over each other thick enough to create firm ground that's no more yielding than topsoil. Beyond me is an absolute eyesore: bridges of interwoven ribbons in a dozen colors crisscrossing over a bottomless pit like spider's thread, lit by sourceless roaming spotlights. Overhead is a big top tent in signature white-and-red, like the kind you'd see at a circus.

In every direction it all stretches into infinity, and I can see that same curvature trick that gave the Mourner's realm a sense of dimension despite the lack of any real border to the worldspace. I suspect that if I walk for a while, I'll start getting more of those scene transitions that became scarce in the city proper.

I slowly clamber to my feet—or at least I *try* to move slowly, but I lift up too fast and nearly pull a muscle. The atmosphere in the Mourner's bubble was oppressive and choking, like swimming through tar, and it took extra effort just to move. But here, inside the Reveler's maze, there's an odd buoyancy underlying every movement that makes every motion too easy. I feel like there's static electricity crackling over my limbs.

I stretch my body carefully and try to get acclimated to the new atmosphere. "Well, that was unpleasant," I groan to Cheshire, who flickers into view next to me.

She winces sympathetically. "Yeah, that did not look fun."

I glance up, looking for the mirror that I fell through, but I can't find it. I frown, but before I can ask Cheshire about it I hear echoing hyena-like laughter coming from multiple directions. A quick sweep of the area shows me the source: four humanoid creatures—more than humanoid, *human*, but animalistic in movement—loping on all fours, sprinting at me from separate ribbon-bridges.

From a distance, I can tell that they're wearing even less than the last pack of monsters were: strips of gauzy cloth in many colors wrapped around only the most necessary areas to maintain their decency. Cheshire hisses, "Celebrants!" and I have a name for these new creatures. "Don't let them touch you!"

"Yeah, remember that from the Lost," I mutter. "Gods I hate this place. I literally just got here!"

Okay, running time. Those fuckers are moving fast, so there's no time to get fancy or clever. I call [Swarmheart] to one hand and point at the Celebrants with my other hand. "[Carrion Swarm]: bury them in centipedes!" I unleash the spell and watch a mass of horrid, wriggly, creepy-crawly centipedes appear at the intersection where the ribbon-bridges my opponents are on meet mine. I don't stick around to see how that pans out.

I race away from the Celebrants, picking the direction that seems furthest in opposition. I start running. I am *still* not in shape—we really need to get a spell that'll fix that—and my bruised ribs hurt with every step, but I ignore my body's protests and move as fast as I can.

While I run, I swap the bug-stone for the knife I infused with a tracking spell. Running aimlessly might get me away from the Celebrants, but it definitely won't help me escape the maze and evade Averrich's hunters. But though I'm clutching [Hunter's Marker] in my hand, I don't sense my quarry anywhere.

I hiss at the knife and try to reach for its spell effect in my mind. I can *feel*, in that strange intangible way, the knife trying to point me toward Averrich, but it comes up blank like a 404 error. "Cheshire, what the fuck?" I ask between gasping breaths. "Why isn't it working?"

Cheshire, who is gliding alongside me because the cheating bastard doesn't have a corporeal form right now, looks at the knife and winces again. "Ah, that's because we're in a dream bubble. The spell you copied can't track targets while they're in another world."

That nearly gets me to stop in my tracks, though luckily I restrain that impulse. "What?" I need my lungs for running, so I have to hope she gets my meaning from that alone.

Cheshire seems to pick up on the unspoken part, as she winces for a third time since arriving in this wretched space. "Right, Dara was your guide. His explanation was technically correct but misleading if you lack context."

I spare a glance back at the Celebrants and find that they've collided with the centipedes and begun *eating* the bugs. They're all laughing, but two of them are fighting over the same insect—actually, wait, centipedes are a different class of arthropod—and clawing at each other with overgrown fingernails. One of them is ignoring the centipedes clinging to them and still charging at me full force, but it stumbles and nearly falls into the pit, only barely scrabbling back onto the bridge.

"Dream bubbles are just nested, subordinate throne worlds. This whole place is the Reveler's soul, which can manifest a stable worldspace indefinitely because the Labyrinth isn't trying to reassert its own reality—why would it, when the Reveler is just a piece of a piece of the Maze-Maker?"

I am a piece of a piece of me. The phrase from the school, scrawled on the walls in the room with the doll. This new revelation is maddening, but I don't have time to analyze it because the Celebrants are *gaining on me.*

The pack of four is loping toward me, one in the lead, all the centipedes swept aside or eaten. None of them seem to be bleeding from the centipede bites, damn it, but the two that were scratching at each other *are* bleeding. I can work with that, but first I need to take out the front-runner.

I whirl to face the monsters, trade [Hunter's Marker] for [Swarmheart], and call out, "[Carrion Swarm]: stag beetles! [Swarmheart]: Madame Hornsby! CHARGE!"

In rapid succession I see a swarm of stag beetles burrow out of the ribbon-bridge, melt into buggy goo, and reform into a much larger stag beetle. Madame Hornsby, iridescent and majestic, immediately charges the leading runner at full speed.

The crazed, half-naked, ghoul-like Celebrant merely laughs and pounces on the charging stag beetle as it gets close. The mad monster keeps laughing as Madame Hornsby keeps charging, momentum and mindless obedience sending both of them soaring off the side of the ribbon-bridge and down toward the infinite pit below.

You were the best of us, Madame Hornsby. Your sacrifice will not be forgotten. The remaining three are gaining fast, but two of them have given me an opening. I reach a hand in the direction of a bleeder and cry, "[Exsanguinate]!" I clench my fist to punctuate the cry, because that seems like the kind of thing this magic system would appreciate.

A dozen shallow cuts rupture and widen into brutal lacerations, and the wounded Celebrant immediately stumbles and collapses, bleeding profusely but *still laughing*. Its fellows halt their running, turn sharply to look upon their fallen peer, and pounce. The Celebrants tear into their comrade with jagged nails and filthy teeth, grasping and biting in ways that seem disturbingly close to sexual, and through the whole process they're all still laughing.

I watch the carnage in undisguised horror. I let out a deep, nervous breath, and I realize that the pain in my side is gone. I poke at where the wound used to be and feel nothing out of the ordinary. *Parasitic transfusion at work. Absolutely worth the cost.*

"We shouldn't stick around," Cheshire reminds me, and I nod.

"Yes, right. Back to running. Somewhere." I set off at a more comfortable jog, still just aiming to get away from the Celebrants. It feels *wrong* to jog, though, like my body could go faster and thus should go faster. That static feeling, the buoyancy, it's pushing me to push my *body* to its limits. "Ugh, how is this maze *worse* than the last one? The atmosphere, the horrid circus aesthetic, and the bastardfuck fast zombies. That's the worst kind of zombie! Legitimately, why are these so much more violent than the Lost?"

Cheshire, who is *still* gliding alongside me like a cheater—and now that I think about, there are practical reasons as well as petty that I should manifest her first chance I get—responds, "Well, think about it: are you usually more destructive when you're manic or depressed?"

I roll my eyes. "Bah, I can ruin my life in any mood. Wait." Click. "Oh, you're kidding me. Oh, fuckshit dammit. That's what the 'Beast of Lamentation and Euphoria' is, isn't it? Of course it is, because all this throne world shit comes back to psychology and belief and mindset. Magic and meaning, 'cause magic *is* meaning. So the Mourner makes depression zombies, and the Reveler makes mania zombies, because those are the two halves of the Beast behind them both. Motherfucker."

I'm still swearing when I cross the arbitrary threshold into a new zone of the dream bubble. Gone are the ribbon-bridges and big top tent, replaced by giant wooden blocks that are colored and engraved like children's toys. The toy blocks are stacked in infinitely recurring piles and some of them are stuck frozen in the air to form pathways from pile to pile. Some are frozen in the act of tumbling down toward the pit or tumbling *up* toward the ceiling. The background of this room—I suspect it would be accurate to think of it as the skybox of a video game level—is the inside of a toy chest.

I come to a stop at the edge of one block and take a seat, already feeling the strain of all this physical exertion. "Okay. Quick pause to figure out what the fuck we're going to do, and also to get you a body." I summon the charm bracelet and manifest Cheshire, who luxuriates in the act of stretching her limbs. "Ideas?" I ask the catgirl.

"I mean, there's the obvious: your artifact may not help, but you still *have* a spell that's perfect for the occasion. You've used it for this exact scenario before."

I hiss at her and clutch the brand on my right hand. "I've already used it twice! This is the last one, and I can't just waste it. I sold my *name* for this spell. At some point I'm going to have to kill a fae because of this spell, and that's entirely separate from the *other* fae that I have to kill. It's such a waste to burn two out of three uses on navigating a maze."

"Okay, then get caught by the hunters or the Reveler and die here. Those are your options." Cheshire's voice is firm, and her expression is serious. "You can't deal with Averrich or Eirdryd if you never escape the maze."

"Argh, I know that . . . but it's just so inefficient. If I could—wait, idea. If I ask it to lead me to something *outside* the maze, rather than just leading me to the exit, I'll get a path to freedom and still extract value. There's just the question of what I ask for."

"Something to help you beat Averrich," Cheshire suggests, "since that seems like your immediate goal. A weapon uniquely suited to killing him, or an ally that'll be good in a fight with him."

"Good idea. Hmm." I hold up my branded hand and burn my last spell charge. "[Find the Path]: lead me to that beyond the maze which would be most helpful in defeating Averrich."

The wheel of flame spins to life, spokes forming into an arrow, and then the brand vanishes from my hand, leaving my porcelain skin smooth and unblemished. I have my path, and I have a goal. And maybe, just maybe, I have a shot at killing that bastard fae who threw me in this maze.

Cheshire stiffens and points at something off in the distance. I glance in that direction and catch sight of the reaver with a crossbow and dog. He's just finished clambering over a tricky block and has definitely seen me, because he's loading his crossbow.

"Fuck. [Carrion Swarm]: crows for the eyes!"

My summoned crows fly at the reaver and peck at his eyes, but he gets a shot off first and it nails me in the shoulder, piercing right through my cape and blouse. I scream and pain floods my nervous system, that arm immediately going dead. I clutch at the bolt, hesitate for only a moment, and then do the one thing you're never supposed to do: I pull it out.

The bolt hurts even worse leaving than it did entering, and I nearly double over with pain. Blood flows freely, staining my blouse, and my knuckles go even whiter from clutching the crossbow bolt.

At the same time, I see Cheshire shapeshift into a hawk and begin flying straight for the goblin dog. The hideous monster dog takes off at a run, horrible human eyes locked on me, but Cheshire flies up to it as a hawk and transforms into a lion at the last moment. The lion slams into the dog and both careen perilously close to the edge. They scrap, trading bites and scratches.

I try to split my attention between their fight and the reaver's struggle with the crows, an attempt made more difficult by the awful, awful pain that is now partly self-inflicted. "[Carrion Swarm]: another round of crows," I croak out. The reaver draws his sidearm and slashes at the crows, but with the arrival of the second batch he cries out in pain and one of the corvids *swallows* something. I see blood, and I immediately exploit that opportunity with a shouted "[Exsanguinate]!"

Blood ruptures from the reaver's face, and I feel the wound in my shoulder begin to knit close. It's not instant like the bruised ribs, but this is definitely a far worse wound. The healing starts to slow before it's finished, and I see another pair of crows die by the sword, so I cast another "[Exsanguinate]!" and hope it'll be enough. Blood flows and flesh knits.

In her scrap with the goblin dog, I see Cheshire finally grapple the mutt and put all her leonine weight into rolling off the side of the giant toy block. Both lion and dog fall toward the pit below, but only one of them vanishes into the dark. Cheshire flies out of the pit as a crow and joins my summons, transforming into a wolf as she arrives.

She's bleeding from a few wounds, but still looking strong, and she easily pins the reaver to the ground. He's in bad shape, far worse than Mahiri was after my spell, and I race to get the kill before he becomes ineligible for my coup de grace.

Cheshire knows what I'm after and injures without killing, focusing her efforts on crippling his limbs. I reach the still-shouting reaver, crouch down, and cast "[Prey Upon]: all mana."

The Abyssal darkness takes hold, and the reaver breathes his last.

And just like that, with almost callous ease, I have taken another life.

IV

Satisfaction and discomfort war within me as I stare down at the mangled face of what used to be a person.

There was something very different about this fight compared to my last scrap with a reaver. It was so much quicker, and there was so much less preamble. We exchanged, what, two lines of dialogue? I didn't even know his name. His only distinguishing feature was that he acted smug.

As the adrenaline fades from my system I keep expecting guilt to take its place, but it never does. But then, was it guilt that I felt when I killed Shane Murtagh? I felt horror, certainly, and I felt the twisted need to justify my actions, but is that really the same thing as guilt? Did I feel *sorry* for taking that man's life, or was it fear of how others would respond to the act? Is it selfish or selfless to feel that kind of guilt?

Regardless, I don't feel that way, not this time. No effort of contrivance is needed to justify my actions; the terms of the hunt left no ambiguity as to its "kill or be killed" nature, and he willingly volunteered. If we are to view my actions in a legal sense, neither killing was a murder. If we are to view my actions in a moral sense, at least this killing is firmly self-defense. He tried to kill me, and my only way to survive was by killing him first.

So no, I don't feel guilt. I feel vindication that I proved him wrong after his annoying comment in front of the other reavers. I feel relief that I'm not the one lying dead on the ground. I feel fascination at Cheshire's clever tactics in that fight. I feel pride in my own use of spells.

I have no reason to feel bad about killing this man, and I have every reason to feel good about my success, and I think that's what makes me so discomforted. I feel like I should feel more. Should I not feel some sense of loss? Is there not some inherent sanctity of life that I have violated? Philosophically, those ideas come to mind, but though they carry intellectual weight they lack *emotional* weight. I may *ought* to feel guilt or loss or regret, but they find no purchase in my heart.

And amid all that, perhaps because of that, one terrifying question surfaces in my mind: if this is how I feel about my second kill . . . how will I feel about the third, or the tenth, or the hundredth? Will there come a time when I feel no remorse over the taking of even an innocent life? Is such a mindset inevitable, when one commits to a path that is by necessity paved in bone and soaked in blood?

And if or when that day comes . . . would it not be a relief, to be free of confusion and turmoil? From the most cynical point of view, morality is merely an obstacle to be circumvented, for what need has a god to care for the morals of mortal minds? From a more idealistic perspective, I should be doing everything I can to cling to my humanity and sense of ethics, lest I become no better than the Demiurge I seek to one day overthrow.

My mind whirls with questions and scenarios, abuzz with consideration and doubt. What kind of monster do I want to become, and where will I draw the line? My conversation with Cheshire echoes through my thoughts, and I finally turn to face the creature that has become so important to my survival and development here in the Labyrinth.

Cheshire has been watching me as I stared down at the corpse, smiling and human again, though I see a few bite marks here and there from her scrap with the goblin dog. When I finally look up at her she asks, "Anything you'd like to share? You seem to be deep in thought."

I shake my head. "No, there's not much to say. I mean, I could talk philosophy for hours, but it's all just scattered impressions, nothing concrete. The facts of the situation are obvious: he was a threat, and we neutralized that threat. There will be more like him, in this maze and beyond. I can't afford regret."

"Mm." I can tell she's not entirely satisfied with that answer, but she doesn't press. "Then let's loot the body and keep moving. Oh, and sorry I couldn't nab the dog's anchor. That would have been useful to have."

I wave a hand dismissively. "It was an efficient disposal technique. No need to apologize. Also, on the subject of anchors and manifestations: how do we fix all that?" I ask, gesturing vaguely at Cheshire's wounds.

"Oh, that's easy. When it's just minor damage, you can refresh my form by canceling the manifestation and casting it again."

"Convenient." I resummon Cheshire and then see about looting the dead guy.

He's got what I take to be the standard reaver kit: a crossbow, a sidearm (a sword, in this case), and a belt lined with pouches and a quiver. I rifle through the pouches and find some beef jerky and a vial of green liquid. Cheshire identifies the latter as a healing potion, which in this setting's context means a potion that will slow my wounds from getting worse but not actually heal me. I send it to my throne world anyway, along with the jerky and the sword.

For the crossbow, I have other plans. I want to experiment with my Gift more. I didn't see the reaver cast any spells, but I cast [Exsanguinate] twice, and I'm hungry to turn that into an artifact. I grab the crossbow, focus on a mental picture of crimson energy flowing into it, and will it to do something cool and lifesteal-y.

"[Scarlet Repeater]!"

The magic sinks in and the crossbow crackles with red electricity. I grin and load the crossbow with a bolt, which takes me like a minute because I've never used a crossbow before and I'm kind of nervous. The electricity builds, getting redder and faster and strangely hot.

I aim at the corpse, pull the trigger, and somehow manage to miss, which is vaguely humiliating. Nothing happens to the ground or the bolt, though, and the electricity continues to build on the weapon. It, uh, it seems be getting quite hot, actually. Like, about to burn my fingers. I hiss at the crossbow and will the artifact to turn off, but it just keeps getting hotter, the electricity crackling more and more, and now I'm the slightest bit panicking.

Cheshire looks at the crossbow with concern. "What's going on? Are you doing that?"

"Nope!" I toss the crossbow away from me back the direction we came and try to cool my singed fingers. The crossbow hits the wooden block, wobbles a few times, and then it explodes into tiny pieces. A few bits of shrapnel graze me but do no real damage.

I blink a few times at the scorch mark left behind and the scattered fragments of crossbow. A few more sparks of crackling red electricity arc between pieces, but then they die down and the shards lie still.

"What the fuck was that!?" I protest. "How the hell does that happen? Why!?" I glare at the ruins of my crossbow artifact.

Cheshire takes a few cautious steps toward the pieces and strokes her chin. "Interesting. I think I have an idea of what went wrong, but I'll need you to run a test. Can you try to make another artifact?"

I give the catgirl a suspicious look but do as she asked, popping the reaver's sword into my hand and holding it out. I create the mental picture of bugs flying into the sword and name it, "Carrion Blade!" Nothing happens, and I send the sword back to my throne world. "Huh. Ah, now I think I have the same idea as you. Area's out of resonances, which means—"

"—they all got sucked into the first artifact," Cheshire finishes. "And I'm betting those contradictory resonances had some kind of mutually annihilating effect on the artifact."

I grimace. "Well, that's unpleasant news. That makes the aftermath of basically any fight worthless, artifact-wise. There's got to be a way to discriminate between resonances. Bah."

Hmm. I wonder if I could learn to see resonances the same way I can see souls. I flicker on soul-sight and glance at the fragments of the crossbow, but it's just scribbles. *Something to think about after our next fight, then.*

"Alright, time to get moving." I summon the compass and follow its lead.

We follow a winding path through the toy chest, sometimes having to clamber or jump where the connection between wooden blocks is uneven. I am lucky for Cheshire's presence, as she is far more physically adept than I am and she helps me with both moral and practical support.

At one point, I catch sight of more Celebrants, but they're feuding with each other atop a pile that has no clear path to the one I'm on. Since I doubt I'll get a better opportunity to observe them safely, I flicker soul-sight and take a look.

Two details immediately stand out: most of the Celebrants are figments, and all of them have their souls streaked with the same white-hot ecstasy I saw in Averrich.

The figment-Celebrants are red meat, jutting glass, and flowing fabric, but their meat is leaner and the glass is cracked and the fabric is torn and tattered. Veins in meat and cracks in glass burn bright white, and blank-faced masks have had smiles drawn on in blood. When I follow the strings wrapped around their limbs, I see not the black glass tower but only an endless horizon of burning white. The white is featureless and uniform but it pulses and moves, and it burns with joy and need and exultant hunger. I can feel it reaching for me, grasping at me. A hand. An infection. An ocean.

I look away from the figments. The toy chest around us is black charcoal and white ink, sketchy and indistinct, but there's something unnerving about the background. The longer I look, the more I get phantom images at the corner of my vision, tricks of perception that make it seem like the whole world is smiles and laughter and watching eyes. It's the same presence as the burning ocean, just another form.

I focus on the one Celebrant that doesn't match the others: a human, not a figment. There are no strings here, and when I peer deeper I see the remnants of a vibrant inner world: flowery meadows and quiet candlelight, reverence for the divine and the satisfaction of toil, all suffocated by joyous thorns.

They're all infected by the same plague of mania, the twin to what I saw and felt in the Mourner's maze. And somehow, disturbingly, Averrich carries that plague without fully succumbing to it.

I turn off soul-sight and turn to Cheshire to hear her take on the matter, but she's in danger mode again: body stiff, face drawn.

"*Mahiri*," she warns, and then she shifts into a hawk and takes off.

I follow the arc of Cheshire's flight and catch sight of the reaver a number of blocks away. Mahiri has her crossbow at her side, goggles strapped over her eyes, expression smug. I conjure up a flock of crows to harass her while Cheshire closes the distance, but their pecks don't seem to even scratch Mahiri's goggles, and the reaver seems entirely unbothered by their presence.

My changeling-geist flies above Mahiri and transforms from hawk to bear, mimicking the owlbear's trick, but the reaver moves in a blur and dodges out of the way. In the same motion, Mahiri draws her blade—the fancy sword with the animal-carving hilt—and slashes at Cheshire. Her sword cuts through bear-flesh like it isn't there at all, and wherever the blade passes I see Cheshire's form distort and start to melt into wisps of shadow.

Cheshire wastes no time in retaliating. She makes use of her quick-change trick to dodge Mahiri's second swipe in bird form before switching to wolf form for a rapid lunge at the reaver's leg. Mahiri is a moment too slow and Cheshire's powerful jaws close around tender flesh, but when Cheshire flits away as a bird to dodge the next attack I don't see any blood. The cloth is torn and I can see skin, but instead of blood and muscle all I see marring her leg is something strangely shiny.

Why is there no blood? I can't use [Exsanguinate] if there's no blood! My crows are doing nothing, so I command them, "Go for the sword!"

The summoned birds abandon Mahiri's impenetrable goggles and dive for her sword arm, but with a single sweep she cuts through all of them and they melt away like smoke in a gust of wind. Cheshire takes advantage of the distraction to claw at Mahiri in bear form, but again no blood is drawn. Mahiri counterattacks before Cheshire can get away, striking in a blur of motion and cutting right through the whole of Cheshire's form.

The animal melts away, and the charm bracelet falls—seemingly whole—at Mahiri's feet. The reaver picks up the bracelet, pockets it, and laughs. At my side, Cheshire reforms, and I quietly begin to panic.

What do I do!? What do I do!? She countered all my moves! That's cheating! "How did she do that?" I ask Cheshire, trying to keep the panic from slipping into my voice.

Mahiri, now moving leisurely and unblurred, takes a seat at the edge of a wooden block. She sheathes her blade, picks up her crossbow, loads it, and sets it in her lap. Then she calls over to me, "What, was that really the best you have? No new tricks?"

Cheshire grimaces and turns to me. "The goggles look alchemically made, expensive components but nothing rare. The wound-sealing, that's [Gold-Leaf Scales], it's a Glory spell. And the sword—"

"—Is an artifact," Mahiri interrupts. "Top of its class."

Cheshire's grimace deepens. "The second variety of fae artifact: an investiture of stockpiled power by an elf. This one seems to disrupt phantasms and homunculi."

"Did you think I wouldn't adapt?" Mahiri jeers at me. "I'm a reaver, demon girl. We hunt monsters much, much bigger and badder than you could ever hope to be. And every reaver knows that the key to a successful hunt is *preparation*. If you're hunting a bear, come armed for bear."

Cheshire crosses her arms at the reaver and asks, "And how much did it cost you, for that bit of preparation? How many debts do you owe Averrich for that sword? Imlashi, for the invocation?"

Mahiri shrugs. "It was worth it for the look on her face."

I bristle. "Why? Why do you care so much? Is this about your eye? About Murtagh?" I'm half-curious, half-stalling. How do I beat someone who's prepared for all my moves?

Thunk. A crossbow bolt sinks into the wood just in front of my feet, and Mahiri lazily reloads. The implication is clear: warning shot. "Oh, believe me," she says, "you'll pay for both of those. But, no, that's not really what's driving me."

The fear is rising in me, the panic and terror and dread that *I am about to die.* "Then what do you want?" I ask, voice too shaky, too rough. I don't know what to do, and I am about to die.

Mahiri sighs happily. "That. I want that fear coming off you in waves. It's about showing you your place, you stupid bitch. You waltz into our territory, you steal our prey, and you act like you're the big shot predator here. But you're not a predator, you're just a two-bit scavenger playing at being strong."

What do we do? What do we do? We can't make her bleed, she'll just banish any swarms, and there's no way I can recite the manifestation phrase before I take a bolt to the throat. I've got nothing that can touch her.

"You don't deserve to make me feel afraid. You don't *get* to make me feel vulnerable. You're the prey, and I'm the hunter, and I'm gonna make damn sure you understand that for the rest of your short, miserable little life."

She still has human limits, right? If I summon enough targets, maybe I can overwhelm her. But I can't give her lead time, so I have to distract her and prime multiple castings at once. Can I do that? I have to try.

"Okay," I say to her, holding my hands up in a surrendering gesture. [Carrion Swarm], [Carrion Swarm], [Carrion Swarm]. "You got me. I feel small. I feel powerless. I feel like prey." I *can* prime multiple spells at once, it would seem, but the strain on my mind increases dramatically with each new casting. I'm already approaching serious migraine level. "You're the big bad wolf, and I'm just the scared little girl who woke you up on the wrong side of bed. Point proven. So how about—"

A crossbow bolt lances my left hand and I scream in pain. Porcelain cracks and blood splatters, and the bolt pierces through to the other side but doesn't quite pass all the way out, stuck lodged in my hand. I clutch at my fresh injury and glare murder at the reaver. My primed spells vanished with the shock of the hit, and I try to call them up again but with the agony hitting me in waves I can't manage more than two before the strain becomes overwhelming.

"You wretched fucking animal," I snarl. "Can't spare even a moment to hear me out?"

Mahiri calmly reloads her crossbow and asks, "Sorry, do you think I'm stupid? Do you think I'm going to underestimate you just because I have the upper hand? I watched you snivel like a pathetic worm right before you killed my friend. You may really be a worm, but you're just as much a killer."

Fuck. Fuck! There's nothing I can do. I have no outs. This is a hopeless fight.

So I turn and run. I sprint away from Mahiri, back the way I came, and of course I immediately take a bolt in the side for my troubles. Another cry of pain claws its way out of my throat, but I keep running. I can hear her laughing at me, toying with me, relishing in my helplessness, but there's nothing else I can do. I have to get away. I have to keep running.

Cheshire glides beside me, expression urgent. "I think I know a way we can beat her. It'll work, I know it will, but you might not like it. Do you trust me?"

"No!" I hiss. Another crossbow bolt strikes me, piercing my left shoulder and deadening that arm. I clutch at it, stumble, hiss again. "But I obviously don't have a choice, so just spit it out."

"There's a way around her sword's enchantment. If—"

Echoing, manic laughter interrupts her. It is the innocent giggling of a delighted child, the raucous cheers of a frenzied crowd, and the uncontrollable howling of sanity's fraying edge. It is euphoria itself distilled into a many-layered sound, and I know exactly what that means: the Reveler is near.

Cheshire breaks off into swearing and I hear Mahiri swear behind me, but then both of them are drowned out by the laughter getting louder, louder, louder—

—and the Reveler rises from the wooden block in front of me. A hundred grasping hands from a hundred too-long arms spill out of a porcelain mask that resembles the mask of comedy from Greek theater. Its smiling eyes bleed red, and more blood is splattered across its many twitching fingers.

I skid to a halt and try to course-correct, try to turn back and run the other way, any other way, but another crossbow bolt slams into my ankle. I stumble and fall and hit the ground, my head, everything stars and darkness and grasping hands, and then I feel a great and terrible shudder and the whole block I'm on *unfreezes* from its fixed point in space.

The block tumbles and I tumble with it, sliding from it, falling into the darkness below.

I fall through darkness, fear and exhaustion choking me, environments and backgrounds changing at a pace too rapid to keep track of, and then I hit water. I hit the surface and break through, still falling, sinking now, the water cold as ice a shock to all my senses.

I gasp for air like a fool and water rushes in, filling my lungs, and I close my mouth but I can already feel myself beginning to drown. Blood diffuses from three wounds, and bubbles escape my lips. My chest pounds. My lungs ache.

"Alice!"

I am drowning. I am drowning. I am drowning. I kick and struggle, but I keep sinking, down, down, deeper, drowning. My limbs weaken, my vision blurs. Everything is so cold.

"Alice! Alice, you need to stop holding your breath."

Cheshire is hovering over me, floating in the water. Cheating bastard. I almost laugh, but I stop myself. I'm running out of air. I'm drowning. What's she saying? Why would I do that?

"Alice, listen to me: your body isn't real! Your lungs, your blood, all of it, they're all just constructs! *You don't need to keep breathing.*"

The water is dark, and cold, and there's no escaping it. No swimming for air. Nothing to do but let go. I open my mouth and breathe it in . . .

. . . and I don't drown. Water fills my lungs completely, but my vision stops blurring and my chest stops hurting. I drift, and I taste the ocean, and I do not drown.

I laugh, the sound warped by water but somehow still traveling. My panic leaves me in fits of erratic cackling, and I double over, fetal position. I nearly drowned. I nearly died so many times in just a few moments, but I'm alive.

I look around, and the dark depths of an infinite ocean remind me that I still have reason to be afraid. I shiver, from both the terrifying sight before me and from the ever-present cold. There's nothing out there, just darkness and water and murk. But it still terrifies me.

I can feel the water surrounding me. I can feel the cold, wet dark. I can feel the pressure pushing on me, another reminder that I should not be here. Where am I? Is this really part of the same dream bubble?

I look to Cheshire for answers, and she seems relieved, but then a new expression crosses her face: absolute terror. She screams and reaches out for me, and then I feel something wrap itself around me and pull.

I glance down and see a tendril of skinless, bloody, pulsating flesh wrapped around my torso. It's a tentacle of raw meat, but meat in the sense of ground beef or sausage outside a casing; there's no sense of anatomy, no muscle or structure, just a hyper-flexible limb of pure gore.

It pulls me down into the deepest depths of the vast ocean. I pull at it, punch at it, scrape at it, but the most I get is blood beneath my nails. It drags me down and the pressure gets stronger, the force of the water pushing against me, pushing in on me.

I hear a crack, and then another, and I see cracks in the porcelain spider-webbing across every visible bit of my skin. I scream and the tendril drags me deeper and I watch in horror as my chest caves in and then one-by-one each of my limbs shatters into pieces, and those pieces shatter too, my whole body crumbling to bone and porcelain, the water filling with blood and glass, everything shattering, splintering, fracturing—

—and I'm shielding my eyes from the glare of a burning sun, washed ashore on a sandy beach. The sand beneath my hands—my hands, whole and unbroken, unshattered, unmarred—perfect grains of white and black. The red tide, gentle, washes in and out.

My body is whole. I can breathe air. The crossbow wounds are gone. I am alive.

Am I? I stare at my shaking hands. The sun is warm against my body and the sand. My annihilation plays in mind on repeat. I shattered. I broke. I died. Was that death? Is this death?

I vomit blood and seawater onto the white-and-black sand.

"Oh my. Well now you could *definitely* use a drink."

A voice. A new voice. A strange voice. Many voices, or maybe no voice, just sound and meaning. I push off the sand and stumble to my feet, and I look around.

The beach stretches forever, and the red ocean beyond, both broken by only one landmark: a massive beached whale, the size of a skyscraper on its side, ripped open and ribs exposed. Built between the ribs is a ramshackle bamboo bar, and standing behind the counter is a roughly human-shaped mass of roiling skin and glass.

It has no facial features, or maybe it has many faces, all familiar and all a stranger. It has no limbs, or maybe it has many, the exact number changing with every shift of my attention. Shards of glass jut from it oddly, or it is the glass, and the skin flows from it; a glass face, glass hands, a glass heart beneath translucent skin.

It laughs, sounding just like the Reveler's laugh but somehow twice as intense, and my skin crawls and shivers and I feel an awful euphoric energy seize my heart and then pass just as quick. "Come, come!" it cries. "I've prepared your favorite drink!"

I keep staring at the abomination. I feel like my brain is full of static. But . . . I don't see anything else to do, so I slowly pad over to the bar and take a seat on a bamboo stool. I blink, and it's holding out one of those coconut cups from tiki bars on television. Something sloshes within, and there's a crazy straw sticking out.

"Take it!" the creature insists. "You'll love it, I just know it."

Hesitantly, I reach out and grasp the cup. The abomination's limb holding the cup flickers, and for a moment a bit of glass touches my skin, and then the whole creature starts to shift and change. I set the cup down and watch in dull fascination as it begins to take a more human shape and more human features.

My shape, and my features. My porcelain skin, my dark red lips, my raven hair done up in a bun. My red eyes, pointed ears, and fangs. It's my face, down to every detail. The body is mine, the exact same shape and size. The only difference is that she's wearing a crisp three-piece suit instead of my weird vampire magician ensemble.

My doppelganger rolls her shoulders, cracks her knuckles, and grins. "Much better. Oh, I quite like this form. You have a lovely body." She holds a hand—my hand—in front of her face and marvels at it. "Now, go on. Please, take a sip. Tell me you like it! Oh, I do hope you like it. Please, you simply must like it." Her last words gain an almost despairing tone, echoing with a hundred kinds of melancholy, and her expression falls.

"I . . . uh . . ." I slowly raise the cup to my lips, hand still shaking, and take a sip. "It, um, it's nice," I answer honestly. "Fruity."

Immediately her expression switches back to unbridled joy and she claps her hands excitedly. "Oh, wonderful, simply wonderful! I'm so glad I made it right. I've been so nervous about this moment, you have no idea. I'm so happy to finally meet you in person."

"What the fuck," I breathe, because at this point I really have no idea what else to say. I stare at my doppelganger, utterly dumbfounded.

She laughs and makes a little half-bow. "Oh, my apologies. I completely skipped over introductions. I know your names, of course, even the ones you've forgotten. And I . . . well, it would not be inaccurate to call me 'Katoptris,' as in my heart I am a piece of she, but I think that would cause quite a bit of confusion with the more *important* Katoptris. So, please, you may address me by my title: I am the Beast of Lamentation and Euphoria."

V

"You don't look happy to see me," the Beast pouts. "And after I went to all that trouble to save you from the hunter."

I blink a few times, still incredibly disoriented. "You what? You did what?"

The Beast grins and gives me a conspiratorial wink. "Just a finger on the scales, really, but more than enough. I gave the Reveler a nudge to come and find you, and then I plucked the ground from beneath your feet before it could catch you! With luck, it'll even take care of the hunter." The Beast pauses and tilts its—her?—head, staring vacantly past me, before continuing, "Oh, but that one's a survivor. Very well done, little hunter."

I can barely register whatever it is the Beast is saying about Mahiri, because I'm too hung up on the first half of that speech. "You . . . you can do that. You did that. You threw me into the ocean. You drowned me." Vivid, horrible memories flood my mind, flashes of suffocating darkness and deep, deep pressure. "The tendril. Was that you, too? Did you—" I break off, shivering, remembering the weight of a vast and terrible horror wrapping itself around me. "What did you do to me?"

The Beast laughs. "Oh, that? I killed you."

"Oh," I say softly. *Oh? Is that all you have to say?* I don't understand.

It pats me on the shoulder and I flinch away. It laughs again. "Don't worry, you're alive now. You were only dead for a few minutes at most. Just long enough for you to feel it when you woke up."

"Why?" I croak. "Why would you do that? Why did you kill me? What's wrong with you?"

The Beast raises an eyebrow. "What's wrong with me? Oh, oh that is *delightful*. But, to your more reasonable question: I killed you to offer perspective. It's something I think you are in dire need of, in this terrible maze. You have made so many decisions without truly understanding what drives you and what the consequences of your actions might be."

I start to laugh. "Perspective? *Perspective!?* Hahaha. You've gotta be fucking kidding me. You're mad. You're absolutely mad."

The Beast just smiles. "We're all mad here."

"No, fuck you. Fuck that. Fuck all of this." I knock the cup off the table and hiss at my doppelganger. "You crushed me to death at the bottom of the ocean! You can't just toss around some cryptic bullshit and drop a literary reference as if that's any kind of explanation. I want actual answers, now!"

The Beast watches me, unfazed by my outburst. "You have a choice to make, girl of many names. And unlike your cat-eared harlot, I believe in the principle of *informed consent*. You must understand the choice before you can make it."

"What choice?" I demand.

My doppelganger removes a shard of glass from its suit and places the shard on the bar. "Tomorrow, everyone in this city is going to start killing each other over who gets to lay their hands on this shard of glass, this piece of Katoptris' mirror shattered so long ago by the Emissary. All those who dwell within my city—Myriad, Carnival, Voidhearts, and Guild—will sacrifice everything they have to walk through the gates of my amphitheater and claim this prize." She pushes the shard toward me. "Unless *you* claim it first."

I stare at her, uncomprehending.

"Take the shard and become a pretender to the Lady's throne. They call themselves Nobility, because they are not quite Royalty and never will be. They are the squatting lords of the Labyrinth, ruling over its scattered cities and feuding over land rights in paradise."

"You just murdered me and resurrected me and now you're expositing about the hierarchy of this stupid fucking hell dimension?"

The Beast sighs and leans against one of the whale ribs. "It's only hell because you make it hell. We gave you, all of you, a world where you could be happy. A world where all your needs would be taken care of. We raised you a garden, and you keep choosing to set it on fire."

I bare my teeth and lean forward, hands pushing against the bar. "You didn't make a garden, you made a slaughterhouse. You filled a pen with sheep and invited the wolves. What about this outcome is surprising? It's human nature to kill and lie and ruin."

The Beast cocks her head. "Is that really human nature, or just your nature projected onto the whole?"

I flinch and rear back. "That's not . . . I'm not a killer. I'm a liar, definitely, but I'm not a killer. Every act of violence I've committed has been for a higher purpose. My actions have been self-defense. I just want to survive. I just want to be safe."

The Beast smiles. "Liar. You *enjoy* the act of killing; you just can't admit it to yourself. You want to take lives, because it makes you feel powerful. When you butchered the woman in white, you wanted to make her scream. You laughed when you killed Shane Murtagh. You felt pride in your victory over the hunter whose name you never learned."

I clench my teeth. "You're ignoring context. My laughter was a response to the chemical rush of a spell. My pride was about survival."

"And the first?"

"That one only looked like a person. It was just another beast of the Labyrinth."

There's a tap on my shoulder and I whirl, panicked, to stare into Lena's big soft eyes. "Like me?" she asks. Blood drips down her neck from two familiar marks.

"What are you—" I blink and she's gone, like she was never there. My hands won't stop shaking. "Stop it. Stop."

"Perhaps a more familiar environment would make this easier for you. Let's reset." The Beast snaps her fingers and the beach vanishes, the bar and the whale with it, and for a brief moment we are suspended in darkness before the world reforms around us.

It's another tea party. A fancy tablecloth, painted white chairs, an expensive-looking tea set. And all around us, stretching to the horizon in every direction, is a series of alternating black-and-white squares like the world's largest chess-board. The Beast sits across from me, sipping her tea, still wearing my face and dressed in a three-piece suit. Lena stands at her side, now unbloodied, smiling placidly.

"Much better. Now, allow me to begin again: I have brought you here, Maven Alice, to offer you a choice. If all you truly desire is to be safe and feel loved, then you simply have to take up the shard of Katoptris' mirror and you shall have both safety and companionship. The shard shall keep you from aging or falling ill, though that is something your demonhood already provides. You shall have the love and care of any figment you desire, though again that is something already within your reach." She gestures at Lena, who waves at me.

I frown at the monster. "Why are you undermining your own points?"

"Oh, I'm simply making a different point than you think. But, regardless, there is another thing the shard can offer that you do not already possess: power. Within the Labyrinth, only a handful can match the raw power of a shard-holder. You will not be Royalty, but you will be closer than most, and you will have a degree of control over the Labyrinth itself while within your sphere of influence. Take up the shard and it would become child's play to strike down Averrich and all his hunters."

"Okay. That's a bit more tempting, sure. So what's the catch? What am I giving up? What's the other option in this choice?" I give the Beast a hard look.

She smiles and takes another sip of tea. I haven't touched mine. "The other option is that you stay with Cheshire and attempt to become God."

I narrow my eyes. "You're framing that as mutually exclusive with the shard of glass. Why?"

"As a Noble, your power will be stagnant; glass cannot grow. You will become a fixed existence, far more powerful than you are now but far less powerful than your theoretical potential as a demon. And in becoming a Noble, you will give up your demonhood and turn your back on your geist. Those are the terms of my offer."

I suck in air. "You can't be serious. That's absurd. Do you know what I've sacrificed already to get this far?"

"You're reciting the sunk cost fallacy," she chides me. "What you have sacrificed is irrelevant; what you stand to gain or lose is all that matters. Take the shard and you lose Cheshire and your chance at ever becoming Royalty, but you gain immediate and guaranteed security, companionship, and power. Reject my offer and return to Cheshire, and you put your life at risk at the side of a creature that you do not and cannot trust. It would seem an easy choice. So why do you hesitate?"

"You just said I won't be able to reach Royalty—"

"Why do you *care?*" she interrupts me, suddenly vicious. "If your greatest drive is a fear of death, then why do you balk at the easy road to immortality? If you feel alone and unloved, then why would you not reach for those you know cannot betray you? If you take the shard, you will only ever rule a piece of the Labyrinth, but is that not enough? Is my paradise *lacking?* What is missing for you to be happy here?"

I look away from her, down at the cup of tea in front of me. I don't have an answer.

"You want control. That's the real root of it all. You cut yourself for control. You manipulate people for control. You're desperate for it. Back on Earth, you felt like you couldn't control anything; you couldn't control your emotions, you couldn't control your behavior, not who liked you, not your financial situation, not your success or popularity, none of it. And at the end of it all, you knew, no matter what you did to turn your life around, no matter what scraps of control you managed to scavenge, you would still never be in control of your own mortality."

I hug myself and mutter, "Cheshire already tried this, okay? I've already had my fear of death used as a cudgel to beat me with."

"It's not *about* death," the Beast insists. "It's about *pride*. When you were a teenager, when you realized that you were never going to invent a dozen miracle solutions to stave off your own inevitable demise, do you remember what you fantasized about next? You dreamt of *killing the world*. You sketched out plans of how you would become the president of the United States so that you could trigger a *nuclear fucking holocaust*. If you were going to die, then damn it, at least let the Earth die with you. You thought that maybe, just maybe, you could feel some satisfaction if you died knowing that you had taken out every other human being first—that of all humanity, you were the last human standing. What the fuck is wrong with you?"

"I was just a kid! I was just a stupid, sad, angry teenager, okay?" I cover my ears, hating all the words she's saying. *Just stop, just stop, just stop!*

"Did you ever stop being that kid? Can you honestly tell me you don't still harbor that desire to burn the whole world lest it outlive you? That you're not, deep down, still just a scared, hateful little girl? What difference is there, really, between you and Homura?"

Like a bucket of ice water, I'm shocked completely out of my stupor. "How do you know that? How do you know about her? Does . . . does Cheshire know about Homura?"

My doppelganger shrugs. "I know many things that Cheshire doesn't, and she knows many things that I don't. I highly doubt she's aware of the visions you've been seeing in your dreams. And I do know why you're having those visions, and what they mean. But if you want to know what I know that you don't . . . take the shard." The piece of glass appears on the table, taking the place of the teapot.

I curl my lip. "You want that so fucking badly, huh? Why? What do you get out of this?"

She smiles. "I'll tell you, if you take the shard."

"Ugh. Okay, different question: what happens to *you*, if I take the shard and become a Noble? You said I'll rule this city, but didn't you call it your city?"

"Correct. The mirror fragment is my animus, what you might call my animating principle. When you take my animus, my existence as the Beast of Lamentation and Euphoria will end. From one point of view, I will die. But in other ways, I will live forever by your side, through you and part of you."

I narrow my eyes. "You'll replace Cheshire. Trading a geist for a phantom reflection. Why the hell would I agree to that? Cheshire may secretly be plotting to backstab me, but at least she's trying to be appealing. You are *infuriating*."

The Beast laughs. "You have no idea how funny that is. Ah, that's delightful. But, please, let's get back on track. You want answers, and I can provide them. Answers about why I'm so interested in you. Answers about why you were brought to the Labyrinth in the first place. Answers about Homura, and Reska, and the world of your dreams. Answers to questions you've forgotten. I can answer all your questions, even the ones you don't know to ask. Take the shard, and I'll tell you everything you've forgotten. Take the shard, and I'll tell you all you want to know."

Everything I've forgotten? That sounds like more credence to my Alice in Wonderland *theory. Hypothesis. Whatever.*

"I can give you back the names you've forgotten. I can even break Eirdryd's hold over you." She leans in, expression full of sincerity that could so easily be faked. "I want to free you, Maven. Cheshire? She wants to make you into a hungry animal she can pull around on a leash."

"How can you say you want to free me when your shard would put me in a cage? Forever bound beneath Katoptris, beneath the Demiurge."

"You can't beat the Demiurge, Maven. I'm not sure you really understand how impossible that feat would be. She is the guiding will and living avatar of the Dreamweaver. You can't usurp Nyara without usurping Azathoth, and Azathoth is the entire universe—all universes, all realities, all of everything. The hard road only leads to suffering and despair. There will be no victory at the end of it. Please, choose the easy road instead. Stay with me. Take my shard. Rest."

"You're asking me to give up. To just abandon everything I've worked for."

"Let this be your story's end. It doesn't need to be a tale of all or nothing. Accept compromise and walk the easy road. Let yourself find happiness in comfort and safety, surrounded by people who love you. Or, you can take the hard road, and struggle and strive like one of those wretched Leviathans. Destroy yourself, again and again, in pursuit of an unattainable dream. The choice is yours."

I will have all the world, Huntsman, or I will have nothing at all. That's what I said to Eirdryd, right before making one of the most costly decisions of my time in the Labyrinth. I sacrificed my name and gave a faerie hold over my free will, all for the sake of a single magic spell. There's a temptation to call that decision foolish, idiotic, a monumental fuck-up.

But it *worked*. The compass bought me a path out of the forest, and it led me to my first ally in this world. Anyone who would have balked at that deal would have died in that forest, from starvation or spider-dogs or just a whim of the Huntsman. Being reckless saved my life. Hell, even before Eirdryd, my all-or-nothing approach is how I won my first fight. And my second, come to think of it.

I bet on Bashe when I broke the circle, and for all that our relationship went south, it *worked*. He turned out to be a better man than I had even hoped for, and his sense of obligation earned me spells, information, and crucial guidance.

If I hadn't taken so many risks in my conversations with Bashe, I think I would have been in a much worse position going into Sanctuary 7.

And when the Mourner caught me and infected me with despair, my recklessness saved my life yet again. My callous risk-taking has been downright adaptive in this environment. All my victories have come from being willing to go all-in on a crazy, reckless, dangerous plan.

And sure, maybe those victories will come with scars. But I'm already wearing a tapestry of them, inside and out. What's a few more to add to the collection?

"The hard road," I finally tell the Beast of Lamentation and Euphoria. "I'll take the hard road."

VI

The Beast sighs. "I was afraid of that. You do realize this may be your best opportunity to rid yourself of Cheshire, don't you? If you take my offer, you'll never have to worry about her betraying you. Isn't that peace of mind worth it on its own?"

"Hey. I may not trust Cheshire, but I don't trust you either; there's no 'peace of mind' in your deal. And you know, maybe you're right about me. Maybe the core of me isn't fear, or hunger; maybe it's pride. And I have too much pride to accept your gilded cage."

"Mm." She seems oddly pleased with that answer for someone I've just denied. "Remember that, then, when she leads you to water."

What does that mean? Is that literal or metaphorical? "Whatever. Let me leave."

The Beast gestures and I see an empty doorframe in the middle of the chessboard. "You were never my prisoner, Maven. But, please, before you go: I have a parting gift, to be offered in good faith. Will you hear me out?"

I raise an eyebrow. "Perhaps. If you'll swear by the Weaver that it really is good faith, whatever it is."

"Of course. I offer you a gift in good faith, and my words to follow contain no trap or will to harm. I offer you something that you have desired, in the manner that you have desired or more pleasing to your desires. This and these I swear by Azathoth, Dreamweaver, All-Mother, Origin. Weaver take me if I forswear."

I feel Azathoth's touch, the sign of her passing interest and acknowledgement of the Beast's vow. I breathe it in. "Okay. What's this about?"

My doppelganger points at the anatomical heart around my neck. "That locket: it's a clever idea, but it won't work. Constructing an artifact that precise and complex would take a level of proficiency you're nowhere near approaching.

At least, not in the kinds of conditions you'd be consuming your first soul. But I can help."

I blink a few times. "Wait, what? Why and how? And what do you mean, why won't it work?"

The Beast gives me a chiding look. "Do you remember what happened with your last artifact? How about the artifact two tries before that? You've made four artifacts so far, and only one did exactly what you wanted it to. I'm sure you can piece together why."

I frown, and now I'm actually interested. "It's the resonances," I guess. "The crossbow was too contradictory. The hive-rock had a coherent focus, but it wasn't the one I wanted. The seeker dagger worked because I was copying an exact effect. I don't have precise enough control to make the resonances do what I want, so I have to rely on finding or making the right resonances."

"And what resonances do you think you'll find, when you first cut at your soul and shape its growth?"

I consider the question carefully. "Hunger. Consumption. Change. The process of carving. Interaction with the soul. Which . . . admittedly, does not seem perfectly correspondent to the preservation and safekeeping of soul fragments."

"And *that's* assuming your artifact isn't being contaminated by whatever resonances are left over from the fight that earned you that soul. Face it: you don't have the capacity to create that locket, and you can't afford to restrain your hunger until you do have that capacity. You'll need every scrap of power you can get on the hard road."

I cross my arms and lean back in my chair. "So what's your solution, then?"

The Beast lifts the mirror-shard and I'm about to complain, but then it twists and cracks and reshapes itself into a flawless glass tuning fork. She withdraws a golden needle from her suit jacket and taps it to the tuning fork once, twice, three times, each tap producing a beautiful and harmonious series of notes. "The metaphysical space around us is now vibrating with resonances that perfectly match the spell effect you're seeking to achieve. Simply name the artifact and give it life."

I hesitate, because I'm skeptical that it could be that simple, but I can't exactly choose now to start doubting the veracity of Weaver-sworn oaths. I breathe deep, hold up the anatomical heart locket, and give it a name. "[My Heart]." The locket warms in my hand, and after a moment I begin to hear a very faint bump-bump, like the beating of a heart.

"You changed the name," the Beast says, head tilted quizzically.

"Future-proofing," I explain. "I came here with one name and traded it away, then set Malice behind to be Alice. I may have even been Homura, once upon a time. No reason to think I'll be an Alice forever."

The Beast chuckles. "What a clever animal you are."

I poke at the locket. "I can feel something, but how do I know it actually does what it's supposed to do? Short of, y'know, carving off a piece of my identity and seeing if it comes back."

"You could trust my oath," she says pointedly, "but barring that, I think you'd best start learning how to read artifacts like you read souls."

Interesting. That seems like a very worthwhile avenue of exploration.

"In any event, thank you for your time, and I sincerely hope you don't die again any time soon."

I open my mouth to deliver a snarky reply, but she's already gone, and everything but the door with her. I sigh, muster myself, and walk through.

I step through space and emerge into a yellow-walled room with a single wooden door, and immediately I'm being hugged by a catgirl.

"Oh, thank the Weaver you're okay," Cheshire cries, voice muffled from her mouth being shoved into my shoulder.

"Hey, uh, hi. Good to see you too. Uh, what did that look like from your perspective?"

Cheshire looks up at me, still clinging tightly, eyes full and slightly reddened. There's a tension to her, a full-body nervous energy that I can see in every motion. Another trick of manipulation, or was she actually scared I might not come back? "I . . . I saw you die, Alice. For a moment you *were* dead, and I was terrified. But then I felt you again, alive yet distant; separated from me by a power I couldn't contest. It was the Beast, wasn't it? What happened to you? What did it do to you?"

I gently extricate myself from Cheshire and look away from her, gathering my thoughts. Do I test her? Do I lie? I'm certainly not going to tell her everything, considering some of what the Beast and I talked about. But . . . I have to extend *some* measure of trust, or I'll miss out on an opportunity to gather information—and besides, the plan is still to guarantee Cheshire's loyalty, right? I look back at the catgirl, seeming so small and vulnerable. I hate it. I hate not knowing what she's really thinking, how much of this is an act.

We made our choice; we're with Cheshire for the hard road. Come hell or high water, it's us against the universe.

"The Beast wanted to talk. She took my form, then made me an offer. She offered me her 'animus.' She called it a shard of Katoptris' mirror." *And we really need to interrogate that further, at some point. If Reska became Katoptris, was she sealed in a mirror somehow? Our first vision saw Reska shatter a mirror, was that foreshadowing? Symbolically, thematically resonant?* "She said it would make me Nobility, a shard-holder, and that the factions of the city are going to start murdering each other to get that shard in just a day or two."

Cheshire stiffens, then bares her teeth. "They're going to call a Game of Glass. It's a custom in the Labyrinth, a way to determine which lucky soul gets to claim the shard of a Beast and ascend to join the ranks of the Nobility. The rules are different every time, but the Games are always violent, and they don't always have a winner."

I frown. "Why not? Do they end in a lot of mutual kills?"

She shakes her head. "It's not even that, though that has happened. The real problem is that whoever wins the Game of Glass still has to confront the presiding Beast before they can claim its shard; see, the Nobles don't actually control the shard or hand it out, they just control access to the Beast's lair. Claimants to the shard compete for the right to approach the Beast, and the Nobles guarantee that whoever challenges it is given a fair chance to join their ranks. It's . . . you could call it a privilege of Nobility: the Beasts allow the Nobles to call the Games and dictate the terms of selecting the next shard-holder, though it's still up to the final candidate to prove capable enough or worthy enough or however the shard is gained. But just giving it away before the Game's even been called . . . that doesn't happen." Cheshire looks even more nervous now. "What exactly did it say? What kind of offer did it make?"

Again I have to carefully consider how I'm going to phrase this. "She was . . . evasive about her motives. But she wanted me to become a Noble, and to leave the path I'm currently on. She seemed very interested in making sure I didn't become an archdemon, and she asked me to turn my back on you. That was the offer: become Nobility and forsake Royalty."

Cheshire scoffs. "What an absurd deal to present. Did it take you for a fool?"

"Perhaps. Regardless, I learned much from the encounter. I don't know *why* this Beast is so interested in me, but we may be able to leverage that. And now I think I know what Averrich was talking about, when he mentioned a 'big event' come tomorrow."

Cheshire's gaze sharpens. "Yes, I think you're right. Averrich must have a Noble backer, and he's been given advance notice of the Game of Glass. That makes it more important than ever that we win this little hunt."

I walk over to the room's single door and push it open. "Then let's walk and talk."

I step out into a hallway with plain white walls and doors as far as the eye can see. Cheshire follows me out and glances around critically. "This is a bit much," she says. "Summon the compass; we're not going to make much progress otherwise."

"Agreed." I call the burning wheel to my hand and follow it to a door with dandelions painted on it. I open the door into an identical hallway, down to every door. "Oh, okay, I hate this. This is some Hanna-Barbera bullshit."

I'm pretty sure this would have been impossible to navigate without the compass, but with the spell active I can just go through doors on autopilot and trust that eventually one of them will lead out of this horrible space-warping hallway. In the meantime, I have room to think, and to worry about what's going to happen tomorrow.

"Something's bugging me," I tell Cheshire. "If Averrich knows he's going to war tomorrow, and if he wants to become Nobility and rule the city, then why is he throwing lives away? Why take the risk that I might kill all his hunters and emerge stronger for it? He has to know I'm a rival—he definitely knows, because that concern is probably what he messaged 'Kasumi' about."

Cheshire walks alongside me, manifested through the toy sword she picked out during our shopping trip. "He could just be mad; we saw it in his soul, that ruinous joy. I can imagine that driving him to self-destructive ends."

I shake my head. "Madness is a cheap justification. I can believe the infection has some influence over him, but he wasn't acting on random whims in that throne room; that show was calculated, the beats premeditated, all driven toward some goal in mind. I don't believe it was idle madness to call this hunt."

"Mm. I think you're right. There's an interesting contradiction in this hunt he's called: reavers like the first one we fought are being thrown to the wolves, but one has been armed with a wealth of power. Why? What does he gain, from any of this? What are the possible outcomes to this hunt, and how do they benefit Averrich?"

I hold up a finger. "Outcome the first: a hunter kills me and takes a trophy from my corpse; Averrich eliminates a rival and adds a new artifact to his faction's trove. But what's stopping him from doing that himself, aside from it maybe being less interesting?"

"Power disparity," Cheshire answers quickly. "As you are now, a fight with Averrich would be horribly one-sided in his favor, and that's not what earns hunting trophies. It's part of what slows progression for scions of all stripes: as they get stronger, they face fewer and fewer real challenges, which means fewer opportunities for advancement. Killing you personally would remove a contestant from the Game of Glass, but it wouldn't meaningfully strengthen his position."

"Whereas his cronies are all hovering much closer to my power level, hmm. But then, why not stack the deck further in their favor? The Reveler doesn't seem to discriminate targets, and we utterly destroyed our first reaver opponent. If the goal is to get one of his minions to kill me, why not arm all of them to the degree he's armed Mahiri, or at least send only the strongest of his forces to do the deed?"

Cheshire taps her chin thoughtfully. "Think about who he sent into the maze: volunteers, one and all. What kind of person volunteers to go fight a demon inside the lair of an eldritch horror?"

I snort. "Someone with more ambition or arrogance than sense."

"Exactly!" Cheshire says with a clap. "The hunters who signed on—barring Mahiri—are hungry for power and overestimate their own abilities. In a Game of Glass, those hunters are liabilities, not assets. One of them might get the bright idea to try and seize the shard for themselves and end up jeopardizing a critical operation."

"This is a culling," I realize with horror. "Averrich is using me to get rid of the weak links in his organization. They're sacrifices. That's awful."

"It's worse than that. Think about how he presented the hunt: like it was a—"

"A gift," I interrupt, the implications unfolding before me. "His gracious offering to his followers. He talked about it like he was sharing the spoils. He's trying to reinforce his image as a generous leader who offers fair prospects for advancement."

"And if they all fail, that just reinforces the gulf between him and them. It reminds them how much they need Averrich and how they can't survive without him. And then, when you've glutted on his followers and proved their inferiority, he gets to swoop in and kill you to prove his superiority—and your triumph over his minions might be enough to earn him a hunting trophy out of the act. That's the second outcome to this hunt: you eliminate his liabilities, then he eliminates you, and he improves both his control over his faction and his personal power as a scion."

"Ugh, what a conniving bastard. I really hate dealing with fae. Clever plan, though, I'll give him that. The only real risk point is if one of those liabilities actually kills me and becomes a much bigger problem."

"And *that* is probably why he's given Mahiri so much support; she's his guarantee that outcome number one doesn't backfire on him. She's his champion pick, the only reaver in the running really allowed to beat you, because she's so tied down with debt that she'll have no choice but to behave herself if she does win the grand prize."

Well, that gives us a good segue. "Which brings us back to the question of the hour: how do we beat Mahiri? You had an idea for that, didn't you?"

"I did!" she exclaims cheerfully. "And there are parts of my idea that you'll like, and parts that you may not like, so let's start with the good stuff: have you ever wanted to be a werewolf?"

That stops me in my tracks in the middle of another identical hallway, hand outstretched to open a lilac-patterned door. "Sorry, what? Like, an actual werewolf? Are you going to make me a werewolf?"

"It doesn't have to be a wolf, but I know you like them and I thought that might get your attention. Put simply, our greatest obstacle to killing Mahiri lies in that sword of hers: the sword banishes summons, and you are primarily a summoner. But if we could get you an extra visceral edge, you could triumph. And anchoring a homunculus isn't the only way to manifest a geist."

My confusion and curiosity last for only a moment as I quickly put the pieces together. "You mean to manifest through me. You want to use my body as an anchor, or something like an anchor. You're talking about possession." My voice is soft, hollow, almost questioning. I stare at her, lips tight and eyes unblinking.

Cheshire notices my discomfort and rushes to reassure me. "Possession has a lot of negative connotations, I don't think it's a useful point of comparison. You'll still have full control of your body, and you'll have the power to end the merge at any time." I keep staring, and she barrels on. "Alice, you've seen what my shapeshifting can accomplish with a good anchor. Your form, though, it's something special. Give me any old body and I'd be able to fight Mahiri without getting banished, but your essence is more potent—more real—than any mortal anchor. You are a scion, an existence above the masses, and with my Gift in your hands you could do things I can't even begin to attempt. You could become an all-consuming demonic wolf and turn the tables on Mahiri. She made so much noise about being the predator to your prey, so flip the script and hunt her like she's hunting you. Chase her down, rip her limb from limb, and devour her soul. She framed herself as your rival, your nemesis, your antithesis, and that makes her a perfect target for your first throne duel. Become the god-eater wolf, hunt your prey, and take the next step on the path to your *ascension*. This is a golden opportunity, Alice."

I am silent, my mind buzzing with paranoid ideation. Is this the moment my dreams have been warning me about? Is this the fatal choice? If I manifest Cheshire through my body, if I let her possess me, will it give her power over me? Was this outcome her plan all along?

Lines of actions, plots and schemes, the flow from decision to decision. Our first deal, the need to feed, a fateful encounter, everything spiraling out. Did she lead me to the club to forge a conflict with Mahiri that would lead me to this moment? Are even my Truths a clever trap, driving me toward the predator/prey dichotomy and a life as a hungry wolf?

"What parts of it won't I like?" I ask when I find my voice.

"Well, you'll be sharing a body with me, and . . . I know you don't really like me. Not like I like you, at least."

The melancholy in her tone elicits a twinge of sympathy that I brutally suppress. This is manipulation. She doesn't really feel sad, or if she does, she's still playing it up to incite a particular response. "The werewolf blood. Were you plotting this, when you urged me to drink from the lycanthrope instead of the fae?" *Are you ever not plotting?*

"It was the option with the highest utility value," she says instead of answering plainly. "Averrich was too dangerous, most of the others would lack the same kick, and between the various retainers she had the highest synergy. Her blood was powerful on its own, but resonant if transformation became a necessary condition of success, which I believe it has." She's calm, confident, explaining the steps in her logic in a way that makes perfect sense.

Liar. Betrayer. Untrustworthy. Plotting, scheming, deceiving. "The Beast warned me about you, when she had me in her lair. She told me you were going to turn me into 'a hungry animal on a leash.' I didn't realize how distressingly literal she was being. If I had, I wonder how that would have changed the calculus of her offer."

Cheshire acts alarmed, concerned, cautious. "The Beast will say many things, if it can get you to listen. You shouldn't take it at its word, love, it's not—"

"Don't call me 'love!'" I scream. Fists clenched, breathing heavy, tension boiling over. "Don't call me that, don't call me that, don't call me that! I don't know you! You know me like nobody else knows me, but I don't know you. You say you know me, but you say you love me, and I don't believe you."

Frightened. Wounded. Pleading. *Lies, lies, all of it lies.* "Alice, I—"

"No!" I bark. "No, no, no. No more lies. You've been lying to me over and over, using me, manipulating me, taking advantage of me. You're guiding me toward some horrible sinister end and I don't know what it is and I don't understand why. I don't know what you want! I—" I break off, choking back . . . I don't know what. "There's always another layer, more secrets, something you're hiding, something you haven't told me yet. You told me she remade you, made you love me, and maybe that's a lie, or maybe that's true and the lie is that you want good things for me, or maybe the lie is that . . . is . . . I don't know. I just."

Sorrow on her face. The appearance of heartache and pain. "Please. Please, just give me a bit of trust and I'll repay it tenfold, I promise."

"I *want* to trust you," I admit, bleak and hollow and pained. "I wish that I could trust someone without qualifiers, without fear. I want to trust you. I want to believe that you really do see me for who I really am and love me regardless, and I want to see the real you and fall in love with what I find. I want to believe that there's something in me to love. I want to believe you'll hold my hand and walk with me through every blasphemy and risk, but how can I believe that when . . . when . . ." I trail off, words not coming. ". . . everything," I lamely finish.

I see the fear in Cheshire's eyes, and I see her open her mouth to say something, to plead or reassure, but then she hesitates, falters, and stops.

She slumps against the door opposite me and laughs bitterly. "Yeah. I mean, yeah, what can I really say to that? You're right: you don't have any good reason to trust me or believe me beyond brute, ugly necessity." She stews in that for a moment, eyes dark and downcast. "Y'know, I was gonna argue about that. Point out all I've done to help you. Try to build on emotional connections, the pathos of moments we've shared. But there's an easy counter for every example, and we both understand that sentiment can be faked. How can I expect the girl with literal trust issue trauma to take it on faith that I'm safe to trust?"

This... this isn't what I was expecting. My thoughts are torn and fractured, conflicted between surprise at this new side of Cheshire and suspicion that it's just another layer of her sick game. "Yeah," is all I say, unsure of what to say or how to react.

Cheshire laughs again, pained and broken. "I hate every part of this. Do you know what she wanted me to do, when she sent me to meet you for the first time? The Demiurge asked me to make my introduction, 'Make a contract with me, and become a magical girl!'" More broken laughter, and a clenched fist. "She stuck her filthy fingers in my brain and made me want nothing more than to be the perfect partner for a girl I'd never met, and then she asked me to poison the well in my first introduction to that girl. She wanted me to sabotage my chances of ever being trustworthy, and all for a fucking anime reference. She still got her way, I guess, with that bait-and-switch stunt."

Whiplash. I'm thrown back to that first meeting with Cheshire, a mere hour or so after my first vision of another life. I registered Cheshire as a Kyubey type on first sight, but I thought that was because Homura's name choice had primed me to think about *Madoka Magica* and look for parallel structures to the story of that show. And now, Cheshire tells me that the Demiurge *intended* for that connection to be made?

Did the Demiurge send me those dreams? Did she set me up to be suspicious of Cheshire, to distrust the woman I have no choice but to rely on? Is it all some sick game to her? It's like Nyarlathotep was winking at me, taunting me, saying, "Look what a bad decision this is, and still you jump at it. Pathetic."

I want to ask what else the Demiurge told Cheshire to do. I want to ask how much of my time in the Labyrinth so far has gone according to her design. "Do you hate me?" I ask instead, the question sounding dumb and petty and absurd as it leaves my lips.

Cheshire is silent for a long moment, still staring into the ground, but at least she looks up at me with soft, sad eyes and admits quietly, "Maybe a little. But not as much as I hate myself. And I love you a lot more than I love myself."

"I can relate to that," I say softly. "But... you already knew that."

"Yeah. I guess that's the real issue, isn't it? Hard to have a relationship this one-sided."

I hesitate, paranoid brain screaming that I'm about to make a mistake, but then I say, "How about . . . how about this: I don't know you, but I think I'd like to. Whatever you are, you *are* fascinating, and appealing, and you may really be my perfect other half. So why don't we start over? I'm . . . not really good at this stuff. A lot of things, really." I laugh awkwardly. "Gods, I don't actually know where I'm going with this. But, um . . . yeah. I want to be able to trust you. I want to go on more dates with you, too, because as messy as this whole situation has been I have really enjoyed your company at times. But I'm not ready to trust my body to you."

She smiles sadly. "That's . . . understandable. And thank you. I look forward to going on more dates with you, Maven. I do love you, even if that didn't come about organically. I love the way your mind is always so full and frantic. I love the way you dig into systems and try to unravel them like puzzles. I love your yearning for adventure and your reckless impulsivity. I love the way you cry when you think no one can hear you." Her smile turns wry as she finishes, "And I love the way you flaunt your ego but can't stand it when someone else starts complimenting you."

I ignore the blush on my face and cough awkwardly. "Ahem. Yes. Well. Let's keep moving, and, uh, maybe figure out an alternative to the Mahiri situation. We do still have a hunt to win, after all."

"Of course." She rises to her feet, and together we proceed farther into the maze.

VII

I mull over ways to deal with my current nemesis, Mahiri, as we continue through the endless series of hallways and doors. It's frustrating to face someone who can counter my abilities so perfectly, and I'm beginning to feel the painful outer bounds of my limited existing toolkit.

Part of my problem is that I only have three spells—plus the invocation from Bashe, but I don't think that'll really help me here—and I can't get more spells until I kill Mahiri. The other half of my problem is the actual content of those spells.

[Prey Upon] is a classic example of a "win more" spell, a term from card games back on Earth that I'm happy to apply here. It's a great way to refill my mana and in the long run it's making me stronger, but having to kill an opponent before you can see any benefit is as "win more" as it gets.

[Exsanguinate] only needs an enemy wounded, not dying, and with the recently added lifesteal it's an incalculably valuable spell, but that condition of use does still matter. I wouldn't really describe [Exsanguinate] as "win more" because it doesn't need me to have the advantage, just an opening, but it'll still never be the first spell I cast. I also doubt Mahiri will be the last enemy I fight that doesn't bleed; fantasy is full of creatures like ghosts and golems that don't have any blood to spill.

So that puts the onus of initiation on [Carrion Swarm] and on Cheshire. At its base level [Carrion Swarm] is only good for harassment and crowd control, not carrying damage. [Swarmheart] changes the math on that, thankfully, but even boosted bugs are still vulnerable to anti-summoner abilities, and just like with [Exsanguinate] I doubt Mahiri will be the last enemy to optimize in that direction.

I need to expand my toolkit and add more spells capable of raw damage output, preferably spells that work as initiators and are as unconditionally effective as possible. Of course, to add new spells I need to beat Mahiri first, so it's something of a vicious cycle. Cheshire offered me [Soulfire], back when I first got to pick my spells, and now I'm kicking myself for not taking it. There'd be no fuss about how to beat Mahiri if I could just burn her soul to ash.

I mentally flip through the inventory I have saved up in my throne world. If I try to bring a sword to a crossbow fight I think Mahiri might just laugh me to death. Cheshire's "caltrops" might buy me a few seconds, if that, but I have no faith in them making a difference. Toys, food, medical supplies—all things to make my life easier after I win, not things that can help me achieve that win. I could put the reaver's gambeson back on, but it might actually impede my "rip the bolt out and regenerate" tactic if the projectile gets caught (and it'll harm my magic, if I understand this system right). My throne world is full of random bullshit I've collected, but none of it's actually helpful.

... Hmm. Idea: my inventory isn't helpful, but the throne world itself might be. If the plan is to engage Mahiri in a scion's duel inside my throne world, and if I have the capacity to create figments within my throne world and command them, could I then use those figments in the place of my normal summons? "Cheshire," I ask aloud, "would Mahiri's sword banish figments? You said it disrupts phantasms and homunculi, are figments part of the same category of being or something distinct?"

"Distinct," Cheshire says with a thoughtful expression. "Figments are essentially made of the same 'stuff' as mortals, same goes for night horrors, and all three are fundamentally corporeal or 'real' in a way that phantasms and homunculi aren't. The sword wouldn't be able to disrupt a figment because there's nothing to disrupt."

I'm torn between revealing my genius plan and asking follow-up questions about night horrors, but all my plans are derailed when the scenery flickers and a man in reaver garb runs his blade through my gut.

My brain short-circuits and I try to make sense of scattered impressions—a looming figure framed by neon lights, splashes of contradicting color—as I'm overwhelmed by sensory data and pain, pain, horrible pain. For a hundred eternities I am frozen in that moment of excruciating agony arcing through my body like lightning from the freshly made hole in my chest, staring horror-struck into the dark eyes of the man with the arming sword lodged in my stomach.

He pulls the sword free, blood seeps from the open wound, and fear swallows me like Pinocchio in the mouth of the whale.

[Carrion Swarm], [Carrion Swarm], [Carrion Swarm]! I scream the spell in my mind, too panicked to form polysyllabic sounds. A flock of crows takes shape from churning shadow, and the summoned avians dive at the reaver, but

I don't see what happens next; the flight instinct sends me stumbling back past the threshold point, back into the eternal hallway, clutching at my wound and desperate to get away.

Run run run, we have to run, we need to run, run! I pick a door at random and barrel through, then another, not taking the time to close them because I just need *distance* between myself and the man who put a hole in my stomach that's still bleeding. The pain wracks my whole body but is strongest in my core, my nervous system screaming at me that I am wounded and I am weak and I am dying, I am dying, I need to fix this.

What do I do? What do I do? Enough rational thought breaks through the haze of panic that I think to grab the not-quite-healing potion from my throne world. I uncork the vial and down the green liquid, immediately feeling a wave of strange prickling over my body that concentrates around my gut wound. The pain eases but doesn't go away, and the bleeding slows but doesn't stop. *Fuck!*

The sound of metal parting flesh and feathers alerts me to the hunter's pursuit, and I whirl to see the reaver hot on my trail. He bears a few superficial scratches on his face but nothing significant, nothing deep enough to be worth exsanguinating, and there are already fewer crows than I summoned.

He holds his shield high, limiting targetable space for the avian attackers, and when they come at him his blade cuts through them in a blur of movement I recognize as that same bastard reaver trick they all seem to know. He's coming for me, undeterred by my first and only line of defense, and I don't know what to do. I'm paralyzed, watching death approach and not knowing how to stop it.

Then a tiger pounces on the reaver from behind, Cheshire come to save me once again. A spike of relief pierces the miasma of dread clouding my mind, and I force myself to move. *Create space, then ideate tactics.*

I pick more doors at random and run, hoping Cheshire will give me the chance I need to think of something actionable. I remember to close the doors behind me, this time, which with luck should slow down the hunter.

[Exsanguinate]?

Healing needed, but mana-effect ratio too inefficient with current enemy wounds. Cheshire may change math, can't guarantee. Need another hitter.

[Swarmheart]? Giant centipede, giant wasp?

Too squishy, can't contest in strength. Has to be something that can punch above its weight class. Something mean and quick and dangerous.

Cheshire reforms at my side, incorporeal once more, her latest homunculus body already slain by the reaver. "Sorry, weak anchor; couldn't do more than slow him down."

I nod and pop the bug-making chunk of amber into my hand. I step into another hallway, throw my back against the far wall, and cast, "[Carrion

Swarm], [Carrion Swarm]: praying mantises. [Swarmheart]: Sergeant Slicer!"

Mantises of all shapes and colors are conjured up by my spells and then melted into goo by my artifact. The resulting giant mantis, which I have named Sergeant Slicer, stands at the ready with vicious spiked forelegs pointed toward the door I last came out of.

There is a tense moment as I wait for the reaver to come bursting through the door, but the moment passes, and then another. Was my "blindly run away" tactic more effective than I thought? Shouldn't [Hunter's Mark] let him narrow in on my location? Maybe it's not as precise as [Find the Path].

I resummon Cheshire with the weird toy drone I found at the mall, since it seems I have enough breathing room to get through a full incantation. I consider digging through my inventory for the sketch of me, to try casting [Indulgent Vitality] before the potion wears off, but will it still work now that my appearance is different?

The question is made irrelevant by the arrival of Sword-and-Board, who kicks open one of the doors of the hallway with shield up and blade pointed forward.

"Kill!" I order my minions, and they move. Cheshire keeps pace with the stalking mantis, having shifted into wolf form, and they try to flank the reaver despite the narrow hallway.

Cheshire pounces from one side as the mantis strikes from the other, but the reaver raises his shield to block the mantis while simultaneously repositioning to drive the point of his sword through the skull of the oncoming wolf. Cheshire shifts into a hawk at the last second, but the reaver blurs again and carves the bird in half, causing Cheshire's manifestation to dissipate. The toy drone, now in two pieces, falls to the ground at his feet.

The mantis, meanwhile, has successfully gotten one of its spiked, grasping, almost pincer-like forelegs around and over the shield. As the reaver turns his attention to his remaining opponent, the mantis pierces his shield arm with its spines and pins the arm in place, locked within the vice grip of an ambush predator whose grip strength has presumably increased proportionally to its growth in mass.

The reaver grunts his pain and grits his teeth, pulling back his sword arm for another devastating stab, but now it's my turn. All the little cuts on his face from my flock of crows aren't much, but they're not nothing, and I catch sight of one more serious-looking wound on his leg—Cheshire's handiwork, from their first scrap. Taken together, that's more than enough for a right proper "[Exsanguinate]."

His leg buckles, his face bleeds, and his lunge is thrown off just enough for the mantis to land a strike of its own. The mantis pins the reaver's sword arm, spikes sinking in and grip holding it in place. For a moment the two are locked in a contest of strength, and I take that chance to dart behind the reaver, wrap my arms around him, and sink my fangs into his vulnerable neck.

His blood hits my throat, hot and savory, and I drink it down with eager, vicious glee. He struggles, still grappled by the mantis, and manages to take a few stumbling steps toward the nearest wall, shoving me against it. The impact makes me cough up blood, and my lungs ache from the sudden force, but *I don't need to breathe anymore*. I keep my hold on the reaver and bite down harder, tearing into his flesh and drinking liquid essence.

The pulse of life flows through me, his heartbeat pounding beneath my porcelain skin. I can't feel my own heartbeat, not after my modifications, but I can feel his and it tastes so vulnerable. Like a flickering candle-flame in the dark, so easy to blow out with just a puff of air.

The reaver struggles against me with all his might, but I feel a strength in my limbs that I have never felt in my life. I feel a fire deep within me, something dark and terrible and all-consuming, and it makes me feel alive.

His efforts weaken, his mortal flesh failing him as all flesh inevitably fails. He screams his rage and pain and fear, and it becomes just one more flavor to the banquet of sensation that I am devouring.

With a final effort of will he manages to free his arm just enough to stab the mantis and shake me off, but it's far too late for him. Another casting of [Exsanguinate] and he collapses, but instead of finishing him off with [Prey Upon] I climb on top of him and return to my feeding.

His life ebbs out within my grasp, and his faltering heartbeat is music to my ears. When at last the song stills, I am filled with a sense of joy and power that eclipses anything felt previously.

I keep drinking until I can't drink another drop, the tap run dry. I slide off of his body and lie on the ground next to him, sighing pleasantly, glutted.

I remember the words of the Beast, castigating me for my joy. I remember Bashekehi, telling me not to be a monster. I laugh at their vain, petty judgment. Fuck the both of them. I enjoyed that kill, and I won't feel guilty about it.

He was in my way, and he tasted delicious.

I bask in the afterglow of my first true feeding. The others feel so paltry now, so restrained. I freaked out over the difference in mana between Lena and Cameron, but both of those feedings now pale to the flood of mana that just poured into me.

My whole body feels warm and satisfied. There's a strange energy to me, like an oddly calm mania; I feel like I could sprint up a mountain or fistfight a god, but the energy is coiled without tension, patiently waiting to be called upon.

All that, from just a single life taken. How much power could I have at my fingertips if I did it again, and again, and again? Would I receive the same multiplier if I drank a figment to death?

You enjoy the act of killing; you just can't admit it to yourself. You want to take lives, because it makes you feel powerful. Well, Beast of the Labyrinth, I admit it. That felt good. And maybe, when the high of my victory fades, I'll start to feel doubt once again.

For now, I think I deserve a bit of joy.

"Someone had a good meal," comes Cheshire's voice from elsewhere in the hallway. I don't bother looking around for her, content to let my gaze wander across the ceiling.

"Better than any before it. Mm. When I asked Bashe if sleeping with him would kill me, he said his kind didn't kill 'with every sexual encounter.' I'm beginning to think that was something of a lie of omission. They might not have to, but I bet they get more out of the act if they do. I'd say the same for all imps, and everyone under Shadow. It's baked into the Throne, isn't it?"

Cheshire walks into view, smiling down at me. "Dara is, as ever, the exception to the rule."

"Yeah, that tracks." I sit up and glance at the body of the reaver, my eyes half-lidded. "Well, this was an interesting lesson. Hot-girl figment acting human: good amount of mana. Boy figment not acting human: less mana. Werewolf woman: more mana. Draining a man until he dies: insane amounts of mana. I think I got more from that than Lena and Cameron combined, though admittedly I'm going purely on vibes here."

"No, I think that's about right." Cheshire pokes at the reaver's corpse with her foot, though she can't actually affect it right now thanks to being unmanifested. "It's the difference between snacking on a bagel and sitting down for a full-course meal; both give energy, but one'll last you a lot longer. To kill by feeding is the natural culmination of conflict and consumption's intersection. In other words, it is the essence of Shadow."

"Makes sense." I crawl over to the dead body and inspect it more closely, rifling through pockets and searching for loot. I send his sword and shield to my throne world, and I find an empty potion bottle, but there's nothing else of note.

I push off the ground and clamber to my feet. There's a hole in my vest-and-blouse combo, which is annoying, but the wound underneath has completely healed. [Exsanguinate] continues to prove its worth, despite its glaring restriction.

"You know," I complain, "this world has been lousy for loot. Why aren't my enemies dropping weapon upgrades, or spell scrolls, or at least a few coins?"

Cheshire grins at me and answers, "Probably because you don't know how to use a weapon, spell scrolls aren't a thing here, and nobody in the Labyrinth uses money."

"Bah! Get out of here with your fancy 'logic' and 'reason.' I want my murderhobo D&D power fantasy, dammit." I stick my tongue out at her, then giggle. "Alright, let's keep moving."

I summon the compass and follow its lead back through the maze of doors. We make good time, and in short order we're back at the threshold and crossing into a new zone of the Reveler's domain.

The jump between areas is stark. The maze of doors was claustrophobic, but the enclosed spaces were a relief after the horrible heights of this place's first two areas. This newest region doesn't *appear* to have any dramatic pitfalls, but I can't say for certain because most of it is pitch-black.

The parts of the scenery that aren't black are glaring neon colors, glowing splashes of purple, green, red, blue, orange. Streaks of sharp light form twisting contoured paths across an endless black canvas. The texture of it all is like paint, and I'm reminded of the body paints that glow under blacklight.

"So tell me about your idea," Cheshire prompts as we start moving through the strange new space. "You asked if Mahiri could banish figments, which makes me think your plan to defeat her involves using figments in some way."

"Right, yeah. Okay, so: when we declare a scion's duel, it's going to be fought in my throne world, right? So what if I filled my throne world with figments and used them to fight her? If they can overwhelm her while I keep my distance, it shouldn't matter that I can't use [Exsanguinate] on her. And hey, do you know what the conditions of that stupid gold spell are, anyway? Like, if I hit her enough times, does she start bleeding again?"

"Hmm." Cheshire chews her lip and considers my long list of questions. "That may work, though I wouldn't put a guarantee on it. A big part of this fight is going to be Truths and Thrones: Mahiri has Summer at her back because she's established a narrative where she's the big scary predator putting a frightened prey animal in its place, and hiding behind walls of minions might just strengthen her position. There's a chance that any figments you throw at Mahiri will fold like tissue paper thanks to the weight behind her. You need some weight of your own to match her in a fight."

"Okay, how do I get that? What's the Throne of Shadow looking for?"

"A Leviathan," she says simply. "Your powers are at their strongest when tapping into consumption, conflict, will, and want. Mahiri has made a declaration of the way that she thinks the world works, and you need to respond to that. You need to make it into a true clash of beliefs, a battle where the loser is devoured and the winner grows and evolves, incorporating the greatest strengths of the fallen and cutting away your own weakness. Mahiri says you're just prey pretending to be a predator, a scavenger hiding behind cheap tricks. What is your response, and how does it tie into your personal Truths?"

I frown, and give the thought due contemplation. From the framing that Mahiri's set up and Cheshire's explained, I can actually see how my minion strategy would backfire: I'd be like a wounded animal hiding within the herd. If I could get into the fray and fight with my own two hands that would be different, or even just slinging spells, but she's countered everything I have too effectively.

I can imagine how that scene would play out: I hang back and unleash a horde of figments, but she cuts through them all and chases after me, merciless and unrelenting. I run for my life, desperately trying to put more bodies between me and my pursuer, but it's not enough. She catches me, she cripples me, she kills me.

"What about her gold spell?" I ask.

"[Gold-Leaf Scales] is an invocation she must have acquired from Imlashi, the imp of Glory. For any normal caster of the spell, it works like this: it stops wounds from bleeding by sealing them with gold, keeping the caster in the fight, but the gold doesn't act like flesh and disabling or lethal blows will still disable or kill. Running water washes away the gold, which allows for treatment of injuries but also makes the spell less useful when near any sizable body of water. As someone who is not a diabolist, Mahiri will be further limited by needing to carry precious metals on her person to leech from for wound sealing. Those metals don't have to be gold, but gold is most efficient. If you could find whatever chunks of shiny rock she's keeping in her pockets, and if you could then get it away from her, the spell would stop sealing fresh wounds."

Ah. Opportunity. "Okay, new plan: I'll use the figments, but as a distraction rather than a sincere offensive measure. While they're tarpitting Mahiri, you can use a smaller shapeshifted form to find whatever she's using as fuel for [Gold-Leaf Scales] and remove it. Then we're back in business with the [Carrion Swarm] into [Exsanguinate] train."

Cheshire taps her chin. "That might have a higher chance of working. Still, it leaves the question of Truths: what will your framing be, going into this fight? How will you respond to Mahiri's claims about who and what you are?"

"I don't know," I murmur. "Blood, Gluttony, and Fear, but what do they really mean? Should I wish to be a predator and inherit the Eternal Conflict, or should I wish to be a scavenger like Azathoth? When given the choice and the power is in my hands, what kind of monster do I want to become? All these questions are echoing around my head like so much noise, but I don't have answers."

"I think you have more of an idea than you're willing to admit." Cheshire bites her lip and looks away for a moment, then turns her attention back to me. "Listen, Alice: the Throne of Shadow is about *the self*. Not the world of natural laws, or the world of shared identity, but the world of individual identity. Beneath every mask you wear, beneath layers of irony and insincerity, beneath the lies you tell to others and to yourself, there's something there. Deep down, I think you know what you really are."

I grimace. "Let's just hope my plan works."

We fall silent for the next part of our trek, just following the burning compass, until the echoing layered laughter of the Reveler fills the air. I track the sound and see that horrid mass of grasping hands off in the distance, laughing and swimming through air. There's a scream, much more human than the cacophony of the Reveler, and then the monster dives down into the black canvas and vanishes once more.

I freeze up at the Reveler's first appearance, but my moment of panic turns to confusion as it leaves just as quickly as it came. Was the Beast directing it once more, or was this a more random act? What was it doing here?

Where the Reveler left, I see what must have been its quarry: a reaver, the woman with all the knives, doubled over and clutching her head in her hands. Her body is shaking, and strange noises are emanating from her, something somewhere half between crying out in pain and . . . laughing.

Shit, is this what it looks like when someone turns Celebrant? And me without a convenient ledge to shove her off.

The reaver shudders and suddenly screams out, "No, no, it's too much, it's too loud!" She draws a knife in one hand and stabs it into her arm once, twice, thrice. She stabs at her leg, into her stomach, carving at her own body wildly. And she laughs and cries all the while.

I stare, stunned and disturbed, until her motions slow and stop. For a long pause she just breathes and bleeds, at last silent, but then she freezes up, twitches, and turns to face me. She raises her head and smiles at me with an utterly vacant expression.

The reaver-Celebrant takes a step toward me and I immediately shout, "[Exsanguinate]!"

Blood pours from her many self-inflicted wounds and she collapses like a puppet whose strings have been cut, but then she starts crawling toward me and I cast the spell again, panicked. She shudders and gasps and stops crawling, instead just lying there on the ground, shivering and half-dead.

"That," Cheshire murmurs from my side, "is what happens if the Reveler catches you: your mind will be consumed by a joy so bright and hot that it drives out all rational thought. At first, new Celebrants try to cut it out, to break their bones, to burn it away or freeze it away, but the curse won't let them die or give them relief. Inevitably, some quicker than others, they turn their frenzy outward."

"Horrifying." I look on nervously at the still-twitching body of the fresh Celebrant. "Is it . . . is it safe to use [Prey Upon] here? If I take a bite of her soul, will I get that infection inside me?"

Cheshire shakes her head. "No, that spell is safe. It's using Abyssal magic as an enzyme to break down the complex structure of a soul into raw energy that can be more easily absorbed. That's why you can use it on souls that would be incompatible if consumed conventionally through a scion's duel, but that's also why you get less growth from it compared to such a duel."

"Interesting." I take a few nervous steps toward the shuddering form.

"Oh," Cheshire adds, "you should still avoid touching it with any part of your body. Poke it with a sword or something."

I walk over to the dying Celebrant, careful to keep a good distance so it can't suddenly lunge at me and grab my ankle. I summon the sword I appropriated from my last foe and gingerly poke at the reaver with the blade's tip. "[Prey Upon]," I incant.

Shadows crawl down the length of my blade and bite into the reaver-Celebrant, finishing her off and giving me another tasty meal. I drink in the flow of energy, and the gears in my head begin to turn.

That Abyssal magic that lets me digest souls . . . could that be weaponized? Cheshire offered me the spells [Soulfire] and [Prey Upon] as separate abilities, but what if I were to combine them? Could I create a spell that steals soulstuff at a distance and feeds it to me?

Hmm. Food for thought.

VIII

I keep thinking about my upcoming duel as Cheshire and I walk through the black-and-neon landscape, following the lead of the burning compass. I also remanifest Cheshire while I think, using a scavenged sword since I'm running out of suitable selections.

I have hope that my plan will work, and that I'll be able to kill Mahiri without having to fuse with Cheshire. But, if I fail . . . it's my very soul at risk. I don't entirely understand what that means in this world, but I can't imagine it being pleasant—and besides, it'll entail me dying first.

So I have to examine every possibility, even those that make me uncomfortable. Whatever Cheshire is planning, whatever hidden trap might lie within her offer of transformation, it can't be *worse* than dying at my enemy's hands. Maybe.

The uncertainty is driving me mad, but what can I do about it? I don't have any way to . . . well, that's not entirely true. I may have one way to end the uncertainty, but I've been avoiding thinking about it: an oath.

If Cheshire swore by the Weaver, and I felt the Weaver's presence verify her words, then that could very well prove her intentions. From everything I've seen of this setting so far, from many different sources, the Weaver's contracts are inviolate. So, unless I am to embrace radical doubt, I have to believe that a Weaver-bound oath *could* exonerate Cheshire of malevolence.

Or it could prove that malevolence, with my soul still shackled to hers—or however this demon-geist relationship works. And there's the rub: asking her to swear that oath would mean collapsing the quantum wave function and producing a single undeniable answer, and I am afraid of what that answer might be.

But with my life and soul on the line, and the duel fast approaching, I guess I don't have a choice anymore.

I clear my throat and ask, "Cheshire, would you be willing to swear by the Weaver that what you said about manifestation is true? That I'll keep control of my body, if we were to share a form?"

"Yes," she answers automatically, and for a moment my hopes soar, but then she grimaces and my heart plummets. "But I don't think it'll work. Nyarlathotep warned me before our first encounter that I wouldn't be able to take that 'easy out.'" Cheshire quickly adds, "I'll still try! Just, don't be surprised if something goes wrong."

That is extremely convenient for you, but also makes total sense from what little we know of the Demiurge. "Okay. Let's try, then. Swear your truthfulness."

We both stop walking. Cheshire takes a few steadying breaths, inches a few steps back, and lowers her head. "If you, Maven Alice, choose to manifest me, your geist, through the anchor of your body, then you will retain full control of your form and faculties. This and these—"

As Cheshire speaks, I feel the presence of Azathoth gather around us. I feel her infinite eyes watching me, loving me, dissecting me. I feel that alien, unknowable intelligence, something so far beyond me that I could never hope to understand it. I feel the pressure in the air and the prickling on my skin and the vanishing of everything that is not Cheshire, Azathoth, and me.

And then, as Cheshire begins to swear her truthfulness by the name of the Weaver, a horrible formless thing pours itself down my throat and slips inside my skin.

At once the presence of Azathoth vanishes, as if banished by this new entity, but the pressure only gets stronger. I feel black tar coating my brain, ink sluggish in my veins, black ichor dripping from porcelain seams. I try to scream but my lungs bloat with bile. I try to vomit, to run, to claw my skin open and dig out the sludge, but my muscles are paralyzed, stone-like, inert. I want to cry, and this I am allowed; black ichor drips down ashen cheeks.

And somehow, through that sixth sense of the divine, I can feel that my impotent struggles make this new presence *happy*.

Gone is the love of a mother's caress; now is the hand that plucks wings from a fly. Gone is the lens that would study the bug; now is the glass that burns ants under sun. Cruelty scours my veins as contempt calcifies my bones, and yet my face can't help but smile, lips and cheeks twisted by the invader's vicious glee.

All this happens in a frozen instant, the flow of time stilled on Cheshire's next word. I am imprisoned within my own body between the flutter of a hummingbird's wings, and when the second hand of the clock finally ticks forward, the name of my captor sears itself into my mind like a burning brand:

Nyarlathotep, the Lucid Demiurge, She Who Shapes Firmament From the Formless Sea; Crawling Chaos, Soul-Sculptor, Divine Architect, Star-Snuffer,

Night Mother, Fate-Spinner, Toymaker; Nyara Albaoth Zereth Gremory Lazotep, the God of Death.

    I lunge forward and wrap my hands around the changeling's throat, cutting off whatever she was about to say. I slam her down into the snow, the red from her wounds staining the pristine white, the cold seeping in. I pin her there, grip tightening, choking the life from her while my knee digs into the gash across her abdomen. She pulls at my hands in vain, too weak to separate even a finger from her throat. I squeeze harder and laugh.

    Her blue and yellow eyes are bloodshot and teary, gleaming with blind panic and mindless fear. Her mouth gapes, desperate for air, like a fish on dry land. I keep choking her, feeling her frantic pulse beneath my hands. What a wonderful feeling. Droplets of black ichor splatter against her face.

    Strength fills my arms and I squeeze the changeling's throat tighter, thumbs pressing into skin and *puncturing*, pushing through into vulnerable flesh. Her warm blood stains my fingers, such a comfort in the freezing cold. Not long now.

    Her struggles weaken. Her arms fall to her sides. Her eyes turn glassy. The changeling's body dies. And as she dies, I lower my head next to hers and whisper, "No spoilers. No shortcuts. Trust is a leap of faith."

    My strings are cut and I collapse. Control of my body returns in spurts and spasms, and I vomit black bile onto the neon ground. My hands, still only half-mine, clutch at a twisted piece of metal that must be whatever remains of the sword that I used to summon Cheshire.

    When I stop heaving and finally regain full control of my limbs, I toss aside the useless blade and stare down at my hands. The blood is gone, and the snow, like it was never there, but I can still feel her insides, her vocal chords and vertebrae. I touch my face, and my cheeks are still sticky with black ichor.

    Cheshire reforms in front of me, disheveled and rubbing her throat where I choked her to death. Her eyes are dark, haunted, and she rasps, "Yeah, that's . . . that's about what I thought might happen."

    I look up at her. "Why?" There's something pleading about that question. "Why would she do that? Why do all of that instead of just telling us to stop, or banishing Azathoth and leaving it at that? What was the point of that? Why?"

    Cheshire laughs darkly. "Why else? To entertain herself."

    I can't think of anything to say to that. I sit there, just trying to grapple with the enormity of what I just experienced. The divine authority of this universe just poured herself down my throat and puppeted my body into murdering Cheshire's. She overwhelmed me, and she made me feel like it was me, like I was the one laughing at Cheshire's pain even as I cried black tears.

    It is a sense of violation far worse than Azathoth's nudges in ritual. I can't bring myself to care even an iota about the Weaver putting words in my mouth after what the Demiurge just did to me. Night Mother, Toymaker, Soul-Sculptor. What a horrible, monstrous being.

I want to kill her. I want to bleed her to death. I want to take a knife to her soul and carve my name into it.

I slowly rise to my feet, still feeling unsteady and frail after the usurpation of my form. Cheshire watches me, expression somber, and when I have my balance I turn to her and tell her, "First the Beast, then Katoptris, then Nyara. I'll settle for nothing less."

The catgirl smiles sadly and says, "I hope you win. I really do."

I summon the compass and remanifest my geist, and we trudge along in silence.

After a bit of walking we pass into a new area: a mess of steel beams and platforms suspended in the air like the rafters and catwalks of a theater. Spotlights shine from above, and far below I can make out the distant impression of a wooden stage and shadows dancing.

There are fewer paths here than the ribbon-bridge zone, and while they branch out at places they usually meet back up. In the distance, two brightly lit signs point in opposite directions: one is labeled "Exit," and the other is labeled "Backstage."

This is much, much worse than the first two zones; on those bridges I could at least stay at a comfortable distance from any terrifying death-drop ledges (aside from the drop that killed me), but the catwalks are much thinner and I am surrounded by empty space and great heights. I clutch the metal railing tightly.

"Why did it have to be heights?" I hiss as I start to carefully walk forward. "I hate heights. I'm afraid of heights. Can't this wretched Labyrinth take pity on a poor demon? No, of course it can't, because the God of Death delights in seeing me suffer."

Cheshire backwards-walks in front of me, unconcerned with the risk of falling. "Do you wish you could fly? We could see about working toward that, if it would help."

"Hmmph. Maybe? I'm surprisingly fine with planes, but those aren't, y'know, open to the rushing air. Might solve the problem, might be terrifying. Wings would be cool, though. Magic wings, obviously, since I have too much mass to be lifted by ordinary wings. Wait, could we adjust my mass?"

Cheshire chuckles, and I am thankful for the distraction to keep my mind off the dizzying heights below us, but then her demeanor shifts into serious mode and she points ahead. "Reaver. It's the woman with a spear."

I grimace. "This is the worst arena yet, but at least it's not Mahiri. Alright, how best to kill this whelp . . ."

Cheshire's expression darkness. "Shit. Mahiri's *also* near. Farther out, but moving steadily."

I hiss. "I hate the Labyrinth, I hate the Labyrinth, I hate the Labyrinth! Argh! Okay, go slow the boss, I'll clear the trash mob."

Cheshire nods and transforms into a crow. "Spear lady is waiting by the exit!"

The sign is big and obvious, and the compass points the same direction. *We're almost out of the woods.* I pick up the pace, still nervous about falling but now faced with the equal-or-greater danger of Mahiri catching me.

The reaver comes into view quickly, lounging against the catwalk's railing in a way that is just begging for it to come loose and send her falling into the vast depths below. I suppress a shiver and force myself not to clutch at the railing again, needing to project confidence in front of my opponent.

She has her spear out, but pointed at the ground, and she waves at me as I approach. "Evenin', prey. Enjoy scurrying your way past hounds and hedges?"

I stop a good distance from the hunter and cross my arms. "What, no scurrying on your part? Have you been waiting here all this time?"

The reaver grins. "I've played this game before. Why chase the rat through the maze when you can lay a mousetrap at the cheese?"

Interesting. "These hunts are a regular event, then?" I don't know why I'm talking to this woman instead of just killing her. Cheshire won't be able to hold Mahiri for long, so this is just wasted breath.

There's always a choice. Ah, I see. Damn moralists.

The huntress shrugs. "Regular enough. We try to recruit first, so these hunts really only get called when someone doesn't wanna play nice. I guess I should thank you for that." She raises her spear, still grinning.

"If you fight me, you'll die," I tell her calmly.

The reaver scoffs. "Weren't you criticizing Cooper for arrogance just a few short hours ago?"

Cooper. Noted. "I'm nothing if not an inveterate hypocrite, but . . . Cooper's dead. So is the woman with knives, and the man with a shield. They tried to kill me, and I killed them first."

She narrows her eyes, and her grip tightens around her spear. "I see."

"But please, don't take that as a threat; it's a warning. Averrich is the one who sent you to die. You're a sacrifice, just like your friends."

She scoffs. "I volunteered."

"He knew you would. You've done it before," I point out. "He knew you'd volunteer, just like he knew the others would volunteer. And he never intended for you to win. He doesn't want you to win. So, please: just leave. Walk through that exit, and I'll walk after you, and we can both walk away from this without blood on our hands. There is no prize at the end of this game, only death."

"Bold words." The reaver settles into a fighting stance. "But I can take you."

Next to me, Cheshire coalesces from black mist. The hunter doesn't react to her arrival. I grit my teeth. "She'll be here soon," Cheshire murmurs to me. "You're running out of time."

"Maybe," I respond to the reaver. "But can you take Mahiri, too? You saw her new toy: a gift from Averrich himself. She has a spell from Imlashi, and a story at her back. She's the one that Averrich wants to kill me, the only one he'll allow to claim that prize. If you stand even a chance of taking me down, Mahiri will stop you. She'll kill you, if she needs to."

For the first time in our conversation, the reaver looks uneasy. "That . . . no, that's against the spirit of the hunt. Averrich wouldn't interfere like that."

I laugh. "Oh, you poor fucker. You think he cares? All of you are just means to an end. He'll sacrifice every one of you to get his hands on the Beast's shard."

Immediately she's back in hostility mode, and internally I swear at myself. "So you *do* know about the big event."

"Yes, but—"

"That shard is the only way that any of us can escape the Wolf Queen's shackles! Don't think the boss is the only one with cause to claim it. I won't let you stand in the way of my freedom."

I sigh. "Fine. The easy way it is."

She lunges at me and I don't try to dodge. I can heal whatever wound I take as long as I dish out a wound of my own, so I'll just get in close and bite, then [Exsanguinate] until she's dead and I'm whole.

Instead, the reaver takes a crossbow bolt to the eye. She crumples without ceremony, momentum carrying the tip of her spear to scrape against my chest but only barely draw blood. I blink a few times, then crouch down and tap her side. "[Prey Upon]."

The reaver finishes dying, and as I rise I start looking for Mahiri. She's not hard to find, as she's leaning against the railing of another catwalk not far away from the one I'm on. Her crossbow is loaded, and pointing at me. "Just you and me," she says with lazy contempt.

Showtime. I roll my shoulders and crack my knuckles. "Guess it is. Gonna shoot me like you shot her, or do you want to make this more interesting?"

Mahiri raises an eyebrow. "I'm listening, dead girl."

"Let's make this more than just a hunt: I challenge you to a scion's duel." A wave of force immediately surges out from me, rocking both my catwalk and Mahiri's. I grip the metal railing tightly and try to recover my composure. "My soul wagered against yours. Then we can see which of us is really the predator and which of us is the prey."

"Heh." Mahiri lifts her crossbow and scratches her chin, but doesn't seem impressed. "Why should I make that wager, give you a chance to bring more power to bear against me, when I could kill you right now and claim the prize I was after from the start?"

Cheshire steps up beside me and I see Mahiri's gaze flicker to the changeling. "That prize won't get you out from under Averrich's thumb," my geist says. "You know he's giving you this opportunity because he thinks he can control you. If you kill us now, he will. But if you can beat us in a scion's duel, you'll have the soul of a demon as leverage to escape your contract . . . and maybe more."

Mahiri smirks cruelly and curls her lip. "And will you become my geist, cat?" I tense up, but let Cheshire answer.

"No. I belong to Maven Alice and no other soul. If you kill her, I go with her. But perhaps some other geist will take pity on you."

The look on Mahiri's face gets uglier. "No one pities me. And no one beats me, either. You're on, bitch: I accept your scion's duel."

The air crackles with potential, I breathe deep, and then my soul becomes the world.

IX

The world of my soul comes to life in sharp streaks of bursting color. The Reveler's maze is swallowed by darkness, then lit by a bleeding black sun. The sky paints itself in browns and grays, and a bleak mountain rises like a spear thrusting into the heavens.

Beneath and below, tumor-trees pulsate and a forest of animalistic vegetation sprouts to life, the details hidden by a thick, clinging mist. The painting completes itself with a worn path winding its way up the mountainside, and a sharp-crowned castle at the highest point on that path.

I find myself standing atop the frontmost rampart of the castle within my soul, overlooking the entrance archway, hands clutching at stone parapets. Before me and below me, where the far end of the winding path vanishes into mist, stands the hunter that wants so badly to make me bleed.

She is, I note, in the process of aiming her crossbow.

Mahiri pulls the trigger and a bolt shoots toward me faster than my reflexes can catch up to, still disoriented by the shift in scenery. For a frozen instant it seems the projectile will strike me true, but then Clavicus—one of the skeletal servants I shaped and named on my prior visit to this realm—pushes me out of the way just in time.

The bolt strikes the skeleton's skull and passes right through, shattering it. I stumble away from the servant and fall back, landing hard on my ass, head ducked low to stay behind the safety of the parapet wall. I stare dumbly at my creation as he collapses into a lifeless pile of bones.

The part of my brain that holds all my coping mechanisms tries to crack a joke. "I thought skeletons were supposed to be resistant to piercing damage," I attempt, but my words come out so wavering and breathless that the sentence is completely unintelligible.

What if that were me? I can't stop envisioning it: the bolt hitting my skull, the cracking, the bleeding, the cerebral fluid spilling. Would it pierce through my forehead, or would it lodge in my eye? Would I die in seconds, or in minutes? How badly would it hurt?

"Alice!" shouts Cheshire. She's standing over me, shaking my shoulders, her expression urgent and intense. "You need your figments. You had a plan, remember?"

I blink a few times and shake my head to clear it. "Right. The plan. Yes. Uh, should I manifest you first?"

"You don't need to, not in here." Cheshire places her hand on Bonehilda, my other skeletal servant, who I only just notice has been standing with us the entire time. "Let me borrow this one, and I'll slow that reaver down." Cheshire melts into wisps of black fog that curl around the skeleton and pour into its skull. The skeleton forms muscle, fat, skin, hair, and clothing, and then Cheshire is standing in its place.

The newly reformed catgirl stretches the limbs of her new body, then shifts into a white-feathered raven and takes off.

We should give her some support now, since gathering our figments might take a while. I crack my knuckles and start casting. "[Carrion Swarm], [Carrion Swarm], [Carrion Swarm]: an unkindness of white ravens to distract and dismay." Pale corvids coalesce from shadow and circle above me. I give them their marching orders: "Strike in ones and twos at the hunter down below. Tear at her flesh and interfere with her vision, but move in scattered fashion and evade when you can. Go."

They fly off as a flock, and I have to trust that they'll be enough. Now for the hard part.

I take a few deep breaths and try to steady my shaking hands. I'm anxious about this battle, downright terrified if I stop and think about it, but I can't let that get in my way. I have to do this. I have to succeed.

I retreat deep into the recesses of my soul, searching for that click I felt when I reshaped this world the first time. The sights and sounds fade around me, until I am alone in the dark with only my thoughts for company. I reach inward and keep reaching until I find that sense of malleability, that connection between my will and my throne world.

When I learned from Cheshire that I could populate my throne world with figments, it took me time to get it right. My sense of time's passing isn't the best, but there was at least a half hour's gap between the inception of the idea and finishing the process. I don't have the luxury of that kind of time now that Mahiri is here, hunting me inside my own soul.

So instead of creating new figments, I reach for the ones that are already here. The skeletons were good for a laugh, but they weren't what I spent the bulk of my time on; that went to the creation of the hungering beasts that now wander the forest of flesh at the base of the mountain.

I grab hold of as many as I can, and then I speak to them. I hear my voice, echoing dimly, like heard from the far end of an incredibly long hall. "Beasts of my soul, of shadowbound bone, rise from your forest and protect me. Be . . ."

Thoughts of my conversation with Cheshire interrupt my speech. I remember the concern I had when she emphasized the importance of framing: *I'd be like a wounded animal hiding within the herd.* I can't allow that. I need every possible advantage.

"Be . . . be my packmates. Be my hunting hounds. Where my enemy . . . where my would-be hunter sees a wounded animal, vulnerable like prey, let that instead be the bait that draws her into our trap. Pounce, my creatures of night, and feast on this paltry interloper."

I can sense them responding to my call. They bound across the forest floor and sink bony claws into the side of the mountain, and they climb it with supernatural speed and agility. *Distance is conceptual,* I remember. In one sense they could be miles away from me, but in another sense they are exactly as close as they need to be.

I let go of the beasts and return to my body. My physical senses rush back to me, once more disorienting me with a flood of visual stimuli. I hear the flapping of winds, and a noise like howling wind but sharper and layered with growling.

I start to rise from the floor to try and get a look at what's happening, but I stop myself before actually poking my head over the parapet. I am frozen by the memory of bolt shattering bone.

We need protection. We still have that reaver's shield, right? It should be here, somewhere. That raises an interesting question: can I conjure objects from my throne world while inside that same space?

I concentrate on my mental impression of what that shield looked like, the part of the castle that I sent it to, and how it felt for the brief moments that I held it. I will it to appear in my hands, like I have for other items. It does appear, but instead of simply popping into existence like normal, it forms from shadowy mist the same way that Cheshire appears and vanishes when acting as a geist. It's an interesting difference, but I don't have time to examine the implications.

I grip the shield tightly and stand up, ready to raise that shield and duck down the second I see Mahiri's crossbow aimed my way, but thankfully my caution proves unnecessary; when I survey the field, I find the reaver engaged in pitched battle with all of the creatures that I have called.

My ravens circle the hunter and divebomb her at random intervals, but Mahiri barely seems to notice them; she draws a few lazy swings of her sword through ravens that didn't move away fast enough, but otherwise she seems completely focused on the growing ranks of skeletal wolf-monsters.

My monstrous servants are as I designed them: they have skeletal frames like stretched-out wolves, and they are skinless and fleshless but dense shadow stretches between bone like spider-silk webbing, forming the emaciated suggestion of mass. They are claw and fang and baleful red eyes, and they are mine. I feel the strangest sense of pride, witnessing my handiwork.

The beasts arrive in twos and threes, drawn by my call across strange, conceptual distances. Their trickling arrival gives Mahiri time to react to each new pack of foes. When a group climbs over the cliffside, she responds with a burning bolt that explodes into wild green flame and makes that whole side of the path treacherous for my minions—and I witness one shadow-beast take the bolt directly to the chest and be knocked off the side of the cliff by the explosion.

When a beast gets through, the reaver holds her crossbow at her side and draws that dreadful artifact blade with her free hand. She blurs out of the way of the monster's assault and carves into it. The creature's body doesn't fade and melt like the bodies of my summons, but Mahiri's blade cuts through bone like the softest of butter. The first slash takes a claw, the second its head, and the third opens its shadowed ribcage for good measure.

Still, they are *demanding* her focus, especially as more join the fray. Though the fire keeps many at bay—the flames shift and writhe, alive in their hunger for any beast that draws near—each creature that gets through and reaches Mahiri stops her from spreading the flames. The beasts that reach her still die, and rather quickly, but those moments where she is forced to use her sword to carve open beasts and bat away birds are moments where she is not shooting at the new arrivals, and the horde of beasts doesn't stop growing.

I don't know how, but I can tell which of the white-feathered ravens is actually Cheshire in her shifted form. She hangs back from the divebombing, watching and waiting for the right moment to strike, and when two shadowbound beasts break through the barrier of flames, Cheshire seizes the opportunity. Two summoned ravens dive at Mahiri, and Cheshire shadows them, keeping their bodies between her and the hunter.

The summons peck at Mahiri's arms, which is barely an inconvenience to the hunter, so she keeps her focus on the gathering beasts. Cheshire slips past the other birds and alights on Mahiri's belt, using her beak to tear open the bottom of one specific pouch. Something gleaming and golden falls from the pouch and Cheshire dives for it, catching it before it can hit the ground.

Immediately, Mahiri realizes what's gone wrong and whirls from her fight with the shadowbound beasts to turn her full attention on the pilfering raven. Mahiri blurs into motion to strike the thief out of the air, but Cheshire just barely doges the first strike with a harsh swerve. The raven loses a few feathers and her form waves, but she keeps moving, forcing Mahiri to push herself to move even faster. The second strike catches Cheshire and cuts her in half, form melting away.

The shining piece of gold falls and Mahiri lunges for it, dropping her crossbow to free up a hand, but a beast's frenzied assault forces her to blur out of the way instead. The gold hits the ground, and with more beasts closing in I see a narrow window where we might just be able to claim our prize.

"Grab the bauble!" I shout at all my gathered minions. "Grab it and bring it to me!"

The ravens dive from above and the shadowbound beasts leap through the flames to get at that glimmering chunk of gold. Mahiri cuts down the beast she was engaged with and darts for the bauble, but a raven reaches it first and snatches it up, immediately taking off and flying toward me. The rest of the monsters converge, every one of them ready to seize the gold and keep it moving if Mahiri cuts the holder down.

"[Wheel of Life and Death]!"

The reaver shouts a spell, panic seeping into her voice, and the space around her erupts with green-gold light. The light swirls around Mahiri like the petals of a curled flower, forming a pristine bulb for a single instant before exploding outward in the shape of thorny vines and jagged branches. Limbs of green-gold light sweep across the battlefield and impale every creature that isn't Mahiri; every raven is caught by vines and crushed into smoke, and every shadow-beast is stabbed through with branches that sprout green-gold flowers and crush bone into shards.

In seconds, my entire army is destroyed. When the light fades, the vegetation withers, and it leaves behind only fragments of bone and a golden bauble that falls to the dirt halfway between me and the reaver.

Mahiri stands there, breathing heavily, and I see the faintest bit of blood on her leg where one of the shadow-beasts must have nicked her. She slouches, head lowered, seeming overcome by exertion. Whatever the hell that spell was, it seems to have taken a toll on her. *Maybe I still have a chance.*

I let the shield slip from my fingers and curl them back, claw-like, as I begin casting spells. With luck, a bit of framing might do something to counteract the cost of not casting out loud, and my silence will grant me an edge of surprise. I cast [Carrion Swarm] thrice, keeping the prior configuration, and a new unkindness comes to life around me—fewer of them, but hopefully still enough.

I murmur to them, "Get the rock," and they take flight.

The ravens I summoned all fly for the bauble, and I see another raven soar out of the castle gates: Cheshire, returned to the fight in a new body. Mahiri sees all this and shakes off her weariness. She grits her teeth and blurs forward, determined to reach the object first.

The flock converges on the shiny piece of gold just a second before Mahiri reaches it, but the reaver moves faster than I've ever seen her move before and sweeps her blade through the swarm of birds, the sword catching fire midswing and parting the flock like so many grains of wheat before the thresher—all except a single raven, Cheshire, who swerved *away* from the prize and instead maneuvered behind Mahiri.

The changeling shifts into a bear and takes a swipe at the reaver that Mahiri has to contort to avoid, but for once the hunter's not quick enough and she takes a nasty-looking slash to the arm holding her sword. It's not brutal enough to make her drop the sword, but she cries out in pain and stumbles, finally thrown off-balance.

"[Exsanguinate]!" I shout as soon as I see that glistening red. Her arm ruptures and hot crimson paints the dirt, but she pushes through the pain and dives for the gold.

The bear becomes a wolf and leaps at Mahiri to try and stop her, but the reaver's fingers curl around the bauble, and with burning blade she slices the wolf in half midair. When Cheshire's smoke fades, Mahiri stands triumphant, wounds sealed with gold, amid a field of my failures.

She takes a moment to straighten out her posture and rise to her full height, and then she raises her sword and points it at me with a smirk. She calls out, "Is that all you've got? I would say I was expecting better, but that would be a lie."

I hate the smug look on her face. I hate the way she drips with confidence, like this was inevitable, even after all the pain I put her through. I bare my teeth and clench my fists, but what can I say to her? My plan didn't work, and nothing I have left will even scratch her. *Literally!*

Mahiri's smirk only intensifies when I don't immediately respond. "What, no pithy retort? No begging for me to spare your miserable life? Have you finally run out of words, just like you've run out of fodder?"

I lean forward, hands clutching at the castle stonework. "This isn't over! Don't think you've won yet. This was just a warmup."

Mahiri laughs at me. "You're out of bigger, stronger monsters to hide behind, little demon girl. I've reduced your protective herd to shards of bone, and your shapeshifting geist knows she can't beat me in a straight fight. You're cornered, prey. All that's left is the killing blow."

"I won't stop fighting. I won't give you an easy victory. I won't give you the *satisfaction* of making me feel small."

"Oh? That's funny, because that's really not the impression you gave all those times you folded like a paper crane at the slightest promise of pain. No, I think you'll make very entertaining noises when I'm cutting you open. Prey animals like you make the most adorable squeaks when they're in mortal danger."

The reaver chuckles to herself and turns her back on me, leisurely strolling toward where she left her crossbow after Cheshire first stole that piece of gold. My grip on the stonework tightens as I watch her move with such arrogance and disregard, and then I stumble and nearly fall as the stone crumbles beneath my hands.

I take a cautious step back and stare at the damaged parapet with wide eyes. I'm not strong enough to break stone. I sweep my gaze around and see more cracks appearing all over the stonework of the castle ramparts. It's all eroding right in front of me.

Cheshire appears next to me, forming from black mist. "You need to answer her," she urges me. "Your foundation is crumbling. You have to tell her why she's wrong."

"But she isn't!" I hiss at Cheshire. "I threw everything I had at her, and I failed. I hid behind all my minions, and she tore right through them. My clever plots were for *nothing*." More cracks spread through stone, spiderwebbing. "I'm just . . . I'm just too fucking weak."

In the distance, Mahiri picks up her crossbow and starts loading it.

Cheshire stares at me, intense and intent. "Then what are you going to do?"

The fear is rising. The panic, the dread, the loathing. I failed, and I'm going to die, exactly like I feared would happen from the moment I first realized this world had *consequences*. I am staring down at the woman who is going to kill me, and it's all my own damn fault.

"What are you going to do?" Cheshire asks me again, fear creeping into her voice as she grabs at my hand. "Come on, you have to do something. If you don't want to merge with me, then what else do you want to try? What are you going to do?"

Mahiri starts walking back toward us, crossbow in one hand and sword in the other, grinning. *What do I do? What can I do? If I try to summon more minions, she'll cut them down. If she doesn't bleed, I can't trade blows with her. And if I let Cheshire possess my body, it might mean the only thing as terrifying as death of the body: death of the mind.*

I'm going to die. I'm going to die unless I do something, but there's nothing that I can do.

So I run. I sprint for the nearest entrance that leads inside the castle, reasoning that maybe I can use that extra-dimensional interior to hide within some kind of maze. Maybe I can wear Mahiri out, fight a war of attrition.

Instead, before I can even reach the door, the entire castle collapses and the mountainside crumbles with it. I fall, stone falling around me, the distant ground coming closer, closer, closer—

—and I'm lying on slick earth, surrounded by stony rubble and meat-moss trees. I'm afraid to move, paralyzed by dread and uncertainty, but I shake my limbs and find them all functional. I'm alone in the dark, mist shrouding me from the light of the red-limned eclipse.

Weakness. Failure. Just as inadequate as ever.

Ah, of course. Never truly alone. I clamber to my feet and start moving away from the rubble, mindful of the reaver likely still hunting me. I have to get away. Have to put distance between myself and where I was. If I just run far enough, she won't follow me, and maybe I can slip back to the Labyrinth and get out of the maze.

You're going to die here. You're going to die here and it's all your fault.

I can hear whispers through the trees. Voices, all my own. Reminders of failure, weakness, inadequacy. My own loathing, so familiar, but now echoing through my soul.

Every choice you made was the wrong one. You're a fool. An idiot. A crying child.

I cover my ears and keep moving, keeping forward, just have to run far enough and I'll survive. I have to survive.

You turned down your only way out, and now it's time to crash and burn.

The forest catches fire.

The fire comes from everywhere, all at once. It's red in some areas and green in others, gold and orange and blue and black. It's a rainbow of flame, and it burns the world. Mist gives way to smoke, and meat blackens to bark-like husks.

I run through the burning forest, and behind me I hear the reaver's mocking laughter. A crossbow bolt tears a hole in my cape and I run faster, pushing my body to its limits and past them. I need to get away. I can't die here.

The forest around me continues to blacken, and overhead the flames form a twisted Aurora Borealis effect. The smoke burns my eyes and lungs, but I fight through it. The ground beneath me is ash and dead leaves and blood-soaked mud.

My foot snags on a blackened root and I trip, no time to correct my movement. I land amid more roots, big and small, bursting from a tree larger than the rest. I am covered in ash and mud, and I scrabble to get up but keep slipping and falling, the mud almost seeming to drag me down, to grasp at me.

Mahiri steps into view and I immediately call my pilfered shield back to my hands, the object forming from shadow just in time to take a bolt that still pierces nearly the whole way through. Mahiri strides toward me, calmly, leisurely, and I back up against the tree as best I'm able, still unable to find my footing in the ash and mud.

What do I do? How do I get away. I need to run. I need to run. Damn it, why can't I run? I shout "[Carrion Swarm]!" and raise the shield to protect myself, but Mahiri easily carves through the summoned ravens and then brings the sword down on my shield, cutting clean through and severing it in two.

The two halves of the shield fall from my hands, and I stare up at the woman who is about to kill me. She points the sword at my chest and grins. "Any last words? You know, before the screaming."

"I don't want to die," I whisper, and then the blade is moving and I fall backward through the roots of the blackened tree, swallowed by darkness.

I fall through dim fog past burning roots, through a world of fire and shadow. I fall until I slam hard against the ground, against flooring, against... carpet? Above, distant, I still see root and fire, but beneath me is oddly familiar brown carpet, and around me are beige walls that stretch upward into darkness. I see the impressions of a book pile, and a closet, and two closed doors.

On shaking legs I rise and look around. *Where am I? What is this?* I see indistinct figures, shadows cast against the walls, but they're like giants looming over me, looking down at me. They're all watching me, but they're clustered around the edges of this vast chamber to leave space for me in the center.

Me, and one other: in the heart of this dark hollow there is a great bed, and upon that bed lies a woman. Her face is blurry, giving the impression of detail but no discernable specifics. Her body is sickly, and she is dying. A single emaciated hand trails off the side of the bed, palm open, fingers outstretched like she's reaching for me, but she lacks the strength to move her hand any closer.

I know this scene. I know why those shadows all look like giants, and why I can't see her face, and why this room is so familiar: because this was what my parents' room looked like on the night that my mother died. They look big because I was small; when it happened, I was only four years old.

I feel tired, and terrified, and weak. I stumble forward and collapse by the side of the bed, reaching out for that withered hand, but it turns to ash the moment I touch it. The body of my mother fades away, now ashes that I have long since scattered, and the room seems to get smaller, down to its real size.

I lean my back against the bedside and close my eyes, still feeling the ashes on my fingertips and the mud on my legs. I laugh, the sound piteous and broken. "Ironic, isn't it?" I ask the ghosts. "Not cancer like took her, or age that's taking him, but the inevitable consequences of my own desperate attempts to stave off the end."

The ghosts don't respond, of course. I am, as I have always been, alone.

I feel wetness growing in my eyes, and I hate it. Can't I die with some dignity? Do I have to relive this stupid fucking moment? All the pain and the hate that I've never really outgrown? The loss, the regret, and all the masks to cover it up.

"Why did you leave me?" I ask the ashes. "Why didn't you stay?"

I hear footfalls, soft against the carpet. I open my eyes, expecting to see my executioner, but instead it's Cheshire. Cheshire, who says she loves me. Cheshire, who says she can save me. Cheshire, who lies.

I laugh again, but it turns to a coughing fit almost immediately. "What?" I rasp. "Come for one last attempt to convince me? Well, go on; I'm vulnerable, and I'm afraid, so do what you do best."

The girl with mismatched eyes looks at me with sorrow and care. I hate it. I hate her stupid face and all her stupid expressions. I hate when she pretends to feel empathy for me. I hate it all.

Cheshire murmurs, "This was the first memory of yours that Nyara showed me, when she made me your geist. She called it your animus: the 'animating principle' of your soul. She said that everything you are is built around this one moment. The very heart of you."

"I wish I could burn it out." I stare up at the flaming roots far above. "I guess I'm getting my wish."

Cheshire kneels down in front of me and reaches out to cup my face in her hands. I don't stop her. "I know you're worried that I'll betray you or abandon you like they did. I know you have just as many logical reasons as emotional reasons to distrust me. But I won't betray you. I won't abandon you. Please, Alice. Please, let me help you. Let me in."

Logic says that Cheshire has kept me alive. Logic says that Cheshire has put me in danger. Logic says that I lack sufficient evidence to put my trust in Cheshire's claims. Logic says I don't have a choice.

But human beings don't make their decisions based on logic. We are irrational, emotional, impulsive creatures, and I'm a better example of that than anyone. So none of my logic is why I'm hesitating.

The real reason, the emotional reason, is the room we're sitting in and everything it represents. This is the heart of me. This is my animus.

I whisper to Cheshire, "I'm scared."

Her expression softens, and her eyes seem so full and warm, and I hate that I want to believe her. "Hey. Do you want to know a secret? I'm scared too."

I believe her. It may damn me, but I believe her. "Okay. You have my consent. Do the merge."

Cheshire fades into black mist that pours down my throat and fills my lungs. I breathe it in, and it's like I've been cold all my life and finally found warmth. It spreads from my chest down my limbs to the tips of my fingers and toes, pleasant and relaxing like a full-body high.

I feel . . . strength and surety, a sense of coiled power waiting patiently to be unleashed, like I felt after eating that reaver. I raise a hand in front of my face, take off my gloves, and flex my fingers, feeling skin and flesh and bone with a greater awareness than I have before. There's more than just strength hiding inside this body; it feels like . . . potential. Malleability.

There's another set of feelings in the back of my mind, not mine but not entirely separate and getting less separate by the second. I feel Cheshire's joy at having a real body again. I feel her hunger to test our new capabilities against the arrogant hunter that dared to challenge us. I feel her gratitude that I put my trust in her.

There's a sense of light pressure against my raised arm, questioning, asking permission. I grant it, and my arm moves by Cheshire's will, outstretched finger drawing a circle in the air in front of me. The circle becomes a disk of reflective glass suspended, a mirror fixed in place, and I see myself. I see us.

Our hair is mostly black, but streaked with white, and the bun has come undone to let my hair fall loose. Skin just as pale, fangs just as pointy, lips and nails still dark red. But while one of my eyes is still red, the other is now blue, and both pupils have turned golden.

"Interesting," we speak with my voice.

May I shift? Cheshire asks inside my head.

You may. You promised me a werewolf, and I want to see it with my own eyes. Our own eyes. Blue and red, gleaming.

Your wish is my command.

The skin on my hand sprouts white fur, and my nails harden and lengthen into claws. Then fur becomes feathers, then scales, then fleshless bone, and then fur once more.

The white fur travels up my arm, and where it reaches clothing that clothing turns to black mist and fades away. It spreads across my torso, my other arm, down to my legs, and I feel my bones crack and reshape themselves as my whole body gets *bigger*. Muscle forms where before my limbs were twig-like in their delicacy, my limbs stretch longer, and my clawed nails blacken.

When it reaches my head, the changes are dramatic. My face reshapes to be more wolf-like, jaw jutting forward and filling with sharp teeth fit for piercing and tearing. My pointed ears broaden as they become furry, and my eyes glow bright as the irises swallow the sclera.

I expect it to stop there, but Cheshire adds one final detail to my new form: a pair of curling black ram's horns that burst from my skull. I feel her amusement, and she whispers to me, *I promised a demon wolf, did I not?*

"It's perfect," I say aloud, my voice now deeper and perpetually growling. "Now let's use it, and make her pay."

I reach with my will for the burning roots far above, and then we leap. The roots that were far away are now right in front of me, and we sink our claws into them and climb up past the flames. We emerge into the forest, the fires gone out, the trees all blackened husks.

There, wandering between the trees with sword in one hand and a crossbow in the others, is our target: Mahiri.

"Come out, come out, little prey," she calls, not having spotted us yet. "You can't hide forever."

I have an idea, Cheshire tells me.

Do it, I tell her without hesitation.

Above, the black sun swallows the sky, the red halo vanishing, and the forest is plunged into darkness. My eyes can still see clearly, though color turns grayscale, but I see Mahiri immediately swear and set her sword aflame to produce light.

"I don't know how you broke my [Hunter's Mark]," she shouts, "but it was a cute trick! It still won't save you."

We laugh, the sound cruel and echoing. "Oh, we don't need saving."

The hunter whirls and fires a bolt at where the noise came from, but we're already moving, sprinting across the forest floor on all fours. We dash past her, raking a claw along her leg before she can retaliate, and then we're safe behind a tree husk. Mahiri cries out, but that damnable invocation keeps her from bleeding.

"Do you know the difference," we growl, "between a hunter and a predator?"

Mahiri fires a bolt in our direction that explodes into green flame, but it hits the tree and we leap to another point of cover before the flames can reach us. She makes a noise of agitation and demands, "Stop hiding, you little wretch! None of your tricks are enough to beat me."

"Ah, but that's just it." We dart from one tree to another, then leap out and score another slash on the hunter from behind. She whirls with her flaming sword and nicks us, but it's a shallow wound and the flames don't cling as we rush behind another tree, slipping from shadow to shadow. "A hunter uses tricks and tools to make up for weakness and limitation, like you with your kit. But a predator is a thing of pure killing ability."

"Weakness?" she scoffs. "I beat you on the bridge, and outside your castle, and now I'm going to beat you here. [Wyldfire Shot]." She fires her crossbow, the bolt once again exploding into flame, but the tree doesn't burn; it actually starts to regrow, dark leaves sprouting from seemingly dead wood—wood that was once flesh, but no longer. "It's not weakness to use the right tool for the job."

"You bargained for those toys because you knew you couldn't kill me without them. You knew you didn't have the *strength* to overcome me, even in my fledgling state." We keep moving as we growl, evading every shot and watching the forest grow back stronger and thicker. "Because you are just a human, and I am a demon."

Mahiri grits her teeth, drops her crossbow, and wields the flaming sword with both hands. "I'll bleed that arrogance from you, drop by drop."

We laugh. "Is it truly arrogance if we really are better than you? I am more than you will ever—could ever—be in your sad, sorry life. You are just the first rung of the ladder I'm climbing. You're a footnote in *my* story."

The reaver puts her back to a tree and looks around warily, trying to track our movements and voice. "I'm more driven than you. I'm more capable than you. I'm *worthier* than you."

"Then why weren't you chosen?"

We cease being a wolf and turn into a dragonfly, and in that small-but-speedy form we zip to the newly grown branches of the tree she has her back to. We shift back to wolf form, and in that instant we pounce.

Mahiri blurs to raise her blade against us the moment she realizes where we are, but even with super-speed she's too late. We slam into her and knock her to the forest floor, claws digging into her flesh. She manages one final cut with the blade, scoring us along our side, but then we bite at her wrist with crushing force and break her bones.

She screams, and the second we release her wrist the wounds fill with gold, but the damage is done; though she struggles with all her might, she cannot move that hand. She tries to push us off with her unbroken arm and with her legs, but we are so much stronger than her now.

We bite at her again, and again, and again, each time taking a chunk of flesh that seals with gold, until finally one bite does not seal, and her blood flows. [Exsanguinate] to seal our wounds, and then we stop toying with her and start *eating* her.

We taste her flesh and her blood, and as we tear into her, ripping apart to get at bone and organs, we begin to taste something more: her very soul. It tastes like spite and springtime and wounded ego, and like a hundred arrows carved by hand. It tastes like promises made and hatred sworn, and it tastes of pumping blood in a human heart.

It tastes like power, and I swallow it whole.

X

Mahiri's soul is the most filling meal I've ever had, and yet paradoxically I find myself getting hungrier and hungrier as I eat. I keep feasting on her corpse long past the point where I stop tasting her soul, a manic energy stirring me on. When I finally feel satisfied and content to stop eating, there's barely any of her left beyond the clothes she was wearing and a few pieces of gear.

Her magic sword, regrettably, seems to have vanished. I send the crossbow, belt, and goggles to a storeroom.

I allow myself to bask in the glow of victory for a few moments, but soon enough my throne world begins to fade away. I rise from the tattered remnants of my foe, once more standing amid the familiar lights and walkways of the maze's last zone.

My body returns to its porcelain vampire doll form, and a moment later black mist flows from my mouth and takes the form of Cheshire. I feel a cold prickling sense of loss as she leaves me, like the crash after a high, but it's not enough to break through my post-meal delight.

"Congrats on the win, Allie. How's it feel?" She leans against the walkway railing, seeming happy.

"Exceptional," I breathe. "Very viscerally satisfying. I want to do it again."

She smiles. "I'm glad. You deserved a real win, after all you've been through in this Labyrinth. Once we're somewhere safe, I'll tell you all about the benefits of that soul you ate, though I imagine you remember most of them from our last talk on the subject. Come on, let's get to the exit." She waves a hand and starts walking in that direction, but I don't follow her.

"No. I'm not done here yet."

Cheshire turns back to me and frowns. "What do you mean?"

I look to the other pathway, the one leading to the Reveler's lair. "I'm tired of running scared. I just had my first real taste of victory and it was *intoxicating*. I'm not leaving this maze until I've gotten one over on everyone standing in my way, and that means vexing the bastard who threw me in here. Averrich schemed to make this a game where every outcome benefits him more than me, but there's one outcome he can't have predicted: I'm going to kill the Reveler."

Cheshire pales. "That's . . . uh, I mean, he certainly wouldn't expect that, but *how* do you plan on doing that? The Reveler is still a bit above your power level, even with your latest boost. You do have a plan, right?"

"You said that I get new spells by eating souls, right?"

Cheshire nods slowly. "That's right. With the soul you just ate and everything else you've done since becoming a demon, you have the resources to make a new spell. What did you have in mind?"

I grin. "I've been going over a lot of pieces in my head, and now I think I understand how they all click together. Take us back to my throne world; I want to do this with flair, like when we assembled my Truths."

The world shifts again, and we're back in my soul, standing at the entrance to my thankfully reconstructed castle. I take us to one of the unused rooms and conjure a table into the center of it. I drum my fingers on the table, mind buzzing with ideas, and think about how to word this.

"Okay. So, this idea really started forming when we talked about [Prey Upon] and you explained how it 'digests' souls. I started thinking: could that property be applied to a spell like [Soulfire]? And then, then I thought about [Abyssal Armament], and how I used it to save myself from the Mourner's touch. I thought about what would happen if I combined all those traits." I reach into my throne world and shape a dagger of black stone, setting it on the table.

Cheshire strokes her chin and hums. "Interesting. A weapon purpose-built for killing something like a Reveler that relies on corrupting your soul. If you carved off the corrupted part of your soul with every casting, and gained back more than you lost by consuming part of their soul—avoiding further corruption through digestion—that might actually work. Maybe."

"There's more." I shape a bloody fang next to the black dagger. "[Prey Upon] eats souls, but it can also grant me mana. [Exsanguinate], meanwhile, has been modified to have a lifesteal effect. Both are useful, but both have restrictions that limit their usefulness: the latter requires a wounded foe, while the former requires a dying foe. But what if I had one spell that could feed me soulstuff, feed me mana, *and* heal my wounds, all while working on any foe—wounded or whole, bloody or bloodless?"

Cheshire frowns. "That would be an absurdly costly effect. Prohibitively so. If a spell like that was easy to cast, I would have offered it in the first place instead of a bunch of lesser options."

I nod. "I figured that'd be the case. But then, in that dark hollow deep inside my soul, I found the final piece of the puzzle. I saw my own animus: the fear of death and abandonment that sprung from the loss of my mother. And I *defied it* by taking your hand and choosing to trust you. I took a risk, and it paid off. And that's what I've been doing ever since I arrived in this world.

"When I sold my name to the Huntsman, it was a risk that came with sacrifice, but it got me the compass that led to my first ally in this world. When I freed the incubus, it was a risk, but I earned his gratitude and that carried me through two days of pissing him off. When I stabbed my own hand with a soul-devouring dagger, it was risk and sacrifice, but it saved my life. And when I chose to trust you, when I took that risk, it won us the duel. Risk and sacrifice, and through that, power."

I add a vial of blood to the table, and next to it a blood-red twenty-sided die.

"I want to make a spell that will be my *new* animus: the will to rise through sacrifice and risk. A spell with an incredibly powerful payoff, but an incredibly dangerous cost: with every casting, it will sacrifice a portion of my mana, my life essence, and my very soul—not just when it's been corrupted, but every single time, taking as much as it needs to fuel the spell. Every casting would be a gamble, a wager that I would gain back more than I spent."

Cheshire whistles appreciatively. "Damn, girl, but you really don't do half-measures. Hmm." Cheshire raises her hands and conjures an orb of blood, an orb of darkness, and an orb of black flame, all levitating in front of her. "A spell like that . . . it's possible, but only for you. You have the right Truths, and you've built the right meaning, and we have power to work with. I can make it, but I'll have to deconstruct both [Prey Upon] and [Exsanguinate] *and* use up all the power we just gained from that duel. You'll be left with just this spell and [Carrion Swarm] until, in all likelihood, your next duel victory."

"I'm okay with that. This spell is worth the investment."

Cheshire nods. "There *is* one restriction that I won't be able to get around: if you're just trying to harm a soul, something like [Soulfire] is sufficient, but to feed on a soul and take from it you need some form of contact. Physical contact is conventional, ranging from skin-to-skin to casting at the point of a sword like you did to finish off that corrupted reaver. Since you're a demon, anything touching your shadow qualifies as touching you for the purposes of a spell like this. And lastly, you'll be able to cast it through any tethered object; I count as one of those, when manifested, and I can modify [Carrion Swarm]'s phantasms to be tethered as well, though doing so would add a range restriction on how far from you they can move before disapparating."

I consider that briefly, but it's not a hard choice. "Make the change. I'm not really a long-range combatant anyways, at this point."

"Noted. Also, and this should go without saying, but I do want you to be aware that every casting of this spell is going to cause you *excruciating pain*. Even if it's carving off a damaged or corrupted piece of your soul—and I intend to set its default to target those areas—you're still losing a part of your soul, and that's going to hurt."

I laugh and grin. "Please, a little pain never stopped me. I'll gladly bear it."

"Okay." Cheshire brings the three orbs together, the trinity melding into a single orb of shifting color. "Then give it a name, and I'll give you this spell."

I take a deep breath, and I start speaking. "This spell is my animus. It is the culmination of who I want to be, of the choices that I have made and am going to make going forward. Every risk I've taken on the path to this point has given me the strength to keep moving, so I'll risk it all: my power, my body, and my very soul. Every casting of this spell will be the line between darkness and the divine. The ultimate risk, and the ultimate reward. With this spell in hand, I will overthrow the Demiurge and take her place on the Throne of Creation, or I will fall from grace and be taken by the hungering Abyss. There is no other path that will suffice, no lesser road that still leads to the usurpation of God herself. She who is not willing to give everything will be forever left with nothing. I'll make that creed my whole life, my whole being, my whole reason to exist: [Feast or Famine]."

The orb vanishes and a new spell matrix appears in my mind's eye.

This matrix is more complex than those I've looked at previously, by a fairly wide margin, but it also seems very rigid for a spoken spell. I see the sigil for the Abyss in multiple places in the configuration, which I think may be the first time I've seen an individual glyph appear more than once in a single matrix?

I really want to note down this matrix and compare it to the others, but that's something I can do later. Right now, I have a monster to kill.

I dismiss the spell without unleashing it and we return to the Reveler's maze once more. At my lead we follow the path leading to the sign marked "Backstage."

In short order we pass into a new region of the maze, but there's something familiar about this place: it's the wooden stage I saw far below the catwalks. Red curtains are drawn in front of the stage, and spotlights are pointed at it, while behind me stretches an audience of swaying shadow-figures.

Cheshire looks to me as I walk toward the stage. "Do you want to manifest me for this fight?"

I shake my head. "I have a different idea. You told me some geists take care of spellcasting in a fight, and I want to try that out. Prime castings of [Feast or Famine], and unleash whenever I make contact."

Cheshire nods, then melts into my shadow. I take another few steps forward and stop at the edge of the stage.

I spread my hands and call out, "Well, Beast? Going to let me fight your manic little splinter, or will I have to force it to come out?"

On cue, the curtains are pulled to either side of the stage, and the Reveler is unveiled. The horrifying mass of limbs is curled up like a sleeping cat, but as the curtains draw back it raises its smiling mask and unfurls.

The Reveler laughs—the giggling of a child, the cheers of a crowd, the howling of the mad—and I laugh right back at it, grinning and ready. "Gimme your best shot," I dare the monster, and I reach out my hand and make a "come at me" gesture.

The creature lifts a few limbs with fingers delicately outstretched, and it gently moves those limbs to graze it fingers along my hand. For a single instant I am overwhelmed by joy so bright and sharp it hurts to feel, like sex and drugs and feeding all compressed into a chemical overdose in my brain. It's strength so intense I feel like my muscles will tear themselves apart, and a sense of suicidal invincibility that tells me I could break the world with my bare hands.

Then black mist swirls around my hand, and the intrusive thoughts scatter like petals, replaced with searing pain that stabs my insides and blanks my thoughts—and then that pain is salved by the heavenly taste of fresh soulstuff.

The Reveler recoils as if burned, mist clinging to its fingers and withering them. The creature tilts its masked face at me, blood dripping from its empty eyeholes, looking almost like a confused puppy. It untangles another limb from its mass, and this one extends a single finger to poke my arm.

The wheel of sensations repeats: unbearable euphoria, soul-rending pain, and the satisfaction of a good meal. It's disorienting, and I have to take a few deep breaths to steady myself, but the Reveler seems to take it worse; the monster hisses, the first time I've heard it make a noise other than laughter.

It backs away slowly, so I climb onto the stage and advance, pulling myself up with more ease than I was expecting. Am I stronger now? Like, permanently?

The Reveler rises out of my reach, clinging to the far wall of the stage and watching me with unknowable emotion. I smirk. "Cute. [Carrion Swarm]. Get close."

White ravens spring forth and fly at the Reveler. A limb twitches to life for each raven and moves with lurching speed to swat them out of the air, but in the instant before each raven disintegrates they are wreathed in black mist that clings to the Reveler's limbs. More grasping hands wither until they are emaciated husks.

This time there's no euphoria to contrast with the pain, so I'm shotgun-blasted with a myriad of fresh agonies only partly blunted by the food high that follows. I double over and my vision briefly goes black, but with gritted teeth and fierce will I force myself to regain my composure.

Above me, the Reveler scratches at its own mask, and the limbs I bit with my spell are getting worse. As I watch, two of them fall from the main mass and shatter into black glass against the wooden stage. Another falls, and another, and I see hands that never touched me or my creatures beginning to rot away.

The Reveler laughs again, a cacophonous chorus, but this time tinged with panic. It gathers its fullness and lunges at me, all remaining arms spread wide as if to crush me to death in its embrace.

I lunge right back at it, arm outstretched, and lay my hand on its mask. Cheshire unleashes my magic, and I cast it myself for good measure. "[Feast or Famine]!"

Black mist swallows its mask and courses down its mass of limbs, rotting them to nothing, and the Reveler dies.

When the pain and the mist both fade, I'm left standing surrounded by glass dust and larger shards. Amid all that, two objects stick out: the mask of the Reveler, smiling and bloody; and a weapon that I recognize as a war rapier, with a swept hilt and a broader blade than a standard rapier. The blade of the weapon is also, oddly, a deep crimson hue.

I reach for the mask first, then hesitate. Cheshire appears next to me and gives me a warning look. "Careful, they might be cursed in some way."

"Mm. But I *want* them. Let's try something." I flick on soul sight and the world goes ink-and-charcoal.

The mask appears almost identical to its physical form. The only real difference I can see is that the white of it seems brighter, but it doesn't feel like the veins of corruption I saw in Averrich. I peer closer, and I try to reach for whatever part of my soul contains my Gift of creation.

My sight sharpens, and it's like I can hear vibrations coming from the mask. Resonances. I know that the mask does nothing on its own, but that it is made of resonant materials which I could tap into, harness, and make a very strong artifact out of. I just need the right something to fill it with.

I turn my gaze on the rapier and it *blazes* to my sight. Where to my physical sight the blade was merely red, to my soul sight it is drenched in blood. The hilt and cross guard, corded leather and metal in realspace, are bleached bone in the realm of meaning. This is a killing instrument, and it is full of power, and it is very, very old.

I hear the name of the weapon, and I know that it yearns for me to wield it.

I flicker off my soul sight and grab the hilt, heedless of Cheshire's shouted concern. I raise the blade, finding it so natural in my grip. I swing it lightly through the air, watching the red arc. Perfectly balanced.

I murmur, "Vorpal, the Bloodstained Blade," and I feel it seethe with power as it wakes to life.

Cheshire stares at the sword, eyes wide. "That . . . that's not a Throne-made artifact. That's not even Gift-made. That's a *Crest*. Alice, that sword . . . it's older than Firmament."

"And now it's mine."

I take the mask and send it to my throne world, but the rapier I keep in hand, clutched gently. *Vorpal. A name so fitting it can't possibly be a coincidence, built around an affinity that I possess as a Truth. And, if I am to take the ultimate risk and trust in my companion, the blade's presence here was a surprise. I wonder . . . was this an act of the Beast? Of Katoptris herself?*

Or of the monster pulling all our strings?

Our journey to the maze's end is brief and uneventful, and when I cross the final threshold and emerge back into the city it comes without fanfare. From there, it's easy to find a figment and get directions back to the district I first woke up in.

We walk together, silence quickly giving way to idle chatter, and eventually we reach the apartment that Bashe acquired for us. We head inside and I lock the door, and then I collapse gratefully onto my bed. I manifest Cheshire so that she can cuddle me in cat form, and then I drift comfortably to sleep with her in my arms.

And then, I dream.

INTERLUDE

SHADOW & GLASS V

The day we put our plan into motion was a celebrated one, both between ourselves and among the court.

For them, it was a much-welcomed change in familiar routine; it's not every day, after all, that a mysterious sorcerer with strange affectations arrives from a faraway clan. Rarer still when that sorcerer's introduction is being rescued by the royal pariah.

For us, it was the culmination of months of effort. We delved into ancient crypts in search of your gift to the clan, and we battled terrible monsters to acquire the bloodstone ore that your Crest was forged from. Every step on our path was paved with great effort . . . save the last; the final key to making your Crest, the affinity that would have to be sacrificed, came not from either of our souls but from a strange needle of red glass that you attained through means you never spoke of.

"Introducing to the court, Lady Homura Annatar Bloodfallen."

Courtesies and formalities were observed, and then you stood before my father's throne and knelt. I knew by then, from all our time together, that you burned with hatred for every aspect of that act, but you kept your face smiling and serene. Grateful, even.

"I thank you for your generosity, Your Majesty," you spoke without a hint of insincerity. "After the tragedy that has left me bereft of lands, titles, and kinfolk, it restores my spirit to see that there are those who still retain their humanity."

He gestured for you to rise, and even that you performed with careful grace.

"If you will allow me," you continued, "I would thank you for taking me in with the only two gifts I have left to give: one material, and one immaterial." You withdrew from your jacket pocket a dull golden jewel streaked with prismatic color. "First, I offer a Titan's Eye gem, the only treasure I was able to take with me when I fled the destruction of my clan—aside from my Crest, of course. I regret that it is bereft of stored power, but all our resources were expended in our desperate efforts to stave off our vanquishers."

My father peered at the gem with a keen eye, then slowly nodded. "A worthy gift, indeed. Though your titles were torn from you, I see you still have a noble nature. And what of this immaterial gift?"

Luka takes the Titan's Eye from you and sets it by the throne. You smile at him, red eyes warm, and then you return your attention to the king. "Perhaps it is discourteous of me to frame it as such, Your Majesty. Rather, I should say that I wish for a request to be granted: I wish to enter into your service as a retainer, and perhaps with time earn a full position in your court. I know that clan Bloodfallen can never again exist as it once did, but it would bring me joy to raise a new Bloodfallen within the grace of your dominion."

The king leveled a piercing gaze at you. "You must have become quite attached to our kingdom in the scant time you have been here."

"Well, your daughter was quite compelling in her praises."

"Was she, now." He leaned back and gestured to the old crone. "Zdenka, you are requested."

Zdenka came forth and took her place next to the throne. "Your Majesty, I possess no record of a Bloodfallen sorcerer line, but if she is truly from distant lands then this is only expected; the Crawling Chaos takes great pains to restrict our knowledge of realms beyond the Glass Tower's reach. To be truly certain of her identity as a blooded sorcerer, I would request permission to examine her Crest."

"I would consent to such an examination," you told the king. You carefully drew your rapier and held it out, presenting it with both hands. "I present the Crest of my family: Vorpal, the Bloodstained Blade."

Zdenka placed a single finger upon the blade and called upon her affinities, weaving a spell of such complexity that even I felt envious at the level of skill on display. When her spell was complete, she slowly nodded. "It is as she says, Your Majesty: this is a true Crest, and it has a deep connection to the woman before you. It is my belief as your loremaster that Lady Bloodfallen is indeed the rightful wielder of this sorcerer Crest."

"Thank you, Zdenka." The king dismissed his advisor, and then he spoke to you: "I believe that your request can be accommodated, Lady Bloodfallen. Welcome to the Kingdom of Sun and Sword."

The whole court watched you, interest or excitement on every face. Courtiers already plotting how they would make use of you and manipulate you, or wondering how you would change the game. The Master of War was looking at your blade with curiosity, while the Masters of Coin and Letters were conversing in hushed tones. Even Luka was looking at you warmly.

Everyone wanted to meet you and figure you out. Everyone was intrigued by your presence in court. They were all giving you their full attention.

And in my heart, I felt the first twinge of jealousy.

ABOUT THE AUTHOR

J. M. Alexia was born old and proceeded to make that everyone else's problem. She always struggled to find the kind of story she most wanted to read—an eclectic mix of psychological horror, queer romance, and brutally honest depiction of mental illness—so she decided to write it herself. When she's not writing, Alexia is usually menacing friends and readers with blatant lies and bad memes on Discord or in the comments of her web serial. You can find her under her handle VoraVora, short for Voracity Maledictus, because she's never quite outgrown her teenage edgelord phase.